# JASON JUPITER

## LOST AND FOUND

ALBERT M. MANAFORD

ARCHWAY PUBLISHING

Archway Publishing books may be ordered through booksellers or by contacting:

Archway Publishing
1663 Liberty Drive
Bloomington, IN 47403
www.archwaypublishing.com
844-669-3957



ISBN: 978-1-4808-9039-8 (sc)
ISBN: 978-1-4808-9037-4 (hc)
ISBN: 978-1-4808-9038-1 (e)

Library of Congress Control Number: 2020908813

Print information available on the last page.

Archway Publishing rev. date: 08/19/2020

# CONTENTS


1 The Strange Object ........................................1
2 The Surprising Communication ........................................16
3 Jason Leaves the Spaceship ........................................30
4 Jason Contemplates Michael's Predicament ........................................46
5 A Joyride in the Spaceship ........................................62
6 Jason's Mom's Curiosity Rises ........................................78
7 An Evening at the Creek ........................................99
8 One of Jason's Secrets Exposed ........................................122
9 Surprising Tests at the Los Alamos Labs ........................................144
10 Jason's Secrets about to Be Exposed ........................................174
11 Jason's Parents Finally Meet Michael ........................................188
12 A Trip into Outer Space for the Jupiter Family ........................................203
13 A Walk on the Moon ........................................221
14 The Unimaginable, Highly Advanced Race ........................................240
15 Secrets about Michael from the Geneticists ........................................273
16 Deeper Secrets about Michael Are Revealed ........................................295
17 The Main Medical Lab ........................................324
18 The Visit from the Chief Engineer ........................................353
19 Picking Michael Up from the Lab ........................................378
20 A Celebration Dinner to Remember ........................................399
21 The Mother Ship's Magnificent Plantatrium ........................................435
22 A Surprising Conversation in the Lounge ........................................467
23 Leaving the Mother Ship ........................................486
24 Returning Home ........................................505
25 The Jupiters' First Evening Back on Earth ........................................525
26 The Following Day ........................................540

Abbreviations ........................................563

# 1

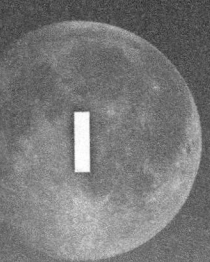

## THE STRANGE OBJECT

Ten-year-old Jason Jupiter stared quietly into the heavens from the swing on the front porch. He was always dreaming of space travel. On this particular night, the myriad stars twinkled in the clear sky like light bulbs on a Christmas tree. Suddenly, one of them darted across the sky, moving like a comet. Then, just as quickly, it stopped. In amazement, Jason watched as the object fell to Earth, glowing blue and red in intensity, its movement defying known laws of physics. And then it vanished along the western horizon.

Jason felt an unusual urge to investigate the object, which seemed to have fallen in fairly close proximity to his house. Since his parents were inside watching one of their favorite television programs, *Star Trek: Voyager*, he did not think they would notice he was gone. Without a second thought, he stood up and walked across the wood deck porch, filled with immense curiosity about what he had just seen, as there had been no sound whatsoever of anything impacting the ground. He continued down the steps, jumped to the ground, and quickly headed toward what had fallen out of the sky.

On this night, the moon shone brightly, and along the western horizon, there was a strange glow. Passing by the compost pile, Jason continued down the same trail his family used many times when hiking into the woods. The two-foot-high bushes on each side of the trail did not worry him in the least bit, or the possibility something might jump out from behind them.

Continuing down a small embankment, he entered the small forest of oak and piñon trees, and it naturally became darker, especially under the oak trees. The strong moonlight filtered through their leaves, allowing him to focus his spellbound attention on the glow in the distance. His heartbeat of excitement finally started to slow down. He was still not scared at all, regardless of the thought that he might be approaching something unusual—maybe even from outer space.

As he walked out from under the trees into a clearing, he spotted the object! It had to be over two hundred feet long and about forty feet in diameter. It was hovering above the ground, lit up like a multicolored fluorescent light bulb. The closer he got, the brighter it grew. He stopped in his tracks as the object moved, touching down on the ground. It had landed!

He continued toward the object through a haze of gray smoke, now a little cautious. He could not believe his eyes. It was a spaceship! He walked up to the tubular, cigar-shaped spaceship. Its outer hull appeared damaged, having taken on the shape of an accordion. The mysterious spaceship caused him immense curiosity. He surveyed its outer hull but found not a soul or any occupants whatsoever—only the trees of the surrounding forest and the moon shining down like a large spotlight.

Jason decided to investigate the strange spaceship, as if driven by some unseen force. He hesitated at first but finally walked up to the side of the spaceship. To his surprise, an open doorway appeared in front of him, seemingly from out of nowhere. Feeling a little braver, he entered the spaceship and looked around but again found no crew members. He now wondered if it had been abandoned, as no one appeared to have been in command. *Maybe it was remote controlled,* Jason thought.

He continued down a rectangular corridor nearly fifteen feet tall, though the size of the corridor was like an optical illusion, changing shape, becoming larger and then smaller about every four feet, matching the accordion shape of the spaceship. Even the floor seemed to be getting longer and then shorter, as though Jason were walking up and down on a hill, yet he was not struggling or using any more effort than if he were walking on a flat surface—very strange. Continuing farther into the ship, he entered a large cargo hold, which seemed much larger than what he'd viewed from the outside of the spaceship. It was easily over a hundred feet high—another optical illusion? To his eyes, the floor, walls, and even the ceiling had more depth to them but still matched the accordion shape of the spaceship's outer hull.

When Jason turned his head to his left, something amazing caught his eye: a partially visible circular glass container, similar to a soap bubble. The transparent object was disappearing and reappearing. Then it started to flicker like a clear light bulb and finally turned into a solid object.

A small spaceship that had been previously cloaked was now visible. It was a circular craft, at least twenty-five feet in diameter and flat on its bottom with a silver hull shaped like a half-domed football. There were numerous round and oval windows along its sides. At the very top was a strange-looking, silver-tinted window nearly six feet in diameter and perfectly matching the curvature of the outer hull. Its tint had an unusual depth, similar to a two-way mirror, yet was still reflective.

Jason immediately became excited, as he had always wanted to travel into outer space, visit the moon and Mars, and even journey beyond Earth's solar system. He walked within a few feet of the spaceship but did not see the outline of a door anywhere. Without warning, dozens of small circular lights appeared on the hull in front of him, glowing red and then blue in surreal intensity. They looked like reflections—mirages—and started to blink on and off in unusual sequences. This surprised Jason, as he had not touched anything. The lights seemed to have activated when he had gotten in close proximity. Gingerly, he reached out and touched one of the blue lights, and an open doorway, about seven feet in height, appeared just to his left.

For a few moments, he could hear only the excited wisps of his breathing as he thought about what might be inside the small craft. Finally, making his ultimate decision, he walked up a small ramp, continued inside, and then stopped. The interior was very bright, but he could not see any lighting fixtures anywhere. The space also appeared twice as big as viewed from the outside, as though he were inside a holographic deck like in the *Star Trek* science fiction movies.

There were three seats at the front of the spaceship, with curved windows in front of each seat, matching the curvature of the ship's outer hull. There was a square instrument panel in front of each seat, as well as instrument panels to each side of the outer seats. All the instrument panels were blank. In front of the two outer seats were what appeared to be control wheels, or yokes, similar to what would be found on jet-powered or propeller-driven aircraft, but they looked remarkably different. Jason calmly sat down in the left chair, which was extremely comfortable, as if sitting on air. With all the instrument panels apparently turned off, he wondered how he was ever going to get the small craft out of the cargo bay.

He studied the interior of the spaceship, which he now thought of as *his* spaceship, because he'd found it first and it had been abandoned on his mom and dad's 640 acres. When he stared back down at the instrument panels, there were still no etchings of life whatsoever. *I wonder how I can get this ship to fly,* he thought. *This might be my chance to see the stars.*

Jason continued his inspection of the spaceship in silence. When he looked back toward the doorway, it had disappeared, causing a feeling of anxiety to come over him—a feeling of being trapped. He was startled as a humming sound filled the air. He turned in his seat in the direction of the sound. On the wall, the outline of a small door, approximately three feet tall, had appeared. "Hmmm," he mumbled out loud, "that sure is strange." He fixated his eyes on the small door, wondering what would happen next.

Just as quickly, the humming sound abruptly stopped. The door started to open upward from the floor with a *psssshhh!* Jason figured the compartment may have been pressurized. He watched in fascination as a cold white vapor appeared, followed by a bright rectangular flash of light at the small opening. Jason was again startled. The door finally rose all the way.

Jason's eyes remained riveted on the doorway. The vapor finally cleared, revealing a small robot or humanoid android. It was three feet tall and standing upright, its eyes closed. In a way, it looked very much like a little Earth boy, maybe around five years old. Its outer covering was flesh-colored skin, the same as Jason's, yet something seemed different about it. If it had mechanical joints, it was not obvious.

As Jason stared at the small humanoid, it suddenly opened its eyes and made eye contact with him. "Sc-gnu Lxoktj Eub …" it said in an extremely strange language. Jason had not the faintest idea what it just said to him.

"I do not understand you," he replied. "Can you speak English?"

The humanoid boy analyzed Jason's reply with extreme intuition and then said, in perfect English, "Okay. Are you my new friend?"

Jason was surprised by how quickly the humanoid had adapted to the English language and decided to go along with it, because surely the humanoid did not know he was an Earth boy. "Yes, I am," he answered.

"Good," responded the little humanoid, and it walked out of the wall opening like a human boy—nothing like a robot with mechanical joints. The small door closed behind the humanoid. Jason did not know for sure whether it was a robot, an android, or maybe even a real alien boy who had just woken up from suspended animation. He decided, though, that the humanoid was a *he*, not an it.

The little humanoid turned to Jason and asked with a calm demeanor, "What do you want to do now?"

Jason was quiet. He knew the humanoid would probably answer any question and do anything asked of him—maybe even teach Jason how to fly the small craft—but he wanted to remain as inconspicuous as possible. He wanted to conceal not only how naive he was about the ship but also the fact that he was a human. "How do we power up our ship?" he finally asked.

The humanoid stared directly at Jason, as if confused by the question, and became particularly quiet. "Is not this your spaceship?"

Jason thought about a reply the humanoid would understand yet would not reveal that he was an Earth boy. "I haven't flown on a ship like this one," he said.

The humanoid boy duly analyzed Jason's reply. "Okay, I understand," he said. He sat down in the far right seat, leaving the middle seat empty between them. He touched a green button on the right console in front of him, and all the lights on the front and side instrument panels lit up.

Jason looked down at his front instrument panel. He did not have a clue of what anything meant. He turned back to the humanoid boy, again curious. "I do not know this ship," he said. "Can you teach me?"

"Sure, I can," the humanoid answered, after analyzing Jason's unusual question for a moment.

Jason stared at the humanoid boy, who was dressed in a short-sleeved light-gray one-piece outfit that fit tightly against his body. He had an extremely thin armband on his left forearm with multiple buttons, all of them flush with the surface of the armband. The humanoid boy did look very much like a human, having thick, dark-brown, partially curly hair, though his hair had an unusual luster in the lighting of their spaceship.

"What is your name?" Jason asked.

"My name is Michael," he answered, understanding Jason quickly. "What is your name?"

With how extremely open and friendly Michael was, he reminded Jason of his little brother, Kyle. "Well, my name is Jason, Michael," he replied.

"Okay, Jason Michael."

Jason grinned a little. "You can just call me Jason. Okay?"

"Okay," Michael said.

Jason now felt extremely relaxed. It suddenly felt as though the humanoid boy were his best friend, but he did not know whether Michael had emotions.

Jason knew the military could very well show up at any time to secure the cargo ship and everything inside, including their small spaceship. If that happened, it would place him in a very precarious situation, so they needed to get their ship out of the cargo bay as soon as possible. He made direct eye contact with Michael. "Is there any way we can get this small craft out of the cargo bay?"

"Yes, we can," Michael replied.

Jason was surprised, as there was no open cargo bay door through which they could leave. "How?" he asked.

Michael continued to stare directly at Jason. "Well," he said, "we would first have to go into gravity propulsion. Once in propulsion mode, we could burn a hole through the side of the cargo ship using one of our spaceship's weapons."

Jason was amazed. "Okay, let's do it," he said.

Michael touched a red button on the center console. The cockpit grew a little darker, and their instrument panels lit up even more brightly.

When Jason looked back through his side window, he realized they were now hovering above the cargo bay floor, as evidenced by the containers below their vantage point. It was an invigorating and surprising realization, because he had not heard a sound or felt any movement whatsoever.

Michael next grabbed his control wheel with both hands and began maneuvering their spaceship. He ever so slightly moved his control wheel horizontally to his right, and the spaceship immediately moved to their right and then stopped.

"What weapon are we going to use to get out of here?" Jason asked.

"A gravitational laser beam ring," Michael answered. "It will easily cut a hole through the reactive hull material of this particular cargo ship."

Jason had not heard of a *gravitational laser beam ring* from any of the science fiction books that he had read. "Okay," he said and closely watched Michael's next course of action.

Michael touched a red button on his front display, and another screen appeared. Now both of their displays showed the interior of the cargo bay, along with a set of intersecting crosshairs. The crosshairs turned blue, as if their ship had vectored in on the wall, and Michael touched the display again, activating their ship's gravitational laser beam.

Fascinated and amazed, Jason watched as a reddish-yellow beam of light projected out from their spaceship. When the circular beam of light hit the wall, the wall started to glow white, then turned red momentarily. A few seconds later, the beam of light disappeared. A round, curved piece of the hull fell outward onto the ground. It actually sort of looked like a crinkle-cut potato chip. Jason was excited as he saw moonlight shining through the open hole. "Let's get out of here!" he said.

Michael began analyzing Jason's unusual emotions and his lack of understanding about the spaceship. It confirmed to Michael that Jason was a young Earth boy. He pushed his control wheel forward, and they quickly accelerated through the open hole, missing its edges by only centimeters. Their ship stopped and hovered in place just outside the tubular cargo ship. "Turn our ship around, Michael," Jason said.

Michael pulled the left yoke handle toward him while pushing the right handle away. Their spaceship quickly rotated counterclockwise

180 degrees and stopped. After Michael let loose of his control wheel, it instantly reverted back into its original position, as if spring-loaded.

With the tubular spaceship now about forty feet below them, Jason could see more clearly how bad the damage to its outer hull really was. Its crumpled accordion shape was much more pronounced. It looked as though someone had placed the entire spaceship in a vise. The circular piece of hull that they'd just cut out of the side of the cargo ship had the same ripples but was slowly changing into a smooth disk. Within moments, the ripples in the cut-out piece had disappeared entirely, and the disk now appeared larger than the hole in the side of the cargo ship. The rest of the cargo ship remained in the shape of an accordion. Jason was puzzled.

Their small spaceship was not detecting any signs of biological life, not even signs of deceased bodies. Michael knew the cargo ship surely would have had a crew. There were also no skid marks to indicate that the ship had impacted the planet at an angle, so it must have fallen out of the sky vertically and then touched down with minimal ground impact force.

Without warning, the cargo ship started to break apart, cascading into circular sections about four feet in length. Each section then instantly flexed out into a perfect ring, matching the high-point diameters of the previous accordion shape. The entire ship completely broke apart from end to end. When the collapse finally stopped, all that remained of the hull were two conical end sections, about four feet long, and what had to be over sixty smooth tubular sections, each of them forty feet in diameter and also about four feet long. Most of those forty-foot-diameter ring-shaped sections were lying on top of each other in every conceivable direction, as if someone had dropped a loaf's worth of round bread slices. Items from the ship were scattered everywhere, including consoles, chairs, equipment, and a multitude of other items, as if a series of small explosions had just occurred. Because of the hole they had just cut, some of the hull sections looked as though someone had taken a bite out of them. Four of the forty-foot-diameter ring-shaped hull sections that had broken apart remained standing upright in the deconstructed frame of the cargo ship, located in what would have been the center of the spaceship. A few objects inside those rings had also not moved in the least bit and were partially visible through the small crevices in between the upright ring-shaped sections. One of the objects partially visible was a large disk, maybe ten feet in diameter by a few feet thick, located at the very center of the ship. A flat-bottomed dome appeared to have previously encompassed the disk but was now broken in half like an eggshell, the two halves lying on their sides.

The disk was part of the quantum gravity drive. Encased inside were highly radioactive heavy elements unknown to Earth science. The broken dome was the interactive dome that allowed highly directional quantum gravity propulsion. Michael knew the structural changes just witnessed were a result of the hull reverting back to its original shape, but he did not understand how the ship could have ever taken on the crumpled accordion shape in the first place. It seemed to indicate an encounter with an advanced weapon of unknown origin, well beyond the capabilities of the race that had designed the ship.

The hull had been created inside a large energy chamber where the molecular energies were traveling above the speed of light. It should have never been able to permanently retain a different shape while located inside a normal plane of space-time, especially when it was referenced against light speed. Since above-light-speed, hidden molecular energy bonds still existed across the entire hull surface, the hole they'd just cut had released the compression bands, which had already been near a state of collapse. Michael thought some more, but he still did not understand what could have damaged the spaceship's highly reactive, extremely lightweight crystal-metal alloy hull in the manner in which it had been compressed. Under normal circumstances, the cargo ship would have impacted the planet with a hull completely undamaged, due to its above-light-speed design.

Off to the west, bright headlights and flashing red lights were traveling across the open field toward them. The screen in front of Jason showed a remarkably clear video of two helicopters also headed their direction. The video appeared lit up as though it were daylight, nothing like infrared vision used on Earth. The helicopters were almost certainly the military coming to retrieve the spaceship. They were approaching awfully fast. Jason turned to Michael, who was also watching the helicopters on his front screen, a strange look on his face. "Take our ship to a thousand feet, Michael," Jason finally said, "and watch what they do next."

"Okay," Michael replied. He grabbed his control wheel and lifted up slightly, and their ship quickly accelerated straight up at a ninety-degree angle. Jason felt no acceleration forces whatsoever with this magnificent maneuver. Michael let go of his control wheel, and their ship suddenly stopped, hovering at one thousand feet.

Jason glanced down at his front display and was surprised to see their altitude given in English, using both the imperial system (1,000 feet) and the metric system—304.80 meters—as though it had been adjusted for his viewing. The race who had built this ship must have known about Earth for years.

Down below, the military vehicles had finally arrived at the spaceship. The vehicles were displayed on Jason's front display as clearly as though it were daylight. There were six semitrailers, two with flatbed trailers and four with box trailers, and the two helicopters were now flying around the cargo ship. The helicopters were completely black, and Jason did not recognize any of their modifications. They were very mysterious looking, not only for the way the tail rotor was shrouded, but also for the shrouding below the main rotors. Jason figured the military would secure the site and try to remove as much of the spaceship as possible before sunrise.

*At least they didn't get this ship*, he thought.

A red light began flashing on their displays. Two small white objects then appeared on the screen, causing Jason to look out the top dome window. Off to the west, two faint white lights were traveling in their direction. "That is strange," he said and turned to Michael. "What are those?"

Michael touched a few buttons on his front display and saw that the jets headed in their direction were armed with active Sidewinder missiles and 20-millimeter machine-gun cannons, but those weapons could have no possible effects on their spaceship with its active force field and highly reactive hull. "They are military fighter jets you call F-16 Falcons," he said.

"Can we outrun them?" Jason asked.

Michael nodded in the affirmative. "Yes, no problem. They are limited to a speed of around Mach 2, or a sound factor according to your planet's atmospheric altitude bubble."

That would make the F-16s' maximum speed nearly 2,200 feet per second—at least at sea level. "I understand," Jason said. "Let's leave them in the dust, then."

"Okay." Michael grabbed his control wheel again and rotated it toward his body. Their ship quickly rotated clockwise 135 degrees and stopped. Michael then pushed his control wheel way forward.

The stars in the night sky changed position, yet Jason again did not feel any movement whatsoever as they quickly sped away. The lights from the F-16 fighter jets quickly grew dimmer, so Jason knew they must be traveling much faster than Mach 2. Suddenly, the lights were gone, and even the lights from the cities and houses below them became a blur. After what seemed only a few seconds, the lights below them were no longer a blur, indicating they had come to a halt. Jason's front console now displayed a map of the north-central United States with all the state borders outlined in light blue. He recognized South Dakota, Nebraska, Kansas, Oklahoma, Colorado, Missouri, and Arkansas. There were also partial outlines for the adjoining states. Jason turned to Michael, who was no longer holding on to his control wheel. "How far did we just travel?"

"Seven hundred miles," Michael replied. He knew that, despite greatly surpassing the sound barrier, their spaceship would not have created even a single sonic boom due to its ability to remove all collapsing trailing edge airstreams.

Amazed, Jason contemplated just how far they had just traveled and how quickly. It had seemed almost instantaneous. He mumbled to himself, "We must have left New Mexico and crossed at least two states." He looked over to Michael again. "Can you take us back to where we just came from? I live near a town called Los Alamos."

"How fast do you want us to return?"

Jason wondered how fast their ship could actually travel. "How about Mach 10?"

"Okay," Michael replied without hesitation. He rotated his control wheel left toward his body, and their spaceship immediately rotated counterclockwise 135 degrees. With both hands still on the wheel, he pushed forward a small amount.

Like before, Jason could tell they were traveling at a high rate of speed by the movement of the stars, but they did not seem to be traveling even remotely as fast as before. Knowing they were traveling at ten times the speed of sound, Jason calculated approximately how long it would take them to return home. He estimated it would take them about six minutes. It seemed almost inconceivable they could travel seven hundred miles in less than six minutes.

On the way back, he reflected on everything that had just happened and the fact that he was now flying aboard a real spaceship—*a UFO*. He turned to Michael with immense curiosity. "Where did you come from?"

"From a galaxy nearly 194,689 light-years away," he said. "At least, that is what my memories tell me."

Jason was puzzled. "What do you mean by that?" he asked. "Don't you know for sure?"

"No, I don't," Michael said. "I do not believe I've ever seen the planet where I was created or even the galaxy—at least not with my own eyes."

Jason thought his answer strange. It appeared Michael had never been consciously awake, only filled with memories from his home world. Jason continued to stare into Michael's blue eyes. His dark, round pupils seemed to be glowing slightly, almost as if they were glistening, and then the glow suddenly went away. He did seem so much like a real alien boy. "Will those who created you now be looking for you?"

"I do not know," Michael said, continuing to stare into Jason's face. Michael understood a multitude of advanced sciences, and he also understood how most humans on Earth would react to meeting an alien being for the first time, even if it was a child—paranoia. Jason seemed much different, though.

Jason remained quiet, unsure what to think about Michael's last answer. Though Michael might not know whether or not the race that had created him would come looking for him, Jason was sure they would.

They were now less than a minute from reaching Los Alamos, reminding Jason that they had not only the race that had created Michael but also the military, especially the F-16 fighter jets, to worry about. *I figure we are about fifty miles from the crash site,* Jason thought, *and the military definitely knows about our spaceship. We can't outrun their jets forever, and besides that, how are we going to keep this ship without them finding it?*

Jason finally turned to Michael, who had been watching him daydream. "Is there any way for us to become invisible to the military?"

"Yes, there is."

Jason was excited at the amazing prospect. "How?" he asked.

Michael noticed Jason's excitement and now understood that human emotion. "We could cloak our ship," he said. "We would then be completely invisible to Earth's primitive radars."

Jason realized how much Michael must understand. *This is too good to be true,* he thought. *They will never be able to find this ship now.* He gave a small, distant grin. "Let's cloak our ship, then," he said.

"Okay, Jason," Michael replied and touched his front display.

The front displays showed what appeared to be Earth's magnetic dipole field with field lines. Michael touched the screen again and then said, "We are now cloaked and invisible to Earth-based radars as well as all visual sighting."

Jason was again excited, as they could now go anywhere without fear of being seen or detected. "Take us back to the crashed spaceship," he said, "and let's watch the military for a while."

"Okay," Michael replied. He accelerated them toward the cargo ship at a twenty-degree angle of descent. Again, Jason felt no acceleration forces or any roller-coaster effects. He watched the altitude display in front of him as they dropped—five hundred feet, four hundred feet, two hundred feet, and then one hundred feet before finally leveling off in their southwesterly path, the cargo ship just ahead of them.

The military had set up huge spotlights, making it extremely bright around the cargo ship. The lights were pointed away from the cargo ship, yet inside the ring of spotlights, it was lit up like a room with a 100-watt light bulb. Jason knew the lights would make it hard, if not nearly impossible, for anyone to see inside the perimeter of bright spotlights. Near the edge of the brightly lit perimeter, the two black helicopters were flying in a circular pattern, seemingly overseeing and protecting the site. Jason finally looked back to Michael, who was also watching the helicopters. "Take us to within about forty feet of the cargo ship, and let's hover over them for a while," he said.

2

# THE SURPRISING COMMUNICATION

Michael grabbed his control wheel again, pushed it forward, and guided their spaceship in a westerly direction to within forty feet of the now destroyed cargo ship. After entering the brightly lit perimeter, he loosened his grip on the control wheel, and they hovered quietly, undetected. On their front displays, clearly illuminated, were dozens of armed military personnel, including individuals dressed in black attire. Michael and Jason watched as the military personnel meticulously wrapped the spaceship's contents in packages. Some of the personnel were dressed in gray suits and carrying what were possibly Geiger counters. All the items were placed in large plywood crates and marked with either green or red stickers. The plywood crates were then loaded into the forty-foot-long box trailers. Most of the crates were marked with green stickers. Michael knew the crates marked with red stickers were lined with lead.

The semitrailer engines were running, their exhaust gas vapors cascading in a light fog against the cool night breeze. To Jason's and Michael's surprise, another red light started flashing on their front displays, followed by a message in a strange language that only Michael could read. The message indicated that four additional helicopters were traveling in from the north on a direct collision course with their ship. Grabbing his control wheel again, Michael lifted up slightly, and their spaceship quickly accelerated up at a ninety-degree angle to an altitude of 1,500 feet. There was now no chance of the helicopters running into the side of their cloaked spaceship. Michael knew such a collision would have resulted in the deaths of the pilots and everyone aboard. The four helicopters finally arrived at the site and systematically hovered over the circular sections of the cargo ship. Metallic cables were dropped out of their bellies and carefully positioned around some of the four-foot-long, forty-foot-diameter circular hull sections. The helicopters then began lifting the hull sections out of the pile. Their spaceship had identified the helicopters as heavy-lift helicopters, two Boeing XCH-62s and two Sikorsky CH-53Es.

Jason wondered what the military might be talking about and turned to Michael, curious about what other advanced technologies they had at their disposal. "Is it possible to listen to what is being said at the crash site?"

"Yes," Michael said.

Jason was thrilled about their ability to eavesdrop on the military without them ever knowing. "Okay, let's listen to the highest-ranking officer."

Michael touched his front screen, and dozens of small white lights appeared, with faint lines between some of them. Some of the lines were different colors. There was a single red line between two white dots.

Jason figured it was a strange communications display. His curiosity was immense, but so was his deduction ability. "I suppose those small lights represent people and the colored lines between them represent verbal and nonverbal communications?"

"Yes, that's correct," Michael said. Their ship's computer identified one of the lights connected by the red line as the highest-ranking officer—a major—speaking on a satellite phone. Michael touched the light, and suddenly, the conversation between the major and a general in Dayton, Ohio, filled the inside of their spaceship. Jason and Michael remained extremely quiet.

"Yes, General," the major said. "The tubular spaceship touched down within a quarter mile of our projected impact point, as calculated by our satellites and deep space radar, as well as the strange restricted military radio transmission of unknown origin that pinpointed the impact for us. The fact it slowed down in a controlled fall after entering our atmosphere is strange and still makes no sense. No occupants were at the site, so we have no idea what really happened. The spaceship also broke apart into over seventy-five smaller circular sections that are scattered everywhere. Believe it or not, General, but those nearly fourteen-meter-diameter, two-meter-long circular hull sections are paper thin and lighter than hell, yet we cannot cut them, nor can they be affected in any manner whatsoever."

"Is that right?" the general said, sounding surprised.

"Yes, it is, General," the major said. "Our diamond bits immediately snapped within seconds, our carbide wheels came apart and then exploded, and our acetylene torches popped and were quickly extinguished. It's as though the hull material is highly reactive to all external stimuli, even our high-powered $CO_2$ lasers were burned out and rendered inoperative. I could swear that an intense beam of light was reflected back into the lasers."

The general was quiet, appearing to contemplate this surprising information. "Why did the ship break apart into smaller sections, then?"

"That is a very strange mystery, General," the major said. "It could be related to a hole we found cut through the back section."

"Is that right?" the general said. "Did you locate the spaceship's gravity drive?"

"Yes, we did," the major said. "It was located at what appears to have been the center of the ship, just where we suspected it would be, but it is heavier than normal. It has much-higher levels of radiation than normal and is shaped like none of the gravity drives we have ever seen. There is also a broken spherical dome that once encased it, and there appears to be a strange power feed collector we've never seen before in any other craft."

The race associated with this spaceship was highly advanced to a level they had never before encountered, aside from an event that started back in 1982. That encounter would probably never be surpassed. Still, with the level of technologies they were currently dealing with, the current scenario was not good, for surely the race would want to retrieve their spaceship and all associated technologies—regardless of where they were hidden away.

The major knew the general was contemplating what he had just told him. "We should have a large tent erected over the entire site well before sunrise, General," he said. "There is just one small problem, sir."

"What would that be, Major?"

The major paused. "A small craft, possibly from the large ship, left before we got here."

The general raised his eyebrows and leaned back in his chair. "How do you know that for a fact, Major?"

"Our radars picked up a small craft directly above the large ship when we first arrived. We believe that it may have been responsible for the hole cut through the large spacecraft before it broke into smaller sections, because there is a single perfectly shaped curved disk on the ground that matches the hole outlines in over a half dozen of the ring-shaped sections. When our F-16s tried to engage the craft, it quickly accelerated away toward the northeast at a speed we have never seen before and then vanished out of the pilots' visual sight and radar. According to NORAD, the craft traveled up to northeastern Nebraska in twenty-seven seconds and stopped. It then traveled back to the vicinity of the crash site at nearly Mach 10 and disappeared less than fifteen minutes ago using what we believe is some type of cloaking."

The general was overwhelmingly surprised to hear this, especially after learning they could not affect the hull of the large ship with diamond bits, torches, $CO_2$ lasers, or anything they had at their disposal. The small craft must have a highly advanced weapon to be able to cut a hole through the hull as if it were paper. They were definitely dealing with a race that had technologies more advanced than anything *directly* encountered to date. The small craft speeding away seemed to be a panic maneuver and did not make sense. Returning and then watching them while cloaked was cause for additional concern. "I understand, Major," he finally said. "Have you been able to locate the small craft at all?"

"No, we haven't," the major said. "We've been modifying the signature patterns of our mobile quantum radars across various subspace compression frequency bands, but with no luck."

"Okay, Major," the general said. "Keep me informed of the situation, and if you determine anything else about the small craft, let me know immediately. It appears we have a situation here of the highest order, a Mother Hen protocol. I'll call Colonel Peterson later tonight to let him know we will be assembling two high-profile field teams. Also monitor all land- and air-based communications within a hundred-mile radius around Los Alamos. I am sure there will be some chatter of interest."

"Will do, sir," the major replied.

"Goodbye, Major," the general said.

"Bye, sir," the major replied and then hung up his phone.

Jason and Michael's cockpit went silent. Michael was unusually quiet. "We need to be careful now," Jason said.

"Yes, I know," Michael said.

They watched as the military continued to place items from the cargo ship into plywood crates—consoles, chairs, even structural pieces from the ship that had been scattered in every conceivable direction. Some of the workers were erecting large, tubular frames, attached to poles, around the perimeter of the ship—most likely for the large tent the major had told the general about.

Jason suddenly realized he had completely lost track of the time. His parents must be immensely worried about his whereabouts, as there were wolves, mountain lions, and even venomous diamondback rattlesnakes in New Mexico. He checked his wristwatch. It was 12:11 a.m. He had been gone for almost three hours from the time he'd first walked off the porch. When he looked up, Michael was staring at him. "Take us about a half mile to the east, Michael," Jason said. "That's where I live."

"Okay," Michael said.

With the ship still cloaked and invisible, Michael again grabbed his control wheel. He moved it in a counterclockwise motion, and their ship rotated 180 degrees. He pushed the control wheel forward, just slightly, and they accelerated toward Jason's home. Michael then pushed down, ever so slightly, and they began to drop in altitude.

The bright lights at the crash site dimmed behind them, and Jason spotted the telephone pole light near one of his family's barns and pointed at his house. "Right there, Michael," he said, excited. "That's where I live."

Michael quickly analyzed the intonation change in Jason's voice. He could tell Jason was relieved to arrive back home, but he did not understand the full reasons for his reaction. All he could do was continue to analyze Jason's excitement while slowly guiding their ship to within about fifty feet of the house. Their ship now hovered at an altitude of forty feet just north of Jason's house.

Jason's mother was standing on the front deck porch, but Jason did not see his father anywhere. *Maybe he is out looking for me,* Jason thought, *especially since they have not seen or heard from me in almost three hours.*

He turned to Michael, who was staring down at his mother with a look of puzzlement. Jason wondered again who may have created

Michael. "That's my mom standing on the porch," he said, pointing at her. "Her name is Barbara Jupiter."

Michael continued to look puzzled and made direct eye contact with Jason. "What's a mother?" he calmly asked.

Jason now knew for sure Michael had never had a mom, just as he had thought. Michael must have been created as a humanoid android that only looked like a human child. Jason thought some more about Michael's question and how to answer him in a manner in which he might understand. "She is kind of like the one who created you," Jason said.

Michael nodded. "I think I understand," he said.

Compassion filled Jason's mind and heart. "Go ahead and land our ship just east of my house," he said.

"Okay, Jason." Michael grabbed his control wheel and methodically guided their ship just east of the house. He rotated the control wheel clockwise, and their ship softly dropped until touching down with only the slightest of a bump. Their ship now pointed in a northwesterly direction and faced the front porch.

Jason's mother was staring out into the darkness just beyond the porch lighting. Jason knew she had to have noticed the bright lights in the west and must be immensely curious about what was happening. Suddenly, his father, carrying a flashlight, walked out from the darkness and into the porch lighting. He continued toward the front porch. Jason knew he would be carrying his M1911 Colt .45 pistol on his right hip.

Michael stared at Jason's father, a look of puzzlement mixed with curiosity on his face. Jason realized again that his humanoid friend was unique. "That's my father there, Michael," Jason said, pointing. "His name is Dan Jupiter. He was out looking for me."

Michael still looked puzzled. "What's a father, Jason?"

Jason knew Michael must not have any recollections whatsoever of who had created him. Jason thought about how to answer his extremely smart friend so that he would again be able to understand.

"He is kind of like the one who gave you the energy to function," he said.

Michael duly analyzed Jason's answer. "I think I understand," he said.

Jason glanced at his father, who was walking up to his mother. Jason was curious whether his father had been down to the crash site. "Let's listen to what my parents have to say," he told Michael.

"Okay," Michael said. He reactivated the communications screen and selected a parameter of human bioelectrical signatures inside a fifty-foot circle. Three white lights showed on the screen. Jason recognized the two lights next to each other as his parents and the third light, slightly smaller and just southwest of their ship, as his younger brother, Kyle, asleep in his bedroom. Michael selected the verbal communication between Jason's mom and dad and remained completely quiet.

Jason's father finally stopped in front of his mom.

"Dan," Barbara said, her voice quivering. "Where is Jason?"

Dan recognized her deep emotional concern. "I do not know, dear," he said. "I've looked everywhere. I have been down by the creek and through the small forest. Remember the loud popping sounds that sounded like a series of explosions?"

"Yes," she said.

"Well," Dan said, "about a half mile west of here there is some strange, brightly lit military operation."

"So what is going on?" Barbara asked, her voice no longer trembling.

"I don't know," Dan said. "When I started toward the bright lights, armed military guards stopped me and asked me why I was out by myself at night. Some men in dark suits showed up soon afterward and took me inside a tent, where they grilled me with even more questions. I in turn told them that they were on my land, and I showed them my credentials—my military CAC card—and explained that I have a high-level, top-secret clearance because of my work at the Los Alamos labs. I finally revealed to them that I was actually out looking for my ten-year-old son."

"Then what happened?"

Dan paused briefly. "I believe they ran a quick check on me. They logged onto a laptop, and my picture appeared on the screen. A few minutes later, they gave me my pistol back and warned me to stay away from the area, as an aircraft carrying radioactive material had crashed. They also reminded me that talking about the crash site or my having met armed guards, especially to any news media, would be an NSA violation and cause my top-secret clearance to be revoked."

Barbara was very surprised to hear this and took a deep breath. "You don't think Jason was there, do you?"

"I do not know, dear," he said and gave her a big hug. "Well, we had better call the authorities and report our son missing."

"Okay," she replied, audibly holding back tears.

Jason's parents walked inside.

Michael was extremely quiet and turned to Jason with an inquisitive, distant look. "Your mother and father are worried about you," he said.

"Yes, they are," Jason agreed.

"Are my parents worried about me?"

Jason was surprised, not knowing for sure how to answer him. "I do not know, Michael," he finally said. "If they did not spend time with you when you were much younger, probably not."

Michael understood, as he truly did not know who had actually created him, only the race responsible, so he had to surmise that what Jason said was correct. "Okay, I think I understand," he said.

Jason, filled with compassion, felt sorry for Michael, who reminded him even more of his little brother, but his parents had to know their oldest son was okay. He stared into Michael's pretty, unusual-looking eyes. Michael did not look a bit tired. "I must sleep in my house," Jason finally said. "Otherwise, my parents will remain worried the rest of the night."

Michael understood, especially after seeing the way Jason's parents had acted on the porch. "I understand," he said. "I will leave this ship sitting right here."

Jason exhaled. He was about to leave Michael all alone. "How can I keep in contact with you?"

"We have communication devices," Michael said.

Jason was thrilled. "That's good," he said. "Where are they?"

Michael turned around and pointed at a console behind them. "In the bottom drawer of that console."

Jason walked over to the console, which had two drawers nearly two feet wide and flush with the cabinet. He turned back to Michael, confused. "How do I open the drawer?"

"Just touch it," Michael said.

Jason touched the drawer, and it suddenly appeared open, as though it had slid out on rollers. The nearly eighteen-inch-deep drawer was momentarily transparent before becoming solid. *What strange technology*, Jason thought. Inside the drawer were six silver-and-gray rectangular devices. He picked one up, and as soon as his hand left the drawer, the drawer appeared closed, as though by magic. He shook his head a little over the strange technology and returned to his seat. "Okay, explain to me how this communicator works," he said.

Jason seemed open and sincere to Michael, similar to the child companion Michael was supposed to have met after first becoming conscious. Jason was polite and friendly, not afraid in the least bit. Michael's memories told him that this was not how most humans would normally react to meeting an alien being for the first time. "Hand it to me, and I will show you," he said.

Jason handed the communicator to Michael, who held it up in the air and pointed at the top right button of the eight light-blue buttons, and explained, "When you push this button here, it will open communication to this spaceship anywhere within this planet's geomagnetic field."

"That's anywhere on Earth, right?" Jason asked.

"Yes," Michael said, "anywhere, and it would be nearly instantaneous."

Jason acknowledged with a small nod. "Will our spaceship also be able to pinpoint where I am?"

"Yes, it will," Michael said. "Since our communications use unique subspace quantum signals that travel much faster than the speed of light, each communicator can easily be triangulated within this planet's dipole magnetic field—kind of like ripples in a large body of water that form when an object falls into it."

Jason was amazed to hear about subspace signals traveling faster than the speed of light, and it reminded him again of how much Michael must understand. Curious about the secret military division looking for their ship, Jason asked, "Will the military be able to detect our communications?"

"No, they cannot," Michael said. "Our subspace quantum signals travel too fast for the relaxed space quantum receivers they're using."

Jason was relieved that the military would not be able to eavesdrop or locate them. The term *relaxed space* was interesting, as was the fact that the military was using quantum receivers. "Good," he finally said. "What are the other buttons for?" he asked, since Michael had not explained any of the communicators' other functions.

Michael knew the communicators had an assortment of highly directional electronic countermeasures, offensive and defensive weapons, and a multitude of other capabilities. "Certain buttons can create holographic and optical illusions," he calmly explained, "while others create energy beams."

Jason was surprised. "Is that right? Energy beams for what?"

Michael noticed Jason's keen interest. "Many things." Michael answered vaguely, at least at first, because Jason was a young Earth boy, but then he revealed, "The beams can be used to cut holes, vaporize objects, and even momentarily stun living organic matter. The beams can also be used to cause electron energy disruption to both organic and inorganic matter." Michael paused.

Jason was now starry-eyed. "So they're powerful weapons too, huh?"

"Yes, they are," Michael confirmed, "with the ability to also hypnotize living beings, even put them to sleep."

Jason was again overly impressed. Michael finally handed the device back to Jason, who placed it in his front jeans pocket. "I will be sure to only use the communication function," Jason said. "What other devices do you have that might help me?"

Michael knew Jason would only be using the communication function because the weapons and countermeasure functions on the communicator would not be active until Michael activated them. "There is a metallic armband that will allow you to become invisible and even walk through solid objects," Michael said, seeming a little hesitant.

Jason noticed Michael was wearing such an armband on his left forearm. There was a variety of buttons on the extremely thin silver-colored armband. "Would it work on me?"

"It should," Michael said, "but the armband would have to be reconfigured to the physiology of the host and exact bioelectrical physiology of your nerve cells."

"I want one, then," Jason said without a second thought. He wondered why Michael would be wearing an armband if he were some kind of humanoid android or robot. "What kind of humanoid robot android are you?"

"I am *not* a robot android, Jason," Michael replied. "I am an organic android … I think."

Jason was surprised to hear this and did not understand Michael's term *organic android*, but he said no more about it, because it appeared Michael did not even know for sure himself. "That's why you have on one of those armbands, then, huh?" he said.

Michael did not remember when he received his armband, but for some reason, he fully understood everything about it in both nuclear and physical elemental construction, including its interfaces with the organic host body. "Yes, it also works on me," he said.

Jason knew for sure he wanted an armband and was excited, especially for the opportunity to experience what it would be like to walk through a solid object. "How long would it take you to reconfigure one of the armbands for me?" he asked.

"A few Earth hours," Michael answered, "only after your hand is placed inside the organic-matter analyzer."

Jason was surprised. "Where's the analyzer?"

"Here, I will show you."

Michael led Jason to a small table toward the back of their spaceship. Jason looked with fascination at a rectangular slot in the wall above the table. "Place your hand in that slot there," Michael said, pointing, "and your organic cellular DNA and complete biophysical configuration pattern will be recorded."

Jason's heart sped up a little, but he did not hesitate to place his hand inside. There was a sudden white flash of light inside the slot, followed by an undetectable, at least to Jason, millisecond halo of blue light that encompassed his entire body, and then his hand went momentarily numb. The numbness quickly went away, and the white light vanished right afterward.

Michael knew the test was now complete, with a complete recording of Jason's biophysical body—his organs, muscles, nerves, skeletal construction, cerebral cortex, everything, down to each individual cell of his body. Jason was still holding his hand in the slot. "Your organic cellular configuration is now recorded," Michael said, "just like mine. You can now remove your hand from the slot."

Jason removed his hand, feeling unusual knowing their ship's computer now knew how he was biophysically designed, including having his DNA configuration in its data banks. His anticipation for receiving the armband was high. "You said it would be a couple of hours, right?" he said.

"Yes," Michael answered. "It will take the ship's computer a few

Earth hours to reconfigure the armband for your exact molecular configuration."

Jason was amazed. "Okay, I understand. Well, I need to let my parents know I am all right. I will see you in about eight hours or so, okay?"

"Okay, Jason."

Michael touched a button on his armband, and an open doorway out of their ship suddenly appeared. Jason now knew that was another function of the armband. Jason could see the moon still shining down on the ground through the open doorway. He turned his attention back to Michael. "Are you going to keep our ship cloaked all night?"

"Probably not," Michael said.

"Why not?"

"Because," Michael answered, "our ship's cloaking field is too close to your house and will start disrupting all electrically powered appliances inside your house."

Jason was now even more curious. "Why is that?"

"Earth's magnetic lines of force that are used as the medium for their power generation are now having inverse magnetic polarity induced into them, causing the appliances to struggle to run properly."

Jason still did not fully understand. "Okay, bye, Michael," he said anyway.

Michael continued to stare at Jason, who was now looking through the doorway. "Bye, Jason," he replied. "See you after sunrise."

# 3

## JASON LEAVES THE SPACESHIP

Jason finally walked down the ramp and planted his feet on the ground. He turned around and could see only a brightly lit opening into the spaceship and nothing else. It was like a hole into another world. The ramp suddenly vanished, followed by the entrance, and no matter how hard he strained his eyes, he could not see an outline of the ship. It had to be there, though. He stretched his arm out and walked forward a little. Sure enough, he felt the outer hull.

*That is so weird,* he thought. He turned around and started toward the front porch. As he approached the stairs, his father opened the driver's door to his SUV, as if about to leave. "Dad!" he yelled out.

His father turned around, extremely surprised and filled with sudden relief. "Jason!" he called out. "Where in the world have you been? Your mother and I have been worried to death about you!"

"I've been *around,* Dad," Jason said. He briefly turned around to make sure the spaceship was still invisible.

Dan Jupiter was somewhat speechless. He closed the door to his SUV and quickly walked up to his son, not knowing whether to punish or hug Jason, because he did not yet know what was going on. "Never do this again without telling us," he sternly warned. "Your mother broke down crying from worrying about you and then started bawling after we found our landline had no dial tone and our cell phones had no service."

Jason felt compassion for his mom and wondered whether the phones were dead because of the spaceship's cloaking field, or maybe the crashed cargo ship had caused it. He and his father returned to the house, and he said not a word about the small spaceship or Michael.

✦ ✦ ✦

Inside the spaceship, soon after Jason left, Michael activated the voice communications menu. He listened to Jason and his father's conversation with keen interest. Analyzing their verbal communication, he thought he had a better understanding of what Jason meant about having a mother and father. As far as Michael could remember, he had no parents, and that fact caused him to wonder again about who might have created him—who had given him his energy to function, as Jason had said. No matter how hard he thought about it, he could not recall any of those exact memories.

What Jason's dad said about the landline and cell phones not functioning was a direct result of the dampening effect from his ship's cloaking field. Michael touched a series of buttons on his front console and studied the standing wave values and frequencies of his ship's inverse-resonance cloaking field, noticing right away the cell phone operating frequencies that were being dampened. Methodically, he phase-shifted the cloaking field so that it would allow the cell phones to operate properly inside their moving dual-path transceiver configurations. Next he analyzed the primitive two-wire paired phone circuits and wiring inside the house and modified the cloaking field so that it would not inject inverse energy into the low-current 48-volt DC positive ground circuits. As soon as he had accomplished this task, with a little help from his ship's computer, he leaned back in his chair with unusual interest in what was about to be said inside Jason's house.

✦ ✦ ✦

Inside the house, Jason and his dad entered the dining room, where Barbara sat at the table with a sad face and tears in her eyes. When she saw Jason, she quickly stood up with an immense feeling of relief and walked to meet them. She leaned down and placed a kiss on Jason's cheek, followed by a big hug. "Jason," she said, staring into his eyes, "you've been worrying us to death. Where in the world have you been?"

"I was around, Mom," he answered.

Jason looked up to his father briefly, curious about what he might have seen at the crash site, already knowing the military had detained him. "Did you see all those lights over to the west, Dad?"

Dan was curious about his son's question. "Yes, I did," he said. "You didn't go down there, did you?"

"Yes, I did," Jason said. He added with a little excitement, "There were semitrailers and helicopters—even F-16 fighter jets!"

Dan was puzzled, not to mention surprised. "How could you ever know there were F-16s?"

"I saw them, Dad."

Dan thought his son's comment a little strange, but regardless, he was happy as could be that this oldest son was safe. "Well, I am glad you're okay," he said.

Jason knew his parents didn't have a clue how he'd determined the jets were F-16s.

Dan continued to stare down into his son's face and wondered how Jason had managed to remain hidden from the military, but he did not want to get into that conversation so early in the morning, especially anything about the armed guards at the crash site. He only leaned down and placed a small kiss against Jason's forehead. "Let's go to bed, Son," he said. "I have to be at work by seven. If I do not see you at breakfast, then I will see you after work. We are going to talk some more about this incident and the consequences of your worrying us like you did. You also need to stay away from that area until the military has the site cleaned up."

Jason's father had worked at the Los Alamos labs for quite some time, even before Jason was born, but Jason did not know what his work actually entailed, because he would not talk about it. His dad was one of the labs' lead scientists and had a top-secret clearance, according to his badge. Jason wondered what his father might say to him after work and what kind of trouble he was in, including how long he might be grounded. "Good night, Dad," he said.

Dan was again thankful his oldest boy was okay. "Good night, Jason," he said and turned to his wife, who wanted to talk more with Jason. "I will see you in a little bit," he told her.

"Okay," she answered.

Dan left for the master bedroom. He could not wait to talk to Barbara more about Jason and the active ongoing military operation on their land.

Jason's mother still looked happy and relieved after thinking something terrible had happened. She sighed deeply while staring down into Jason's pretty eyes. "Please do not ever worry us like that again, Jason," she stressed. "I could not stand it if something bad would have happened to you."

Jason's mother also used to work at the Los Alamos labs full-time as one of their research scientists. She now worked part-time from home using a secure internet connection, so that she could raise and homeschool her two sons. She only visited the labs for classified meetings. From previously looking at her badge, Jason knew she also had a top-secret clearance. "Okay, Mom," he said, realizing her concern. "I promise to never do this again."

Barbara believed her oldest son. She placed a small kiss against his lips, followed by a warm hug. "Good night, Jason," she whispered into his ear.

Jason felt good inside to receive his mom's kindness, just as it had always been. "Good night, mom," he replied and watched her leave the room. He stood in the dining room for a moment longer and thought about how much fun it had been to fly around with Michael in their little spaceship. His mom and dad would have never believed he'd been aboard a spaceship almost the entire time and that he now had a new friend who was naive in some ways but extremely smart and friendly.

He finally headed toward his bedroom and thought about the armband that should be ready in a few hours. Not only would it allow him to walk through solid objects, but it would also allow him to become invisible. Getting to experience those magnificent feats was exciting to think about. Entering his bedroom, he turned on the lights. His four-year-old brother's bedroom was next to his, just across the hallway from their parents', and Jason realized that his brother would have slept through the whole ordeal of Jason being gone for almost three hours.

Jason quickly turned off the bedroom light and noticed the etchings of moonlight shining through his window. Since the spaceship was next to the house, just outside his window, he walked over, unlocked the window, and raised it all the way up. A cool breeze immediately gushed through the screen and across his face. It gave him a strange feeling to know a cloaked spaceship was about fifteen feet away.

He removed the communicator from his pants and placed it on top of his bedside table. He set his alarm clock to go off at 3:30 a.m., climbed into bed, and lay flat on his back, his eyes closed. In the darkness of the room, he thought about the trip he had just taken into another state while leaving the F-16 jets in the dust. He soon found himself not tired at all, especially as he thought about how easily their spaceship had outrun the jets. Adrenaline was still pumping through his veins as he relived every detail of their fantastic, mind-boggling trip into northern Nebraska. Then they'd traveled back to Los Alamos at the amazing speed of Mach 10.

He opened his eyes. He could not wait to find out if his communicator worked, so he picked it up, noticing its buttons were glowing, and touched the top right button. "Michael?" he softly called.

"Yes, Jason?" Michael responded a few moments later.

Jason gave a small grin and was now curious whether Michael was lonely on the spaceship. "How are you doing?"

"Good, Jason," Michael said.

Jason felt better now, especially hearing Michael's calm voice. "I'm returning to the ship in a few hours. Okay?"

"Okay, Jason. I will be waiting."

Jason's anticipation for flying around in their spaceship again was high. If not in a few hours, then surely after sunrise, he would be back in the spaceship. "Okay. I will see you later," he said.

"Bye, Jason."

"Bye, Michael."

Jason suddenly realized he did not know how to turn off the communicator and surmised he would either touch the same button or do nothing. The button he had just touched seemed to be glowing a little brighter, so he touched it again. Sure enough, its intensity diminished, and he placed the communicator on top of the bedside table. His wristwatch's its phosphor-coated hour and minute hands were now showing 1:18 a.m. He pulled the bedcovers all the way over his head. Closing his eyes under the darkness of his bedsheets, thinking about the armband he would soon receive, he was not able to fall asleep.

✦ ✦ ✦

In their bedroom, Jason's parents talked about the strange events of the evening, especially Jason's temporary disappearance. Dan mentioned seeing strange helicopters making very little noise—as if they were stealth helicopters.

They also talked more about the military cleanup operation about a half mile west on their land, including the fact that Jason had been gone for almost three hours while watching the military. Barbara finally turned to her husband, puzzled, and stared into his shadowy face. "Why did Jason walk in from the east side of our house if he was watching the military operation that was west of here?"

Dan thought about her question. "I truly do not know," he said. "Maybe he walked around our fenced backyard? He is not afraid of the dark."

"True," she agreed, "but how could he have ever known in the darkness that the jets were F-16s?"

Dan also thought that was a bit strange. "Honestly, I do not know that answer either," he said. "Maybe he saw their lights and just assumed they were F-16s by the sound of their engines. He is very perceptive."

Barbara agreed that their son was perceptive. Jason's maturity did seem to be blossoming into that of around a fifteen-year-old. She sighed again deeply, happy that their oldest son was safe. "Good night, dear," she said and planted a soft, sensual kiss against Dan's lips.

Dan returned the warm kiss, a glow filling his body. "Good night, honey," he replied.

Dan and Barbara lay next to each other, sharing their feelings of comfort that their two sons were now safe, especially Jason, who had been gone for over three hours. He was their first precious child, born in August 1993, almost three years after they were married. At the end of the spring semester in 1989, Barbara had received her particle physics doctorate from Cornell University in Ithaca, New York, and later that year, she'd met Dan at a seminar he was presenting at the university titled "Topological Momentum Energy Transients in Electron Energy Shells."

She remembered how interesting his presentation had been, not to mention his good looks, with his distinct forehead and firm chin, complemented with a soft, sexy smile. After the seminar, she found out he was single and began flirting. He asked her out on a dinner date the next evening before his scheduled return flight to Los Alamos. They enjoyed lobster at Lucatelli's Ristorante and talked about their personal lives, their families, and their college degrees over a bottle of Marchesi di Barolo red wine. They hit it off and could both feel the immense physical, emotional, and spiritual chemistry between them. During dinner, she'd made arrangements to travel to Los Alamos the following week for a job interview, but deep down inside, she'd known it was really to see Dan. What became of her visit was a job at the Los Alamos labs, a happy marriage to a highly respected scientist, and two wonderful sons. Their marriage was now going on thirteen years. She finally fell into a deep sleep, dreaming of that memorable time nearly fourteen years ago when they'd first met.

Dan was also reminiscing before he fell asleep. He remembered the nine years he'd spent in college starting at age sixteen. During those years, he'd been awarded a doctorate in astrophysics in 1986 at twenty-three, followed by a doctorate in high-energy particle physics at twenty-five, both from the University of Illinois at Urbana-Champaign. Soon after obtaining his particle physics doctorate, he had become highly sought after by the scientific community, but he'd decided to work for the government at the Los Alamos labs. He'd never imagined that nearly a year after accepting the government job, he would travel to Cornell University to present a seminar that would result in meeting his wife. He remembered the first time he set his eyes on her. He'd thought she was extremely pretty, and her inner being had seemed intoxicating. He'd been surprised she was not married. Knowing he would be waking in less than five hours to go to work, he fell into a sound sleep beside his wife.

✦ ✦ ✦

Michael sat quietly inside his spaceship, not sleepy in the least bit. The Jupiter family had been asleep for quite some time now. Jason and Kyle were already in a level five sleep, drifting in and out of rapid eye movement. Michael's front display showed their fairly smooth multipath electroencephalograph brain wave patterns. Michael realized this REM state of human physiology was also a normal characteristic of the race that had created him—a direct relation to the electrical impulses generated across synaptic cell junctures.

Jason's and Kyle's low-amplitude REM frequencies ranged between 12 and 18 hertz, but the race that had created Michael had much-higher low frequencies. Michael changed his front display from their REM brain wave frequencies to the multitude of radio and television information his ship's advanced receivers had loaded into its data banks soon after powering up, information from not only the United States but the entire planet, from standard broadcasts to secret and top-secret data that his spaceship's computer easily decrypted. Three holographic images were now displayed in front of him, allowing him to learn much about the human race, from its many different cultures and societies, to internal conflicts within the United States and abroad, to conflicts between countries, conflicts of religion, and conflicts of ethnicity. The planet where he came from did not have any of these conflicts. The human race had a long way to go before their many different societies and cultures could attain the same level of peace.

Michael continued to pore through all the data like a supercomputer, soaking up the information like a dry sponge in water, analyzing the physiological, genetic, and scientific advancements of the human race. He quickly understood the level of Earth's technological advancements, in both the private sector and top-secret governmental agencies. He then decided to focus his ship's eavesdropping back on the crash site. He touched one of the holographic images, and his ship's computer spherically extended a teardrop-shaped subspace field nearly 2,800 feet to the northwest, encompassing the military operation. Numerous small lights appeared on his front display, and the computer identified that there were sixty-seven human beings at the site and nine aboard two top-secret Black Hawk helicopters still circling around the site using infrared detectors for any would-be intruders.

His ship's computer also analyzed all the communications and identified the conversation of most interest, a satellite-link conversation between two military officers—a major at the site and a colonel inside a highly secured structure on the East Coast of the United States, located south of Suffolk, Virginia. Displayed on the screen were the two officers full names, ranks, ages, dates of birth, and their entire histories since they'd been alive. Michael was extremely quiet as he listened to their conversation inside the cockpit, especially after his ship's computer registered that their satellite-link communication was using a primitive form of subspace compression.

"Yes, Colonel," the major said. "I talked to General Parker a few hours ago about the small craft we suspect is still in the vicinity of Los Alamos. He told me to put together two high-profile field teams and that we had a Mother Hen protocol of the highest order."

Colonel Peterson paused with the receiver to his ear, as it had been quite a number of years since there had been a Mother Hen protocol—a protocol for when a small ship left a larger ship prior to or after it crashed. Their two field teams would be comprised of highly seasoned, experienced agents, because they were dealing with a highly advanced race. "I understand, Major," Colonel Peterson finally said. "You were correct to call me. I will alert the Pentagon of our situation and have them follow all the proper channels to the governor of New Mexico, the Los Alamos mayor, and all law enforcement agencies so that our field teams have full, unabated authority. I'll brief the president tomorrow."

Major Henderson was quiet after what his boss had told him. He knew their field teams would use their deemed authority, outside the normal laws of the land, ready to act quickly in case the small craft ever crashed or made its presence known to the general public, for it would surely have technologies far more advanced than any they'd encountered to date for a firsthand encounter. "I understand, sir," he finally said. "Talk to you later."

"Goodbye, Major," Colonel Peterson said. He hung up his satellite phone receiver and leaned back in his chair. This incident of extraterrestrial origin near Los Alamos caused him to become extremely mentally alert, even at 5:29 a.m. on the East Coast. General Parker should also be calling him within the hour.

Back aboard the small spaceship, Michael knew he would have to be even more careful now and checked the status of his cloaking field. It was still taking into account all electrically driven motors inside Jason's house, allowing them to function normally. He then noticed the time. Jason would be waking up anytime now.

✦ ✦ ✦

In Jason's bedroom, a buzzing sound suddenly filled the air, as if a hive of irritated bumblebees were looking for someone to sting. Jason immediately opened his heavy-laden eyes and shut off the alarm. It was exactly 3:30 a.m. The time made him feel as though he had not slept at all. He grabbed the communicator. "Michael, are you there?" he called out.

"Yes, Jason, I am here," Michael replied.

Jason was delighted to hear Michael's voice and wondered whether Michael needed sleep. "Is my armband ready?"

"Yes, it is."

"Okay," Jason said. "Open the door to our ship, and I will be there shortly."

"Okay, Jason."

Jason slipped the communicator into his pants and lifted his arms high above his head in a mind-tingling stretch, gaining more of his mental senses. He sat on the side of his bed and slipped on his tennis shoes. After tying the laces, he walked over to the open window, unlatched the screen, and gingerly pushed it open. He climbed feetfirst out onto the windowsill. His feet and legs hanging down, he turned over, positioning his stomach against the sill, and jumped to the ground. The window screen frame fell down and smacked the window with a bang.

Jason was briefly worried that his parents may have heard the noise, but he ignored that possibility, especially after seeing the brightly lit open doorway of the invisible spaceship. Without further hesitation, he hurried toward the spaceship, up the ramp, and all the way inside. When he turned around, the doorway had already disappeared, so he headed straight to the cockpit, where he found Michael sitting in the same copilot seat. Rays of light from the telephone pole security light projected down into their ship through the top domed window. It seemed strange to Jason that he could still see those light rays and everything, as if the ship were not invisible. "Hi, Michael," Jason said.

"Hi, Jason," Michael replied. "Ready for your armband?"

Jason was again excited. "Yes, I am."

"Good. Follow me."

Jason followed Michael to where he'd previously placed his hand inside the organic-matter analyzer. On a table was a small, paper-thin, silver-colored armband that had the exact same number of buttons as Michael's armband. Jason turned to Michael, eager with anticipation. "So that's my armband?"

"Yes, it is," Michael replied.

Jason picked up the armband, which was practically weightless. It was about three inches wide, with six light-brown square buttons about a quarter inch wide on its top. Above those six buttons were ten smaller light-green circular buttons about an eighth inch in diameter. All the buttons were smooth and the same thickness as the armband, which was shaped like a C, as though its ends had been bent outward. The ends were too far apart for the armband to fit securely on his arm. It looked like it would quickly fall off. It made no sense. Jason turned it over, revealing three thin, gold-colored needles on the bottom. They had very sharp points and were about a quarter inch in length, about the same diameter as sewing needles. He knew the needles must have to prick through his skin and finally looked down at Michael. "How exactly are these needles used?"

Michael noticed Jason's slight concern and answered, "They have to pierce the outer layers of your epidermal skin and myelin sheaths, Jason, so that the dorsal radial nerve cells in your arm make electrical contact with the armband. That's the only way your body can be altered like I mentioned earlier and not be affected by planetary magnetic fluctuations."

Jason thought about his response. "Will the needles hurt much?"

"I do not know," Michael said.

Jason was somewhat confused about Michael's answer, and he didn't have the slightest idea how the armband would be able to alter his body. "Okay, do I just stick it on my forearm wherever I want?"

"Yes, you can," Michael said. "It will take around five Earth minutes for it to become fully adjusted to your body's chemistry. That particular armband will also only work for your body and no one else's."

Jason was excited to try out the armband, especially the two functions Michael had mentioned, but he was still curious about the other buttons. "What are the other buttons used for?"

Michael decided to explain a few of the armband's other capabilities, including the two already mentioned. "Touching these two circular buttons on the left side at the same time will activate the invisibility function," he explained, pointing. "Simultaneously touching the two buttons one position over from those two will activate the molecular vibratory function and allow you to walk through objects. Touching the third square button to your left will allow our ship to know exactly where you're located for space transports on or off the ship, in case you do not have your communicator. There are other functions that we can talk about later."

Jason was again amazed. The term *space transport* sounded similar to the transporters used in the television series *Star Trek*. He now wanted to install his armband more than ever. "How do I turn off the functions when I use them?" he asked.

"Touch the original buttons," Michael said.

"Okay, I am going to place it on my arm," Jason said.

Michael remained quiet as Jason slowly and meticulously positioned the armband over his left forearm, about midway between his elbow and wrist. Jason was now hesitant, for fear of the needles, but it did not matter, for as soon as the needles brushed his skin, the armband immediately changed shape, tightening around his forearm and forcing the needles deep into his arm. Jason grimaced. "Ouch!" he said. "That smarted."

Michael analyzed Jason's facial reaction. It was an emotion he did not understand, but he did know what *smarted* meant. "Did you feel pain, Jason?"

"Yes, I did."

"Why?"

Jason was surprised at the question and suddenly realized the pain had subsided. Michael was still waiting for an answer, so Jason explained, "Humans feel pain whenever they are hurt or injured."

Michael analyzed what Jason had told him. He did not recall ever experiencing any pain, but his body did have the physical sensation of touching objects, like pressure on his feet when walking or his butt resting against a seat. He also had mental and emotional sensations, like when talking to Jason, including a feeling of emotions deep inside his chest. "I think I understand what you said, Jason," he finally said. "I know humans are fragile."

Jason was curious about Michael's latest comment and wondered whether Michael had any sensory nerves. "Have you ever felt pain?"

"I do not know," Michael said, "but I do feel myself standing here with a sensation of pressure against my feet. I also feel my fingers touching other objects and can feel wind blowing across my skin."

Jason was again curious about Michael's response and did not fully understand it, especially with Michael being an organic android. Whoever had created Michael must have added feeling receptors across his entire body. Jason glanced down at his wristwatch and realized it had been over five minutes since he'd installed his armband. Experimenting, he touched the two buttons that would allow him to pass through solid objects. With a sense of excitement, he moved his hand quickly toward the tabletop, but it smacked hard on the table's surface. "Ouch!" he said and looked at Michael in confusion. "I thought it only took five minutes to work."

"It does," Michael replied, "but the invisibility function for altering your body's cellular configuration, so that you can even walk through objects, cannot work while inside our spaceship, at least not without special command overrides."

"Why is that?"

Michael noticed Jason's keen interest. "Because the ship controls the functions of the armband and its interfaces with your body while inside this planet's magnetic field. The gravity field inside our spaceship is focused much differently than the planet's."

Jason thought he understood part of that explanation and touched the same two buttons again, shutting off the molecular vibratory function.

Michael continued to stare into Jason's tired face. "You'd better get some sleep," he said.

Jason smiled a little at the fact that his new friend could read his facial expressions. "Okay, I will," he said. "My mom homeschools my little brother and me, so I can pretty much see you anytime during the day, at least after I finish my studies."

"Okay, Jason," Michael said. "See you sometime after sunrise."

Michael touched a button on his armband, and the open doorway suddenly appeared. They both started toward the doorway, but then Jason abruptly stopped. "Good night, Michael," he said.

"Good night, Jason," Michael replied.

Jason walked down the ramp and scampered over to his bedroom window. He briefly turned around, and the doorway into the ship suddenly vanished again before his very eyes, matching the rest of the invisible spaceship. Lifting the screen frame, he jumped up into the windowsill. After struggling a bit, he finally made it back inside while holding the window screen to stop it from banging again, but this caused him to fall down on the floor. The top of his head noisily bumped against his bedside table.

"I'm going to have to move that over a little," he whispered to himself. "I hope I didn't wake Mom and Dad."

He relatched the window screen, removed the communicator from his pants, and placed it in the top drawer of his bedside table. He then removed his tennis shoes and crawled back into bed with his clothes still on, now thinking about the armband and his new abilities. It was exciting to know that in less than eight hours he would have the opportunity to try them out. According to his alarm clock, it was now 4:15 a.m. Realizing how truly late it was, Jason felt tired again, and he closed his eyes, quickly falling into a deep sleep.

# 4

## JASON CONTEMPLATES MICHAEL'S PREDICAMENT

Later that morning, when Jason woke up, the sun was shining into his bedroom. It was a familiar sight from the multitude of sunrises over the years, but it seemed brighter on this particular morning. Looking at his alarm clock, he was surprised to find it was already eleven o'clock, which explained why it was so much brighter, because he did not sleep in that late very often. The number of hours that had passed caused him to wonder about Michael. He rolled out of bed and walked to the window but did not see their spaceship. He then removed the communicator from the top drawer of his bedside table. "Michael?" he said.

There was silence. "Yes, Jason?" Michael finally replied.

Jason felt relieved hearing Michael's voice. "Are you still beside the house?"

"Yes, I am," Michael said. "Your dad left for work at six thirty, and at seven o'clock your mom walked to the road, picked up the *Los Alamos Monitor* newspaper, and then returned inside. She read the newspaper at the kitchen table while drinking a cup of coffee."

Jason grinned at the fact that Michael was keeping track of his parents. "Well, I had better eat breakfast. My mom is helping me with geometry today. I will talk to you later. Okay?"

"Okay, Jason. Talk to you later."

Jason placed the communicator in his jeans and stared up at the wall calendar directly above his bed. The picture for this month—September 2003—was a nice photograph of two gray wolves standing next to each other, surrounded by evergreen trees and lush vegetation. The wolves were staring directly into the camera lens, more than likely keeping a watchful eye on the photographer. Jason's birthday had been nearly a month ago, on August 8. His birthday party had been lots of fun. The kids of some of his dad's coworkers had come over to help him celebrate, and he'd received a lot of presents. Today was Tuesday, September 9, so Michael had become Jason's new friend exactly one month after his birthday.

Jason grabbed some fresh underwear from his dresser and headed straight to the bathroom attached to his bedroom. Stripping down, he stared at the armband on his left forearm. He did not know how to remove it but figured it was probably waterproof, so he jumped into the tub, closed the shower door, and turned on the water. The armband repelled the water as if it were coated in Teflon. Strangely, the water seemed to jump off of its surface. Considering this, Jason wondered whether Michael had ever bathed. He'd never seen any perspiration on Michael's forehead, but then, the environment aboard the ship seemed perfect, extremely comfortable, with a feel of mind-warming humidity.

Jason finished his quick shower, dried off, slipped into his new underwear, and then returned to his bedroom. After he was dressed in his same jeans, a new pair of socks, and a new short-sleeved shirt, he sat down on the side of his bed. He tied his shoelaces while staring at the armband and then stood up with a small sigh. His mother would probably think it strange that he would be wearing anything other than the wristwatch she and his dad had bought him for his birthday. He finally exited his bedroom. He figured his little brother was already up and around, and sure enough, when he entered the kitchen, he found his mom holding his little brother and reading a book to him.

Barbara paused when Jason entered the kitchen and showed him a kind, relaxed smile, especially considering how worried he had made her feel last night. He was also getting up kind of late, but she didn't say anything about it. "Did you sleep well, Jason?" she calmly asked.

Jason recognized the kindness in his mom's voice. "Yes, I did, Mom," he said. "I slept very well."

"Good," she said. "Want some Cream of Wheat, eggs, and toast?"

"Cream of Wheat is fine, Mom."

Barbara immediately noticed the unusual-looking, finely detailed thin armband on his left forearm. "Can you read to your little brother while I start your breakfast?"

"Okay," Jason answered and walked over to the kitchen table. His mom stood up and placed a small, motherly kiss against his lips. Jason willingly returned the kiss and then sat down at the table while she handed him his little brother. Holding his little brother, he stared at the children's book his mother had been reading. It was intended for at least an eight-year-old, but then, his parents had taught him and his little brother to start reading at a very young age. In fact, it was not just reading skills but also math, sciences, and general education. His mom had helped him with trigonometry and Algebra II in last semester's homeschooling course that had ended in May. He was now getting ready to learn some geometry.

✦ ✦ ✦

Inside the spaceship, Michael listened intently to Jason's conversation with his mother before she started his breakfast. He could tell from the small, subtle changes in her voice that she was still relieved her son was okay—even after he had slept in the house the rest of the night. This was something Michael did not quite understand. Why would she still have a feeling of relief after the events of the night before were over? He continued to analyze her emotions and tried to understand it but found he could not. He wondered again about who had created him and whether they were worried about his welfare—his mother and father, as Jason had told him, the ones who had given him the energy to function. He tried again with all his might to remember who they were or what they even looked like, but he found no memories of them whatsoever. He strangely knew about the race that had created him, including the fact that they had a bodily appearance and a biophysical stature very similar to the human race on Earth, but even they seemed like a distant dream.

Michael now listened to Jason reading to his little brother while their mother cooked two eggs in a skillet. His ship's sensors found the temperature of the stove's burner to be 389 degrees Fahrenheit—according to Earth's temperature scale. Michael knew the human race had determined that water boiled and started to turn into steam at 212 degrees Fahrenheit and froze at 32 degrees Fahrenheit. By what his ship's computer was telling him, the human race had not yet come to understand the exact molecular bond paths between the hydrogen and oxygen molecules and why they formed crystalline structures in specific six-fold hexagonal symmetry, but the two-scale temperature range between hot and cold and the associated advanced sciences still intrigued him. The only temperature he had experienced was the surface of the seat he was sitting on, the front console as he touched it with his fingertips, and the control wheel as he grabbed it with both hands. He had never endured either of the temperature extremes—at least not that he could remember.

His ship's sensors had detected the stove's burner was now cooling down, and he heard a beeping sound from a radiation-powered device humans called a microwave oven. It was the same sound he had heard earlier in the morning for Kyle's Cream of Wheat cereal. His ship's sensors again detected the heating elements of a toaster. Suddenly, a spring actuated, and two pieces of toasted wheat bread popped up vertically out of rectangular slots. These primitive devices were intriguing. He then heard Jason's mother open and close the microwave oven door. By what his front console was now telling him, based on what his ship's sensors had detected, she was carrying a bowl of Cream of Wheat cereal, two eggs, and buttered toast on a small plate over to the kitchen table where Jason was still holding his little brother. She placed the food down in front of Jason and then picked Kyle back up in her arms. "Thank you, Jason, for reading to your brother," she said. "Here's your late breakfast."

Michael continued to listen with keen interest to everything said inside the house.

✦ ✦ ✦

At the table, Jason stared at his hot, steaming Cream of Wheat, the two pieces of toast, and the two eggs over easy—just the way he liked them. He had a glass of milk and a jar of grape jelly in front of him as well. He finally began his breakfast by first cutting one of his eggs in half. His mom sat down across from him, holding his little brother. Jason wondered whether Michael had ever eaten anything. He wished there was some easy way he could introduce Michael to his parents. It made Jason sad that Michael did not know who had actually created him, his mom and dad.

Barbara looked up from the children's book and again noticed the unusual-looking armband. Jason was also daydreaming with a somber look. "Jason," she finally asked, "where were you all those hours last night?"

Her question snapped him out of his daydream, and he paused while staring up into her eyes. "I was watching the military clean up that crashed ship," he said truthfully.

Barbara was concerned, especially after what Dan had told her, but then, she was also taking Jason's usage of "crashed ship" to mean an Earth-based military aircraft. "You shouldn't have been near that," she said. "Your dad told me that military guards stopped him when he approached the site and told him to stay away because an aircraft carrying radioactive material had crashed."

Jason quietly acknowledged the falsehood the military had told his father, except for the fact there probably really was radioactive material. He thought about what had really happened—the existence of a large cargo ship from an entirely different galaxy. He also thought about Michael, who had been secretly hidden away in a compartment aboard a smaller ship in the cargo bay. He just could not get it off his mind that Michael was inside a cloaked spaceship in very close proximity to their house. He had an urge to tell his mom everything at that very moment, but what he'd heard the secret military talking about last night worried him. *Would she have to tell the government about Michael and our spaceship?* He thought. *Would the government then take Michael and our spaceship away, for me to never see him again?*

That possibility caused him to stay quiet about what had transpired, including his meeting Michael. His parents being aware of the existence of Michael and the small spaceship might cause them undue burden, not only because of the military, but also because of their top-secret security clearances, especially since the government was their employer. He placed a spoonful of Cream of Wheat in his mouth and continued his silence.

On the other side of the table, Barbara noticed that Jason was not volunteering additional information about what he might have seen at the crash site. She knew there had to be more behind it, especially since Dan had told her there were armed military guards. Jason must have been secretly hidden away the entire time. "Jason," she said, "do not ever worry us like that again, and do not approach any crashed aircraft without first telling your dad or me. Otherwise, you may end up grounded for a month."

Jason thought about her warning. "Okay, Mom," he said. "I will never do it again."

Barbara believed her oldest son and decided not to say any more about it, at least not while he was eating breakfast. She looked again at his unusual-looking armband. She wondered where he'd gotten it. It was extremely thin, had a lot of square and round buttons, and looked to be of high quality. Jason might have made it, but it looked too realistic and had the appearance of being finely detailed metal.

Jason was relieved she did not ask any more about the events of last night, as it might have placed him in an awkward situation of trying to keep Michael and his small spaceship secret. He did notice his mother glancing at his armband, so he ate breakfast a little faster than normal, just in case she did start asking more questions. He sipped his milk, using his left arm out of habit, openly exposing the device firmly encircling his forearm. He hoped she would not ask about the armband, because he did not know how to take it off to show it to her.

As he took another bite of his Cream of Wheat, his mother began reading to his little brother again. He glanced briefly at his armband, admiring it. It was a very unusual piece of advanced alien technology. The luminous silver armband was so thin that it practically matched the surface of his skin. He knew it had to look strange to his mom, especially for it to have so many buttons on such a thin device, but then, the armband was nothing compared to his traveling at Mach 10 from Nebraska back to Los Alamos. What speed they'd traveled at to reach Nebraska originally, he had no idea, but it had to be much faster.

Jason finished his breakfast, gulped his milk down to the last drop, and began staring at his mother, who was still reading to his little brother. She had done the same with him when he was that age. "I'm headed to my room to grab the geometry book, Mom," he said.

Barbara looked up from the children's book and thought about how smart her oldest son was becoming at the young age of ten. She knew he really liked math and the sciences, something she and Dan had stressed and taught to him at a very young age. "Okay, Jason," she said. After he stood up, she began staring again at his armband with even more interest.

Recognizing this, Jason quickly picked up his dishes and carried them over to the sink. He rinsed them off, dried his hands, and walked back over to his mother with appreciation. "Thanks for breakfast, Mom," he said.

Jason's kindness made Barbara feel good. "You're welcome, Jason," she said.

Jason smiled a little and quickly left the kitchen without giving her a chance to ask about the armband. He returned to his bedroom, closing the door behind him. He knew Michael had probably been listening to everything, and he was eager to contact his new friend. He sat down on his bed, removed the communicator from his jeans, and let out a deep sigh. "Michael?" he said.

It was quiet inside his room. "Yes, Jason?" Michael finally replied.

Jason sighed again. "I am going to be studying geometry for the next few hours or so," he said. "I will see you later this afternoon. Okay?"

"Okay, Jason. I will be right here."

"Okay. Bye."

"Bye, Jason."

Jason slipped the communicator back into his pants, antsy to return to their spaceship and fly around again with Michael, but he had to be patient. After all, he had lots of time. He reached over to the bedside table and picked up the Prentice Hall high school geometry book he had just started looking at a few days ago. It was actually a neat-looking book, especially with the sleek, futuristic blue car on the front cover. At the bottom of the cover were the words "New Tools for a Changing World," and across the center was the formula $A=\pi r^2$. He knew about that formula from his trigonometry schooling. He set the book down and grabbed his notebook, opening it to the written set of instructions and assignments from his mother. He carried both the notebook and the textbook out to the living room. He was the only one in the living room, so he sat down in one of the soft chairs and opened the book to page 12, section 1-2 of chapter 1.

This chapter was about points, lines, and planes, as well as connecting points of an object. It gave the constellation Leo the Lion as an example—a constellation composed of ten stars. Jason grinned a little since Leo was his zodiac sign. It was as if the book were written especially for him. He read over the "Think and Discuss" section that defined a point, space, and line, even though he already understood their scientific notations. He understood the collinear and coplanar concepts and turned to page 14, which mentioned the four basic postulates for points, lines, and planes. He found this material interesting. He finally opened the notebook to see what set of exercise problems his mom had assigned from pages 15 and 16. He would have to get at least 85 percent of the exercise problems correct, or he would have to do the assignment over again with a new set of problems created by his mother. She had done that in the past in other courses, but Jason was not going to let it happen today, as it would cause him to see Michael even later in the day. Grabbing his pencil, he worked through exercise problem numbers 1, 3, and 5 on her list, becoming entranced in his studies.

Barbara walked into the living room carrying Kyle, and Jason looked up. She set Kyle down on the floor, and he quickly headed in Jason's direction, climbed up into his chair, and sat next to him, staring with fascination at his open textbook. Jason knew his little brother was already studying second-grade arithmetic. He gave Kyle a little hug, because he knew how much his brother admired and looked up to him.

Barbara sat down in a chair across from her two sons, feeling good inside after seeing Jason's affection toward his little brother. She picked up the September issue of *Discover* magazine and opened it to the index. One of the articles—"They Came from Outer Space: Does the Very Existence of Cosmic Rays Defy the Laws of Physics?"—sounded interesting, so she flipped to page 44.

Barbara began reading the article but then paused, looking over at her two boys. Jason's armband was starting to become even more of a mystery, especially since it was paper thin and had a metallic appearance. She was pretty certain Jason could not have made it, but she decided not to ask about it while he was studying his geometry, as it would be a distraction.

✦ ✦ ✦

On the spaceship, Michael listened as Jason asked his mother a question about problem 17 and she answered his question with a question of her own, prompting two-way communication between them.

He was Intrigued with this mother-to-son interaction. He could tell Jason's mother was much more educated than Jason, but what they were talking about was extremely elementary. That fact caused him to realize again the multitude of advanced sciences he understood. He knew humans had to study and learn at a young age to gain knowledge and understanding as they grew older. He did not know why he had such a vast knowledge of sciences that encompassed an array of fields—quantum gravity, faster-than-light compression schemes, subspace, a multitude of cloaking technologies, advanced particle and quantum physics, and even molecular and physical biology, both real and quantum. He still could not remember who had created him or for what purpose. Jason was the first carbon-based living being he'd met upon opening his eyes for the first time after what had seemed a long sleep. Strangely, he could remember the galaxy and planet from which he'd originated, but he still could not remember any actual living beings from the planet. He knew names and people from its history, but they all seemed like a figment of his imagination. While listening to Barbara's kindness toward Jason, he felt a warm, reverberating feeling inside his chest toward her that he did not quite understand.

✦ ✦ ✦

Inside the house, Jason was working on the last problem on his mother's list—number 46. He had to determine if the points (0, 0), (0, 3), (0, –10) were collinear by graphing them. He had just started the graph. The point (0, 0) was a single point; the point (0, 3) caused a line to the right, from 0 to 3; and the point (0, –10) caused a line to the left, from 0 to –10. After he had graphed the points, Jason saw right away that they were collinear, because they all fell along the axis of 0. He wrote "Yes!" next to the graph and explained, in a scientific manner, exactly why they were collinear, because it would give him extra brownie points. After finishing his detailed explanation, he looked down at his little brother, who was now playing with a small toy spaceship on the floor. Jason grinned a little, because he had a full-size spaceship to play with, including an armband that looked like a toy but certainly was not. He then looked over at his mother, who was quietly reading a book. After writing his name and date at the top of each page, he slowly walked over to his mother and handed her the completed exercise problems. "Here, Mom," he said. "I know I aced it."

"You did, huh?" she replied with a grin.

"Yep," Jason said.

Barbara took his completed assignment, knowing that he did ace it if he said so. "Thanks, Jason."

Thinking about Michael and the spaceship next to their house, as well as the special capabilities of his armband, Jason said, "I am going outside for a few hours, okay, Mom?"

"Okay," Barbara replied.

She glanced down at his armband, which wrapped at least 240 degrees around his forearm. Jason walked away in a hurry before she could ask about it. She might want to see it, and he still did not know how to remove it. It was much too tight, and it definitely could not be turned, especially because of the three gold needles punctured deep into his arm.

Jason opened the front door to the sun shining brightly in a partly cloudy sky. As he shut the door behind him, he realized his little brother must be entranced with his toy spaceship. Otherwise, he would have surely followed. Jason turned to his right and continued east across the porch and down the steps. Looking toward the southeast, he could not see the cloaked spaceship but knew it had to be there, hidden to everyone else. He walked south, staying as close as possible to the side of the house, because he would surely bump into the ship otherwise, like running into a brick wall.

After he had cleared the ship, he continued south toward one of their wooden barns, knowing Michael was probably watching him. He glanced briefly to his right at the six-foot-tall cedar fence that encompassed their large one-hundred-by-two-hundred-foot backyard. His father had installed the fence about ten years ago, mainly because of their in-ground swimming pool. The pool had a small slide and a diving board, and Jason had lots of fun swimming around in it almost every day this summer. His parents used the pool as a bargaining chip whenever they wanted something done or a chore completed, as the threat of being grounding and not allowed in the pool was worse than any spanking and something that he did not let happen.

Jason continued toward the barn, noticing the old metal weather vane on the northern peak of the roof. The rooster weather vane's arrow was currently pointing toward the north due to a light breeze blowing in from the north. The rustic-colored barn had been on the land when his parents bought the 640 acres. There had also been an existing old farmhouse, which his parents had replaced with a newly built ranch-style house. Since that all had happened before he was born, he knew his parents had already been planning to start a family and raise their children on the property. Their house faced slightly northeast, so they could all sit on the front deck porch together and enjoy the beautiful sunrises. The sunsets were also magnificent, with soft rays of light against the forest trees. Jason spent a lot of time on the front porch, watching the stars at night, daydreaming about the chance to visit them someday. After what had happened last night, those dreams could now become a reality.

Jason finally stopped in front of the barn and thought about his armband's capabilities. His heart sped up slightly, because he was about to see what it was like to walk through a solid object. He was still curious how Earth's gravity might affect him, since the molecules of his body would surely not be as rigid as the barn's wood siding. After looking down at the armband, he lifted his arm and, with two fingers, touched the appropriate buttons. Nothing appeared different, and the barn still looked the same. He was also not sinking down into the soil, so there must be safeguards in place for that not to happen. When he turned back around, he could see his house and the cedar fence, but he still could not see the spaceship. "Strange," he mumbled to himself and turned back to the barn. He walked toward it but then stopped again.

"Okay, here I go," he whispered. He walked directly into the wall, expecting to bounce off of it, but he continued straight through it. He found himself standing inside the barn, the sun shining through small cracks and crevices between the barn's wood siding. He had successfully walked through the solid wood wall! In the experience, he'd walked from out of the sunlight into the barn's dark interior, and his pupils were still trying to adjust to the sudden change. He walked toward the wall a second time and traveled straight through to the other side into the shining sunlight. He squinted, his eyes having to adjust to the brightness. "That is so strange," he said out loud.

He touched the same buttons, shutting off the armband's vibratory function, and next touched the two buttons for invisibility. The sunlight changed, seeming brighter. It was as if the sunlight were now passing through his body, yet he did not have to squint. *Hmmm,* he thought, *this is also strange. I wonder what it would be like to be invisible and walk through objects at the same time.*

Jason glanced over in the direction of the spaceship and still could not see it. *So what does that mean?* Jason asked himself. *What is invisible, especially in relation to the ship's cloaking field?* He wondered if he would still appear invisible if he was on the spaceship. He would definitely be asking Michael that exact question.

Jason knew Michael probably had seen him disappear, but he thought about maybe trying to surprise him with his invisibility. Then the thought of playing a game on his mother was all he could imagine. He headed back toward the house to test out his cloak of invisibility, again staying as close as possible to the house.

He stopped at the front door and knocked three times, his heartbeat speeding up a little. He stepped back a few feet. He still did not know if he was really invisible, but he stood quietly smiling nevertheless.

About ten seconds later, his mother opened the door, took one step outside, and looked around but saw no one in sight. She was at first confused but then shook her head a little with a small smile. She figured Jason had run off the porch and hidden. She closed the door.

On the porch, Jason giggled, as his invisibility had worked perfectly. "This invisibility is great," he mumbled to himself. "I bet people can still hear me walking, though. I will have to be careful with that."

Jason headed back across the porch and down the stairs. He removed the communicator from his jeans when in close proximity to their spaceship. "Michael?" he called out.

"Yes, Jason?" Michael replied.

"I am returning to the ship."

"Okay. I will open the door for you."

About five feet away, an open doorway and a ramp suddenly appeared. Jason figured there must be strange gravity manipulations going on for what he was now witnessing between the spaceship and his cloak of invisibility. He walked up the ramp, quietly as possible, hoping to surprise Michael. Once he was inside, the door reappeared behind him. He continued to where Michael was sitting in the same copilot seat. Michael suddenly turned around, staring directly at him. "Hi, Jason," he said.

Jason was surprised. "Are you also invisible with your armband?"

"No," Michael replied.

"How are you able to see me, then?" Jason asked.

Michael continued to stare at Jason. "Remember what I said earlier about using the armbands inside our ship?"

Jason remembered what Michael had told him about the armbands' functions for altering the host body and their not working inside the spaceship, because the spaceship controlled those functions. "Yes, I remember," he answered, understanding he was not invisible while inside their spaceship. "Were you able to see me when I was outside the ship?"

"No, I couldn't," Michael said, "but I could have easily adjusted the ship's cloaking field if I wanted, and you would have then been completely visible."

Jason was amazed to hear this and touched the same two armband buttons to shut off the invisibility function. He now wanted to know more about how he'd been able to walk through objects so easily. "So when I used the armband to walk through objects," he said, "what stopped me from sinking down into the ground from gravity, as surely my body was not of solid matter anymore?"

Michael thought about Jason's good question. "Because," he answered, "like I told you before, the ship controls the armband's functions. As a result, the ship polarized both the molecules on Earth's surface and the molecules of your body to match. Since the molecules of your body still had molecular cohesion and the molecules on the bottom of your feet were repelling the planet, it was impossible for you to ever sink down toward the center of the planet."

Jason somewhat understood and sat down in the captain's chair. He glanced at his wristwatch. His father would not be home from work for at least two more hours. The thought of how much fun it had been flying around in their spaceship last night came to mind. "How about we fly around for a little while? I would like to learn more about this spaceship."

"Okay, Jason," Michael replied.

# 5

## A JOYRIDE IN THE SPACESHIP

Michael grabbed his control wheel and tilted it up and away from his body. The spaceship quickly accelerated away in a northerly direction, as evidenced by the fact Jason's house suddenly disappeared from his side window. Jason's front display registered an altitude of five thousand feet as they continued to rise toward the north. Michael finally let loose of the control wheel, and their spaceship stopped, hovering north of Los Alamos at an altitude of eighteen thousand feet. Michael noticed the amazed, excited look on Jason's face. "Okay, Jason, it's your turn to fly," he said.

Jason, flushed with additional excitement, firmly grabbed his control wheel with both hands. He now knew that pushing the control wheel forward made their ship accelerate forward, pulling it toward him made it accelerate backward, pushing it to his left away from him made it accelerate forward in a left bank, and pushing it to his right away from him made it accelerate forward in a right bank. Pulling up on the wheel made their ship rise, and pushing down caused it to drop.

Jason pushed his control wheel nearly five inches forward and slightly to the right at the same time. Their spaceship quickly accelerated toward the northeast at an immense speed. Looking at his display, he was amazed to see they were already traveling 80,000 miles per hour! He pushed the control wheel forward a little more, taking them up to 120,000 miles per hour! Jason was absolutely flabbergasted at the speed of their ship. His concept of speed was his parents' Lincoln Navigator traveling at eighty miles per hour on the interstate. He was thoroughly amazed and curious how many high-altitude sonic booms their ship might have just created in greatly surpassing the speed of sound many times over.

"The speed of this spaceship is almost inconceivable," Jason said, staring at Michael. "What will everyone down below think after all the sonic booms that were just created?"

"They won't hear a thing," Michael said. "This ship creates an atmospheric gravity vacuum in front of its direction of travel and then quickly fills in the backside with an atmospheric gravity pressure wake, as though traveling on ice and inside a vacuum of pressurized space."

Jason thought about Michael's explanation. "That is interesting," he said. "I think I somewhat understand."

Michael remained quiet as Jason continued to hold his control wheel forward. They were traveling northeast at a velocity that would soon have them leaving the United States and entering Canada. Though Jason didn't realize it, his sudden acceleration had caused their ship to uncloak before quickly reacquiring Earth's magnetic field lines to maintain its inverse polarity field.

Jason finally let loose of his control wheel, and their ship quickly slowed until their speed was zero. He grabbed the control wheel again with both hands and pushed straight down, putting their ship into a dead drop. He paid extremely close attention to their altitude—six thousand feet … three thousand feet … two thousand feet … one thousand feet—and finally let loose of the control wheel. Their ship quickly decelerated and hovered in place. Jason was thrilled. Their ship had just dropped nearly seventeen thousand feet in what had to be just a few seconds, yet he had not felt a single negative gravity force like you would experience aboard a roller coaster or an airplane dropping out of the sky from an air pocket.

Michael continued to analyze Jason's excitement. Jason apparently understood the dangers of altitude loss, but Michael also knew their ship's computer would have taken command of the ship if it had detected a dangerous flight condition, like an impact to the planet.

Jason grabbed his control wheel again and pulled it evenly to his left. Their ship rotated counterclockwise. By the time Jason let go, their ship had rotated seventy-five times, according to the front display, yet Jason did not feel dizzy in the least bit. The control wheels were very sensitive. He looked over at Michael, amazed. "I think I understand somewhat how to control this ship," he said.

"Yes, you're doing pretty well," Michael said. "Do you know how to return to Los Alamos?"

Because their ship had just rotated dozens of times, Jason actually had no idea which direction to go, especially since it was midday and the sun's position did not offer very many clues. "I do not know, Michael," he admitted. "I've lost my sense of bearings."

"Look at your front display," Michael said. "Your house's magnetic field location is now in our ship's data banks."

On Jason's display was a picture of Earth, including its magnetic field configuration, as though their ship's computer had been listening to them, but what he saw did not make any sense. "I do not understand the display, Michael," he admitted.

"Right here," Michael explained, pointing, "is the equator of Earth, dividing its magnetic dipole field into north and south halves." Michael paused to see Jason listening intently and continued, "Since your Earth uses Greenwich, England, for its solar time base reference, our ship's computer, at least for this planet, will also use it as a vertical magnetic-zero time base. As a result, your planet will now have a zero magnetic reference, in relation to our ship's computer to any point on Earth, in both longitudinal and latitudinal bearings, according to the north and south poles, which are considered vertical zero points, and Greenwich, England, which is also a vertical zero point. In other words, Jason, our spaceship's computer will instantly know all vertical and horizontal magnetic field strength inclinations and declinations across the entire surface of your planet, using a triangulation of three points and two lines, even as its magnetic north pole fluctuates in an elliptical pattern of up to twenty-two degrees from its rotational axis."

Michael clearly understood a lot about Earth planetary sciences, even if it was less than twenty-four hours ago that he'd first become conscious. "That is amazing," Jason said.

Michael pointed down at Jason's screen a second time and further explained, "As a result, this spaceship knows exactly how far your house is from the vertical zero line through Greenwich, England; the horizontal zero line of the equator; and the north and south poles, depending on which half of the planet you're located. Because of our ship's magnetic vector computation capabilities, your house will now have east-to-west and north-to-south magnetic field vectors, plus a magnetic field strength vector in direct relation to Earth's equator that our advanced gravity technologies then nullify through Earth's lines of force and their toroidal movements."

Michael was giving Jason a crash course on some type of magnetic field celestial navigation he had never heard about—even from his father. "I think I understand some of what you're saying," he said.

As Michael stared over at Jason, a warm sensation filled his chest, as though Jason had been his friend his entire life. In reality, Jason really had been his friend for as long as he could remember, which was less than fifteen Earth hours. Even if their meeting in the first place had been a mistake, their friendship was one that could never be broken. "You can let this ship fly itself back to your house if you want," he said.

Jason raised his eyebrows. "Oh, really, so it is kind of like autopilot, huh?"

Michael analyzed Jason's *autopilot* terminology. "Sort of," he answered. "Our ship's computer calculates the most efficient magnetic field path to where you want to travel and will then automatically take us there."

"Where's that button?"

Michael leaned over again and pointed to a blue-and-green touch button on Jason's display. "Right there," he said. "It will activate once you've entered a magnetic zero point coordinate or a location that is already in our ship's computer."

Jason also noticed their ship's current magnetic field coordinates and vectors were displayed on his front screen, but he did not fully understand many of the strange values. What he did recognize were the longitudinal and latitudinal values for their current location, which indicated their ship had to be somewhat north of the United States, possibly somewhere in Ontario, Canada, north of Michigan and Lake Huron. He finally looked back to Michael, again curious. "How do I display the magnetic field coordinates of my house?"

"Your house is listed under 'Captain, Jason Jupiter,'" Michael answered.

Jason grinned, as Michael must have entered his house that way into their ship's data banks. After he touched the blue-and-green button, sure enough, his name was displayed. He touched his name on the screen, and another blue-and-green button now showed. "Is that all there is?"

"Yes," Michael said.

Jason touched the second blue-and-green button, and their ship rotated counterclockwise 145 degrees and quickly accelerated along a sixty-degree southwestern vector. They would return to Los Alamos within minutes at their current speed.

Their current velocity was 23,000 miles per hour, and they were still at an altitude of 1,000 feet. Next to the imperial units were the metric values—37,000 kilometers per hour and an altitude of 305 meters. Jason was amazed their ship could travel so fast and noticed

Michael was now kind of quiet. "Can you display a map for our current location in the United States?"

"Yes, I can," Michael said. "Do you want it on our front screens or as a holographic image we can both view?"

Jason was again thrilled. "How about a holographic image?"

"Okay," Michael said and touched his front display.

Suddenly, a flat holographic image, nearly three feet long by two feet tall, appeared directly in front of them, displaying Nebraska, Kansas, Oklahoma, Iowa, Colorado, Texas, New Mexico, as well as parts of the adjoining states. Their ship was shown on the holograph as a small blue dot, moving across the display at an extremely fast rate. They had already exited Nebraska and entered northwestern Kansas, and they were about to cross into the eastern plains of Colorado.

Through the cockpit windows, Jason could clearly see the Rocky Mountains in the far distance. "Look over there, Michael," he said, pointing. "Those are the Colorado Rocky Mountains."

Michael stared at the mountains and surmised they were called *Rocky* because they were either solid rock or rocky in shape. "They are magnificent, Jason."

Jason was a little surprised at Michael's comment. "How about we admire them for a while?"

"Okay," Michael said. He pulled back slightly on his control wheel and then let go. The ship's autopilot system disengaged, and they quickly slowed to a stop in what seemed a matter of seconds. They both now gazed at the mountains about ninety miles west of their spaceship. The peaks were much higher than their spaceship's current altitude, and Jason felt an overwhelming urge to view them up close. "How about we fly over the mountains?"

"Okay," Michael said. "Do you want me to fly the ship or you?"

"How about I fly it?" Jason replied.

"Okay," Michael said.

Jason grab his control wheel with both hands. He nudged it a little, pulling it back to his right, and then let go. Their ship rotated clockwise, facing due west, so that the Rocky Mountains were directly in their line of sight. Jason gripped his control wheel as though holding on to the steering wheel of a dragster, ready for a quarter-mile race. He then pushed the control wheel forward while lifting up, because they would need to rise above the mountains. Their ship quickly accelerated toward the west at ten thousand miles per hour while their altitude increased at about a half mile (2,600 feet) per second.

Jason, like before, did not feel any acceleration forces whatsoever as they moved quickly toward the mountain range. The mountains were magnificent, even as they approached them at over three miles per second. All Jason could do was to continue staring at the mountains and the flat holographic map displayed in front of them. Less than thirty seconds later, they were already passing over the easternmost peaks, so he pulled back on the control wheel and slowed their ship to five hundred miles per hour. They cruised over the top of the first mountains. There was ice and snow on the highest caps—similar to upside-down snow cones. According to their holographic display, the mountaintops were 1,250 feet below them.

A momentary red light flashed on Michael's front screen when Jason slowed their ship from ten thousand to five hundred miles per hour. It meant their ship's countermeasures had temporarily broken down, uncloaking the ship before the ship's computer quickly reacquired Earth's magnetic field and then recloaked. It was a direct result of decelerating too quickly, but Michael didn't say a word to Jason, even after their ship was also briefly radiated by powerful Earth-based radars near Colorado Springs and registered electronic inflections from orbiting satellites.

Jason finally let go of his control wheel, and a new holographic map appeared, showing Colorado and the major surrounding cities within a sixty-mile radius. Jason recognized Colorado Springs, which was 55.5 miles to their northeast, because the US government facility NORAD command was near that town. He turned to Michael with an exhilarated feeling. "This is fun," he said.

Michael briefly analyzed Jason's term *fun*. Though he knew what it meant, he did not think he had ever experienced it until now. Flying over the mountaintops had seemed to give him an invigorated feeling inside. He continued to stare directly over at Jason. "What do you want to do now?"

It had already been over an hour since Jason left his house, and his mother might have gone outside looking for him. If that was the case, she might be wondering where he was hiding, especially if she had been calling for him. "We'd better return home," he said.

"Okay," Michael said.

Jason looked up again at the holographic map and saw Canon City 15.125 miles north of their position. The Royal Gorge Bridge was near that town, and it reminded him of the time two years ago when his parents had taken him and his little brother to see it while on summer vacation. He thought about flying there, passing over the bridge and looking down at the Arkansas River over a thousand feet below them, a vantage point he'd never believed possible, but he realized he had better return before his father arrived home. Grabbing the control wheel again, he pulled it back toward his left slightly, and their ship rotated counterclockwise nearly ninety degrees. They now faced directly south. He pushed his control wheel forward, and they quickly accelerated toward New Mexico at over forty-one thousand miles per hour, while maintaining an altitude of fifteen thousand feet.

Michael again saw the momentary red light on his display and turned to Jason. "Do not overshoot Los Alamos," he said.

Jason knew Michael's warning was smart, because at their current speed of over eleven miles per second, they would enter the airspace of New Mexico in less than eight seconds and it would only take seven seconds after they crossed the border to fly right by Los Alamos. He glanced at the holographic map, which was still listing cities within a sixty-mile radius of their spaceship. Los Alamos was fifty-five miles to the southwest, mostly west of their position, so he let loose of his control wheel. Their ship suddenly slowed until coming to a complete stop.

Again grabbing his control wheel, he pulled it slightly back to his right, and their ship rotated clockwise until pointing due west. He pushed the control wheel forward again, and they quickly sped off toward Los Alamos, accelerating to a velocity of eight thousand miles per hour in a split second. Jason stared at the holograph, watching their ship move across the map, the map also moving within the image. The map appeared to have unusual three-dimensional depth. To his surprise, Los Alamos had a green dot, different from the rest of the cities, as if their ship had designated it a point of reference. Jason turned to Michael, amazed. "How did you do that?"

"I didn't," Michael said. "The ship's computer designated it as our home base."

After traveling west for less than thirty seconds, they were within ten miles of Los Alamos. Since they were traveling over two miles per second, Jason let loose of his control wheel, not wanting to overshoot his house. Their ship quickly came to a complete stop, hovering in place two and a half miles east of Los Alamos. Jason could see the town in the far distance. He pushed down hard on his control wheel, and the ship quickly dropped at a rate of six thousand miles per hour straight down. He felt the ship override the pressure on his control wheel, suddenly stopping at an altitude of five hundred feet. He suddenly realized that he had dropped much too quickly, so the ship's computer had completely overridden his control wheel. "This ship is amazing," he said, thrilled.

"Yes, it is," Michael agreed. "It has a full complement of fail-safe measures."

Jason looked through his side window and saw the Los Alamos Highway (State Road 502) just to their south as it traveled straight through Los Alamos and ended at State Road 501—a north-south blacktop. He also saw aircraft to their south taking off and landing at the Los Alamos Airport. This caused him to wonder whether the military had removed all traces of the cargo ship. He turned back to Michael with immense curiosity and said, "Let's go back to the crash site."

Michael knew that, like before, their ship had been momentarily radiated numerous times by Earth-based radar on their trip back to Los Alamos because Jason had accelerated and decelerated their ship too quickly. The military would now be trying to vector their ship from those sporadic radar signatures. "Okay," Michael said, "but I will guide the ship this time."

Jason did not disagree. Like a master, Michael grabbed his own control wheel and pushed it forward slightly. They quickly accelerated up to 1,500 miles per hour within only a few seconds, their ship remaining cloaked 100 percent of the time.

They flew by Jason's house and the two barns and then approached the crash site. Sure enough, the cargo ship was completely gone. Michael let loose of his control wheel, and their ship came to a complete stop, hovering directly over the crash site at an altitude of five hundred feet. There were still a few military vehicles parked nearby, including two flatbed semitrailers, a bulldozer and loader, and two dump trucks. A few military personnel dressed in green camouflage were walking around carrying what appeared to be metal detectors, Geiger counters, and strange detectors of some kind that Jason did not recognize.

Michael knew most of the instruments were Geiger counters but was somewhat surprised a few were uniquely shielded, highly directional high-energy radio frequency generators, able to ping for fragments or items from the spaceship not detectable by normal metal detectors or Geiger counters. These advanced detectors were ahead of Earth's twenty-first-century scientific advancements, but Michael gave no more thought to how the US military might have acquired the technology. As the military cleaned up the area, the only evidence of an object falling out of the sky and a ship ever being there was some smashed and broken trees. Quite a number of the oak and piñon trees, as well as surrounding shrubbery, had been destroyed, some broken off like toothpicks. There was also a small crater where the ship had come to a stop, but the bulldozer was covering this up and leveling the ground, even pushing some of the damaged trees into large piles. Jason and Michael continued to watch in quiet fascination as the military removed all evidence of a spaceship ever having crashed.

✦ ✦ ✦

Near Colorado Springs, the NORAD command center's radars sporadically picked up the small craft as it flew north out of Los Alamos and up into Canada at a velocity of over one hundred thousand miles per hour. It appeared on their radar screens in short, intermittent bursts, during the initial acceleration and deceleration. This allowed them to calculate a fairly accurate speed based on the amount of time the ship had taken to travel to Canada. No nuclear ballistic missile or airspace violation warnings were issued, as they knew without doubt it was a craft of extraterrestrial origin. It stopped just north of Lake Huron in Ontario, Canada, near the town of Elliot Lake, at an altitude of eighteen thousand feet, before it again quickly disappeared. It reappeared briefly for a split second when it started to drop in altitude, and then the next time it was seen on radar was in the southeastern plains of Colorado at an altitude of one thousand feet.

According to the speed and altitudes surmised by predictive vectors, the ship had maintained velocity and acceleration speeds never before encountered. No prior unidentified object had ever registered a velocity over eighteen thousand miles per hour while inside Earth's atmosphere. Such immense speeds were especially noteworthy considering the low-altitude flight. There had been no sonic booms, so the craft must be able to remove or dampen the collapsing air pockets—similar to other craft encountered.

Because of the craft's speed, the radar operators knew it was the same craft from last night, except last night it had been visible on their radars 100 percent of the time as it traveled to Nebraska and then returned to Los Alamos, before completely vanishing from their radars a few miles north of Los Alamos. Since it had not been detected for the remainder of the night, it had either landed or been cloaked. Surprisingly, today, it had appeared intermittently on their radar screens, during daylight hours too. Why it would travel into Canada, they had no idea. The craft eventually traveled back to New Mexico at a velocity of thirty-seven thousand kilometers (twenty-three thousand miles) per hour, maintaining a low altitude of one thousand feet while crossing the states of Wisconsin, Iowa, Nebraska, Kansas, and then into Colorado, where it stopped in the eastern central plains about eighty miles southeast of Colorado Springs. This information was again determined from angular vector paths calculated after the ship stopped and briefly radiated. NORAD and their radar operators wondered if the craft might be playing cat and mouse, testing the capability of their radars and the tracking capabilities of their geosynchronous and low-Earth satellites.

After the craft stopped in the plains of Colorado, it was briefly radiated again when it accelerated west in their direction at ten thousand miles per hour while also rising in altitude. It then stopped over the mountains of the San Isabel National Forest at a new altitude of fifteen thousand feet, just fifteen miles south of Canon City. It remained over the mountain range for nearly five minutes before heading south at close to forty thousand miles per hour, again known because of another brief radar reflection right before it sped off toward New Mexico. It appeared briefly again seventeen seconds later, fifty-five miles east of Los Alamos. The craft covered nearly two hundred miles in less than eighteen seconds.

Once it was back in New Mexico airspace, the NORAD operators, now glued to their radar screens, were curious where it would next appear. There was then another brief detection when it started traveling toward the west at eight thousand miles per hour. It stopped two and a half miles east of Los Alamos but then quickly vanished again. A few seconds later, they saw it for one final time when it dropped from fifteen thousand feet to five hundred feet in just a matter of seconds. Like all the previous times, their radar screens were blank during the descent phase. The sudden g-forces such a quick descent would have normally created for its occupants was almost inconceivable. The operators additionally knew, as did their superiors, that the craft was more highly advanced than other craft they had directly encountered. The short blip on their screens right before the craft stopped at an altitude of five hundred feet, just south of Los Alamos, was their last radar detection.

NORAD contacted the extremely secretive Majestic 12 (MJ-12) organization again about the day sighting of the same craft from last night. The same highly compartmentalized, top-secret protocols were followed to make it seem the event had never happened. All recordings and all records were secured and turned over to the top-secret MJ-12 organization. The radar operators and their superiors who had witnessed or were aware of the incident would be immediately debriefed—secrecy for the sake of national security was mandatory under full penalties, up to and including treasonable offenses.

✦ ✦ ✦

On the spaceship, Jason and Michael continued watching the activity at the crash site. The military was making its presence well known with two Peterbilt 378 dump trucks, one large Caterpillar 928 loader, and a D6 bulldozer. Even some of the dirt where the ship had touched down was loaded into the dump trucks. Jason finally turned to Michael, who was still staring at him. "Are you ready to return home?"

"Yes, I am," Michael said. He grabbed his control wheel again and pulled it back to his left, causing their ship to rotate counterclockwise 180 degrees. He then pushed his wheel forward slightly and down at the same time. Their ship accelerated toward the east at a low velocity of ninety miles per hour while dropping to an altitude of seventy-five feet. Their ship traveled directly over Jason's house and toward the barn with the rooster weather vane.

Jason noticed Michael was not landing next to the house, but he remained quiet about it as they continued south of the barn to an open field. Michael pulled the wheel to his right, and their ship rotated clockwise ninety degrees, now pointing due north. He softly pushed down on the control wheel but then let loose as the ship's computer took control. Their spaceship softly touched down a few moments later.

Finally back home, Jason took a deep breath and exhaled. "Why did we land here?"

"Because," Michael answered, "our ship intermittently uncloaked a few times when traveling back to Los Alamos."

"What do you mean?" Jason asked.

Michael continued to stare at Jason. "What I mean, Jason," he said, "is that when we traveled up into Canada, then to Colorado, and returned home, we were sporadically detected by Earth-based radars in Colorado Springs."

"That's bad, huh?"

"It's not good," Michael said, "because the military will now be trying to vector our spaceship and locate its final position."

"Why did our ship uncloak?" Jason asked.

"If it accelerates or decelerates at a too-high rate or makes a sudden change in direction beyond a certain threshold, it temporarily uncloaks before its computer can reacquire its inverse magnetic field vectors and recloak."

Jason was thoroughly amazed. "I think I somewhat understand," he said while glancing at his wristwatch. His father would be home in less than forty-five minutes. "Well, I better get back inside the house," he said and stood up while thinking about his armband. "How do I remove my armband?"

"Push the two square buttons on the left side at the same time," Michael said.

"Okay," Jason said. Using his index and middle fingers, he touched the two indicated buttons. The armband flexed outward and changed shape, immediately releasing its grip. He felt the three gold needles pull out of his skin, and he pulled the armband off, revealing three small holes now in his forearm.

Michael stood up and noticed Jason staring at the three holes. "You will need to install the armband in the same place on your arm," he said. "Otherwise, it will take another five minutes to readjust to your body's electrochemical nerve impulse configuration."

"Okay," Jason said. "Well, I better return before my mom really starts to wonder where I am."

"Okay, Jason, bye," Michael replied. He touched a couple of buttons on his armband, and an open doorway into their ship suddenly appeared.

Jason started toward the doorway alongside Michael but then stopped. Michael also stopped, and Jason stared down at Michael, wondering again whether Michael was lonely on the ship all by himself. It caused him to feel compassionate toward Michael.

Michael noticed this. "Aren't you leaving the ship?"

Jason came to his senses. "Yes, I am." He took a short, deep breath. "Do you get lonely for companionship, Michael?"

Michael quietly analyzed Jason's question. "Yes, I do," he finally answered.

So Jason's suspicions had been correct. "I will call you on my communicator in a few hours," he said.

"Okay, Jason."

Jason finally exited their ship and walked down to the planet's surface. He turned around to watch the doorway into the ship slowly fade away until it vanished. The entire spaceship was again completely invisible, and all he could now see was an open field of juniper trees, Indian parsley plants, yellow ragweed wildflowers, and a pasture full of buffalo grass—as though their invisible ship had never been there. After passing through the gate west of the barn, he continued under a large Dutch elm tree over forty feet tall and toward the house carrying his nearly weightless armband—it felt like a feather. As he approached the front porch, he looked down again at his left forearm. The three small holes now looked like mosquito bites. As he headed up the east porch steps to the front door, he wondered whether his mother was waiting for him.

He slowly opened the door. She was not in the living room, so he headed straight for his bedroom without telling her that he had returned. Once inside, he closed the door behind him and put the armband away in the top drawer of his bedside table. He sat down on his bed, daydreaming about what he had just experienced aboard the spaceship with Michael. It had been extremely invigorating to fly up to Canada and then back to Colorado, witnessing a magnificent view of the snowcapped mountain peaks from a vantage point not many people would ever get the chance to experience in their lifetimes. The fact the military was looking for their ship was of concern, and Michael not knowing who had created him—his mom and dad—and being all alone like an abandoned child was also starting to weigh heavily on Jason's mind.

# 6

## JASON'S MOM'S CURIOSITY RISES

Jason's father would be arriving home anytime now from work, where he managed many of the Los Alamos research projects. Jason's parents had taken him and his little brother to the Los Alamos labs about a year ago. They hadn't been allowed into some labs, but what they had gotten to see was interesting stuff. All the workers had been friendly and nice, though his little brother had gotten most of the attention, especially from the women, probably because he was so much younger.

The cloaked spaceship behind the barn came to mind, and Jason wondered when he should reveal the existence of the ship and Michael to his parents. He was not sure how they would react. He decided not to tell them about either the ship or Michael, at least at this time, and wondered how Michael was doing all alone on the ship.

✦ ✦ ✦

In the kitchen, Jason's mother, Barbara, was preparing dinner. Her husband hadn't called about having to work late, so he should get home in less than fifteen minutes, at his usual time of about five fifteen. She paused from cooking and noticed her youngest son was playing in the dining room. She wondered again why Jason had been outside for almost two hours. When she'd called for him, he hadn't answered, and his little brother had also begun to ask about him. When Jason had returned a few minutes ago, he had headed straight to his bedroom, not letting her know he had returned. That was not usual behavior for him.

She decided to check on her oldest son and headed toward his bedroom. She found his bedroom door closed. Quietly curious about what might be wrong, she lightly knocked a couple of times. "Are you okay, Jason?" she softly asked.

"Yes, Mom, I am okay," he called out.

Barbara was hesitant to say anything else. She knew something was bothering him, but she decided to let it go for now. "Well, get cleaned up," she said. "Dinner will be ready in less than twenty minutes."

"Okay, Mom," he replied.

Barbara exhaled, filled with unusual curiosity. Her oldest son had never acted like this. *I wonder what is behind it,* she thought as she returned to the kitchen, now concerned about what was bothering her ten-year-old.

✦ ✦ ✦

With Michael's predicament still weighing heavily on his mind, Jason headed to his bathroom. Stopping in front of the mirror, he pulled his shirt off and then stared down at the three small puncture wounds in his left forearm. The wounds, which were still a little red, formed a perfect equilateral triangle. His mother would surely see them and recognize that they were located exactly where his armband had been. "What should I tell my mom if she asks?" Jason mumbled to himself.

He continued to think about the three small holes, as well as what his parents might have talked about last night after he'd been gone so long. He figured Michael had probably heard everything. He finally turned on the faucet. Grabbing a bar of soap, he cleaned his face, hands, and arms. He stared at his reflection in the mirror as water ran down the side of his face. It made him wonder again whether Michael had sweat glands and the ability to perspire. He dried his face and hands and returned to his bedroom, wishing Michael could join them at the dinner table.

✦ ✦ ✦

On the spaceship, Michael was intrigued by Barbara and Jason's conversation, with Barbara telling Jason through a closed door to clean up for dinner. Michael instinctively could tell Jason did not hide secrets from his mom, especially ones that affected his entire family. The concern in her voice over the way Jason was acting was something he was still analyzing, but he knew Jason was acting differently because of having him as a new friend. He wondered how Jason's parents would act toward him and whether they would act much differently from Jason.

Michael's front display was now registering the characteristics of Jason's father's vehicle, which was on the way home. His ship had computed the exhaust gas emissions from the vehicle when it left the drive earlier this morning, including all variable exhaust frequencies, while taking into account the atmospheric temperature and pressure in Los Alamos. The carbon monoxide emission level from the vehicle registered 98.633 parts per million in relation to an atmospheric envelope between his spaceship and the city of Los Alamos, at least while taking the rotational and toroidal movement of Earth into account. The ship's computer additionally knew the exact heat and energy signatures for the 5.4-liter V-8 combustion engine, including the exhaust gas signatures. There were tens of thousands of poisonous gas emitters in and around Los Alamos and the world, constantly polluting the planet's atmosphere. This was something that did not make sense to Michael, but he quickly surmised it was only because these poisonous gas emitters were the most viable form of transportation for Earth's primitive society that allowed its societies and economies to function, survive, and prosper. He knew no two combustion engine vehicles and their exhaust could be exactly 100 percent alike, due to intake and exhaust flow mechanics. There would always be minute carbon monoxide molecular differences when the exhaust gas molecules scattered and mixed in with the billions and trillions of nitrogen and oxygen molecules. In addition to those variables, the ship's computer also computed the small force-line ripple changes in the vehicle's alternator system in direct relation to the planet's magnetosphere, via a weak magnetic field. All these variables allowed the ship's computer to pinpoint the exact magnetic field location of Jason's dad's Lincoln Navigator, as well as the vehicle's arrival time based on its current velocity.

According to Michael's front display, Jason's dad was now 2.937 kilometers away. All he could do was continue patiently waiting, just like Jason, yet his anticipation for the Lincoln Navigator to pull up into the driveway was much different from Jason's.

✦ ✦ ✦

Jason sat on the side of his bed with new shirt, clean hands, and a clean face. He felt his right pants pocket for the communicator and lifted his left arm again, examining the three small holes. They were no longer pure red but still visible as reddish-brown dots. He was not sure how to go about explaining them. He headed out into the hallway with a feeling of uncertainty about what the evening might have in store. He knew he had to say something to his mother since he hadn't acknowledged her when returning from outside. He found her in the kitchen, standing in front of the stove. "Hi, Mom," he said.

Barbara turned around. "Hi, Jason, how are you doing?"

"Good, Mom."

Barbara noticed Jason was no longer wearing the armband. "Dad should be home in less than ten minutes," she said.

Jason nodded slightly. "Okay, I will be in the living room until then."

"Sure," Barbara replied and watched her oldest son leave the kitchen. She could again tell there was something on his mind and that he was trying to mask it. She watched her four-year-old leave the dining room, following after the older brother he admired, and then turned back to the stove.

In the living room, Jason sat down in the recliner. For a short-lived moment, he was alone, and then Kyle entered the room and headed directly toward his chair.

"Want to sit up here, Kyle?"

"Yes," he answered.

"Come up here, then," Jason said.

Kyle crawled up in the recliner next to his brother, sitting so that their rib cages touching each other. As his little brother leaned his head up against his left shoulder, Jason realized again how much Kyle looked up to him. Michael was about the same size as Kyle, maybe a few inches taller. *I bet Michael would like Kyle,* Jason thought.

Jason wondered how Michael might react to meeting Kyle for the first time. Michael had a light complexion, so he could easily pass as their brother, but his hair seemed somehow different.

Jason slowly exhaled. At some point, he would have to let his parents know about Michael and their spaceship, especially since the military was looking for the ship. He picked up the Dish Network multifunction remote control and turned on their thirty-six-inch picture tube television. The TV was on the Sci Fi channel, and *The Incredible Hulk* was showing. Jason began watching the movie with his little brother, with strange anticipation for his father arriving home.

✦ ✦ ✦

Outside the Jupiters' house, Dan was on his way up the gravel drive after stopping to grab the mail. There was not much of interest, mostly advertisements. He laid the mail on top of his briefcase as he thought about some of the conversations he'd had at work. He hadn't been able to find out even one shred of information about the military aircraft that had supposedly crashed on his land, even after talking to a few of his friends in the upper echelons of the Pentagon. He wondered what was going on, and a strange thought went through his mind that the craft could have possibly been of extraterrestrial nature, especially since some people at work had mentioned strange lights being seen around Los Alamos last night. His oldest son being gone for almost three hours made the event seem even stranger, because if it was a craft of extraterrestrial nature and Jason knew something, why would he not have mentioned it?

After pulling up in front of their two-car garage, he shut off the ignition, grabbed his briefcase and the mail, and exited his SUV, wondering what his wife might have cooked to go along with roast beef brisket he'd placed in the refrigerator before leaving for work. Walking up the west porch stairs and to the front door, he continued inside. He placed the mail and his briefcase on the small foyer table and closed the door behind him. In the living room, his two sons were sitting next to each, watching television. "Hi, kids," he calmly said, continuing into the living room.

Kyle was happy to see his father. "Daddy!" he replied.

"Hi, Dad," Jason also replied.

Dan knew from Jason's tone that he had something on his mind or was not feeling good. He continued to where they sat and picked Kyle up, giving him an affectionate kiss on the lips. He then leaned down and placed a small kiss against Jason's forehead. "Are you okay, Jason?"

"Yes, Dad, I am okay," he said.

Jason had something on his mind, then. "Have you both been good for your mom today?" he asked.

"Yes, we have," Jason said.

"Good," Dan said. "Maybe we'll all have some fun after dinner."

Jason perked up. "What, Dad?"

Dan grinned a little. "I will let you know after dinner," he said and left the room with Kyle still in his arms. Jason turned off the television and followed his father into the kitchen.

Dan placed a soft kiss against Barbara's lips. "Hi, dear," he said.

Barbara felt warm inside. "Hi, honey," she replied.

Jason's parents gave each other a hug with Kyle still in his dad's arms. Jason could not remember a day going by when his parents were not hugging or kissing, except for when they were separated when visiting a relative or his dad was away on a business trip for the government.

"How was work?" Barbara asked.

"Busy," Dan said. "Believe it or not, but there was talk of strange lights being spotted near Los Alamos last night and then a few times late this afternoon."

Barbara was surprised. "Is that right?"

"Yes," Dan said. "Was there anything mentioned in the newspaper?"

"No, there wasn't," she said. "Did you find out any more information about that aircraft that crashed?"

"No, I couldn't," he said. "I made a few calls to some friends at the Pentagon, but either they did not know anything or would not talk about it."

"I understand," Barbara said.

Jason listened intently to his parents, especially what they said about the strange lights, because they were almost certainly from his and Michael's spaceship.

Dan noticed Jason's keen interest and placed Kyle down on the floor. He turned back to his wife with a relaxed, peaceful spirit. "I'm changing clothes and freshening up," he said.

"Okay," she replied, and he left the room.

Jason's mother had neatly arranged the dining room table for a family of four. Jason wished it could be a family of *five*, instead of *four*, as it would be cool to have a brother from another world, but he would have to convince his parents of that being a good idea or a real possibility.

The steaming-hot food caused a sudden appetite for Jason. His mother was an excellent cook, and her food was always delicious. Without hesitation, he headed toward the table, trailed by his little brother.

Jason helped Kyle into his booster seat and then sat down across from him in the same chairs they had always used since Kyle was old enough to sit at the table. Jason's mother would sit to his left, his father to his right, and before their dinner, they would hold hands, just as they had always done, and his dad would say a prayer, blessing their food and praying for their welfare, for their relatives, and military personnel around the world who were helping to preserve their freedoms. He would also pray that the leaders of the many nations would make decisions in the best interests of all humankind.

Jason's mother walked into the dining room and set another plate of food on the table. She again stared at his left forearm, but she did not say anything about the three holes that formed a triangle. She went back to the kitchen. Jason had no idea what his mother thought about the three small holes.

His father entered the kitchen, briefly glanced Jason's direction, and continued over to the stove. He was probably curious about how Jason had acted in the living room and what might be behind it, even more so after everything that had happened last night with the crashed aircraft, Jason's being gone so long, the meeting of armed military guards, and especially the government agents dressed in black attire.

His dad carried a ceramic bowl of hot green beans into the dining room, set it down on a metal coaster, and returned to the kitchen. His mother turned off the stove, removed a large pan with their main course of meat, and placed it on the granite countertop. His father removed a metal bowl from the oven, and then his parents came back into the dining room, his mother carrying hot rolls and his father, the pan of sliced, tender roast beef. His mother set the hot rolls down, and his father meticulously placed the roast beef on another large metal coaster.

Barbara then sat down while Dan placed a half dozen slices of roast beef on an empty plate. He then walked around Kyle, sat down to Jason's right, and looked around their table, feeling blessed to have a loving wife and two kind-mannered kids.

They all grabbed hands. As Jason extended his left hand to his mom, she again noticed the three small holes located exactly where he'd been wearing the unusual-looking armband. The puncture wounds formed an equilateral triangle and seemed odd, as if caused by something mechanical. She did not know what to think about it and gently squeezed his hand a couple of times. Jason did not know what she might now say to him.

His parents and little brother bowed their heads and closed their eyes, so he did the same. He remained especially quiet as his father prayed for their food, blessed his wife for preparing it, and prayed for the welfare of their family and relatives and for those in the world who were not as fortunate and those who labored in the fields. He prayed that the world leaders' decisions would be for the goodness of humankind. He prayed for military soldiers, both in the United States and throughout the world, to keep them safe from harm, and lastly, he made a wish for world peace. He ended his prayer in the name of Jesus Christ.

"Amen," Dan said. He lifted his head and opened his eyes.

Barbara, Jason, and Kyle also opened their eyes and let go of each other's hands. Barbara gave a gracious nod to her husband and placed a piece of roast beef on her plate. She handed the platter to Jason, who placed a large, delicious-looking, tender piece on his plate and watched it fall apart. Jason passed the platter to his father, who set it down in front of him. Dan placed a piece on his plate and a smaller slice on his young son's plate. The family continued to pass food until their plates were full, with Dan filling Kyle's plate with a child's portion.

On his plate, Jason had roast beef, mashed potatoes, gravy, green beans, and a hot roll. Everyone savored their dinner, making it unusually quiet at the table all of a sudden. As Jason took a sip of his iced tea, his mother again stared at his left forearm. He had the feeling she was about to ask about the three puncture holes.

"What happened to your left forearm, Jason?" she asked, just as Jason had suspected.

Jason was silent and set his tea down. "It must have happened when I was playing," he said.

Jason's response seemed a little vague and out of character to Barbara, and she knew the holes were in the same spot where he'd been wearing the armband earlier, but she decided not to mention anything more about it—at least during dinner. Jason had been a little hesitant in answering her question, and she thought the holes might have something to do with what was bothering him. Her question may have also ruined his appetite.

Jason was relieved she did not pursue her line of questioning about the holes or the armband. It would have put him in an awkward position of not knowing what to say and possibly causing him to fib a little. Lying to his parents was something he had never done. Taking another bite of food, he slowly chewed his tender roast beef, wondering whether Michael was again listening to their conversations.

Dan was also becoming curious about the three puncture wounds in Jason's forearm, especially with his son's vague answer. He looked at Barbara on the other end of the table. "Dinner is excellent, honey," he said, "as always."

Barbara gave a flirty grin in response to Dan's charm, and he gave her a look only the two of them could know the meaning of. Jason grinned about it, knowing that what his parents were now expressing toward each other usually led to additional affection between them later in the evening, ending in the privacy of their bedroom. He had noticed this interaction many times before but still did not understand why it would be started so early in the evening.

✦ ✦ ✦

Aboard the spaceship, Michael was listening to the entire dinner conversation, especially the question about the three small holes in Jason's forearm. Michael had not eaten anything since becoming conscious yesterday, waking up from what had seemed a very long dream.

Jason's parents were talking about the nice weather they were having in Los Alamos and about events from around the planet. Jason's dad mentioned Hurricane Fabian, a Category 3 hurricane that had traveled west of Bermuda a few Earth days ago, battering the island with winds over 140 miles per hour, ending in a lot of flooding. It had been the most powerful hurricane to hit Bermuda in eighty years, and four lives had been lost. Michael briefly thought about the four lives lost. He scientifically understood every detail about extratropical cycles, including their associations to naturally occurring hurricanes. Previous information in his ship's computer told him the human race did not have the ability to redirect hurricanes nor revamp their pressures to dissipate them. The race from which he had originated did understand how to control this powerful, natural planetary atmospheric wonder of nature.

Jason's parents also talked about NASA's plans to return to manned space travel after the catastrophic disaster of the space shuttle *Columbia*. Michael checked his ship's data banks and found the disaster occurred on February 1—almost seven Earth months ago. Jason's parents talked about how it would be at least a few years before the government would allow another space shuttle launch. Michael knew that, because of the primitive rocket technologies the human race was using to propel their spaceships and satellites into outer space, even the most basic initial stages of gravity propulsion would not be developed and openly used for up to a century, maybe longer. Even if they wanted to focus on this new technology, they wouldn't be able to because of wars active in numerous regions around the planet. Without world peace, there would always be those who would use gravity technologies for weapons of mass destruction. Jason's parents then talked about a massive car bomb almost a week ago that had killed the prominent Shiite cleric Baqir al-Hakim and around ninety other human beings. It only reinforced what Michael thought about gravity technologies becoming common public knowledge and used as a simple form of transportation, because some still had no regard for other human beings.

There was sadness in Jason's parents' voices as they talked about this crime against humanity and the human souls lost in the car bombing. Michael could not comprehend why humans would want to kill one another, having no regard for each other—intelligent sentient beings that had to be from the same or similar DNA genus class of the race that had created him. His memories told him to be careful with most humans because of their barbaric ways, as they might treat him in the same manner—like a lower-class entity. Jason's family seemed much different, as they believed in a higher force or intelligence, as clearly evidenced by Dan's prayer before dinner.

Michael found himself fascinated with Jason's mother and father, especially in relation to their two sons. They were just as Jason had told him a mom and dad would be. It helped him better understand the role of a parent, reminding him again that he had no mother or father that he could remember. His fascination for Jason's parents triggered a strange feeling deep inside his chest, something that he was now trying to understand.

✦ ✦ ✦

Inside the Jupiters' house, Kyle had eaten most of his food, enough that would allow him to be excused from the table, and Jason had eaten everything on his plate, even using a roll to mop up the remaining cream gravy, which was especially delicious. Jason's anticipation was now high, because his father was about to tell them what they were going to do later that would be fun. He turned to his mother with sincere appreciation. "Thanks for dinner, Mom," he said.

"You're welcome, Jason," she replied.

"Yes, Mommy," Kyle blurted out. "Thanks for our food."

Barbara grinned at her four-year-old. "You're both welcome," she said again, and Dan gave a subtle grin to their polite kids.

Jason looked briefly to his mother and then back to his father with anticipation. Dan noticed this. "How about we go fishing down at the creek?"

Jason perked up. "Sure, Dad," he said.

"Me too," Kyle said.

"Good," Dan said. "Maybe we'll have fresh fish for tomorrow's dinner—that is, if either of you can catch any."

Jason smiled at his father. "Dad, I will catch enough for all of us."

Dan shook his head with laughter. "How about getting our fishing poles ready, Jason? I'll be out there in about fifteen minutes after I help your mom clear the table and put away the food."

"Okay," Jason said.

As Jason and Kyle left the room, Dan noticed his wife watching them and knew she had something on her mind.

At the front door, Kyle followed his brother onto the front porch, thinking about all the fish that they were going to catch. After Jason closed the door, he looked down at his little brother. "Stay right here, Kyle, while I get our fishing equipment ready, and then I am going to show you something."

"What?" Kyle asked.

"You'll see," Jason said. He quickly headed west across the porch, down the stairs, and toward the garage at a much-faster pace than normal. In the garage, he quickly grabbed four fishing poles, a tackle box, and a fishnet and returned to the porch, where his little brother was patiently waiting at the west steps. Jason set the poles, tackle box, and fishnet down on the porch while staring at his little brother. "Can you keep a secret?"

Kyle gazed up at his brother, intrigued. "What kind of secret?" he asked.

"A secret about a new friend," Jason said.

Kyle was confused. "Yes, I can keep a secret about a new friend," he finally said.

Jason knew his little brother did not understand, but Kyle had always kept secrets in the past when asked. Jason pulled his communicator from his pants pocket and led his little brother down the east porch stairs and toward the barn with the rooster weather vane.

Kyle was again confused. "So where are we going?"

"To see our new friend," Jason said.

"Okay."

Jason pushed the left button on his communicator. "Michael?" he called out.

"Yes, Jason?" Michael replied.

Kyle was surprised to hear another little boy's voice on the small box in his brother's hand. Jason noticed this. "Michael," he said, "I'm headed to the ship with my little brother."

There was silence. "Okay, Jason," Michael finally said. "The door to our spaceship will be open."

As they approached the west side of the barn, Kyle continued to show fascination for the small box in his brother's hand. It reminded him of his father's cell phone. The mention of a spaceship was confusing, though. "Where did you get that?" he asked.

"I got it from my friend," Jason replied.

"I want one," Kyle immediately said.

Jason thought about his little brother having a communicator. He for sure did not want their parents to know about them—at least not yet. "We'll see, Kyle," he said.

"Okay," Kyle replied.

They continued around the barn, under the shade of the large elm tree, and then up to the gate. Jason opened the gate, followed his little brother through, and closed it behind them. When Jason turned back around, his brother was staring up at him with a puzzled look, clearly wondering where they were meeting their new friend. Jason looked out into the open field, now able to see the opening into the invisible ship about fifteen feet away. As he walked toward the spaceship with his little brother tagging alongside, Jason knew his brother was still confused, especially after seeing the brightly lit opening into the invisible ship—it was like a hole into another world.

Kyle looked up briefly at his older brother and then back at the strange rectangular column of light. "What is that?" he asked.

"A doorway into an invisible spaceship, Kyle."

Kyle was suddenly excited and now walked ahead of his older brother, unafraid. Like a trooper, he marched up the ramp and straight into the spaceship, where he stopped. As soon as Jason followed his little brother into the ship, the open doorway behind them vanished. Jason and Kyle continued toward the cockpit, where Michael was again sitting in the far right seat. "Hi, Michael," Jason said, Kyle at his side.

"Hi, Jason. Hi, Kyle," Michael replied.

Kyle stood with a small grin, delighted their new friend already knew his name. Michael was about his same size too. "Hi, Michael," Kyle softly said.

Kyle seemed extremely kind and friendly, just like his older brother, and Michael turned to Jason with puzzlement. "What is a brother, Jason?" he asked.

Jason looked down at Kyle and then to Michael, trying to figure out how to answer him. "Did the ones who created you build any more organic androids like you?"

"I do not know," Michael said.

Jason paused. "Well, if they did, they would be like brothers."

Michael analyzed this answer. "I think I understand," he said.

Jason glanced at his wristwatch, because he definitely did not want his father to come looking for them. It had been about five minutes since they'd first left the house. Believing they still had plenty of idle time, Jason sat down in the left cockpit chair, and Kyle sat down between him and Michael. Fascinated, Kyle unabashedly stared over at Michael and finally placed his right arm around Michael's shoulder. "You're my friend," he declared.

Michael did not say anything at first while Kyle's arm remained on his shoulder. Jason wondered whether Michael would have an emotional response to his little brother.

"You're my friend too," Michael finally responded.

Kyle beamed from ear to ear and finally removed his arm.

Jason looked over at Michael and thought about what Kyle had asked him on the way toward the ship. "Kyle asked if he could have one of your communicators too," he said.

"Okay," Michael said. "Just grab one before you go fishing at the creek."

Jason figured Michael had been listening to the conversations inside the house. He then thought about the three small puncture wounds in his forearm, including the fact that his mother had already asked about them. He continued staring at Michael. "Since my mom questioned me about the holes in my forearm, what if she asks where I got the armband?"

Michael paused. "Just tell her you found it," he said. "You did find it on top of the table inside this spaceship."

Jason realized that was a true statement. "What if she wants to see it?"

Michael analyzed what might happen if Jason's parents were to see the armband's three gold needles. "I understand what you're saying, Jason," he said. "I'll have the ship create a fake armband without the three interface pins, any working buttons, or system interfaces to our ship."

"That's a great idea!" Jason said, excited.

Michael touched a couple of buttons on his display and turned to Jason. "Your simulated armband will be ready shortly."

Jason was surprised the ship's computer could create it so quickly. "Okay," he said.

While the three boys waited for the simulated armband, Michael touched the screen again. Jason recognized it as being a communications display. Two lights were visible, which had to be his parents.

Michael selected the lights, and inside the cockpit they heard Jason and Kyle's parents in the kitchen, putting plates inside the dishwasher.

Dan said, "We'll be down at the creek for a few hours. If you change your mind, grab your fishing pole and come join us."

"Okay, I may just do that," Barbara said. "I want to call my mom first."

"Sure," Dan said. "I'll talk to Jason about the armband after we return from fishing."

"Okay, dear," she said.

Michael leaned forward, touched the display again, and shut off the eavesdropping function. He stared over at Jason with a strange look. "You were correct about the armband, Jason," he said. "Good thing we're creating a fake one."

Jason quietly agreed. "Yes, that was a close one. Well, we had better return to the house before my dad wonders where we are."

"Okay, Jason," Michael said.

The three boys stood up together and started toward the doorway, which was again suddenly open. Jason stopped after seeing another armband on the table where he had picked up the original. He was amazed it had been created so quickly, but then, it did not have any interfaces. Its shape was also different from the original. "Why does this armband look different from the real armband?"

Michael stared up at Jason. "It is shaped like it would be installed on your forearm, matching how your mom would have viewed it."

"I understand," Jason said, realizing Michael was exactly correct. He picked up the fake armband, studying it closely. It was light as a feather, just like the original, and he turned it over to find it was smooth on the interior, with no interface pins. It had the exact same number of buttons and was identical to the original in every respect, except for the interface pins and its current shape. "This does look exactly like the real one," he said.

"It is, Jason," Michael said. "It is exactly like the real one in every elemental respect, *except* with no interface pins or any functional biological system interfaces with our ship."

Jason slipped the fake armband into his other pants pocket, opposite the communicator, and glanced over again at the open doorway. He looked back down at Michael and walked over to the cabinet with communicators. He touched the drawer, and it suddenly appeared open again, just like the previous time. Inside were the remaining five communicators. Jason grabbed one and handed it to his little brother, who was now standing directly behind him. The drawer suddenly appear closed. "Kyle," he admonished, making direct eye contact, "do not let Mom or Dad see your communicator. It is also our little secret."

"Okay," Kyle said and slipped the communicator into his pants pocket.

Jason had a strange comforting feeling inside now that Michael had finally met his little brother. In his mind, it was one down and two to go. "Bye, Michael," he said. "I will call you on the communicator later tonight."

"Okay, Jason. Bye. I will be waiting."

Kyle hugged Michael, their little chests touching. "Bye, Michael," he said.

Kyle had obviously taken a strong liking to Michael. Though Michael hugged Kyle back, it seemed no one had ever hugged him before. That was probably the case, as Jason had never thought about giving him a hug. After the two boys stopped hugging, Jason followed his little brother's lead with a special hug of his own.

After they quit hugging, Michael had a much-calmer, relaxed look on his face. "See you later," Jason said.

"Okay, bye," Michael replied.

Jason and Kyle walked down the ramp to the planet's surface. Michael touched a button on his armband, and the doorway into the ship, on this particular occasion, slowly faded away instead of disappearing instantly.

Outside the ship, Jason also noticed this and knew they had better return to the front porch in a hurry, before their father came outside and began looking around. After the doorway completely vanished, all that was visible was again an open field.

Staring down at his little brother, Jason reminded him, "Michael is our secret, including the spaceship."

"Okay," Kyle replied, vigorously nodding his head up and down.

They walked back through the gate, under the elm tree, past the barn, and quickly toward the house, but before they could reach the porch, their father walked down the east steps and spotted them heading toward the house at a fast pace. "Where have you two been?" he called out.

Jason glanced down at his little brother and then back to his father. "We were just playing, Dad," he said. He noticed his father wearing his M1911 Colt .45 pistol on his right hip, just as he always did when they were hiking on their land or out in the woods, even while fishing and especially when there was a possibility of a dangerous situation, such as a mountain lion or wolf.

Dan thought it a bit strange his kids would walk off when they knew good and well they were about to go fishing. "Okay," he only said. "I've got our bait ready, including a Styrofoam cup of worms. Let's go fishing."

Jason grabbed his fishing pole and the plastic bag of chicken liver, while Kyle picked up his little fishing pole and the Styrofoam cup of worms. Their father grabbed his two fishing poles, the tackle box, the fishnet, and the fish basket. They headed toward the creek about a quarter of a mile away, Jason on their father's right and Kyle to their father's left.

Along the western horizon, the sun was shining with a magnificent, beautiful orange hue Jason had not seen in quite some time. He knew the sun's atmospheric display was caused by the dispersion and refraction of the sunlight into its longer wavelengths of light. Based on the time on his wristwatch, the sun would be setting in a few hours.

Dan also noticed the beautiful sunset and realized again how important its radiant energy was to Earth's ecological and taxonomic systems, including the nitrogen oxidation cycle. If not for this cycle, plants' photosynthesis would be inefficient, and their ability to convert carbon dioxide into oxygen would be extremely limited, but at the moment, spending quality time with his sons was all that mattered.

After entering the small forest of oak and piñon trees, they continued down the same trail Jason had used the previous night. Some of the oak trees were at least forty feet tall, their trunks easily over two feet in diameter. The piñon trees were not quite as big, but they helped support an abundance of wildlife—squirrels, birds, rabbits, lizards, toads, even snakes. Two weeks ago, Jason had seen a huge bull snake, over five feet long, coiled around a rabbit. Suddenly, two deer—a doe and a buck—took off running. "Dad, look over there!" Jason said.

Dan and Kyle also saw the deer. "Yes, I see them," Dan replied.

They continued out of the small forest. The creek was just to their left, the bristling of water running across the rocks clearly audible. Jason suddenly thought about the crash site a quarter mile away to the northwest. Looking in that exact direction, he could not see any military vehicles or personnel, but then again, trees were obscuring most of his view. His father occasionally glanced over in the same direction. As they finally arrived at the shoreline, the spaceship quickly vanished from Jason's mind. The creek was flowing fairly fast and looked very nice for fishing. One of the main reasons Dan wanted them to go fishing was that last week he'd secretly discovered a fairly deep hole—directly in front of where they now stood. They had fished the area many times before and caught some fairly nice catfish. Maybe this evening they would have even better luck.

Jason continued looking around at the abundance of trees and large rocks at this particular location. Over by one of the larger rocks, about fifty feet to the west, was a good fishing hole. He had caught nice perch, crappie, and even bass worth keeping there. Maybe they would have good luck this evening, as there were not many clouds, only a nice breeze blowing in from the west, and his dad always told him, "When the wind is out of the west, the fishing is the best."

# 7

## AN EVENING AT THE CREEK

Dan laid his two fishing poles down, along with the tackle box, fish basket, and fishnet, while Jason quickly reached inside the Styrofoam cup to find the fattest, juiciest worm. It began squirming around, so he grabbed his fishhook, barbed the worm, and slid it all the way onto his hook. Since his fishing line already had a bobber, he was now ready to catch a really big fish.

He had convinced himself that he would catch the first fish, especially since he had gotten a head start on his father and little brother. As he was about to walk away, he noticed his dad had cut a piece of chicken liver about the size of a silver dollar for one of his poles. He would be fishing for catfish with that pole, and since his other pole had a bobber, he'd be using it for top fishing. His dad cast his line with the chicken liver out into the creek nearly twenty feet away, as if he had directed it to a specific location. It broke the surface about three-quarters of the way across and quickly sank to the bottom. Jason's father then installed a worm on the hook of his other line and cast it out in the water. The bobber floated about ten feet away, stopping nearly four feet from the shoreline, the line stretched out tight.

Jason's father next helped Kyle place a worm on his hook. Since Kyle's pole was also using a bobber, their father helped him cast his line into the water, the same way he had done for Jason when he was Kyle's age. Jason suddenly realized his dad and little brother had actually gotten a head start on him, but it really did not matter, as he knew where all the fish were hiding—in his secret fishing hole. He continued to the west down the north shoreline with no worries in the world, oblivious to his surroundings. Nearly fifty feet later, he finally became cognizant of his surroundings, especially after seeing the large gray-and-blue rocks just ahead that had his secret markers. Next to the rocks were large oak, walnut, and juniper trees, which helped him pinpoint his secret fishing hole. His true identification, though, was his initials—"J. J."—inscribed into the surface of one of the large rocks.

Jason stared down at the running water and then up into one of the large juniper trees. A rock squirrel was watching him, shaking its tail and squawking while chewing on a walnut. When he looked back down at the shoreline, he quickly caught a glimpse of a nice perch and even a medium-sized bass. *The fish are waiting for me*, he thought and immediately cast his line into the water. His bobber floated for a moment but then quickly disappeared out of sight. Jason pulled hard and hooked a fish. "That was quick," he mumbled under his breath. He reeled his catch to the shore and pulled it out of the water. It was a small bluegill, about four inches long, and the pesky little perch had stolen the entire worm that he had so carefully shish-kebabbed! "This isn't going to be fun," he mumbled under his breath, "especially if they're going to take the worms that easily."

Jason now had to retrieve another worm or use a lure, so he headed back up the shoreline toward his father. Along the way, he heard a familiar bird in a nearby oak tree. Sure enough, it was a purple martin, just as he suspected, its reflective purple color displayed magnificently against iridescent, glossy blue-black feathers. He loved these popular birds because their insect diets included wasps and other venomous stinging bugs. Yellow jackets had stung him in the past. Their stings smarted, but he was fortunately not allergic to their venom. Their stings were actually more painful and lasting than the armband's needles that had pierced deep into his forearm.

He finally arrived where his father and brother were now sitting next to each other. His father immediately noticed the small bluegill dangling from the end of his fishing pole. He smiled. "You caught one, huh?" he joked.

Jason laughed. "Yes, I did," he said. "I'm sticking it in the fish basket, so I won't catch it any more this evening."

Dan shook his head with additional laughter at his son's snappy retort.

Jason carefully removed the hook from the fish's lower jaw and placed the perch inside the fish basket. He then carried the basket over to a small tree branch hanging out over the water. Using the attached nylon rope, he tied the basket to the branch with a quick-release sailor's knot that his dad had taught him. He let go of the basket, and it dropped into the water with a splash. The rope tightened, and the basket disappeared, so the water must be fairly deep there. Jason walked over to the tackle box, opened it, and looked for the perfect fly lure. After finding what he felt was a perfect red, green, and blue mayfly, he removed the hook and bobber from his line, slipped the mayfly lure onto his swivel, and snapped it into place, ready for some serious fishing. *Now I will catch lots of fish,* he thought.

Jason turned back to the west and started to walk away, but then he saw one of his father's fishing poles—the one with chicken liver on the creek bottom—suddenly bend way over. "Dad, look at your fishing pole!" he yelled.

Dan also saw his fishing pole bend over farther than ever before. Suddenly, the pole turned toward the creek, the end splashing into the water. He quickly leaped to his feet and grabbed the pole before it disappeared into the creek.

Jason stood there, amazed. He had never seen a fishing pole bend so much or head toward the water so quickly. As soon as his father turned the lever on the reel, the line tightened, and the reel began to whine. *Dad must have caught a really big fish this time,* Jason thought.

Dan stood patiently, slowly playing with the clearly large fish, not wanting to take the chance of it breaking the twelve-pound-test fishing line. He slowly reeled the fish toward the shore, and it swam off again, causing his reel to whine with a high pitch. By this time, Kyle had come over next to Jason, and they both watched as their father patiently reeled in what seemed to be a very large fish.

Dan continued to patiently, calmly, yet vigorously play with what he figured was a large flathead catfish that easily exceeded his twelve-pound-test line. He gave it every bit of slack that he could while trying to wear it out. He got it within eight feet of the shore, but then, like the times before, it pulled his fishing line out once again. Surely the old fish had to be getting tired, as Dan was getting a little exhausted in his arms and shoulders. For now, he was still filled with a shot of adrenaline, but he hoped the fish was not too awfully big, because then it would still have plenty more fight and would be extremely hard to land from the creek. He glanced briefly at his wristwatch to see six minutes had already passed, and he was not any closer to bringing the fish ashore than when he'd first started. He glanced at his sons, who were intently watching, and placed his attention back on his rod and reel, hoping to land what might be the largest catfish he'd ever latched on to using rod and reel.

✦ ✦ ✦

Inside the spaceship, Michael listened intently to Jason, Kyle, and their father. He heard Jason get excited after his father hooked a large fish and heard the reel whine numerous times. Whenever Jason's father reeled the fish toward the shore, the whine would stop, but it would begin again after the fish pulled the line back into the creek.

He found himself curious about what was happening visually, but he was over a quarter mile away, and trees blocked any direct line-of-sight optical viewing using his ship's advanced telescopes. He decided to improvise using some of the advanced technologies of his spaceship. He touched a series of buttons on his front console, and a secondary electronic countermeasures menu displayed. He selected the optical dispersion menu. He took note of the barometric (atmospheric) pressure outside the ship as well as the planet's nitrogen level inside a three-kilometer radius, which was exactly 78.045679148 percent of the total atmosphere. The carbon-based heat signatures and the dissipation values for Jason, Kyle, and their father, as projected up into the air, were slightly west of Michael, 1,298 feet away. The ship's computer would also take that into account, as well as the nitrogen free-molecule line frequency of just over 28 MHz, as realized along Earth's lines of force and their electron-ionic flow toward the north magnetic pole, all within a space-light-time plane equal to the speed of light. The ship's computer would additionally compensate for the west-northwestern wind velocities varying in intensity between ten to fifteen knots.

Michael touched another button on his display, and a thin three-dimensional holographic image, one meter in diameter, appeared directly above his front console. He touched another button on the console, and a short, fixed-wavelength, polarized beam of energy projected out from his ship, 1,300 feet to the west and up to an altitude of 88 feet above the creek. This fixed-length energy beam immediately repolarized Earth's atmosphere inside a localized three-meter-diameter disk, causing all the nitrogen molecules within this small area to be immediately brought down to their ground state. The ship's advanced molecular optical system and molecular computers then reconstituted all wavelengths of light being reflected up into the atmosphere from the shoreline of the creek inside a fifty-foot circular pattern. The ship's advanced molecular optical dispersion system then took the space curvature of Earth's lines of force into account, within the same fifty-foot circle, both temporally and spatially, and applied it to a ninety-degree refraction of light according to a plane equal to the speed of light.

Jason, Kyle, and their father—their reflections reconstituted in a conical form of panorhombic image (a modification of panoramic space, with its depth flattened out to form true three-dimensional remote viewing)—appeared on the thin holographic image in extremely fine detail. It was as though Michael were watching a television in 3-D without needing special 3-D glasses. What he was now viewing was the same as if he had been looking down at Jason, Kyle, and their father from eighty-eight feet above them, except he could also now zoom in if he so wished using the panoramic optical viewing system. He did just that and was now viewing them from about twenty feet away. Jason and Kyle were standing beside their father, who was still attempting to reel the fish to shore. Michael envisioned himself standing alongside Jason and Kyle and remained extremely quiet, listening and watching every detail as though in slow motion.

✦ ✦ ✦

At the creek, with a bit more ease than before, Dan reeled the fish closer one more time, within about six feet of the shore. The fish suddenly pulled the line out once again for what had to be at least the thirtieth time. The fish hadn't surfaced yet, so there was no way of knowing how big it might actually be—it was large, though. After Dan reeled his line in again, the fish finally started to approach the surface, its dark shadow clearly evident. The catfish appeared larger than what he had first expected, and he looked over to his oldest son. "Get the net, Jason. This is an extremely large catfish."

After seeing the surprised look on his father's face and the large shadow just below the surface, Jason grew excited, knowing the catfish had to be huge. He quickly grabbed the net and walked up to the shoreline, ready to scoop the catfish into the net, just as he had done in the past for other fish.

Dan reeled the fish a little closer and felt a sense of relief, as he knew without a doubt, by the shadow in the water, that he was about to land the largest catfish he'd ever caught on rod and reel—and by quite a few pounds too, as the catfish's girth was huge. He did not know yet whether it was a channel or a flathead—maybe a blue cat?

The catfish's top fin and forked tail finally stuck up out of the water, revealing it to be an extremely large channel cat. Then it suddenly splashed water high into the air. "That's a big fish, Dad!" Jason yelled.

Dan knew he had to be careful with his twelve-pound-test fishing line. "Yes, I know, Son," he calmly replied while reeling the catfish closer to shore, making sure there was tension on the nylon line.

Jason glanced at his wristwatch. His father had been trying to land the fish for almost twenty minutes. He stared down at the dark, shadowy figure just below the surface. The catfish splashed more water high into the air. Jason got wet, grinned about it, and immediately placed his attention back on the water.

The large catfish was now within a few feet of the shoreline. "I've worn him out, kids," Dan said. "Now, as long as we do not get him out of the water too soon, he won't break our line."

Jason understood that the weight of the fish out of the water would be much heavier than the twelve-pound-test line. Kyle did not think much about it.

The water was still fairly deep where the catfish now swam nearly motionless, resting itself against the tight nylon fishing line. Because of the depth of the water, Jason would not be able to easily jump into the water and net the fish. Dan reeled the fish a little closer, so that it was next to the shoreline. "Okay, Jason, net the fish," he said.

Excited, Jason stretched the fishnet out into the water, just behind the catfish's tail. He pulled the net toward the shoreline, slowly scooping the catfish inside. It suddenly splashed more water up into the air, as if giving one last strong fight. Jason held on tightly, though, getting wet again in the process. His father could not help but start laughing.

Jason grinned, as he was having fun and did not care how wet he got. He finally managed to ensnare the brownish-gray catfish most of the way inside the net and excitedly turned back to his father. "Okay, Dad, I have him," he said.

"Well, bring him ashore," Dan said.

Jason pulled the fish up onto the bank. The catfish's head stuck out of the end of the net, and Jason struggled while pulling it a little farther up the bank. "He's heavy," he said, noticing that the catfish had also swallowed the hook.

Dan dropped the pole, grabbed the catfish by its lower jaw, and pulled it farther up the bank to level ground. He then removed his pocketknife, cut the line, and lifted the catfish high into the air, surprised at its weight and girth. "Very good, Jason," he said. "We've just landed a possibly thirty-pound channel cat. Go get your mom and have her bring the camera down here."

Kyle stared aimlessly at the large catfish, which appeared bigger than him, as Jason quickly walked away to tell their mother about the catfish they had just caught.

✦ ✦ ✦

Back on the spaceship, Michael continued silently listening and watching everything that was transpiring. He saw Jason's and Kyle's excitement and watched for nearly fifteen minutes as their father patiently and relentlessly reeled the feisty catfish to shore. After Jason pulled the catfish from the water, Michael recognized the Earth creature as *Ictalurus* genus class with the ability to survive in fresh water. It had no multicellular chloride cells in its body to help rid its plasma of excess salt like saltwater species.

Michael continued to gaze at the highly detailed holographic image of Jason's father and Kyle staring down at the catfish, having a dawning realization of what it was like to be part of a family, to have a mother and father. He thought again about who his parents were—who had created him—but could not recall any memory of them, so he made the logical conclusion that he'd never had a family or fully understood the concept prior to his observations of the Jupiter family. He continued to listen with real interest as Jason's father talked with Kyle about the fish they'd just caught. Simultaneously, he also listened to Jason excitedly tell his mother about the catfish inside the house.

Curious to see the front porch, Michael touched his front console, creating another remote-viewing, optical-dispersion beam at a thirty-four-degree angle of incline into the atmosphere, projected nearly eight hundred feet due north at an altitude of five hundred feet. With this new energy beam and phase angle in relation to Earth, the ship's computer began adjusting for a reflected light wavelength that would now have a four-degree spatial phase shift along the ground state of the nitrogen molecules. As soon as the ship's molecular optical dispersion system locked onto the proper reflected-light phase shift angle across the nitrogen molecules in relation to a speed-of-light space plane, he touched another button on his console. Suddenly, another panorhombic image, one meter in diameter, appeared just to the right of the other image. This new light-reflection-scheme, remote-viewing holographic image was referenced from the atmosphere as if Michael's ship were hovering at an altitude of five hundred feet just north of Jason's house. Michael now patiently waited for Jason and his mother to exit the house.

✦ ✦ ✦

Inside the house, fascinated after her son's enthusiastic account of the large catfish, Jason's mother quickly grabbed their Minolta 35 mm camera and followed Jason toward the front door. Jason opened the door for his mother, closed the door behind them, and headed west across the porch. They continued down the west porch stairs while being secretly watched by Michael on the secondary panorhombic holographic image.

Due to Jason's excitement, Barbara had to surmise the fish was pretty big. She found herself walking a little faster than normal to keep up with her son's pace as they walked through the small forest of oak and piñon trees. Barbara paused to catch her breath as they neared the creek. Exiting the forest, she saw Kyle and her husband standing near the shoreline next to an extremely large catfish. When she reached them, she was astounded by the catfish, which was the largest live channel cat she'd ever seen. "That fish is huge!" she said.

"Yes, it is," Dan said, still amazed. "It weighs a surprising thirty-two pounds, if you can believe that. You know, this could very well be a state record for a channel cat."

Barbara was even more surprised. "Are you going to contact Fish and Game?"

"Nope," Dan said. "I don't want anybody finding out about that deep hole in the creek."

Barbara understood.

Jason could tell how surprised his mother was at the size of the fish. He walked over next to his father and little brother while staring down at the catfish.

Barbara removed the lens cover from the camera and looked up at her family. "Let me take a picture of you three fishermen next to the catfish," she kidded.

Dan knew it would be a great picture and grabbed the fish by its lower jaw, lifting it into the air with his right arm. Kyle stood to the right of the catfish, and Jason was just to the right of his little brother. The catfish was almost as long as Kyle was tall.

Barbara focused her camera with what little sunlight remained. "Do not move," she said and pressed the button, which was followed by a flash. "I'm taking another picture," she said, looking through the lens at her husband and boys standing with relaxed grins. She pressed the button again. It seemed to her that Jason was acting his normal self, even though something was still not right with the puncture holes in his forearm and the way he was previously acting.

Dan continued to stare at his wife with a cheerful face and then noticed Jason looking up at him. He turned back to his wife. "Let's get a picture of Jason holding the catfish," he said, "since he did help catch it."

Barbara agreed that was a great idea. Her husband handed the catfish to Jason, who grabbed it by its lower jaw using both hands. He was having a hard time holding its tail off the ground, which made Barbara giggle. "Kyle," she said, "stand just to the right of your brother."

Barbara briefly looked to her husband. "How long is that catfish?"

"Thirty-seven inches," he replied.

"Wow!" she said.

Dan walked behind his two sons, standing directly behind the large catfish with Jason and Kyle on each side of him. Jason turned the catfish a little to his right while struggling to keep its tail off the ground. Barbara giggled again while looking through the camera lens. Dan placed his hands on his sons' shoulders, and she finally pressed the button, triggering an immediate flash. "Let me take one more," she said.

"Hurry, Mom," Jason said. "This fish is wearing me out."

"Okay," she said with a slight grin, again looking through the camera lens. Jason was still struggling to hold the fish off the ground, Kyle had a fascinated look, and Dan displayed a subtle grin. She pushed the button, and the camera again flashed. She knew the last picture would carry a lot of great memories. "I'm done," she said.

Jason immediately handed the catfish to his father, who grabbed it by its lower jaw. The boys were transfixed on the catfish. "We probably have enough meat here for at least a dozen or so meals," Dan kidded.

Jason understood exactly what his father meant, knowing they would have fresh catfish for tomorrow evening's supper and many more to come.

Dan noticed his oldest son daydreaming and also noticed that there was less than an hour of sunlight left. "Go ahead and reel in my other pole, Jason. We're calling it an evening so I can get this monster cleaned before dark."

"Okay," Jason said. He grabbed his father's other pole and had begun reeling it in when suddenly the bobber disappeared. He quickly pulled the pole toward himself, and the line tightened. A fairly good-sized fish soon jumped out of the water, followed by a big splash. "I caught one, Dad!" he called out.

Jason's parents, his brother, and even Michael noticed Jason's excitement. Dan set the catfish down, and they all watched as Jason began reeling in the extremely energetic fish. The fish broke the surface a couple more times, revealing itself to be a fairly good-sized bass. Jason reeled the fish closer to shore, just as his father had done with the catfish, except it was less than a minute later when Jason landed it. He grabbed its lower jaw and lifted his prize catch high above his head. It was a largemouth bass, as clearly evidenced by its large lower jaw and the black band traveling down its sides, from head to tail. Flushed with excitement, Jason turned to his parents and his little brother with pride.

Dan noticed his son's reaction. "Very good, Son," he said.

The next business at hand was to remove the hook from the fish's upper jaw. After unhooking the fish, Jason opened the tackle box and grabbed their Rapala digital fish scale. Carefully hooking the scale on the fish's bottom jaw, he read the weight, becoming flushed with even more excitement, as it was the largest bass he had ever caught. "It weighs five pounds, nine ounces, Dad!" he said. Dan and Barbara could understand his excitement.

Jason pulled the fish basket out of the water and untied it from the tree branch. He returned the small perch he'd caught earlier to the creek and placed his bass inside the basket.

Kyle stood in admiration of his older brother and walked over to his little pole. He began to reel it in but found he'd also caught a fish. "I have a fish too!" he called out excitedly.

Jason, Dan, Barbara, and Michael watched Kyle attempt to reel in his fish. Based on the amount of play in the line, it was a small fish, but it was big to Kyle, just as the bass was to Jason. When he finally reeled it up to the shoreline, it was another largemouth bass, though a very small one. Lifting it out of the water, he gazed up into his father's face with a big, wide smile.

Dan looked down at his young son with compassion, realizing the fish was well under a half pound. "Very good, Kyle," he said, "but your fish is too small to keep. Go ahead and throw it back into the water."

Kyle understood they only kept fish of a certain size to help maintain the populations. "Okay," he said and slowly removed the hook while thinking about the large catfish his father had just caught. He stared at his own fish and finally walked up to the shore and gently placed it into the water. The small fish quickly swam away out of sight.

Kyle walked over to his brother and parents. Jason had his hands full, holding his pole, their father's two poles, the fishnet, and the fish basket with his five-pound bass. Their mother was holding the tackle box, and their dad held the large catfish and plastic bag of chicken liver. Kyle then picked up the Styrofoam cup of worms.

The Jupiter family began the trek back to their house with Dan firmly gripping the thirty-two-pound catfish. Jason and Kyle, beside their father, were still fascinated by the size of the catfish, whose tail occasionally dragged on the ground. After entering the small forest, Dan made eye contact with his wife and held the bloody bag of chicken liver up in the air. "How about carrying this?" he kidded.

Looking at the blood dripping from the bag, Barbara said, "No, not tonight."

Dan shook his head with laughter. Barbara had grown up on a small farm, enjoyed fishing, and had baited many hooks as a kid, with worms, shrimp, and even liver, but Dan knew she probably did not want to get her hands bloody. Jason noticed his parents joking around. It meant they were in extremely good moods. He looked back toward the creek, seeing the tree shadows behind them, and wondered whether Michael had been listening to their conversations at the creek, especially everything that had happened with catching the large catfish.

As the Jupiter family walked closer to the house, Michael sat quietly, watching them on his panorhombic holographic display. All the while, his ship's computer was continually changing the endpoint, or length of the panorhombic energy beam in a moving pattern to match the Jupiters' relative angular positions to his spaceship. The computer modified and projected the beam higher in altitude the closer they approached the house. The image slowly matched the secondary image north of the Jupiters' house, projected down on the porch. The two panorhombic images started to overlap one another, creating panorhombic holographic stereovision. The Jupiter family finally walked up the west stairs onto the porch, and the two images became identical. In response to this unsuspected aspect of advanced remote viewing, Michael grabbed a pair of optical dispersion eyeglasses. When he put the glasses on, his visual acuity was projected into the image itself. He was able to view everything with 360 degrees of rotation, as though standing on the porch next to them.

On the porch, Barbara set the tackle box down in preparation for the abundance of meat. "I'll get the pans ready," she said.

"Okay," Dan said and stared down at his two sons. "Put everything away, boys, while I get a tub and a bucket."

"Okay," Jason said. As his father headed toward the garage, Jason removed his bass from the basket, laid it down next to the catfish, and picked up all four fishing poles, the fishnet, the fish basket, and the chicken liver while Kyle picked up the tackle box and Styrofoam cup of worms. They both walked down the west stairs toward the garage as quickly as possible. Their father had already left the garage carrying a rectangular ten-gallon metal tub and a five-gallon white plastic bucket. This only caused them to hurry even more so they could watch their father prepare the large catfish.

Inside the garage, Jason set the poles back on their stand and hung the fishnet and basket on the wall. Kyle placed the tackle box on the table and then followed his older brother to the refrigerator. Jason placed the chicken liver back inside the freezer, and Kyle gently placed the Styrofoam cup inside the refrigerator. Jason shut the door while staring down at his little brother. "We'd better hurry," he said.

Kyle vigorously nodded his head up and down.

The two boys hurried out of the garage to find their father had already turned on the water and was pulling the garden hose toward the porch. They followed close behind him, up the west stairs and back onto the porch, where Dan placed both fish inside the tub. He latched the water nozzle open, set it in the tub, and noticed his boys staring aimlessly at the fish. "Jason," he said, "I'm grabbing my knives, pliers, and hammer, so shut the water off when the tub is about half-full."

Jason knew exactly why his dad was retrieving those items. "Okay, Dad," he replied and watched his father enter the house.

While the boys watched the fish, the large catfish suddenly flipped its tail, splashing water high into the air, getting Jason and Kyle's wet, but neither of them cared, as it was fun seeing the power of the catfish. The bass could barely swim around due to the enormous catfish, which could not straighten its body inside the tub. Jason watched intently as the catfish opened and closed its gills, curious how it was able to remove oxygen from the water so easily. When the tub was about half-full, he pulled the nozzle out of the water and shut the hose off.

Dan walked out onto the porch carrying an extremely sharp filet knife, a hunting knife, pliers, a sixteen-ounce claw hammer, and a large pan. He set everything down on the small wood table next to the porch stairs and picked up the hammer, firmly grasping it in his right hand.

Jason and Kyle knew exactly how the hammer was to be used—you could not have a fish alive when skinning and cleaning it. Dan reached down into the tub, picked up the bass, which was already in shock from a lack of oxygen and near death, and set it down on the wood deck porch. He hit it squarely between the eyes and placed it back in the tub. Jason, Kyle, and secretly Michael earnestly watched as Dan next lifted the large catfish out of the tub, laid it down on the wood deck, and then whacked it with as much force as humanly possible, two times squarely between the eyes.

The large catfish flopped around for a few seconds and was then motionless, just like the bass, its gills no longer moving. Solemnly witnessing this, Jason's and Kyle's hearts saddened for the large, old fish—even though it would provide lots of food. Their father would sometimes release large fish, like the channel cat, but not this time, possibly because it had swallowed the bait or maybe because of where it had been caught.

Michael also felt something after witnessing Dan Jupiter remove the life force from the old catfish and did not fully understand this new feeling. It was as though he felt sorry for the fish, but he quickly understood it was a lower-order, nonsentient species class that provided food with high protein, low levels of potassium, and sodium supplements.

Dan next picked up the bass. Using his hunting knife, he held it over the five-gallon bucket and began removing the overlapping ctenoid scales, brushing the sharp blade back and forth at an angle toward its head. The scales overlapped each other in the direction of the bass's tail, so when the knife traveled toward the head, the nearly colorless scales easily popped off.

With all the scales finally removed, Dan cut and removed the dorsal and side fins, followed by the tail. He then made a spiral cut behind the gills, the eyes, and around the circumference of the fish's body to its bottom. He then made a slit at the bottom of the bass, starting at its vent opening and connecting up to the spiral cut he had just completed. Now the bass's internal organs and innards were exposed. Dan grabbed and bent the bass's head, breaking its spine in half just behind the head. He then gently pulled its head, along with its innards, from the body and tossed them into the five-gallon bucket.

Among the innards was the bass's white air bladder. Jason and Kyle knew the air bladder was not a lung but a hollow organ used as both an emergency air supply and swim bladder. Michael knew even more about air bladders and the other anatomy of fish species, including that the filaments in gills helped remove oxygen from the water. The gills had arches that housed the filaments, and their folds greatly increased the surface area of the water across the gills, allowing fish to remove oxygen from water by a process called diffusion. The human race did not have the technology to use fish gill $O_2$-$CO_2$ diffusion exchange biology for scuba diving, which they could not do without the use of external air tanks, but the race he'd come from did have that ability.

Kyle suddenly reached down into the bucket, picked up the bass's innards, and pulled the air sack loose. He threw the head and guts back into the bucket, stared at the air sack, just as he had done many times in the past, and then squeezed—it popped like a small balloon. The fun was short-lived, and he tossed the airless air sack back into the bucket. Meanwhile, Dan had finished preparing the bass and had placed its edible meat portions inside the pan.

Next came the large catfish. Since Kyle and Jason had never seen their father clean so big of a fish, they both were extremely eager to watch. Michael also continued to watch intently, intrigued, as it was another new experience for him that would become forever ingrained in his memories.

Dan set the catfish on the small table, and Jason and Kyle again noted its lifeless body. For the second time, a little sadness crept over them, as they had to acknowledge that the fish that had put up such a valiant fight was now dead.

Dan, using his extremely sharp hunting knife, made a shallow, superficial cut just below the skin that traveled over the catfish's head, behind each eye. He rolled it over and continued this superficial cut all the way around the circumference of the fish, just behind the head. Using pliers, he slowly removed the gray epidermal skin and membrane, starting at the spiral cut and pulling it toward the tail until completely removed. This took him less than a minute and exposed the succulent, translucent white catfish meat. The boys were still watching, and Dan knew they would now have a rough idea how to prepare a really large catfish.

With his hunting knife, he cut around the catfish's fins and pulled them loose with the pliers. He then made a circular cut down to the backbone, just behind its eyes, and partway around the head. He rolled the catfish over and made another carefully located, deep cut on its underbelly, through the soft tissue, taking care not to cut any of its innards. Turning the catfish over on its back, he carefully slit the fish, starting at its vent and continuing through its outer myelin sheath up to the spiral cut just behind the head. The catfish's innards were now eviscerated, visible for the boys, including Michael. Dan firmly held the fish on its side and hit the exposed backbone with the sharp blade of his hunting knife until the bone finally cracked. He then grabbed the head, snapped the backbone in half just behind the head, and slowly and methodically pulled the head and innards loose from the body. He placed them on the table, cut the head off, and threw the innards into the bucket.

Jason quickly grabbed the large white air bladder before Kyle had a chance. He pulled it loose from the guts and stared aimlessly at the enormous air sack with two distinct sections, wondering not for the first time why it looked so much like two balloons. Just as Kyle had done with the bass's air sack, he squeezed them. Pow! Pow! The two sections popped like small firecrackers. Again, the fun was short-lived, and he threw the punctured air sack back into the bucket, turning his full attention and keen interest to his father, curious what he would do next.

Dan placed the large catfish on its side, grabbed his filet knife, and proceeded to cut four- to six-inch-long, even filets from the exposed meat. After he'd cut dozens of filets, half the fish was stripped to the bone, so he turned it over and did the other side, placing the filets in the pan. Before long, the dozens of boneless fish filets formed a heaping pile. He looked forward to trying some for tomorrow night's dinner and many more in the future. On the table now sat a nearly fleshless bone structure, as though an animal had eaten the meat off of it, and he threw the headless skeleton into the plastic bucket. They now had less than ten minutes before sunset.

Dan noticed his sons staring at him and said, "Boys, we probably have over twenty pounds of meat."

Jason looked up with curiosity. "How much meat did we get from my bass, Dad?"

"Maybe two to three pounds," he answered.

Jason stared off with a distant look.

Dan noticed his oldest son was daydreaming. "Jason," he said, "can you carry the large pan of meat to your mother while Kyle and I clean up the porch?"

Without hesitation, Jason walked over to the table, and his father handed him the pan. "This is heavy," Jason said.

Dan grinned a little while opening the front door. Jason walked inside, and Dan closed the door behind him. Dan turned to his young son. "Go ahead and rinse off the porch, Kyle."

"Okay," Kyle said. With the garden hose, he rinsed off the porch and table, spraying until all the fish scales were washed away. Dan then rinsed off his pliers, hammer, and knives in the ten-gallon tub and noticed the large catfish head still sitting on the table. Kyle also noticed and was now curious about it.

Dan removed a sixteen-penny nail from his shirt pocket and

grabbed his claw hammer. After positioning the nail between the catfish's eyes, he hammered it partway into the catfish's skull. He then positioned the head against one of the wood porch posts, glanced briefly at his young son, and drove the nail the rest of the way through the skull. With a ping, the nail buried itself into the post. The catfish head was now nicely displayed about six feet off the porch.

"There," Dan said, looking back down at his little boy. "Now whenever you and your older brother see this catfish head, you'll always know the story behind it."

A dreamy look filled Kyle's face. He wished he could catch a big catfish like that someday, so that he could nail its head on the post next to his dad's prized catch. Dan recognized his son was daydreaming. "Go ahead and finish rinsing off the porch, Kyle," he said.

"Okay," Kyle said and turned the nozzle back on.

Jason walked out of the house, and the first thing he noticed was the large catfish head nailed to one of the wood posts. In amazement, he noted again the catfish's extraordinary size and girth and continued staring at the head, daydreaming and remembering how valiantly the fish had fought for the better part of twenty minutes before finally losing its battle. Jason knew exactly why his father had nailed the head to the post—to serve as a memory and conversation piece to go along with the pictures his mother had taken.

Dan picked up the ten-gallon tub and carried it over to the front porch railing. Resting it on the rails, he slowly dumped the water out onto the rare, mature Pecos sunflowers growing just below the railing. New Mexico Fish and Game were very much aware of the sunflowers' presence here. Dan and his wife also had a verbal agreement with the New Mexico Forestry Division to keep their existence somewhat secret, and as a result, seeds were given to the forestry division each year. All he had to do was maintain them—keep them watered and properly fertilized—something he would never fail to do, since they were beautiful plants. "Jason," he said, "rinse out this tub."

"Okay," Jason replied. He grabbed the nozzle from Kyle and

began rinsing out the tub, thinking about how much fun they'd had fishing, though he really wished Michael could have been with them.

"That's good," his dad said. Jason shut off the nozzle, and Dan lifted the tub off the hand railing. "Spray a little water into the bucket too, Jason."

"Okay, Dad." Jason started filling the bucket, still thinking about Michael and what his mom and dad had talked about in the kitchen after dinner, while he and Kyle were aboard the spaceship.

"That's good," Dan said again, and he picked up the bucket. "Wind up the hose, and, Kyle, put away the tub while I dump the fish guts into our compost."

"Okay, Daddy," Kyle said.

As Dan walked down the west stairs and across the gravel driveway, he thought about the fun he'd had with his two sons. With a quick glance back in their direction, he noticed Kyle carrying the ten-gallon tub toward the garage and Jason not far behind, headed to the faucet on the side of the house. Dan then continued toward the compost pile.

At the house, Jason slowly wound the hose up and thought again about how much fun they'd had fishing but how he wished Michael could have joined them, as it would have no doubt been a new experience for him. As he finished winding up the hose, his little brother came over and stood next to him.

On the other side of the driveway, Dan dumped the fish guts into the five-foot-by-ten-foot compost with a three-foot-high fence and then headed back toward the porch to see his sons patiently waiting. After crossing the driveway and peeling off toward the faucet, he rinsed out the bucket and laid it against the house. He then returned to his two waiting boys. "Well, we're done, kids," he said.

Jason and Kyle had solemnly observed their father's preparation of the fish, which had also included quite a bit of cleanup. Michael had also observed this, all while his ship's computer adjusted the light sensitivity of the photons across the ground state line frequency of the nitrogen molecules. His view of the porch was as bright and clear as if it were still daylight. Shortly, though, he would lose sight of Jason, Kyle, and their father when they entered the house. He could easily adjust the energy beams to look through the north wall of the house, by molecularly changing the vibratory states of the vinyl siding, Styrofoam insulation, plywood sheets, Sheetrock, and their painted surface compositions, but he decided against it, because any solid object that touched the wall would also pass through to the other side. Consequently, he just remained quiet, watching and soon only listening.

Dan grabbed his knives, pliers, and hammer, opened the front door for his sons, and followed them inside. They continued toward the kitchen to find Barbara had already placed most of the catfish filets into vacuum-sealed containers, except for a few that were encased in plastic wrap for dinner the next day. She turned around and saw her family standing quietly. "Yes, there is quite a bit of meat," she said. "We'll have fresh filets tomorrow night."

"Great!" Dan said. "I look forward to trying them. Twenty minutes to land that monster will make it taste even better—not too bad a price for fresh catfish."

Barbara and Jason laughed, and Kyle grinned.

Dan and Barbara thought about what they'd talked about after dinner in the kitchen while Jason and Kyle were getting the fishing gear and bait ready. Jason fixated his eyes on his little brother and then turned his attention back to his parents. He looked as though he was about to say something, but he only said, "We're headed to the living room."

"Okay, Jason," Dan said. "We'll be there shortly."

Dan and Barbara noticed contentment on their oldest son's face as he left the kitchen with his little brother. In the living room, Jason picked up the remote and turned on the television. The Dish Network receiver was on The History Channel. A surprising special was on: *UFOs: Best Evidence Ever Caught on Tape.*

Jason and Kyle sat down together on the couch and quietly began watching the documentary about UFO sightings and the possibility of their existence, both knowing without any doubt whatsoever that UFOs from another world were real. It caused Jason to think about Michael, who was all alone. He gazed down at his little brother. "I wish Michael could be here with us," he said.

"So do I," Kyle said.

About that time, their parents walked into the living room and noticed their boys watching the UFO documentary. It was a very unusual coincidence, with the talk of a UFO being spotted in the vicinity of Los Alamos, not to mention the fact that Jason appeared to be keeping a secret from them. They continued over to the love seat and sat down just across from their boys. Seeing how close their two sons had bonded made their hearts swell. They looked briefly at each other and then back to the television, quietly watching the documentary—at least at first.

# 8

## ONE OF JASON'S SECRETS EXPOSED

Dan and Barbara quietly watched the documentary for only a short moment before Dan made eye contact with his wife—a nonverbal communication that went unnoticed by their boys. She returned a silent nod. Dan then looked directly over at Jason, who was entranced by the UFO documentary special. Dan thought about what to say, knowing they had never bought Jason an armband, especially one that was extremely thin and as realistic looking as his wife had described. Besides that, Jason did not normally wear any type of jewelry or toys beyond the expensive waterproof phosphorescent wristwatch they'd bought for his birthday about a month ago.

"I heard you were wearing an armband earlier, Jason," Dan finally said.

Jason turned toward his parents. He'd known that question would pop up sooner or later—he just hadn't been sure when. He thought about a response. "Yes, I was," he said.

Dan noticed Jason was not saying much. "May I please see it?"

"Okay," he said, somewhat reluctant, and then stood up. He removed the fake armband from his pants, walked over, and handed it to his father.

Dan looked at the armband with unusual curiosity. It was extremely light and thin as paper, and its surface had the appearance and texture of a metallic composition he had never seen. He turned it over, revealing a plain-looking underside. Naturally curious, Jason's mother also looked at the armband, closely scrutinizing the underside, which was extremely smooth. The top side did appear to have the same buttons she'd seen before. Dan touched a few of the buttons and then attempted to bend the armband, but no matter how hard he tried, it remained solid and inflexible. He finally turned back to Jason, who still stood quietly in front of him. "Where did you get this?" he asked.

"I found it," Jason quickly replied.

Dan paused at his son's strange answer and asked, "Where?"

"I found it on our land," he said. "Can I have it back?"

Dan knew his son did not realize the uncharacteristic insistence in his voice. He then thought about the military activity he'd seen, including the armed guards that had told him about a crashed military aircraft, and a strange thought about the whole incident came to mind. He now did not know what to think about it all, especially considering that their cell phones and landline had all gone dead soon after the supposed military aircraft crash. There was talk of a UFO in the vicinity of Los Alamos last night and today, and somehow, the armband was a part of that equation.

He made direct eye contact with his oldest son. He wanted to get to the bottom of this secret without causing his son unwarranted duress, especially as he did not know the circumstances behind what had caused the three holes in Jason's forearm that formed the points of a perfect equilateral triangle. "Okay, Jason," he finally said. "I will give it back to you for now, but tomorrow I'm taking it to the labs to determine what material it is composed of."

Jason did not know what to think about his dad having possession of the alien artifact. "I'll leave it on the table before I go to bed tonight. Okay, Dad?"

"Okay, Son," Dan said, looking down again at the puncture wounds on Jason's forearm. "So what happened to your left forearm?"

Jason figured his father had already seen the three small puncture holes, but he hadn't said anything until now. "It must have happened when I was playing, Dad," he said.

Dan immediately knew his son was hiding something, but he did not have the faintest idea what could be behind it. "Is that right?" he only said. "Did this armband cause them?"

"No," Jason truthfully answered.

Dan could tell from his son's quick answer and intonation that he was telling the truth. He handed the armband back to his son.

Jason turned around and walked back over to the couch, relieved his father had not questioned him further about the three small puncture holes. He did not think he could give another answer without being trapped in a lie. He thought about his dad's line of questions and sat back down. *That was a close one*, he thought.

While the Jupiter family continued to watch the UFO documentary, which was talking about the many hoaxes versus true unexplained visual sightings, Jason started to wonder about Michael and his welfare on the spaceship all by himself. He felt an immense urge to call Michael on his communicator and noticed his parents seemed to now have a lot on their minds besides just the History Channel special. "Mom, Dad," he said across the room, "Kyle and I are going to my bedroom. Okay?"

"Sure, you guys," their father said.

Jason and Kyle headed to his bedroom, where they sat down on his bed, Michael and the spaceship clearly on their minds.

Kyle wondered what his older brother wanted to do now. Jason knew this and said, "Let's get our communicators out, and I'll show you how they work."

"Okay," Kyle said, quickly removing the communicator from his pants pocket.

Jason also removed his, and they both quietly stared at their communicators, which Jason knew were much more than just communicators; they were also weapons and had advanced countermeasures, such as image displacement and synaptic disruption. He was not going to mention those capabilities to Kyle, though. He held the communicators next to each other and pointed at the button on the left side of Kyle's communicator. "Okay, if you push that button there, the communicator becomes active, and you can speak freely to Michael," he explained. "Understand?"

Kyle saw the button mentioned. "Yeah, I understand." He quickly touched the button and paused, looking up into Jason's eyes.

"Go ahead and talk into the communicator," Jason said.

Kyle stared down at his communicator. "Hi, Michael," he said.

"Hi, Kyle," Michael quickly responded.

A big grin appeared on Kyle's face.

"Fun, huh?" Jason said.

"Yes, it is," Kyle said, excited to now have his own little communicator box, similar to his dad's cell phone.

Michael quietly listened while Jason and Kyle talked back and forth. "When are you two coming back to the ship?" he asked.

Jason looked down at his little brother's communicator. "How about midnight?" he replied.

"Okay, I will be waiting," Michael said.

Jason thought about the spaceship hidden behind the barn. "Michael," he said into the communicator, "can you bring the ship over to the east side of the house again about ten minutes before midnight?"

"Yes, I can," Michael responded.

Jason stared down at the communicator one more time. "Okay. We'll see you at midnight, then."

"Okay, bye," Michael said.

Jason shut off Kyle's communicator while making direct eye contact with his little brother. "I'm telling Mom and Dad that you'll be sleeping with me tonight."

Kyle was visibly excited. "Oh, goody!"

Jason glanced at his wristwatch. It was 9:35 p.m. He reached over to his alarm clock, adjusted the alarm to go off five minutes before midnight, and then stood up along with Kyle. He stared down at his little brother again. "Let's go tell Mom and Dad good night," he said.

"Okay," Kyle said.

They returned to the living room, where Jason caught his parents kissing each other on the lips. They'd been flirting at the dinner table earlier, and he had seen this behavior in the past. It always seemed to lead to additional affection later that night.

Realizing they'd been caught passionately kissing, Dan and Barbara sat silently with slightly embarrassed, short smiles. Jason recognized this. "Mom, Dad," he said, "Kyle is sleeping with me tonight."

"Okay, Jason," his mother said. "Are you two also going to bed, then?"

"Yes, we are," Jason said.

"Come and give us good night kisses, then," she said.

The two boys said their good nights, which included hugs and kisses. Jason was about to leave the room but then stopped. He turned around, removed the fake armband from his pants, and placed it on the coffee table in front of his parents. He then looked directly into his father's eyes with a sincere expression, again worrying about his parents working for the government with top-secret clearances, not to mention what could possibly happen to Michael. "Dad," he said, "would you please only show this armband to someone you completely trust?"

Dan was surprised by the unusual request from his ten-year-old. "Why, Jason?" he asked.

Jason paused. Even though the armband was fake, he knew there was a possibility his father might determine strange characteristics about it that indicated it came from outside of this world, and that could lead to their family being closely scrutinized by the government. "Can I explain it to you tomorrow after you get home from work?"

Dan turned to Barbara, who now had an unusual look on her face. Jason saw this, and Dan, with an honest face, made direct eye contact with his son. "All right, Son, I will," he promised. "Tomorrow, then."

Dan and Barbara noticed a sense of relief appear across Jason's face. Jason then left the room with his little brother trailing closely behind. After they entered his bedroom, Jason closed the door behind them and noticed Kyle already on top of his bed. He sat down next to Kyle, knowing his little brother was thrilled getting to sleep with his older brother. "Let's leave our clothes on," Jason said, "because when we wake up in just a few hours, it will seem like we never slept."

"Okay," Kyle said.

Jason pulled off his tennis shoes and his little brother's shoes. He then walked over to his door, turned off the light, and returned to the bed, where he crawled in next to his little brother, pulling the bedcovers up to his neck. His little brother stared into his eyes, his face cast in shadow. Kyle had slept with him hundreds of times, though they hadn't been allowed to sleep together overnight until Kyle was about two. Jason took a deep breath and gently whispered, "Michael and I flew to Canada in the spaceship earlier today."

Kyle was quiet, because he knew Canada was far away, another country that was north of the United States. "I want to go to there too," he said.

"We'll see," Jason said. "Maybe tonight we can even fly to the stars."

Kyle now daydreamed of them flying to the stars and could think of nothing else, but it also caused him to start becoming extremely tired.

"Yes," Jason said, "we then flew over the Colorado mountains and saw their snowy peaks, which looked like upside-down snow cones." Jason paused and looked down again at his little brother, whose eyes were now closed. "That was a lot of fun," he said, "but what was even more fun was when I used my armband to walk through one of the walls of our barn. I even played a joke on Mom while I was invisible."

Jason looked down into his little brother's face again. "Are you still awake, Kyle?"

Kyle did not respond, having fallen asleep.

Jason thought about his father having the fake armband and taking it the Los Alamos labs, which had an abundance of equipment to test it. "Good night, little brother," he softly whispered and placed a small, affectionate kiss against Kyle's cheek.

Jason soon fell asleep in anticipation of seeing Michael at midnight and having the chance to again fly around in the spaceship.

✦ ✦ ✦

In the living room, Barbara and Dan watched television for only a short moment longer after Jason and Kyle left the room. They were eager to talk about what Jason had just said to them and even more so about the object he'd left on the table. Neither of them could fathom what would motivate their son to say what he had about not showing the armband to anyone they did not trust. Dan turned to his wife. "Wasn't that a strange question from Jason?"

"Yes, it was," she said, fully agreeing. "What do you think is behind it?"

"I do not have a clue."

Barbara again thought about the three puncture wounds in their son's left arm. "You know," she finally said, "those three small holes in his forearm are located exactly where he was wearing the armband earlier this morning."

Dan was a little surprised by her comment, even though she had already alluded to it. "Is that right?" he said.

"Yes," she said. "Let's take another look at the armband."

Dan picked up the armband, again amazed at how extremely light it was. He leaned back and studied the armband with unusual curiosity, examining it much more closely. Barbara grabbed his hand, gently tilting the armband just a bit. "Yes, this looks exactly like what he was wearing," she said. "Might it have retractable needles?"

A strange look came over Dan's face at this question, and he continued to scrutinize the armband from different angles. "Good question," he said, "but then that would mean Jason knows how the armband is used, since the needles are now gone. Look how thin it is—paper thin yet so strong I cannot bend it. I have a hard time believing there could ever be retractable needles with its extreme thinness."

Now more curious, Barbara gently grabbed the armband from her husband, also noticing its extremely light weight. She also tried to bend it with all her might but found she could not. She gave her husband a long look. "Honey," she said, "there is definitely more going on here. The armband could be more dangerous that we realize. Could Jason have another device similar to the armband that caused the three holes?"

"Another good question," Dan said, "and as far as this armband being dangerous, I would not have the faintest idea, but I am extremely curious what the metallurgy lab can determine about its basic atomic structure."

Barbara remembered what Jason had said to them before leaving the room. "Do you fully trust Frank?"

She was referring to their longtime friend Dr. Frank Andrews, whom she also used to work with at the labs about ten years ago before transitioning to a part-time consultant working from home soon after Jason was born. Frank had been a college buddy of Dan's before either of them had accepted jobs at the Los Alamos labs. "Yes, I do trust him," Dan finally answered.

"Good," Barbara said, "because I do not want anyone, any government agency, meddling in our family's personal lives, especially if that armband turns out to be much more than a toy."

Dan could understand his wife's firmness. "I understand, dear," he said. He found himself wondering again about the reports of a UFO being spotted in the area of Los Alamos as well as the armed military guards he'd met, including the men dressed in black who had detained him when he was looking for Jason. When he tried to put all the pieces together in his mind, it did not add up. Jason's armband was a part of the puzzle. That thought alone caused him to let out a deep sigh. He decided not to say anything more about it to his wife. He laid the armband on the table and looked into Barbara's big, pretty blue eyes, filled with never-ending love. He wanted to get everything that had just transpired with their oldest son off his mind. "Let's go to bed," he said with a slight grin.

Barbara giggled at Dan's suggestion, knowing that, like her, he also did not want to keep dwelling on the armband at the moment, including what unusual circumstances Jason might have gotten their family into. What that might be, they both still did not have a clue. She leaned over for another wet kiss.

Encouraged, Dan held his wife tight while returning a passionate kiss. For a short moment, they were oblivious to the world around them, thinking only about how much they loved each other and their family. They finally stood up, Dan turning off the living room lights, and they left the room holding hands, heading directly to their bedroom, where Dan closed the door behind them. Leaving the bedside lamp on, he removed his shoes and socks and began kissing his pretty wife on the neck and behind her ear.

Barbara's body tingled all over, and she briefly shivered. As Dan looked into her eyes, his heartbeat increased slightly, and he began passionately kissing her on the lips. They slowly removed each other's clothes, meticulously, thoughtfully, until completely naked.

Dan held his wife tight, again realizing how much he truly loved her, both physically and spiritually. It was an attraction as if she was his chosen soul mate. Catching his breath, he pulled the covers back with a feeling inside reserved especially for him. Under the covers, their passion heated up, and in the privacy of their bedroom, they proceeded to finish one of love's most rewarding dances—a dance that had begun earlier during dinner.

✦ ✦ ✦

Michael moved the spaceship from behind the barn to just east of the house—the exact location as yesterday. He thought about his new friends Jason and Kyle and how he would get to see them again shortly. While waiting for them to show up, he wondered again about who had created him and what they might look like, but he could not visualize anybody in his mind, real or living, from the planet from where he'd originated. The only living beings he could now see in his thoughts were Jason, Kyle, and their parents.

He looked up through the top dome window. The moon was shining down, lighting up the side of Jason's house and the two barns. The light from the telephone pole, just south of the ship, was also shining down on the ground, its rays reflecting against the sides of the barns, the cedar fence, and the house, all seemingly in concert with the moonlight.

According to the front console, the solar time on Earth in reference to Los Alamos was 11:54 p.m. Michael touched a few buttons on the front console to check the status of the cloaked ship and make sure it was still harmonically adjusted to allow for the proper operation of all phones inside the house, as well as the 60 Hz, 120 VAC–powered devices, such as the cold-storage units inside the house and garage, what he now knew were called "refrigerators" and "freezers." The ship's computer was still compensating for the magnetic-flux variations in Earth's magnetic field in relation to the cloaking field. Since there were now small pockets of harmonic energy inside the house and the garage directly associated with 120 VAC devices, he created new algorithms that would null out the small pockets of reversed potential energy, because he now knew the military might be able to detect those uncharacteristic harmonics using their highly sophisticated spy satellites. After successfully accomplishing these tasks, he leaned back in his chair, quietly waiting for Jason and Kyle.

✦ ✦ ✦

In Jason's bedroom, a buzzing sound filled the air, and Jason immediately woke up. He remembered the same alarm clock going off at 3:30 a.m. the night before, but this time the alarm seemed to take on more meaning, because his little brother was joining him and Michael and they were planning to travel into outer space. He shut off the alarm after slowly opening his sleep-laden eyes.

Kyle was still sound asleep, conked out, so Jason gently shook his shoulder. "Kyle, wake up," he whispered. "We're going to the spaceship."

His brother moved around and fussed, wanting to wake up, but then he went back to sleep. Jason insistently urged him awake again, nudging his shoulder a little harder. "Wake up, Kyle," he said again.

Jason knew he would have a hard time waking Kyle up and turned on his bedside lamp. He walked over to the window and felt a cool breeze blowing in from the east. Outside, the telephone pole light was shining down on the ground, but there was no sign of the spaceship, which was most likely cloaked. Returning to the bed, he slipped on his tennis shoes. After tying the laces, he removed the communicator from his pants. "Michael?" he called out and placed the communicator next to his brother's left ear.

"Yes, Jason?" Michael replied.

Kyle had to have heard Michael's reply, as he finally aroused a little, barely opening his eyes. "About time, sleepyhead," Jason said. "Are you ready to go to the spaceship?"

Kyle opened his eyes a little more. "Yes, I am," he said, still half-asleep.

"I'm still here, Michael," Jason said into the communicator.

"I know," Michael said, instinctively knowing Jason was having a hard time waking up his little brother.

Jason slipped the communicator into his pants pocket and helped his little brother out of bed. Kyle stretched a little, and Jason also stretched, trying to gain more of his mental senses. Kyle then sat up on the side of the bed, and Jason grabbed his little brother's tennis shoes. He slipped the tennis shoes onto his brother's dangling feet and tied the shoelaces, as it would have taken forever for his little brother to do it. Kyle crawled out of the bed, now standing next to his older brother.

They continued over to the window, where Jason unlatched the screen. He then slid a small table in front of the window and stared down at his little brother. "I'll go out the window first, so I can help you down to the ground. Okay?"

"Okay," Kyle said.

Jason gently pushed the screen open and placed his legs through the opening first, sitting on the bottom of the window. He then turned around on his stomach. Holding on to the windowsill for a short moment longer, he looked up into the room. "Hold the screen, Kyle," he whispered, "so that it doesn't bang shut."

Kyle climbed on the table and held the screen. Jason then quietly jumped down to the ground and stared up toward the window. "Okay, come on," he said.

Kyle crawled out of the window the same way Jason had, carefully turning onto his stomach while holding the window frame. His feet now dangled outside the window. Jason grabbed his legs, and Kyle let loose before Jason was fully prepared. There was a small crackling sound from the metal screen slamming into the window frame, and Jason immediately felt the full weight of his little brother, plus gravitational momentum, and lost his balance. He held on tight to his brother as he fell backward. Not wanting Kyle to get hurt, Jason kept his little brother shielded on top of him, taking the brunt of the force. They lay tangled on the ground for a moment. After they both finally stood up, Jason gave his little brother a small grin. "I guess you're a little heavier than I thought," he said. He then removed the communicator from his pants and told Michael, "We're right outside the ship."

"Okay, Jason," Michael said. "I watched you fall to the ground. Did either of you get hurt?"

"No, we're both okay," Jason replied.

A bright opening soon appeared from out of nowhere—like a hole into another world—revealing the exact location of the spaceship. A ramp appeared just below the doorway.

Jason gently nudged Kyle toward the ship with a hand on his shoulder. Kyle sped off without hesitation, heading up the ramp with Jason close behind. After they were inside, the open doorway disappeared behind them. They continued toward the cockpit to find Michael still sitting in the right seat. He calmly turned around.

The three boys greeted each other, and Jason and Kyle sat down in the two open seats, Kyle again between Michael and Jason. Kyle was clearly fascinated with all the brightly colored lights on the consoles. Jason turned to Michael. "How about we fly into outer space?"

"Are you sure?" Michael asked.

"Yes," Jason said.

"Okay," Michael said, noticeable concern in his voice, "but I will have to pilot the ship when traveling through the ionosphere."

Jason knew a little about the ionosphere, the invisible sphere that shielded Earth from the sun's intense energy that would be otherwise dangerous. "Okay, Michael," he said.

Michael grabbed his control wheel with both hands.

Jason felt immense anticipation for traveling into outer space, as it was something only astronauts had the chance to do. It reminded him of how much he wanted to become an astronaut when he was older. Michael pulled up on the control wheel and then removed his hands. According to Jason's front console, they were now hovering at an altitude of 250 feet. Kyle stood up and looked out one of the side windows. Their two barns and house were visible down below against the mercury-vapor telephone pole light. Even more fascinated, Kyle sat back down. In some respects, Kyle felt they were flying like in an airplane, but it was also nothing like an airplane, because they were motionless and did not hear or feel a thing while moving.

Jason noticed his brother's rapt silence and fascinated expression. "Neat, huh?" he said.

"Yes, it is," he said while looking around the spaceship.

Michael also observed Kyle's interest, which seemed mixed with even more fascination than Jason had experienced the first time. Michael gazed over at Jason and said, "We are now traveling into outer space."

Jason's and Kyle's excitement increased, especially after Michael grabbed his control wheel again with both hands and lifted straight up. Their ship rose even higher at an extremely fast but exponentially even rate to ensure their cloaking field did not break down. According to Jason's front console, their rapidly changing altitude had just surpassed fifteen thousand feet and was still rising.

Michael pulled his control wheel back toward the right, just a bit, and then pushed it forward while continuing to apply upward pressure with very little effort. Their ship traveled both up and away in an easterly direction at eighteen thousand miles per hour, rising at a rate of one thousand feet per second, yet Jason did not feel any movement or acceleration forces whatsoever. He pointed down at his display. "See, Kyle, we are now traveling at eighteen thousand miles per hour. Mom and Dad can only travel around fifty-five miles per hour in their car. We are traveling over three hundred times faster."

Kyle knew what Jason had told him was true, but he had a hard time comprehending how fast eighteen thousand miles per hour was in relation to fifty-five miles per hour. He knew it was a big number, though, because of Jason telling him it was over three hundred times faster.

Michael idly listened to Jason and Kyle talk back and forth and pulled up on his wheel with additional pressure. Their ship was now rising upward at an eighty-eight degree angle while traveling farther away from Earth. Jason glanced at his display a third time. They were already at an altitude of 140,000 feet and rising at a rate of 22,000 miles per hour. The altitude indicator was changing by over six miles per second. Jason was amazed the ship had that much gravitational propulsion power, to overcome Earth's gravitational forces so easily, especially at their current angle of incline, which was almost straight up.

Michael looked briefly at Jason and Kyle. "We are about to enter the ozone layer," he announced, "and will soon into the mesosphere."

Jason was surprised. "Oh really?"

Kyle was quiet, not knowing what "ozone layer" meant.

Suddenly, red and white electrical flashes appeared outside the cockpit windows and then stopped as they continued farther away from Earth. Only Michael knew the reason for the flashes: they had traveled through Earth's ozone layer and its atmospheric effects at too steep of an angle to Earth's gravitational tug, but their ship's highly advanced hull material would not have felt any gravitational torsional effects.

Jason did not think much about the flashes of light. All he could do was stare mesmerized, almost hypnotic, at Earth's brilliant blue. "Look, Kyle," he said, pointing through one of the side windows.

Kyle also saw the beauty of Earth as well as the peering face of the sun starting to show along the western horizon. "That is pretty," he said.

Michael listened with real interest to Jason and Kyle's conversation and finally removed his hands from the control wheel. Their ship gently came to a stop just a few miles below the lowest layer of the ionosphere, and the three boys sat motionless inside their ship. Michael nudged the right side of his control wheel slightly forward, and their ship turned ninety degrees. They now faced Earth, as if they were about to torpedo back to the planet.

The three boys sat quietly, held in their seats by the spaceship's gravity field. They stared at the brilliant blue Earth, admiring its magnificent beauty and the abundance of clouds, some churning with a tremendous amount of power in the Atlantic Ocean, just off the East Coast of the United States. It was a tropical storm in its birth stages, Michael knew, and they were all amazed at the atmospheric phenomenon.

Jason noticed their altitude was continually changing by a few feet. He thought he understood what might be happening and glanced over to Michael with a slight grin. "I bet we're not rotating at the same speed as Earth, huh?"

"Very good, Jason," Michael said. "That is correct. We are not orbiting at all but locked inside a gravity stream to this planet and its sun."

Jason was surprised by the term *gravity stream* and did not understand it, but he ignored it for now. He stared down at Earth again briefly and then back to Michael. "Is our ship still cloaked?"

"Yes, it is," Michael said.

Jason now wondered about the flashes of light in the ozone layer. "Did those flashes of light occur because our ship was still cloaked?"

"Partly," Michael answered, "but the torsional movement and rotational bulge of Earth against our ship's reactive hull was the main reason, resulting in a high-energy electrical path discharge across the $O_2$ and $O_3$ oxygen molecules."

Jason became dreamy-faced.

Michael took a deep breath and exhaled. "Are you two ready to travel deeper into outer space?"

Jason was surprised to hear Michael exhale, as it seemed to indicate that he had lungs or some apparatus similar to lungs to process air. Whether Michael breathed oxygen or nitrogen, Jason did not know. "Yes, I am," Jason eagerly replied.

"So am I," Kyle said, undisguised excitement filling his voice.

"Okay then," Michael said, "but we need to fasten our seat belts."

Jason did not see any seat belts. Then suddenly, shoulder straps, waist straps, and even leg straps, just above the knees, appeared from out of nowhere. Michael did not touch his front console or armband, so it had to have been a voice-activated response from the ship's computer.

Without warning, the straps tightened. Jason felt them around his waist and legs and crisscrossing his shoulders like would be found in a fighter jet. Surprisingly, none of the straps had buckles. Michael and Kyle were constrained in the exact same manner.

Michael nudged his control wheel forward a little and to the left, and their ship rotated 180 degrees. They now pointed out into deep space. With both hands, he pushed the wheel forward, and their ship quickly accelerated through Earth's mesosphere and toward the ionosphere at a high rate of speed. There was a bump as they entered the first invisible sphere and then a few more bumps as they traveled from one invisible sphere to the next.

Their spaceship's velocity was forty-one thousand miles per hour, and there was another bump right before it became smooth. Jason looked back at Earth, which was becoming much smaller very quickly. When he turned his attention back ahead, Earth's moon was visible in the far distance like a large white light bulb. Michael then let loose of his control wheel, and their ship slowed until their velocity was again zero. They now sat motionless in outer space, less than one-quarter of the way between Earth and the moon.

Jason's front display was still registering their distance to Earth—2,300,795 feet, 2,300,792, feet, 2,300,810 feet—and continuing to change. "That is so strange," he mumbled to himself, "that this ship can tell its distance to Earth so accurately and quick."

"Yes, it is very accurate," Michael said, "because like I told you, our ship's field of gravity is encapsulated inside a gravity stream."

Jason was now even more curious. "So what exactly is a gravity stream?"

Michael answered, "Since gravitational forces exist between your planet and its moon, they also exist in unseen frictional form between those same bodies, as well as other planetary bodies in this solar system, as they orbit around the sun. As a result, there are moving streams focused back to a series of Lagrangian points, as your race calls them, or zero points of curved gravitational space. Our spaceship's computer easily senses those vibration changes in the form of gravity streams, similar to ripples created from a rock thrown into a body of water."

Michael's explanation involved technological understanding of gravity mechanics that Jason was clueless about. Regardless, their ship's computer would have to be extremely powerful to calculate the gravity-stream changes that were probably traveling at the speed of light. Jason looked toward the magnificent stars in the heavens. Their majestic brightness and brilliance were much more pronounced than what he had seen before with his telescope.

Michael noticed Kyle and Jason appeared to be in distant daydreams, their pupils dilated, seemingly totally mesmerized by their trip into outer space. "Do you want to travel farther away from Earth?" he asked.

Jason felt immense anticipation for traveling the rest of the way to the moon, but it was getting close to three in the morning, and they might not be able to return home before his dad left for work. His little brother also looked tired, so Jason decided that they'd better return home. Besides, there was plenty of time to travel to the moon and maybe even visit Mars. "Let's head back home," he said.

"Okay," Michael said. He nudged his control wheel to the left, and their spaceship rotated 180 degrees.

Magnificently displayed against the heavens was Earth, the sun partially exposed and starting to shine its face even more around Earth's horizon. It looked similar to a solar eclipse, except with the moon behind them and with them inside the envelope of Earth's shadow. It was a strange sight to behold, a visual display that had before been possible only in their dreams. Michael pushed his control wheel way forward, taking their velocity up to two hundred and thirty thousand miles per hour. Again, Jason did not felt any acceleration forces whatsoever—it seemed instantaneous. "Is that our maximum speed?" Jason asked.

"No," Michael said. "In the current configuration, yes, but if I were to readjust the energy system's interface to the gravity element, I could increase our speed to a fraction under the speed of light."

Jason was amazed again. Earth quickly came into full view. There was a slight bump again after entering the outer ionospheric layer and then a few more bumps before it was smooth again. Michael pulled back on his control wheel, slowing their ship to twenty thousand miles per hour, and Jason knew what would probably soon be evident. Sure enough, white flames mixed with a red-and-yellow glow appeared around their ship, passing directly across the top bubble-shaped window and their side windows. The flames suddenly extinguished, and they continued their descent, getting to witness firsthand the North American coastlines—the Atlantic and Pacific Ocean shorelines for Canada, the United States, and Mexico—from an amazing vantage point not possible from jet aircraft.

Kyle was still thinking about the ozone layer previously mentioned. "What is the ozone layer, Jason?" he asked.

Jason knew the level of his little brother's inquisitive nature. "The ozone layer, Kyle," he answered, "is a layer of oxygen that absorbs the sun's ultraviolet rays. Without it, most life on Earth would quickly die, especially humans."

Kyle took in this new information like a dry sponge in water. "That is interesting," he said.

Michael showed keen interest in Jason and Kyle's verbal interaction as their altitude approached forty thousand feet and still dropping. Jason understood astronomy quite well for his young Earth age of ten.

Jason studied their bearing and distance on his front display, which showed a map of the southeastern United States. Blue lines marked the state borders, and amazingly, their ship was pinpointed as a small red dot, now over Texas and traveling toward New Mexico at ten thousand miles per hour. They would arrive back home in a matter of minutes. Jason watched as they exited Texas and quickly entered New Mexico.

Once they were within about ten miles of Los Alamos, Michael pulled back on his control wheel, and they slowed to one hundred miles per hour. He expertly guided them directly toward Jason and Kyle's house with a strange feeling, as though he'd also arrived home. Jason was the first to spot the mercury-vapor light on the telephone pole. "There's our house," he said.

"Yes, I see it," Michael said. He let loose of his control wheel and stopped their ship, which quietly hovered fifty feet above the house. He then pulled down on the wheel and slightly to the right. Their ship moved east of the house and hovered again. After pulling down just a bit, Michael let go of the wheel, and the ship's computer guided the ship down in altitude, until they gently touched down where the ship had previously landed. Michael then touched a couple of buttons on his armband, and an open doorway into the ship suddenly appeared. "You two better get some sleep," he said.

Jason agreed with a tired smile, while Kyle could express only an extremely sleepy face. Their seat belt contraptions had disappeared, and Jason stood up, along with Kyle and Michael. The three boys walked together toward the door opening, but then Jason stopped. He stared down at Michael and remembered what had happened earlier with his father. "Did you hear the conversation with my dad in the living room about the armband?"

"Yes, I did," Michael said.

"My parents know something is not right," Jason said. "I can't lie to them, because they're too smart."

"Yes, I know they are," Michael said. He then wistfully asked, "Do you think your mom and dad would be kind and friendly to me?"

Jason was speechless for a brief moment, even knowing he wanted his parents to meet Michael and accept him as one of their own. "They should be," he said, "but I don't know what they would do."

Michael quietly acknowledged Jason yet still wondered whether Jason and Kyle's parents would view him as an outsider, an extraterrestrial that had no place within a human society.

After thinking more about Michael's last question, Jason said, "I'm going to tell my parents about you later this evening and then introduce you to them afterward. Okay?"

"Yes, Jason, that's okay," Michael said. "I've never had a mom or dad before."

Jason grinned a little, realizing Michael thought that by just meeting his parents they would become his mom and dad. "I hope they can accept you," he said. "I want them to."

"Okay," Michael said. "Bye."

Jason noticed anticipation on Michael's face, another surprising emotional display. "Goodbye, Michael," he said.

Kyle realized they were about to leave the ship and forced himself a little more awake. "Bye, Michael," he said and then gave Michael a big hug. Michael, who was a few inches taller, returned the hug.

After the two boys quit hugging, Jason led his little brother down the ramp back to the planet. After walking a short distance, they both turned around. The ship was still invisible, and Michael was silhouetted against the brightly lit door opening. The rectangular opening slowly vanished, and Michael disappeared from sight, the ship again completely invisible.

"Let's crawl back inside, Kyle," Jason said.

"Okay."

The boys returned to the side of the house, just below Jason's bedroom window. Jason then locked his fingers together, turned his palms upward, and leaned down just a bit. "Okay, Kyle, I want you to grab my neck and step into my locked fingers. I will then lift you back inside."

"Okay," Kyle said. He placed his arms around Jason's neck and his left foot inside Jason's locked fingers, and Jason lifted him up to the window. Kyle gently lifted the window screen and pulled himself inside, crawling onto the small table by the window. Back inside, he held the screen open while Jason jumped up into the opening and pulled himself inside. After crawling across the table, Jason gently let the window screen fall back in place and locked it. He returned the table to its original position, and after carefully inspecting the room, he told his little brother, "We'd better get some sleep."

Kyle became even more tired after sitting down on Jason's bed. Jason removed his little brother's tennis shoes and then his own tennis shoes. They crawled into bed, and Jason pulled the covers over them. He thought about the trip they'd just taken into outer space. He looked forward to when they would finally travel to the stars, but the thought of seeing Michael again, during daylight hours, and introducing him to his parents later in the evening gave him an unusual feeling of mixed anticipation. His mom and dad loved him and Kyle dearly, so he could not see them not loving Michael, who was like a lost little boy. Jason, with his eyes now closed, quickly fell into a deep sleep, hoping and wishing that his parents would have an open mind and be sensitive to Michael's current situation.

# 9

# SURPRISING TESTS AT THE LOS ALAMOS LABS

When Jason woke up, it was 10:58 a.m. He'd slept in again for the second day in a row. Kyle was still soundly asleep, so Jason gently rolled out of bed. Their mom had probably already checked on them and was likely curious why they were sleeping in so late. Without further ado, he headed straight to his bathroom and turned on the tub faucet. After making a few adjustments, he had the water nice and warm, just the way he liked it.

He went to the bedside table to check on the real armband. He opened the top drawer, and sure enough, it was still right where he had left it. Luckily, his parents had not found it, not that they would have been looking for it. He sat down on the side of his bed, removed the communicator from his pants, and activated it. "Hi, Michael," he said.

There was silence. "Hi, Jason," Michael finally replied.

Jason glanced down at Kyle briefly and then said into the communicator, "That was fun earlier, huh?"

"Yes, it was," Michael agreed.

Jason wondered how Michael could know it was fun, but Michael was a very unique organic android, having a wide range of human emotions. "I'll talk to you later, Michael. I am going to take a bath."

"Why are you taking a bath?" Michael asked.

Jason grinned a little at Michael not knowing why he bathed. "It is how I clean odors off my body," he said.

Michael now knew Jason was referring to the sweat glands and pores in his epidermal skin layers that opened and closed to release biological energy, a requirement of the human body to help regulate internal body temperature, but he did not know whether he had real pores in his skin like Jason and other intelligent beings. His skin texture showed signs of having pores, but when he checked the ship's computer for more information about the characteristics of his body, there was no information to be found. There was also nothing about how old he was or the exact time period or year he had been created. "Okay, Jason, I understand," he finally said. "I will talk to you later, then."

"Bye, Michael," Jason said.

Jason placed the communicator inside the drawer and again saw the real armband, with its three interface pins clearly exposed. He retrieved the second communicator from his brother's pants pocket and placed it next to his own communicator. After closing the drawer, he was confident their parents would not find the communicators. He especially wanted to avoid his mother finding Kyle's communicator in his pants, because that would require additional explaining and place him in a precarious situation of having to figure out what to tell his mother, answers that would fall along the lines of what he was planning to tell both of his parents later this evening.

Jason removed his clothes and wondered about the fake armband his father had taken to work. He then headed to the bathroom, found the water level almost eight inches from the top of the tub, and quickly turned off the faucet. He stepped into the water and completely submersed himself, enjoying the tantalizing warmth across his entire body. The sound of his soft-beating heart made him wonder whether Michael had a heart or some type of mechanical device to simulate a heart, such that he could have placed a hand on Michael's chest or checked his neck or wrist for a pulse. He lifted himself out of the water, opened his eyes, grabbed a bar of soap, and slowly washed his body. He had to be careful not to spill any water over the sides of the tub, because his mom would make him mop it up.

✦ ✦ ✦

About that time, Barbara entered Jason's bedroom and saw Kyle still sound asleep. It seemed Jason had kept him up kind of late. She heard Jason in the bathroom and gently opened the bathroom door halfway, briefly peeking inside to see Jason hidden down in the tub. "You must have kept your brother up late," she said.

Jason nodded with a small grin. "Yes, we were up pretty late," he said.

With Jason's humorous attitude, what seemed to be bothering him yesterday was not quite as noticeable. "Well, you shouldn't have done that," she said. "Remember, he is only four."

Jason knew she would have never believed why they were up so late. "Okay, Mom, I won't do it again," he said.

Barbara believed her kindhearted son. "Well, once you finish your bath, come into the kitchen, and I'll make your breakfast."

"Okay, Mom."

Barbara turned around, and on her way through the bedroom, she picked Jason's clothes up off the floor. She removed the belt from his pants, placed it on the bed, and glanced down one more time at her sound-asleep little boy before heading straight to the laundry room.

In the bathtub, Jason thought about the fact that his father had taken the fake armband to work and wondered again what he might find out about it. Maybe he'd find nothing at all, but then, maybe he'd find something very surprising—something out of this world.

As Jason continued to wash his body, he wondered whether

Michael could sweat and whether his body created odors. He hadn't smelled any so far and remembered Michael telling him, "I am an organic android … I think," which could only mean Michael did not know how his body had been created or what it was actually composed of. "That is still strange," he mumbled to himself. "I would not like it if I did not know who created me, who my parents were, or even what my body was made of."

Jason started playing with the bar of soap, squeezing it between his hands, propelling it high into the air, and then watching it fall back into the water like an object falling to Earth. It was interesting to think about, as the near-frictionless surface of the wet soap was kind of like Teflon. Grabbing the bar, he squeezed it again between his hands, this time more rapidly, propelling it higher into the air like a missile. Like the last time, it quickly fell down into the tub, causing the water to explode—like a meteor hitting a planet.

Realizing he had been in the tub long enough, he rinsed his hands off, pushed the drain lever down, and climbed out of the tub. Grabbing a towel, he began drying off. He thought about how extremely coincidental meeting Michael was.

Jason finished drying off and remembered when he'd walked toward the spaceship, in near darkness, with only the lighting of the moon. Not everyone would have been as brave, especially other kids his age, but he had not been scared one bit. He'd actually been filled with a lot of adrenaline, his mind strangely focused. Returning to his bedroom, he saw his little brother was still asleep and noticed his mother had picked up his clothes. He continued over to his magnolia triple dresser. He removed underwear and a pair of socks from the middle right drawer and a pair of Levi 501 jeans and a dark-blue cotton polo shirt from the next drawer down. He started to get dressed for the day. Tucking in his shirt, he looked down again at his little brother. "Kyle must really be worn out," he whispered to himself and grabbed his belt.

As he cinched his belt tight, he realized Michael had not changed out of his clothes since yesterday—at least they appeared to be the same clothes. After slipping on his socks and tennis shoes, he tied the laces and wondered again what his dad might have found out about the fake armband, especially since Jason had told him to show it to only someone he completely trusted.

Jason felt he was now ready for breakfast, but he first had to make sure the communicators and real armband were still undisturbed. He opened the top drawer of the bedside table to see they had not been moved around. He grabbed one of the communicators and then laid a piece of paper over the other communicator and real armband. Placing the communicator in his right pants pocket, he closed the drawer and finally left his bedroom and headed toward the kitchen. He wondered whether his mother would ask him about the armband his dad had taken to work. If she did, he would not know for sure how to answer her, only that it would be something like "When dad is here" or "After dinner." Entering the kitchen, he found his mother sitting at the kitchen table reading a book.

As her oldest son walked into the kitchen, Barbara glanced at the wall clock to see it was now 11:25 a.m. and turned back to her son. "Good morning, Jason," she said.

"Morning, Mom," he said and gave her an affectionate hug.

Barbara accepted his hug without hesitation. "Looks like you'll be studying your history and geography most of the afternoon," she said.

Jason had known that would be the case, but he did not care. "That's okay with me, Mom," he said.

Barbara grinned at her son's response, as that was the way it had always been since she could remember. He was interested in many different subjects, though especially science. She'd known since he was a young boy of two that he would be gifted and have a brilliant mind. "I will make your breakfast," she said.

"Okay," Jason replied and sat down at the kitchen table. He could not recall ever being spanked by his mother, but he did remember being grounded, and that was worse than any spanking. Besides that, it was better not to get into trouble with his mom, because then he would have to answer to his dad and suffer the possible consequences.

His mother removed eggs and bacon from the refrigerator and started his breakfast. Watching her in front of the stove, he contemplated how he should go about introducing Michael. Should he bring Michael to the house or take his parents to the spaceship?

Kyle suddenly walked into the kitchen rubbing his eyes. Seeing her youngest was finally awake, Barbara picked him up and gave him a small kiss and hug. "Did Jason keep you up late?" she softly asked.

"Yes, he did," Kyle said, still half-asleep, and looked over at Jason, who was staring directly at him. His older brother's look meant to stay quiet about Michael and the spaceship.

Barbara set Kyle down on a barstool next to Jason. "I guess I can make you both breakfast now," she said and walked back to the refrigerator to get more eggs and bacon.

At the kitchen table, Kyle turned to his older brother with a distant grin about the trip they'd just taken into outer space. Both boys were now daydreaming about what it would be like to travel to the moon and beyond. Jason stared at his mother again and thought, *I wish Mom and Dad could travel with us to the stars.*

✦ ✦ ✦

On the invisible spaceship in the open field behind the barn, Michael again listened intently to everything happening between Jason, Kyle, and their mother. He recognized her kindness and how caring she always seemed, and like before, he wondered whether she would be kind and caring to him. She was extremely nice to her sons, always hugging and kissing them, showing them unwavering affection. This was something he was certain he had never experienced from a grown-up in the race that had created him, let alone a human being.

He began daydreaming about what it would feel like if she were to hug and kiss him. It made him feel strange inside, and there was a sudden palpitation in his chest that he did not quite understand. He took a deep breath and exhaled, now curious about Jason and Kyle's father, who had arrived at the Los Alamos labs earlier that morning. Michael adjusted the ship's sensors to locate him about six miles north of the ship, but the advanced computer could not distinguish him from the hundreds of other bioelectrical heat signatures inside the Los Alamos complex, even after adjusting for his exact body mass and cellular configuration.

He attempted to make precise adjustments of the ship's sensors in order to eavesdrop on the exact frequency spectrum of Jason's father's vocal cords, but it was too hard of a task from so far away, especially since the ship's computer had registered active electronic countermeasure jamming devices inside some of the labs. The computer had also identified extremely high-powered devices throughout the complex.

Michael instinctively knew Jason's father would be extremely secretive about the fake armband because of the promise he'd made to Jason last night. All Michael could do now was sit quietly, listening to the conversations inside the Jupiters' house while attempting to adjust his ship's electronic eavesdropping capabilities to overcome the countermeasures at the Los Alamos labs.

✦ ✦ ✦

Inside the house, Jason and Kyle were eating bacon, egg, and cheese omelets, daydreaming about their trip into outer space. Their mother was sitting beside them with a glass of iced tea. She took a sip and set the glass down. This sound of the glass contacting the countertop brought Jason out of his daydream. His little brother was sipping on his milk, and his mother was staring at the three small puncture wounds in his forearm. She did not say anything, though.

Barbara opened her book and began silently reading. She still did not know what to think about the puncture wounds in her son's forearm. She could not get them off her mind, because the reddish-brown holes did not seem to be scabbing and healing over as they should. She made direct eye contact with her oldest son. "Did you clean your forearm good, Jason?"

"Yes, I did," he said.

Barbara stood up, gently grabbed his left forearm, and examined the three puncture wounds more closely. They were not just small pricks but fairly deep puncture wounds, perfectly spaced about one-half to three-quarters of an inch apart. They were not from any insect, like a spider bite, and she stared again into Jason's eyes. "What caused these?"

Jason knew he could not lie to his mom. "Can we talk about it when Dad is here?"

"Why?" she quickly asked.

"Because I want Dad here when I answer the question," he said.

Barbara took a deep breath and exhaled, filled with curiosity about what Jason had to tell them about the three holes in his forearm and, better yet, what he was hiding. She was not going to press him any more about it and now wondered what Dan might have found out about the armband at the Los Alamos labs, especially its elemental properties.

✦ ✦ ✦

At the Los Alamos labs, Dan Jupiter waited with anticipation all morning with the armband secretly hidden in the lower left pocket of his suit jacket. After a vague phone call to Frank around eight thirty that morning, in which Dan said he needed to check the nuclear and molecular composition of an object, with a requirement of the utmost confidence and secrecy, Frank had agreed to help.

Dan was currently sitting behind his desk and looking out into his high-energy particle physics lab. The lab was vacant because he had sent all his employees to a three-hour seminar (from 1:30 to 4:30 p.m.) that he and Frank Andrews had arranged earlier in the morning, a seminar that also included Frank's employees, to ensure the metallurgy lab was also vacant.

He glanced at his wristwatch. It was 1:55 p.m. He was still surprised by how easily he'd entered the extremely secretive section of the complex without the metal detector making a single beep. The armband had to be composed of some type of metallic material or element. He slipped his suit jacket on and felt the pocket to ensure the armband was still there. He left his office and walked down the hallway to the metallurgy lab, where Frank was waiting.

Dan's anticipation increased as he wondered what might be discovered about the artifact. His wristwatch showed 2:00 p.m.—the exact time he'd told Frank he would arrive.

He walked up to the door, entered the cipher lock number, and heard the electromagnetic locks unlock. He opened the door and continued into the lab to find it was vacant, except for Frank Andrews, who was sitting in his office on the far side of the room. Dan continued through the lab to Frank's office.

Frank noticed Dan had arrived. "Hi, Dan," he said.

"Hi, Frank," Dan replied and shook his hand. "How are you doing?"

Frank returned the handshake, clearly curious about Dan's mysterious request. "Good, Dan. So what's up with the object?"

Dan, even knowing no one else was in the lab and that there were no cameras, still looked around before turning back to Frank. He reached into his pocket, pulled out the armband, and handed it to Frank. "Here, take a look at this," he said.

As soon as Frank took hold of the device, his facial expression and demeanor immediately changed, because the object was light as a feather and paper thin. Its many buttons were not painted on its surface as he'd first suspected. He turned it over to see the bottom side was extremely smooth and plain-looking. He examined the topside one more time. There were six light-brown rectangular buttons, and directly above them were ten smaller light-green round buttons. Based on the object's size and shape, it looked like an armband for a child. He finally looked up with extreme curiosity. "What is it?"

"I do not know, maybe an armband," Dan said.

Frank was mildly surprised to have his suspicion confirmed and again noticed the object was practically weightless. "I take it that the metal detector did not make a single peep?"

"That is correct," Dan said.

"Where'd you find it?"

Dan remembered what Jason had asked of him last night. "On my land," he vaguely answered.

Frank was again surprised and began thoroughly examining the metallic-looking armband in more detail. The silver material seemed to be a metal type he'd never seen, even after conducting thousands of tests on everything from metal alloys to plastics to advanced carbon composite fibers to polymers. He tried to bend it, but no matter how hard he pressed, it would not budge. He turned to Dan with a strange look. "Not only is this device almost weightless," he said, "but I've never seen a base metal alloy with this texture, not to mention its tremendous strength for being … what? Maybe ten to twenty mils thick? Which I am sure you were already aware of."

Dan did know that to be the case. "Yes, and I was just as surprised after seeing it for the first time."

Frank was very curious about the device and understood now why Dan had brought it to his lab to be secretly tested. "How about we first irradiate it with our advanced x-ray fluorescence spectrometer? I am extremely curious about its base structure composition."

"That's fine, Frank," Dan said. "That was going to be my first suggestion, and yes, I am also extremely curious."

They left Frank's office with Frank carrying the armband device, feeling an anticipation like never before. When they arrived at the metallurgical and elemental analyzer, an energy-dispersive x-ray fluorescence (EDXRF) spectrometer, Frank opened a small door, placed the armband inside, and then closed the door. They stared at the armband through the tempered glass before Frank sat down in front of the computer and logged onto the system, entering his user ID and password. A few seconds later, the computer was up and running, waiting for a command, and Frank entered a few parameters, including approximate size, shape, surface area, and thickness, and then pressed the Enter key to activate the EDXRF spectrometer.

The EDXRF spectrometer started to run, emitting x-ray energies directly at the armband in an attempt to ionize it—to get a "fingerprint" of its elemental composition. Dan stood quietly behind Frank, extremely curious about what they might determine, especially since it was his son that had given him the armband. Less than a minute later, the spectrometer suddenly shut down, almost prematurely, so it seemed.

The computer screen displayed in big, bold letters: **UNKNOWN?**

Frank turned around, surprised. "Look at that, would you, Dan," he said.

Dan was also surprised at what the spectrometer had told them—nothing.

Frank turned back to the computer screen, where a small red light was flashing. A brief message indicated the armband's internal temperature was minus 225 degrees Celsius, but then just as quickly, the red light went away, indicating the armband had returned to room temperature. Frank raised his eyebrows and turned to Dan. "Did you see that?"

Dan had not seen the momentary flashing light or message. "See what?"

"I do not know for sure," Frank said, "but the spectrometer's sensors said the armband's internal temperature momentarily dropped to minus 225 degrees Celsius and then just as quickly returned to room temperature. Maybe it was just an XRF malfunction?"

Dan thought it unlikely. "Are you sure? The device could have been reacting to the x-ray energies?"

"Maybe," Frank said. He typed a few keys to check the line

analysis for any elemental compositions. The monitor displayed a flat line across the keV spectrum—zero. Frank shook his head, bewildered, and typed a few more keystrokes to see what the multipoint analysis screen might show them. On the screen again was another flat line—zero. It was as though the strange device's atomic structure was nonexistent, even though it was surely not. Frank was now shaking his head. It was possible the device had an internal structure that repelled energy. He turned around to see Dan also shaking his head at what they had just witnessed on the computer screen. "Care if I try to cut it?" Frank asked.

Dan snapped out of his thoughts about the armband. "Not at all, Frank."

Frank stood up, grabbed a temperature probe, opened the door of the spectrometer, and touched the probe to the armband's surface. The probe registered 68 degrees Fahrenheit (20 degrees Celsius), and Frank shook his head again upon finding the device was indeed at room temperature. He was still hesitant as he picked the armband up. He and Dan walked over to the upright heavy-duty band saw that could cut a variety of materials, including hardened steel. They both put on protective goggles, and Frank turned on the band saw with the assumption that the armband might be extremely hard, considering it could not be flexed whatsoever, despite how extremely thin it was. Using a small guide, he placed the armband in front of the band saw so that its curved top surface pointed toward the blade. He then set the band saw speed to one hundred feet per minute.

He slowly moved the armband toward the band saw. As soon as the armband touched the blade, sparks appeared, almost electrical in nature, and pieces of metal flew up into the air. Some of the hot metal fragments hit Frank's fingers, feeling like small, sharp needles. A high-pitched screeching noise filled the lab, and Frank could not believe his eyes or ears. He quickly pulled the device back after realizing the band saw was not going to cut it.

"What the ...?" he said. There was not even a scratch on the armband! Not only that, but the oil residue on the armband from the band saw blade quickly dispersed off its surface, as though from a static discharge. "This is an extremely hard metallic alloy," he mumbled and turned off the band saw. When the band saw blade finally came to a stop, Frank noticed most of the teeth on the blade were completely broken off, as if the armband had caused them to fracture and explode. He stood stunned that this had happened to their tungsten-carbide-tipped blade. "Well, that's a first," he muttered.

Dan also noticed the damage to the band saw blade. "So what happened?" Frank stared with a long look. "This device appears to be harder than a diamond," he said, "and extremely reactive."

"How can that be?" Dan asked, surprised.

"I do not know," Frank said. "Let's place it in our hydraulic press and see how much pressure it takes to bend it."

"Okay," Dan said. "That's fine."

They walked over to the Greenerd open-gap C-frame 50-ton hydraulic press with a two-post guided ram. Frank placed the armband on the platform, with only the two ends touching the flat surface, leaving the square and round buttons of the device clearly visible on top. Frank pressed the On button, and the 230-volt AC three-phase motor came up to speed and the hydraulic pump started to run. Slowly, he manually brought the ram plate down against the armband, so that the plate was now barely contacting the armband's top surface. The amount of contact pressure between the armband and the ram plate was very light—barely touching. Frank turned back to Dan. "What do you think?" he asked with anticipation. "About a quarter of an inch or less of this device's total surface area contacting the ram plate?"

Dan leaned down and looked under the ram plate to see that only a minimal amount of the armband's surface area was contacting the ram plate. The hydraulic press was registering 100 pounds per square inch (psi), and the armband had not budged whatsoever, probably already having well over five hundred pounds of force on it and easily over 2,000 pounds psi of load bearing to its contacting surfaces. Dan leaned back up and looked directly at his friend. "Yes, Frank, you're probably pretty close," he said. "Strange how there is probably already over 2,000 psi on the device's contacting surfaces, and it hasn't even budged in the least bit, huh?"

"Yes, it is," Frank agreed, having already surmised that the armband would not buckle under a few thousand pounds of force, especially after what he'd just witnessed at the band saw. He glanced down at the armband, the ram plate, and then back to Dan. "Okay, here we go," he said.

Dan remained especially quiet.

Frank turned the knob to increase the hydraulic ram pressure. The pressure on the armband was now 200 psi. The armband remained firm and unchanged. He adjusted the hydraulic force pressure to 300 psi—nothing … 500 psi … 600 psi … and then 800 psi. The armband still remained unfazed and unbent. Frank turned to Dan, astonished. "That is totally amazing!" he said. "There's … what? Easily over 15,000 pounds per square inch of force against the contacting surfaces of the device now?"

"Probably," Dan agreed, standing in awe of what they were witnessing.

Frank adjusted the force pressure on the armband even higher. The gauge of the hydraulic press now registered 1,000 psi, yet the armband remained solid and in original form. He began adjusting the tonnage force pressure at a higher rate, and the gauge registered 1,200 psi … 1,500 psi … 1,800 psi … and now 2,000 psi. The armband was still unbent. Frank had to catch his breath and stood flabbergasted while glaring at Dan. "Would you look at that, Dan!" he said. "This is unreal. That object has more strength than anything currently known or possible—especially for its extreme thinness and shape."

Dan didn't say a word. At the ends of the armband and the small bit of contacting surface area on the top, the armband had to have over 40,000 psi.

Frank applied even more hydraulic force pressure. The gauge registered 2,200 psi … 2,400 psi … 2,600 psi … and Frank began worrying whether they might break a hydraulic line or burn up the electric motor. They were now at 2,800 psi … 3,000 psi … and then 3,200 psi. The hydraulic pump started to whine and make a high screeching sound. When it reached 3,300 pounds per square inch of force, the armband finally buckled, and the ram plate traveled its full distance, completely flattening the armband.

Frank could not believe it. "My God!" he said, excited. "No doubt that object is not from our world!" He then adjusted the hydraulic force pressure to zero and raised the ram plate off the platform table to see the armband was flat as a pancake. Before their very eyes, it suddenly returned to its original shape.

They both stood in a quiet daze, as though in a dream, completely and totally fascinated by this molecular scientific phenomenon. After finally buckling at well over 70,000 psi of pressure to its contacting surfaces, the device had just returned to its original shape. Frank picked up the armband to find it was still at room temperature. He closely inspected it and found no apparent damage whatsoever. He turned to Dan with a long, assessing look. "We had better not tell a soul about this, Dan, or our lives will never be the same."

"I totally agree," Dan quickly replied. "Do you want to try any other tests?"

"How about we see if it has any electrical conductivity properties?"

"Okay," Dan said. "That should be interesting."

"Yes, it will," Frank agreed. "The elemental composition of this armband has to be metallic in nature."

Dan again agreed and followed Frank over to the electrical conductivity bench. Frank flipped the power on to the workbench and then grabbed a Fluke 189 multimeter and set it to the lowest resistance scale possible. When Frank clipped the lead wires to each end of the armband, the resistance was infinite. Not fully believing what he saw, Frank wondered whether one of the leads might be defective. He unhooked one of the lead wires, touched it to the other lead, and the resistance immediately went to zero, so the lead wires were good and the meter working properly. He reconnected the lead wire to the armband, and again nothing registered—infinite. Frank turned to Dan, puzzled. "That is extremely strange and doesn't make sense," he said. "The device appears to have no resistance, yet it just has to be somehow metallic in nature."

"Yes, it is strange," Dan said, "seemingly a physical violation of science as we understand it."

Frank now wondered what Dan really knew about the device, since he had it in his possession. He looked back down at the conductivity electrodes plugged into the high-powered unit. "Let's apply a high-voltage current and see what happens," he said.

Dan thought about what Frank had told him about how the device had turned extremely cold when trying to ionize it inside the EDXRF spectrometer. "Are you sure the armband won't react somehow to the high voltage?" he asked, concerned.

Frank paused. "I do not see how with infinite resistance," he said.

Dan did not say another word as Frank unhooked the multimeter leads from the device. Frank then connected the negative and positive power lead wires to each end of the armband. He grabbed a current transformer, with a 50-ampere analog meter, and clamped it around the middle of the armband.

Frank looked briefly to Dan and then back to the control console. He turned on to the high-voltage AC power supply. "Okay, here we go," he said.

Dan held his breath a little, still concerned about how the device had reacted to the EDXRF machine. "Let's install wrist ground straps as a precautionary measure," he said.

Frank knew it was probably a good cautionary measure, so he grabbed a couple of wrist straps, plugged their ground cords into the bench unit, and handed one of the straps to Dan. They each slipped a strap around their wrist and snapped a ground lead wire to the strap. "Okay, I think we're now ready," Frank said.

Dan stood in quiet anticipation.

Frank adjusted the voltage output and first applied 115 volts AC across the armband. No current registered on the 50-amp current transformer gauge or the milliamp meter on the console for the source. He increased the voltage to 230 volts … then to 450 volts … 600 volts … 1,000 volts. Still no current draw was evident on the current transformer or a single milliamp of current on the console's meter. "Hmmm," Frank mumbled under his breath and increased the voltage output even higher … 2,500 volts … 5,000 volts … 10,000 volts … 20,000 volts! Suddenly, a blue glow appeared on the surface of the armband, and the current transformer's 50-ampere meter quickly pegged out. *Bang!* It sounded like a double-barrel shotgun blast. All the circuit breakers on the console's high-voltage control unit, including the main AC breakers feeding power into the metallurgy lab, popped. Equipment throughout the entire lab went dead, and the emergency lights immediately came on. Frank and Dan could now smell burnt varnish and electrical wire, most likely from an overheated transformer.

Frank looked over at Dan standing beside him in the darkened lab with only the emergency lighting to illuminate their faces. He shook his head in disbelief. "I do not know what this device is for," he said, "but it has some of the strangest properties beyond belief, well beyond our imagination. It had to have easily momentarily registered over a million-watt output back into all the power supplies, as if the device turned into a high-voltage, high-current power supply generator and then discharged. At what harmonic, I would not have the faintest. I bet the main power transformer feeding our equipment is now fried."

Dan knew what Frank meant by his million-watt power output comment, as they were applying 20,000 volts to the armband, and the current transformer's 50-ampere meter pegged out—the basic equation of power equals voltage times current gave a power output of

1,000,000 watts. "I do not know what to say, Frank," Dan finally said. "I guess we should have been more careful when testing something that was already violating many of our known principles of physics, huh?"

"That's for sure," Frank said and unhooked the electrodes. He removed the current transformer from around the armband. The needle was bent over, actually smashed up against the side of the scale beyond the 50-ampere indication, so that meant the current generated was well beyond 50 amps. He briefly touched the armband, again surprised it was at room temperature, especially after generating and propagating such a tremendous amount of power, and then picked it up. After thinking about everything they had just discovered about the device, he stared directly at Dan with another long, mind-riveting, assessing look. "It's a good thing we did not place this device in the high-voltage electron microscope in your lab. Its reactive state may have very well taken out the power grid for the entire Los Alamos complex and, who knows, maybe even the city of Los Alamos."

Dan was amazed at Frank's comment, true as it might have been. "Yes, that could have been a very good possibility," he said and unhooked the ground strap from his wrist to find his wrist aching.

Frank unhooked his ground strap and found that his wrist also ached. "Does your wrist hurt any?"

"Yes, it does," Dan said. "Does yours?"

"Yep," Frank said. "Probably a good thing we had them on, or we might not be among the living."

Dan agreed with a silent nod.

Frank, still holding the armband, headed toward the lab's main AC breakers alongside Dan. Frank was still curious how the armband had come into Dan's possession. "When did you find this, anyway?"

Dan wanted to keep his son out of the conversation, now more than ever. "A few days ago," he said.

Frank arrived at the lab's main AC breakers, surprised the 460 VAC breakers had also been knocked offline, meaning voltage from the device had jumped phase circuits. He looked back to Dan under the shadow of the emergency lights. "You know," he finally said, "supposedly there was a military aircraft that crashed on your land a few days ago. Maybe it was not an aircraft at all but a spacecraft of extraterrestrial origin. There have been reports of a UFO being sporadically spotted in the area the past few days."

Dan had a sudden strange feeling inside. Jason had told him he was watching the military clean up the crash site, and he had never actually said where he'd found the armband. Dan also thought about the three small puncture holes in Jason's forearm where he had been wearing the armband. Dan did not know what to think about it all, and an uncomfortable look crossed his face. "Please do not mention this armband device to another soul," he sincerely asked.

Frank flipped the 460 VAC breakers on, waited a short moment, and then flipped on a half dozen 230 VAC breakers, followed by resetting about a dozen 115 VAC breakers that had also popped. The overhead fluorescent lighting started to come back on, and the emergency lights shut off. "Sure, Dan, never," Frank said. He handed Dan the armband and removed his goggles.

"Thank you," Dan said. He removed his goggles and slipped the armband back into his coat pocket. "Well, I better get back to my lab. I am sincerely sorry about what happened to the transformer that was probably fried."

"That's okay, Dan. Don't worry about it. I'll come up with some elaborate explanation. What we just witnessed makes me realize even more just how much we have yet to learn about our universe."

Dan managed to muster a small smile. "That's for sure," he said and shook Frank's hand. "Talk to you later."

Frank noticed Dan was acting a little strange and knew he was hiding something, which was understandable, because it could have been one of his kids that had found the alien artifact. There could also be much more going on than Dan was letting on. "Bye, Dan, and do not worry about me," Frank said.

Dan smiled a little, knowing he would not have to worry about his longtime friend ever saying anything. Frank walked with him to the exit, and Dan continued alone back to his particle physics laboratory, thinking about everything that had just transpired in the metallurgy lab.

✦ ✦ ✦

Inside the metallurgy lab, Frank walked over to the main transformer, which he suspected was fried. Sure enough, the putrid smell of burnt varnish and copper wire was even more intense by the transformer. Even the outer casing appeared discolored from intense heat. He grabbed a couple of aerosol cans of Febreze air freshener and Lysol from a supply cabinet and liberally sprayed the entire room, especially around the transformer, in an attempt to knock out some of the stench. He emptied both Febreze cans and part of the Lysol can and returned to the transformer to further assess the situation.

Staring at the outer casing more closely, he was surprised to see an iron bolt attached to the transformer, as though glued in place. He tried to pry it loose but had a hard time. With a little more physical energy and some twisting, he was finally able to finally pull it loose. He then let go of it from about twelve inches away, and the bolt quickly flew back against the transformer, as though attached to it with a rubber band. The transformer's core—its case and surrounding sheet metal—must have been highly magnetized by the strange energy burst, no telling at what frequency harmonic. It was without doubt an energy propagation in the millions of watts of power. How high the actual gauss value was at the transformer's core had to be beyond Earth's capabilities. Why he and Dan had not been shocked would probably always remain a mystery, but then, his wrist was hurting a little, which was probably directly related to the ground straps that had taken their bodies down to a zero static ground state.

With the transformer's intense magnetic field and everything he and Dan had just witnessed, he knew he had better get in touch with the electrical maintenance shop as soon as possible to have them replace the transformer. He needed to figure out how to keep possession of the current transformer, though, to help safeguard its unusual magnetic properties, not to mention stop anyone from asking questions.

He returned to his office, sat down behind his desk, and leaned all the way back with a deep sigh as he thought about the alien artifact his friend had in his possession. Picking up his desk phone, he called the electrical maintenance shop, knowing there was a high possibility an outside bonded company might have to replace the large transformer. The maintenance shop answered his call after a few rings.

✦ ✦ ✦

Dan Jupiter, now sitting behind his desk, could not get the strange properties of the armband off his mind, especially the unforeseen amounts of power it generated. The time was 4:22 p.m., and his employees would be getting out of their seminar shortly. Afterward, many of them would gather their personal effects and leave for the day, so he decided to leave a little early himself. He grabbed his desk phone, dialed home, and stared at the picture of his wife and two sons on his desk.

"Jupiters' residence," his wife answered.

"Hi, honey," Dan said. "How's it going?"

"Fine," she said. "The boys are in the living room watching television, and Jason did well on his geography and history."

"How is he doing otherwise?"

Barbara was puzzled. "What do you mean?"

"You know, is he still the same old Jason?" Dan asked.

"I am not following you."

Dan did not want to say anything over the phone. "I'll tell you more when I get home, sometime after dinner."

"Is this related to what Jason gave you?"

"Yes, it is," he said immediately.

Barbara paused with immense interest. "Okay, I've started dinner. We'll of course be having fresh catfish."

Dan managed to muster a small smile at the mention of catfish. "I look forward to it, as will our boys."

"Yes, I know they will too," she said.

Dan felt contented, as though he would soon have closure on a mystery. What kind of mystery, he did not know. "Bye, honey," he said. "I'll be leaving in about ten minutes."

Barbara suddenly felt good inside, even knowing Jason was hiding a secret that could affect their entire family. "Okay, love, see you in a little bit," she said, "Bye."

"Bye," Dan told her and hung up the phone with Jason still on his mind. Jason had been acting his old self while fishing down at the creek last night and even before he and Kyle went to his bedroom to sleep together. He had to suppose that, whatever secret Jason was hiding from them, he might have now gotten Kyle involved, since the two boys were pretty close. "Maybe tonight we'll find out what's really going on," he mumbled to himself, "including what is behind those three puncture holes in his forearm."

Dan picked up his briefcase, stood up, and turned off the lights to his office before closing the door. He was leaving the lab before any of his employees returned from the seminar, but his office door being closed would be a clue he'd left for the day. They did have his cell phone number if they needed to contact him.

As he exited the lab and continued out into the hallway, he thought about his sixteen employees who worked in the high-energy particle physics lab and the additional eight in another highly secretive lab, code-named the Black Quadrant. Most of the employees who reported to him had master's and doctorate degrees, but there were also a few with bachelor's degrees who were pursuing higher degrees at either the University of New Mexico in Albuquerque or the Institute of Mining and Technology in Socorro. All his employees knew before he ever considered hiring them that they would be required to advance their studies until receiving a master's or doctorate. They respected him for it, because they knew exactly where he stood on higher education before ever being hired. Besides that, the government paid for their higher education, making it a win-win for everyone.

Dan turned the corner and noticed the armed guard and walk-through metal detector just up ahead. He wondered whether the armband's internal molecular composition might have changed as a result of the tests in the metallurgy lab, especially with the energy burst it had generated. If its composition had changed, would the metal detector now pick it up? He would be finding out that answer shortly. If the detector did sound, would he have to surrender the armband and explain to his superiors why it was at the Los Alamos labs, including where it came from? It would put him in a precarious situation, unless he was able to explain it off as a toy of one of his sons.

As he approached the metal detector, he noticed the guard behind the desk was someone he had known for over a decade. Walking up to the counter, he set his briefcase on the conveyor belt. "Hi, Ken," Dan said.

"Hi, Dan," Ken replied.

Dan placed his car keys, pocket change, and cell phone in a large bowl and handed it to Ken, who stared up at Dan as he walked through the multipoint Garrett PD 6500i Magnascanner. Suddenly, all the lights lit up, followed by a high-pitched tone, and then the detector completely shut down. "What the ..." Ken said. "Hold on, Dan."

Dan stopped, surprised at what had just happened. He wondered whether the armband had possibly transmitted a strong multiphased frequency and overloaded the detector's thirty-three zones. That would be very unusual and only possible if the armband's characteristics had indeed changed, because it had not been detected earlier this morning.

Ken looked down at the computer display and did not understand it, as it was indicating that none of the multizone coils was working properly. He picked up his hand wand and walked over to Dan. "Looks like I am going to have to wand you, Dan," he said. "You don't have anything on you that you shouldn't?" he asked, grinning a little.

Dan remained calm. "Nope," he said, returning a small smile. "I'm not carrying anything that I did not have with me earlier this morning."

Ken ran the wand along Dan's waistline, coat, pants pockets, and up and down his legs. The hand wand remained completely silent.

Dan was only a little surprised the armband was not detected by the hand wand, because it was operating at a different frequency than the walk-through detector. After the malfunction of all thirty-three of the walk-through detector's zones, it was almost as if the armband had gone into a defensive mode. It was probably reacting to the electromagnetic frequency energy that had been previously directed toward it, such as it had been with the walk-through detector earlier. If that was the case, the hand wand would no longer work if used again on the alien artifact. Dan then made eye contact with Ken. "Has the walk-through detector ever done that before?"

Ken shook his head in the negative. "Not that I am aware of," he said, "especially for as dependable as it's supposed to be. I guess when it malfunctions, it really goes bad."

"Possibly," Dan said. He picked up his car keys, loose change, and cell phone, which he snapped back on its belt holder. He then picked up his briefcase. "Good night, Ken."

"Good night, Dan," Ken said. "Have a wonderful evening, and tell your gorgeous wife hello."

"Thank you, I will," Dan said while walking away, knowing without doubt that the coming evening of events with his family would be strange, especially now that he knew the armband was of extraterrestrial origin. He greatly anticipated discovering how the armband had come into Jason's possession. Neither of his sons was prone to telling lies, so getting to the truth should be fairly easy.

Continuing toward the exit, he wondered whether anyone would ever suspect him of having caused the metal detector malfunction. It was still strange to him that the device had not affected the hand wand, as if it had smart circuitry. Perhaps the high voltage it had experienced had caused it to go into some bizarre defensive mode.

At the main entrance/exit to the building, there were two more security guards and additional metal detectors, but Dan would not have to pass through them, since he was leaving a highly classified area and had already gone through security. He continued around the detectors, out of the complex, and toward his Lincoln Navigator at a faster pace than normal. After remote unlocking his vehicle, he sat down behind the wheel and closed the door behind him. The vehicle now running, he thought about the armband and Jason. He wondered what Jason knew about the alien artifact, including where he'd found it. Finding it in the dark seemed totally unlikely, unless it happened to be glowing. Finally shifting into drive, he left the parking lot and headed toward home, not understanding why his son would keep the extraterrestrial armband secret from him. It was totally out of character.

✦ ✦ ✦

Inside the Jupiter family home, Jason and Kyle sat next to each other in the living room watching the movie *Sphere*, starring Dustin Hoffman and Sharon Stone. They were also quietly daydreaming about Michael and the spaceship, even more so since the movie centered on a spaceship that had been on the bottom of the South Pacific Ocean for years. They knew the movie was make-believe, yet parked behind their barn was a real spaceship. Kyle had not talked to Michael all day, and Jason hadn't talked to him since this morning but figured he was listening to all their conversations inside the house.

Their mom was in the kitchen cooking fish filets, and Jason looked forward to trying some of those scrumptious tenders. He stared down at his little brother and said in a low voice, "I'm going to my bedroom for a little bit."

"Can I go with you?" Kyle asked.

"Not to my bedroom," Jason said, "but you can follow me into the kitchen. I need to talk to Michael in private."

Kyle did not question his older brother. "Okay," he said.

Jason turned off the television, and the two boys headed straight to the kitchen, where the aroma of fresh catfish filled the air. Their mother was standing in front of the stove. "Hi, Mom," Jason said. "That fish sure smells good."

Barbara turned around with an appreciative grin and could tell Jason was acting more relaxed—somewhat like his old self. "Yes, it does," she said.

"I'm headed to my room for a little while before dinner, okay?"

"Sure, Jason," she said. "Your dad is on his way and should be home anytime."

Jason again wondered what his father might have discovered about the armband. "Okay," he said. He made direct eye contact with Kyle and then left the kitchen. Kyle knew what Jason was telling him.

Barbara noticed Kyle now standing with a sincere, open face. "Do you want to help bread fish, Kyle?"

"Yes, I do," he said.

"Okay," she said. "Come sit at the kitchen table, then."

Kyle climbed up into one of the chairs, and she placed three pans on the countertop directly in front of him, one with catfish filets, one with cornmeal flour, and one that was empty.

"Dip the first filet in the cornmeal flour," she said. "Turn it over a few times until its completely covered, and then place it into the empty pan."

"Okay," Kyle said. He picked up the first catfish filet, which was about four inches long, and dutifully dipped it into the cornmeal flour. He liked helping his mother.

✦ ✦ ✦

In Jason's bedroom, the door closed, Jason sat on the side of his magnolia sleigh bed, thinking about the events later this evening that might very well entail introducing Michael to his parents. He removed the communicator from his pants and activated it. "Michael?" he softly called.

"Yes, Jason?" Michael replied.

Jason sighed in relief at Michael's voice. "Is our ship still behind the barn or next to the house?"

"It's behind the barn."

Jason was quiet, and Michael noticed. "What's wrong, Jason?"

Jason sighed again. "It's my dad, Michael, and the fake armband he took to work."

"I understand," Michael said.

Jason wondered whether Michael knew anything about what his dad had discovered. "They probably found out strange things about that fake armband, huh?"

"Yes, they almost certainly did," Michael said.

"What might they have discovered?"

"That it is indestructible to all Earth's technologies," Michael said plainly, "and has the capability to generate a tremendous amount of power, especially if high voltage is applied to it."

Jason was soundly surprised. "Why is that?"

"Because," Michael explained, "any high voltage that is applied to it in a manner to cause current flow will force it to become extremely reactive."

Jason was now concerned and fearful. "It could not have hurt them, could it?"

Michael picked up on Jason's concern. "Only if their power supply was extremely powerful," he said. "I do know that high-voltage power was applied to it, because my ship's sensors detected a planetary magnetic field disturbance in the form of a specific harmonic energy. It was centered at the Los Alamos labs north of our house and was an energy type that could have only been generated by the armband."

Jason wondered whether or not his father was injured. "Well, I hope my dad is okay. He is on his way home, and I am sure he will be questioning me thoroughly about the armband."

"I'm sure he will, Jason," Michael said.

Jason thought again about introducing Michael to his parents and how to go about it. He came to a decision, knowing that introducing Michael was now a requirement, because his dad must now know the armband was of extraterrestrial origin. "I'm going to introduce you to my mom and dad after dinner, Michael," he finally said.

Michael was quiet, wondering what it would be like meeting Jason's parents for the first time. It caused a warm sensation in his chest, something he did not fully understand. "Okay, Jason," he finally said. "I want to meet them. If they created you, they also must be kind and friendly."

Jason grinned slightly, as he knew Michael was thinking about what he'd said earlier about who had created him—who had given him the energy to function. "Yes, Michael, I know they are," he said. "Well, my dad should be getting home anytime now. I'll see you after dinner, okay?"

"Bye, Jason. See you after dinner."

"Bye, Michael."

Jason placed his communicator back inside his jeans, opened the top drawer of his bedside table, moved the papers back, and saw the real armband exactly where he'd left it. He closed the drawer and headed to the kitchen, wondering what kind of trouble he might be in later over the fake armband and his meeting Michael and then keeping his existence secret.

In the kitchen, his little brother was sitting at the kitchen table, and his mother was standing at the stove. Jason walked up behind her. "Hi, Mom," he said softly.

Barbara was startled, because she had not heard him enter the kitchen. She turned around with a mother's instinct that there was something on his mind. She figured it was related to what had been bothering him yesterday and especially what his dad might have discovered about the armband. "Hi, Jason," she said.

Jason stood for only a short moment longer before giving his mom a big hug. Barbara hugged him back, secretly enjoying the spontaneous affection from her oldest son. Jason was no dummy. He was getting her prepared for the questions his father would surely be asking him about the armband and his surprising answers. He was also trying to soften her up for the introduction of Michael after dinner. *One parent down and one to go,* he thought, continuing to hug her.

Barbara, of course, noticed her son was hugging her a little too long and wondered what was behind it. Being no dummy herself, she instinctively knew it was his uncertainty about what his father might have discovered about the armband. "Thank you, Jason," she said with a warm, kind heart. She thought she understood a little more why Jason had been acting differently, though not the full reasons. "You're not in trouble over that armband," she said.

Jason felt relieved. "Okay," he said.

Barbara planted a small kiss against his cheek and turned back around to the stove.

Jason, now with a good feeling inside, looked over at the dining room table, which was already set with hot, steaming food, including a small platter of catfish filets. He headed toward the dining room, as though drawn by a magnet. Seeing the delicious catfish filets made him even hungrier. "I can't wait to try those," he mumbled under his breath.

Kyle, seeing his older brother leave the kitchen, crawled out of his chair and headed straight toward the dining room. Jason saw his little brother had followed him, and he figured they might as well sit down. Jason pulled his chair out and sat, and Kyle climbed into his chair, just across from Jason. They both now waited like little lion cubs for their parents to bring them their food—in this case, the rest of the catfish filets. Jason also had additional anticipation inside regarding what his father might say about the armband.

✦ ✦ ✦

While Jason and Kyle waited patiently for their father, he was nearing the house, about a half mile away, thinking about the armband in his coat pocket. He could not conceive what Jason might know about it, especially regarding the three holes in his forearm and what might be going through his mind right now. "I have to remember that he's only ten and not mention anything until after dinner," he mumbled.

He noticed his driveway just up ahead, slowed down, and pulled up to the mailbox. After lowering his electric window, he opened the mailbox and grabbed all the mail, spotting the latest issue of *Physics World* magazine. A small caption on the front cover mentioned the possibility of a subatomic number series triangle that could possibly breed new mathematical expressions, via triangular limit functions between energy shells, but then, there was a big question mark beside the caption. *How interesting!* he thought. He closed the mailbox and placed the mail on top of his briefcase. Raising the window, he continued toward his house.

Turning onto his gravel drive, his mind adrift over the armband, he stared at the rows of oak trees lining both sides of his driveway. He remembered first planting them nearly twelve years ago. They had been about six feet tall then. They had now reached maturity and were easily over thirty-five feet tall, which added a nice touch to his ranch house. Finally pulling up in front of the garage, he turned off the engine and turned his thoughts to the fresh catfish filets. Thinking about catching the catfish last night did help get his mind off the armband of extraterrestrial origin.

Removing the ignition key, he picked up his briefcase and the mail. He headed toward his house with a sense of unusual anticipation never before felt. On the way, he pressed the remote lock button. The headlights of his Lincoln Navigator flashed, and the horn beeped.

# 10

## JASON'S SECRETS ABOUT TO BE EXPOSED

Jason heard the horn to their Lincoln Navigator and knew his dad would be walking inside anytime. He continued to wait patiently and stared across the table at his little brother. "Well, this is the moment of truth," he mumbled to himself.

Their father entered the house, set his briefcase and the mail on the foyer table, and continued toward the kitchen. After walking by the dining room, where his boys were sitting at the table, he continued into the kitchen, up to where his wife stood at the stove.

Barbara turned around, and Dan placed a small kiss against her lips. "Dinner smells good," he said.

"Thank you," she said.

The kiss was followed with a hug, and Dan gently squeezed her right shoulder. He headed into the dining room, where the two boys quietly waited. Extreme kindness suddenly filled his face. "Hi, guys," he said.

Jason was speechless for a moment and wondered what his father might say next. "Hi, Dad," he replied softly.

Kyle didn't think a thing about what was going on with Michael or the spaceship. He was simply thrilled to see his father. "Daddy!"

Dan planted a small kiss on Kyle's cheek and then walked around the table to deliver a small kiss to Jason's forehead. He looked across the table to his young son and then down to Jason. "Are you two ready for fresh catfish?"

"Yes, I am," Kyle said.

"Yes," Jason said, feeling a little more relaxed.

"Okay then," Dan said. "After I change clothes, we'll try some of that delicious catfish." He left the dining room, turned the corner, and then disappeared out of sight.

Jason sighed deeply, relieved that his father had not mentioned anything about the armband. He now figured it would be brought up after dinner.

Barbara walked up carrying a bowl of green beans, set them down on the table, and noticed her boys still sitting quietly, Jason in a daydream. She could not imagine what might be going through his mind at this very moment, especially since he was keeping a secret that affected their entire family. Keeping secrets of that nature was not something he would do under normal circumstances, so she was filled with anticipation for him to fully explain the reasons for his latest behavior after dinner. She walked away from the table to retrieve the last platter of catfish filets.

Jason, after staring at the filets, grabbed a small piece and took a bite. His mouth watered at the soft, scrumptious, delicious meat. Kyle was staring at him behind soft eyes, like a hungry little puppy. "Go ahead and try some, Kyle," he said.

"Okay," Kyle said. He leaned forward a little and tore off a small piece. He sat back down and began chewing on the tender white meat. "This is good," he said.

Jason nodded slightly. "Yes, and I helped catch it."

Kyle stared off with a distant look, remembering his brother scooping the large catfish up into the fishnet before pulling it ashore.

Barbara walked back into the room with the last platter of filets, along with a basket of hot rolls. She had heard her two boys talking about the catfish filets and noticed they had already sampled them. She set the last platter down, followed by the hot rolls, and returned to the kitchen with a good feeling inside because of her polite, good-natured kids.

Dan walked by the dining room to the kitchen and then up to Barbara. "Need any help?" he asked her.

Barbara turned around. "No, everything is ready," she said.

Barbara made sure the stove's burners were off, checked the amount of time left for the apple pie in the oven, and headed to the dining room with Dan following directly behind. Their two sons were patiently waiting, and Barbara sat down to Jason's left, Dan to Jason's right—similar to assigned seats.

Dan looked around their table and thought briefly about Jason and the armband. "Let's hold hands," he said.

The Jupiter family grabbed each other's hands. Jason again noticed his mother staring at his left forearm, and Dan noticed Jason give a slight reaction to her looking at his forearm. "Let's bow our heads," Dan said.

They all bowed their heads and closed their eyes. Dan began his prayer, and from the spaceship, Michael listened in. "Our heavenly Father, thank you for the food set before us, and bless those who have prepared it and those who have labored in the fields, allowing it to be eaten in the privacy of our homes. We also ask that you bless this family and that we may always remain as one—a family that will continue to be respectful to one another and truthful to one another, no matter what the situation. We know there are many mysteries in this world beyond our comprehension that we do not fully understand, and we ask for your grace that we might gain the understanding. Be with those who are less fortunate, that they might have their aching stomachs filled and their pains comforted. Always be with the leaders of this land and of foreign lands, that they might always keep you in mind and make decisions according to your will, in the best interests of humankind. Help them come to understand what is required to strive forward on a path toward world peace one day. In closing, I pray that you might be with this family and always keep us safe from harm. This we all ask in your son's precious, dear name, Jesus Christ … Amen."

When Dan opened his eyes and lifted his head, his wife was staring at him. She knew part of his prayer had been direct related to Jason and his secret about the armband. They all finally let go of each other's hands, and Dan turned to Jason with a relaxed, kind face. Jason, after seeing this, also understood that part of his father's prayer had pertained to him. With no doubt in his mind, he knew his father had determined something strange about the armband, but he also knew his dad would be kind to him, no matter what was revealed about the armband, the spaceship, and especially his organic-android friend, Michael. A good feeling now filled his spirit.

Barbara placed two filets on her plate and one on Kyle's plate. Meanwhile, Dan placed mashed potatoes on his plate and Kyle's. Jason seemed to be in a much-better attitude, and Barbara thought his father's prayer might have had something to do with it.

Dan stared directly at his kind wife. "Dinner looks and smells really good, honey," he said.

Barbara smiled a little. "Thank you," she said, knowing her family was always appreciative of her cooking.

As she took a bite of her catfish filet, Dan looked around the table and then directly to Jason. "Good catfish, huh?" he said.

Jason knew his father was trying to break the ice of uncertainty that must still be showing on his face. "Yes, it is," he said.

Dan sipped on his tea while looking at his wife and calmly turned back to Jason. "You know," he said, "I bet there's more large catfish where I caught this one."

Jason finally completely relaxed. "Yes, Dad, I bet there are."

Dan smiled a little. "Well, maybe this weekend we'll have to try and catch them."

Jason quietly acknowledged his father, who looked over in Kyle's direction and said, "And you too, Kyle."

"I want to catch one, Daddy," Kyle said.

Dan turned to his wife, and they both started laughing, because they knew Kyle could not have reeled in a catfish even half the size of the one Dan had caught last night.

Dan picked up his iced tea, and after a couple of gulps, he set his glass down while again making eye contact with his wife. "I looked up the state record for a channel cat earlier this morning," he said.

"Oh, really?" she said. "Would your fish have broken the record?"

"Nope," he said. "The record is thirty-six pounds, eight ounces and was caught nearly four years ago in Stubblefield Lake. I bet mine was a record from a creek or river."

"I bet it was," Barbara said.

Dan continued, "Yeah, that old catfish had been around for quite some time, possibly living near that deep hole the entire twelve years we've lived here. If anyone knew about the hole, I am sure they would have snuck out at night to fish there."

"Probably true, dear," Barbara agreed.

Kyle and Jason stared up at their father with real interest, almost glued to him, because the catfish was older than them. Jason now showed curiosity. "How deep do you think that creek is, Dad?"

Dan paused at his son's interest. "I measured it not too long ago," he said, "and found it nearly fourteen feet deep where we caught the catfish."

Jason started daydreaming about the deep hole he'd known nothing about and took another bite of his filet. There were surely other large catfish there, just as his father had mentioned. He now wondered whether his dad had measured the creek last week when he, his little brother, and their mom had flown to Albany, New York, to see their mom's parents. It had been his grandpa's sixty-fifth birthday, and there had been a big surprise party. It truly had been surprising, especially with them showing up unannounced. He remembered his grandpa's reaction when he'd seen his daughter and two grandsons. It had been a fun party, and Jason had met a lot of his cousins, but his father had not been able to join them because of important meetings with government officials that week.

Dan continued to eat at a normal pace but noticed his sons eating their food a little faster than normal, especially Jason, almost as if they were itching to go play or something. He looked around their table and realized that today was September 10, one day before the two-year anniversary of the September 11, 2001, terrorist act on New York's Twin Towers and the Pentagon. Over three thousand innocent souls had been lost at the Twin Towers alone, and there had been a lot of news about it lately, in the newspaper, on the radio, and on television. He looked across the table at his wife. "Remember what tomorrow is?"

"Yes," she said. "The two-year anniversary of the Twin Towers' destruction. What a terrible, despicable attack against humanity."

Dan sighed. "Yes, it was," he said. "At least the chances of them ever using our commercial airliners against us again are close to zero."

"True," Barbara said.

Dan continued, "We now have ways to preempt any future terrorist attack."

Barbara knew he was referring to some of the top-secret transceiver systems now at the government's disposal. Portions of the subsystem architectures had been designed in the Los Alamos computer sciences lab, but she did not comment any further on it. She simply nodded to agree, because the NSA, CIA, FBI, and Homeland Security were using those transceivers.

Jason lifted his iced tea to his mouth, exposing his left forearm, and it caused Dan to wonder more about the armband, including its strange, almost surreal properties, characteristics well beyond Earth's twenty-first-century capabilities. He could not wait to find out what his son could tell him about it.

Kyle and Jason were about done eating, both having eaten a little faster than normal, even with Kyle having eaten quite a lot. Barbara figured Kyle was probably following his older brother's lead, because of how much he looked up to Jason as a role model. When Barbara had been pregnant with Kyle, Jason had kept telling her that he wanted a little brother. After the sonogram indicated she was carrying a boy, Jason had been all excited. When Kyle was finally born, he had been happy as a lark and had always looked after Kyle like a guardian babysitter.

Jason set his spoon down, grabbed his napkin, and wiped his face. "Kyle and I are going to my bedroom for a while. Okay, Dad?" he asked.

"Sure, Son," Dan said. "In twenty minutes, I want you to come into the living room, and we are going to talk about that armband you gave me." Dan paused and made eye contact with his youngest son. "I want you to join him too, Kyle."

Kyle silently acknowledged this, feeling as if he were in trouble. Jason, though, now had a feeling of immense relief that his secret about Michael was about to come to an end. He and Kyle stood from his chairs and walked up to their mother. Jason stared into his mother's eyes. "Thanks for dinner, Mom," he said, followed by a small hug.

Barbara appreciated his kindness. "You're welcome, Jason."

Still standing there quietly, having observed what Jason had done, Kyle looked up into his mother's pretty eyes. "Yes, Mommy," he said. "Thanks for the catfish."

Barbara giggled at her four-year-old. "You're welcome too, Kyle," she said and received a little kiss and hug from him.

The boys headed to Jason's bedroom, Kyle following closely behind his brother. After they entered the bedroom, Jason closed the door behind them, removed the communicator from his pants, and activated it. "Michael?" he said.

"Yes, Jason?" Michael replied.

"Looks like the conversation with my dad about the armband will happen in about twenty minutes."

"Yes, I know."

Jason figured he'd been listening. "Michael?" he said a second time.

"Yes, Jason?"

Jason thought about Michael meeting his parents for the first time. He knew it was something his parents would have never dreamed of in their lifetimes. He took a deep breath and then exhaled. "I'm coming to the ship after talking with my dad, and I'll bring you inside to meet my parents."

Michael was quiet and showed an unusual reaction of uncertainty at the prospect of meeting adult human beings, even if they were Jason's parents. "Okay, Jason," he finally said. "I would like that."

Jason noticed his little brother was antsy to talk to Michael. "Kyle wants to talk with you, Michael."

"Okay," Michael said.

Jason handed the communicator to his little brother. "Hi, Michael," Kyle quickly said.

"Hi, Kyle."

A big smile formed across Kyle's face. "I want to go to the stars again," he said.

Jason's bedroom suddenly became quiet while Michael analyzed Kyle's statement. "And so do I," he finally replied.

Jason sat down on his bed next to his little brother and listened to them talk back and forth. He then thought ahead to his coming conversation about the armband, what he should say, and how to answer his dad in a method that would lead up to his introducing his parents to Michael.

✦ ✦ ✦

At the dining room table, Barbara and Dan had also finished dinner and were now talking about the armband tests in the metallurgy lab. Dan gave her a long look after explaining what had happened when the armband knocked all the power out in the lab.

Barbara was extremely quiet, even more so than before, because she now knew the armband had extremely dangerous properties that could easily be lethal. "How did you two keep from getting hurt?"

"Possibly because we were wearing ground straps," Dan said. "Our wrists did hurt afterward."

Barbara took a deep breath and exhaled. "Where do you think Jason got the armband?"

"I do not know," he said. "I'm under the suspicion it was a spaceship of extraterrestrial origin that crashed, not a military aircraft as I was led to believe. Maybe the armband flew out of the spaceship after impact and Jason found it glowing on the ground?"

"Why would there be three small holes in his forearm, then?" she asked, puzzled.

"I have no idea," Dan said. "That is very strange."

Dan and Barbara were both quiet again, wondering what Jason would tell them in less than ten minutes about the armband. The three holes in his forearm were now of more concern than ever. Barbara stood up and began clearing dishes off the table while Dan took leftovers to the kitchen. The catfish would make great filet sandwiches for a late-night snack. They cleared the table a little faster than normal, due to the anticipation of hearing what Jason had to tell them about the armband and his explanation for the three puncture holes in his forearm. Dan carried the last of the dishes and leftovers into the kitchen, passing by his wife as she returned to wipe off the table. As Dan put the food away in air-tight plastic containers, Barbara returned to the kitchen to remove her finished cinnamon-crumb apple pie from the oven. She then turned the oven off and set the pie on the countertop to cool.

Dan walked over to where she stood. "That pie will go good with filet sandwiches later," he kidded.

Barbara giggled at Dan's humor, even knowing they were about to find out something unusual from their oldest son—what, they could not yet imagine. She knew Dan was trying to break the ice and help keep them in a relaxed frame of mind for the coming conversation.

Dan noticed his wife's slightly somber look and grabbed her hand. "Well, let's go find out what's going on with our sons," he said.

Barbara consented yet felt relief as they entered the living room only to find it empty. Their sons were probably still in Jason's bedroom. She and Dan sat down in the love seat, just across from the couch, patiently waiting. Their sons were always prompt when told to do something or given a time for a family get-together or conversation, so they should be arriving anytime.

In Jason's bedroom, Jason and Kyle still sat on the bed, Jason again thinking about how he would be revealing something to his parents they would have never ever expected or dreamed. Kyle had talked with Michael for almost five minutes nonstop, and Jason knew his little brother's attachment to Michael was real. Jason's thoughts turned to the fake armband he'd given his father, and he opened the top drawer of his bedside table and removed the *real* armband, placing it in the front pocket of his jeans. He glanced down at his wristwatch and noticed they were about a minute late to meet their parents. "Let's go, Kyle," he said.

Kyle was daydreaming, most likely about Michael and the spaceship, but he snapped out of his thoughts at Jason's voice. "Okay," he said.

Jason grabbed his communicator from Kyle. "Talk to you in a little bit, Michael," he said. "Bye."

"Okay," Michael said.

Jason placed the communicator in his other pants pocket, and he and Kyle both stood up. They headed out of the bedroom, Jason opening the door for his little brother, and continued down the hallway to the living room, neither of them knowing for sure what to expect. When they finally entered the room, their parents were patiently waiting on the love seat, and the television was turned off—it was especially quiet at that very moment. The first thing Jason noticed was his dad's calm face.

"Boys," Dan said, "please have a seat on the couch."

"Okay," Jason said and followed his little brother over to the couch, where they sat down next to each other, straight across from their parents.

Dan pulled the fake armband from his pocket, holding it up in the air. "All right, Jason," he said. "I know from tests at work that this armband is not from Earth. What do you know about it that you do not want to tell us?"

Jason quietly contemplated his answer. "Yes, Dad, it is not of this world," he said.

Dan and Barbara were now especially quiet. Not only was Jason being careful with his answers, but he'd also agreed the armband was not from Earth. Dan thought about how to phrase his next question to his clever son, who had obviously thought ahead about his replies. He held the armband up in the air again. "Did this armband place those three holes in your forearm?"

"No, it didn't," Jason said.

"What put them there, then, Jason?" Dan asked.

Barbara remained quiet.

Jason's father had asked him the one question that he could not answer without telling everything, including introducing them to Michael. He was not going to lie, as one lie would lead to another. He thought about the large spaceship that had crashed a few days ago, the small craft he'd found inside, and his organic-android friend, Michael, who was on that small craft all by himself. His thoughts next focused on the special abilities of the real armband in the pocket of his jeans. With all of that in mind, he finally reached into his pocket, pulled out the real armband, and then stood up from the couch. He walked over to his parents, handed the real armband to his father, and stared directly into his eyes. "Here, Dad. This is the real armband," he said.

Jason turned around without saying another word and sat back down next to his little brother. His parents quietly looked over the new armband just handed to them.

Dan and Barbara were more than just quiet, as the new armband was different from the other one. Still not knowing what to say, Dan turned the new armband over and immediately saw the three small, thin, gold-colored needles on the underside, as though they were interface pins. Barbara also saw the sewing needle–sized pins and recognized they were in the same pattern as the puncture holes in her son's forearm. She also noticed, as did Dan, that the ends of the new armband were different, as if it would have to reshape itself. They both looked over at their boys again with strange stares.

Jason noticed this. "Mom, Dad," he finally said, "I have someone I want you to meet. I'll return in a little bit."

Dan and Barbara were surprised to hear this. "Who, Jason?" Dan asked.

"I will bring him back to the house. Then you'll see."

Barbara and Dan remained quiet while Jason stood up from the couch. Kyle was acting antsy and asked, "Jason, can I go?"

"No, you stay right here, Kyle," Jason said. "I'll be right back."

"Jason," his father quickly said, "I'm coming with you."

"No, Dad," Jason said. "It will be all right. You have nothing to worry about, because he is extremely nice."

Dan and Barbara remained especially quiet again with strange feelings inside, wondering whom Jason was about to have them meet.

Jason glanced at his wristwatch while walking by his parents. It was 6:22 p.m. There was over an hour of sunlight left. He continued toward the front door without hesitation, peeking back at his parents, who were still quiet. He'd never made them speechless before. It was probably partly because they were now well aware that Kyle knew who Jason was about to bring back to the house.

Jason opened the front door, closed it behind him, and stood on the porch. He removed the communicator from his pants. "Michael?" he quietly called.

"Yes, Jason?" Michael said.

"I am coming to the spaceship now."

"Yes, I know."

Jason grinned a little and continued off the east porch stairs, toward the barn, wondering whether Michael had any anticipation for meeting his parents. Michael had been listening to all their conversations inside the house, so that had to mean something. While approaching the barn, Jason slipped the communicator back into his pants. The weather on this particular evening was actually quite mild, with only a light breeze out of the west. Finally walking around the west side of the barn, he continued under the large elm tree and finally up to the gate. Opening the gate, he continued into the open field, and about twenty feet away, he saw the door into the invisible spaceship. It again looked like a brightly lit hole into another world. He continued toward the opening without hesitation to find Michael waiting near the doorway, looking quite eager. "Are you ready to meet my mom and dad?" Jason asked.

"Yes, I am," Michael quickly responded.

He sounded anxious, which was a surprise to Jason. Spotting the armband on Michael's forearm, Jason thought, *That will become a topic of conversation for Mom and Dad.* "Okay, let's go then," he said.

Michael walked down the ramp to the planet's surface and planted his feet firmly on the ground. He then touched a couple of buttons on his armband, and the doorway suddenly vanished, leaving nothing visible but an open field of grass, shrubs, and a few juniper trees.

Jason and Michael walked away from the invisible spaceship, passing through the gate and then under the large elm tree. Jason glanced over at Michael, who had a look on his face that Jason had never seen or ever expected to see. Michael was looking around at his surroundings and up at the leaves on the elm tree as if he had never seen them up close and personal. A subtle, relaxed smile filled his face.

This was surprising because Michael was supposed to be an organic android and Jason still didn't know whether he actually had a full complement of emotions. "Have you ever been off the ship before, Michael?" Jason asked.

"No," he replied.

As they continued toward the house, Jason grew curious about how his parents would react to meeting Michael. Would they have to contact the government to see what they wanted to do, or would they want to keep Michael secret even from them? He hoped it would be the latter and did feel his parents would not want their family subjected to governmental bureaucracy associated with Michael's origin and his spaceship, including the possibility of Michael becoming a guinea pig, forever locked away in some top-secret lab. The existence of extraterrestrial spaceships was not something openly discussed in Earth's society, just as had been mentioned in the UFO documentary special on television last night.

Jason and Michael finally walked up the east stairs onto the front porch, with Jason still leading the way, and then stopped at the front door. Standing quietly, Jason looked down at Michael with unusual anticipation. "Okay, here we go," he said.

# 11

## JASON'S PARENTS FINALLY MEET MICHAEL

Jason turned the knob, opened the door, and noticed Michael with a happy look on his face. "Go on in, Michael," he said.

"Okay," Michael said.

Jason's parents heard Jason talking to what sounded like another young boy. They had not bothered asking Kyle where Jason had gone, because they knew he did not fully understand the implications of what was going on with his older brother's secret.

Jason and Michael finally walked into the living room and stood quietly. Despite having heard another boy's voice, Barbara and Dan were still surprised to see Jason standing alongside a nice-looking little boy who looked about the same age as Kyle, possibly a little older. Jason glanced down at Michael and then back to his parents. "Mom, Dad," he said, "this is my friend, Michael."

Michael stared directly at Jason's parents and calmly raised his left hand in a wave, openly exposing his armband. "Hello," he said.

Barbara and Dan were at first startled, mainly because Michael had on an armband like the one that had started this evening's conversation, but nevertheless, both still managed small smiles at Michael's sincerity. "Hi, Michael," they replied in unison.

"Hi, Michael," Kyle said.

Michael turned his head. "Hi, Kyle," he said.

Dan and Barbara now knew both kids had been playing with the little boy without their knowledge. For how long, they did not know and could only speculate that it had likely been for a few days. Dan looked briefly at his wife, who still had a small smile on her face because of how sincerely the little boy had presented himself. Dan turned back to Michael, quite curious, especially since their closest neighbors lived nearly a half mile away and did not have a little boy. "Where do you live?"

Michael stared directly at Jason's father with a sincere, open face. "I used to live in the stars, but now I live here," he said.

Dan and Barbara were more than surprised and could not tell any characteristics other than his hair that would distinguish him much from their own kids. Dan turned briefly to his wife and then back to Michael. "Where are your parents?"

"I do not know," Michael answered truthfully.

Dan and Barbara were both surprised at his answer. Barbara was silent for only a short moment longer. "Jason," she said in a calm, soft voice, "you and your friend have a seat on the couch next to Kyle."

"Okay, Mom," Jason said.

Another small smile appeared on Michael's face at this request, because it seemed to be an open invitation. Jason followed Michael over to the couch, where they sat down on each side of Kyle. The three boys quietly stared over at Dan and Barbara, and in the new lighting, Dan and Barbara could see Michael looked physically the same as their two sons—his skin texture, his eyes, his hands, and even the shape of his body—but there was just something about his hair. Even though it was as thick as Kyle's, maybe a little thicker, it seemed to shine with unusual luster. Dan and Barbara knew Michael was somehow related to the crash of what had to be spaceship and could not ignore the fact that he was wearing the same type of armband that Jason had in his possession—an armband that had caused three puncture holes to his forearm and had dangerous molecular properties. Michael continued to stare over at Barbara and Dan, and the room got particularly quiet, especially since Dan and Barbara knew the little boy was not from Earth.

Dan now figured Michael must have a spaceship nearby and looked briefly at Michael's left arm. "What is your armband for?" he asked.

Michael paused and answered truthfully, "It opens the door to my ship but can be used for many other things."

Dan felt strange having his suspicions confirmed.

Michael turned to Jason and said, "Your mom and dad are kind and friendly just like you."

Barbara's and Dan's hearts softened hearing this, and they looked more closely at Michael.

"Where is your ship?" Dan asked.

"Behind the barn," Michael answered.

Dan remembered Jason and Kyle walking from that direction last night, right before they went fishing. "Is that where you two were last night?"

Jason paused. "Yes, it is," he replied.

Dan again stared at Michael's armband, knowing it had strange and very dangerous properties. Though the fake armband did not have the interface pins, it was real in many other aspects. He picked up both armbands and held them up in the air, curious what Michael knew about them. "Are these dangerous?" he asked.

"They can be," Michael said, "especially if a high-voltage, high-current source is applied to them, like what happened at your Los Alamos labs."

Dan was surprised Michael knew that event had occurred. "How about for humans wearing them?"

Michael knew he was referring to Jason, who had worn the armband for a short while. "No, they're not dangerous to wear," he said, "but must be reconfigured to the physiology of the host body's limbic nervous system, just as it was for Jason."

Barbara and Dan both sighed deeply, as they knew they were talking to a young alien boy, possibly a very high-quality, realistic-looking android, who was extremely smart, probably smarter than both of them combined. Though they knew he must be organic because of his armband, he still looked somewhat different because his hair strands seemed extremely robust and healthy, filled with strange luster. They both now wondered why his hair was different.

Jason noticed his parents' puzzlement and revealed, "He's an organic android, Mom and Dad."

Dan and Barbara thought they now understood a little more about Michael, but it was strange for them to be talking to a calm humanoid-android boy with a sincere demeanor yet having emotions—much like their own two sons.

Barbara was still staring at Michael, and Dan knew she had compassion for the little android boy since he was alone and did not understand why he was not with the ones who had created him. Dan turned back to Michael with curiosity. "Can you take us to your spaceship?"

"Okay," Michael said quickly. He eagerly stood up from the couch. For a moment, he stood in front of the couch by himself. Noticing this, Jason and Kyle also stood up, and the three boys stood next to each other, waiting for the grown-ups.

Jason's parents also stood up, slightly giddy yet full of anticipation to see Michael's spaceship. Though they both had always believed in spacecraft of extraterrestrial origin, they had never thought they would get to see one up close in their lifetime, let alone walk aboard one. With how willing Michael was to show them his spaceship, they had to assume it was part of his programming to look up to adults for guidance.

Jason took the lead, Michael and Kyle following close behind, and bringing up the rear were Dan and Barbara, who could not help but notice the way Kyle and Michael were acting, as if they were twin brothers. Their youngest had an attachment to Michael.

Jason opened the front door and walked out onto the porch, followed by Michael and Kyle, then Dan and Barbara. Jason had an unusual grin on his face, and as Dan closed the door, he wondered what was behind his son's grin.

Michael turned around. "This way," he said.

They all continued across the porch, down the east stairs, and south toward the barn. Dan and Barbara looked down again at Michael and wondered how any intelligent race would abandon a young organic-android boy, especially one designed with emotions. They looked forward to finding out those answers, as well as discovering how Jason had met Michael.

The five of them walked around the west side of the barn, under the large elm tree, and through the open gate. They all walked about fifteen more feet, and then Michael stopped. Dan and Barbara stopped behind their two boys, confused, because they saw no spaceship. They continued to stare into the open field of juniper trees, Indian parsley plants, yellow ragweed wildflowers, and buffalo grass. Puzzlement filled their faces.

Jason noticed their confusion and explained, "The spaceship is cloaked, Mom and Dad."

Barbara and Dan looked at each other in surprise and then down at Michael, who was staring up at them. "I am going to open the door to the ship now," he told them.

Michael touched a few buttons on his armband, and a brightly lit doorway suddenly appeared from out of nowhere—like a hole into another world. Dan and Barbara now knew the ship was in the open field, completely invisible. A small ramp below the door was also now visible, and Dan was curious about the size of the spaceship. "Michael," he said, "can you uncloak the ship so that we can see what it looks like?"

"Okay." Michael touched a few buttons on his armband, and the spaceship slowly came into view.

Dan and Barbara stood amazed. The ship seemed like a mirage for a moment before fully transitioning out of its cloaking field. The circular, flat-bottomed spaceship was at least twenty-five feet in diameter and twelve to fifteen feet tall. The top was domed, its curvature shaped like a football cut in half lengthwise. There were small viewing windows around its sides and a larger circular window, similar to a bubble, on the top that matched the curvature of the spaceship's domed shape.

Michael stared up again at Jason's parents. "I will cloak the ship again after we are all inside," he said.

Dan and Barbara were still speechless but quietly acknowledged Michael while following the three boys up the ramp into the spaceship. Once inside, Michael touched another series of buttons on his armband. Nothing seemed to happen, but Dan and Barbara had to assume he had recloaked the spaceship. He touched additional buttons on his armband, and the open doorway behind them suddenly disappeared. Surprisingly, there was not even an outline of a door remaining.

Michael continued to stare up at Jason's parents. "The ship is cloaked again," he announced.

There was fascination on Dan's and Barbara's faces. They were absolutely flabbergasted to be aboard a spaceship from another world—a spaceship that, when airborne, would definitely be considered a UFO to everyone on Earth—even if it was fairly small.

Michael, Jason, and Kyle walked up to the cockpit area and quickly sat down in the same seats as earlier in the day, Jason in the left captain's seat, Michael in the right copilot's seat, and Kyle between them like an observer.

Dan turned to his wife, who had an unusual expression on her face, and they finally walked up to the cockpit, just behind the three kids, and again stood quietly. There were two control wheels, one in front of Jason and one in front of Michael. The wheels appeared to be mounted directly over pedestals, and the pedestals looked to be mounted on large omnidirectional ball joints, except the pedestal bases seemed to also have the ability to telescopically move up and down. It was very strange-looking, and Dan did not understand the mechanics behind the setup. He finally looked directly at Michael with curiosity. "Do those control wheels fly this ship similar to Earth aircraft?"

Michael turned around. "Sort of," he said, "except they have direct control of the spaceship's gravity drive for propulsion movement in any direction, and movement is almost instantaneous."

Dan was fascinated and became extremely curious about the spaceship, as it must also have inertial dampening. It did not appear to be a spaceship that would be used to fly from star to star or from galaxy to galaxy. After staring down at the lit consoles in front of the three cockpit seats and the side consoles, one to Jason's left and the other to Michael's right, Dan wondered whether the ship was possibly a child's spaceship. He also realized just how much more complicated their lives had become after meeting Michael.

Michael turned around again and noticed Jason's parents still standing. He touched his front console, and two seats suddenly appeared out of nowhere directly behind them. "You can both sit down now," he said.

Dan and Barbara sat down, Barbara continuing to stare into Michael's unusual but human-looking eyes. "Thank you, Michael," she said.

"You're welcome," he softly replied.

She again noticed Michael's sincere politeness and calm demeanor. All she and Dan could do now was look around the spaceship and cockpit area, not knowing for sure what to say or do next. During those few moments of silence, Jason thought about what Michael had told him about not having a mom and dad or even knowing who had created him. He was pretty sure Michael's only understanding of a family was what he'd observed of Jason's family. Jason sighed and wished his parents would raise Michael as their own, as his brother. He remained quiet, wishing and dearly hoping in his heart.

Barbara and Dan were still lost in their thoughts while looking around the spaceship. Dan thought about all the reports of a UFO in the area and wondered whether it had been Michael's spaceship that everyone had seen. He just had to know. "Was this the UFO reported near Los Alamos?" he asked.

Michael turned around. "Yes, it was."

Dan noticed his two kids staring at him with honest faces. "Have you two flown on this ship?" he asked.

Jason paused. "Yes, we have, Dad."

Dan was surprised. "When did you do that?"

"After midnight," Jason said. "Kyle and I snuck out my bedroom window and then flew into outer space. We made it back before sunrise, though."

Dan and Barbara were again quiet, as they now knew why Jason had Kyle sleep in his bedroom. Barbara also realized that was why they'd slept in later than normal. "What time did you get back?" she asked.

"About four this morning," Jason answered truthfully. "We flew outside the ionosphere and to around forty thousand miles away from Earth—right, Michael?"

"That is correct," Michael said.

Dan and Barbara were quiet again. It seemed Michael had been educating Jason. They just had to know how Jason had come about meeting Michael in the first place, as it just was not making complete sense, especially since the military, for some reason, had been at the crash site of the spaceship fairly quickly.

Dan directed his attention to Jason with intense curiosity. "Jason?"

Jason turned around. "Yes, Dad?"

"Tell your mom and me how you came about meeting Michael."

Jason looked briefly over at Michael and then back to his parents.

"Remember when you started walking toward your car right after looking for me two nights ago?"

Dan thought about it. "Yes," he said.

Jason continued, "Well, I had just walked off this spaceship, which was cloaked and invisible just east of our house."

Dan remembered his son walking in from the east side of the house. "Yes, I remember that," he said. "I never would have dreamed you were aboard a spaceship."

Jason grinned a little. "Well, we'd been flying around for a few hours just before that."

Dan turned to Barbara and knew she had to remember Jason walking into the house about twenty minutes after midnight after being gone for almost three hours, making them worried something bad had happened to him. Dan then remembered the military personnel he'd met at the crash site. The site had been highly secured and for what he now knew was good reason, since it was not actually an aircraft carrying radioactive material but a spaceship of extraterrestrial origin that had crashed. He continued to stare at his oldest son and wondered how the ship they were currently aboard could have ever left the spaceship that had crashed. "Did this ship come from that crash site?" he asked.

Jason looked briefly at Michael and then back to his father. "Yes, it did."

It still did not make complete sense to Dan. "How did you come into possession of this ship, then?"

Jason paused and gave a small sigh. "All right, Mom and Dad," he said. "I'm going to tell you the whole story of that night from the very beginning, including how I met Michael. Okay?"

"Sure, Son," his father quickly answered. "Your mom and I want to hear all about it."

Jason noticed his parents' interest, briefly looked at Kyle and Michael, and then turned back to his parents. He proceeded to tell them how he'd been on the front porch watching the stars and had seen what he thought to be a shooting star—an object with a brilliant white tail behind it. The object stopped in the sky and was stationary for a moment before it started to fall toward Earth really fast, glowing blue and red and then disappearing along the western horizon.

Jason paused to gauge his parents' reactions and found them glued to what he was telling them. He explained that there was a glow along the western horizon, so he had no problem tracking where the object had fallen. When he finally approached the object, he was surprised to find it was a large, tubular spaceship. Its hull was damaged and took on the shape of an accordion, as though it had been placed in a vise. There was an open doorway, and when he found no occupants, he entered.

Jason paused again to see his parents staring at him as though in a hypnotic trance. He calmly continued his story and told his parents that he continued farther inside the cargo ship and found a large cargo hold with the same spaceship they were aboard, except it was blinking on and off, disappearing and then reappearing. Then it turned into a solid, and another doorway appeared. He went inside and then sat down in the cockpit to find all the instrument panels turned off.

Jason paused for a third time and noticed his parents still entranced by his story. So he explained that he next heard a humming noise coming from behind the outline of a door in the wall. There was the sound of pressure releasing, followed by vapor rising out of the compartment. After a bright flash of light at the bottom of the doorway, the door finally opened all the way. After the vapor cleared, Michael was standing there with his eyes closed. After his eyes opened, he walked out of the compartment, and he and Jason had been friends ever since. Jason paused from his story.

Dan and Barbara were amazed at Jason's detailed story. They'd always known he was fascinated by outer space and wanted to be an astronaut when older. He had been awfully brave to walk by himself in the dark and enter a strange alien spaceship. They were not sure they could have done it. Dan continued to think about the fact that the military had arrived at the site soon afterward and been able to remove the cargo ship, which had to have been fairly large, and its contents before sunrise. He glanced briefly through the bubble-shaped window, noticing the sun had already set in the western horizon, and turned back to his oldest son, still not understanding how the smaller ship had been able to exit the larger damaged ship. "How did you get this spaceship out of the cargo bay?"

"Michael did it," Jason said. "He activated our ship's gravity propulsion and, after hovering inside the cargo bay, cut a large, circular hole through one of the walls."

Dan was again surprised. "How was that accomplished?"

Barbara remained especially quiet.

Jason glanced over at Michael. "By using a gravitational laser beam ring—right, Michael?"

"Yes," Michael said. "It is one of the many weapons this small ship possesses. It burned a hole through the hull of the cargo ship using a tangent-line-vector gravity wave projected along a rotational ring of laser energy traveling above the speed of light. There is no other weapon that could have successfully cut a hole through the highly reactive crystalline-metallic hull material of the larger ship."

Dan and his wife were surprised to hear about weapons, especially a rotational gravity wave laser beam capable of burning a hole through the hull of an alien spaceship, not to mention that the laser energy traveled above the speed of light. They both now knew Michael had come from an extremely advanced race that was able to manipulate gravity and could also probably travel magnitudes above the speed of light in their spaceships.

Dan turned to Jason filled with overwhelming curiosity. "What happened next?"

Jason paused. "Well, we left the cargo bay and stopped just outside the crashed ship. It suddenly broke apart into smaller circular sections along the high-point edges of its accordion shape. The sections that were slightly bent immediately flexed out into perfectly shaped round rings."

"Why did the ship break apart all of a sudden?" Dan quickly asked.

Jason did not have the faintest idea and turned to Michael, who was already staring at his dad. "The cargo ship's hull collapsed," Michael calmly answered, "due to a cascading decompression of its ground zero base nuclear structure, because of it being deformed and compressed out of its original configuration. When we cut the hole, it released the compression that was near a state of collapse and started a decompression sequence back to its original state, which was no longer sustainable." Michael paused as though what he'd just explained was common knowledge.

Dan and Barbara did not know how to comment on Michael's explanation, and Jason recognized this. "Mom and Dad," he said, "are you ready for the rest of my story?"

They both came out of their transient states of thought at their oldest boy's question. "Yes, we are," Dan said.

"Okay then," Jason said. "When Michael turned the ship back toward the west, we saw vehicles with flashing red lights headed in our direction as well as a few helicopters. Michael took our ship up to one thousand feet." Jason paused while staring at his father. "Remember when I told you about the F-16s, Dad?"

"Yes," Dan answered.

"Well, there were two of them headed straight toward our spaceship, and we left them in the dust. We stopped around seven hundred miles away in Nebraska."

Dan grabbed his wife's hand after the full realization of what had happened hit him like a brick wall. She also found the story amazing but realized there might be possible ramifications with the military and the secret government agencies that oversee extraterrestrial events, to keep them safeguarded from the public. They both knew the spaceship they were currently aboard could travel at tremendous speeds. Dan turned back to Jason, knowing there had to be more to his story. "Is there anything else we should know about?"

Jason paused again. "This ship can eavesdrop on all Earth-based communications," he said, "even secret military groups."

Dan was puzzled. "What do you mean?"

"What I mean, Dad," Jason said, "is that we went back to the crash site cloaked and watched them clean up. They loaded crate after crate into box trailers, and they even had cranes to load some of the larger items onto semitrailer flatbeds. We hovered a few hundred feet above them, undetected, and heard a major speaking to a general on a satellite phone." Jason paused. "They know about this spaceship, Dad, and I think they're looking for it."

Dan leaned back in his chair and looked over at his wife, who had already slumped back in her own chair. "What do we do now?"

Barbara perked up and sat up in her chair. "Well, they can't detect the ship, right?"

"Evidently not," Dan said.

Barbara knew Michael was like an innocent little boy, even if he was an organic android, and if the government were to get their hands on him, they might lock him away like a lab animal, and she and her family would never see him again. "Well, they are not getting this ship or Michael," she determinedly declared.

Dan could understand his wife's firmness, as he also thought Michael was like a lost little boy, a unique humanoid organic android who seemed to be carrying an immense amount of knowledge yet did not even know the identity of who had created him. Dan wondered how his knowledge was being stored, whether it was a unique organic synaptic brain cell configuration or some advanced aspect of solid-state circuitry on the molecular level. Dan continued staring at his wife. "I know what you're thinking," he said.

"Yes, I knew you would," she said.

Michael, Jason, and Kyle all remained quiet, listening to the grown-ups talking back and forth.

Dan noticed the three kids sitting with innocent faces and knew his family's lives could never be the same, especially since his kids had an emotional attachment to Michael. He stared directly into Michael's calm, humanlike eyes. "You're going to stay with us, Michael," he finally said.

Jason and Kyle broke into happy grins, and Michael stared up at Dan and Barbara with confusion. "Are you my mom and dad now?" he suddenly asked.

Dan looked over at his wife, who was smiling a little and calmly gave Michael an affirmative nod. "Yes, we are," Dan said.

A small grin appeared on Michael's face, and Dan and Barbara were surprised again that he could show such emotions as an organic android, reacting much like a human boy would. They both still could not believe that any advanced race could ever leave a young android boy behind, especially one with emotions designed into him. Now they were curious just how much emotional behavior he had and whether it was something he would have to learn by example.

Michael continued to stare up into their faces. "Can I call you Mommy and Daddy like Kyle?" he asked, his face sincere.

Dan and Barbara now had small grins, because they knew Michael was indeed learning and mimicking their own two kids. It might be part of his learning process, as it was very possible that he'd first become consciously awake just before meeting Jason.

"Yes, you may," Dan said, and Barbara gave a small nod to reaffirm his answer.

Michael continued to stare up at his new parents. He now truly believed they were his parents. They would become permanent markers in his memory, deeply embedded, both physically and emotionally.

Dan was curious about the race that had created Michael. He wondered whether Michael's isolation from other living beings was for a reason and, if so, what the underlying rationale was. "Michael," he finally said, "do you remember anyone on the planet from where you originated?"

"No," Michael said, "only from their history."

Dan quietly nodded. *Hmmm,* he thought. *My assumption was correct, as it appears he has never had any physical interaction with any living being. He now seems to have bonded to our family.*

"Where is your home world?" Dan asked.

"In another galaxy 184,262 light-years away," Michael answered.

Dan and Barbara were again amazed and quietly contemplated their current situation. Another of Dan's assumption had been confirmed: that whoever had created Michael evidently had spaceships that could travel magnitudes greater than the speed of light. Why they would ever bring Michael to Earth was a very strange mystery.

Jason and Kyle were all smiles, because Michael was now like their brother. Their mom and dad had accepted him as their own, just like Jason had hoped and wished for all along. Jason stared over at his *two* younger brothers and turned around with a good feeling inside, especially since he knew their spaceship had highly advanced capabilities. "Do you want to travel into outer space with us, Mom and Dad?" he asked.

# 12

## A TRIP INTO OUTER SPACE FOR THE JUPITER FAMILY

Jason's question gave Dan and Barbara mixed emotions, but they still felt immense anticipation for accomplishing something they'd never thought possible. Neither of them had believed in their wildest imaginations that they would ever get to leave Earth's atmosphere, let alone travel past its outer reaches as Jason and Kyle had done—only astronauts had that opportunity. Dan turned to his wife, who nodded in the affirmative, and looked back to the three boys. "Sure, why not?" he said.

Michael touched his front console, and the general lighting throughout the ship dimmed a little. The three front consoles as well as Jason's and Michael's side consoles lit up brightly, and Michael grabbed his control wheel with both hands while looking back at his new parents. "Okay, here we go," he said. He lifted straight up on his control wheel, and their spaceship rose quickly away from the planet.

Dan and Barbara glanced out their side windows and noticed their house getting farther away very quickly. They could see the top of their house, the fenced backyard, the swimming pool, and the gazebo over their Jacuzzi. Parked in front of the garage was the

Lincoln Navigator, and off to the east, aircraft from the Los Alamos Airport flew below their current position. Dan looked at Jason. "How high are we now?"

Jason looked down at his front console and back to his father. "We are now at fifteen thousand feet and still climbing, Dad."

Dan and Barbara were somewhat surprised, because neither of them felt any acceleration forces whatsoever, despite climbing at such an extremely fast rate of speed. Dan glanced at his wristwatch. Their ship had to have easily accelerated over fifteen thousand miles per hour to get to their current altitude so quickly. Through the bubble-shaped window, stars shined brightly in the night sky. Michael knew they were also traveling slightly toward the east, flying at an angle of eighty-nine degrees while approaching the upper reaches and boundary of Earth's atmospheric pressure differential to the vacuum of outer space.

Jason looked down again at their altitude and turned around with a wide smile. "We are now at 190,000 feet and rising," he informed his parents.

They were already in the upper levels of the stratosphere and approaching the ozone layer. The sun was shining along the western horizon, on the sunward side of Earth, visible over the tops of cirrocumulus clouds that had to be at least twenty miles below them. Dan was curious about their spaceship leaving pressurized space at such a high angle of climb—basically straight up. "What will the extreme gravitational forces and pressures do to our ship, Michael?" he asked.

Michael had been staring straight ahead, but realizing the concern in his new father's voice, he turned around. "Nothing will happen, Dad," he said. "This ship's highly reactive hull material won't feel any effects."

Dan had to smile a little at hearing Michael call him "Dad" and realized how fast Michael had adapted to him as his father. He also was not going to ignore how much Michael probably understood about highly advanced sciences from the race that had created him. In Dan's mind, it seemed as though Michael had been born only a few days ago and he and Barbara were his new adoptive parents. They had been the first adults he'd set his eyes on and physically interacted with, so it could be more of his child-bonding programming. Barbara was still staring at Michael with a subtle smile. Dan knew how good of a mother she was to their two biological kids, so a third child should be no problem, even if he was an organic android who was brilliant yet naive in many ways.

Dan gently squeezed his wife's hand as more of the sun's face peeked around the horizon. Suddenly, white flashes of light appeared outside the windows, almost as if lightning were arcing across air molecules, some of the streams with a touch of blue tint. Dan had to suppose the ship might have entered the ozone layer and lower ionospheric layers at an abnormal angle, but he did not know. Suddenly, the bluish-white streaks of light ceased as they continued farther into space.

Dan was curious about what he'd witnessed and knew they were still traveling extremely fast in relation to Earth's magnetosphere and electron-proton current flow. He looked over at Michael again. There would be some getting used to having another child. Even though he and his wife had accepted Michael as one of their own in just the past hour, Dan found himself already attached to the young, sincere humanoid android. "Michael?" he gently called.

Michael turned around. "Yes, Dad?"

"How fast are we going, Son?"

"We are traveling at twenty-one thousand miles per hour, Dad, or about Mach 30."

Jason and Kyle looked to each other with small smiles, as Michael was now their brother, a humanoid-android brother of all things, a brother who Jason knew could teach them much about advanced sciences that were unknown to Earth.

All Dan and Barbara could do was sit with amazed faces at the reality of the *three* boys they now had. Equally amazing was the speed at which they were traveling away from Earth.

Michael, after looking briefly at Jason and Kyle, touched his front console and turned around to his new parents. "We are about to leave the planet's mesosphere and enter the ionospheric regions," he announced. "Everyone should have their seat belts fastened."

Dan and Barbara did not see any seat belts, but then suddenly they appeared on all the chairs, each seat belt having a shoulder harness, a waist belt, and leg straps. Dan and Barbara knew the ship's computer must somehow be controlling the seat belts. Dan looked up to Michael. "Why are we using seat belts, Michael?"

Suddenly, the six-axis seatbelts latched themselves around their bodies. Dan's shoulder harness crisscrossed his chest, attached to his waist belt, but there was no buckle to unlatch it. There were also straps across his thighs that were attached to the waist strap, which was attached to the seat. He felt very secure and definitely would not be standing up, but he strangely found that he could lean forward, as though the shoulder harness were elastic.

Michael turned around to answer his father's last question. "We have seat belts, Dad, because the gravitational field of this small ship, while cloaked, can get momentarily interrupted by this planet's geometric ionic-energy field fluctuations."

Dan was quiet. Even though he understood there were electrical charge paths for the ionization of atoms in the ionospheric regions, Michael's understanding made his seem elementary. Michael's explanation made some sense, but he had no idea know a cloaked spaceship would interact with Earth's ionosphere. His only guess was that the cloaking field might be creating some strange inverse polarizing field to Earth's magnetic field to cause those electrical charges. They were experimenting with that type of cloaking in the highly secretive Black Quadrant section of the Los Alamos labs, but they had not been very successful, due to a space–light-speed time lapse. "I would like to talk to you more about that some time, Michael," he said.

Michael nodded. "Okay, Daddy."

Barbara gave Michael an encouraging smile. When Michael looked straight ahead again, she looked back to her husband. "Do you think we can teach him how to show love and affection?"

"Good question," Dan said. "I hope so. If not, we'll show him by example."

Barbara knew how true that would be and looked forward to showing Michael love and affection. She wondered how Michael might show and return affection, since he had never had any physical interaction with adults before. She didn't have the faintest idea how she and Dan would go about explaining Michael's sudden appearance in their lives to their friends and family. They would have to figure it out when they returned back home.

Dan noticed his wife daydreaming and realized he was also starting to daydream about Michael, who was now a part of their lives. It would be an interesting challenge to explain him to their friends and relatives. As Dan sat idly, there was a sudden bump, followed by a series of smaller bumps, and then one more profound bump before the ship was again completely smooth.

Michael let loose of his control wheel, and the ship quickly slowed to a stop. He turned around with a calm look. Dan and Barbara were especially quiet, as they did not know what to say.

Michael blurted out, "Well, we've left Earth's ionosphere, and there are now very few gravity effects. What do you want to do now?"

Jason turned around, excited. "Can we travel to the moon?"

"Yes, Mommy," Kyle chimed in. "I want to go there too."

Noting the excitement in his kids' voices, Dan glanced at his wristwatch: it was 10:33 p.m. He looked directly at Michael, who was still calmly waiting for their answer. "How long will it take us to travel to the moon, Michael?" Dan asked.

"Less than one Earth hour," Michael answered.

Dan stared briefly at his wife, surprised, and she gave an affirmative nod. He turned back to the three boys with anticipation like never before. "Okay, let's visit the moon, then," he calmly said. "Getting up early to go to work will just have to wait," he joked.

Barbara laughed under her breath at her husband's lightheartedness, especially for the situation they were now in. Jason, Kyle, and even Michael perked up, excited at the prospect of traveling to the moon. Because of Michael's excited expression, Dan and Barbara felt confident they could teach him any type of emotion, even love and affection. They found themselves looking forward to teaching him how to express affection between family members who dearly loved each other.

Michael grabbed his control wheel and pushed it forward with more pressure than when they'd left Earth. Dan wondered whether Michael was taking their spaceship to its maximum speed, since it had to be traveling over two hundred thousand miles per hour to arrive at the moon in one Earth hour.

As their ship quickly accelerated up to speed, the stars outside the ship seemed to change their apparent positions like a blue haze, yet Dan and Barbara again felt no inertial forces. It was strange not to feel any movement as their ship increased to an extraordinary speed within only a few seconds. They both remained quiet, admiring the twinkling stars just beyond the moon.

Dan finally looked forward to the boys. "Michael," he asked, "how fast are we currently traveling?"

Michael turned around. "Two hundred and thirty thousand miles per hour," he answered.

Dan noticed everyone's seat belts had disappeared. Until that point, he hadn't even realized that his own seat belt had vanished. He made eye contact with Michael. "Are we traveling at our ship's maximum velocity?"

"In its current gravity element energy configuration, yes," he said, "but if I were to modify and override its current power supply interface, I could redistribute the application of additional harmonic energy across the gravity element, and we would then be able to travel much faster." Like before, Michael acted as though what he had just said was basic common knowledge.

Dan was amazed. "Okay, thank you." He thought about the armbands Jason had given him. He removed the two armbands from his shirt pocket and studied them in more detail, curious about their internal properties. The ends of the real armband bent outward, the three small, thin gold needles clearly visible. He remembered what Michael had told them about how the armband caused a bioelectrical interface to the organic host body and looked over at Michael's armband again. "Michael?" he called out.

Michael turned around. "Yes, Dad?"

Dan had to again grin, as Michael probably really did believe he was his dad. He held the armband with the needles up in the air. "What are some of the properties of this device?"

"Do you mean how it is designed or what you can do with it?"

Dan turned to his wife, surprised. Michael clearly had an extreme amount of programmed information, especially to be able to understand the nuclear properties of the armbands, considering even the fake armband had been indestructible to all tests at the Los Alamos labs. He turned back to Michael, who was waiting for an answer. "What can you do with it?" he asked.

"You can become invisible and walk through solid objects, for a few of its properties."

Dan raised his eyebrows. "How's that possible?"

Michael's face remained sincere and open. "This ship controls it," he said. "The ship must also be inside the same magnetic field polarity of the object you want to walk through or where you want to become invisible."

Dan looked briefly at his wife, who had an amazed look, and slowly turned back to Michael. "That is amazing," he said. He knew Jason must have had the armband interfaced to his body—a host, as

Michael called it—as the three holes on his forearm clearly matched the interface pins. Dan looked directly at his oldest son with immense interest. "So, Jason, did you ever use any of those armband functions?"

Jason turned around with a small grin. "Yes, I've tried out both of those functions, Dad."

"You did?"

"Yes, I did," Jason said while giving his mother a look that made her curious. "Mom," he said, "remember when you opened the door yesterday after someone knocked on it?"

"Yes," she said.

"Well, it was me who knocked on the door," he revealed.

Dan knew nothing about it, but Barbara suddenly started to laugh. "Is that right?" she said.

"Yes," Jason said, grinning. "I was standing in front of you the entire time. You looked around and then closed the door about five seconds later."

"You know," she said with a distant look, "I thought it might have been you that knocked on the door. I thought you were probably playing a game."

"I *was* playing a game, Mom," Jason said immediately. "I was testing the invisibility function of my armband."

Dan was surprised again by the technological advancements of the race that had created Michael and just could not believe an alien race with that level of advanced technology would ever purposely abandon a small android boy like Michael. He looked down at the two armbands again and placed the circular one without gold pins on a side console. He knew it was a fake that Jason had given him to sidetrack him from the truth, but based on the tests at the Los Alamos labs, it was only partially fake. He continued to stare at the real armband. With the way its ends were bent outward, he realized that the indestructible material had reshaped itself to his son's forearm and reconfigured itself to his son's physiology and electrochemical configuration. He was now curious about that exact thing. "Michael?" he said.

Michael turned back around. "Yes, Dad?"

Dan paused. "Will these armbands have any long-term effects on the human body from wearing them too long or using their advanced attributes?"

"No, none at all," Michael said.

"Okay, thank you," Dan said and glanced at his wife.

Barbara instinctively knew what Dan was thinking: to have armbands created for them so that they could also become invisible and walk through solid objects. Since their new organic-android son, Michael, and their oldest son had them, why should they not also have them?

"Michael?" Dan said.

Michael turned around. "Yes, Dad?"

Dan paused with anticipation. "How long would it take to have armbands created for your mom, myself, and your brother Kyle?"

"A couple of Earth hours," Michael answered, "after your hands are placed inside the organic-matter analyzer."

Dan and Barbara could hardly believe it was possible that the molecular construction of the organic host body, including its limbic nervous system, could be analyzed so easily and quickly by just placing a hand in a slot, but then again, the race that had created Michael did not appear to be your normal race, which meant they'd likely been around for quite some time. Dan was curious about the analyzer. "Where is the analyzer?"

"Here, I will show you," Michael said. He touched a button on the control wheel that placed their ship on automatic propulsion (autopilot). There were biometric field sensors on the control wheel, so only his fingers back on the wheel could change their spaceship's path.

Jason followed Michael and his parents toward the back of the ship, where they all stood next to each other.

In the cockpit, Kyle sat by himself and felt as though he were flying their ship, not knowing it was on autopilot and had a full complement of flight safety measures, including the capability to evade any object directly in their path.

At the back of the ship, Michael stared up into Dan's and Barbara's faces. "You both must position your hands in that slot there, and your biophysical body and molecular configuration will be recorded."

Dan looked briefly to his wife, amazed to hear this, and stared down at the slot. He placed his hand in the slot without hesitation. There was a bright flash of light inside the slot, followed by an undetectable, at least to Dan, short millisecond halo of blue light that encompassed his body, and then his hand went momentarily numb. The numbness quickly went away, as did the white flash of light. Once the flash disappeared, Michael knew the test was complete. "Your organic biophysical configuration is now recorded, Dad," he said, "just like mine. You can now remove your hand from the slot."

After he removed his hand, Dan turned to his wife with a small grin. "It's not that bad, honey," he said. "You'll feel a little numbness, and then it'll go right away."

Barbara believed him and could have sworn she'd seen a momentary flicker of blue light around his body right before the white flash of light vanished. She slowly placed her hand into the rectangular slot. There was again an immediate bright flash of white light. Her hand felt momentarily numb, but then it went away. When the second white flash of light disappeared, Michael knew his mother's cellular organic matter recording was also now complete. "Mom," he said, "your organic biophysical configuration is also recorded, just like mine. You can now remove your hand from the slot."

"Thank you," she kindly replied and removed her hand while staring down at Michael with compassion. He was looking up at her with a sincere, innocent face, like that of a lost little boy who had just found his family. She felt an urge to hold his little body and did just that, reaching down to pick him up in her arms. Michael suddenly reached for her in return. After he was in her arms, she noticed he had a body temperature like that of a living human boy, maybe a few degrees warmer. She placed a small kiss against his soft, humanlike cheek while looking into his pretty blue eyes. It was somewhat surprising for her to see that he had eyes like that of a human being, with colored irises and pupils that were dilating with her physical interaction. For a short moment, his eyes appeared to glow a little under the lighting of the ship, but the glow then faded away—it could have been a reflection.

Michael analyzed this new experience of his mother hugging and kissing him, just as he had heard her doing with Jason and Kyle. He quickly understood this motherly affection and hugged her around her neck.

Barbara turned to her husband with a small smile, Michael's spontaneous return affection another surprise. She then handed him to Dan, who also quickly realized Michael's body temperature was nearly the same as his, possibly to help maintain fluids in his android body. His weight was comparable to Kyle's at around fifty pounds, what would have been expected for a little boy four to five years old. No vibrational or frictional movement was evident at any time in any of his mechanical joints—his arms, his legs, or his neck. The degree of detail the advanced race had put into creating Michael was amazing and made Dan realize even more that the race that had created Michael could very well now be looking for him.

Dan gave him a small hug and a kiss on his cheek. Michael then returned a small hug to his dad. Dan knew without doubt they could teach him love and affection. He finally set him down on the floor. Michael and Jason then returned to their original seats in the cockpit.

A few moments later, Kyle headed toward the back. When he arrived where his parents stood, he looked up with a curious, innocent face. "Michael wanted me to put my hand in the rectangular hole too," he said.

"Okay, Son," Dan said and pointed at the rectangular opening. "Place your hand inside that slot there."

"Okay," Kyle said. He reached up and placed his little hand inside the slot without a second thought. There was a bright flash of light, followed by a short millisecond halo of blue light encompassing his little body, and his hand went numb. The white light suddenly vanished, and the numbness also went away. "That tickled," Kyle said.

Dan and Barbara giggled a little at their little boy, who was still holding his hand inside the slot. Dan was mesmerized, seeing a brief halo of blue light around his young son's body, right before the flash of white light vanished. When the blue halo had encompassed his wife during her test, he hadn't been sure it happened. "You can remove your hand now, Son," he said, "and return to the cockpit with your brothers."

"Okay, Daddy." Kyle removed his hand and returned to the cockpit.

Dan turned to his wife, curious about their cellular recordings. "Did you notice a brief glow of blue light around my body when my hand was in the slot?"

"Yes, I did," she said. "I thought at first I was imagining it, until I noticed it again around Kyle's small body."

"Weird," Dan said. "The blue light was almost like a snapshot. I see no other way our body's molecular construction could have been fully recorded. It's still amazing to be accomplished so quickly."

Barbara fully agreed, and they began walking around inside the spaceship while waiting to arrive at the moon. They noticed strange-looking writing on the walls that did not appear even close to any language on Earth, including any hieroglyphics. There also appeared to be art, some of planetary systems, others of red and white dwarf stars. Dan turned to his wife with an amazing realization. "You know," he said, "this race appears to have a very similar culture to ours."

"Yes, it does," she agreed.

They walked over to where there was a console, couple of chairs, and a rectangular display similar to a flat monitor, though it appeared thinner than a pane of glass. The area had to be a small workstation, similar to what would be found on Earth. There were a couple of drawers, and Dan was curious what might be inside, but there were no handles. "Strange," he mumbled under his breath. He touched the flat, extremely thin monitor at least thirty inches across. It suddenly lit up, startling Dan. "Surprising, huh?" he said.

"Yes, it was," Barbara said, "and evidently touch activated."

"True," Dan said. "The ship's computer does have our cellular biological configurations in its data banks now." He was now eager to find out what the ship's data banks might reveal to them, but the menus and symbols on the screen were in a language he did not recognize, nor did he have the faintest idea how to decipher them. Suddenly, before his very eyes, the menus and symbols reverted to letters and numbers of the English language and other known languages on Earth, some in Greek, others in Hebrew. There were over fifty menu selections. Dan looked briefly to his wife, who was staring ahead toward the three boys. "Look at this, would you?"

Barbara turned to her husband. "What?" she asked, a bit surprised.

"Look at the display," he said. "It is now showing a menu in a few Earth languages, mostly English."

Barbara stared at the screen. "Yes, that is strange," she said. "How could it have known?"

"Good question," Dan said, "but I expect the ship's computer is a smart computer, listens, and knows our language."

Barbara nodded to agree, as that was a real possibility.

Out of curiosity, Dan touched the Greek omega symbol on the display, and a holographic image suddenly appeared directly above the console, filled with submenus. The holographic image had a surprising, unusual clarity like Dan and Barbara had never before seen, even in Earth's science fiction movies and series.

Dan noticed the new menu appeared to have a historical database, with a complement of submenus—philosophies, theological teachings, even mythologies. "Simply amazing," Dan said under his breath.

Barbara also was staring at the submenus with the interest of a little girl. She glanced forward again at the three boys. Through the front cockpit windows, the moon seemed much closer. "We'd better return to our seats," she said.

Dan looked at the holographic image one last time and then back to his wife. "Okay," he said. The holographic image suddenly vanished, and the monitor turned off.

Dan followed his wife back to their seats and had to surmise that the ship's computer had again picked up their verbal communication. He and Barbara stood directly behind the boys while watching the moon increase in size, the sun lighting up its surface like a large light bulb. Michael also noticed they were quickly approaching the moon and turned around. "Mom and Dad, here comes the Moon," he said.

Jason, Michael, Kyle, Dan, and Barbara all watched as they continued to approach the moon at an extremely fast pace. Dan and Barbara felt that, at their current speed, they might crash into the moon like a meteor, but they could not see the ship's computer ever allowing that, especially with the level of technological advancement of the race that had created Michael. Indeed, Michael knew their ship was being methodically slowed as it neared the moon. Their current velocity was forty thousand miles per hour (a little over sixty-seven thousand kilometers per hour or eleven miles per second) and continuing to slow down. When their ship approached within four hundred kilometers of the surface, he grabbed his control wheel with both hands before the ship's computer had a chance to take complete control and slow the spaceship to a complete stop. Within a few seconds, their velocity dropped to three hundred kilometers per hour, and Michael manually guided the ship parallel to the moon while looking for a good landing site. When they were within one kilometer, he stopped the ship in a stationary pattern, gently pushed down on the control wheel, and then let loose. The ship's computer took command, and they slowly descended until touching down on a flat, level surface.

Dan and Barbara felt only a very light bump as the ship came to a complete stop. They stared out the side windows to see what looked like a rocky, barren wasteland desert without any sign of vegetation. It suddenly came to their full realization they'd just landed on the moon! Their three boys still sat calmly yet with faces filled with excitement, showing signs of expecting one of the grown-ups to say something. Dan finally looked briefly to his wife and then to the kids. "Now what?" he said.

There was silence, and Jason turned to Michael, wondering more about the multitude of advanced technologies at their disposal. "Is there any way we can all walk on the moon without space suits?"

Dan and Barbara were surprised at their son's question, as there was no atmosphere or air to breathe, not to mention the dangerous radiation outside the spaceship. They both waited anxiously for Michael's answer.

"Yes, there is," Michael finally said.

Jason was excited. "How?"

Michael turned around, faced his new parents, and explained, "If Jason were to reinstall his armband, then using his armband and my armband together, we would be able to create a small atmospheric pressure bubble around us. It would then allow us to walk on the moon without any harm." Michael paused, as if waiting for a question from his new parents about the possible dangers. He added, "Jason and I would have to maintain a perimeter outside of everyone else inside the bubble."

Jason looked away from Michael and directly at his parents with additional excitement. "Could we?"

Dan turned toward Barbara and then back to Jason. Finally, he stared directly at Michael with noticeable concern. "Is it possible for the armbands to ever quit working?"

Michael shook his head in the negative. "No, it is impossible, Dad," he said, "unless our ship was destroyed. Our armbands, while inside the bubble, would be impossible to remove."

"How about the sun's radiation?" Dan asked. "Would our atmospheric bubble completely shield us from all dangerous radiation types?"

"Yes, it will," Michael said, "because the atmospheric bubble is also a gravity bubble with its own unique ozone and ionospheric layers that would dissipate all radiant energy back into space."

Dan and Barbara did not understand gravity formed into a bubble, especially when the bubble also housed ozone and ionospheric layers. Dan briefly glanced outside again and looked around the ship at his family of five. "Okay then, let's see what it is like to walk on the moon."

Jason and Kyle moved around in their seats, visibly excited. Michael also appeared excited, his eyes gaping open a little wider. Dan and Barbara thought this to be another unusual expression for a little organic android. The three boys quickly stood up, and Jason walked by his parents to pick up his armband. After aligning the three small needles with the previous holes, he slightly pushed the armband down. As soon as the needles touched his skin, the armband immediately changed shape and tightened around his forearm, pressing the interface pins deep into his arm, but he did not feel any pain.

Dan and Barbara stood amazed after witnessing Jason's armband change shape before their very eyes. Dan knew whatever elements the armbands possessed reacted directly to the organic host's body, and the armband was clearly highly flexible. It was interesting to think about how it had taken the maximum limit of a fifty-ton hydraulic press to finally flatten the fake armband, which was surely made of the same elemental composition as the real one. Now Jason, by simply touching three small gold needles to his forearm, had caused the armband to change shape.

Michael touched a couple of buttons on his armband, looked up in Dan and Barbara's direction, and calmly revealed, "I just activated an energy field so that we can walk off our spaceship without the moon's lack of oxygen affecting the air pressure inside our ship."

Dan and his wife were amazed to hear more technological secrets of the advanced race. "Okay," Dan said.

Michael looked over at Jason, whose armband was again interfaced with his body and fully functional. "Okay, Jason," he said, "activate your armband for the other polarity half of our atmospheric gravity bubble by touching this sequence of buttons." He showed Jason the appropriate buttons.

"Okay, I understand," Jason said and immediately touched the button sequence on his armband. Nothing appeared to happen.

Michael touched a very similar button sequence on his armband and then looked briefly at the display in front of his seat. Dan and Barbara also looked down at the display, quite curious. There was a strange set of equations, some for atmospheric pressure, some gravitational, and even some that were molecular and chemical in composition, but they did not recognize or have the faintest idea what many of them meant. They did notice steradian functions with pi values, both used in a manner that made no sense.

When Michael saw that their gravity bubble would now become fully operational after walking off the ship, he instinctively looked back up at his parents. "Our atmospheric gravity bubble is now active," he announced, "and will start to form as we leave the ship."

Dan was curious about the equations on the screen, especially as related to their gravity bubble and the pressure differential that would exist inside versus outside the bubble. "What did our ship calculate for, Michael?"

Michael noticed his dad's real interest and answered, "It calculated for an oxygen and nitrogen pressure atmosphere, Dad, using an Earth-force gravity bubble, in direct relation to this solar system's gravity streams and the moon's weak moving gravitational space-time pressures. It also took into account our biological and mass configurations."

Dan and his wife smiled a little hearing this, as it only reminded them again how much Michael must understand. "Okay, Son," Dan said. "Thank you for that information." He added with a little humor, "I look forward to our father-son talk on that subject sometime."

Barbara laughed at Dan's comment, and Michael, after observing this exchange between his new parents, started to laugh himself, just like a human boy would. Jason was again surprised to hear and see such an emotional response from Michael.

Seeing the human reaction of laughter from an organic android gave Dan and Barbara strange feelings. They both sighed deeply, realizing how truly attached they had become to Michael, similar to their attachment to their biological children. They felt as though they had raised Michael his entire life from a little baby, which, in reality, was a pretty close assessment.

The three boys were eagerly waiting, so Dan inhaled and slowly exhaled. "Okay then, let's all take a walk on the moon."

# 13

## A WALK ON THE MOON

Jason, Kyle, and Michael were again visibly excited because they were about to walk on Earth's moon. Dan and Barbara also could not help but be excited, and it caused them to think back to July 20, 1969, when Neil Armstrong walked on the moon. It had been Earth's first moonwalk, and Dan and Barbara had both been six years old at the time. It was hard for them to grasp that shortly they would be walking on the moon, just as Armstrong had done thirty-four years ago, except they would not be using any space suits.

Michael looked over at Kyle. "Kyle," he said, "you will need to stay between Jason and me. Okay?"

"Okay," Kyle said.

This exchange made Dan and Barbara realize Michael also had concern programmed into his memory cells. It was another mild surprise but also reassuring.

Michael touched a series of buttons on his armband, and an open doorway out of their ship appeared, followed by a ramp contacting the moon's surface.

It seemed very bright through the doorway, much brighter than what was showing through the windows, and Dan knew there had to be some ultraviolet filtering inside their spaceship. He was now more curious about the characteristics of their bubble. "How much oxygen will there be in our atmospheric bubble, Michael?"

"Enough for three Earth hours, Dad," Michael replied.

Dan nodded a little. "How much daylight for our current position?"

"Six hours," Michael said.

Dan turned to his wife, who had a small grin on her face. Michael must know the moon continually showed its same face while orbiting around Earth. In six hours, they would be in the shadows on the dark side of the moon, where the temperatures would get very cold, but then, Dan and Barbara figured their gravity bubble might be immune to temperature differentials.

Jason walked down the ramp first, followed by Kyle and Barbara, who was now holding Kyle's little hand. Dan followed his wife's lead, with Michael trailing close behind. Unusually, they did not feel any changes when walking through the organic matter shield to the moon's surface. Once they'd all finally planted their shoes on the moon, they began looking around its barren surface.

Michael touched a couple of buttons on his armband as they all continued about ten feet farther away from the ship, following Michael's lead. When they turned around, their ship was no longer invisible, so Michael must have just uncloaked it. Michael was now about six feet away to Dan's left and staring up at him with an expression of not knowing what they wanted to do next. It made Dan realize again that Michael still needed emotional guidance from an adult, especially in decision-making. To Dan's right, Jason was about ten feet away, and his wife and Kyle were nearly three feet away. Michael was now about ten feet away in the opposite direction from Jason. Dan stared ahead at the moon's barren surface, and it came to his full realization, like in a dream, that he was now standing on the moon. He just had to feel the moon's surface, so he kneeled down and ran his fingers through the dust to find it was only a few inches deep. More surprising, the moon's surface seemed to be around sixty to seventy degrees Fahrenheit, not a temperature for a planetary body that, without an atmosphere, could not help but dissipate radiant energy. The gravity bubble must have cooled the moon's surface, especially since they were in direct sunlight.

Dan grabbed a handful of moondust and watched it fall through his fingers. After witnessing this gravity effect, he stood back up, somewhat surprised, while staring over at Barbara. "Not only are we in an unusual atmospheric gravity bubble," he said, "but a gravity bubble with internal gravity similar to Earth's."

To test the gravity, Barbara moved her arms up and down. She was able to move them as easily as if she were standing on Earth—clearly not as would have been expected where the moon's weak gravity caused a body weight about one-sixth of Earth's. "This is amazing," she said.

"Yes, it is," Dan said. He glanced at his wristwatch to keep an eye on when they needed to return to the ship, based on the amount of oxygen inside their bubble, even though Michael would surely be keeping track. He wondered again about the characteristics of the gravity bubble itself, including whether a small meteorite impact might puncture a hole through it, and looked over at Michael with immense curiosity. "Michael," he asked, "what would a meteorite do to our bubble? Would we be in danger?"

Michael understood his concern. "Nothing, Dad, unless extremely huge. Small meteorites would be slowed and bounce off. For large meteorites, our spaceship tracks them, and if they're determined to be on a direct collision course with either our spaceship or our gravity bubble, our spaceship will vaporize them into smaller meteorites with its high-energy particle laser beam." The particle laser beam was a laser beam traveling faster than the speed of light carrying subatomic particles.

Dan was quiet at the surprising reply, especially the part about another powerful weapon in their spaceship's arsenal. The term *particle laser beam* didn't make complete sense to him. "Interesting!" he said to himself. "Let's continue out farther away from our spaceship, then."

Michael walked about fifteen feet away from Dan, increasing the size of their gravity bubble, while Jason walked in the opposite direction, until they were separated by about thirty feet. They all continued as a group farther away from the spaceship, with Jason and Michael maintaining their separation distance of about ten meters. Seeing the moon was a magnificent experience for all of them, especially because they were getting to walk on the moon inside an atmospheric gravity bubble and got to look at the moon without needing a space suit face mask. Directly in front of them, something suddenly caught Kyle's attention. He reached down and picked up a small, unusually shaped gray-and-silver rock. To Dan and Barbara, it appeared to be an igneous rock, possibly quartz or granite.

Kyle looked up with a sincere face at his prize find. "Can I keep this?" he asked.

Barbara grinned at her little boy. "Sure, honey," she said.

Kyle continued to admire his moon rock and quickly slipped it into his pants pocket. Michael saw this and knew if their ship had detected any radioactivity in the rock, it would have immediately transported it out of Kyle's pocket and back to the moon's surface.

Dan and Barbara continued alongside their three boys and thought about the unusual moon rock Kyle had just found. It was nearly two inches long and looked to be of a type usually formed by volcanic activity. They did not believe it would be radioactive. If so, surely their ship's sensors would have detected it and not allowed him to keep it. Dan suddenly stopped and had to take a long look up at Earth. Barbara, Kyle, Jason, and Michael also stopped, and they, too, stared at the planet from which they had traveled.

The five Jupiter family members continued to stare at Earth. What a truly magnificent sight it was—even through their atmospheric gravity bubble. Though the bubble had a very slight haze, it was still extremely clear, as if sunlight were being reflected off the air molecules. Dan looked across the desolate moon, seeing more detail than could have been witnessed with any photograph. His eyes ratcheted across the landscape, taking in hills, valleys, and even small distant mountains, as well as small, medium, and large rocks within about a thousand feet of their position. It was extremely evident there was no water where they now stood.

As Barbara, Jason, Michael, and Kyle continued to stare at Earth over two hundred thousand miles away, Dan finally looked over in Michael's direction and then Jason's. "Let's walk about another two hundred feet or so and then return to the ship," he said.

Michael and Jason slowly proceeded farther away from the ship, with Michael keeping a watchful eye on his little brother and parents, even though he knew that if any of them were to walk up to the edge of the bubble, it would be like running into an elastic wall—an automatic safety measure.

Continuing farther away from their spaceship, Dan was curious about how much distance there was to the outer spherical shell of the gravity bubble, including its possible resilience factor. "Michael," he calmly called out, "how far does our gravity bubble extend beyond your armbands?"

Michael looked up with real interest. "The bubble extends away from our armbands the same distance to its center, Dad."

Dan felt reassured hearing this. "Can the bubble ever be breached from the inside?" he asked.

"Not very easily," Michael said, "as it would take a gravity force pressure greater than the bubble, and then the bubble would immediately gravitationally seal itself."

Dan paused at this amazing answer, realizing there must be some sort of internal north-south dipole polarity field that used the two armbands as internal poles, possibly wrapping around each other to form some strange toroidal bubble. This was especially true since the bubble was twice as big as the distance between Michael's and Jason's armbands. "Hmmm," he said quietly under his breath, "what an extremely strange and advanced technology." He could not even begin to understand the creation of a gravity bubble with internal poles, as those poles would have to be lying down flat in relation to the armbands.

All the Jupiter family could do now was savor the moment of their first moonwalk together. Michael, though, was still thinking about what his father had asked him. The atmospheric gravity bubble was actually a quad-pole field, using the moon's weak magnetic field and its lunar core to set up the other two reference poles in relation to the lunar surface and crust. This allowed a moving gravity bubble according to the locations of their armbands, but he did not volunteer this advanced understanding to his parents.

Dan noticed a small crater just up ahead and glanced over at Jason and then to Michael. "Let's not go near the edge of the crater," he warned. "Let's not take a chance of anyone falling inside."

Michael and Jason nodded their agreement. "Okay, Dad," Jason called out. Michael briefly looked over at their father before walking about two meters to the right of the crater's edge and looking down inside. It was about forty meters deep. Michael knew their bubble extended in a perfect sphere below the moon's surface and the same distance above the surface, which meant it protruded into the crater. Even if one of them were to fall into the crater, it would only be to the bubble's edge and would be like landing on a trampoline. Again, Michael did not volunteer this information. They continued around the crater, and then suddenly Michael stopped and turned his attention to his new parents. "Well, we are now nine hundred and sixty-two feet from our ship," he said.

Dan, Barbara, and Kyle turned around and looked at their spaceship, which was extremely evident and visible against the moon's barren surface, nicely silhouetted against the horizon, with no large rocks in its immediate vicinity. Dan grinned slightly at how well Michael seemed to have estimated their distance, as the ship did look to be about three football fields away. "Okay," he said to everyone. "Let's head back."

Jason nodded a little. "Okay, Dad."

Michael turned to face their ship. "Okay, Dad," he also replied. Jason also turned around, and they began the trek back toward their ship, around the edges of the crater again. Only Michael knew their spaceship had just swapped the horizontal polarity parameters of their gravity bubble.

Jason smiled as he relived in his mind the experience of being on the moon. He and his little brothers were the youngest astronauts from Earth to ever walk on the moon. He looked forward to visiting it again and turned his attention toward Earth and its magnificent blue atmosphere. Dan and Barbara also stopped to admire the planet of which they were occupants. This in turn caused the other two boys to stop, and the Jupiter family of five enjoyed a quiet, surreal, catatonic moment together, staring at Earth—its brilliant blue atmosphere, its landmasses, and its large bodies of water that helped to sustain its life.

Dan finally turned to his wife with a relaxed, calm face. "You're kind of quiet," he said, having noticed that she'd not said much.

"I'm just taking it all in," she said. "You know, as a kid, I always dreamed of walking on the moon."

Dan grinned in understanding, as he'd also dreamed about that very same thing. "Well, your dream came true, didn't it?"

"Yes, it did," she said with a big smile.

Their ship was now about a 150 meters away, and they all took off walking again. Dan found himself strangely antsy to return to their ship and back to Earth so that he and his wife could figure out how to explain having Michael in their lives. His and his family's lives would never again be somewhat normal and would be extremely complicated, especially since he and his wife worked for the government and carried top-secret clearances. He suddenly stopped again and thought some more about the moonwalk he had just enjoyed with his family. Barbara, Kyle, Michael, and Jason also stopped, curious, and Dan turned to his wife with a humorous look. "I'm taking some moondust with us," he said, "to serve as a memory of our family together here for the first time."

Barbara grinned, and Dan leaned down and scooped up a handful of dust. After straightening, he packed as much of it into his pants pocket as possible. He then made direct eye contact with Barbara. "Do not wash these pants until I've removed the dust," he kidded.

Barbara giggled with a relaxed, strange look at Dan's candor and their current situation of standing on the moon, an event neither of them would have ever thought possible, not to mention now having an organic android from another world in their lives.

Michael recognized how kind his parents were to each other. "Mom, Dad," he said, "ready to continue to the ship?"

Dan looked down at Michael. "Yes, we are."

"Okay," Michael said and stared over in Jason's direction.

Jason instinctively knew Michael wanted him to walk up the ramp first, so he started toward the ship ahead of everyone else. Dan, Barbara, Kyle, and Michael followed, with Michael now walking a little slower. Jason headed up the ramp into the ship, followed by Kyle, his mother, his father, and Michael bringing up the rear. Dan and Barbara turned around to see Michael was also now inside the ship. It gave them a sense of peace to see everyone was back inside the safety of their ship.

On the way toward the cockpit, Michael touched another series of buttons on his armband, and the open doorway to the ship suddenly disappeared. He looked over in Jason's direction. "Okay, Jason," he said. "Touch the same button combination on your armband as before to shut off your half of the atmospheric gravity bubble."

"Okay," Jason replied and touched the same button sequence.

Michael did the same to completely shut off the gravity bubble.

They all sat down in the same seats as before and were again quiet, even Michael, all of them reveling in the experience they had just shared together on the moon. It was so quiet that everyone could almost hear each other breathing.

Dan looked directly at Michael, curious about his past recollections and memories. "Michael," he asked, "do you have any memory of ever walking on a moon or a planet, such as your home world?"

"No," Michael answered.

So their moonwalk had indeed been a new experience for Michael. Dan now knew almost for certain that Michael had never been consciously awake prior to meeting Jason. He glanced at his wristwatch, saw it was already 2:51 a.m., and mumbled under his breath, "Am I ever going to be tired at work!"

Dan's comment made Barbara look at her wristwatch. "Why not just take a day off from work?" she calmly said. "It would allow you to spend more time with our new son, get to know him a little better, and give you some time to search through this spaceship's data banks for more information about the race that created him."

Dan thought her suggestion was a more than great idea. "You're right, honey," he said. "I don't have anything of extreme importance that can't wait a few days. In fact, I'll take vacation Friday as well, maybe even take the kids fishing at the creek."

Barbara knew their three boys would like that, especially Michael, since it would be a new experience for him. She might have to spend time down there herself, maybe take a basket lunch and lawn chairs. "I am sure they would all like that," she said.

Dan gently took hold of her hand and noticed Michael pointing down at his front console, showing something to Jason and Kyle. Dan then twisted his body around in his chair, facing the organic-matter analyzer. To his surprise, three armbands were on top of the table, two larger ones and one small one, all with their ends bent outward. "Look, honey," he said.

Barbara turned around. "Yes, those must be our armbands," she said. "Michael?" she called out.

Michael turned around. "Yes, Mom?"

Barbara grinned a little. "Looks like our armbands are ready," she said.

"Okay," Michael said and stood up, as did Barbara, Dan, Jason, and Kyle. They all walked to the table and their waiting armbands.

Dan looked down at Michael, curious. "Okay, what now?"

"Just place it on your forearm," Michael said.

"That's it?"

"Yes."

Dan picked up the largest armband, assuming it was his.

"It will sting the first time you put it on, Dad," Jason said.

Dan looked at the three gold needles on the underside of his armband. They were about the diameter of sewing needles, maybe a little smaller, and they appeared a little longer than the needles on Jason's armband. To Dan, it still seemed strange how the armband could reshape itself and cause an internal elemental structure change, especially when it was indestructible to Earth's twenty-first-century technologies. "Well, here goes," he said.

Dan placed the armband against his left forearm, about midway between his elbow and wrist. When the needles touched his skin, the armband suddenly changed shape and tightened around his forearm. He grimaced a little as the needles pierced deep into his arm, through his myelin sheath nerve fibers, creating an interface between his body and the spaceship.

Dan regained his composure and looked directly at his wife after the pain had subsided. "That wasn't too bad," he said.

"Did it just sting a lot?" she asked.

"That was kind of how it felt. Sort of like a bee sting, except without a lingering effect. Are you ready to try on yours?"

Barbara had been stung by a bee before, so she knew exactly what he was referencing. "I guess ..." she said, looking at her armband with uncertainty, zeroing in on the three gold needles, about a quarter inch or so in length. She decided to also install her armband on her left forearm, about midway between her wrist and elbow. Mentally bracing herself, she slowly placed it against her forearm, the same way Dan had done. As soon as the needles touched her skin, the armband immediately changed shape, tightening and puncturing three holes deep into her arm. "Ouch!" she said. "That does sting, doesn't it?"

Jason grinned a little. "It wasn't that bad, Mom."

Barbara looked down at her son. "Maybe for you," she said and then realized there was no longer any stinging sensation, just as Dan had assured her.

Barbara, with what she'd felt from the needles, knew Kyle would probably start crying for a short moment when his armband was installed. She looked down at her little son with compassion. "Kyle," she said in a soft voice, "I'm going to install your armband after you fall asleep. Okay?"

Kyle, having seen his mother's reaction to the armband, was not going to disagree. "Okay, Mommy," he said.

"It will take about five Earth minutes for the armband to adjust to your body's chemistry," Michael said. "If you take them off, they have to be installed in the same location; otherwise, it will again take five minutes to readjust. The armbands will also only work for the host body for which they were designed."

Dan and Barbara were fascinated and realized they were now electrochemically interfaced to their ship—via some kind of bioelectrical connection on the molecular level that they could not even imagine. Michael saw the fascination on his parents' faces and explained, "The armbands' functions for altering your body's molecular structures, such as for invisibility and walking through solid objects, won't work inside this ship without special command overrides."

Dan and Barbara continued to be amazed and could not wait to learn more about the functions that would let them become invisible and walk through solid objects. Dan was also curious why a race so advanced would need armbands with interface pins. He just had to know. "Why not use armbands without interface pins?"

Michael knew the answer. "Because," he said, "those armbands would only be accurate and safe within a distance of a few miles from our spaceship. Armbands with interface pins are one hundred percent accurate and safe to use anywhere within the geomagnetic field of the planetary body for which they are being referenced, at least as long as the ship is inside that same field."

"Why is that?" Dan asked.

"Because of planetary magnetic fluctuations," Michael answered plainly.

Dan and Barbara nodded a little, though they thought the other armband types would be much better, at least when near the ship. Exactly how far away they would maintain their accuracy would be interesting to determine.

Barbara picked up Kyle's armband, and they all returned to their original seats. After sitting back down, Dan and Barbara stared at their armbands. They would now have a better advantage against the secret government if anyone were to figure out what had happened at the metallurgy lab, as such a discovery would lead directly back to their family. Dan thought about that possible future scenario and glanced at his wristwatch again to see it was now 3:10 a.m. He stared down at his three sons. Kyle still looked fascinated at getting to walk on the moon, but his sleep-laden eyes were starting to close. Michael suddenly turned around. "What next, Dad?"

Dan grinned a little at Michael's continued sincerity and the way he looked to him for guidance. After glancing briefly at his wife and then back to Michael and Jason, he focused his attention on his youngest son, who had now fallen asleep. Barbara also noticed this and whispered, "I'm going to install his armband."

"Okay," Dan whispered back.

Barbara stood up and leaned forward into the cockpit. Jason also looked tired, but Michael had no tired expression whatsoever. Her youngest son was still soundly asleep. Michael understood exactly what she was about to do and knew it would work only because the ship's computer had already temporarily adjusted the composition of the armband for Barbara's bioelectrical signature, to allow her to place it on Kyle's forearm. Without this adjustment, the armband would never reshape itself or pierce the interface pins into Kyle's arm. Barbara lifted Kyle's arm, gently positioned the armband about midway between his left elbow and wrist, and slowly pushed down until the needles touched his skin. The armband immediately changed shape, quickly tightening, and the three gold needles pierced deep into his arm. Kyle suddenly fussed but then went back to sleep. "There," Barbara said, "that wasn't so bad." Now all her kids had armbands. She then thought about the invisibility function. "Michael," she asked, "if two or more of us were invisible at the same time, would we be able to see each other?"

"Yes," Michael said.

Barbara stood quietly amazed, and Michael continued to look up at his new mother. "We also have communicators to keep in contact with each other," he said.

Barbara was mildly surprised. "Oh really?" she said. "Where are they?"

Michael pointed to the back of the ship, near the console where Dan had accidentally turned on the extremely thin display. "They are in the top drawer of that console," he said.

Barbara left the cockpit area and went to the console. She reached down to open the drawer but found no handle. Confused, she looked back at Jason and Michael, who were both staring at her. "How do you open the drawer?"

Jason turned briefly to Michael and then back to his mother. "Just lightly touch it, Mom," he said.

Barbara wondered what was behind her son's small grin and lightly touched the drawer. To her mild surprise, before her very eyes, the drawer suddenly appeared open, first transparent, then solid. There were four rectangular communicators, and she grabbed two of them. After she removed her hand, the open drawer suddenly vanished, as though it had never been open. She had to shake her head. She carried the two communicators back to her seat, handed one to Dan, and then sat back down.

Dan studied the silver-and-gold-colored device. It was about three inches long and extremely thin, maybe a quarter inch thick. It had eight small light-blue buttons that appeared to be touch activated and a very small black dot near its top, possibly a transceiver microphone.

Michael watched his parents as they studied their communication devices. "The button on the left side activates two-way communication," he said. "There are other buttons that will allow individual communication between each communicator once the ship has activated that function. Our spaceship will also be able to pinpoint each communicator's exact location anywhere within the magnetic field of the planet in reference, as well as anywhere within the entire magnetosphere of this solar system's sun."

Dan and Barbara were surprised, and Dan raised his eyebrows, filled with overwhelming curiosity. "Oh really?" he said. "How does it do that?"

"By gravity streams," Michael said. "It is almost instantaneous too."

"Amazing," Dan said. "What communication technology is that?"

"Gravitational space transmissions," Michael said, "similar to what the human race is currently calling subspace but at a factor many times the speed of light."

Dan and Barbara were amazed by the technology, as they knew *gravitational space* meant much more than just radio transmissions, because radio waves from Earth traveled through space while inside gravity waves from many different sources, which in turn were similar to ether. The transmissions mentioned would more than likely be undetectable to Earth technologies. Dan looked directly down at his new son and kidded, "Sounds like we'll need another father-son conversation on that too."

Michael smiled a little, as he understood what his dad meant. "Yes, Dad, I look forward to it."

A grin spread on Jason's tired face at this exchange between his father and Michael, yet he thought it strange Michael would be the one educating his really smart dad. He then stared over at Kyle and knew it would be hard to wake him.

Dan also saw Kyle was asleep like a log and turned his attention to Michael. "Let's head back home."

"Okay," Michael said with hidden anticipation, as he was looking forward to living on Earth with his new brothers and parents. He touched his front console, and a seat belt suddenly appeared around Kyle's body, adjusting his slumping body more upright. Michael then grabbed his control wheel and lifted straight up.

As their spaceship quickly accelerated away from the moon at a magnificent speed, Dan and Barbara again felt no inertial forces. Jason looked down at his front display and saw that they were already traveling almost seventeen thousand miles per hour.

Michael repositioned their ship directly toward Earth and then pushed his control wheel way forward. Within a matter of seconds, their ship's velocity increased to 230,000 miles per hour. Michael glanced over at Jason. "Well, we should arrive back to Earth in about an hour," he said.

Jason's display indicated Earth was currently 230,000 miles away. He was amazed, as the speed they were traveling was inconceivable, even if it was the same speed at which they'd traveled to the moon. He was intrigued but suddenly felt himself getting tired, like when riding in a car down a flat, smooth, straight highway during a trip. He yawned, and after he looked over at Kyle, how tired he truly was hit him like a lead weight.

Dan and Barbara continued to stare at their three kids, all while their ship flew at a tremendous speed back toward Earth. Through the front cockpit windows, Earth was clearly visible in the distance. It made them realize again that they would be arriving back to the blue planet in less than an hour.

The Jupiter family of five, one of them asleep, patiently waited as they returned to their home, located on 640 peaceful, beautiful acres of mature trees with a really nice creek. Dan and Barbara started wondering again how they would go about explaining Michael being in their lives, when suddenly, a strange bump rumbled throughout the entire ship, causing it to momentarily shake. Surprised, Dan looked at his wife and then at Michael. "Michael?" he asked, concerned. "What just happened?"

"I do not know," he said, watching on his front display as their gravity-propulsion speed quickly dropped. "Our ship is starting to slow down," he said. "Maybe our gravity drive failed."

Dan was clueless about gravity-drive technology and surprised by Michael's suggestion. "What do you mean?" he asked.

"I do not know, Dad," Michael said again. "Our ship's propulsion system seems to have just died."

Dan and Barbara stood up, standing behind the three boys. The front instrument panels indicated they were continuing to slow down in a controlled yet steady manner … sixty thousand miles per hour … forty thousand miles per hour … twenty thousand miles per hour … five thousand miles per hour … ten miles per hour … zero!

They now sat motionless in outer space.

Everyone was very quiet, and Jason, who had been partially asleep, perked up and was now wide-awake. Even Michael was confused by what had just transpired. He touched his front console to see if he could figure out what had happened.

Dan looked down at Michael, who was still puzzled. "Is our ship's gravity-propulsion system still active?"

Michael looked up. "Yes, it is."

"Then why aren't we moving?"

"I do not know," Michael said, sounding perplexed.

Dan and Barbara were surprised to hear "I do not know" coming from Michael, especially with as knowledgeable as he was about the advanced race's technologies. Suddenly, a strange language appeared on the front screens. Dan, Barbara, and Jason had no idea what it said, but Michael did. He stared quietly at the screens, reading everything that was flashing and appearing on the displays.

"What is it saying, Michael?" Dan asked, curious and concerned.

"They're coming," Michael said.

"Who's coming?" Dan asked.

"I think the ones from where I originated," Michael replied.

Dan and Barbara stood especially quiet. Michael touched another series of buttons on his front display, possibly a long-range scan menu. Suddenly, a holographic image appeared in front of Michael, indicating dozens of spaceships traveling their direction, each ship shown as a small white dot at a distance well outside Earth's solar system. One dot was larger than the others, likely a mother ship, with smaller ships traveling both ahead and behind the large ship—like a small armada. Dan and Barbara shook their heads, especially after noticing the ships on the display were registering a velocity over 3,500 times the speed of light, or +3,500c.

Dan turned to Michael again, absolutely flabbergasted, not fully believing it. "Is that indicating those ships are traveling over thirty-five hundred times the speed of light, Michael?"

"Yes, it is," Michael said.

Barbara had a strange look on her face. The race heading their direction appeared more advanced than Barbara and Dan had first imagined. Dan peeked at the screen again. He and Barbara were additionally surprised to see the display indicated the mother ship was possibly five thousand meters (three miles) in diameter.

Dan thought about what had just happened. "Did they deactivate our ship from afar, Michael?" he asked.

"Yes, they did," Michael answered.

Dan turned to Barbara, not knowing what to think. For the race to have deactivated their ship's gravity drive from such an immense distance, well outside the reaches of Earth's solar system, was a feat in itself, as amazing as the approaching ships' immense speed, thousands of times the speed of light. Dan had already known this race was extremely advanced, and this feat only showed more of their technological advancements. Dan and Barbara continued to stand quietly, knowing there was nothing they could do but wait to see what happened next. Dan looked down again at Michael, who had a strange look on his face that Dan had never seen before. "Is the race that created you friendly, Michael?"

Michael made direct eye contact. "Yes, as far as I know."

Barbara and Dan felt sudden, immense relief but still did not know what to think about it all, when suddenly spaceships started to appear from out of nowhere all around them—like a spider surrounded by hornets. Even the smaller ships in the armada were bigger than their little ship. They were at least two hundred feet in diameter and shaped much differently. According to their ship's front displays, the metallic-silver spaceships had stopped 3,200 feet from their spaceship. The mother ship was so large that it filled the entire view of their cockpit's front windows. It had an assortment of smaller and midsized windows around its outer hull, which was shaped similar to a football.

Suddenly, another bump momentarily shook their ship, and Dan took a deep breath. "What was that, Michael?"

Michael was still calm yet concerned and looked up at his father. "The mother ship locked a gravity tractor beam on us, Dad," he said, "and they're taking us aboard their ship."

Jason had a strange look on his face, probably out of concern for Michael. Dan laid his hand on Jason's shoulder and gave him a little encouragement. "It will be okay, Jason."

"Dad," Jason immediately said, "I don't want them taking Michael."

Neither Dan nor Barbara said anything, because they knew they were powerless in the face of this advanced race. Dan looked down at Michael and then over to Jason, realizing he could only give his oldest son further words of encouragement. "We'll talk to them," he said.

"Okay," Jason said, still concerned.

With deep sighs, Dan and Barbara sat back down, figuring they might as well get mentally prepared for whatever was to come. They remained quiet, watching, waiting, as their ship continued toward the mother ship. There hadn't been an outline of a doorway previously, but now there was an opening in the bottom of the massive mother ship, revealing a brightly lit interior. Dan sighed deeply, turned to Barbara, and whispered, "Well, we always wanted to meet extraterrestrial beings. I just never thought it would be under these circumstances."

Barbara returned a small, agreeable nod and gently grabbed his hand. Dan took his wife's hand into his lap.

Their ship entered the cargo bay, and the door opening behind them suddenly disappeared. The wall looked completely smooth and unbroken, as though there had never been an opening.

Their ship finally came to a stop and softly touched down on the floor. Looking out through the cockpit windows, Dan, Barbara, Jason, and even Michael did not see any of the ship's crew members, only hundreds of spacecraft like the smaller ships in the armada. "This is strange," Dan said.

"Yes, it is," Barbara agreed.

# 14

## THE UNIMAGINABLE, HIGHLY ADVANCED RACE

All the Jupiter family members, except for the sound-asleep Kyle, stared out into the cargo bay that was vacant of all life. Thinking it strange, Dan and Barbara stood and walked up behind their three kids.

Barbara looked down at her sound-asleep four-year-old. His seat belt had vanished, so she gently picked him up in her arms. Dan now stood with keen curiosity, observing the empty cargo bay, which was still void of any living beings. It made no sense for an advanced alien race of such stature, and he wondered whether they might be invisible.

Dan looked down at Jason and then over to Michael. He could tell from the look on his new little boy's face that even he did not know what was about to happen. "Michael," he softly asked, "are they normally invisible?"

Michael was already staring up into his face. "No, I don't believe so."

"Then why are they not visible?"

"I do not know," Michael said. "Maybe they're not sure if they want to show themselves."

Dan and Barbara did not understand his answer but had to figure the alien race was scrutinizing them, possibly even analyzing their ship's records, trying to figure out why they were with Michael. Dan could see puzzlement on Michael's face. "Let me hold you," he said.

Without a second thought, Michael reached for his father, and Dan picked him up, holding him close to his chest. Instinctively and with the emotions of a child that needed affection, Michael put his arms around his father's neck just like a human boy. Dan and Barbara now held Michael and Kyle in their arms.

Jason understood exactly why his father was holding Michael. It was a message to the alien race that Michael was now a part of their family. Jason left his chair and stood beside his parents and *two* brothers—at least that was how he viewed it.

While Dan, Barbara, Jason, and Michael continued to stare into the cargo bay, it suddenly became pitch black, the only lighting coming from their spaceship. A few moments later, the cargo bay lit back up, and there were hundreds of crew members throughout the cargo bay and around the other ships. A small group was standing just outside their spaceship, about ten meters away, and staring directly at them. Dan and Barbara wondered whether the crew members had been standing there the entire time, unbeknownst to them.

Physically, the crew members looked the same as humans—two arms, two legs, elbow and shoulder joints, similar facial features, knees that bent the same way as humans', an abdomen, and hands with four fingers and a thumb. Most had light-complexioned skin, but some were dark-complexioned, similar to African Americans, and some had a light-brown complexion. All of them were dressed in similar garments—long-sleeved one-piece outfits that were tight against their bodies. The suits, in contrasting shades of silver, stopped at the neck and appeared to have mysterious properties, almost as if they were holographic. The outfits had attached boots, but no weapons, handheld or otherwise, were visible. The outfits had insignias on them, possibly denoting levels of a command hierarchy. One of the crew members did appear to be giving instructions to the others and was possibly a high-ranking officer, maybe even the captain or commander of the mother ship.

Dan and Barbara knew the advanced race could see them holding their two boys with their oldest son standing beside them. They had *three* sons as they viewed it, and they were determined to keep it that way, but they also knew they could not stop the alien race from doing whatever they wanted or had in mind.

Suddenly, an open doorway into their ship appeared, making it clear that the alien race was in complete command of their spaceship. Dan and Barbara were not going to forget the fact that their ship actually belonged to the alien race. The crew members had probably completely downloaded their ship's data banks, and if that was the case, the alien race now had their molecular DNA configurations and knew who they were and possibly everything about them historically.

Barbara stared down at the crew member who appeared to be directing the others next to him. She looked over to her husband with a sigh. "Well, let's go meet them and find out what is going to happen."

Dan nodded to agree and looked down into Michael's pretty eyes. "Is that what they want, Michael?"

"Yes, it is, Daddy."

Jason still looked concerned, so Dan said, "You lead the way, Son. Maybe a young boy walking out of the ship first will mean something—a sign that we mean nothing bad."

"Okay, Dad," Jason said. Without hesitation, he walked toward the open doorway. Dan and Barbara followed, Dan carrying a wide-awake little boy and Barbara, a sound-asleep little boy. As Jason exited the ship, he thought about his family getting to meet real-life alien beings and became a little excited. He continued down the ramp with his parents right behind him until they were all standing in the cargo bay next to their ship, about twenty feet from the group of beings who were waiting for them. They weren't sure what to do next or what would happen. Five of the beings with light-complexioned skin, including the one who had been giving instructions, broke away from the larger group and headed their direction. The aliens really did look like humans. In fact, the more Barbara and Dan stared at them, the more they realized the aliens looked exactly like them. One of the aliens appeared to be a female, as she had slightly longer hair and her body was shaped like a human female's, with breasts. The real distinction between this alien race and humans was their size. All the males appeared to be seven feet or taller and had large frames, with no obesity. The female was also tall—well over six feet and taller than Dan, who was six feet two inches. They were all extremely handsome, even by Earth standards. So they were not only a tall race but also a beautiful race of beings.

The five beings walked up to within three meters of the Jupiter family and stopped. They already knew quite a lot about what had happened with Michael and his time spent with the Jupiter family, especially Jason, as determined from what they'd retrieved from the small ship's data banks, but there were still a lot of mysteries surrounding those events that had them concerned. Regardless, they all displayed calm, personable faces, and the one who had been giving instructions smiled a little at Michael in Dan's arms. He immediately began speaking in a strange tongue. Michael replied back in the same strange language, and a conversation ensued.

Jason recognized this language as the one Michael had first spoken after walking out of the small wall opening of their spaceship. Dan, Barbara, and Jason were extremely curious what Michael was telling the captain of the mother ship. They heard the words "English" and "Earth," followed by the names Dan, Barbara, Jason, and Kyle. The conversation ended after Michael said, "They are my mom, dad, and brothers."

Suddenly, all became quiet.

The one who was talking with Michael looked directly at Dan Jupiter and his family, now showing a kind, open expression on his face. He was at least six feet, ten inches tall and was clean-shaven, with wavy, dark-brown hair nearly two inches long. He was wearing an unusual-looking armband, easily six inches long, on his left forearm, over the sleeve of his light-blue outfit with silver contrasts.

As the five advanced beings continued to stand in front of the Earth family, even they were a bit awed, as their current predicament was unexpected, especially after what Michael had just told them. The chances of them ever meeting a human being who was consciously awake or knew they were an extraterrestrial race was normally zero, but Michael's current situation and his bonding with the Earth family required them to change their normal protocol and procedures.

Their mother ship's computers had downloaded the complete data banks of the small ship. With this information, the mother ship's highly computational molecular computers had checked the Jupiter family's DNA configurations against known DNA sequences of humans on Earth and found a match, and they had verified this information with Michael. His calling Dan and Barbara Jupiter his mom and dad was a problem their race had never expected and might be hard to resolve.

While Dan and Barbara continued to stand quietly, the five beings looked at the armbands on their forearms. Suddenly, one of the males was holding an unusual-looking contraption in his hand that had not been there previously. The silver-colored device was extremely thin, like paper, and about four inches wide by ten inches long. He touched it a couple of times and tilted it in their direction. A few moments later, there was a light beeping sound.

The tall male nodded to the one who had spoken with Michael. "They're clean," he said in plain English.

Dan looked to Michael, surprised, especially after the crew member spoke English. "What was that all about, Michael?"

"They were checking to make sure we did not have unnecessary viruses or bacteria, Dad, that may not have been removed from our bodies after we entered their cargo bay," Michael said.

Dan was amazed and could only stare, along with his wife and oldest son, at the alien beings standing in front of them. Although, in reality, *they* were actually the alien beings aboard the mother ship.

The officer who had initially spoken to Michael made direct eye contact with Dan and Barbara. He knew they were Earth physics scientists who worked for the United States government, Barbara as a consultant, both with above-average intelligence for Earthlings. It could make any decisions about what to do with them much easier.

"Welcome to my ship," he said in plain English. "In your language, I am Captain Don Donaldson."

Dan, Barbara, and especially Jason felt relief hearing "welcome" spoken to them in the English tongue. It was also extremely well spoken with no accent whatsoever. "Thank you," Dan replied while Barbara graciously nodded.

The captain continued with a kind face, "Michael told me that you spent some time with him, especially your oldest son, Jason."

Dan was now curious what Michael might have told him. "Yes, we have," he said.

"Good," the captain said. "Let's all talk. As Earthlings, I know you probably have many questions. It is not every day that intelligent sentient beings from such a primitive race get to see and experience an assortment of technologies thousands of years ahead of them. Quite the breach of our protocols for nonadvanced races, I might add."

Dan and Barbara understood exactly what the captain told them, especially if one of those technologies was the atmospheric gravity bubble they'd used to walk on the moon. Dan glanced briefly at Barbara and then back to the captain. "Is that now a problem for us?"

Captain Donaldson thought about the possible level of bonding Michael had now with the Jupiter family and whether his active synaptic patterns could ever be corrected to a pre-stasis state prior to meeting them. "Maybe not," he said, "but let's talk about it, as I am sure you're also curious about the history of Michael, a precious creation of our most brilliant scientists, a one-of-a-kind organic-based humanoid prototype, you might say. Once you hear and learn more about him, you'll understand why we came diligently looking for him."

Dan and Barbara nodded slightly. Dan's suspicions had been correct, as Michael was no doubt a very unique, intelligent organic-based humanoid life-form with emotional learning capability, a regulated body temperature, and an immense amount of advanced technological understanding. Not hearing "android" was confusing. Dan held Michael a little tighter. "Okay, we look forward to it," he said.

Dan, Barbara, and Jason walked alongside the five beings toward the outline of a large closed door, not knowing what to think or what might now happen to them. The large double door instantly vanished, exposing a hallway nearly five meters wide by around four meters tall. They continued as a group into the hallway, Dan and Barbara still holding Michael and a sleeping Kyle tightly in their arms.

The captain was to Dan's left, and Barbara and Jason were to Dan's right, with Jason between his mom and dad. The other four beings followed behind them, staring at the Jupiter family and analyzing their facial expressions and body language, especially from a spiritual-bonding point of view. The female sensed Dan's and Barbara's bonding to their two biological sons and their emotional bonding attachment to Michael.

Captain Donaldson turned his head to Dan and Barbara with a kind face and could again see the way Michael had bonded to the Jupiter family. "Michael told us your names are Dan and Barbara," he said, "and your children's names are Jason and Kyle."

"That is correct," Dan said.

Captain Donaldson became even more personable. "You can call me Don," he said.

Dan noticed again how well spoken the captain was in the English tongue, not to mention his extremely personable attitude. It caused Dan to relax a little bit more. "Okay, Don, we will," he said. "Thank you."

Captain Donaldson turned around briefly to his four crew members, slightly surprised at how calm Dan, Barbara, and Jason were acting for their current situation. He figured it was partially because of them being somewhat desensitized after meeting Michael and riding aboard his ship, followed by walking on the moon and getting to experience some of his race's advanced technologies firsthand.

An outline of another door appeared just up ahead. He was escorting the Jupiter family to a conference room for a short, private meeting and to reveal a little more information about Michael's unique characteristics, essentially why it was highly possible he would not be able to stay with them. The military, of which he was a member, would have full jurisdiction over decisions directly related to Michael and the Jupiter family, regardless of the wishes of the civilian sector and the genetic scientists who had created Michael, some of whom were currently aboard his vessel. As captain of the military starship, he had broad veto powers, especially due to the current protocol breaches of human beings being aware of their race and advanced technologies.

The door to the conference room appeared open, and they all walked inside. The oval room was at least fifteen meters wide, with a vaulted ceiling nearly seven meters tall, and there was an assortment of magnificent pictures on the walls, a few directly above some side tables. There were portraits, flowers, mountain scenes, and even one picture of a beautiful tan-sand beach and waves from a deep-blue ocean. The slightly curved walls were made of a highly polished wood similar to walnut. There were six rectangular windows on the far wall, around a meter high by two meters long, located maybe two meters from the floor. Outer space was clearly visible on the other side of the glass. A large oval table in the middle of the room, at least seven meters long by two meters wide, with more than twenty chairs, nicely complemented the surroundings. Additional square tables with chairs lined the walls, and next to some were two-meter-tall, eye-catching plants fitted nicely inside silver-and-gold pots. With bluish-green iridescent leaves, the plants did not appear to be of Earth origin.

Everyone sat down. Dan and Barbara sat next to each other on one side of the table, with Jason to his mom's left. The female crew member sat to Jason's left, and Captain Donaldson and his three officers sat directly across from the Jupiters. Kyle began to stir in his mother's arms.

Captain Donaldson stared directly across the table, an extremely kind spirit still filling his face. "Can we get you anything to drink?"

"Sure," Dan said, "we are a little thirsty."

Captain Donaldson touched his large armband, and suddenly, before their eyes, three transparent drinking glasses with clear liquid appeared in front of Dan, Barbara, and Jason.

Amazed, Dan picked up his drink, which looked like crystal-clear water. He did not believe the race would drug them, especially with the attachment Michael had to them, but he was not 100 percent sure.

Captain Donaldson noticed Dan was hesitant to take a sip and knew what he was thinking. "Your drinks are not drugged," he calmly said.

Dan finally took a sip. It was not 100 percent water, as there was a slight taste, possibly vitamin C. He gulped a couple more times and set the glass down while staring at Captain Donaldson. "How did our drinks appear?" he asked. "Was it anything like the transporter dispensers on the science fiction series *Star Trek* back on Earth?"

Captain Donaldson smiled a little at Dan's question and the current predicament he was in. His officers chuckled, and he laughed along with them. The female officer next to the Jupiters was also now grinning a little. Dan, Barbara, and Jason could not help but be curious about their reactions. "What's so funny?" Dan asked.

Captain Donaldson stared directly at Dan, knowing he had the curiosity of a child physics professor on Earth. "That's primitive technology, Dan," he said. "Your drinks appeared using a technology known to us as IMT, or instantaneous matter transport, a transport scheme that moves the total mass of an object between two points in space while in resonance—a bridging of those two points, you might say. Our ship's computers in fact first created your drinks, similar to matter reconstitution, but then their transport to the table was by instantaneous matter transport. For space transports, such as transmitting organic bodies, we no longer use the matter breakdown, transmission, and molecular reconstitution as simulated in your science fiction movies and imaginative television stories, such as *Stargate SG-1*." Captain Donaldson paused and calmly added, "Why molecularly break down something that's already known inside the curvature of zero-point gravitational space and then reconstitute those billions upon billions molecules, when you can bridge two points in space like a portal?"

Dan, Barbara, and Jason thought about everything the captain had just told them and realized the advanced race was keeping track of Earth's progression in the sciences, including what was being imagined in science fiction stories and movies. The race obviously understood a vast array of advanced technologies, and Dan just could not stop thinking about how the race's mother ship and support ships were able to travel thousands of times the speed of light. It was seemingly a violation of the laws of quantum physics, such as Einstein's $E=mc^2$ and many others. He felt strangely intrigued all of a sudden, like a child in a candy store. "Is that how you also transport your ships through space above light speed?" he asked.

"Not completely," Captain Donaldson said, opening up a bit. "It is not an instantaneous-matter-transport process when outside the gravity field of the reference ship while in outer space, especially when you deal with the many variable fields of gravitation from stars, planets, and solar systems." Captain Donaldson had opened up a bit about their faster-than-light space-travel techniques but was still being vague.

Captain Donaldson knew how the Jupiters must be feeling in their current predicament, having uncertainty for their future and what might now happen with Michael, who was maintaining his silence, only staring around the room, analyzing everything being said, including everyone's physical behaviors, facial expressions, and reactions.

Captain Donaldson looked around the table one more time. This initial meeting with the Earth family had been reserved for his highest-ranking officers, so they could gauge the current situation and Michael's level of bonding to the Earthlings. Naturally, there was already much talk on his ship regarding a human family being aboard. While a few knew the history about Michael and his creation, most had only heard rumors of his existence. The details of his creation had been kept extremely secret and hidden from their entire race for decades, and nobody knew for sure why he was with a human family from Earth. Captain Donaldson paused while staring directly at Dan and Barbara and decided to introduce his officers before revealing anything about Michael's secretive past and history.

He raised his right hand and pointed with an open hand to the male directly to his right. "This is my first officer, Jeremiah," he said. "He also goes by the name of Jerry."

"Hello," Dan and Barbara said.

"Hello," the first officer replied in perfect English.

Captain Donaldson next pointed to the male to Jeremiah's right. "This is my chief science officer, Jonathan," he said. "He also goes by the name John."

"Hello," Dan and Barbara again said in unison, staring directly across the table at the chief science officer.

"Hello," the chief science officer replied, also in perfect English.

Captain Donaldson then pointed to the male sitting directly to his left. "This is my chief medical officer, Darryl Randish," he said.

Dan and Barbara looked across the table at the chief medical officer. "Hello," they chorused.

"Hello," the chief medical officer replied, again in perfect English.

Next, Captain Donaldson indicated the female sitting to Jason's left. "And this is our spiritual advisor and counselor, Josephine," he said. "She also answers to Jose."

"Hello," she said with a soft, kind smile, also speaking in perfect English. Her soft-spoken voice had an unusual catatonic, relaxing effect.

"Hello," Dan and Barbara replied.

Jose stared down at Jason, who still had a sincere expression on his face, and read his inner being, as well as those of Dan, Barbara, Kyle, and even Michael. "Hello, Jason," she said.

Jason now felt even more relaxed. It suddenly seemed as though she were a close relative he'd known forever. "Hello," he calmly answered.

Dan already knew Captain Donaldson and his officers spoke perfect English, and he had a feeling they spoke a multitude of other Earth languages. He stared across the table with a curious face. "How many languages do you speak?" he asked.

Captain Donaldson could understand the question. "Most of our race speaks over a hundred languages," he said, "including over twenty of Earth's languages."

It was starting to dawn even more on Dan and Barbara just how intelligent this race was in relation to Earth, confirming this race had been around for quite some time, as they'd suspected. Dan, again curious, asked, "How many other races are you aware of?"

"We know about many races," Captain Donaldson replied.

Dan and Barbara realized he was again being vague, and the room suddenly became quiet as a mouse.

Captain Donaldson again assessed their current situation and thought about what Dan and Barbara didn't know concerning Michael. Michael was still sitting calmly in Dan's lap, contentment filling his face. Barbara was holding their youngest son, who was now partially awake, and their ten-year-old, Jason, looked partially tired yet intensely fascinated. Captain Donaldson turned back to Michael one more time and noticed the calm, happy look he had being with the Jupiter family, which only reinforced what they already knew: Michael had bonded to Dan and Barbara as his parents and Jason and

Kyle as his brothers. He stared briefly to his spiritual advisor, knowing she was analyzing, both spiritually and telepathically, the honesty of the Earth family sitting in front of them, especially since it was the first time for any Earthling to know about their race, especially while conscious.

Captain Donaldson let out a silent sigh. The Jupiter family were in for a surprise with what was about to be revealed, but they had to know why Michael could probably not stay with them. He finally explained, "Michael was the work of over forty of our years, or eighty Earth years of painstaking research, development, and creation by our most brilliant scientists. He was designed to learn all the natural emotions of an intelligent being—a meticulous, precious work in the field of DNA matter matrices genetics. Michael will now physically grow normally, starting from the moment he came out of his stasis."

Captain Donaldson paused to gauge the Jupiters' reaction, including Michael's, and continued, "I guess you might say he was born as a boy five Earth years of age while also having a knowledge base that encompasses all of our race's current technological understanding." Captain Donaldson paused again. He knew what the Jupiters were thinking, so he decided to let them lead with a few questions.

Dan and Barbara relaxed back in their chairs, amazed to hear Michael was actually a biological alien boy with amazing knowledge, which they'd already witnessed firsthand. Dan turned to his wife for a short moment, knowing she also realized Michael was a living, breathing intelligent being, a carbon-based humanoid, as Captain Donaldson had just alluded. He turned back to Captain Donaldson, even more curious. "How long will he live?"

Captain Donaldson calmly answered, "Currently his metabolism is extremely slow, and his life span is well over two thousand Earth years."

Dan shook his head, slightly bewildered, as did Barbara, while Jason continued to listen with even more interest. Michael remained quiet.

Captain Donaldson continued, "Michael has a body temperature of 101.3 degrees Fahrenheit by your Earth standards, a temperature our race also possesses. He carries the DNA patterns of some of the brightest kids on our planet yet has his own unique DNA pattern and fingerprints, just so you know to what detail our race went to create him." Captain Donaldson paused again to assess the Jupiters' reaction. "Presently, his hair is also partially synthetic in nature," he said, "as it contains secret transpondence markers that allow us to always know his exact location." Captain Donaldson paused again and now remained quiet.

Dan and Barbara were again extremely surprised by all the information being revealed to them so quickly, not fully understanding the underlying reasons for the sharing of this information, unless it was to show why they could not have Michael in their lives. They were also puzzled about the use of "presently" in relation to Michael's hair follicles. Dan was additionally curious about Michael's DNA pattern. "Is Michael some type of unique clone?" he asked.

Captain Donaldson shook his head in the negative. "No, he is not a clone by any standard of science whatsoever. He is a bioengineered organic-based intelligent being with his own unique DNA yet is also a descendant of the brilliant young children from whom he obtained the gamete stem cells."

Dan saw his wife had a strange expression. Captain Donaldson and his officers noticed this silent exchange between Dan and his wife. Captain Donaldson looked briefly to Jonathan, his chief science officer, and understood his telepathic message.

Jonathan stared directly across the table at Dan and Barbara, making eye contact. "Michael," he explained, "was on his way to be field-tested on your planet and begin a life in secret away from our home world, to grow up with one of our two families currently living on your planet, families who also have natural kids."

Dan and Barbara realized the advanced race might have known about Earth's residents for many years, possibly even before Earth had much understanding about the universe, before the times of Nicolaus Copernicus, René Descartes, Galileo Galilei, Johannes Kepler, Isaac Newton, and many other astronomers and physicists of past centuries.

Dan, Barbara, Jason, and even Michael were listening intently. After seeing Michael's reaction to what was just said, Jonathan wondered whether they should even be talking about all of this in his presence. Jonathan, too, like others, wondered what adverse emotional and spiritual reactions Michael might have if they were to remove him from the Jupiter family and place him back into another stasis for a reconstruction reversal back to his original pre-stasis condition. Jonathan finally continued, "Our cargo ship that impacted Earth was supposed to have left Michael with one of those two families, along with other advanced technologies to help intrigue him and advance his understanding. We are not sure what happened when the cargo ship entered Earth's magnetosphere." Jonathan paused and added, "We have not yet checked your small ship's data banks for what would have been recorded in its inertial gravity field logs, or its receivers, including the exact circumstances of how Michael came out of his stasis to become so attached and bonded to your son Jason, but we look very much forward to learning more about this."

Dan and Barbara were quiet again, with Dan now wondering about the term *bonding*. He wanted to make sure his understanding was the same as the advanced race. "What do you mean, 'bonded to our son'?" he asked.

Jonathan looked around the table and then back to Dan and Barbara. "What we mean," he said, "is that Michael was supposed to have been a child companion and brother to one of our young boys on your planet. The ship you were riding aboard is a child's spaceship that was specifically created for Michael. He was biologically and synaptically designed to permanently bond to the first child he met. That child is now your son Jason." Jonathan paused again.

Dan and Barbara were again quiet. "Synaptically" implied Michael had a cerebral brain, but he had to have immense modifications to hold such a vast amount of knowledge within his young internal core.

Jonathan added, "It also appears that Michael has permanently bonded to your young son, Kyle, as a brother and to both of you as his mother and father."

Michael was remaining quiet in Dan's lap, his head resting against Dan's chest, still listening, taking in everything without any noticeable reaction. Jason was also still listening, while Kyle was quietly staring around the room, not having any idea where all the strange people had come from, but he stayed calm since his father was beside him and his mother was holding him.

Dan and Barbara continued to be puzzled over what Jonathan had just told them regarding the plans for Michael. They did not understand how they fit into the picture after the mention of the bonding issue, and it caused them to feel uneasy, especially with Michael's life span projected to be over two thousand Earth years.

Josephine sensed their puzzlement and uneasiness. "Michael," she said, "was supposed to have bonded physically, emotionally, and spiritually with one of our families on your planet, as Jonathan told you. He was supposed to have bonded to their son, first as a companion, then as a brother, and then bonded to the little boy's parents as their son. Since that did not happen, both of you and your sons have substituted for them, you might say, and we are pretty certain you are now deeply ingrained within his unique synaptic cell matrices. It may be irreversible."

Dan looked briefly to his wife, now having a good idea why they were being told everything, but it sounded like the advanced race had not conceded to Michael remaining a part of their family and retaining his newly created synaptic cell memories of their time spent with him. Dan stared across the table to Captain Donaldson and sighed deeply. "Now what?" he asked.

Captain Donaldson looked around the table and then back to the Jupiter family. "We may have to talk about that again, Dan," he said, "with only you and your wife, if everything my officers discuss with the geneticists ends in your favor."

Jason could not remain silent. "I want to be present if you're going to talk about Michael," he blurted out.

Captain Donaldson and his officers grinned a little at the determination in Jason's voice, already knowing he was above average intelligence for his young Earth age of ten. "Okay, Jason," Captain Donaldson calmly replied. "You can be present if a new meeting with your parents does indeed happen."

Jason nodded with a calm, tired face.

Dan checked his wristwatch. It was already 6:29 in the morning, so he definitely would not be showing up for work. He glanced over to Captain Donaldson. "Michael mentioned that you have communication technology in the field of gravity streams—gravitational space transmissions, a form of subspace. Is that communication by chance ever detectable by Earth-based receivers?"

Captain Donaldson looked briefly to his science officer and then back to Dan. "No, it is not," he said. "Earth cannot detect our harmonic pulses traveling multitudes faster than light."

Dan was quiet again. He always promptly called in whenever he would not be showing up for work. If he did not make that call, it might raise suspicions from the secret government if they were ever to investigate any strange occurrences at the Los Alamos labs, specifically the tests conducted on the simulated armband in the metallurgy lab. Wondering about his strange request, he decided to ask it, as surely the advanced could easily accomplish it. "I work at the Los Alamos labs in New Mexico," he finally said, "and I need to call to let them know that I won't be in today. Is there any way that can be accomplished from this ship?"

Captain Donaldson glanced briefly to his officers and then back to Dan. "We know where you work, Dan," he said, "and yes, we can transmit a focused beam directly to your home just south of Los Alamos, easily accessing the dial tone for your Earth's primitive

48-volt DC system, including dropping the line voltage for the required momentary 90-volt AC pulse to ring the phone on the other end of the line. If so wished, we can also enter your wireless cell phone carrier's switching circuits using Earth's satellites, and that would never be recognized by Earth technologies either."

Dan and Barbara were amazed to hear about these possible spectacular feats, especially since the mother ship had to be around two hundred thousand miles away from Earth. Dan turned to his wife and then back to Captain Donaldson. "Okay then," he said, "can you access my home phone?"

Captain Donaldson knew Dan would not say anything about being aboard a large mother ship or his family's time spent with Michael, especially since he carried a top-secret clearance and was aware the highly secretive governmental agency that oversaw extraterrestrial events and encounters was looking for the small ship they'd just used to fly to the moon. The mother ship's computers could have easily mimicked Dan's voice in a perfect, unnoticeable smart artificial intelligence conversation with the Los Alamos labs, but Captain Donaldson decided against it. He turned to Jonathan. "Let's have him do it," he said in English.

Jonathan lifted his left hand, and a small gold-and-silver device suddenly appeared in his palm. The rectangular device looked very similar to the communicators in the Jupiter family's pockets, but it had noticeable differences, including being longer yet very thin. Jonathan touched a series of buttons, entered his command authorization codes, and waited for the mother ship's sensors and computers to finish the parameters. The device would lock onto Earth's geomagnetic field lines, take into account its North Pole dipole field strength, including the zero point along the equator, and then pinpoint Los Alamos, New Mexico, with everything calculated as it was related to the sun's magnetic field, including all associated planets and moons within the same field of resonance. The device's small display indicated that the mother ship's computers had accomplished this task, including isolating the Jupiters' home phone circuits to the city of Los Alamos switching circuits. The computers set up the final parameters for the gravity-stream transmission beam, via satellites, and a phone link was established. Jonathan looked directly across the table to Dan. "The communicator in your pocket is now active for talking over your home telephone landline," he said. "It will be as though you're inside your house. Just touch the second lower button to your left and then talk freely after the other phone is answered."

Dan and Barbara were only mildly surprised Jonathan knew about the communicators in their pockets. They were more amazed at how easily he had accomplished the communication interface link to Earth from so far away. The level of signal propagation in the field of gravity streams was amazingly intriguing, highly advanced beyond imagination. Dan pulled his communicator out of his pants pocket and touched the button Jonathan had mentioned. He immediately heard a dial tone throughout the room, as if over a loudspeaker, but did not have the faintest idea how to dial the number.

All the officers knew this, and Captain Donaldson nodded his head a little. "Just talk the number you want to call," he said, "including area code."

"Okay," Dan said and spoke the cell phone number for his lead employee at the high-energy particle physics lab.

The number was heard being dialed, a phone started to ring, and the cell phone on the other end intercepted the signal. Everyone inside the room remained completely quiet. "Los Alamos Labs, Nuclear Research Department," they all heard. "Dr. Doug Johnson."

Dan looked down at the communicator and then around the room. "Good morning, Doug. This is Dan," he said.

"Hi, Dan, what's up?" Doug said.

Even knowing he could speak freely, Dan looked around the room a second time and then stared down at his communicator. "I won't be into work today, Doug," he said, "and will be taking vacation the next two days to spend time with my boys."

Doug had met Dan's two sons and knew they were smart beyond their years. Little did he know, though, that Dan was secretly referring to three sons, not two, at least if the advanced race decided to not reverse Michael's synaptic memories, allowing him to remain a part of the Jupiter family. "Sure, Dan," Doug said.

"Thanks, Doug," Dan said. "I should return to work on Monday."

"Okay," Doug said. "I'll let everybody know."

An amazed grin filled Dan's face because his conversation with Doug seemed instantaneous, without any delay. "I'll talk to you later," he said.

"Sure, Dan, have fun with your family."

"That is a good possibility," he said. "Take care."

"Bye, Dan," Doug said and hung up.

With that, Dan touched the same button on his communicator, amazed at how easily he'd carried on a phone conversation over such a vast distance of space, not to mention using his home-phone landline while the phone was still on the hook. He looked across the table at Jonathan and felt a little humorous, even in his current predicament. "That sure seemed easy enough," he said. "I wish it were always that easy for a perfect high-speed internet connection."

All the crew members chuckled a little, and Barbara, Jason, and even Michael grinned.

Captain Donaldson and his officers found Dan personable, even in this unusual situation. They also noticed Michael had developed a sense of humor. Of course, to them, the Earth technology Dan referred to was quite primitive.

Captain Donaldson leaned back in his chair. Dan and his family appeared unusually relaxed aboard the mother ship. It was not something Captain Donaldson or any of his crew would have expected, especially since the Jupiters were from a race over two thousand technological years behind them, but then, the Jupiters had sort of been primed by their meeting Michael and riding aboard his small spaceship. Captain Donaldson stared over to Dan and Barbara with a relaxed feeling inside. "I know you're tired after being up all night," he said, "so I want you to spend the day on our ship with Michael, resting and relaxing. Later on, let's say around five o'clock Earth time, we may tell you more about Michael, his future, and your possible futures, if it comes to that, after my officers and I have a chance to speak with the geneticists who created Michael. I will forewarn you that if we decide against you keeping Michael, you will never see any of us again, nor will you ever remember being aboard this ship, the smaller ship, or having spent any time whatsoever with Michael."

Dan and Barbara were very surprised to hear this. They had no idea what the captain meant by their "possible futures." The fact the geneticists who had created Michael were aboard the mother ship implied Captain Donaldson was on a retrieval mission for Michael. Dan and Barbara were also very much aware that if the coming meeting with the geneticists did not go in their favor, they would probably have their memories of Michael and everything they'd experienced wiped clean, but they were much too tired to think any more about it. "Okay," Dan said, "we look forward to a little rest until then, and I sincerely hope our friendship can continue."

"Yes, thank you," Barbara said. "I also hope everything turns out in our favor."

Captain Donaldson suddenly felt good inside and looked forward to his meeting with the geneticists. "Jose will now take you to your room," he said.

Jose stood up, so Dan and Barbara also stood, still holding Michael and Kyle. Jason stood as well. It felt strange to him to know Michael was some unusual bioengineered alien boy and not an android in any aspect whatsoever. Captain Donaldson and his other officers remained seated, and the Jupiter family finally turned away from the table, following Jose toward the doorway. The conference room door suddenly disappeared, and they continued out into the hallway, the door reappearing behind them.

Inside the conference room, Captain Donaldson looked around the room again and then to Jonathan. "Let's contact the chief recombinant geneticists and their team of scientists," he said. "Have them meet us here in two hours for what I know will be an extremely important meeting about Michael. Michael's level of bonding to the Jupiter family is much more serious than what we first thought would be the case."

Jonathan nodded in agreement, knowing the two hours mentioned was actually four in relation to the Earth family. The geneticists to whom Captain Donaldson referred were the nonmilitary generative recombinant geneticists who had come aboard their ship specifically to retrieve Michael and reverse any problems that might have occurred with his synaptic cell matrices configurations that should have never happened. As the ship's chief science officer, Jonathan knew, as did the captain and other high-ranking officers, the agenda of the geneticists if Michael were to awaken prematurely from his stasis, especially if there was any interaction with any intelligent beings other than their race. It looked as though what they feared the most had happened. "Okay, Don, will do," Jonathan said in their alien tongue.

Captain Donaldson also realized what the geneticists had in mind for Michael, regardless of the wishes of the Jupiter family. He turned to Jeremiah, his first officer. Knowing how good Jeremiah's intuition had always been in the past, he asked, "What do you think about the Earth couple, Jerry?"

Jeremiah thought about what he had observed so far. "They seemed levelheaded with a good family atmosphere," he said. "It does appear that Michael has bonded with them from a perspective of needing parental affection. He probably believes in his own mind that Dan and Barbara Jupiter really are his parents, even after hearing about how he was actually created."

"True," Captain Donaldson agreed. "His synaptic cell bonding to the Jupiter family could even be on a spiritual level."

"Very possible," Jeremiah agreed. He'd read in reports that

Michael did have an aura, and even the geneticists who had created him believed he possessed a soul or spirit like other sentient beings.

Captain Donaldson paused before making direct eye contact again with his first officer. "It will be interesting," he said, "to see what the degenerative recombinant experts say about Michael's DNA matrices and the neural pathways that were created since waking up almost three Earth days ago, including whether or not they believe the changes are completely reversible."

Jeremiah agreed 100 percent. *Yes, it will,* he replied telepathically. He then said out loud, "But I hope it doesn't come down to their attempting a reversal of those pathways, for I can foresee problems arising in some of his higher-order brain functions."

Captain Donaldson also foresaw those possible problems. *So do I,* he said telepathically. *Forty years of painstaking research and highly detailed cerebral synaptic mapping wasted, but at the moment we have the agenda of our armadas.*

Jeremiah nodded in full agreement, and Captain Donaldson looked to his other officers. "Thank you for being present in this unusual circumstance of a first-contact meeting with the Earthling family," he said. "I will see everyone back here in two hours."

The chief medical officer and chief science officer both stood up and left the room while the first officer remained seated to talk about the incoming classified communiqué from their armada in the far reaches of the Milky Way galaxy, including what their race had just discovered near a nebula that appeared to have some strange disruption of space.

✦ ✦ ✦

After being instantly transported up 474 levels to level 18, Dan Jupiter, his family, and Jose exited the transporter elevator into another hallway. The projection of their bodies had seemed instantaneous, and only Jose and Michael knew what had actually happened. Dan,

Barbara, and Jason had thought it strange to walk into a small room, have Jose say "Level 18," and then have the transporter-elevator door in front of them appear open again right afterward, exposing a new floor. Though Dan, Barbara, and Jason knew they had just traveled up 474 floors, they did not know how far that was. Jose did explain that they were eighteen floors from the cockpit on level 1, the top main deck of the spaceship. Dan and Barbara did not bother to ask how many levels the mother ship had in total.

While Dan and Barbara continued down the hallway, they were still surprised not only at how fast they'd just traveled up to level 18 without feeling any movement whatsoever but also at how the doors kept instantly appearing open or closed in front of them like the entrance door on Michael's ship.

The hallway ceiling appeared to be at least twelve feet high, and Barbara wondered about the exact size of mother ship, since it had completely filled the windows of their small spacecraft and made their ship look like a small insect. She turned to Jose with a small, constrained smile. "This mother ship is huge, isn't it?" she said.

"Yes, it is," Jose said, "a unique elliptical double-saucer shape nearly 5,200 meters in diameter and half that size at its center."

Dan and Barbara were again amazed, as Jose had just verified what their small ship's sensors had told them right before being intercepted: that the football-shaped mother ship was massive. For it to be able to travel thousands of times the speed of light truly was an astonishing, mind-boggling feat. The size of the ship also meant they had probably been instantly transported over a mile while inside the elevator.

Dan and Barbara were suddenly curious about the lighting in the hallway, as it did not resemble anything they'd ever seen. Neither were there any physical fixtures. They now realized their small ship had not had any noticeable physical lighting fixtures either.

Jose noticed Dan and Barbara looking around the hallway and knew they were curious about the hallway's general lighting. She slowed down near a door on their right with a strange marking on the wall next to it. Michael and Jose knew it read "Room 18." The door suddenly appeared as open. Jason entered first, followed by Dan and Barbara, then Jose. When Dan and Barbara turned around, the door had already reappeared as closed behind them, and they began looking around the room. It appeared to be a family quarters with four beds, three for kids and a larger bed off to the side inside a small room. There was also a lounge area and a room that looked to be a bathroom with a sink but no kitchenette. On one of the far walls were two circular windows about a meter in diameter, and outer space was visible beyond the clear glass.

Jose noticed Dan and his family staring around the room, fascinated, and she pointed at a table with six chairs. There were flush-mounted displays in front of each chair, with each display built into the tabletop. "On that table," Jose said, "in front of each chair, are touch-activated displays to choose anything you wish to eat or drink. The menu is in English, and your selections will appear on the table in front of you."

Dan and Barbara were amazed at how quickly the advanced race had arranged everything for them, as though one step ahead. Barbara also recognized Jose's continued kindness. Her being the mother ship's spiritual advisor was understandable, as her voice was catatonic, peaceful, and relaxing. "Thank you," Barbara told her.

"You're welcome," Jose calmly replied. "Everyone have a restful sleep, and enjoy yourselves as our guests."

Dan and Barbara again acknowledged her continued kindness, not knowing she was a strong telepath, continually reading their minds and hearts. She was also reading the young hearts and minds of Jason and Kyle and knew how emotionally and spiritually attached they were to Michael. She was surprised how deeply attached they had become in such a short time span, but then, no one had been around Michael to know what kind of personality traits he would develop once consciously aware of his surroundings. "Bye, everyone," she said again and walked over to the exit. The door was suddenly open, and she continued out into the hallway, turned around, and now faced the Jupiter family.

Barbara stared into Jose's peaceful-looking face. "Bye, Jose," she said.

Jose smiled a little. "Bye," she said a second time, and the door slowly faded into a solid, different from the previous occurrences. Jose proceeded slowly down the hallway and thought about everything she'd read and felt from the Jupiter family. Captain Donaldson wanted her to take telepathic readings of their spiritual states of mind, something normally not done freely, except when someone was spiritually disturbed or had come to her for guidance or in emergency situations. Continually reading the minds of intelligent beings, without regard to your own self-awareness, could be detrimental to one's own state of mind and its balance between sanity and insanity. Due to this spiritual-balance factor, most of their race, who were all telepaths to some degree, did not use their telepathic abilities that often, but Jose, being a strong telepath, controlled incoming thought emanations much more easily. Others in their race were accustomed to using their telepathic abilities mostly with friends or relatives, and even then, they did not use their abilities 100 percent of the time.

Jose continued toward the transporter elevator and thought some more about what she'd felt from Dan, Barbara, and their two kids toward Michael. Her readings from Michael were confusing because his thought-pattern emanations were not fully understood. It was as though they were distant, like he was in a dream, and she now wondered if there had not yet been a full adjustment of the new synaptic cell pathways being created inside his cerebrum, which was more densely compacted than those of other children in their race.

At the transporter, the entrance door vanished, she entered, and the door reappeared behind her. She then stared down at the control panel. "Level sixty-four," she said, "Theological Studies Library."

✦ ✦ ✦

In the guest room, Jason was already lying down on one of the small beds, conked out. He hadn't even pulled back the bedcovers, but his tennis shoes were on the floor. After Dan and Barbara set Michael and Kyle down, neither of them looked tired, so they sat down together at a small side table.

Dan walked over to where Jason slept, lifted him up, and, while holding him with one arm, pulled back the covers. He then repositioned him in bed correctly, covered him up, and noticed the armband on his forearm. He was now curious how they were removed, since they wrapped almost three-quarters of the way around their forearms and there were gold needles pierced deep into their flesh. "Michael," he asked across the room, "how do we remove our armbands?"

Michael turned to his new father. "Touch the two buttons on the left side at the same time," he answered.

"Okay," Dan said. He touched the two buttons on Jason's armband, but nothing happened. He turned back to Michael, puzzled. "Why isn't his armband releasing?"

"Only the one the armband is configured to can remove it, Dad."

Dan grinned a little, amazed. He lifted up Jason's right hand and placed two of his fingers on the two buttons while Jason remained asleep. Jason's armband suddenly changed shape and then released. Dan grabbed the armband, removed it from his son's forearm, and set it down on a small bedside table. He next reached into Jason's pants pocket, removed his communicator, and placed it on the table next to the armband. Dan thought about his own armband and decided to remove it before resting his mind and getting prepared for what the future held in store for his family. Then again, he could very well be waking up on Earth not remembering a thing. With his right hand, he touched the same two armband buttons. The armband immediately changed shape, releasing its grip. Barbara noticed what Dan had done, so she did the same. Her armband also flexed outward, and she quickly pulled it off, noticing her forearm now had three slightly red holes forming the points of an equilateral triangle. It was strange to think about how the armband could so easily interface to the host body using three gold needles. She turned to Dan, curious. "What are your thoughts on how the armbands are molecularly interfaced to our bodies using three small needles?"

Dan was clueless. "I truly do not know," he said. "Let's ask Michael? I am sure he knows."

"That is a good idea," she said.

Dan stared over in Michael's direction. "Michael," he asked, "why are our bodies interfaced to the armband with three gold pins?"

Michael saw his parents staring intently at him. "Because, Mom and Dad," he said, unabashed, "it is a three-state energy system, where the host body is taken down to a zero resonance before it can be molecularly modified within two fields of gravitational space-time."

Dan and Barbara were amazed by the answer. Dan still could not visualize the transfer method of molecularized data. "Do the three small pins also transfer molecular data?" he asked.

Michael stared directly at his curious father. "The smooth underside also transfers molecularized energy data, Dad."

The answer was more than Dan and Barbara had expected or dreamed. There was a lot to be learned in the field of matter-to-energy conversions on a molecular scale, but they had plenty of time to find out those answers and more, provided the race allowed them to raise Michael. If not, it would not matter, as the advanced race would remove all their memories and experiences with Michael.

Dan and Barbara finally walked inside the small separate bedroom and placed their armbands on a small bedside table. Dan turned to his wife, who was grinning as if in a dream, possibly related to being aboard a mother ship from another world—from an entirely different galaxy. Dan noticed again Michael did not look tired at all and stared over in his direction. "Michael," he calmly said, "your mother and I are getting some rest. You and your brother can play, but make sure you stay in our quarters."

Michael continued to stare at his kind father. "Okay, Daddy."

Kyle felt brotherly love and respect for Michael and turned to his father, knowing he would not leave their family quarters.

"Thank you, Michael," Dan again.

Michael touched the display on the table in front of him, and a holographic image appeared. He began pointing at the image, explaining to Kyle what was now visualized. This only reminded them again how much knowledge Michael must have inside his cerebral cortex, and they stood for a moment longer, contemplating everything that had transpired over the last almost six Earth hours. They'd just met Michael, who they'd thought to be an organic android, only to find out he was actually a genetically altered little alien boy. They had then ridden aboard his small ship to the moon and even had the opportunity to walk on the moon without the use of any space suits while inside an atmospheric gravity bubble. Then on their way back to Earth, they'd had their sudden, unexpected meeting with the race that had created Michael—an event they would have not believed possible in their lifetimes. Just the previous morning they'd woken up to another typical day, never in their wildest dreams believing the armband taken to the Los Alamos labs would lead them to their current predicament.

Dan removed his communicator from his pants, curious what the advanced race might talk about in their coming meeting about Michael. He placed his communicator on the table next to their armbands, and Barbara did the same with her communicator. On their bed, light-blue two-piece outfits suddenly appeared, and Barbara turned to Dan in surprise. "Look what just appeared on the bed, dear," she said.

In addition to outfits for the two of them, there were three outfits for the boys. Dan picked up the outfit that seemed to be sized for Jason and rubbed it between his fingers. It felt much like silk yet had a much-softer texture and appeared to be extremely durable. He carried it out of their room, over to where his son slept. He pulled the covers back and removed Jason's jeans, shirt, and finally his socks. He then dressed Jason in the nightwear that had been graciously provided.

Michael and Kyle solemnly watched their father dress their older brother, Michael showing unusual interest, because he did not understand why his dad had not just woken Jason to have him change his own clothes. With his keen sense of insight, he figured it out, realizing his father did not want to wake his tired son. Michael had not yet slept since first meeting Jason almost three Earth solar days ago, and he still was not tired one little bit. He did not understand the reasons but did now know that his metabolism was extremely slow and that he would live much longer than humans, just as the captain had mentioned in the conference room.

Over at Jason's bed, Dan finished fitting Jason into the nightwear and then covered him back up. As he stared down at his firstborn for a moment longer, his wife carried their nightclothes to the bathroom. He followed her into the room, and a closed door suddenly appeared behind them, so they began changing out of their clothes.

Michael quietly observed this behavior from his parents, not understanding why they were changing in privacy. Continuing to analyze this behavior, he thought he knew the answer—it was because grown-ups did not normally show their naked bodies in front of young children. Kyle didn't think a thing about his parents changing their clothes and continued staring into the holographic image, thinking about what Michael had previously explained to him.

Michael turned his attention back to the holographic image and touched another series of console buttons. The image changed, now showing a spaceship similar to the mother ship. All the ships in the armada, including the mother ship, were capable of quantum gravity propulsion and able to travel thousands of times the speed of light in look-ahead altered flight paths, but then, those velocities were magnitudes slower than their quantum jump straight-line velocities. Michael gazed over at Kyle, who was still staring at the holographic image. "That is what the smaller spaceships and the mother ship look like," he said.

Kyle was fascinated and reached up into the image, his fingers traveling through the metallic-silver spaceship. He quickly removed his hand. "What kind of television is this?"

"It isn't a television, Kyle," Michael said. "It is a spatial multidimensional holographic image."

Kyle still did not fully understand and continued to stare up into the image with fascination. He reached up into the image again. Michael saw this and touched his console, and an even larger holographic image of the spaceship appeared.

The door to the bathroom suddenly disappeared, and out walked Dan and Barbara dressed in the alien nightwear and carrying their Earth clothing. The nightgowns were extremely comfortable, feeling soft and cushiony against their skin. When Dan stared over at their bed, he felt even more tired, but he managed a quick peek over at Kyle and Michael, who were staring at a large holographic image of a spaceship. He was tempted to join them but was pretty sure resting his weary mind would not happen if he did. He wanted to be as sharp as possible if the meeting with the geneticists who had created Michael turned out favorable for them, since they would have an opportunity to find out what the captain meant by "possible futures." When he glanced over at his sound-asleep son, he noticed the Earth clothing he'd just removed was gone. "Jason's clothes are gone," he said.

"Yes, that is strange," Barbara said.

"Yes, it is," Dan said and was momentarily startled when their own Earth clothing also vanished. "Look at that, would you?"

Barbara turned around. Sure enough, all the clothing they'd just changed out of was gone. "Strange," she said. "Do you figure this race will be providing our clothing while aboard their ship, then?"

"Possibly," Dan said, "provided we're not back on Earth in a few hours with no memory of anything about this ship or Michael."

"True," Barbara said.

Dan looked over in Kyle and Michael's direction. "Boys," he said, "we're getting some rest now. Good night."

Kyle stood up and dutifully walked over to his parents, with Michael in tow. When the two small boys arrived, Barbara immediately picked Michael up and placed a small kiss against his lips. "Good night, Michael," she said.

Michael stared intently into his mom's eyes. "Good night, Mommy," he replied.

Dan had already given Kyle a good-night kiss. He and Barbara exchanged kids, and she immediately delivered a kiss to Kyle's lips. "Good night, honey," she said.

"Night, Mommy," Kyle replied.

Dan gently held Michael up against his chest, gave him a fatherly hug, and placed a special kiss against his lips. "Good night, Michael," he whispered.

"Good night, Daddy," Michael said while staring into his eyes.

Dan turned to Barbara with a warm feeling inside at Michael's spontaneous affection and finally placed him down on the floor next to Kyle. The little boys headed back to the table with the holographic image. Dan grabbed his wife's hand, and they returned to the small bedroom, noticing the nightclothes for Kyle and Michael had vanished. Dan pulled the bedcovers back with a small sigh of finally resting his mind after everything that had just transpired in the last almost twelve hours. He tried to stop thinking about what might be said about Michael in the coming meeting with the geneticists and the possible follow-up meeting, if they were given that chance; otherwise, for all they knew, they could be waking up in their own beds in Los Alamos, not having the slightest idea about the existence of Michael or his ship, their experiences with him, or why Dan had taken a vacation from work, unless the alien race were to implant new memories. If all that happened, there probably would not be a single scar remaining from the holes in their forearms, but then, what the captain had said about their "possible futures" was truly a strange comment. Dan now wondered whether the captain was speaking for his entire race or purely from a military point of view.

Dan and Barbara finally crawled into bed. Dan pulled the covers up to their necks, still thinking about Captain Donaldson's comment about their possible futures. He leaned over and placed a soft kiss against his wife's lips. The lights in their room suddenly dimmed, and Dan realized again there were no incandescent lighting sources anywhere, not in the ceilings or any sidewalls. The rest of the quarters, where Kyle and Michael sat at the table, was still brightly lit. There even appeared to be a slightly curved vertical wall between the darkness of their bedroom and the lighting where Kyle and Michael sat. The light around the boys' table was not bleeding into their bedroom as it normally should have according to hyperbolic light reflection and shadow laws. It seemed similar to looking through a curved two-way mirror. "Strange," Dan mumbled under his breath and finally closed his eyes while holding his wife.

Under the darkness of their eyelids, they both thought about everything that had happened while aboard the mother ship until they succumbed to deep sleeps, all while Michael and Kyle continued staring up at the holographic images being controlled by Michael. Michael touched the console in front of him again, and now showing was a video recording of them inside their small spaceship on their way to the moon. Michael, Kyle, Jason, Dan, and Barbara were visible in the cockpit area, staring at the moon as they quickly approached it at a high rate of speed.

15

# SECRETS ABOUT MICHAEL FROM THE GENETICISTS

Early afternoon on Thursday, September 11, Earth time, almost everyone from the advanced race who was allowed to hear about Michael was now present, patiently waiting in the same conference room where Captain Donaldson and his officers had met earlier with the Jupiter family and Michael.

Sitting at the oval table as full command military authority and governor of the meeting was Captain Donaldson. He would also be providing direct oversight over the second meeting and possibly a third, if the final determination about Michael included the possibility of the Earth family raising him. To Captain Donaldson's left sat his first officer, Jeremiah. To Jeremiah's left was the chief science officer, Jonathan, and to Jonathan's left was the chief medical officer. Their spiritual advisor, Josephine, sat to Captain Donaldson's right. After the brief meeting with Dan Jupiter and his family, there were now many uncertainties and questions left unanswered. The biggest uncertainty was what to do about Michael and his attachment to the Earth family. Captain Donaldson was given immense leeway whenever something of potential military or humanitarian value to their race was deemed a high possibility, regardless of the civilian sector. If his initial suspicion about Michael's newly created synaptic pathways held true, he might be using his veto powers in favor of the Jupiter family. If the third meeting did happen, the entire Jupiter family would have to be willing participants, and there would be no turning back to the life they once knew.

Captain Donaldson looked again around the room, which was getting fairly full. This classified meeting could be a historic moment in their race's future. It could result in a decision that might effectively change certain protocols in relation to nonadvanced races that had not obtained worldwide peace or the open use of gravity-propulsion technologies in their society. But then again, those protocols would really only apply to one family of that entire race. With the geneticists aboard his ship, he was very much aware and understood the liaison interfaces the military had with the civilian sector. Such interfaces only made their race stronger and much more resilient, especially when it came to starting new treaties with other advanced races that had also achieved their level of peace and quantum gravity, even if it was a few notches below them.

It was now less than ten Earth minutes before the meeting would be closed, and he glanced around the room one more time. In addition to his three military officers and spiritual advisor, over near one of the far walls were two of his ship's secret security agents dressed in civilian clothing. They were unknown to the civilian populous and most of the military personnel on the ship, except for his highest-ranking officers. Also in the room were lower-ranking military officers, and from the civilian sector, there was a large assortment of genetic interface engineers, organ function analysts, degenerative recombinant geneticists, and regenerative recombinant geneticists. The chiefs of those four divisions, who also gave direct oversight and played a big part in Michael's creation, were also sitting at the table, directly across from Captain Donaldson and his officers. Next to those chiefs were some of their project managers. All the geneticists were aboard the ship because it was considered a retrieval mission for Michael.

That retrieval, with the help of the military, already had the alien race at a disadvantage. The retrieval mission had been a complete mystery before leaving their galaxy less than one day ago (two Earth days). Some of the military personnel had been on yearlong sabbaticals after their last tour, and those vacations had all been cut short due to the priority level for the retrieval of their race's most precious creation. Captain Donaldson had been enjoying himself back on their home world when the urgent communiqué came in about what had happened to the cargo ship near the planet Earth. He, along with his officers, had left for the small planet Earth without hesitation, especially after it was determined Michael had come out of his stasis. The spaceship carrying Michael was also of the upmost concern to Captain Donaldson and his officers, as it had encountered a strange energy fluctuation when it was about nine hundred thousand kilometers from Earth. The fluctuation had been from an energy beam that appeared to have originated not from Earth but from a nebula over two thousand light-years away—information that was now classified at the highest of levels. All communications to and from the cargo ship, even its subspace transponder beacon, had ceased transmission when the ship was radiated by the beam. What was even stranger was that the ship had uncloaked right afterward and transmitted a signal to Earth on a secret Earth-based military frequency band that would have allowed the United States government to detect and easily track it, which was very unusual. That did not include the fact that none of the sixty crew members aboard the cargo ship had yet been located. They were not down on the planet Earth, as verified from all the radio chatter they were intercepting from top-secret and above-top-secret government organizations, which included the Majestic community—the organization that oversaw and ensured extraterrestrial technologies from crashed craft were kept out of the hands of the general public. Before daylight early Tuesday morning, the entire cargo ship had been gone from the crash site, under the control of those same government organizations. But then, as Captain Donaldson knew, sometimes not all of Earth's radio chatter could be trusted or believed. Secret governments that had intergalactic or highly advanced extraterrestrial devices in their possession, well beyond Earth's technological advancements, were always under the impression their communications could be compromised by other advanced races, so misleading and inaccurate information was sometimes used, including a vast array of top-secret code words.

Captain Donaldson paused and thought some more about the cargo ship carrying Michael. It had impacted the planet in a controlled landing similar to being under the control of a strange gravity tractor beam, all while its hull, having faster-than-light molecular and nuclear energy bonds, was compressed and deformed during the space deflection. A communiqué earlier with Captain Gary Randolph from their large armada of twenty-four mother ships and thousands of support ships, all with highly advanced weaponry, had told him they would soon be at ground zero of the beam's origination. The beam transmission was considered a hostile act against their race, and even though they were a peaceful race with a society having no wars or violence, what had happened was over the line, and their advanced weapons would be used to the fullest extent in any intergalactic conflict. Captain Donaldson realized most nonadvanced races, such as the human race on planet Earth, still had violence ingrained within their society but were not an intergalactic threat. When races with intergalactic capability tried to spread their barbaric ways throughout the universe, his own race would staunchly defend their territories, the races they had treaties with, and even the races they did not have treaties with, if the acts of barbarism included trying to enslave a race or destroying its existence. Some of the advanced weapons in their arsenal included above-light-speed gravity beams, high-energy gravity-laser particle beams, and neutrino explosive emissions, which could be used over small or even large regions, killing all living matter in the exposed focused regions. They also had the ability to create magnetic reversion fields that would disrupt power and the natural frequency resonances of any planet with a magnetic field, and they could completely isolate large surface regions of a planet using highly resonant EMPs. These and many other powerful weapons allowed them to completely neutralize an entire planetary race within minutes, if they so wished, even a race hundreds or a thousand technological years ahead of Earth. But even with all this science and sophisticated, technologically advanced weaponry, not one of their scientists back on their home world understood what type of beam had radiated the cargo ship. All they knew was that the beam had been carrying unknown energy-type properties that had disrupted the highly reactive hull material of the spaceship. Michael being secretly hidden away inside a small spaceship on the cargo ship could have had something to do with the damage to the cargo ship and it becoming known to Earth's radars, as his existence was classified at the highest levels.

Captain Donaldson remembered what Captain Randolph from the other mother ship had told him. Captain Randolph would also keep him apprised of what they found at ground zero, but at the moment Captain Donaldson's highest priority was what to do about the Jupiter family and Michael—their race's most precious creation. He looked around the room one last time. Everyone was now present, and the talk and whispering throughout the room started to subside. The doors to the conference room were now closed and locked and could only be opened by his command authority. He finally stood up and it became especially quiet. Even telepathic communications ceased. "Okay, everyone," he said in their alien tongue. "Let's begin our meeting."

Everyone became extremely attentive. "This meeting today," Captain Donaldson continued in their alien tongue, "is about our cell-replicate organic being, Michael, and the Earthling family of Dan Jupiter, which consists of his wife, Barbara, and their two sons,

Jason and Kyle. As everyone may have heard, this Earth family came aboard our ship with Michael about two hours ago. My three officers, our spiritual advisor, and I met with them, and we had a surprisingly relaxed visit. It appears Michael has emotionally and spiritually bonded to the Earth family as his parents and their two sons as his brothers."

Surprised looks crossed the geneticists' faces, and Captain Donaldson sat back down, knowing he'd kick-started the meeting into high gear. He glanced briefly at Jose again, as it was no mystery to everyone aboard the ship that she was a strong telepath, easily one the most powerful telepaths in their armada, in the top 0.0001 percent of strong telepaths for their entire race. "Isn't that correct, Jose?" he calmly asked.

Jose looked around the room. "Yes, it is," she said. "According to what I've felt and read telepathically about the Jupiter family, all four members have spiritually and emotionally bonded with Michael."

Phil, the chief regenerative geneticist, knew right away that could be a huge problem, but Jose had not mentioned Michael's state of mind. "How about Michael's bonding to the Earth family?" he asked her. "Did you read Michael's emotions and his possible level of bonding to them?"

A strange look briefly crossed Jose's face. Captain Donaldson had never seen her make that expression before in the many years he'd personally known her. She looked around the room and turned back to Phil. It was no mystery to anyone that he was one of their race's top geneticists. "Yes, I did," she said, "but I could not correctly understand his telepathic signature emanations as they were projected from his mind, as they seemed more like a dream state. For his actual level of spiritual bonding to the Jupiter family, I am not completely certain of that either, but I did sense he was extremely relaxed around them and had what appeared to be an immense feeling of love toward the Jupiters."

Phil shook his head in a negative manner. He did not have a good feeling about what he was hearing. "We always wondered about those emotional traits," he said and then looked around the room. "It might now be impossible to properly analyze all his newly created synaptic junctures as related to emotions since first becoming cognitively aware of his surroundings almost three Earth solar days ago, not to mention his awareness of all those past events, including what he is currently recording and experiencing. Already, he must have amassed a vast amount of memories and experiences that are now ingrained within his unique cyclic-votonic synapses for both his intelligence and child emotions—synaptic markers that could easily already number over a hundred billion."

Neill, the chief degenerative geneticist, nodded in agreement. "That would be a correct statement, Phil," he blurted.

Phil glanced across the table to Captain Donaldson, remembering him being one of his brightest students in his genetics classes from years ago. He then turned back to Neill. "What do you think, Neill? Is it possible to successfully reverse all of Michael's ingrained memories from the time he first became consciously awake?"

Everyone in the room was extremely quiet, very interested in Neill's answer. Neill consulted with a few degenerative geneticists, engineers, and organ function analysts, including Brian, the chief organ function analyst. Captain Donaldson and most everyone in the room knew they were contemplating the chances of a complete and successful removal of Michael's memories of the Earth family altogether, including all newly created synaptic pathways so that he could live the life he was supposed to have with one of their two families secretly living on Earth.

All Captain Donaldson could do was remain quiet and wait for the decision from the geneticists, as he did not have full, unrestricted jurisdiction over Michael's welfare at the moment. Michael's fate was mostly in their hands. If their decision was to destroy Michael's latest memories and start over with a 100 percent pre-stasis configuration, he would normally have to abide, but since the military was now involved, they had a chance to voice their opinions. The geneticists were also very much aware that Captain Donaldson's chief science officer, Jonathan, had a lot of respect and pull within their race's scientific community, having been one of their race's top scientists before he began serving with Captain Donaldson on the flagship. Captain Donaldson and Jonathan had served together for almost eight years, and both continued to sit quietly, listening, waiting, and wondering with extreme interest about the side conversations still going on in the room.

The room finally got quiet again, as the chief organ function analyst, Brian, who was sitting next to Neill, looked around the table and finally said, "Even if you were to successfully remove his memories of the past few days, there has already been multiple synaptic juncture pathways created for his facial reactions in relation to both sight and sound, pathways that have now been intermixed with the main primer and parent synaptic cells for the motor functions. Their interface patterns back to the secondary dendrite and axon roots would now be extremely complex." Brian paused. "Well," he calmly added, "all those newly modified parent cell interfaces back to those roots could be extremely hard to find and map out into their correct sequences prior to his becoming consciously awake. We have heard that Michael has already smiled and shown affection to the Earth family, which means there are now parent synapses intermixed to both the sight and sound synaptic pathways, regardless of the safeguards we purposely designed into his cyclic-votonic memory synapses. I see no way of guaranteeing he won't have some problems controlling electrical impulses to both his facial skin and muscle cells, including tissues anywhere on his body for that matter, if these parent cells are not completely modified to their original state and we missed even one synaptic connection reversal. While his eyesight-oriented synaptic juncture interfaces of the parent cells should be able to be isolated to their pre-stasis configuration, we could have a problem finding all the parent neuronal patterns associated to his hearing, as directly associated to the olfactory cortex system. This hearing pathway problem, if even one sequence is missed, could cause Michael to not fully comprehend many of the current fifty-nine thousand languages he speaks and understands."

There was light whispering at this revelation about Michael's language ability.

Neill nodded to Brian in full appreciation of his sincere, detailed explanation. "What are our odds of a successful synaptic degeneration considering what you've just mentioned?"

Brian turned around, quietly conferring with other organ function analysts behind him, and the room became quiet again in anticipation of his answer. He finally turned back to Neill. "We estimate about a thirty percent success rate in relation to Michael's synaptic cell motor organ interfaces, as directly associated to his cellular impulse controls."

The room immediately erupted with additional whispering and light conversation, including light telepathic conversation.

Surprised by Brian's answer, Neill turned to his longtime friend, chief regenerative geneticist, Phil, now curious of his final opinion. "Phil," he said, "let's say we go ahead and remove Michael's memories of the past few days and start over, taking the chance that Brian and his group just mentioned. What are the odds of Michael's initial memory, intelligence synaptic pathways, and his cyclic memory programming before meeting the Earth family being compromised and in severe jeopardy of failure if we try to regenerate them back to his pre-stasis configuration?"

Phil gave him a long look and calmly answered, "There is no doubt in my mind that all of those would be compromised. While the effects could be minor, Michael would then have to overcome and outgrow those minor effects."

Neill knew the underlying meaning behind "minor effects" was not good. He also knew Phil had more to say about attempting a regeneration of Michael's synaptic pathways, if they were to first accomplish a degeneration of his cerebral core to a pre-stasis configuration. "What are the possible minor effects?" he asked.

Phil had known Neill was going to ask that question and answered without hesitation, "Well, there is the possibility that some of the synaptic junctures could be slightly out of sequence in relation to the root base structures of the secondary dendrites and axons, as associated to the parent synapses, including those in the hypothalamus region. This out-of-sequence synaptic configuration could lead to verbal sentences occasionally not making sense, as Brian already alluded. The worst possible scenario of having even one out-of-sequence synaptic connection would be that Michael might have an epileptic-type seizure, due to a spontaneous emotional parent memory associated to the Earth family that we failed to remove."

Everyone in the room was especially quiet.

Neill stared directly at Phil for his final opinion. "What do you believe the overall odds for success are?"

Phil thought about the question. "I would say fifty-fifty," he answered.

Neill leaned back in his chair and shook his head, as he was certain they would be in trouble and risk failure attempting any degenerative and regenerative process of Michael's highly advanced synaptic cell cerebral core to return him to a pre-stasis configuration.

The top geneticists had a huge decision on their hands, especially after some of them had invested over forty years of their life in the top-secret project of creating Michael, a project called New Life Force Intelligence. For the first thirty-five years of work, the project had been secret to nearly everyone.

There was light whispering and side conversations in the room, and nobody was clearly leading the meeting anymore. To get it moving along, Captain Donaldson said, "Okay, everyone, so now we know where we are headed in our decision regarding Michael. In addition, we should not forget that Michael is still an intelligent organic being five biological years of age emotionally, even if he is forty physical years (eighty Earth years) old. This five-year-old child has bonded with a human family and that family back to him, especially their four-year-old son. We all know that the memory regression of a four-year-old human could very well have aftereffects later in his life, due to his imaginative state still being in its early stages of development."

Phil and Neill appreciated Captain Donaldson's insight about the young human boy, because it was completely accurate. The boy's current age was one of the most critical times of learning development.

Phil looked briefly to Neill and then around the room. "I recommend we not disturb Michael's new emotional state of mind," he finally said, "and this includes all memories that have been developed over the last few days with the Earth family. The odds are surely against us that we could successfully degenerate all those memories and successfully regenerate them to his original pre-stasis synaptic base junctures, the parent cells, or the dendrite and axon configurations with greater than a fifty percent success rate, especially without permanently damaging some of his advanced mental capabilities."

"I agree," Neill quickly said and looked across the table at the ship's chief science officer, Jonathan, wondering what the stance of the military's science division was. Since the civilian community had decided not to alter Michael's current synaptic configuration, Michael now fell fully under the military's jurisdiction. Neill was curious how well the Jupiter family would take care of Michael, if the military authorized it. A new set of protocols would definitely have to be created, which was something already known to be a slight possibility before the meeting and which now looked like a more likely possibility, unless the military decided to have them ultimately destroy Michael's synaptic mind and start over again in the lab.

Captain Donaldson continued his silence now that the ultimate decision regarding Michael's future was under military jurisdiction. He waited patiently for what his chief science officer had to say, which could include giving Michael back to the civilian community to destroy his mind and start over. He hoped his chief science officer would be of the opinion not to touch Michael's current synaptic cell configurations, but then, he could override his science officer's opinion.

Jonathan nodded to his longtime friend Neill and looked around the room. "I completely agree with Phil's, Neill's, and Brian's assessments," he said, "and believe we should not take a chance of destroying what a lot of you have spent many years of your life working on." Jonathan paused and turned to Captain Donaldson.

Captain Donaldson nodded his head a little. "I also agree," he said. "Okay, everyone, we are adjourning for thirty minutes before we start our next meeting in relation to new protocols of our race regarding the Earth family. In this meeting we must discuss whether there can be a successful modification of Michael's advanced attributes to live a somewhat normal life with the Jupiter family. If we determine that his body can be properly modified within an acceptable limit, then a third meeting with the Jupiter family will follow."

Captain Donaldson stared directly at the chief geneticists and said, "If a third meeting does come about, only the four chief geneticists—Phil, Neill, Brian, and James—will be allowed in the meeting and only to answer any questions Dan and Barbara Jupiter may have about Michael." Captain Donaldson paused again while still staring at the chief geneticists. "And depending on what the Jupiter parents decide, including how they answer our questions, Michael could quickly go back to you for a decision you will not like and that we will all carry with us for the rest of our lives."

Phil, Neill, Brian, James, and all the other geneticists understood exactly what Captain Donaldson had just told them, as it would amount to destroying Michael's cerebral mind and core. If the Jupiter family did not accept all the protocol requirements of their race, they would not be allowed to raise Michael, and the geneticists knew Captain Donaldson would not take the chance of Michael being mentally and spiritually devastated by that turn of events. Most everyone in the room finally stood up and began stretching their legs. All the geneticists, except for the four chiefs, left the room before the second meeting.

Captain Donaldson and his high-ranking officers remained seated, except for Jose, who also left the room but would soon return. In the second meeting, there would be some highly classified information revealed about Michael, some of which had already been told in private to the military, but the military officers had been led to believe the geneticists were about to reveal even more information not in any database or report, which was the main reason why the second meeting was highly classified. Captain Donaldson was curious what this new information could possibly be.

Phil, Neill, Brian, and James, top experts in their specific fields of genetics, relaxed back in their chairs. Captain Donaldson touched the flat console display on the table, and a drink suddenly appeared in front of him. Jeremiah, his first officer, knew exactly what his friend was now sipping on, as he could smell its sweet aroma. It was a natural, delicious-tasting tea from a plant back home, genetically engineered with medicinal herbal properties, such as flavonoid glycosides, theobromic hypericin, and polysaccharide molecules, all of them embedded into the plant's molecular structure, which was now a part of its natural growth cycle, passed from plant generation to plant generation.

Jeremiah followed his captain's lead and touched the display in front of him. The same warm tea appeared in front of him, and the two quietly drank tea together—just like the thousands of times in the past. Others in the room also started touching flat screens, and before long everyone was sipping on a vast assortment of drinks—hot drinks, cold drinks, and drinks with crushed ice, even some filled with thick fruit pulps from specialized trees.

Captain Donaldson looked around the room to see everyone relaxed and in good moods. It caused him to think ahead to the next meeting. Jose suddenly returned, and he gave her a small smile and nod, because her spiritual insight and telepathic readings from the Jupiter family would be highly valuable, especially if the third meeting did happen. Jose returned a kind nod and sat down in her previous chair, just to his right.

Six additional military officers entered the room. Two of them were secret planetary security agents dressed in military attire, but Captain Donaldson still had jurisdiction over those agents while they were aboard his ship. Their arrival marked the last of the authorized attendees. Since everyone's bioelectrical configurations were recorded, it was impossible for anyone unauthorized to remain in the room. Those unauthorized would be automatically transported to security to explain why they thought they should have been present.

Standing outside the closed door were additional ship security officers, and anyone trying to eavesdrop would quickly have their attempts squelched by the mother ship's powerful computers, which would block everything from molecular vibratory radio and audio transmission methods to space energy transports varying hundreds to even thousands of times the speed of light. Even dark energy emanations directly associated to telepathy would be displaced, so that any telepathic information transferred in and out of the room would be scrambled, not able to be completely understood. As Captain Donaldson and the others knew, there was no way to block telepathy—only scramble and shift the hidden energy. As a result, even their most sophisticated dark energy scrambling techniques could never be totally effective against extremely strong telepaths, such as Jose.

It suddenly became extremely quiet, as everyone was waiting for Captain Donaldson to start the second meeting. He did just that. "Okay, everyone," he said in their alien tongue, looking around the room, "we are now proceeding to our protocol requirements stage about Michael and a possible new liaison interface of our race with the Earth family of Dan Jupiter. Let it be known that if Dan Jupiter and his wife do not accept the terms of our protocols, to shield their associations with our race from their race, Michael's complete cerebral memories and synaptic pathways will have to be erased, essentially destroying his mind and all brain cell patterns. There are no exceptions to this rule." Captain Donaldson paused and added, "If this happens, there will also be psychoanalysis regressions of the memories of Dan, Barbara, Jason, and Kyle Jupiter of their time spent with Michael, and new memories will be implanted. Does everyone here fully understand this?" Captain Donaldson paused again while gazing around the room.

The chief geneticists—Phil, Neill, Brian, and James—fully understood. Phil looked briefly around the room and then gave Captain Donaldson a long look. "Don, I hope it doesn't come to that," he said. "Mapping the neural pathways for Michael's advanced second-order axon-dendrite configurations to intermix our race's entire knowledge base was quite the time-consuming process. I am sure it would take us at least twenty years to remap and recreate them all again. I'm also not certain how another extended zero-energy stasis might affect him after the first forty-year stasis, especially during the slow growth into the boy he is today. That is a scenario we had not taken into account, so we would have to run new computer model simulations to determine possible issues."

Neill nodded. "I agree," he blurted out, "because with a second extended zero-energy stasis, there is always the possibility that any cellular matter that has changed, such as Michael's advanced neural patterns, might try reverting back to their initial states of progression and not survive a second extended zero-energy stasis." Neill paused, glanced around the table, and revealed, "Besides that, there was an accident ten years and nine months ago in one of our labs where we lost part of the neural pathways data associated with Michael's child emotional base."

Captain Donaldson hadn't known about that incident, which had evidently been kept secret from most everyone, including the military. If not kept secret from the governmental organization overseeing the project, the geneticists would have had to reproduce the information. It would have added years to the project. "I think I know what you're getting at, Neill," he said, "but explain it to me anyway."

"What I am saying, Don," he answered, "is that we'll never be able to recreate Michael's emotional child personality the way it is currently configured, if his synaptic patterns were destroyed and we started over. Basically, his current synaptic personality configuration toward the Jupiter family is now unique to his being, one of a kind, you might say."

Captain Donaldson's assumption was correct. "I understand," he said, "so we definitely do not want to destroy Michael's new synaptic base configuration, if at all possible. Besides that, my observations tell me that Michael has developed a strong bond toward the Earth family, and I can feel their level of bonding back toward him is extremely high."

Phil, Neill, Brian, and James agreed but still wanted to meet Michael and evaluate the situation for themselves. Captain Donaldson would allow them this opportunity, regardless of Michael's future and final outcome.

"Okay then," Captain Donaldson said. "If the next meeting with the Jupiters does happen, we will proceed to plan B, where we let them know what we've decided. Hopefully, they'll accept Michael in their lives, and all the protocol requirements they must adhere to will then be revealed."

The four chief geneticists and Captain Donaldson's officers hoped that plan B did happen; otherwise, they would have to destroy Michael's mind. Phil, Neill, Brian, and James were extremely curious about the plan B protocols Captain Donaldson had mentioned, as they would be unique to an Earth family living within a civilization that was not only over two thousand years behind them technologically but also had not achieved a path toward world peace and was still filled with barbarism.

Captain Donaldson glanced briefly across the table to the chief geneticists and then looked around the room. "The first priority for plan B," he said, "is that Dan Jupiter and his wife must be willing to raise Michael and love him the same as their two biological sons. It will be a short meeting if not, but I am sure that won't be the case." Captain Donaldson paused and continued, "Protocol number one is that Dan Jupiter and his family keep our race unknown to the rest of the human race at all times unless we directly authorize any interactions with their top-secret agencies that oversee extraterrestrial events. Protocol two is that they have a spaceship with fourth-order cloaking and a quantum drive with time-warp-field propulsion. This quantum drive must have the ability of a forward directional maximum speed of 6,900 times light, plus straight-line burst velocities slightly over $63 \times 10^6$ times light, the same as our military ships. This is all mandatory so they have the ability to travel to our home world in a matter of days, if a debriefing is required and we are not able to travel to Earth."

Captain Donaldson calmly looked around the room, knowing Michael would be able to teach Dan, Barbara, and their two biological kids much about their advanced technologies. He continued, "Protocol number three is that Michael be given an identity on Earth, something that should be fairly easy to manipulate, as far as Earth's census, Social Security, and every other database system they have is concerned."

Everyone in the room chuckled a little, as they knew their advanced computers could easily systematically bypass all internal security measures of Earth's computer systems without ever being detected, using what they called smart artificial intelligence programming, a highly sophisticated software that learned and then closed software loop identities behind it, deeply embedding itself within the core of the main system and fooling it into believing it was a necessary operating program. If anyone on Earth discovered and tried to read the hidden program, it would erase and disguise itself in a rewrite, even forcing a new mini backup of the system files and data, overwriting previous information, including the ability to alter prior backup history. Once the required data that the hidden program was originally supposed to have changed was properly modified, it would then remove itself from every system to which it had been propagated and overwrite itself, adding existing redundant information onto the exact same sectors of the hard drives, magnetic tapes, or optical drives on which it had once been stored. All those electronic database manipulations would all be done in the background and completely untraceable.

Captain Donaldson continued, "Protocol number four is that Michael's body temperature and internal regulation be lowered to the Earthling temperature of 98.6 degrees Fahrenheit. Additionally, his metabolism and cell replication rates must be sped up immensely, so that he will age at a rate closer to that of the Jupiter family." Captain Donaldson looked across the table at the chief organ function analyst. "That isn't a problem, is it?"

"No, I do not believe so," Brian answered, "but those changes to his hypothalamus nerve cell junctures, his intrinsic thermoreceptors, and his brain stem metabolic reconstitutions would have to be accomplished by Phil's and Neill's synaptic cell groups, using the genetic markers that the genetic interface engineers oversee."

Phil, Neill, and James all agreed. "That is correct, Brian," Phil said. "We would have to modify both his hypothalamic gland and his synaptic nerve cells at the brain stem accordingly to recognize an Earth body temperature of 98.6 degrees Fahrenheit. We would also have to change the master stem cell regulators in the brain stem to a lower intrinsic metabolic level, so it would allow the chemical-electrical adhesions to fire at a slightly faster rate." Phil paused.

Captain Donaldson thought about what Phil had told everyone. Even though he understood genetics well enough for an above-average conversation in the field, he did not fully understand what Phil had just said about the metabolic changes that would be required at the molecular level. "Okay then," he said anyway. "That brings us to our fifth protocol requirement that Michael's synthetic transpondence hair follicles, at their root base structures, are changed to produce pure organically induced DNA strands from his body's own stem cell regulators." Captain Donaldson paused to see if any of the geneticists would comment on this requirement, as their race would not be able to know Michael's whereabouts after this procedure. That was how they would want it anyway. Captain Donaldson knew silence was concurrence and that the follicle change mentioned could be easily accomplished, so he continued, "The last protocol that I view as extremely mandatory is that Dan Jupiter and his family fall under the same treaty outlines that we have with other races. Essentially, they would have all the same rights as any of our citizens and must adhere to all our laws, having dual planetary citizenship, you could say."

Everyone in the room grinned slightly, as what Captain Donaldson had said would become factual, if the Jupiters agreed to their protocols. Captain Donaldson smiled slightly and hoped in his heart that this agreement did happen, not only for their race's sake, but also for the Jupiter family's, especially considering the possible military and humanitarian value such an agreement could bring to the table. With this agreement, the human race would have some limited intergalactic protection but not full protection, as that would require disclosing their race's existence to the humans. Captain Donaldson looked around the room. "Is there anything anyone wants to add?"

Neill looked to Phil, Brian, and James and then back to Captain Donaldson. "Yes, there is," he said. "There are a few additional cellular changes that would have to be made to Michael's body."

"What?" Captain Donaldson immediately asked.

The changes Neill was referencing were related to some closely guarded secrets about Michael not found in any report or database. "We'll talk about them in our next meeting with the Jupiter family," he said, "and will reveal them at that time, provided they agree to raise Michael as their own and adhere to all our protocol requirements; otherwise, it doesn't matter, as Michael's synaptic cell configuration will end up being destroyed."

Captain Donaldson knew Neill must be referencing information kept out of the top-secret report he'd read. The geneticists had committed a crime in keeping some information and changes hidden from the governmental agency overseeing the project, but they did not say anything about it, as it was now meaningless. It was possible, though, that the high council was aware of those highly secretive changes. If so, it would absolve the geneticists of the crime and only meant the changes truly were of extreme secrecy. "I look forward to hearing about it, Neill," Captain Donaldson said.

Neill did not say anything further.

Captain Donaldson noticed this. "Great!" he said. "Our next meeting with the Jupiter family will be held in conference room twenty-four, located on level ten, quadrant seventeen, in thirty minutes." He paused with a relaxed face and turned to his spiritual advisor. "Can you meet with the Jupiter family and escort them to our next meeting and then take Kyle and Michael to the children's learning center?"

"Sure," Jose softly answered. "I would love to."

Captain Donaldson knew she would let Dan and Barbara Jupiter know that their coming meeting would be extremely favorable for them. Jose stood up and exited the open doorway into the hallway, the door reappearing behind her. Slowly walking toward the transporter elevator, she thought about Dan Jupiter and his family, now filled with a good spirit.

After the door had reappeared behind Jose, Captain Donaldson stood up to stretch his legs in preparation of leaving for the next meeting. Others also stood up and left the room, including the planetary security agents who would again be providing security oversight beyond his ship's own security. He turned to his first officer with telepathic eye contact.

Jeremiah received Captain Donaldson's telepathic message that he was to head to the cockpit before their next meeting so they could check on the retrieval status of the cargo ship and its contents, most of which were no longer in possession of the human race. Their advanced technologies being in the human race's possession, along with Michael's premature biological conscious awareness, was what caused their current incident to be so high of a priority. They had initially been expecting to recover Michael from the United States government, still secretly hidden away inside the wall compartment of the small spaceship, unbeknownst to the humans. After their advanced sensors had detected that Michael was cognizant and flying around on his small ship, they'd known they had a strange, unknown problem on their hands.

Captain Donaldson and his first officer finally left the room. On their way to the transporter elevator, Captain Donaldson thought some more about the cargo ship and the fact that quite a lot of their advanced equipment had already been recovered, regardless of where it had been secretly hidden away on Earth. Whether it was in Nevada at a place known as Area 51; secret labs at Wright-Patterson Air Force Base in Dayton, Ohio; the Bitterroot Mountains complex of Montana; the secret underground facilities in Idaho; the underground facilities deep in the Appalachian Mountains of Virginia and North Carolina; or the numerous top-secret underground complexes in the Colorado Rocky Mountains, it really didn't matter. The US government—or any government on Earth, for that matter—regardless of security measures, would not be able to stop them from taking back what was rightfully their property. After their ship's advanced sensors identified the objects or any piece of the cargo ship's hull material, they could instantaneously space-transport the item off the planet from anywhere around its globe.

The transporter elevator was just up ahead, and Captain Donaldson stared over at his first officer. "The coming meeting with the Jupiter family will be interesting," he said.

"Yes, it will," Jeremiah said. "Do you think they will accept all our protocols?"

"Yes, I do," Captain Donaldson said. "I believe they'll accept them without a second thought or a full realization of how much their lives will change. They will be surprised beyond imagination if they do accept them, especially for the chance to witness and experience sciences they would have never dreamed of."

The transporter-elevator door vanished, and they both walked inside, Jeremiah now grinning a little at Captain Donaldson's last comment. The door reappeared behind them, and Jeremiah looked back to his friend. "Yes, they will be surprised," he said. "I also believe they'll fully accept our protocols."

Captain Donaldson felt content and stared down at the wall console. "Cockpit—level one, quadrant one," he said.

# 16

## DEEPER SECRETS ABOUT MICHAEL ARE REVEALED

Josephine had already taken the transporter elevator to level eighteen and was approaching the Jupiter family's guest quarters. It had been almost nine Earth hours. A small smile filled her face because she knew they would be happy and appreciative for what the geneticists and military division had decided. Her small smile was also related to the fact that she was certain Dan Jupiter and his wife would accept Michael without hesitation, even without thinking through the implications of how much their lives would change. She walked up to the door and touched it, which would activate a soft tone inside the room. She could have telepathically communicated with them that she was waiting outside, but she decided against it, since they did not yet know of their race's telepathic abilities.

Inside the guest quarters, Dan and Barbara heard a light tone. Barbara looked over at the three boys, who were dressed in new attire and sitting at one of the small tables, and then back to the door. "Please, come in," she called out, knowing that the ship's computer would open the door at the voice command.

The door vanished, and Jose slowly walked into the room to

find Dan and Barbara sitting on the couch, dressed in garments that military personnel wore when off duty. The three boys were dressed in similar garments and over at a small table that had a holographic image above it. Jose turned back to Dan and Barbara. "You should enjoy our coming meeting," she said. "The geneticists decided against attempting a degeneration of Michael's new memories that were created after coming out of his stasis, including his time spent with your family."

Dan and Barbara sighed, filled with relief, and were now curious what had been talked about in the previous meeting. Dan continued to make eye contact with Jose. "We very much look forward to it," he said.

Jose knew he was sincere. "Kyle and Michael will be taken to one of our children's learning centers," she said again. "There they will enjoy spending time with other young kids, some who will be close to their age."

Dan and Barbara could understand the alien race not wanting Kyle present at the meeting and even more so for Michael, but to find out there were other young children on the military starship was a mild surprise. Dan and Barbara both stood up, and Barbara stared over at her three children. "Time to go, boys," she said.

Kyle, Michael, and Jason stood up, and Michael turned off the holographic image. They continued over to the doorway, and Jose knew Jason was filled with anticipation to hear more about Michael. Barbara picked Kyle up, and Dan did the same with Michael.

Jason figured they would have a chance to keep Michael, but he did not know how it would be possible, since Michael had a life span of over two thousand years.

Jose again read Jason's mind and noticed Kyle and Michael were still wearing their armbands. "Follow me," she said.

Dan, Barbara, and Jason followed her out into the hallway. The door to their quarters reappeared behind them, and they continued down the hallway toward the transporter elevator. Dan and Barbara noticed again that the ceiling was easily three to four meters high and the doors over three meters tall. It reminded them that the race was a tall race of beings. What was strange was the lack of any visible incandescent lighting sources in the hallways or inside their guest quarters, yet everything was still brightly lit. Dan had an urge to ask about it but then decided to wait, holding Michael a little tighter in his arms.

They all continued around a curved section of the hallway, still kind of quiet. Dan's and Barbara's anticipation continued to rise for the coming meeting. The hallway straightened out, revealing the transporter elevator up on their left. Jose glanced briefly to Dan and then to Barbara, knowing they could not imagine what was about to be said to them at the meeting. At the transporter elevator, the door quickly vanished, and they all entered with Jason leading the way, followed by Dan and Barbara, then Jose. The transporter door reappeared behind them, and Jose turned around to Dan and Barbara with an encouraging smile. "Your two boys will like it at the children's learning center," she said.

Dan and Barbara grinned at her usage of "your two boys." They, too, knew Michael and Kyle would enjoy themselves, but they were also curious how Michael might react to and interact with other children who were surely not only much smarter than Kyle but also more closely related to him.

Jose looked down briefly at the wall control panel, knowing what Dan and Barbara were thinking. "Level twenty-six, children's learning center," she said.

A split second later, the door vanished, exposing a new hallway. They all exited and turned right toward the learning center. Dan was becoming ever more curious about the strange elevator system, in which they moved extremely fast without feeling the effects of any acceleration. He finally turned to Jose with intense curiosity. "What kind of elevator were we using?"

Jose understood his curiosity. "There are no elevator shafts," she explained. "It's a very similar space-transport process for when your food or drinks suddenly appear in front of you."

Dan thought he might understand some of her explanation, but he still could not see how it could ever be possible to space-transport so many molecularized organic bodies at once through the large ship, especially if there were thousands of crew members. "So it's kind of like a transporter system, huh?" he said.

"Sort of," Jose answered, "but not entirely."

Dan glanced briefly at Kyle, then at Michael in his arms. Ahead, there was a tall double door entrance, possibly leading to the learning center—what type of learning center, he did not know, but he now wondered if the term *learning center* meant school. As their group arrived at the doors, they, too, vanished, exposing a fairly large room, and they all walked inside. There were dozens of children, from nearly two years old up to teenage years. There were numerous adults as well, both males and females, probably teachers, and there was a corridor leading to many other rooms—possibly classrooms.

Jose saw Dan and Barbara staring down the hallway. "We educate our children here," she said. "This is our ship's main learning center, what you would call a *school* on Earth, having equivalent preschool, grade school, junior high, and high school teaching levels. College-level and above classes are located on another floor of this ship."

Dan and Barbara turned to Jose, curious whether military personnel had their families with them, especially considering it was a military vessel. One of the adult females in the room walked up to meet them, and Dan and Barbara set Kyle and Michael down. Kyle and Michael knew they were being left in the room, and both of them still exhibited contented faces. Barbara did not expect it to bother either of them being alone with the advanced race. "Mommy, Daddy, and Jason are going to a meeting," she said. "We'll return in a few hours."

Michael and Kyle stared up into their kind mother's face. "Okay, Mommy," they chorused.

Jose gave a kind smile at the love Barbara had inside for the two boys, again recognizing how Michael had taken to her as his mother. Dan also noticed how calm and trusting Kyle and Michael appeared, even after learning they would be staying in a strange room without their parents and older brother, but Kyle's trusting attitude and calmness might have been because Michael was still with him. Michael's unusual calm look could be related to their coming meeting about him and what they would be told, including what was about to be offered. "See you boys later," Dan said.

"Okay, Daddy," they both chorused again.

The female teacher standing next to them had been expecting the two little boys, and Barbara could tell she was kindhearted. The boys would be in good hands.

Jason sighed at his younger brothers because he was about to find out in the coming meeting their possible future—at least that was how the captain had worded it to them. His parents and Jose started a conversation with the female teacher, and Jason grew ever more curious how the advanced race would go about them having Michael in their lives. Jose and his parents said goodbye to the female teacher, and they started toward the door while Michael and Kyle walked away alongside the nice teacher. Jason had to hurry to catch up with his parents and Jose, and they all continued out into the hallway. Before the double doors reappeared, Dan and Barbara glanced back inside one more time and saw Kyle and Michael already sitting at a small table with other young kids about their age. The door suddenly reappeared, causing Dan and Barbara to sigh, and they all continued back toward the transporter. What Dan and Barbara had witnessed made them realize again how similar the alien race's culture was to Earth's—just on a much-higher level of teaching and understanding. They both knew that the race's methods of teaching must be immense, especially for each member to speak nearly one hundred languages, but then again, maybe their cerebral brain cell and cortex configurations were very different from Earthlings', having much-higher memory and retention capabilities.

As they headed to the transporter up ahead, Jose knew what the Jupiter family was thinking but again chose not to reveal she was a telepath or that her entire race was telepathic to some degree, as it could have made them feel uneasy. She remained quiet as they continued farther down the hallway. When they arrived at the transporter, the door vanished, Jason entered first, then his parents, followed by Jose, and the door reappeared behind them. Jose glanced briefly at the three Jupiter family members and then down to the small wall panel. "Level ten, quadrant seventeen, conference room twenty-four," she said.

The door suddenly disappeared after her last spoken word and yet again revealed another hallway. They exited the elevator, Dan and Barbara thoroughly amazed they were now on the tenth level of the large spaceship. Their movement between floors, like before, had seemed instantaneous. They slowly walked beside Jason and Jose, filled with unusual anticipation about what could be their future with the advanced race, especially when it included Michael being in their lives. Dan started to wonder again about the transporter elevator, turned to Jose with the curiosity of a little boy, and asked, "Does your elevator system transport us through space between floors?"

"Good question, Dan," she said. "Our bodies are actually transported through the space inside extremely small, hollow, circular waveguide conduits."

Dan looked briefly to his wife, who was also amazed at this answer, and then back to Jose. "That has got to be some amazing molecular science," he said.

Jose smiled a little and noticed Jason looking up at his father. She sensed how much he respected him for his level of understanding in science, but then, she knew Michael's broad understanding was thousands of years beyond Dan's. As they approached the meeting room door, Jason grabbed his father's hand for reassurance about what was about to be told to them. Dan, after looking down at Jason, understood this and gripped his son's hand a little tighter.

They finally stopped in front of a door with a strange language on a sign next to it. The door suddenly vanished, revealing Captain Donaldson and dozens of other officers sitting around a large oval table, including the first officer, the science officer, and the chief medical officer, all directly to Captain Donaldson's left. In addition to these familiar faces were unfamiliar military officers, dressed in military attire and sitting at side tables, as if observers. Four older-looking men were directly to Captain Donaldson's right, dressed in outfits that were very different from the attire of the military officers. Dan and Barbara had to figure they were civilian scientists, nonmilitary.

The three Jupiter family members finally walked into the room alongside Jose, who led them over to four empty chairs reserved especially for them straight across from Captain Donaldson, his high-ranking officers, and the geneticists.

After they all sat down, Jose was now to Jason's left, and Dan and Barbara were to their son's right. Captain Donaldson noticed Dan, Barbara, and Jason were dressed in the new attire provided. "Did everyone rest well?" he asked with a kind heart.

Dan, Barbara, and Jason relaxed a little more after hearing the captain's kind, catatonic voice. "Yes, we did," Dan said. "Thank you."

Everyone was now present who was allowed, and the same countermeasures were being used as at the last meeting. "Great," Captain Donaldson said, looking around the room and giving a subtle glance to the planetary security agents at a side table next to some of his military officers. After looking around the room one more time, he then stared directly across the table at the three Jupiter family members. "Before we get started," he said, "I want to introduce you to four of our top geneticists who were instrumental in seeing the creation of Michael from his first stages of embryonic molecular conception to the young boy he is today."

Dan, Barbara, and Jason glanced just to Captain Donaldson's right at the geneticists mentioned. Captain Donaldson introduced the four geneticist chiefs to the Jupiters, starting with Brian, the organ function analyst chief; then Neill, the degenerative geneticist chief; James, the genetic engineering interface chief; and ending with Phil, the regenerative geneticist chief. When the introductions were finished, Dan, Barbara, and Jason noted how sincere and well spoken they all were in the English tongue. Like the others of their race, the geneticists were large individuals, all easily over seven feet tall.

Captain Donaldson looked around the room again and thought briefly about the ongoing investigation into how the cargo ship carrying Michael seemed to have impacted Earth in a controlled fall. He also thought about what the ship's flight computers had recorded regarding the damage to its highly reactive hull, as though it had been placed in a vise. Hull damage did not normally happen, due to the fail-safe measures of their spaceships. There were also many unknowns about how Michael had become consciously awake, as it would have taken special command overrides.

He looked directly across the table at Dan, Barbara, and Jason and knew there were mysteries surrounding Michael that were still of concern for their race. Voicing his thoughts, he said, "We still do not fully understand how Michael was released from his stasis, as his activation would have normally taken top-secret protocols known only by our security council back home. Like I told you earlier, he was supposed to have awakened in the presence of one of our two families currently living on your Earth." Captain Donaldson paused, looked around the room, and then turned back to the Jupiter family to gauge their reaction. He continued, "Our scientific community is still investigating this security-code override and security breach, as the only way it could have been accomplished is by a highly sophisticated computer system and master encryption codes at a level equivalent to or a magnitude higher than what we understand. So it could have only been accomplished by someone in our race or another race with a much-higher level of technological understanding."

Captain Donaldson paused again. Dan and Barbara were extremely quiet, as they did not know what to say, but they had to know up front what they might have to contend with in their future by keeping Michael, including why his existence had to be kept extremely secret at the highest of levels. Captain Donaldson continued to stare over at Dan and Barbara, thinking about the sixty crew members on the cargo ship who had yet to be accounted for. Their disappearance did not make sense, and an exhaustive search for their whereabouts continued.

Captain Donaldson smiled a little from across the table. "But enough about our ship that was carrying Michael. I was mostly talking out loud to myself and only letting you know what our race is up against in trying to figure out how Michael was awakened from his stasis. In the next few hours, you three are going to hear amazing highly classified information about Michael and his history, from his initial stages of molecular creation to who he is today as a little boy—that is, provided you are willing to raise him as your own child and strictly adhere to all of our security protocols associated with the Earth race, which still has violence ingrained within its many cultures and societies. No one on Earth can ever know about your association with our race or Michael's true origin without strict approval from me or another officer above my command level. Does that sound like something you might be willing to accept?"

"Yes," Barbara immediately blurted out without hesitation.

Dan nodded in agreement. "Yes, it is," he said and glanced down at Jason, who was looking up at him with a small smile yet serious face.

Personally, Captain Donaldson felt relief upon hearing this—something none of his crew members would have recognized. "Good," he said. "I was hoping you two were going to say that; otherwise, all of Michael's memories and his programmed intelligence at his cerebral core would have been destroyed. Now his field testing as a new life-form can continue." Captain Donaldson paused, knowing his last comment would get a reaction out of the Jupiters.

Indeed, Dan was intrigued. "What do you mean by new life-form?" he asked.

Captain Donaldson turned to Phil, Neill, Brian, and James and then looked back across the table. "You three," he said, "will now have the opportunity to hear highly classified information that I'll let the chief geneticists explain."

Dan, Barbara, and Jason looked across the table to the four geneticists. James, the chief of the genetic interface engineers, gave them a kind look. He knew some of what was about to be revealed was not common knowledge to the military or in any official report. "We call Michael," he said, "a cell-replicate, organic, carbon-based intelligent being only because we do not know how to classify him due to the method in which he was created. We carefully selected individual male and female gametes of our race's origin and then altered their growth patterns accordingly during their initial stages of cell division and enzyme creation. Michael then grew from a zygote under continual cell-structure control and manipulation into the little boy he is today."

James saw that Dan and Barbara were intensely interested and looked to Brian for further explanation about Michael's cellular modifications. Brian said, "Michael has the same bronchial trees and lungs as our race, but his lungs are each the same size, not as it is with our two races, where the left is a little smaller, due to the position of our hearts in the left chest cavity. Michael has an extra organ that was genetically added into his chest cavity, directly opposite of his heart, and we sized his right lung accordingly. We call this new organ an oxygen synthesizer, and it can completely supplement his oxygen requirements for full synaptic brain cell activity, as well as proper function of all cells and organs throughout his entire body. Essentially, Michael doesn't have to breathe, if he so wishes, or eat for that matter, in order to maintain his body mass, at least as long as he is not too overly active."

Surprised amazement appeared on Dan's and Barbara's faces. Captain Donaldson and the other military officers also were surprised, because the addition of the new oxygen synthesizer had not been in the official reports.

Brian looked around the room one more time and then back across to the Jupiter family. "This extra organ is able to supply a full red blood cell complement of oxygen to his entire body's cellular construction, as it works in conjunction with sunlight and uses a unique photosynthesis process of ours called reverse photoautotrophisis. Essentially, we successfully combined two percent plant genetics within this new cellular organ, along with specialized thylakoid membrane cells just below his epidermal skin layers. We then created a unique sixteen-protein-complex thylakoid system far more advanced than the four-protein-complex thylakoid membrane system of plants currently known by your race. These highly advanced additional protein-complex systems are also what help maintain his flesh-colored skin pigmentation and allow photosynthetic chemical energy and oxygen output without the need of expelling the carbon dioxide gas with his lungs. All these photosynthetic energetic cells across his body, which are also pulling carbon dioxide directly out of his capillaries, then feed the synthesizer for processing and blood flow directly to his heart for distribution to his body. At the same time, any leftover carbon dioxide from his body is then returned to the synthesizer, which is interfaced directly with his modified kidneys and liver. So whenever the synthesizer is used, the liver will remove the remaining carbon dioxide from his bloodstream and convert it into a unique aqueous carbonate dioxide solution. This liquid waste product is then sent to his special kidneys for processing before being transferred to his bladder for expulsion, but if he's in autotrophic mode without the intake of food or liquids, this aqueous carbonate dioxide liquid will be reabsorbed back into his body for energy." Brian again paused.

Dan glanced briefly to his wife. The room was extremely quiet. He was totally amazed at what he'd just heard. Michael's liquid waste product would also be high-energy liquid fertilizer, and his autotrophic capabilities were just as amazing, if not more. Dan could not understand how those modifications could have been successfully accomplished. "Does Michael have a normal heart for those processes?" he asked.

Brian paused. "Yes, he does in a small sense," he said, "but then, to a large degree, no. His heart is located in his chest cavity the same as our two races, but it has two extra valves, a pulmonary valve and mitral valve as you call them, and one extra chamber similar to a left atrium, or the return chamber from the lungs, causing two chambers to now be associated with the left ventricle. Of the two new valves, one feeds the right ventricle, and the other feeds the left ventricle, attached to the new chamber. The new valves are genetically associated to only the synthesizer and are normally dormant. They will only become active when his lungs shut down, either after sensing a noxious gas or chemical from his advanced olfactory bulb and filaments in his nose or when submersed in water. If either of those scenarios were to happen, those two heart valves would automatically become active and start supplementing full-loop synthesized oxygen, while at the same time becoming a slave to the oxygen-synthesizer organ while functioning. The normal pulmonary functions, or two valves from the heart to the lungs, would also shut down with only minimal capillary blood flow to keep the lungs alive and functional."

Brian paused again after revealing that closely guarded, highly classified information. "Basically, it is impossible for Michael to drown or perish from noxious fumes or gas. His body's advanced olfactory system is capable of detecting over two hundred thousand odors, and his lung's airways would be shut down before any hazardous molecules could ever enter his bloodstream or lymphatic system. It is also impossible for Michael to perish from a lack of food or water, due to his autotrophic capability, as previously mentioned, at least as long as there is sunlight or oxygen." Brian paused again.

After all the detailed, secret revelations about Michael, everybody in the room, except Phil, Neill, and James, was surprised. Captain Donaldson and his officers were hearing intricate secrets about Michael that had been left out of the top-secret biological-design reports. Even the chief medical officer, Darryl Randish, was amazed to hear about the advanced autotrophic aspect of Michael's molecular construction in direct relation to the oxygen synthesizer. There were some in their race who were autotrophs, just like a few humans, but they all had to breathe oxygen to stay alive.

Barbara was quiet only for a short moment longer. "Will Michael feel pain the same as we do?" she asked.

"Yes, he will," Brian answered, "but he will have to learn it similar to a newborn, since he was essentially born as a five-year-old carbon-based child who was in a zero-energy stasis field for eighty Earth years. He'll have to be taught the difference, such as what is too hot or too cold, maybe even have to experience some of it for himself."

After rearing and teaching their two boys that same thing, Dan and Barbara understood Brian's statement. Barbara stared over at Brian and the other geneticists. "Can Michael cry in the same manner?"

"Yes, he can," Brian said. "He has tear ducts with all the physical actions and emotional responses possessed by our races. His emotional synaptic base, at his cerebral core, is that of a kind, outgoing child." Brian paused and looked over to Phil. "Right, Phil?"

"That is correct, Brian," Phil said while staring across the table. "Presently, Michael doesn't require much sleep, so we would have to reprogram both his hypothalamic and brain stem synaptic juncture interfaces for that correction, including readjusting his metabolic pituitary gland interfaces at the master stem cell level."

Barbara saw Jason had an interested face, though he could not have understood what Phil had just told them. She turned back to Phil. "How often does Michael have to eat?"

Phil looked briefly to Brian. "In his present state, not too often," Brian said. "This is because his metabolism is close to two hundred times slower than humans'. Basically, he has all the same organs and gastrointestinal tracts that our two races possess, except for the oxygen synthesizer. His six-valve, five-chamber heart and modified organs to fully support the synthesizer are unique to only his body."

Dan and Barbara were especially quiet after hearing about Michael's metabolism. Brian, after seeing this, continued, "Michael also has a special red blood cell type and fluid we designate as OZR positive, a type that associates itself and works in conjunction with all the cells in his body, including the new organ and modified organs. The blood type was created from our race's origin and is one of a kind, containing thirty antibody types, some of which are directly related to his synthesizer. His unique blood can be easily synthesized by our computers, using any human blood type or any blood type from our race, and it would be good to have some available in case Michael were to ever sustain an injury that caused severe blood loss. His blood will also coagulate just like any normal blood fluid."

Dan, Barbara, and Jason were surprised to hear about Michael's unique blood type, as were Captain Donaldson and his officers, but for Captain Donaldson and his officers, the real surprise was Michael's thirty different antibody types, as their race possessed only ten different types of antibodies.

Barbara looked across the table and then back to Brian, curious about Michael's immune system. "Is his blood compatible with any human blood types?"

Brian knew she was referring to Michael's extremely powerful immune system and whether it had the ability to transfer any of its antibody properties to a human. "No, it is not," he said. "Even one ounce of his blood or plasma injected into the bloodstream of a human being—or anyone in our race, for that matter—would quickly prove fatal, causing an inevitable massive stroke or heart attack. Even one milliliter of his blood would cause massive side effects, unless quickly neutralized within less than a minute or two. Additionally, any human blood type, even any of our race's origin, if injected into his bloodstream, would be viewed as a foreign agent, quickly isolated, and then destroyed by his powerful immune system."

Barbara thought about what she had just heard and knew Michael's DNA being intermixed with a human would be an interesting scenario—an alien-human hybrid child, or to her and Dan, a grandchild. "Are Michael's gametes compatible with a female human?" she asked.

Brian looked around the table and then back to Dan and his family. "Yes, we believe they are," he said. "He has twenty-three pairs of chromosomes, for a total of forty-six, as does everyone in our race, except his chromosomes, even more than our own, have much-longer nucleic acid gene sequences than humans'."

Dan, Barbara, and Jason were quiet, their eyes starry. Barbara, who had a master's degree in virology, was very curious about Michael's powerful immune system. "Is it possible for Michael to become sick from any known disease on Earth?"

Brian thought about Barbara's good question. For him to answer it, he would have to open up a whole new field of Michael's construction that was not in any official report and had even been kept secret from the governmental agency overseeing their project. He decided to answer her question anyway. "We do not believe it is possible for him to contract any disease or virus from your planet or ours or to become sick from any poisons or toxins. He is essentially immune to all Earth diseases and toxins, as well as many others throughout this galaxy, our galaxy, and many others. This immense immunity is due not only to his thirty different antibody types but also his millions of receptor memory cells—new, advanced, smart cells that would be called leukographyilias in your native tongue, if they existed in your world. These cells exist in our race's genome in primitive form and in higher forms in some of the animals on our home world. We successfully isolated them and were able to modify and then amplify them for Michael's body. Those cells exist in the epithelial lining fluid of his lungs, the gastric walls of his small intestines, and even the mucosa inner walls of his stomach, all of which will detect toxins and poisons that are deemed harmful. Those cells will immediately release what we call neutralizing antibodies, which will break down the molecules of the harmful toxin or poison agents, at the source of invasion, before they have a chance to enter his lymphatic system and cause dangerous chemical reactions to his cells. All neutralized foreign poisons or toxins are then sent to his unique bladder for removal." Brian paused. "Just so you all know, Michael also has leukographyilia cells just below his epithelial skin layers, which act similar to what white blood cells do when they leave the capillaries of the bloodstream to fight external skin infections, except his leukographyilias release tissue-based antibodies, which will again immediately neutralize any poisons or toxins that happen to come in contact with his skin." Brian paused again after this revelation, as it was highly classified information not listed in any official report.

Barbara and Dan were again amazed at what they heard, as were Captain Donaldson and his officers, mainly because Michael's poison and toxin immunity was off the charts, both internally and externally. Dan and Barbara continued to be overwhelmingly amazed by the extent of genetic engineering the race had invested into Michael. They also knew the alien race probably had cures for all current diseases and afflictions on Earth, including HIV, not to mention all forms of toxin poisoning. That briefly caused them sad feelings because they would not be able to reveal any of that advanced virology, biological toxicology, and related immunology understanding to the human race.

Barbara thought some more about Michael's attributes and could not begin to fully understand how the race had been able to control his unique antibiotic-antigen system so precisely with so many different viruses, bacteria, and now what appeared to be new leukographyilia cells that controlled an automatic release of neutralizing antibiotics of toxins and poisons.

Dan continued his silence, as did Captain Donaldson and his officers, after the newly revealed, intricate details of Michael's attributes.

Barbara finally regained her thoughts and glanced briefly at her son and then her husband before finally looking back across the table with a small, subtle grin. "Michael has one heck of an extremely unique antibiotic system, huh?" she said. "One that could essentially cure the human race of all diseases, if synthesized."

All the advanced beings in the room laughed a little, as Michael's antibodies were indeed synthesizable and could cure all diseases that affected the human immune system. "That is correct," Brian said and figured he might as well reveal additional highly advanced secrets that had been kept out of the official reports. "Not only does he have a unique antibody system that is magnitudes more powerful than ours, but we've also successfully isolated the regenerative healing gene of our race's DNA. We designed those DNA matrices into all his cellular structures and then amplified them. Michael now has the ability to heal injuries at a much-faster rate than what our race can, including severe damage to his body, but as it is with any living matter, some injuries can be fatal, even to Michael."

Dan and Barbara were quiet again. This new information seemed to indicate Michael was nearly invincible, at least biophysically.

Brian looked over at Phil, Neill, and James and then back to Dan and Barbara. "In reality," he calmly said, "Michael is a superior being even to our race—a masterpiece, our race's greatest creation. Imagine a five-year-old with all of our race's knowledge yet having the ability to understand even more as he grows older. That is why he is so unique and can be called the first of a new race." Brian paused, glancing over to Jose and then back to Dan and Barbara. "Whether Michael has a soul inside the physical shell body that we've genetically engineered and modified is something we do not know for sure. We also do not know whether his reproductive system will function properly when he reaches puberty, though we highly suspect that it will, since he has twenty-three pairs of chromosomes, as previously mentioned. This is something we very much look forward to finding out in the future." Brian paused again and thought about the greatest secret of all about Michael, which was one of the main reasons why they'd taken on the project and created all his uniquely advanced modifications. He looked over to Phil with a telepathic thought, and Phil replied telepathically, *Go ahead.*

Captain Donaldson and his officers noticed Brian's hesitation and knew there was more secret information about Michael that had been withheld from their reports. Though Brian and Phil tried to mask their telepathic communication, Jose easily picked up on it and knew what they were about to divulge.

Brian stared across the table at Dan and Barbara, looked briefly at Captain Donaldson and his officers, and then gazed around the room with a stern look. "The following information that I am about to reveal can never leave this room," he warned.

Everyone would without doubt follow Brian's request, especially Dan, Barbara, and Jason, as it was yet another revelation that would have to remain extremely secret.

Brian noticed everyone's reaction with confidence. "We believe that in time," he said, "Michael might come to fully understand wormhole technologies—or, if not him, then his offspring, who should carry his immense synaptic DNA advanced learning capability, including dense synaptic cell configurations. We basically designed Michael with almost every characteristic possible so that he or his offspring would live a lives mostly free of harm and injury while at the same time having the ability to unlock the secrets of wormhole technology, potentially revealing some of the deepest secrets of our universe and its creation." Brian paused again and warned a second time, "Only a handful of our race and the high council know this information."

Brian glanced to Phil, Neill, and James. His division worked closely with theirs, and they were three of the handful outside of the high council who knew the information just mentioned. "Do any of you have anything to add?" he asked.

"No, I don't," Phil said immediately. "You've done an excellent job explaining Michael's interfaces to his new organs and related intricacies, Brian."

Brian returned a small nod to his longtime friend.

Neill also quietly acknowledged Brian. "I do not have anything either, Brian," he said.

"Neither do I," James said.

Brian looked over to Captain Donaldson, as he and the other geneticists had nothing further to reveal or say about Michael. Captain Donaldson realized this and stared across the table at the Jupiters, who were exhibiting intense faces, though also amazed small grins. Dan and Barbara continued to think about everything they'd been told, understanding more than ever why the advanced race had come diligently looking for Michael. Not only was he a new life-form, but he'd also been created as a superior being, having unique characteristics that were easily thousands of years ahead of Earth's sciences, possibly even centuries ahead of the race that had created him. They looking forward to raising him and spending the rest of their lives with him as one of their sons. At the same time, they knew they had to protect the many secrets about him, including the fact that he might come to understand wormhole technologies later in life. They also had to figure they might receive a spaceship that would allow them the opportunity to explore their solar system and even travel beyond their solar system to the deepest reaches of their galaxy. Their secret association with the advanced race would continue for the rest of their natural physical lives.

Everyone in the room was rather quiet, and Dan finally looked across the table at Captain Donaldson. "Now what?" he asked.

Captain Donaldson had been waiting for them to ask that

question. "Well," he said, "Michael will have to go to our main medical lab in order to have his hypothalamic nerve cells and master stem cells modified on the molecular level, including changing his intrinsic receptors so they'll recognize a normal body temperature of 98.6 degrees Fahrenheit. All synthetic molecules will be removed from the hair follicles on his head, down to their root bulbs and papillae, so that his hair grows with pure DNA strands. Then there will be adjustments to the metabolism of his pituitary gland so that he will age and consume nutrients with the same frequency as your family. He will also have to undergo a hypothalamic and synaptic adjustment so that his sleep patterns more closely match that of an Earth child of his age."

Captain Donaldson turned to Phil, Neill, Brian, and James. "What do you think, guys?" he calmly asked. "Can all those changes be accomplished in one Earth solar night?"

Phil looked briefly to the chief medical officer and then back to Captain Donaldson, who had been one of his brightest students in his genetics classes years ago. Captain Donaldson carried a broad variety of molecular biology doctorate degrees on top of numerous other degrees across many different fields. There was not a single military officer on the ship that did not carry at least three doctorates per their race's standards, and the higher-ranking officers carried dozens. "With the help of Darryl and some of his medical staff, I believe we can," Phil answered while staring directly at Dan and Barbara. "I will make one comment about changing Michael's sleep patterns and metabolism. Even though we can change his sleep patterns to be close to that of a young Earth boy, he still may outgrow those changes and not sleep much again, maybe two to four Earth hours a day. For his metabolism and life cycle, he will still probably outlive all of us, even if his cell division rate is greatly increased. Those two attributes are part of his genetic configuration that cannot be completely changed, only slightly modified."

Captain Donaldson understood and looked across the table to

Dan, Barbara, and Jason. "Do you have any other questions about Michael?"

Dan and Barbara, even after hearing everything told to them, surprising as it all was, were becoming ever more curious how the geneticists had been able to create Michael from two opposite gametes and then modify them as a zygote during cell structure divisions. They also could not ignore the fact that Michael might outlive even their kids. Dan looked directly across the table at Phil, still filled with curiosity. "Were any of Michael's initial cellular modifications created similar to cloning?"

Phil glanced briefly at Neill and Captain Donaldson and then looked back to Dan. "No, they were not," he said. "Like previously explained, we only used the DNA genetic road map of one of our race's most brilliant male children and made changes accordingly for Michael's unique DNA and cellular configurations, especially his synaptic base growth patterns. As Brian previously explained, we carefully picked a male spermatozoon, as your race calls it, and a female ovule from which his chromosomal orders were sustained, developed, and then modified to allow all his unique molecular and cellular modifications to be successfully accomplished, including all enzymic strain catalysis markers deemed pertinent to those cellular modifications."

Dan and Barbara were again quiet, with Dan becoming more curious about genetic clones, since the advanced race's understanding about DNA sequences, chromosomal order, enzyme creation, and cell divisions on a molecular level seemed immense. He looked back across the table to Phil and asked, "Does your race have clones?"

Phil knew Dan was thinking about Earth's twenty-first-century attempts to clone a human being, which was essentially trying to make an exact duplicate from another DNA-patterned cellular being, except using only female gamete structures. Phil glanced to Captain Donaldson with a telepathic question, and Captain Donaldson replied back telepathically, *Yes, it is okay.*

Phil then turned his attention back to Dan, Barbara, and Jason. "Our ancestors," he said, "attempted to clone our genome system 1,040 of our years ago—2,080 Earth years ago. They tried for hundreds of years, only to create unstable and genetically inferior embryos, all of which were then quickly destroyed before the third gestation period and before existence was viable outside the womb. They finally did successfully clone a female embryo with a 97.3 percent enzyme configuration match, in direct relation to their DNA sequences. It was at a percentile level of enzyme degradation they believed would not allow a new virus or disease strain vulnerability to our genome system, so they allowed the girl to gestate and be born into our world. Unfortunately, our ancestors' genetic model calculations were incorrect. When she was two years of age, she developed a deadly echovirus strain and died less than a week later from a virus that had no cure. What our race discovered about a century later was that when we bypassed the natural order of the enzyme transfers between opposing gametes, during the creation of DNA nucleic acids into their nucleotide chains, it left a door open, or an open seal in Pandora's box, as it is called in your Greek mythology." Phil paused and then calmly added, "Well, as a result, this little girl and her unique virgin DNA nucleotide combinations allowed the introduction of a new virus strain that fell outside our normal molecular DNA gene construction. It ended up causing one of the worst possible catastrophes in the history of our race."

Phil paused again to see Dan, Barbara, and even Jason sitting quietly. He let out a small, softhearted sigh. "Well, that child clone caused a worldwide epidemic soon afterward from a resilient and unstoppable airborne virus that ultimately defeated all normal air-filtering systems and quickly mutated into a whole new family of viruses. These new viruses constantly mutated every two hours. They were extremely virulent pathogens and killed ninety-eight percent of our race's population—seventeen billion beings—in less than two of your Earth years. The other two percent of our population, or about four hundred million, ended up having an immunity to this biologically destructive virus strain. This airborne virus that nearly destroyed our race was similar to HIV, as you call it on your planet, but caused a much-faster reaction, having many similarities to what the hemorrhagic Ebola virus does to the human body."

Phil paused with compassion to the Jupiter family and continued, "Well, that two percent of our population are our only ancestral bloodline now. It took our race over fifty of our years to begin recovering from that catastrophic event. A cremation of those who died was an absolute necessity, but this mass cremation took another toll, spiritually, on those who had survived and was the cause for millions more deaths afterward."

Dan, Barbara, and Jason felt deep sympathy, almost to the point of tears, and Jose telepathically sensed this. It only confirmed what she already knew: that the Jupiter family had a close spiritual bond and were kindhearted.

Captain Donaldson gave Phil a small, appreciative nod for revealing these secrets from their race's history, something now taught to all their children as a reminder of the mistakes made in the progression of science. He turned to Dan and Barbara and sternly warned, "Your race is attempting to head down the same path. One day, maybe they will come to understand the dangers of disrupting or bypassing the natural order of amino acid structure creation during the initial stages of conception. After that incident almost a thousand years ago, our race outlawed cloning attempts of entire individuals with severe penalties for anyone violating this law. Your race should do the same, but there are those who do not seem to care or listen. Maybe your race will have to learn the hard way like ours."

Captain Donaldson paused with a serious face and then suddenly kidded, "But on the bright side, maybe your race will wipe itself out, and our race can then populate your beautiful planet."

The military officers and chief geneticists chuckled a little. They would never wish that on any race, yet they all knew that, with the current path of Earth's scientific community, such destruction could very well happen sometime in the future. Dan and Barbara did not know what to think about what they'd heard or how everyone had reacted to the semiserious joke. Dan finally stared over at Captain Donaldson with a somewhat somber face. "I hope that doesn't happen," he said.

"And so do I," Captain Donaldson said. "Even though we could cure and immunize the Earth race of every disease and virus known to them, including HIV and Ebola, we can't meddle in your race's history in that manner, nor can you with any of the advanced technologies you receive from us."

Dan and Barbara understood.

Captain Donaldson noticed this, as well as Jason's reaction, and after briefly reading their minds, he knew they would strictly adhere to his race's protocols, especially in regard to raising Michael and having him in their care. He glanced around the table and then back to Dan, Barbara, and Jason. "In return for raising Michael," he calmly said, "you'll also receive a spaceship with a quantum drive with transitional time-warp-field propulsion. The ship is circular in shape and has a diameter of nearly thirty meters by Earth measurements."

Dan, Barbara, and Jason were intensely interested, none of them having heard of this space-travel technique. Dan glanced over to the chief science officer and then back to Captain Donaldson. "What exactly is transitional time-warp-field propulsion?" he asked.

Captain Donaldson could understand Dan's question. "Our ship's chief engineer will come to your room later and briefly explain it, along with your ship's gravity-propulsion system," he answered.

"Okay," Dan said quickly, filled with anticipation. "I look forward to it."

Jason was quiet, as though in a dream. His parents would now have a large spaceship, and he wondered about the small spaceship he'd found inside the cargo ship, the one in which Michael had been secretly hidden away in a wall compartment. He calmly stared across the table at Captain Donaldson. "Can we keep the small spaceship too?" he asked sincerely.

Captain Donaldson looked to his first officer and chief science officer with another telepathic communication. He received both positive telepathic replies and affirmative nods. He stared briefly at Dan and Barbara before making eye contact with Jason. "Since your family is raising Michael," he said, "we will allow it, but only because we know Michael understands the extreme dangers of our advanced technologies in Earth's society, something I'm sure you, Jason, will also come to understand."

Jason nodded his head to agree. "Yes, I will," he said.

Dan and Barbara noticed how mature their ten-year-old son was acting, and Dan turned back to Captain Donaldson. "We'll make sure they all fully understand, even Kyle."

Captain Donaldson knew the meeting was about over and glanced briefly to Darryl Randish, then back to Dan and Barbara. "When you take Michael to the main medical lab, we would like to record your brain wave patterns. This will allow you to telepathically control your ship's propulsion system using the ship's helmets. The ship can also be flown using conventional methods or its computer."

Dan and Barbara were amazed to hear this, as was Jason, and Dan stared directly back at Captain Donaldson, now wondering how the race understood telepathy. "Those recordings and the use of telepathic helmets also applies to our kids, right?" Dan asked.

Captain Donaldson looked briefly to his medical officer and chief science officer, and they both telepathically understood that Dan and Barbara's kids would have to be locked out of telepathic control of the spaceship when without adult supervision. Darryl Randish stared across the table. "Yes, it does," he said. "We also want to record Michael's mental signature emanations, including his brain wave cycles, but I have a suspicion we won't be able to accurately understand them at this time, until our computers figure out the working base of his unique fully conscious to subconscious multilaced frequencies."

"Why's that?" Dan asked.

"His highly dense brain wave cycles are unique," Darryl answered, "and our computers have no true reference on how to interpret or understand them since he awoke prematurely from his stasis, as evidenced by the fact that Jose cannot completely understanding his telepathic thought emanations. Prior to the moment Michael first opened his eyes to physically interact with his surroundings, a brain wave cycle recording, or zero-baseline point you might say, was supposed to have been made that would then match what he was experiencing with his five senses in a completely controlled environment. Since that did not happen, we are now in catch-up mode and will have to reprogram our computers to recognize his brain wave cycles that we already know are interlaced with more than twelve times the number of active neuronal paths than even our race possesses. Essentially, Michael has a very active cerebral brain configuration that can multitask like a supercomputer."

Jose nodded her head in agreement. Dan, Barbara, and Jason were very surprised, not only to learn how extremely advanced Michael's cerebral brain really was, but also to learn Jose was a telepath, which could very well mean all of the race, including Captain Donaldson, were telepaths.

Darryl noticed the Jupiters' reactions and did not know if he should have revealed Jose was a telepath, but then, the Jupiters still did not know for a fact that his entire race was telepathic, some stronger than others. He thought no more about it and only smiled across the table at Dan and Barbara. "In time," he calmly said, "our synaptic-cyclic-memory readers will be able to fully understand Michael's unique brain wave patterns."

Dan and Barbara were truly amazed at the term *synaptic-cyclic-memory readers*.

Captain Donaldson noticed this. "In addition to receiving a ship," he said, "one of our mother ships and its contingent of support ships will return to Earth every six to twelve Earth months for a debriefing, including a follow-up on Michael's progress. Whether it is my ship and its crew members for that first debriefing, I cannot know at this time, but I will make every effort to make sure I am there with my ship and crew for your first debriefing."

Dan and Barbara hoped it would be Captain Donaldson. Dan asked, "How will we know when you're returning?"

Captain Donaldson paused. "Your ship will pick up our gravity-stream communication," he said, "and will cause your communicators to sound or vibrate, similar to your cell phones, so it would be good to always keep at least one nearby. If you by chance were to miss the communicator notification and not respond, one of our two families living on Earth would contact you, since they will now be on the same debriefing cycle."

Dan knew that was a good protocol. "I understand," he said.

Captain Donaldson looked around the room again and then back across the table to the Jupiters, as the meeting was now over. "Jose will now take you to your kids. You'll need to explain to Michael why we have to keep him in the medical lab all night, but I am sure he'll quickly understand. I want you all to have a restful sleep, and at noon tomorrow Earth time, there will be a big dinner in recognition of your family's friendship and future with our race."

"Thank you," Dan said, "especially for all your kindness."

"Yes, thank you," Barbara also said.

Captain Donaldson felt contented at their continued politeness and open minds, especially regarding what their future held in store for them. "This historic meeting is now adjourned," he said.

Nearly everyone immediately stood up, with some leaving the room. Dan and Barbara also stood up, noticing again that they were the shortest in the room. The chief medical officer, now standing across the table, glanced briefly at Phil, Neill, Brian, and James and then back to the Jupiter family. "We'll be ready for all of you, including Michael," he said.

"Okay," Dan said. "Thank you."

Darryl looked forward to the Jupiters' arrival within the next hour or so, and he, along with Brian, Neill, James, and Phil, headed to the main medical lab in preparation for their arrival, especially Michael's. Brian, Neill, Phil, and James realized that the computer models they'd brought with them for restructuring Michael's cerebral synaptic cells were now more important than ever, because of the changes at his brain stem and hypothalamus.

In the conference room, Dan sighed after thinking about how fast-paced the last few days had been and stared over at Captain Donaldson. "We'll see you tomorrow, then," he said.

"Okay, Dan," Captain Donaldson replied. "See you all tomorrow."

Dan, his wife, and son finally started toward the exit alongside Jose. Captain Donaldson and his remaining officers watched them leave the room, continue into the hallway, and then vanish out of sight when the door closed behind them. Captain Donaldson stood silently, knowing he was going to have a busy evening. His main priority was returning to the bridge to find out whether their fleet had determined anything new about the source of the strange energy beam that had been generated from the nebula and directed at the cargo ship, setting off the series of events that had put them in their current predicament. He felt anticipation as he thought about talking to Captain Randolph, the captain in charge of the large armada tasked with investigating the beam, as surely something of interest had been determined by now, even if the beam did have unknown wave characteristics well beyond the speed of light and their understanding. How the beam had been generated from one point to another point thousands of light-years away, similar to both a long-range transporter and gravity tractor beam, was a complete mystery. He finally left the room alongside his first officer, and they headed directly to the cockpit.

On the same floor but in a different hallway, Jose, Dan, Barbara, and Jason finally walked up to the transporter elevator. Dan, Barbara, and Jason were still thinking about everything they'd been told. They were in a strange but good situation, they felt, one that entailed a friendship with the advanced race, something they would have never imagined or dreamed possible in their lifetimes. Now they had a lifetime to live a dream like none other.

Jose slowed down, and the transporter-elevator door vanished. The Jupiter family walked inside first, followed by Jose, and the door reappeared behind them. Jose stared down at the wall panel. "Children's learning center, level twenty-six," she said.

# 17

## THE MAIN MEDICAL LAB

After Jose's last spoken word, the transporter-elevator door immediately vanished. Dan still marveled at how fast they moved between floors. Like the previous times, he had not felt or witnessed any visual effects or inertial changes. They exited into the hallway. There was framed art on the walls that had not been there earlier when they'd taken the two boys to the children's center. There was beginners' art, intermediate art, and even some that was fairly fine in appearance, all of the pieces possibly drawn by children. Dozens of the race's crew members lined the hallways, staring at the many pictures. Up ahead in the distance, there seemed to be hanging pictures that were garnering much more attention than the others, with some crew members standing behind others for a glimpse. Dan, Barbara, and Jason passed by the heavy congregation, curious about what was being looked at so intently and with so much interest. Jason continued to look around like he was standing in a land of giants. Barbara was wondering why the crew members were looking at the pictures to begin with and turned to Jose as they approached the children's learning center. "Is that art drawn by your children?"

"Yes, it is," she said. "It was drawn just today by the children in our learning centers. Once a solar month we have a contest for all kids aboard the ship, and everyone has the opportunity to judge the pieces for originality and imagination—today just happens to be that day."

Jose had a small, subtle smile on her face, and Dan and Barbara wondered whether Michael or Kyle might have also drawn pictures and, if so, whether they would be hanging on walls. Barbara had to know. "That's interesting," she said.

"Yes, it is," Jose said, "and yes, two of the pictures hanging on the walls were drawn by Michael and Kyle."

Barbara raised her eyebrows a little, receiving confirmation that Jose was indeed a telepath. "Oh really?" she said. "Which pictures?"

"I am not certain," Jose said, "but they could be where everyone is congregated."

At the learning center entrance, Jose telepathically analyzed the crew members' minds and discovered which pictures Michael and Kyle had drawn. The double door vanished, and they continued inside. Michael and Kyle were sitting at a small table with six other children who looked about their same ages but who were in reality a few years younger than Kyle.

The teacher who had earlier eagerly accepted Michael and Kyle had already known Dan and Barbara were on their way to pick up their two children. She immediately headed their direction. "Your two children are well mannered," she said. "Michael has been continually talking with the other kids after he drew his picture. He has a kind heart, and we can tell he will be a teacher."

Dan and Barbara grinned a little, knowing that to be a fact, as Michael no doubt would be teaching them about advanced sciences while at the same time learning about love and affection from them. Everyone walked toward the table where Kyle and Michael sat. When Kyle finally saw his parents, he quickly stood up, excited, and headed in their direction. Barbara walked a short distance to meet him. "Mommy!" he said, and she picked him up in her arms.

Michael, after seeing Kyle's reaction, understood that emotional response was good, so he also stood up and headed their direction, gravitating toward Dan.

Dan walked a short distance to meet Michael. "Daddy!" Michael said. Dan picked him up and stared over at his wife with a humorous grin. "I guess Michael is going to be a daddy's boy," he kidded.

Barbara laughed, as did Jose and the female teacher, while Jason only stood with a small grin. He did not care whether Michael was a daddy's boy or not, as long as he was his brother.

Dan gave Michael a special hug that only a father could do and looked into his pretty blue eyes. "Michael," he said, "the geneticists told us that you'll have to remain in their lab for a while."

Dan and Barbara remained quiet, not sure how Michael might react. "I understand, Daddy," he finally said. "I know they need to make adjustments to my neuronal structures and hypothalamus gland so that I will have an internal body temperature and metabolism more like yours. The synthetic transpondence molecules, including the papilla cells that generate them, will be removed so that there will be growth of pure-DNA hair follicles. I will be okay, though."

Dan and Barbara were surprised how easily he had surmised the required changes to his body, including his cerebral cortex, from what little he had heard from the captain soon after they'd met the race. They knew he probably had an amazing power of deduction, but then, it all did not matter, as they were accepting Michael for who he was as a little boy, even if he did carry within his brain the entire knowledge base of the race that had created him. They now stood with tender hearts after hearing his reassurance that he would be okay, which was especially endearing coming from such a young child.

Dan turned to Jose and still could not help but have concern for what the geneticists were about to do. "The changes won't hurt him, will they?"

"No," she said. "He will be placed into another zero-motion, absolute-zero stasis and not remember a thing."

Dan and Barbara were amazed to hear "zero motion" associated with "absolute zero," especially in relation to organic matter.

Jason thought he understood part of what "zero motion" and "absolute zero" meant, as absolute zero was an extremely cold temperature, close to minus 459 degrees Fahrenheit or minus 273 degrees Celsius, according to Earth standards.

Dan took a deep breath at what Jose told them and looked toward the exit while holding Michael a little tighter. "Okay then, let's head to the lab," he said.

The female teacher noticed they were about to leave and expressed a kind, relaxed face toward Jose and the Jupiter family. "Bye, everyone," she said.

Dan and Barbara again noticed the continued kindness from the teacher. In fact, everyone in the race they'd met so far had been kind, outgoing, and extremely courteous. "Bye," Barbara said, "and thank you."

"You're welcome," the teacher replied.

"Bye," Jose said.

Kyle and Michael waved their little hands to tell the teacher goodbye.

The five Jupiters and Jose finally exited the learning center and turned left, headed back toward the transporter elevator. Quite a number of crew members were still looking at the same area of the wall as before, evidently paying much more attention to those pictures. Dan and Barbara were naturally curious why there was so much stir over those particular pictures, but they were also wondering about their two kids' pictures.

When they finally arrived where the crew members were congregated, some of them still transfixed on a particular picture or pictures, they stopped with an unusual urge to look at what had caused so much interest, but they could not see over all the tall, large-framed males and females. Suddenly, the crew members began moving out of the way, like the parting of the Red Sea, and created a small path toward one particular section of the wall. The Jupiter family and Jose walked up to within a few feet of the wall. A nearly half-meter-tall-by-one-meter-wide picture was lit by soft white lighting. They stopped in their tracks, amazed, spellbound like never before for any work of art. It was a magnificent masterpiece—an oil-painting portrait of a family with museum-quality detail. Even more amazing was that the painting was of them standing on the moon next to their small spaceship against the backdrop of outer space. In the background, beyond the ship, was a colorful and magnificent-looking spiral galaxy, exhibiting hues of bright blue and sparkling with stars that seemed to almost be glowing. Even Jose was awed at the oil painting's extremely fine details and immense quality. It was easily one of the finest portraits she had ever seen, even in all their museums back home.

They all knew Michael had drawn the oil painting because his name, Michael Jupiter, was in the bottom right-hand corner in plain English, followed by the Earth date of 09/11/2003. Directly below his name and date in English was his name and date in a strange language that was probably the alien race's main language back home. Michael's imagination was immense, and it was amazing for him to have such a steady hand for a little boy. Jason finally looked up at Michael in his dad's arms. "That's a good picture, Michael," he said.

Michael only smiled a little.

Barbara placed a small, soft kiss against his lips. "You're quite the little artist, Michael," she said.

Michael again remained quiet, but he did notice all the ship's crew members standing around them, watching them as if glued to a television set. "It was no big thing," he finally said in plain English.

Dan and Barbara noticed Michael's casual sincerity and that the crew members were staring at them, almost hypnotic. Kyle suddenly pointed over at the painting just to the left of Michael's. "There's my picture," he said.

Kyle had clearly been trying to mimic Michael's portrait, though his was not even close to as finely detailed. Still, it was not bad for a four-year-old Earth boy and was what would be expected, especially when trying to use his new brother's picture as a guide. Kyle's name and the date were also written in the bottom right-hand corner. Dan finally looked over to his four-year-old. "Very good, Kyle," he said. "Your picture is good too."

Jose telepathically thanked all the crew members for letting them view the paintings. "Bye, everyone," she said out loud in English.

"You're welcome," most of the crew members replied in English.

As the Jupiter family followed Jose back to the center of the hallway, the crew members filed back in front of the pictures, like the Red Sea joining itself back together, and started conversations in their alien tongue. Word of Michael's museum-quality painting spread throughout the entire ship, including the fact that the Earth family currently aboard the ship were the ones in the portrait. Michael's oil painting would no doubt win first place in about every judging category.

As the Jupiter family continued down the hallway, Dan turned to Jose, quite curious. "What will become of Michael's and Kyle's paintings?"

Jose paused. "They will go back to our home world," she said, "never separated, most likely placed on permanent display at one of our main art museums for everyone to talk about and enjoy. Michael's painting is no doubt a masterpiece, and Kyle's will be on display as the first painting from an Earth human who is aware of our race, not just any human, but a young four-year-old boy who is also now Michael's brother."

The entire Jupiter family heard this with real interest, and Dan turned back to Jose again. "We look forward to visiting your home world, then," he calmly said.

Jose completely understood their willingness. "We look forward to seeing all of you," she said.

As they were about to approach the transporter elevator, Jason looked around the hallway and then up at the ceiling. Again, like his father, he did not see any incandescent lighting sources anywhere, yet the area was brightly lit. He stared up into Jose's face, filled with curiosity. "How are these hallways lit?" he asked.

Jose grinned at his question and noticed Dan and Barbara had also perked up, as they had been wondering the same thing in the back of their minds. She glanced down at Kyle, then at Michael, and finally back at Jason. "Light is an amazing substance and force of our universe," she said, "and can be generated by many different neutrino methods using gravity."

Michael, who understood every single scientific aspect of the technology, saw that his father was puzzled by her answer. "They piggyback photons onto low-level neutrinos, Daddy," he explained, "and then create a gravitational oscillatory path to force a decay, so that after the decay, all that can exist is the photons in all open areas of space."

Dan turned to Jose, flabbergasted by Michael's explanation. "That must be some amazing science," he said.

"Yes, it is," she said.

At the transporter elevator, the door again vanished, they all entered, and the door quickly reappeared behind them. Jose stared down at the wall console. "Medical lab, second floor," she said.

Like all the previous times, the door immediately vanished, and Dan, Barbara, and Jason again could not be more amazed that they were already on the second floor, near the top of the ship. They again had not felt any movement as their bodies were molecularly transported through extremely small, hollow waveguide conduits.

Barbara led them out into the hallway, but then Dan suddenly stopped, quietly staring down the new hallway. Jose knew he was uncertain about which direction to go. "The medical lab is to our right," she said.

Without hesitation, they continued down the new hallway. As it started to curve to their left, three large-framed males dressed in military attire, two with light skin and one with brown skin, came into view, walking in their direction. They were easily over seven feet tall and had calm expressions on their faces. They all slightly nodded to the Jupiter family and Jose as they passed. Dan and Barbara returned kind gestures as they walked by without a single word. Jose communicated with them telepathically, wishing the three security personnel a good day. Jose knew that the Jupiter family now had a certain level of security protection, both from security personnel and also from the ship's computers.

Jose led the Jupiter family farther down the hallway. After the hallway finally straightened out, there was a sign on the right wall just ahead in the race's alien language. There was also a symbol that was maybe an arrow, though it was shaped differently from the arrows on Earth. Dan turned to Jose, curious. "Does that sign state 'Medical lab this way'?"

"You're mostly correct," Jose said. "The symbol is an arrow, but it states 'Main medical lab.'"

Dan noticed his wife was filled with anticipation for their arrival at the medical lab, which was understandable, since they were going to get to see what advanced contraptions the lab might have and see up close the device that would be recording their brain wave patterns. Michael had continued calmness and contentment on his face. It made Barbara realize again he was still a little boy. He was filled with an immense amount of information, but inside, emotionally, he still had the need for affection.

When they arrived at the double door entryway, the doors vanished. They walked inside to see three of the chief geneticists—Phil, Neill, and James—standing next to other members of the alien race dressed in civilian attire, possibly other geneticists who reported to them. Standing next to the chief geneticists was the chief medical officer, Darryl, and at least a dozen of the ship's medical personnel, clothed in military attire. Standing in front of the entire group was Brian, who was talking to the others in their alien language.

Noticing the Jupiter family and Jose had arrived, Darryl left the group and walked up to meet them. "Welcome to my medical lab," he said in perfect English.

"Thank you," Dan replied, looking around inside the lab at devices and apparatuses he did not recognize, not from the many secret and top-secret laboratories he'd visited over the years or even from Earth's science fiction movies and series. There were dozens of flat beds off to their right, a place where crew members could lie down, either after an injury or some other condition. At the back of the beds were devices that seemed automated. A large, dark, metallic-looking half ring, about two feet long, was attached to each bed and appeared as if it might slide over the bed.

The four chief geneticists—Brian, Phil, Neill, and James—also left the other group and walked up to the Jupiter family, Jose, and Darryl. They saw Dan and Barbara staring at the medical lab beds and knew the two humans did not know the half ring was a biological-interactive ring that was able to extend across the length of the bed. They also immediately noticed how calm Michael appeared in his new father's arms. It was quite an experience for them, as it was the first time they'd seen Michael since he had been transferred from their lab inside a controlled zero-motion stasis to the small ship, where he had been secretly hidden away in a wall compartment while still in stasis. All they could do was continue to stare at him, filled with pride for how good of a job they'd done in creating his child emotional neuronal patterns, including viable associated advanced bodily interfaces to go with his fully functional, highly modified organs. They also saw and felt his level of bonding to Dan and the Jupiter family. It was even stronger than what they'd first thought it would be. Michael's calmness proved the father-son bond he had with Dan. They now knew without doubt that they would have failed miserably, even worse than first estimated, in trying to degenerate and regenerate Michael's synaptic patterns to a precognitive condition. They also sensed the Jupiter family's love toward Michael and knew why he had bonded with them so quickly, as the Jupiters' love was similar to what their race's two families living on Earth would have shown toward him, if he had bonded with them as originally planned.

Phil, who was easily over seven feet tall, was the most senior of the four chief geneticists yet walked around like a young man in his twenties. He stared down at Dan and Barbara with a kind, open face. "Hello," he said in English.

"Hello," they replied.

Darryl knew Phil was the oldest of the chief geneticists at 190 Earth years old, nearing close to half his life span for their race, but Dan and Barbara would have never guessed it. Darryl glanced briefly at his medical staff and the dozens of geneticists who had joined them to check, double-check, verify, and help to set up the computer system parameters for all the required cellular changes to Michael's cerebrum and body. His spirit was suddenly uplifted while looking back to Dan and Barbara. "Before we place Michael into his zero-motion, absolute-zero stasis," he calmly said, "we would like to record your conscious brain wave frequencies and their amplitudes so that you'll be able to use the telepathic helmets on your ship. It is a requirement that everyone in our race have their known brain wave patterns recorded."

Dan was amazed. "How long will that take?"

Darryl paused. "For each of you, it should be no more than five of your Earth minutes," he said.

Dan was again amazed the race could accurately extrapolate patterns so quickly and easily from their cerebral cores. It essentially amounted to mind reading, even more so as it was related to telepathy. That could mean the race possibly understood something about telepathy and the brain's hidden emanations, which seemed very strange. He looked briefly to his wife to see she was also amazed. "I will go first," he told her.

"Okay," Barbara replied and set Kyle down on the floor next to Jason.

Dan set Michael down next to his two brothers. Barbara and their three sons went over to a small wood table surrounded by matching dark wood armchairs with blue cushioned bottoms and backs. They sat down, and Barbara immediately picked Michael up into her lap, since he was about to be molecularly operated on in less than an hour. She began cuddling and hugging her newest little boy and savored the affection he returned to her—like a child that had been lost and found his parents.

Jose saw Barbara holding Michael like a precious little boy she'd raised her entire life and telepathically felt her motherly bond for him was strong, as if she'd borne him into the world like her two biological kids. It caused Jose a strange new level of compassion for Michael, and she looked briefly over at the exit before turning back to Barbara. "I will see everyone at tomorrow's dinner," she said.

Barbara paused from hugging Michael. "Okay, Jose," she said, "and thank you for everything you have done for us, especially your kindness."

Jose smiled a little. "You're welcome," she said and left the main medical lab. While continuing down the hallway, she knew the Jupiter family did not know how strong of a telepath she was, able to read deep into one's mind. She also wondered whether Michael would ever develop telepathic abilities as he aged. She did not sense he was yet a telepath or aware of his telepathic abilities. Even the geneticists were unsure whether he would ever develop that attribute, but their suspicions were if he did, he would be a powerful telepath.

Inside the medical lab, Dan noticed Darryl staring at a strange-looking device about five meters away with a motorcycle-type helmet in front of a chair. It seemed there might be a video projection system, similar to virtual reality glasses, yet this helmet would also cover one's ears, nose, and mouth. "Okay, what do you want me to do?" Dan asked.

"Follow me," Darryl replied, "and place that helmet on your head. It is extremely simple, and no pain is involved."

Without hesitation, Dan followed Darryl to the machine. The

chair appeared to have sensors on it, at least a few dozen, along the seat bottom and the back of the chair. Below the seat, there appeared to be sensors that would rest against his calves. Strangely, there were also sensors on the floor, where his shoes would be. The chair was attached to the brain wave recording machine, and a few feet above the chair, also attached to the machine, was a half-dome contraption at least three feet in diameter. Dan quickly sat down and found the chair extremely comfortable, as though he were sitting on air, and looked up into the large half dome directly above him to find it hollow. He turned to Darryl, intrigued. "Okay, so how does this contraption actually work?"

Darryl noticed Dan's relaxed, fascinated attitude. "Once you put on the helmet," he said, "you will feel it tighten against your head for a completely lightproof, soundproof environment. The helmet will then project a series of rainbow colors through a variety of different spectrums, followed by base mixtures. A visual set of single-dimensional geometric figures will appear in both color and black and white, against different backgrounds of perception and predetermined frequencies, allowing auditory and visual cortex baselines. During all these tests, you will also notice changes in your sense of smell, as well as your taste buds, as if something were placed inside your mouth, completing the olfactory and gustatory cortex baselines. The last sense of touch, of course, is measured by the helmet's pressure against your head and the biometric sensor transceivers up against your body in the seat, along your legs, and at your feet, completing the full array of external inputs into your cortex."

Dan was amazed at this explanation and noticed the helmet had no wires. It looked similar to a motorcycle helmet with a face mask but was much thinner, and the face mask was not transparent. Dan figured the helmet had to be interfaced remotely using wireless transmission technology, but he was still curious about the hollow half dome directly above him. "What is the purpose of the half dome?" he asked.

Darryl paused. "It is a large collector," he said, "serving a similar function as used in your MRI machines on Earth but on a much-higher level for capturing interlaced sight, sound, smell, taste, and touch thought patterns, including measuring the realized and unrealized mental capacities of the test subject, including telepathic strengths."

Dan was thoroughly amazed again and picked up the helmet to find it was extremely light, in fact almost weightless. He lifted it above his head and slowly slid it down until it covered his eyes, nose, and mouth, finally resting against the top of his head. Strangely, the helmet tightened against his scalp, forehead, ears, and eye sockets. He was now in complete darkness, and the only sound he could hear was a slight ringing in his ears. "Okay, I'm ready," Dan announced, yet he could not hear his own words being spoken, only the vibrations from his vocal cords to his inner ears.

Darryl turned on the cerebral cortex recording machine, activating the helmet, and the large half dome dropped down until it completely encased the helmet. He glanced briefly over at Barbara and her children to see the four geneticist chiefs had sat down at the table directly across from them. They would explain in more detail what they were about to do to Michael and how safe it really was—at least for their race. Darryl had to assume that by now Michael, with his level of intellect, knew everything about the molecular changes they were about to make on him.

At the brain wave recording device, as Dan sat quietly, he suddenly noticed the ringing in his ears go away, as though nulled out by noise-canceling headphones. He was now in a 100 percent soundproof and lightproof environment and felt a sudden mental clarity of mind. Before his eyes, red, blue, and green lights flashed, possibly a primer or start of the test, as Darryl had alluded, and then there were intermittent sounds, like the keys on a piano rising in pitch, followed by an unusual sweet taste in his mouth, then a bitter taste, a smell as though he was at a barbeque, and then a scent that made his eyes water. The tears instantly stopped, and the screen turned light gray, followed by a black circle at its very center. He quickly felt vibrations across his scalp, neck, shoulders, back, buttocks, legs, and feet, as though in a full-body vibrating suit. The vibrations stopped, and a heavy white line appeared around the circumference of the black circle. The circle stretched up and down until turning into an ellipse and continued to stretch until it was a single vertical white line. Then it disappeared. A few seconds later, a black square with white borders appeared in the middle of the screen, once again against a light-gray background. It suddenly rotated ninety degrees, becoming a diamond. The diamond then stretched up and down until it, too, turned into a vertical white line. It also disappeared, leaving only the solid light-gray background. The gray background slowly faded away into total darkness, no light. It was completely silent, not even the sound of ringing in his ears.

Dan still felt extremely mentally alert and was quietly intrigued about what might appear next, when the light-gray background reappeared, followed by a black right triangle with white borders. The triangle pointed toward the right and slowly stretched horizontally into a scalene triangle and then a horizontal white line. The white line vanished, again leaving only the light-gray background. Dan waited with anticipation for what strange figure might appear next. Suddenly, a black equilateral triangle with white borders appeared, vertically positioned so that it was standing perfectly balanced on one of its corners. Dan knew the triangle was a symbol used frequently in mathematics on Earth, such as in electromagnetic wave characteristics, Schrödinger's equations, vector differential calculus, and other science fields.

A few seconds later, the upper line of the triangle curved upward to form a shape similar to a snow cone and continued to stretch upward along with the rest of the triangle's sides until it formed another vertical white line. The line vanished, and there was again only total darkness, no sound, not even any ringing in his ears. His senses of smell and taste felt different, as though they had possibly been changing the entire time and he'd not realized it.

He was again quiet, wondering, contemplating, curious whether the test was over, when there was a series of intermixed sounds, another light-gray screen, followed by a piano scale rising in pitch, then a white-bordered black pentagon. He inhaled and exhaled at this new figure and watched a solid white circle appear inside the pentagon, forming a circumscribed polygon.

Dan was even more intrigued, especially when the circle began intermittently changing into a wide range of rainbow colors. The circle turned black, then white, followed by a tessellation of five triangles inside the pentagon. Then, without warning, the borders of the pentagon changed to blue, then red, then green, followed by yellow, then purple. There was a series of intermittent sounds alternating between his ears, ranging between 50 and 15,000 Hz, but then, he could not be certain of the upper frequencies. The pentagon, circle, and tessellation of triangles vanished. The screen was now black as coal, no sound, no ringing in his ears, no inkling of light whatsoever. The sudden pause and blank screen gave him a short time to think about what he had just experienced. Pentagons were unique and extremely important in geometric designs, especially for elemental configurations and their stellations. He further wondered whether what he had just seen had some hidden meaning, whether there were strange underlying depths of perception about the pentagon, circle, and tessellation directly related to the test subject's level of intellect, including their number of active neurons perceiving what was showing on the screen.

While he continued to ponder the previous pentagonal figure configurations, a light-gray screen again appeared, followed by a hexagon. Like its pentagon predecessor, it was black with white borders. Dan was curious about what might happen next. A solid white square quickly appeared inside the hexagon and began randomly changing colors along with intermittent sounds at varying frequencies. The hexagon's six connecting lines next changed colors, the intermittent sounds continuing. Then all sound ceased, and the square disappeared before his eyes, leaving only the original white-bordered hexagon. The moment of silence was intriguing for Dan. Then a tessellation of six white-bordered equilateral triangles suddenly appeared inside the hexagon, they, too, changing colors before reverting back to solid white-bordered black triangles.

A small black hexagon with white borders formed in the center of the tessellation, and it began growing until turning into a six-pointed star. The star continued to grow until forming a circle, and it meshed in with the outer hexagon. Again there was only one hexagon.

Dan took a deep, short breath. He was wondering what underlying depth of perception was now being tested with the hexagonal figures when suddenly the screen turned black, the helmet released itself from around his head, and the hollow half dome quickly returned to its original position.

Darryl said, "Well, that's it. Your brain wave recording in relation to your level of intellect, your thoughts, and any hidden powers of telepathy was successful."

Dan carefully lifted the helmet off his head, amazed by what he'd just heard, and noticed Darryl standing nearby with a relaxed expression. "That is amazing," Dan said.

Darryl knew Dan did not realize some of the geometric figures had also quickly moved farther away and then closer to his visual perception, measuring not only the barrier between his conscious and subconscious states of mind but also his daydream states as well. This information would allow a full understanding of his mind and the ability to differentiate REM dream states and daydream states, including all his subconscious abilities and attributes. The slew of geometric figures, their patterns, and their movements allowed the cerebral core memory extractor (CCME) to measure the number of active neurons and neuronal path densities, essentially registering the overall intelligence or intelligence capability of the test subject.

"Yes, it is amazing," Darryl said. "Our computers will now be able to extrapolate all other geometric matrices and figures, including sound, taste, and smell interfaces, in direct relationship to all your brain wave activity. It will additionally serve as a road map for all synaptic activity of your subconscious, including cerebral activity during daydream states."

Dan now knew for sure that the advanced race could probably record dreams, if they so desired. He finally stood up and returned to where Barbara still sat at the table with the boys, just across from the chief geneticists. "Your turn," he said.

"How was it?" she asked.

"Not too bad," Dan said. "You'll see a various array of geometric figures, as well as hear intermittent sounds and have your senses of smell, taste, and touch put to the test."

Barbara stood up with unusual anticipation and handed Michael to Dan, who took him without hesitation, as he would soon be undergoing surgery for neuronal-synaptic changes and other molecular changes.

Confidently, Barbara walked over to where Darryl stood waiting. "Go ahead and have a seat," he said, "and place the helmet on your head. There is no pain involved."

"Okay," she replied and then sat down to find the chair was very soft. She noticed the hollow half dome directly above her. During Dan's test, it had dropped down to completely encase the helmet, a very unusual aspect, most likely to help capture thought patterns. She grabbed the helmet and slowly slid it down over her head, eyes, nose, and mouth. Suddenly, the helmet tightened around her eye sockets and ears. She now sat in a completely lightproof and soundproof environment with only slight ringing in her ears. "I'm ready," she said and realized she could not hear herself speaking. The ringing in her ears had also ceased.

Darryl turned on the CCME, and the test began the same as her husband's, first showing red, blue, and then green flashing lights.

Dan noticed his wife's test had started and now realized that the half dome dropped down to completely encase the helmet, a very interesting aspect of the machine, especially after what Darryl had told him about it using a highly advanced aspect of the MRI technology currently used on Earth. Dan sat down next to Jason and Kyle and stared over at the four chief geneticists, curious about the zero-motion, absolute-zero stasis previously mentioned, especially since Michael would soon be entering that stasis. He made eye contact with Phil. "What does 'zero motion, absolute zero' actually mean?"

Since Dan and his family were now considered citizens of the alien race, holding dual citizenship, Phil was allowed to reveal some of his race's secrets. He knew the elementary answer and glanced briefly at Michael, who definitely knew the answer, and then back to Dan. "As we told your wife," he said, "zero motion is the zero-motion state of the electron at its molecular ground state. In other words, we create a negative electron movement of the matter in reference while in an absolute-zero temperature environment, thereby causing a true zero-entropy electron state. This zero-electron force can only be applied while in the absolute-zero temperature state, or the residual energy of the matter would end up destroying itself at its normal operating temperature, especially after being returned to the normal room-temperature environment of the test subject's surroundings."

According to Dan's understanding of science, the advanced beings were essentially stopping all time references for the test subject in the stasis field, and anything inside the field should no longer exist, no longer age, because the field would be essentially nullifying the existence of the matter itself, truly placing it into a state of suspended animation. "That is amazing," he said. "Sometime I would like to learn more about how that is actually accomplished."

Phil glanced briefly to the other chiefs and then back to Dan. "Oh, I am sure you'll get the chance," he replied with assurance in his voice, "but then, that it is something you will never be able to reveal to the Earth race."

Dan had to agree. A little disappointment filled his face, but he knew Phil was right, as the advanced understanding would probably be abused by rogue Earth scientists. He glanced over at his wife to see she was still having her brain wave patterns recorded and turned back to Phil again, still curious how they were able to record their brain wave patterns so easily, especially in relation to telepathy. "How advanced are your computers?" he asked.

Phil paused and then replied, "In relation to Earth's most powerful computers, at least those in the public domain, extremely advanced by over twentyfold. Our processors use a three-state electron charge system in relation to the individual protons and neutrons and then force the neutrons into controlled decay loops at the speed of light. The particles that the electrons force energy across, as your race has begun to understand some of them, are called quarks in the neutron-decay cycle." Phil paused to see Dan sitting starry-eyed and added, "Of course, this neutron decay causes a beta decay of the electron's antiparticle, known to your race as the positron, and these are then sent into controlled loops that will directly intersect the neutron-decay loops. If you can visualize and come to understand the quantum-energy-barrier side of the science, as is taught by our race at an equivalent Earth high school level, you will see where there is an immense amount of information that is possible in one single electron-proton-neutron-decay loop across the quarks and the positronic charges. Multiply each loop by billions, even trillions, and you can see why our computers are so powerful. You can actually look at those loops as matter and antimatter rings of information."

Dan raised his eyebrows, overwhelmed but also completely amazed. "That is truly interesting," he said. "Do your processors interface to the memory in the same nuclear-molecular manner?"

Phil looked briefly to Brian, Neill, and James and then back to Dan. "Yes, they do," he said, "but the decay loops and the memory quantum barriers use a different element that is unknown to the human race. Their elemental configurations actually react to the electron point charges of the processor element to cause multinode, dual-path loops, allowing molecular energy charges in both directions."

Dan was again amazed, feeling like a little kid, as Earth had been trying to build molecular computers for years, even in a few of the secret labs at Los Alamos, but they were finding it extremely complex and hard to contain or control the ion traps. Decay loops, using the method described, was something they'd never considered, because quarks and positrons were considered uncontrollable. Based on what Phil had just told him, the advanced race might also understand the grand unification theory, as proposed on Earth, and Dan was now extremely curious about that exact thing. "Does your race understand what we call the grand unification theory on Earth?"

Phil paused. "In terms of what your race believes the unification theory to be, yes," he said, "but for the true grand unification law of our universe, no, because even though we understand the three main forces of our universe—gravity, light, and time—and the associations that all nuclear and magnetic energies must conform to, there is still a force associated with gravity and time that we are missing. This we know to be a fact; otherwise, our race would have already figured out wormhole technologies and how to successfully create a wormhole across vast expanses of space, even between galaxies, using the energy of a sun or other stars."

Dan was amazed by this answer and also by the fact that he was now friends with this race that was extremely advanced in their understanding of genetics, molecular science, particle physics, and who knew how many other fields of science. Of course, one really could not have a broad knowledge in one without having advancements in the others. He glanced over to his wife again to see she was pulling the helmet off. She would now be able to fly their ship using the telepathic helmets, just like him. She spoke briefly with Darryl, then stood up and headed in their direction.

Arriving at their table, she stared down at Jason with a casual grin. "Your turn, Jason," she calmly said while picking Kyle up in her arms.

"There is no pain at all, nothing like when we placed the armbands on our forearms for the first time."

Jason grinned a little at his mom's comment, stood up, and bravely walked over to where Darryl patiently stood. He stopped in front of the brain wave recording machine and looked up with a sincere face.

"Take a seat and place the helmet on your head," Darryl said. "There is no pain. Just watch the visual screen."

Jason then sat down.

Dan and Barbara watched their oldest son place the helmet on his head and realized he would also have the capability to fly their spaceship with only his thoughts, if they were to allow it. They both stared back at the chief geneticists, who seemed to have calm, relaxed spirits, and it gave them contented feelings. They now wondered about the immediate families of the chief geneticists sitting across from them, since they were in a sense partly Michael's fathers, with their cellular structure manipulations of his zygote and enzyme modifications during growth, helping him to become the little boy he was today. Dan stared across the table at Phil, Neill, Brian, and James and asked, "How many kids do you all have?"

Phil returned eye contact. "I have four children, seven grandchildren, twelve great-grandchildren, and twenty-two great-great-grandchildren. One of my grandsons is an officer aboard this ship. As far as my four children, they are teachers back on our home world."

Dan and Barbara realized that if Phil's grandson was an officer on this ship, Phil probably knew Captain Donaldson personally. In reality, all the chief geneticists probably knew the captain of their race's military flagship. Dan and Barbara then stared over at Brian.

Brian paused for a short moment and answered, "I have three children, five grandchildren, eight great-grandchildren, and sixteen great-great-grandchildren. My three children are in the medical field and spend most of their time aboard research vessels exploring and mapping our universe."

Dan and Barbara were extremely interested to hear this and looked to Neill, who said, "I have four children, nine grandchildren, seventeen great-grandchildren, and thirty-two great-great-grandchildren. Most of my children are in the field of medical research. Of my four children, two are back on our home world, and the other two live on a planet that our race populated a few centuries ago, a viable planet that is 2,888 light-years from our home world. It was a virgin planet when we discovered it."

Dan and Barbara were again interested by this information and next looked to James, who appeared to be the youngest of the four. He looked to be in his early forties but was probably much older, considering that the other chiefs looked like they could have been in their sixties but must be well over a hundred years old (or double that, if taking Earth years into account) to have great-great-grandchildren.

James looked directly at Dan and Barbara. "I have three children, six grandchildren, twelve great-grandchildren, and six great-great-grandchildren. Two of my kids are officers aboard other starships, and my other child is in the medical research field back home."

Barbara glanced briefly to Dan, extremely interested to hear about the number of children, grandchildren, and other descendants for each chief geneticist, including some of their occupations. It appeared most of their kids were in the medical field and following in their fathers' footsteps. She stared back across the table. "Are your cultures similar to Earth's?"

"Yes, they are," Phil said. "Surprisingly, our cultures are almost identical. If you were to compare your Earth's twenty-first century to our race as it was over 2,800 years ago, it is almost as if we both started from a similar pattern in the early stages of the pre–Bronze Age. The human race has a long path ahead. You are currently in the most critical stages of your science and cultural evolution, revolution, or however you want to view it, even more so when you have so many diverse cultures and moralities for what is considered right or wrong, seemingly progressing in so many different directions."

Dan and Barbara quietly thought about his statement. "What do you mean?" Dan asked.

Phil paused. "Diverse cultures and moralities that separate too far apart from the norm will never bring about world peace, only increased internal conflicts. Luckily, many thousands of your years ago, our race only had around a dozen different cultures, so bringing them together for one common goal and purpose, regardless of religious beliefs, was not as much of a hardship. That will not be the case for the human race, as great hardships are coming between those cultures and moralities, and if not endured, self-destruction could follow."

Dan and Barbara were a little surprised to hear this but still showed real interest. Barbara glanced over to Jason and then back to Phil. "What is the current population of your home planet?"

Phil noticed Michael listening intently. "Our home planet currently has a population of nearly twenty-five billion," he said.

Dan and Barbara wore amazed faces, and Dan nodded a little. "Oh really?" he said. "How big is your planet?"

Phil paused. "Our planet is five and a half times larger than your Earth and has a sixty-two percent water surface with its lakes and oceans."

Dan and Barbara now knew the advanced race's home world had to have a massive amount of land mass. Additionally, their travels throughout many different parts of the universe, from the Milky Way to who knew how many other galaxies, had to be immense. Dan felt extremely relaxed all of a sudden and asked, "How many other planets does your race occupy or stake claim for that are viable for life?"

Phil noticed the continued interest on their faces and even on the faces of Michael and Kyle. "Our race currently has societies on twenty-four different planets in sixteen different galaxies. Planets for sustaining carbon-based life, such as ourselves—planets with ideal temperature ranges and fresh drinking water—are not as plentiful as you would first think, especially in relation to the total number of stars and planets inside each galaxy."

Dan and Barbara could understand how the advanced race had found those planets, especially since their ships were capable of traveling thousands of times the speed of light in directional velocity to even millions times the speed of light in straight-line bursts, which they also referred to as time-warp space jumps. Dan and Barbara glanced over to Jason to see he was pulling the helmet off his head. He stood up and walked with Darryl in their direction. Arriving at their table, Darryl looked down at Kyle in Barbara's lap and then over to Dan. "We can record your son Kyle's brain wave patterns another time," he said. "It's not like he'll be guiding any spaceships by himself for a few years."

Dan and Barbara, the chief geneticists, and Jason laughed a little, while Michael only grinned. Kyle heard his name and gave a small, innocent grin of curiosity about what the strange man was referring to.

Darryl felt extremely relaxed and stared down at Dan and Barbara again. Their family seemed like a perfect atmosphere for Michael, them rearing him while he grew into an adult. "You can also record Kyle's brain wave patterns in the lab of the spaceship you'll be receiving," he said, "as there is also a brain wave recording machine in its lab, nearly identical to the one on this ship. For Michael's brain wave patterns, as I alluded to earlier, we'll record them before he is placed into the zero-motion, absolute-zero stasis, not that our computers will be able to accurately extrapolate his signatures correctly at this time, but we would still like to have them in our databases for a baseline measurement and future analysis."

Dan nodded a little. "Okay," he said and sighed while looking down, making direct eye contact with his new son. "You'll be okay, right, Michael?"

"Yes, Daddy," he replied.

Dan lifted him up, hugged him, and placed a small kiss against his cheek. "Okay then, we'll see you first thing in the morning."

Barbara noticed Michael enjoying the hug from his father, leaned over, and placed a soft kiss against his lips, followed by a pat on his cheek. "We'll see you in the morning, honey," she said.

"Okay, Mommy," Michael said with a small, trusting smile, feeling as if he'd known his new parents his entire life. In reality, he *had* known them his entire life, at least since becoming cognitively aware of his existence on Monday night in the presence of Jason.

Darryl, Phil, Neill, Brian, and James also noticed how caring Dan and Barbara were toward Michael, as if he'd always been one of their own. They now knew without doubt that Michael would grow up as planned, without stress and surrounded by an immense amount of love. This was something he had to have if he was to advance his understanding of one of the universe's greatest secrets of space-time perception, a perception only dreamed about that could lead to unbelievable space-travel techniques, called *wormhole technology.*

Phil stared over at the Jupiter family. He knew about when the adjustments and modifications to Michael would be complete. "Return at eight thirty tomorrow morning your Earth time, and Michael should be waiting for you as your official new humanoid advanced-being Earth boy."

Barbara smiled a little, especially at "*Earth* boy." "Thank you," she said. "We'll definitely be here."

Dan stood up, and Michael suddenly touched two buttons on his armband. It flexed outward, releasing itself from around his little forearm. He handed the armband to his dad, who passed it to his mom.

Michael had three small red holes on his forearm that looked like mosquito bites, and it made Barbara realize again how much he was like a human. Yet in reality, he was a new-breed alien boy—the first of a new race. Regardless, it did not matter. He was now one of her sons, and she would love him as though she had borne him into the world.

Dan finally handed Michael to Phil, who gladly took him without hesitation, as he had never had the chance to physically hold Michael before. Neither had any of the other geneticists. They'd only watched him slowly grow in the lab from a single-cell zygote to the boy he was today, all while inside a completely sterile and controlled environment spanning nearly eighty Earth years.

Kyle stared over at Michael in the strange man's arms and thought Michael was staying in the medical lab just for some tests. "Bye, Michael," he softly said.

"Bye, Kyle," Michael replied.

Jason saw Michael in Phil's arms and knew in the morning he would officially be his little brother. He would also more closely match Jason's own body temperature and metabolism, but Jason knew he would always have differences that made him unique, such as the additional organ called an oxygen synthesizer, modified organs to accommodate that new organ, and a special blood type. "Bye, Michael," he said. "See you in the morning."

Michael glanced down at Jason and knew he would always be his closest, best friend and now his older brother. "See you in the morning, Jason," he said.

Dan, Barbara, and Jason noticed Michael's continued calmness, in spite of him knowing he would be in a zero-motion, absolute-zero stasis field before long. They finally turned toward the exit, having small feelings of loss, yet those feelings would quickly go away when they picked Michael up in the morning. The door suddenly vanished in front of them. They continued out into the hallway but had to glance back inside one last time. Michael was now receiving lots of attention from Brian, Neill, Darryl, James, and, in fact, the entire medical staff and other geneticists. The entrance door reappeared in front of them.

Barbara set Kyle down on the floor, and the four Jupiters continued back toward the transporter elevator that would return them to their guest quarters. As the hallway curved toward the right, four crew members, all females and taller than Dan, were walking in their direction. One was pregnant, carrying a child in her womb in the exact same manner as a human, reminding them just how similar their two races were biophysically. They did not know how long the advanced race carried their children, but they could find out from their computers. As they were about to meet the crew members, Dan and Barbara additionally took notice of how extremely pretty they were. One had curly blonde hair, and the one who was pregnant had dark hair and brown skin. "Hello," the pregnant female said in English.

Dan and Barbara felt suddenly relaxed, though Dan still perked up at the sight of the four tall, gorgeous females. "Hello," Barbara said with a small grin as they walked by. She noticed Dan's reaction but did not say anything, as the females were very pretty and would cause most any male on Earth to take a second look. In fact, all the males and females they'd met so far were extremely good-looking, even Captain Donaldson, his officers, and Jose. It was a confirmation in Barbara's mind that the race they were now friends with was an extremely intelligent, tall, and beautiful race of beings.

When the Jupiter family arrived in front of the transporter elevator, it seemed a little more exciting, as they were aboard the mother ship without any escort for the first time. The entrance door vanished, and they all continued inside, turned around, and watched the door reappear behind them. They stood in silence before Dan stared down at the simple-looking wall console. "Level eighteen, quadrant twenty," he said confidently.

As soon as he finished his last spoken word, the entry door again vanished. They exited into the hallway and turned right. Dan and Barbara now wondered which door led to their guest quarters, since there were many different closed doors in the hallway, all of them silhouetted against an outline. They'd never bothered counting the number of entryways in relation to the distance from the transporter elevator. They knew their quarters were number eighteen, but the signs next to each door were still displayed in the alien language, and Michael was not with them to read the signs.

Suddenly, all the markings changed to English. A door to their left was marked twenty-one, so Dan figured their quarters might be to the right, assuming odd entry doors were on the left and even entry doors were on the right. If so, the second door ahead to their right should lead to their guest quarters. Staring over at his wife, he knew she also must have noticed the signs change and seen that the numbering system was somewhat similar to Earth societies'. "Almost there," he said. "You know, it's almost as if the ship's computers read our minds."

"Possibly," Barbara said, amazed at the prospect. "They did just record our brain wave patterns. This race is awfully advanced, huh?"

"Yes, they are," Dan agreed, noticing they'd just walked by room twenty. "For a race that has been around maybe five, ten thousand years or so, they definitely seem quite advanced beyond their years."

"True," she said and noticed Jason was kind of quiet.

Dan saw their room up ahead and looked over again to his wife. "This has been some evening, huh?"

"Yes, it has," she said.

They stood outside their guest quarters, and the entry door vanished. Kyle and Jason entered first, followed by Dan and Barbara. The boys formed a beeline straight over to one of the tables in the room—the same table where Michael had pulled up a holographic image earlier. The two boys sat down, and Jason touched a series of buttons on the flat console. A three-dimensional holographic image immediately appeared above the table.

To Dan and Barbara, it looked like a game, possibly something Michael had shown the boys earlier, and they continued over to the couch. After sitting down, they relaxed back and stared over at the spherical holographic image, which appeared to reposition itself in front of Jason. Jason reached up inside the image and then removed his hand. The image relocated itself in front of Kyle. Kyle stared up at the sphere, and Jason pointed at it, explaining something to his little brother. Kyle then reached up inside and removed his hand. The image again changed, and very small, round objects inside the sphere started to flash different colors.

Dan and Barbara continued to watch the colors of the dots inside the spherical image change, all while the sphere moved back and forth in front of their kids. Michael must have taught Jason not only how to use the console but also how to use some of the advanced holographic imagery. Dan and Barbara both gazed over at the far wall, where outer space was visible outside the windows, suggesting that their quarters were close to the spaceship's outer hull. Since the chief engineer would be visiting them later, they both relaxed all the way back on the couch, and Dan grabbed his wife's hand. "I can't wait to see Michael in the morning," he said.

"And neither can I," she said and placed Michael's armband on a nearby table.

Dan and Barbara continued to watch their two boys play the unusual holographic imagery game. They again thought about Michael, their new son, a bioengineered alien boy given to them by the advanced race. They thought about what it would be like having him in their lives. At the same time, they knew they would have to keep his true origin a deep secret. The spaceship they were receiving from the race that had cloaking countermeasures would help in that regard, but they would still have to contend with the supersecretive Majestic 12 group and other top-secret and above-top-secret governmental agencies on Earth whose mission was to oversee extraterrestrial events and prevent alien technology from coming into the hands of the general public. Maintaining their family's secret association to the advanced race would not be an entirely simple task. Barbara laid her head against Dan's shoulder, wondering again about Michael in the medical lab—their third little boy.

18

## THE VISIT FROM THE CHIEF ENGINEER

Barbara was still daydreaming with her head against Dan's shoulder when suddenly there was a light tone inside their room. "Dan Jupiter," they both heard in English, "this is chief engineer Doug Clarke. Are you two ready to hear a little about your spaceship?"

Barbara lifted her head, and Dan looked into her surprised face. "Yes, we are," he replied, to no one in particular, because he did not know from where the voice had originated.

"Okay," they both heard again. "I will be there in about five of your minutes."

Dan noticed his wife still had a strange look. "Okay," he said, again to no one in particular. "We'll be waiting."

It was again all quiet. The voice Dan had heard was strange, as though an echo, and he now wondered whether it had been telepathic communication. According to his watch, it was 8:30 p.m., and they both now highly anticipated getting to meet the ship's chief engineer. "This should be interesting," Dan said. "I bet he is really smart."

"Probably true," Barbara agreed.

Dan leaned to the table in front of them and touched the display a few times, pulling up a menu with an assortment of drinks, displayed in English. Again, the race seemed to be one step ahead of them, as there were a variety of teas, some he did not recognize, as well as vitamin-flavored drinks. He turned to his wife with a relaxed grin. "Want something to drink?"

"Sure, orange juice would be fine," she said.

Dan selected orange juice for his wife and was curious whether the juice was from natural oranges or organically reproduced from their molecules. He then selected one of the advanced race's warm teas that he did not recognize. Suddenly, two drinks appeared on the table, the orange juice inside a clear glass and the tea inside a cream-colored coffee cup.

Barbara picked up her glass and found it was ice-cold, though there was no solid ice in the liquid. She then took a sip and raised her eyebrows, as the juice had her taste buds tingling. "This orange juice is excellent!" she said.

Dan picked up his tea, which was fairly warm, and took a small, tentative swig, savoring its mild, unusual, sweet taste. "This tea has an interesting flavor," he said, "and is possibly the best-tasting warm tea I've ever had." He then held it up in his wife's direction. "Want to try a sip?"

"Sure," she said and took a gentle sip, also savoring the reaction it triggered in her taste buds. "Yes, that is delicious," she said. "Do you think they grow natural tea plants or biologically alter their molecules?"

"Good question," Dan said. "Maybe the chief engineer can tell us?"

"True," she said and took another sip before handing the cup back to Dan.

There was another soft tone inside their room, and this time Dan saw a light-green light flashing above the entry door. The light appeared to be built into the wall, yet there was no outline to designate it as being an incandescent light. It seemed almost like a mirage in free space. The tone and light most likely indicated the chief engineer had arrived. "Please come in," Dan called out.

The door vanished, and in walked a large-framed male who was easily seven and a half feet tall and weighed in excess of 350 pounds. He was also good-looking, just like the rest of the males. His skin was a little darker than the others', as if tanned, but it could have been his natural skin color. "Hello, my name is Doug Clarke," he said in plain English. "I'm the chief engineer."

"Hello," Dan and Barbara replied, still surprised by his enormous size. They both stood up to greet him. Sure enough, he was as tall and large as he'd appeared. He was carrying an open accordion folder with what appeared to be three manuals or softbound books.

Doug looked briefly over at Jason and Kyle, who were staring at a spherical holographic image with white, blue, and green dots, all connected by faint white lines, which eventually connected back to the very center dot, like a nucleus. He knew they were playing a multiplayer game called Capsalon Sphere Challenge, where the object of the game was to capture as many of the other player's pieces (dots) as possible in a specific three-dimensional order. The game was somewhat similar to the Earth board game Othello but was a highly advanced, three-dimensional version. Their holographic game had also existed over three thousand Earth years before Othello had existed on Earth. Doug finally turned back to Dan and Barbara, who now stood in front of him.

Dan also glanced briefly over at his sons and then back at Doug. "Please have a seat," he said.

Doug recognized Dan's kindness. "Thank you," he said and followed them to the couch, sitting down in a chair directly across from them.

The chief engineer noticed Dan and Barbara were sitting forward a little with anticipatory interest, and he read Dan's mind. He touched the flat display on the table in front of him, and a light-blue cup, filled with a dark liquid, suddenly appeared on the table. He laid the folder down, picked up the drink, and slowly placed it against his lips.

Dan and Barbara knew Doug's drink was hot, as heat vapors were rising from the cup. It also had a really nice, attention-grabbing aroma. "Is that coffee?" Dan asked.

The chief engineer set the cup down. "Yes, it is," he said, "a special blend that I enjoy drinking whenever I meet new friends."

Dan felt good inside at his comment and was even more curious about the coffee. "Oh, really?" he said. "What kind of blend?"

Doug noticed their continued interest. "It is a special herbal blend," he said, "that has both medicinal properties and vitamin nutrients."

Dan and Barbara perked up. "Amazing," Dan said. "Is it from a genetically altered plant or a natural plant?"

Doug smiled a little. "Genetically altered, and it's actually the most popular coffee back on our home world."

Dan was determined to give it a try. "I think we'll have a cup too," he said, "and its name?"

Doug thought about how to pronounce the special-blend coffee in the English tongue, according to its molecular properties and place of origin. "It is called herbal beta-glucose Travanian coffee," he finally said. "Travanian is the city on our home world where the coffee plant is mostly grown. It is also where the natural plant originated many thousands of years ago before we genetically altered it into the plant it is today."

Dan and Barbara were genuinely interested to hear more intricate details about the race's past history, and Dan exhibited a fascinated face. "We look forward to trying it, then," he said.

The chief engineer touched the display again, and two cups appeared on the table in front of Dan and Barbara. Dan picked up both cups, handed one to his wife, and stared back across the table. "Thank you," he said.

"No problem at all," Doug said.

Dan slowly sipped on his coffee and watched his wife do the same. "Yes, this is very good," he said.

Doug sipped again on his coffee and set the cup down on the table. "Well, are you two ready to learn a little about your ship?"

"Yes, and with great interest," Dan quickly said.

"Me too," Barbara said.

"Good," Doug said. "Inside the folder is what you would call flight manuals, which have been translated into English. There are paper copies because of your attachment to paper information, but your ship's computer also has a full, viewable copy."

Dan slowly reached forward with an understandable small grin. He picked up the accordion folder, removed two manuals, and handed one to his wife. He then leaned back on the couch. The manual title was "Spaceship 6XA4258: Transitional Time-Warp-Field Propulsion and Its Nuclear-Magnetic Interfaces." He opened the manual and was surprised at the table of contents.

Doug saw this. "The basic propulsion mechanism of your ship is, of course, gravity," he said, "using the $115^{th}$ element of our universe. This element will eventually be known and verified with one hundred percent confidence by your race, provided they are able to figure out its stable isotopes."

Dan and Barbara suddenly laughed a little.

Doug grinned and continued, "Our spaceships also use a unique energy source that propagates and activates the gravity element in an unusual manner by wrapping the binding energy back upon itself, very much similar to the way our molecular computers use controlled neutron-decay paths for information storage and exchange. This wrapping of the binding energy allows our powerful magnetic-flux energy sources to last much longer than conventional radioactive nuclear energy decay or any magnetic energy from the normal planes of space. This also leads to higher-energy output yields, magnitudes beyond what nuclear-based energy can provide. We actually consider radioactive nuclear-based energies a primitive source of energy, and without doubt, they are much more dangerous during their burn cycles whenever exceeding the speed of light."

Doug paused to see Dan and Barbara had amazed looks on their faces. He calmly added, "You can also read about what I've just mentioned in your manual. Anyway, your ship has a maximum gravity-propulsion velocity, in normal space-time, of nearly three-fifths the speed of light. This velocity is only attainable because of our unique energy source. With nuclear-based energies, at even these speeds, against the source drain of the gravity element, the nuclear energy would quickly deplete, due to the isotopic half-life of the gravity element speeding the nuclear-based element used for the energy source past its molecular limits. The nuclear-based element would get extremely hot and not only melt its spherical encasement but also release an immense amount of radioactive poisoning, essentially burning up the ship. We know this from past experience thousands of years ago, and it cost the lives of the scientists who first tried it. Those scientists—or astronauts, you might call them—are well known in our race's history, and a large permanent memorial recognizes them to this day." Doug paused again.

Dan and Barbara were again extremely interested to hear more detailed history and were very much aware the ship's chief engineer was extremely knowledgeable in particle physics, gravity-propulsion manipulation, and no telling what other fields of science, just as they'd suspected would be the case, but at a much-higher level of understanding.

The chief engineer noticed Dan and Barbara were quiet, waiting to hear more and said, "Your ship also has transitional time-warp-field propulsion, which is just what the name implies: a quantum gravity time warp in transition through the domain of space and time, not a fixed time-warp-field jump that uses a tunneling effect. Neither of these propulsion techniques is actual time travel, at least not as proposed by some of your race's physicists, scientists, and science fiction writers. This is because our race also learned over a thousand years ago that it is impossible to go directly into your own biological past or future within a present plane of dimensional existence."

"Why is that?" Dan asked.

Doug paused with a small grin. "To explain that, Dan, would take the rest of the evening. Let's just say that the construction of our universe is infallible and has immense internal compression to maintain its state of space-time in a field of light-speed awareness. To time-travel into your direct biological future or past would be like trying to move a two-hundred-ton boulder with a tiny plastic spoon, so that the tiny spoon can then relocate and occupy the location of the boulder."

Dan and Barbara were now rather quiet, which was understandable after what Doug had just told them, both from a philosophic and scientific perspective. Doug continued, "Our ships with propulsion using time-warp-field jumps make a quantum gravity jump through space to a new position that could not have been reached in normal time for millions or even billions of years at the speed of light. The difference between a time-warp-field jump and transitional time-warp-field propulsion is that a time-warp-field jump can only create a tunnel in space, fixed, you could say, between two mathematically calculated points in celestial space. Even though it is many thousands of times faster than transitional propulsion, it also depletes the magnetic-flux energy system at a faster rate, leading to a possible dangerous situation of a powerless ship, unless a planetary magnetic field is near the end location of the jump. For ships using transitional time-warp-field propulsion, the preferred method of travel, their quantum gravity field can be shifted in altitude during velocity maneuvers, anywhere between zero and 180 degrees ahead of the half-sphere time base."

Dan and Barbara thought about everything they'd heard and did not fully understand it, especially the term *half-sphere time base*. The term was no doubt some advanced technological aspect used in the quantum gravity drives, possibly even beyond the gravity bubble they'd used during their moonwalk.

Dan finally sighed. "That is amazing to hear," he said. "How do time-warp fields and jumps overcome the inertial and acceleration forces?"

"That's not explained in any of those manuals," Doug said, "but it is in your ship's computer data banks. Let us just say that when there is a modification of the binding energy for the 115$^{th}$ element, in relation to its quantum nucleus, reversing its normal isotopic decay, as mentioned previously, then anything inside the newly created quantum field will now have no mass and will automatically follow the path of least resistance—in this case, the outward projected field of gravity or quantum gravity of the gravity drive." Doug paused and added, "Basically, Dan and Barbara, a rift across the space-time continuum is created for the spaceship and its contents, including everyone and everything inside."

Dan raised his eyebrows. "Amazing, simply amazing," he said. "I can't wait to read about how exactly that is accomplished."

Doug grinned. "Yes, I figured you might, especially because of the secret work you and your groups have been attempting lately at the Los Alamos labs, some of which is trying to split elemental isotopic nuclear bases."

Dan was only a little surprised Doug knew about some of the top-secret work he was involved in. "Is my work on Earth known by everyone on this ship?"

"Not everyone," Doug said, "but quite a few. You and your family have become quite the talk on this ship and even back on our home world, Valzar, a planet that is one of sixteen planets in a solar system we call the Andromeda System."

Dan and Barbara now knew the exact origin of the race and where Michael had come into existence. Dan continued to stare over at the chief engineer with a calm sense of stupor. "I guess you would be considered Valzarians then, huh?"

"Yes, we would," Doug answered.

Dan nodded his head a little. "How many light-years away is your solar system from Earth?"

"About 194,689 light-years," he said, "at least after taking into account the slight speed-of-light velocity changes that exist between galaxies. Our home world is actually located inside a dwarf galaxy known to your race as the Small Magellanic Cloud, and even though its white-matter space is not quite as structured as this spiral galaxy, it is still at a sufficient level to allow it to be sustained by its black hole."

Dan sipped on his special-blend Travanian coffee, realizing not only that light velocity differences must exist outside the constraints and boundaries of each galaxy but also that each galaxy must have a black hole, exactly what was believed and theorized within Earth's scientific community. Earth's scientific community also knew some of the characteristics about the Small Magellanic Cloud galaxy, but the term *white-matter space* was intriguing. "That is all interesting to hear about," he finally said. "Earth has your galaxy on its charts."

"Yes, we know," Doug said. "Maybe you'll just have to visit us sometime soon. I am sure there are many on our home world who would love to meet you."

Dan and Barbara wore dreamy faces at his invitation and knew that would probably happen. Barbara smiled across the table. "We would like that very much," she said.

"Just let us know," Doug said, "and there will be a planetwide reception awaiting your arrival."

Dan and Barbara were quiet again, daydreaming about what it would be like to travel to the alien race's home world and be guests of honors for over twenty-five billion of their race. It would be a magnificent journey, and they'd probably be treated like royalty, since they were the only human beings with a secret friendship with their race. It was tantalizing to think about. It was also dawning on Dan and Barbara just how nice the ship's chief engineer was—in fact, how truly nice all the ship's crew members had been.

Doug noticed Dan and Barbara daydreaming and glanced briefly over at Jason and Kyle before turning back to Dan and Barbara. "Since your brain wave patterns were recorded," he said, "all that information will be transferred to your ship's computer. On your spaceship are small, self-contained telepathic helmets either of you can wear that will directly interface your thoughts to the ship's computer for propulsion control, countermeasures, and even weaponry, if necessary. The ship's computer will always have ultimate control in dangerous flight situations and countermeasure determinations for nonthreat races with inferior spaceships and technologies. Of course, that is only if they are able to detect your ship under its many cloaking schemes that are automatically activated depending on the type of energy they're using to radiate the hull. Basically, your ship's computer can override your thoughts and has the ability to assess all threat levels, immediately ignoring races whose weaponry is technologically insignificant. Your ship's computer also has the ability to distinguish your daydreams from mental commands and will, of course, always maintain a safe operation of the ship. That also includes restricting the use of any of its advanced weaponry when not warranted or required."

Barbara thought about what Doug had just told them. She and Dan now knew the race's computers consisted of highly computational molecular computers, and her curiosity about them was still immense. She stared directly across the table at the chief engineer, who was relaxed back in his chair. "Phil," she said, "one of the chief geneticists, mentioned that your computer processors use new elements unknown to Earth and that the memory is something like electron-quark reactions to electron point charges in direct relation to the processor. What do you actually call the memory?"

Doug thought about how to answer in Earth terminology. "I guess you could call them electron-quark trap bubbles," he finally said. "This is because each electron and its associated positronic charges are switched through predetermined longitudinal and latitudinal zero points within the proton- and neutron-decay loops, decays that would also be known as quarks and neutrinos to your race. Because of a special energy source, we are able to make use of these controlled decay-loop energy rings, and in our case, it is the same energy derived from the nuclear binding energy of the processor element. One of our basic handheld computers would have more overall computing power than practically all the computers on your planet."

Dan and Barbara were amazed by this information and then suddenly started to laugh, because it reminded them again just how advanced the race was compared to Earth. Here they were, friends with an extremely advanced race that had unbelievable space-travel techniques, highly advanced molecular computers, brain wave recording devices, extreme advancements in the field of molecular genetics, atmospheric gravity bubbles, space-transport schemes for almost instantaneous projection of any object, organic or inorganic, and even armbands that allowed you to walk through solid objects and become invisible. What other surprising discoveries might they learn from them?

Doug noticed Dan and Barbara daydreaming. "Anything else?" he asked with a slight grin.

Dan and Barbara were totally absorbed, and Dan was wondering about the transporter-elevator waveguide system. "Why don't you just transport directly from room to room, instead of using a transporter-elevator system of hollow conduits?"

Doug could understand his question. "Because," he answered, "you can never be in too much of a hurry, as you might miss something magnificent or of great importance. It always helps to walk from room to room, gather your thoughts, and then see a door appear open in front of you before entering inside, for instance."

Dan and Barbara understood this explanation, as it would be strange always jumping from room to room, never giving one's mind a chance to unwind or take in its surroundings. Dan nodded a little. "That makes sense," he said. He then wondered about their drinks that had instantly appeared and the safeguards of the space-transport technology. “Is it ever possible for transported objects, like our drinks, to end up where they shouldn’t? You know, like inside one of us?”

“Impossible,” Doug immediately answered. “The ship’s computers are too smart and fast during the molecular conversions and reconstitutions of the molecules into their solid forms. Even the space transports of our bodies in free space are one hundred percent fail-safe. It is impossible to end up inside another object, organic or inorganic, because all surrounding objects are mathematically calculated within the space-transport equation against two opposing gravity fields, the starting and ending points, you could say. If the object or objects at the final end point cannot be determined, like a force field that cannot be penetrated, or anything cannot be removed, the computers will not allow the transport. Once the end point of gravitation is successfully acquired and created, even if a hole is successfully punched through an active inferior force field, no biological matter, nonbiological matter, or force field reconstitutions are allowed inside that area of reserved space.”

Dan and Barbara were extremely amazed to hear this. Doug knew Dan and Barbara were running out of questions that could top his latest answer, but he also knew that they could talk all night about particle and quantum physics he viewed as extremely elementary. “Anything else?” he asked.

Dan glanced over to his wife and then back to Doug. “No, I do not think so,” he said.

“Great!” Doug said and calmly held his coffee cup up to his stomach. “If you need any more particulars about your ship’s gravity-propulsion controls or its time-warp-field quantum drive, you can read about them in the reconstituted paper flight manuals you now have or from your ship’s computer. You will also find that your spaceship is configured for a family of five, having four stories and a very nice lab on the second level.”

Dan and Barbara knew that the lab would have a brain wave recording machine, just as the chief medical officer had told them.

"Okay, thank you," Dan said and glanced down at the flight manual in his lap. He looked back to Doug, who gulped down the last of his coffee and put his cup on the table. The coffee cup suddenly disappeared.

Dan and Barbara, after seeing this, placed their manuals on the table. The words on the front cover changed, becoming completely unreadable. Dan looked up to the chief engineer, very surprised and puzzled. "What just happened?"

"They're biologically encrypted, Dan," Doug said. "The manuals will only expose their contents when they are touched and held by a member of your family."

Dan's eyes widened. "That's interesting!" he said. "That includes Michael, right?"

"Yes, it does," Doug said, "and the cryptography encryption is unreadable, even by anyone in our race."

Dan and Barbara thought about the biologically encrypted manuals, Dan becoming even more curious. "How is the biological cryptograph accomplished?"

"Simple," Doug said, "at least by our race's standards. All living entities—whether they're sentient beings, such as our two races, or animals, plants, or even insects—contain a predetermined biological energy signature. This signature shows itself in the form of what your race calls an aura, and there is always a specific dissipation according to the construction of the material or, in our case, biological cellular construction."

Doug paused to see Dan and Barbara quietly and intently listening to everything he told them and continued, "Basically, our cells, according to their genetic double-helix nucleic acid sequences, will dissipate minute energy differences. Your race currently does not have the ability, on the molecular level, to differentiate between these extremely small point energies. In the case of your manuals, the cellulose material used in their molecular construction have four distinct receptors—or receivers, depending how you want to look at it—that will pick up your bodies as if they were transponders. Of course, those receptors are then activated by the exact molecular nucleic heat signatures of only you and your family."

Doug paused again, read Dan's and Barbara's minds, and knew they were wondering what the ink was composed of to allow it to change. "The symbols, letters, and numbers in your manuals," he said, "are formed using a somewhat similar process to the invisible ink methods you currently have on Earth, except in reality no ink is used. For your invisible ink methods on Earth, an external energy source must activate the surface molecules of the ink. The writing in your manuals is formed from molecular interactions using preset point charges, charges that are normally dormant and will only appear in the unencrypted English form when excited. Your bioelectrical energy signatures act as the catalyst and change the locations of those point charges to form new symbols—sort of like a chain reaction whenever you touch the manuals." Doug paused and added, "This chain reaction is also a direct result of the electrons in each molecule changing from one three-dimensional antisymmetric state to another, one a static encrypted state, the other an unencrypted excited state."

Dan and Barbara were quiet for a short moment, and Dan regained his train of thought. "Simply amazing," he said. "That is also one heck of a science."

"Yes, it is," Doug said. "Believe it or not, but you also cannot make photocopies of your manuals, as the light from the copier will cause the vibratory state of the molecules in the cellulose to encrypt, regardless of whether or not you're touching them. It is also impossible to duplicate the precise bioelectrical energies of your body to excite the molecules, such as someone cutting off your hand or finger, like is shown in some of your television shows and movies on Earth. This is because blood flow and oxygen levels are also taken into account during the preprogrammed encryption and decryption sequences."

Dan and Barbara were now grinning a little, and Dan took a short, relaxed breath. "Can your highly advanced computers overcome the manual's encryption-decryption cycles?"

"Not very easily," Doug said. "It would only be possible inside a small temperature-controlled room, and if they did not also know the exact molecular details and point-energy signatures of the biological body or bodies in reference, it would be virtually impossible, regardless of how advanced the computers."

Dan and Barbara were quiet again, and Doug realized he'd better leave, because of a scheduled meeting with his engineering staff. "Well, it was nice to meet you two," he said and then stood up. "I have a meeting to attend."

Dan and Barbara also stood up and, like before, saw how big the chief engineer was in comparison to them. Dan reached across the table and shook Doug's hand. "Thank you for your time," he said.

Doug returned the handshake. "And thank you," he said and reached over to shake Barbara's hand. "It was a pleasure meeting you both."

Barbara felt good inside at his kindness. "And we want to thank you for your time and telling us a little about your planet and its solar system, not to mention schooling us about advanced molecular sciences."

"No problem," Doug said with a kind face. "You both have a wonderful evening." He headed toward the doorway with Dan and Barbara following closely behind. At the now open doorway, he continued out into the hallway and turned around with a brief nod. The door reappeared, and Dan and Barbara stood in front of the closed door, thinking about everything the chief engineer had told them.

Dan finally turned to his wife. "What a really nice guy," he said.

"Yes, he was," she said and followed Dan back to the couch, where they sat back down. Their two boys were still playing their holographic imagery game, and there were now drinks in front of them.

Dan picked up his flight manual and watched as it biologically decrypted itself. He shook his head, amazed, and opened the manual to a random page about three-quarters toward the end, page 343. What was listed was extremely surprising. He flipped back to the start of the section, having a feeling he might not fully understand the contents.

Barbara noticed her husband was already engrossed. "I'm going to see what the boys are up to," she said.

Dan looked up, starry-eyed. "Okay, dear," he said.

Barbara walked over to Jason and Kyle's table and took a seat to Jason's right. "Who's winning, Jason?" she asked.

"I am, of course," he said, "but I'm also still teaching Kyle how to strategically play the game."

Barbara gave a subtle grin and wondered about Michael, especially the advanced changes to his body on the molecular level.

✦ ✦ ✦

On the flight deck of the starship, Captain Donaldson relaxed back in his chair, in the middle of a briefing about what their fleet had just discovered near the nebula. To his right was his first officer, and to his left, the chief science officer. There were sixty-two lower-ranking officers at numerous workstations and consoles keeping watchful eyes on their spaceship's systems and subsystems, especially the short- and long-range sensors, both in normal planes of space and in above-light-speed subspace planes.

Captain Donaldson surveyed his flight deck again and looked back at the three-dimensional holographic projection of Captain Gary Randolph, who had overall command authority of their fleet near the nebula. Their investigation so far had been strange, because even though they now had a direct recording of the energy beam that had locked onto the cargo ship, they still could not successfully break it down for analysis, nor could they reproduce it in any of their labs, even after trying to simulate what they believed to be an instantaneous-transmission energy wave well above light speed, in fact, at light-year speeds. It was strange, as if other energy types were embedded within the main beam like a compressed carrier wave. How the beam was able to control the cargo ship inside a moving-source resonant frequency, especially from thousands of light-years away, had them puzzled. There was a belief that there might be another source frequency wave piggybacked within the same beam that they could not detect with their technologies. If so, it would be violating subspace harmonic laws as they currently understood them.

Captain Randolph, Captain Donaldson's close friend, was just as much at a loss for an explanation. It was frustrating even for their top scientists in the fields of subspace and subplane physics, but some of them did have a theory that the energy beam might have been projected into the Milky Way galaxy from another galaxy, possibly even from a new plane of space-time existence, a completely new universe. This new theory was very surprising to Captain Randolph, who continued to stare into the three-dimensional holographic projection of Captain Donaldson.

Captain Donaldson took a deep breath and exhaled. "What do you mean you cannot find any quantum gravity signature ripple within the last three days, Gary?"

Captain Randolph paused. "That's what we are finding, Don," he said. "There are also no viable planets, besides Earth, that will sustain any life whatsoever within 34,800 light-years of our location."

"Have you thoroughly scanned the resonant interdimensional time-plane worlds?" Captain Donaldson asked.

Their carbon-based physical bodies could not survive in the alternate worlds Captain Donaldson was asking about, but they could look briefly into such worlds using their advanced sensors, optically and nonoptically, at least after the normal space-time continuum resonance line was shifted. "Yes, we have," Captain Randolph said. "That is actually what makes this area of space even more unusual, almost as if the gravitational fields are no longer in true resonance, slightly out of sync with the rest of the galaxy. Because of that slightly shifted gravity resonance near our armada, my communications chief is modifying our subspace gravity-stream transmissions in real time so there is no broken harmonics."

Captain Donaldson leaned all the way back in his chair. What Captain Randolph had just told him was something their race had never encountered—a nonresonant gravity field offsetting normal space-time curvature, directly affecting their subspace gravity-stream communications. Even black holes were in resonance with one of the higher-ordered harmonics of normal space-time curvature, and their spaceship's highly computational molecular computers were able to easily compensate for the space-shift displacements, allowing them to travel around, even through a black hole's event horizon without any effect—at least as long as the black hole had not compressed itself into a new dimension considered interdimensional space-time. "Strange," Captain Donaldson mumbled under his breath. "Is there anything else, Gary?"

"No, that is all for now," he replied.

"Okay, thanks, Gary," Captain Donaldson said. "Keep me informed of anything new of interest."

"Will do," Captain Randolph replied. "Take care, and we'll see you in about two days."

Two of their days translated to one Earth day, and Captain Donaldson thought about the fact that he would be joining the armada soon after his business with the Jupiter family was concluded. "Goodbye, Gary," he again said. "Look forward to seeing you again."

"Bye, Don," Captain Randolph said.

The holographic images vanished in front of Captains Donaldson and Randolph. Captain Donaldson leaned back in his chair. Some of their scientists believed that nonresonant gravity-field manipulation might hold clues to the first stages of wormhole technology. He looked briefly to his science officer and first officer, knowing they were just as amazed at what they'd heard from the subspace communication. He turned his thoughts to the big celebration dinner tomorrow, where the Jupiters would be guests of honor. It would be one step closer to the final bridging of their friendship with his race. After the dinner, he, along with his senior officers, would escort them to their new spaceship for their imminent trip back to Earth a few hours later. He stared off, daydreaming about the Earth family, who must now live in extreme secrecy from the rest of the human race.

✦ ✦ ✦

Inside the Jupiters' guest quarters, less than ten minutes after the chief engineer left, Barbara returned to the couch. Dozens of children's books suddenly appeared on the table, all in English. She quickly picked up one that caught her attention, and Jason and Kyle soon joined her and Dan on the couch. Sitting between their parents, they listened intently as their mom began reading them the story.

The story was about a young boy who found a spaceship and then took it into outer space with his family, visiting many of the moons and planets within their solar system before leaving the solar system and visiting other solar systems and planets throughout their galaxy. One of the newly discovered planets was filled with an abundance of trees and thick vegetation. It was able to sustain carbon-based life but was not populated, not even having any animals or insects whatsoever. Jason stared up into his mother's face, realizing the boy in the story could be him, riding in a spaceship with his family, and he wondered who wrote the story. Barbara paused from reading and stared down at Kyle, who was glued to her like a television set. Dan was still reading the flight manual, totally absorbed, not paying much attention to the children's story. Jason started wondering about Michael. He reached across Kyle and nudged his father's leg. "How do you think Michael is doing, Dad?"

Dan looked up. "Probably okay, Jason," he said. "He may even be dreaming. Remember Jose telling us that?"

Jason did remember. "Yes, I do," he said and was not quite as worried.

Dan noticed his youngest son had a distant look. He glanced briefly over at his wife and then back to Jason. "After we arrive home tomorrow, maybe we'll all go fishing at the creek Saturday. We could take a tent, have a bonfire, and camp out under the stars. How's that sound?"

Jason perked up. "Sounds like fun, Dad. I bet Michael would really enjoy that."

Dan stared over at his wife briefly and then back to Jason. "I'm sure he would. It would definitely be a new experience for him." Dan paused with a humorous grin. "Who knows, Jason, he might even catch a bigger fish than you."

Jason laughed. "Yeah, right, Dad," he said with a grin. "I don't think so."

Dan also chuckled a little and noticed Kyle staring up at him with speculation, especially after hearing about their fishing down at the creek. His young son was probably thinking about the thirty-two-pound channel cat. "Remember that thirty-two-pound channel cat head that I nailed to the post, Kyle?"

"Yes, I do, Daddy," Kyle said.

"Well," Dan calmly continued, "maybe you'll catch one too, and we can nail its head on the post next to mine."

Kyle showed another distant look at that possibility. Dan, after seeing this, glanced briefly at his flight manual and then back to his wife. "This manual is amazing," he said. "There is a reference here how element 115 is quickly forced into an isotopic half-life decay pattern and into its daughter's daughter element—element 111—first as a stable isotope, but only after cycling back through itself from element 117. It is then returned to element 115 and repeated. The ship's computer would have to be very powerful to control the forward and reverse decays so quickly to stop explosive radioactive poisoning inside the ship. My guess is that all the explosive gravitational energy could be what is creating the quantum gravity time-warp-field propulsion to reach the extreme speeds, but how those decays are able to be focused so precisely, I still do not have the faintest."

Barbara now wore a surprised smile, as she knew isotopic inversions in the opposite direction of beta decays, including neutron decays, with any element, were just not possible by any of Earth's twenty-first century sciences, as it would be essentially reversing the electron energy of the element itself—kind of like winding up a spring-driven toy car. Not only that, but Earth's scientific community did not fully understand the isotopic decay pattern of elements 111, 113, 115, or 117, let alone much about their properties. "Yes, that does sound interesting," she said.

Dan looked briefly down at the manual again, knowing the same thing Barbara did about the four elements. Of course, those four elements and their properties, in time and with some schooling, would no longer be a mystery to them. He glanced back to his wife. "I can't wait to learn more about the isotopic inversion-reversion decay process."

"And neither can I," she said. She glanced at her wristwatch, surprised to see it was already 10:18 p.m., Los Alamos time. Kyle looked tired and was fighting to stay awake, either because he wanted to hear more of the story or because he was wondering about Michael and didn't want to go to sleep without him. Barbara continued to stare down at her two boys with a warm glow, realizing that in the morning it would soon be three boys. "Time to go to bed, kids," she said.

"Okay, Mom," Jason said.

"Okay, Mommy," Kyle chorused.

Dan looked up from his manual. "Good night, boys," he said.

Jason gave his father a big hug. "Good night, Dad."

Dan felt proud of his oldest son. If it had not been for Jason's braveness, they would not be aboard the mother ship and friends with the race that had created Michael. "Good night, Jason," Dan whispered. He then picked up his four-year-old and gave him a soft, reassuring hug, knowing he was possibly thinking about Michael. "Good night, Kyle," he gently said.

"Night, Daddy," Kyle replied.

Barbara walked with Jason and Kyle to their beds, where she picked up some alien nightwear that had not been there a moment ago. While Jason changed out of his previously provided clothing, Barbara helped Kyle into his nightwear and again noticed it was extremely soft and relaxing to the touch, as if it had vibratory properties. After her precious little boys had gotten into bed, they snuggled up next to each other. She leaned down, giving Kyle a soft kiss on the lips. "Good night, Kyle," she said softly.

"Night, Mommy," Kyle said.

Barbara then hugged Kyle and dreamed of what it would be like having three little boys in her life. She then leaned over and placed a small kiss against Jason's lips. "Good night, Jason," she whispered.

"Good night, Mom," he replied, hugging her with a feeling of radiant love.

Barbara realized again it was the last night she'd have only two sons in her life. She returned to the couch, where Dan was leaned back with a calm, relaxed spirit. After sitting back down, she suddenly exhaled.

Dan noticed this. "You have to admit one thing, honey," he said. "This arrangement with the advanced race and having Michael in our lives is almost unimaginable."

Barbara nodded to agree. "Yes, I know," she said. "Not only will we have a spaceship to explore our galaxy, even beyond its reaches, but another child in our lives to teach and be taught by."

Dan understood exactly what she meant. They would be teaching Michael love and compassion, and at the same time, he was sure to be teaching them sciences they'd previously only dreamed of. They both deeply exhaled at the thought of those future events and what had happened in the last almost eighteen Earth hours aboard the mother ship. They could not see how their day could have turned out any more intriguing, and tomorrow would be another interesting day, starting with the big dinner, followed by seeing their new spaceship. They would leave the mother ship soon afterward in that same spaceship and return to Earth.

Dan glanced over at their two boys and could hear them talking to each other. He looked back to his wife with an extremely relaxed feeling inside, his spirit immensely uplifted. "Well, I suppose we ought to go to bed too," he said.

"Okay," she said.

Dan set the manual down on the table and watched the front cover again become unreadable, turning into complete gibberish. "Amazing," he mumbled under his breath.

Dan and Barbara both headed to the bathroom, which was very different from an Earth bathroom, with much more automation. Inside the bathroom, extremely soft two-piece nightwear was lying on a table for them. They began changing out of their previously provided outfits. Dan pulled off his top and saw his wife standing half-naked, her fair skin and bare breasts clearly visible. "These outfits are soft, huh?" he said.

"Yes, they are," she said, also noticing Dan's half-naked body, his dark chest hairs and well-toned muscles. "Do you think these new outfits might have properties that affect our auras?"

"Possibly," Dan said, "especially with this race."

"True," she said. She removed her bottoms, now standing naked. She slipped into her new bottoms with attached socks and found the clothing extremely relaxing against her skin. She slipped into her top and saw Dan already dressed in his new bottoms, now putting on his top. When she looked down at their previously worn alien clothing, it suddenly vanished before her eyes.

Dan also saw this and slid his socks back and forth on the ceramic tile floor. To his surprise, they did not slide much at all. Curious, he lifted his right leg to see if the sock bottom was rubberized. It didn't look like it, but when he touched the surface, there was a soft, leathery feel. He wondered whether there might be friction regulators or some type of advanced material whose molecules reacted exactly opposite of Teflon yet remained extremely flexible and soft with a smooth surface. He finally turned to his wife. "These outfits are strange, huh?" he said. "It seems to have a relaxing, calming effect on my body."

"So does mine," she replied. "It is almost as if my muscles are being lightly massaged."

"True," Dan agreed. He followed her out of the bathroom, headed directly toward their bed, but then they both stopped in their tracks upon noticing the strange lighting around their boys' bed. There was a slightly curved shadow around the bed, like a dark cloud, similar to a curved two-way mirror, while the rest of the room remained brightly lit. Dan and Barbara knew what they were seeing had to be another strange aspect of the photon-neutrino technology and continued to their own bed, curious of the method used to block the photon emissions. Barbara pulled back the covers, and they crawled into bed, quickly snuggling up next to each other after what had been a long day. Now in each other arms, their chests touching, they began daydreaming about the events of tomorrow—the big dinner they would be having with many of the ship's crew members, their leaving the mother ship in a spaceship of their own soon afterward, and then followed by having Michael in their lives forever.

While they continued to dream about their future on Earth and having to live with a secret they would have never dreamed possible, the lighting around their bed slowly dimmed until it reached that of a nightlight. Dan then planted a soft, sensual kiss against his wife's lips. "I will always love you no matter what," he whispered.

Barbara grinned at his kind words. "And I will always love you too," she whispered back.

In the unusual darkness of their room, Dan and Barbara sensed warmness between them like they'd never before felt. Maybe it was because they were aboard an advanced race's mother ship, or it could have been because of the new son they would soon have in their lives. The love between them might have been amplified from being in the presence of so many beings who were extremely peaceful and surely highly spiritual. Regardless, it did not matter to them, as there was nothing that could destroy the family bond and love they had toward their natural sons and their official soon-to-be son, Michael.

All those thoughts, musings on their future, and the immense feelings of love they now felt inside their souls relaxed them into a soft, sensual sleep. The next morning would be the start of another interesting day of events.

# 19

## PICKING MICHAEL UP FROM THE LAB

It was Friday, September 12, the last day aboard the mother ship for the Jupiter family, and Dan Jupiter was wide-awake. It was five o'clock in the morning Los Alamos time, and he was feeling extremely invigorated while sipping on a cup of herbal beta-glucose Travanian coffee, the same coffee the chief engineer had introduced them to last night. Dan normally woke up about five each morning anyway, sort of like his body's own internal alarm clock for going to work each day at the Los Alamos labs. On this particular morning, though, he felt unusual anticipation for picking up Michael from the lab, followed by their attending a big dinner a few hours later. Looking over at his bed, he was amazed how there was a controlled light field of around 100 lumens where he now sat, yet where his wife slept, there was a lighting output of a nightlight. In fact, there were three distinct lighting fields in the room—one where he sat, another where his wife slept, and a third where the kids were still asleep. Each light field was separated by a spherical, shadowy wall that cut off bleeding light, similar to darkened, slightly curved, see-through curtains or two-way mirrors. The lack of any light bleeding through indicated that the light was not conforming to normal light wave mechanics as he understood them, especially for shadowing effects.

Barbara was finally stirring, and he wondered whether she'd gotten a whiff of his coffee's aroma, as it did have an extremely pleasing scent. Barbara finally opened her sleepy eyes, turned her head in his direction, and saw him staring directly at her. "Good morning," he said. "Want some herbal beta-glucose Travanian coffee?"

Barbara smiled a little, remembering its delicious, smooth flavor, and stretched. "Sure," she said. She slowly rolled out of bed and continued out of the small bedroom, through a dim, curved curtain of light into the brightly lit room, where Dan was sitting on the couch. Passing between the light fields was mentally captivating.

From the outside, Dan noticed the unusual changes as she passed out of the dim light field of the bedroom and into the bright field of light where he sat. It was very strange to witness firsthand. He touched the console in front of him. Another cup of herbal coffee suddenly appeared on the table in front of him, and he handed it to his wife.

"Thank you," she said. She took a sip and, like before, savored its tantalizing flavor. Around the boys' bed she saw what appeared to be a dark cloud or curved column of darkness, like an oblong sphere that was completely encasing them. It was not pitch black, though, and she could still see Kyle's head up against his older brother's chest. It caused her to think about Michael. After she sat down, she slowly turned her attention back to her husband. "I can't wait to pick up Michael."

"I know what you mean," he said. "I am also anxious. I guess that is when he truly becomes our third son."

Barbara felt warm inside. Not only was Dan's comment true, but Michael would also be 100 percent organic, no synthetic hair follicle molecules with transpondence markers, as Captain Donaldson called them. He should also have a metabolism closer to that of a young Earth boy, though he still might outlive Jason and Kyle, as Phil had alluded—something they would have to accept. She stared down at the flat display on the table, touched a few buttons to find the breakfast menus, and was surprised to find quite an assortment, including what would be served at fast-food restaurants, family-owned restaurants, and even extremely nice restaurants. She noticed Dan had a relaxed grin on his face. "I suppose you've already looked over the breakfast menus?"

"Pretty much," he said. "Again, they are one step ahead to have such a wide variety of Earth breakfasts in their computers."

"Appears that way," she said. "How about we go ahead and have breakfast?"

"Sure," Dan said. "I was waiting for you to wake up."

Dan and Barbara browsed the menus and decided to try biscuits and gravy, bacon and eggs, blueberry hotcakes topped with maple syrup, and, for their drinks, milk and orange juice. Dan touched the Finish button, and before their very eyes, full plates of food, along with their drinks, appeared on their table. There were also metallic-looking forks, spoons, and knives, as well as a bottle of syrup and a container of what looked to be butter. Dan turned to his wife with a humorous face. "Now that is what I call service," he kidded.

Barbara giggled. "For sure," she said, "but I will always enjoy cooking breakfast for my family."

Dan felt good inside at her comment, because she always savored the appreciation her family gave her after their meals. They both quietly started their breakfasts, all while their two natural boys slept. Their third, soon-to-be-official son was surely also asleep, but inside a zero-energy stasis field. During their breakfast, they noticed that the food did not seem as greasy as foods back on Earth and was extremely delicious, seemingly surpassing the flavors for comparable Earth-based products.

✦ ✦ ✦

In the main medical lab, the four chief geneticists, the chief medical officer, and a vast array of their support staffs had been up all night, working nonstop on Michael while maintaining his life force inside a zero-motion, absolute-zero energy field. They had determined that highly sophisticated harmonic changes from the first stasis field had to be created for the new stasis field because of the cellular changes Michael had gone through since becoming cognizant of his surroundings almost two Earth days ago, such as the physical and chemical changes to his cerebral cortex. Their surgical cellular space-displacement lasers, accurate down to junctions less than one nanometer, successfully changed his synaptic brain stem cellular configurations, as well as completing all the required changes to his hypothalamus gland. Their space-displacement lasers, controlled by their ship's highly computational molecular computers, were nearly infinitesimally accurate for making all the proper changes to Michael's cerebral cortex in relation to a new thermoregulation and metabolism. They were nearly 100 percent complete in their cellular changes, with only a few minor adhesions to construct and reconstitute in direct relation to his glial (neuronal support) cells.

The molecules associated with his scalp's partially synthetic hair follicles, including the special sebaceous glands for the generation and growth of the synthetic transpondence-marker molecules, no longer existed. Pure-DNA master stem cells from his body's own chemistry replaced the sebaceous glands. Newly created hair strands nearly six centimeters in length now fully covered his scalp. The thick hair strands were dark brown and partially curly and would now grow proportionally with the new metabolism of his body under normal anagen (growth), catagen (degeneration), telogen (rest), and exogen (shedding) phases.

Michael's sleep patterns had also been adjusted so there would be a closer balance between his conscious and subconscious states of mind. He should now become tired after being consciously awake for a specific amount of active cognitive brain function, similar to other human kids about his age, but then, as Phil, Neill, Brian, James, and the other geneticists in their divisions knew all too well, Michael might outgrow those sleep-pattern requirements as he aged, a direct result of his unique synaptic brain cell junctures and axon-dendrite configurations that incorporated additional button receptors, each receptor having hundreds of fingers. Because of these unique genetic configurations during Michael's creation, his synaptic activity did not require even remotely the same amount of electrochemical energy during active cerebral activity as humans on Earth, or anybody in their race for that matter. It was part of his unique DNA genetic makeup that could not be changed.

For changes related to his chromosomal nucleic acid gene sequences, their computer models predicted his life span had been reduced from what was found to be four thousand years (instead of the two-thousand-year life span) to around four hundred to five hundred Earth years, maybe even a few additional centuries. Michael's estimated life span was something that would always remain highly secret. They would never reveal it to the Jupiter family or even to Michael, as nobody should know when they might take their last breath and pass from this world.

The geneticists continued to observe Michael lying motionless on a horizontal table that was two meters long by one meter wide. He was gravitationally suspended in midair, inside an active zero-energy stasis field. His eyes were closed, and he appeared to be peacefully asleep. Phil, along with Neill, Brian, James, and Darryl, glanced up again at the large three-meter-by-two-meter three-dimensional holographic images in front of them. The images showed Michael's new synaptic brain stem and hypothalamus reconfigurations off to the side in a photolythic (3-D holographic image broken down in both one and two dimensions) cross-sectional view similar to an MRI, but these images were expanded, as they directly corresponded to his higher-order functions, including intrinsic neuronal thermoreceptors in both his spinal cord and cerebral cortex. Their surgically programmed, computer-controlled displacement lasers had just finished the final restructuring of Michael's glial cells and then shut down. In their language, displayed inside the photolythic images, was an indication that the changes were 100 percent successful. The words "Modifications complete" then appeared.

Phil turned to the other geneticists and the chief medical officer. "Yes, you guys," he said in their alien tongue. "Just as we figured, the modifications to his cerebral core and hypothalamus that we programmed into the computer were a complete success."

Neill paused from looking at the holographic images and turned back to Phil. "Yes, they were," he totally agreed and thought about the Jupiter family, who would be picking Michael up in about a half hour (one Earth hour) and accepting him as their official new son.

They all continued to stare at Michael, knowing he would come out of his zero-motion, absolute-zero stasis field soon. The cylindrical stasis field completely encasing his body was one and a half meters in diameter and two meters long. It had a hazy light-blue tint, yet his body was still clearly visible. No one would have ever thought by looking at him that his body was minus 459.67 degrees Fahrenheit and in a zero-energy stasis field where all electron charges and cell divisions had ceased. All the geneticists and medical personnel knew the blue haze was only visible because of their altering the zero ground state of both Michael's cellular matter and associated electron energy. They now stood in quiet anticipation of shutting down the stasis field in less than thirty minutes. Michael would become consciously awake a few minutes later and feel a little stiff, possibly even feeling residual pain throughout his entire body for a few hours.

✦ ✦ ✦

Back in the Jupiters' guest quarters, Dan and his wife had finished breakfast over an hour ago and were sitting next to each other with continued anticipation for picking up Michael, yet they remained patient. It felt as though their son was in an operation after being in a terrible accident and they were in the waiting room. In reality, while he was in an operation, it was not for anything bad that had happened; it was just modifications to his genetically engineered body.

Dan stared over at Jason and Kyle, who were dressed in the new outfits provided to them soon after finishing their breakfasts. They were at the same table as last night, again playing the spherical holographic game. He took a deep breath and exhaled. Noticing it was 8:15 a.m., he stared over to his wife. "How about we go to the medical lab a little early?"

"Sure," she said. "I would love to see Michael before he wakes up."

Dan, too, had anticipation for seeing Michael before he became consciously awake—kind of like seeing one of your kids and being present before they started waking up from anesthesia. "Great!" he said. "Let's go pick up our new son."

There would be no disagreement from his wife, and Jason and Kyle were already staring over in their direction, most likely having heard them mention Michael. "Boys," Barbara said, "let's go pick up Michael."

Jason and Kyle suddenly expressed excitement. "Okay, Mom," Jason quickly replied.

The three-dimensional holographic image suddenly vanished, and the boys hurried over to the exit well ahead of their parents. Dan noticed the anticipation all over his kids' faces as he and Barbara followed them to the exit. Jason grabbed his right hand, while Kyle clutched Barbara's left hand. The door to their guest quarters vanished a little more slowly than normal this time, fading away. They proceeded out into the hallway and directly toward the transporter elevator.

Dan noticed his sons had distant smiles and could not help but have one himself, because it felt as though they were on their way to an adoption agency to adopt a little boy, except this little boy had already become attached to them, as had they to him.

Three crew members were headed their direction, a very tall male and two tall females, definitely military, possibly part of the ship's security personnel. One of the females was a little taller than the other, though both were easily over six feet five inches. They were the tallest females Dan and Barbara had seen so far, which was why they believed the females to be security personnel.

Dan, Barbara, and their kids moved slightly over to the right. "Hello," one of the females said in plain English.

Dan appreciated their kindness, not to mention the female's use of perfect English. She was extremely pretty, her somewhat muscular frame clearly visible against her tight outfit. "Hello," he replied.

The crew members walked by, calm expressions still filling their faces, and the Jupiter family continued in the opposite direction until the hallway straightened out. Dan was still amazed that the brightly lit hallway was not using any incandescent lighting whatsoever and turned his head to his wife. "That photon-neutrino technology is amazing, huh?" he said.

"Yes, it is," she said. "Might they be using neutrino-photon emitters or something similar in nature?"

"Possibly," Dan said.

The transporter elevator was just ahead, and Jason and Kyle suddenly let loose of their parents' hands and scurried up to the elevator. Dan again turned to his wife. "Did you notice our boys are not casting any shadows whatsoever, as though the hallway is not being lit from any particular direction? That makes Michael's statement of low-level neutrino decay into all open areas of space, leaving only the photons, even more amazing."

Barbara thought about this. "For sure," she said.

The boys were still waiting in front of the elevator, the door closed. When Dan and Barbara arrived, the elevator door finally vanished, explaining that mystery. It appeared that adults had to be present for certain preset conditions on the mother ship. Jason and Kyle entered, then Barbara, followed by Dan, and they all stood quietly as a closed door suddenly appeared. Dan stared down at the wall console. "Level two, medical lab," he said.

The door vanished again as quickly as it had appeared. They exited into the hallway, turned right, and began their journey toward the main medical lab with rising anticipation in their souls. Glancing at his wristwatch, Dan saw it was 8:20 a.m.

He saw the same sign pointing to the medical lab that he'd seen yesterday. It was written in the race's language and, based on what Jose told them yesterday, read "Main medical lab." Even with what little Hebrew and ancient Egyptian he understood, he had no idea how the hieroglyphic language was formulated into sentences. The alien language seemed much more advanced than Hebrew or ancient Egyptian, and the symbols flared out with fewer line segmentations.

Jason grabbed his dad's left hand again as they neared the double doors of the main medical lab entrance. One of the signs next to the doorway changed and now read "Main medical lab" in English. Dan and Barbara took deep breaths and exhaled, because they knew Michael would soon be back with them and a forever part of their family. The double doors vanished, and the Jupiter family continued inside, finding dozens of the ship's medical crew, including geneticists, all of them standing next to Phil, Neill, Brian, James, and Darryl. They were staring through a large glass pane window into a smaller room that contained a strange cylindrical column of light-blue light about two meters in diameter. One of the females in the room, possibly a nurse, saw they had arrived a little early and walked up to meet them. "Welcome," she said. "Michael will be coming out of his stasis in less than five of your minutes."

"Okay, thank you," Dan said and felt Jason let loose of his hand.

Darryl turned around after realizing the Jupiters had arrived. "Hello, Dan and Barbara," he called out. "You're more than welcome to come over here and wait with us."

Additional anticipation filled Dan's heart after seeing Michael inside the light-blue cylinder, which he knew to be the zero-motion, zero-energy stasis field. He walked with his family up to the window, now standing next to Darryl, Phil, Neill, Brian, and James. Michael was lying on his back on a horizontal platform nearly five meters away. The platform was suspended in midair, with no supports above or below it, and Michael seemed peacefully asleep, encased in the strange light-blue cylindrical haze. They could only view the right side of his body. His hair looked a little darker and had a few curls. Dan turned to Darryl with immensely curiosity. He knew the cylindrical column of light was the stasis field, but he was hoping his next question might shed some more light on it. "So that's the zero-energy stasis field, huh?" he calmly asked.

"Yes, it is," Darryl said. "It is our unique zero-energy field that takes the reference matter down to the extremely cold temperature of zero degrees Kelvin, as you call it on Earth, at least as referenced against the water molecules, but in reality it is also an energy-temperature stasis field known to us as a zero-electron vibratory state."

Dan and Barbara heard this with surprise. "That is amazing," Dan said.

Phil turned to Dan with an affirmative nod. "Yes, it is," he said. "In less than three of your minutes, Michael will come out of his stasis, and the extremely cold temperature will also immediately go away."

Dan and Barbara were amazed again, especially at the race's ability to transfer carbon-based matter to room temperature so quickly and without any molecular or cellular degeneration. Jason and Kyle didn't think much about what Phil had just told them. They could only continue to stare at their brother, who lay quietly asleep. They knew he must be inside some kind of strange force field.

The mother ship's highly advanced molecular computers started to run a series of final checks before it would shut down the stasis field. There would be instantaneous matter-energy retrieval the likes of which Dan and Barbara had never witnessed or thought possible. Dan glanced at his wristwatch, keeping track of the three minutes Phil had mentioned.

As they continued to wait, suddenly the cylindrical light-blue haze around Michael turned pitch black, hiding him from their view, followed by an extremely bright burst of light expelled out of each end of the cylindrical black force field. The light bursts were directed away from everyone in the lab and focused into two large silver disks at each end of the beams of light. The black force field suddenly vanished, and the cylindrical light-blue stasis field was no longer present.

Darryl glanced over to Dan and Barbara, who had not taken their eyes off of Michael for even a split second. "Michael should become consciously awake in less than sixty of your seconds," he told them.

Dan turned to Darryl with curiosity mixed with anticipation. "What was that bright flash of light all about?"

Darryl noticed Dan's interest and calmly answered, "On Earth, your scientific community has recorded some of the primitive aspects of electron and proton expulsions emitted from neutron stars, including some of their binary x-ray formations. You have just witnessed some highly advanced technological aspects from that field of science in direct relation to energy expulsions while inside an extremely strong magnetic field—a magnetic field greater than fifteen million gauss, as your race terms the units for magnetic flux density. Had our photon sun shield not activated around Michael the moment the energy field activated, we would have all been immediately blinded and sustained permanent optic nerve damage from photon-dispersive radiation. Of course, that blindness would have only existed until we regenerated and transplanted new retinas and optic nerves for everyone."

Dan and Barbara looked at each other in amazement. It felt as if they were in a dream hearing this. The race's level of stem cell molecular regeneration and medical transplantation was extremely advanced, and they had an extremely high understanding of electron and proton energies. Barbara finally turned to Darryl. "Is it okay if we stand next to him?"

"Yes, you can," he said. "Residual static magnetic-flux energies are no longer present."

"Would it also be okay for me to hold his hand?" she asked.

"Yes, you may," Darryl said.

Dan, Barbara, and their two boys entered the small room and stood next to Michael. Suddenly, the platform suspended in midair repositioned itself about one meter above the floor. Barbara reached down and placed Michael's little hand inside hers, mildly surprised that he had the warmth of her own body so quickly.

Darryl, Phil, Neill, Brian, James, and all the other medical personnel and geneticists watched the affection Barbara was expressing toward Michael as well as how Dan, Jason, and Kyle were patiently waiting for him to wake up. They were still amazed how everything had worked out in the end for Michael, his growing up with a family who already had two boys, one about Michael's age, and his new parents being highly educated in science—at least in relation to Earth's twenty-first-century standards.

Michael finally opened his sleep-laden eyes, just a little, and felt the warmth of his mother's hand. "Mommy," he softly said.

Barbara felt an extreme sense of motherly affection. "Hi, little Michael," she said.

Jason placed his hand on Michael's shoulder. "Hi, Michael," he said.

Michael stared up into Jason's face. "Hi, Jason," he said.

Dan knew Michael was okay. "Hi, Michael," he said.

Michael looked up at his new father with a warm attachment of love and tried to smile but found his facial muscles were still a little stiff. "Hi, Daddy," he said anyway.

Kyle finally reached up and tugged on Michael's arm. "Hi, Michael," he said.

Michael turned his stiff neck and could now see Kyle's head just above the platform. "Hi, Kyle," he said.

Dan and Barbara saw that everyone on the other side of the window was staring at them like a television set, for they could surely see the concern they were expressing toward Michael. Dan made direct eye contact with the chief medical officer. "Is it okay if I pick him up?"

Darryl nodded in the affirmative. "Yes, you may," he said, "but he will be a little stiff after our modified zero-energy stasis field, at least until his body fully adjusts to the molecular changes to his brain stem and hypothalamus."

Dan looked down into Michael's pretty eyes. "Do you want to get up, Son?"

Michael let loose of Barbara's hand and reached up for his father. "Okay, Daddy," he said.

With his left hand positioned on the back of Michael's head, as though supporting a newborn, Dan gently picked Michael up in his arms. A small grimace filled Michael's face. Jason noticed this and wondered whether this was the first time Michael had ever felt any pain or at least recognized it as being pain. Dan held Michael up against his chest, and Michael immediately placed his head against the left side of Dan's neck.

Dan took a deep breath while staring at Darryl and the chief geneticists. "We're going to return to our room before the celebration dinner."

"That's fine," Darryl said. "We'll see all of you at the dinner, then."

Dan and Barbara noticed Darryl's continued kindness and exited the stasis room, with Jason and Kyle close behind. After walking up to the double doors into the lab, Dan suddenly stopped and turned around, as did the rest of his family, all of them now staring directly at all the geneticists. "Thank you all so very much for your work on Michael," he calmly said, "and for allowing him to live his life on Earth with our family."

All the geneticists and medical staff were appreciative, and Darryl nodded his head a little. "No problem, Dan," he said. "The pleasure was all ours."

Dan and Barbara turned back toward the double door, which

vanished in front of them, but then Dan again turned around, realizing he did not know where the celebration dinner was being held. "Oh, by the way, what floor and room is the dinner?"

"The main ballroom," Darryl said, "level forty-three, room forty-five."

"Thank you," Dan said, now curious about the ballroom, as it had to be magnificent. His family of *five* finally left the medical lab. He turned left into the hallway and slowly headed toward the transporter elevator, thinking about Michael's current physical condition. It caused him to briefly wonder about the general activities of the race, since they all seemed in excellent shape with no obesity whatsoever. He turned to his wife. "I wonder what type of entertainment and exercise they have aboard this ship."

Kyle reached out for Barbara, and she picked him up in her arms. "You know," she said, positioning her son a little higher on her hip, "I've wondered about that same thing."

Barbara continued to carry Kyle on her left hip, figuring he wanted to be at the same height as Michael. Michael appeared calm with his head still up against the side of Dan's neck. It made her smile, because she could see his attachment toward his new dad and his feelings of contentment. Especially after the advanced molecular changes deep inside his cerebral cortex, his affection toward them would no doubt be the same as their two natural boys and like that of a little baby starting new experiences in the world, except his experiences would be that of a five-year-old with immense intelligence.

When they walked up to the transporter elevator, the door again vanished, but not before suddenly flashing light blue in an autonomous sequence. Jason walked in first, followed by his parents, and they noticed the door had already closed behind them. Dan stared down at the wall console, curious about the door's flashing colors, and stared at his wife and sons with as much visual acuity as possible. "Level eighteen, quadrant twenty," he said. There was a light-green flash in the doorway right before the door vanished. More interesting was that

Dan did not recognize even for one instant the molecular breakdown and reconstitution of their bodies, nor could he recognize his family vanishing before his eyes, as it was much too fast for his cognizance. Out in the hallway, six crew members were waiting—a first—and they moved over while the Jupiter family exited the elevator.

The six crew members, four males and two females in military outfits, noticed Michael in Dan's arms. They knew about him and saw that he now had curly, dark-brown hair. "Hello," one of males said in plain English. "Your new son looks different."

"Yes, he does," Barbara said. "Possibly his hair?"

One of the females made direct eye contact with Michael and said something in an alien language that only Michael understood. Michael lifted his head, replied back in the same strange alien language, and the six crew members giggled under their breath. Dan, Barbara, and Jason only expressed small, curious smiles. The crew members entered the transporter elevator, and the door reappeared behind them, leaving the Jupiter family standing out in the hallway by themselves.

Starting back toward their guest quarters, Barbara turned to Michael. "What did the lady say, Michael?"

"She said I had a nice-looking family, Mommy," he answered.

"And then what did you say in return?" she asked.

"I said, 'Yes, I know.'"

Barbara and Dan laughed a little, and Jason grinned. Kyle thought he understood and continued to feel an intense brotherly love toward Michael.

The hallway curved to the left, and Dan stared down at where the wall met the floor and then up at where it met the ceiling, intensely analyzing the junctions. Where the floor and the ceiling met the walls, it was curved and smooth, as if they were walking inside a somewhat cylindrical, oblong tube. In fact, he had not seen any hallways or surfaces whatsoever, anywhere on the ship, that were joined by a sharp ninety-degree angle or edge. The intersections between the floor and the wall and between the wall and the ceiling were curved, with a radius of around fifty to a hundred centimeters, and he suspected all the rooms on the ship were the same way. Whether those curvatures were related to the immense speeds of the spaceship, he did not know, but he was curious to find out.

They passed by room twenty-two and were again walking down a straight hallway. They walked by another room they knew to be room twenty, which meant their guest quarters were just up ahead. Dan suddenly sighed while thinking about the past two days aboard the mother ship, an amazing two days during which he and his wife had the opportunity to read about highly advanced sciences and even have some explained to them. To think there was even more to come made him feel sort of like a child in a toy store, with the ability to choose any toy he so wished for free. Finally walking up to their doorway, Dan expressed a small, hidden, distant grin at that amazing opportunity. The door quickly vanished in front of them, exposing a brightly lit room.

Dan followed his family inside but then stopped in the middle of the entryway, because he just had to know if it also had curvatures at the corners. Sure enough, it did. He then continued the rest of the way into the room, watching the door reappear behind him. Barbara set Kyle down, so Dan gently placed Michael down next to his brother, making sure he was able to stand and steady himself. Even after seeing that Michael had his balance, Dan continued to hold on to his little shoulder. "Are you going to be okay, Michael?" Dan calmly asked. "Can you walk on your own?"

"Yes," he said. "I am a little thirsty, though."

Dan could understand this. "I will get you some water, then," he said.

Michael continued to stare up into his dad's eyes. "Okay, Daddy."

Dan knew Michael was still a little stiff but figured it would soon go away, especially since his body had amazing advanced healing and regeneration capabilities. The three puncture holes in his left forearm were already completely healed, as if they'd never been there, no scars evident whatsoever, which was amazing to see.

Michael followed his two brothers over to a small table, where Jason sat down directly across from Michael and Kyle. Michael touched a series of buttons on the table, and a glass with a clear liquid suddenly appeared. He took a small gulp, and Dan and Barbara knew he must have been awfully thirsty to not wait for his dad to bring him a glass. He took another sip, and they further realized it could very well be the first time he was taking any fluids into his little body through his mouth—at least by himself. Jason next touched his display, and two more glasses filled with a clear liquid appeared. All three boys now quietly sipped on their drinks.

For Dan and Barbara, what they now witnessed only reinforced their feelings that the three boys would always remain close, not only as the best of friends, but also as brothers, regardless of where they lived as adults, whether on Earth or even on the advanced race's home world, Valzar. It was a real possibility that their kids, when adults, might want to spend time on the advanced race's home planet, now that they had dual planetary citizenship, as Captain Donaldson had told them. One or more of them could even end up having a Valzarian girlfriend, wife, or whatever the tradition was for the Valzarian race. For Jason and Kyle, such a relationship could give Dan and Barbara half-human, half-Valzarian grandchildren. Those children would most likely also carry a new blood type and be immune to all of Earth's diseases. For Michael, any of his children, who would also be Dan and Barbara's grandchildren, would most likely carry his unique genetic and biophysical advanced attributes, regardless of whether they were half-human or half-Valzarian. His kids would probably carry the DNA of his powerful immune system, along with a completely new and unique blood type. Dan finally turned his head toward his wife, who was still staring at their boys. "Want to relax on the couch before the dinner and read more of those manuals?"

Barbara expressed sudden excitement. "Sure," she said and

followed him over to the couch, where she sat down next to him with a warm feeling deep inside her chest. The manuals were still lying on top of the table, encrypted and unreadable. After Dan picked up two manuals, they immediately decrypted. "Amazing," Dan mumbled under his breath. He relaxed back in the couch, handing one of the manuals to Barbara, who also leaned back. Both of them were starting to feel anticipation, as they were getting closer with each passing minute to finally leaving the mother ship in a spaceship of their own. First, though, they had the celebration dinner to attend in a few hours. They could not imagine what kind of celebration dinner the race might have planned for them, especially since it would include the captain and many of his crew members.

Dan opened his manual to another random page and then flipped back a few pages to the start of the section, which was about the gravitational resonances created across the surface of the spaceship's hull in conjunction with the quantum gravity field. The section somewhat explained how the resonance created a frictionless environment for the space around the spaceship, since it was under hidden gravitational compression forces from nearby planets, stars, solar systems, and even galaxies. Even though he did not fully understand it, some of the terms being used were still interesting. For instance, it said a reference steradian space-time sphere played a factor, which implied there was a series of gravitational space-time spheres created in front of the spaceship, even farther in space, especially while in quantum gravity propulsion. He was now engrossed like a little kid, studying not only to pass the time but also to help quell his anxiousness for the days ahead after they returned to Earth.

✦ ✦ ✦

On the flight deck, Captain Donaldson relaxed back in his chair after a status briefing about the recovery of the cargo ship, including its circular hull sections and especially the quantum gravity drive and its damaged, highly radioactive dome encasement. Most of those items had been taken to secret facilities they were very much aware of, even though it was the first time any of their technologies had ever come into the possession of the Earth race. They still did not fully understand how the faster-than-light bond paths of the cargo ship's hull material had been placed into a state of near collapse by the strange energy beam out of the nebula. They did know, though, that the cargo ship had broken into smaller circular sections because of Michael cutting a hole in the hull using a gravitational laser beam ring, resulting in a sudden decompression collapse. It was that compression-and-decompression collapse that appeared to have violated the internal quantum property laws of the metallic-crystalline material that had originally been created inside a faster-than-light energy chamber, where the metallic-crystalline material had been brought down to a ground state of normal space-time gravitation. Once those above-light-speed molecular bond paths were completed, the hull was then brought back into normal light-speed space-time, retaining those unique bond paths. All remaining hull sections and fragments, as well as the complete contents of the ship, had already been identified down on the surface of the small third planet from the sun. Most of the materials were currently hidden at the Kirtland Air Force Base, in the state of New Mexico, near a town called Albuquerque. Some of the more highly advanced objects were at a facility in Nevada known as Area 51, but it did not matter, as all their rightful property would soon be space-transported off the planet and directly into their main cargo hold.

The Earth race could not block these space transports or stop the advanced race from locating all their property. Even if encased in lead, every piece of material that was a part of or on the spaceship radiated unique energy patterns, similar to hidden radioactive dispersion and undetectable by Earth's twenty-first-century technologies, as Earth technologies could not read faster-than-light energy signatures. Since their mother ship had already transmitted an extremely secretive above-light-speed space-energy transmission toward Earth, forming a spherical blanket around the geomagnetic field of the planet, every piece of the ship and its contents, responded like small radio frequency transponders at the same above-light-speed subspace frequency velocity, relaying their exact magnetic field locations on the planet.

Captain Donaldson turned to his first officer. He knew there would be a lot of surprised US government agents and officers after everything started to disappear, sometimes before their very eyes, but the secret government would classify the event as above top secret anyway, never to be known by the general public. The secret agencies would also not feel threatened, because they would realize what was happening, since they already knew they were dealing with a highly advanced race not encountered before. It would be as if the cargo spaceship had never touched down on Earth. The US government would never know what became of the small spaceship that left the destroyed cargo ship before they arrived; they would have to assume it rejoined the highly advanced extraterrestrial race.

Captain Donaldson paused, now wondering about their armada in the outer reaches of the Milky Way, near the nebula, and his first officer telepathically asked, *What is your opinion about the delta-omega-six quadrant, Don?*

Captain Donaldson knew what his friend was referring to. *I'm not sure,* he answered telepathically. *Since Captain Randolph told us there were unstable gravity-stream oscillations affecting our subspace communication, we could very well be dealing with a race unimaginably far beyond our technological advancements.*

Captain Donaldson's answer confirmed Jeremiah's suspicions. "True," he said out loud. "What is your theory for the whereabouts of the sixty crew members?"

"Good question, Jerry," Captain Donaldson said. "The Earthlings do not have the technology to generate any type of force field to hide them, so the crew members may have been transported off the ship inside the same beam that radiated the ship."

Jeremiah was only a little surprised by the suggestion that the strange energy beam, projected all the way across the galaxy into Earth's solar system, was not only an unusual, highly directional tractor beam but also contained some new type of transporter technology within the same beam. If true, it was a feat like none other. Transporting organic or inorganic matter across such vast distances of space, spanning thousands of light-years, was well beyond the capability of their race.

Captain Donaldson knew his first officer was also wondering about those underlying dilemmas, especially the sixty crew members. If they had been transported off the cargo ship, where had they been transported? Better yet, where did they currently reside? Were they alive? Those questions might always remain unknown mysteries. He changed his thoughts to the summation of the friendship between their race and the Earth family, including their new son, Michael Jupiter, by way of the coming dinner and communion together.

# 20

## A CELEBRATION DINNER TO REMEMBER

In their guest quarters, Dan was still reading his manual, totally absorbed in advanced sciences he would have never envisioned, not fully understanding them. For the gravity-propulsion sciences, he somewhat understood how the basic propulsion concepts were accomplished in frames of movement and acceleration against the space-time domain where no inertial forces would be encountered, plus a little more about the quantum gravity field that was formed across the hull of the spaceship, directly in front of its forward velocity path, a quantum field that also encompassed everything inside the same ship. One thing he still could not fully visualize or mathematically understand was how the application of energy could ever be accomplished in an elemental inversion-reversion wraparound scheme to cause the successful generation of immense quantum gravity–propulsion velocities. Some of the mathematics related to the binding energy manipulation seemed awfully complex.

He looked at his wristwatch and saw it was 11:05 a.m., about an hour before their dinner. His wife was sitting at the table next to the three boys. Seeing this interaction between his wife and their three kids gave him a good feeling inside, because he was witnessing firsthand the genetically engineered child emotional base of Michael yearning to hear what his mother had to say to him. They definitely would not be homeschooling him in sciences and math like their other two boys, but they would be homeschooling him in the art of love, affection, and respect and how to fully express those same qualities back to them and to his brothers.

Dan paused again and took a deep breath. The last two hours reading the manual seemed to have flown by. He stared over at the kids' beds and was surprised to see five new sets of garments neatly arranged on top of one of the beds. There were two full-size adult outfits and three smaller outfits, all of them one-piece suits. "Honey," he said across the room, "look at what is on the bed."

Barbara also now saw the outfits. "Evidently for dinner," she said. "They sure look dressy, huh?"

"You're right about that," Dan agreed. He laid his manual down, and like before, its cover turned into gibberish. "Amazing," he said under his breath. He stood up and headed toward the bed with the new outfits.

Barbara met Dan beside the bed. The five light-gray outfits seemed almost as if they were glowing. They all had gold-colored zippers starting at the waist and continuing up to the neckline. Dan picked up his outfit, and Barbara picked up one of the smaller outfits. They examined the suits more closely and found they were soft like felt yet extremely flexible, with medium-blue boots attached. The outfits had a strange elasticity and also seemed durable, as if they were a mixture of leather or a rubberized material.

Dan, still examining his suit, finally made eye contact with his wife. "You know, these suits look very similar to what some of the crew members were wearing, except there were no zippers."

"True," she said, "but the markings and designs on our suits do appear a little different."

The shoulders and sleeves of their suits did not have the insignias that appeared on Captain Donaldson's and his officers' suits.

Additionally, the officers' suits did not have symmetrical colored bands on the sleeves like theirs did. Their suits had two red, white, and blue bands on each sleeve, one set at the wrist and one set just above each elbow. There were also two additional sets of red, white, and blue bands around the waistline and at the neckline. Each suit had a light-silver V across the chest, starting at the waistline and continuing up to each shoulder. Dan and Barbara wondered whether the V might be in reference to the race's home planet, Valzar, or perhaps it meant Valzarian. The suit bottoms were a slightly darker shade of gray, yet there was no break of the material at the waistline, nor were there any seams where the pant legs attached to the boots. The suits were extremely pleasing to the eye and most likely special occasion dress outfits.

Barbara saw her husband still studying their outfits. "Let's go ahead and put them on," she said.

"Let's do it, then," Dan said. "Boys," he called out, "let's get dressed in our new outfits."

Jason, Michael, and Kyle had been watching their father as he studied their suits and were now excited to get dressed in their one-piece *space suits*—at least, that was how Jason and Kyle viewed them. Michael, on the other hand, knew exactly what type of suits they were, including their special attributes, but he did not volunteer the information.

The three boys met their parents at the bed. Jason picked up his outfit and carried it into his parents' small bedroom, out of sight. After changing out of the previously provided clothing, he slipped his legs into the new outfit, his socks sliding down with ease into the soft boots. He stood up and zipped the suit up to his neck. As soon as he let go of the zipper pull, the entire zipper suddenly vanished, and the suit tightened against his body. He felt less pressure on his feet, as though he were standing on foam rubber, yet the boots would not slide the least bit against the floor.

He stood in front of the mirror in the bedroom, admiring himself, and finally returned to the main room to see his parents helping Kyle and Michael into their one-piece suits. "Mom, Dad," he said, "this suit feels strange and is extremely comfortable. I can barely feel any weight on my feet."

Dan looked up from helping Michael into his suit. "Oh really?" he said. "I can't wait to get dressed in mine."

Dan and Barbara noticed Jason's suit did not have a zipper, and when they finally zipped up Michael's and Kyle's suits and let go of the zipper pulls, their zippers also disappeared. "That is so strange," Dan mumbled under his breath. He picked up his one-piece suit, wondering about the suits' characteristics.

Barbara picked up her one-piece outfit and noticed the three boys looked spiffy in their new suits. "You boys all look nice," she said.

Jason, Kyle, and Michael calmly smiled at their mother's kindness. Michael also had a look of wit about him, because he knew everything about the suits, including their advanced molecular properties. Barbara noticed the unusual look on Michael's face and could tell he had something on his mind, but she did not comment on it, at least not at the moment,. She only displayed another kind face. "Boys," she said, "your father and I are changing into our suits now. We'll return in a little bit."

"Okay, Mom," Jason said, staring down in wonderment at his zipperless suit. How to get out of the suit was currently a mystery, but he was certain Michael knew the answer.

Barbara and Dan continued toward their small bedroom, walking around a small wall and up to their bed. Neatly arranged on top of the bed was the original clothing they'd been wearing when first brought aboard the mother ship. The clothes appeared freshly washed, as though dry-cleaned. Dan put his fingers inside the right pants pocket of his jeans, and sure enough, the moondust was right where he'd left it. With a slight grin, he turned to Barbara, who had already changed out of her previous outfit. "Well, the moondust is still in there," he kidded.

Barbara smiled a little while slipping into her one-piece dress suit. Dan removed his two-piece outfit and watched his wife stand up with her new outfit still unzipped. Now exposed, for his eyes only, were her bare breasts and cute belly button. "You look sexy dressed like that," he said.

Barbara shook her head, giggling, and pulled the zipper up to her neck. When she let loose, her zipper also vanished. Her suit became a little tighter against her body, and her breasts were automatically repositioned upward. It felt as though she were now wearing an extremely comfortable bra, even though she was wearing nothing other than her panties underneath. Dan slipped into his outfit, his socks sliding all the way to the bottom with ease. The boots became a little tighter against his feet yet did not feel uncomfortable, nor were they binding his toes in the least bit. He finally stood up, slipped his arms into the long sleeves, pulled the zipper up to his neck, and let loose. Right on cue, the zipper vanished. "That is so strange," he said. He noticed his suit was not binding at all under his arms, as if made of an elastic material.

"Yes, they seem bizarre," Barbara said. "I wonder how we get out of them?"

"Good question," Dan said. "I'm sure Michael knows. He probably knows everything about them."

"Yes, you're right," she agreed.

Barbara began stretching, twisting, and moving around in her suit, and Dan did the same. Squatting down, he could not believe how comfortable and nonrestrictive his suit was against his body. This was especially true at his ankles, knees, crotch, hips, arms, and shoulders. Dan and Barbara also noticed, just as Jason had told them, that it felt as though not much body weight was being transferred to their feet.

Barbara looked down at the suits they'd just changed out of and noticed they were gone. It caused a small grin. "This is like a dream come true," she said. "Our previous outfits have once again vanished, no need for a washing machine, a dryer, even a laundromat."

Dan giggled under his breath. "True," he said. "I'm curious how they're being cleaned—whether their computers are removing all molecular foreign matter to the materials, such as body odors and grime, or whether they are being processed inside a chamber of some kind."

"Good question," she said and followed Dan out of the bedroom to find their three boys quietly waiting.

Michael had a strange look on his face, as if he knew he was about to be asked a question.

"Michael," Dan asked, "what are some of the properties of our suits?"

Michael noticed his father's interest. "They are reactive pressure suits, Daddy," he answered.

"Oh, really?" Dan said. "What do you mean?"

Both Dan and Barbara were staring down at Michael with real interest on their faces, as was Jason. "They will react to most all outside forces and pressures," Michael said.

Dan was intrigued. "What kind of forces?"

"An assortment of energy beams and mass projectiles," Michael said.

Dan stared over to Barbara, again surprised, and then back to Michael. "So they're kind of like bulletproof vests, huh?"

Michael thought about his father's term *bulletproof vests*. "Sort of," he said, "except these particular suits can also repel dangerous forces without any reactive impact to our bodies."

Dan continued to stare down at Michael, simply amazed. "Are they also resistant to corrosive acids and liquids as well?"

"Yes, they are," Michael said. "They are invincible to acids and corrosives."

Dan wondered about the material of the suits. If they had interwoven or attachable gloves and helmet masks of the same material, it would give a certain level of invincibility. "How do we get out of our suits?"

"Just touch the neckline, and the zipper will appear again, Dad," Michael said.

Dan touched his neckline, and sure enough, the gold zipper reappeared. *What strange technologies this race has,* he thought. He removed his finger from the zipper, and it again suddenly vanished. Dan turned to his wife, who had an amazed look on her face. "I hope they let us keep these suits," he said.

"Oh, I'm sure they will," she said.

Their suits would be like wearing full-body armor, probably capable of stopping or repelling any mechanically projected weapon, laser, or energy beam known to Earth. It would be similar to having a miniature force field around their bodies.

The three boys were still calmly standing next to each other, and Dan asked, "Are you boys hungry any?"

"Yes, I am," Jason quickly replied.

"So am I," Michael said.

"Me too," Kyle said.

"Good," Dan said with a slight grin. "Let's head to the ballroom, then."

Dan and Barbara saw anticipation on their kids' faces as they walked toward the exit. Their anticipation could have been for getting to meet other small kids or something else. Dan and Barbara had anticipation for getting to see more of the large spaceship. Then it occurred to them that the coming dinner could very well be Michael's first time eating solid food and using his gastric system. If that were the case, then he would most likely have an empty, sterile intestine, like that of a newborn baby. They'd already been told that he had an extremely powerful immune system, and this made them realize again to what extent the geneticists had gone in creating Michael from two single gametes, all while inside a controlled environment, inside a unique stasis field, and helping him grow into the five-year-old boy he was today—a boy with a truly unique and powerful antibiotic system to go along with a massive number of advanced bodily modifications.

After the door vanished, they continued out into the hallway, turned left, and headed back toward the transporter elevator with the three boys now rushing ahead of Dan and Barbara. As the hallway curved around to the right, the boys started to leave their parents' sight, acting like brothers who had known each other from their infant years, full of the excitement of typical children. "Kids, slow down a little," Dan called out.

Jason immediately stopped and turned around but did not see his father. Michael and Kyle also stopped, and all the boys patiently waited for their parents to catch up. As Dan and Barbara continued around the curved section, the three boys came into view. Seeing the boys quietly waiting, they realized again Michael was acting like a small human boy, following the lead of his brothers with no worries in the world. He would definitely need some adult guidance while growing up into a young man to help him learn the dangers of living in Earth's society, who could and could not be trusted, and how to avoid actions with consequences that might get him into trouble. Aboard the advanced race's military starship, though, there truly was nothing in the world for him to worry about.

The Jupiter family continued together as a group toward the transporter elevator just up ahead. Like the times before, the hallway extended for hundreds of meters, beyond what they could see. Dan figured there were probably dozens of transporters on each level. Otherwise, with what had to be thousands aboard the ship, they would have run into other crew members at the transporter elevators more often, like Grand Central Station. The near-instantaneous movement from floor to floor probably also helped in that respect.

When they reached the transporter elevator, the door vanished again to expose an empty room. They all entered and turned around, and the door suddenly reappeared behind them, but not before momentarily flashing with a soft violet hue—very unusual. Dan looked down at his oldest son. "Jason," he said, "remember where Darryl told us the dinner was being held?"

Jason knew his father was testing his attentiveness and memory, something he'd done many times in the past for conversations deemed important. "Yes, I do, Dad," he said.

"Good," Dan said. "Go ahead and tell the computer what floor and room, then."

"Okay," Jason replied, a little excited that not only was his dad allowing him to speak into the wall console but also that his verbal command would cause their bodies to be transported through small, hollow conduits. "Level forty-three, room forty-five, please," he said.

The door again vanished, following a near-instantaneous movement of their bodies, and the Jupiter family exited to see there were three hallways, one to their left, one to their right, and one straight ahead. There were signs on each wall, but Dan did not have the slightest idea what the alien language was telling them, nor did the signs change into English like before, so all he could do was stare at Michael. "Which way to room forty-five, Michael?" he asked.

"Straight ahead, Daddy," Michael answered.

Dan grinned a little at Michael's continued usage use of the word *daddy* without hesitation. "Okay, thank you," he said. They continued straight ahead down the corridor that had to be three to four meters wide and nearly four meters high. A tall male and female were headed in their direction with two young children about Michael's and Kyle's ages. The male was easily over seven feet tall and large-framed, and the female was maybe a half foot shorter. When they met each other in the hallway, the male and female were already showing kind, open faces. "Hello, Dan and Barbara," the male said in plain English.

Dan and Barbara were only a little surprised he knew who they were. It also appeared that the entire race spoke English extremely well. Dan returned a kind nod. "Hello," he replied.

"Hello," Barbara also said.

The female crew member continued her kind facial expression. "Hello," she said. "Michael's partially curly hair is so cute."

Barbara gave her a small grin. "Yes, it is," she said. "Isn't your family attending the dinner?"

"No," the female crew member said. "We could have, but our family had previous plans. I wish all of you an enjoyable, fun celebration dinner."

"We look forward to it," Dan replied, "and thank you."

The small family walked away. Apparently, the dinner was not mandatory for all the crew members. Besides, surely not all of them could congregate in one large room anyway. The Jupiter family continued their journey toward the ballroom with rising anticipation in their hearts, even Michael's, but they were also now kind of quiet, waiting for Michael to tell them when they were about to arrive at room forty-five or whether they needed to change direction into another hallway. Since Michael had not told them to change directions, Dan assumed the room must still be straight ahead. "Is it much farther, Michael?"

"Just up ahead, Daddy," he answered. "It is the room at the end of this hallway that has two large light-blue double doors."

Dan noticed the double doors, easily over four meters tall, in the far distance. Crew members were filing out of other hallways and up to the double doors, suggesting that the Jupiters' hallway ended at another three-way intersection. Their hallway was starting to widen just a bit, seemingly curving out to meet the other hallways. The double doors vanished, exposing a brightly lit room as crew members entered the ballroom, which appeared to have hundreds, possibly thousands sitting at tables. The doors then reappeared. These glimpses only increased Dan's and Barbara's anticipation.

The Jupiter family finally walked up to the double doors, which again vanished, exposing a magnificent, large banquet ballroom where thousands were indeed present. Some were standing around talking, but most were sitting down at fairly long tables arranged in neat, symmetrical rows. Scattered within the crowd were young children, possibly next to their parents or guardians. Some tables only had children, and Dan and Barbara wondered whether those children might be relatives of some of the military officers.

Dan and his family continued into the room, which had a vaulted ceiling, easily over fifteen meters high, and extended hundreds of meters in both directions. At the far end of the ballroom was a second-floor balcony, and hanging down from the tall ceiling were dozens of large, circular, twelve-tier chandeliers, each tier lined with individual crystal teardrops. The top tier of each chandelier had to be over twelve meters in diameter, with the bottom tier nearly three meters. There were thousands of crystal elements on each chandelier. Surprisingly, nothing was connecting the extremely aesthetic, beautiful chandeliers to the ceiling—no electrical wires, no chains, no cable supports. Neither were there any incandescent lights, yet all the chandeliers glowed with a soft white light, lighting up the entire ballroom, seemingly in a similar convention used on Earth, but no shadows whatsoever were being cast anywhere inside the large ballroom.

Dan and Barbara had to figure some force of gravity was suspending the chandeliers in midair. How, they could not imagine. They also did not have the faintest idea where they were supposed to sit, and neither did they recognize anyone in the room, though many of the advanced race were staring in their direction, surely knowing they were the Earth family. They felt awkward at that very moment but nevertheless privileged and honored to be the guests of honor.

Suddenly, Captain Donaldson stood up from a table about twenty meters away and waved them over to his table. Normally, visitors or dignitaries from other races they had treaties with would have been escorted, but since the Jupiter family was from Earth and a race thousands of technological years behind them, he thought it would be a nice touch for them to walk to the ballroom without escort.

Dan and his family continued down an aisle, passing six tables, each one at least two meters wide by fifteen meters long, and finally arrived at the table where Captain Donaldson was still standing. Dan and Barbara thought it strange there was no food or eating utensils atop any of the tables, only a few drinks in front of some of those in attendance.

At the far end of the table, a few meters away from Captain Donaldson, was a small stage about a meter higher than the rest of the floor. The raised stage was most likely the front of the room. There were five open seats just to the left of Captain Donaldson, obviously intended for them. Jose was sitting just to the left of the five open seats, and to her left, across the table, was a small group of females the Jupiters did not recognize. Directly across from Captain Donaldson was the first officer, and to the first officer's right was the chief medical officer. To his right, opposite the five open seats, were the chief geneticists, Phil, Neill, Brian, and James. To the geneticists' right was the chief science officer, Jonathan, and next to him was a female crew member, possibly his wife, an acquaintance, or his daughter or granddaughter. No spouses or female acquaintances were sitting next to Captain Donaldson, his first officer, or his chief medical officer, and no spouse or male acquaintance sat next to Jose.

Dan and his family arrived at their seats, and Captain Donaldson saw they were dressed in the outfits provided. "Please have a seat, Dan," he said. "I've reserved these seats especially for you and your family."

"Thank you," Dan said and turned around to see his wife had sat down next to Jose. Michael slowly took a seat next to his mother, Kyle sat to Michael's right, and Jason sat to the right of Kyle, meaning he would be next to his dad. Dan pulled his chair back to see there were no legs or rollers. It was suspended in midair, most likely by some gravity source. He sat down and saw flat displays flush with the tabletops, one in front of each seat, explaining the lack of food. Relaxing back in his chair, he felt a tension when he pushed the chair away from the table, which could mean there was also an attractive gravity force at work. He pulled his chair all the way up to the table and looked across at the geneticists and Captain Donaldson's officers, a warm greeting filling his face. It was still a strange sight to behold the empty tables, no food or utensils, but then, everyone would soon be selecting food from their displays, and the ship's computers would instantly generate and transport everything to their tables.

Brian, the chief organ function analyst, watched Captain Donaldson sit down and stared directly across the table at Michael and then Dan. "How's Michael doing?"

Dan turned to Brian. "Seems to have recovered extremely fast from his stasis," he said.

"That's good," Brian said. "We figured his advanced regenerative healing properties might allow that. If he did not have those attributes, it would have been weeks before his body would have fully recovered."

Dan nodded slightly.

Captain Donaldson noticed a small green light on his metallic-colored armband, an indication the ship's computers had determined everyone invited or able to attend was now present. He also noticed everyone in the room was starting to sit down. He glanced briefly at Dan and his family, stood up, and walked the short distance to the stage. He climbed the few stairs onto the stage and then slowly turned around. As he surveyed the large crowd, a huge screen, nearly five meters tall by seven meters wide, suddenly appeared on the wall directly above and behind him, displaying his face similar to a three-dimensional television yet having highly detailed holographic depth. No projector or camera was evident anywhere. The noise in the room started to die down until it was extremely quiet.

Captain Donaldson glanced down at the Jupiter family, looked around the room one more time, and finally said in plain English, "This dinner we are about to have is a very special dinner, a communion—a communion with new friends from the planet Earth. It is a unique friendship. Not only is it our first friendship with members of the Earth race, but this family has willingly accepted a friendship with our race and the beginning of a permanent bond to our race by way of a young child whom they have adopted as their own—a child who will also have his first meal tonight." Captain Donaldson paused and stared down at Michael, who was sitting quietly next to his mother and looking up with intense interest, analyzing everything that Captain Donaldson was telling the crowd. Captain Donaldson then gazed around the room again. "Well, that child is Michael," he said, "our race's greatest genetic achievement. He will also play an important part in the future of our race." Captain Donaldson paused again.

Now on the large screen, in full view of everyone, was Dan and his family, as though a camera were pointed directly at them, though no cameras were evident anywhere. Everyone in the room was either looking in their direction or staring up at the large screen. Some of those in attendance understood exactly what Captain Donaldson meant by Michael playing "an important part" in their race's future, as it was a secret innuendo of Michael understanding wormhole technologies later in adulthood.

Captain Donaldson looked around the room one more time and then back to Dan and Barbara. "We look forward to our continued friendship with Dan Jupiter and his family. May this friendship grow, prosper, and hopefully, one day in our distant future, develop into a friendship and peace treaty with the human race." Captain Donaldson paused again and added, "We are now going to have a brief moment of silence before dinner. Everyone enjoy our communion afterward. Thank you."

The large three-dimensional image disappeared behind Captain Donaldson, and Dan displayed a subtle, relaxed face. He bowed his head and closed his eyes, knowing the advanced race must have some type of religion in their society. It was an interesting thought, as they were highly advanced beyond imagination in a multitude of sciences, philosophies, and who knew what other fields. What might they know or have confirmed about God, an almighty being, the creator of the universe? Barbara, Jason, Kyle, and even Michael also bowed their heads, as did everyone in the room, children alike. A few moments later, Captain Donaldson raised his head and opened his eyes. "Everyone enjoy their food," he said, his voice again thunderous, as if amplified throughout the entire room, though no microphone was evident on his body or near the stage. He walked down the stairs and back to their table and sat back down next to Dan.

Everyone began touching screens in front of them, and food began appearing across the tables throughout the room, some of it unrecognizable to Dan, Barbara, Jason, and Kyle. The food was complemented with napkins, eating utensils, and full and empty glasses. There were platters in the middle of some tables like a large feast, some holding meats ready to be carved. Also on the tables were pitchers of clear and dark liquids. Dan figured the pitchers were so the guests could refill their glasses, especially the children's, so that the computer did not have to keep reconstituting the liquids into empty glasses.

Dan finally looked down at his display, noticing it was in English. He touched a series of menus and decided to select foods he recognized, not sure he was ready to take the chance of any of the race's foods having adverse effects on his body, such as an upset stomach, even though he did not think the advanced race would ever allow that to happen. Surely the Earth food items would be molecularly bonded the same as or very close to what would be found on Earth, so he selected tender roast beef, cooked medium, as well as mashed potatoes filled with garlic and cheese, corn on the cob, green beans, okra, brussels sprouts, a garden salad with Thousand Island dressing, and iced tea—a very nice selection. All those items instantly appeared on a large plate in front of him, alongside eating utensils and napkins. When Dan looked down the table at his family, he noticed his wife had already selected her food and drink, but he did not recognize her main course. It appeared to be a casserole of some type.

Barbara had chosen a dish that Jose had recommended to her. She was curious about the ingredients, as the dish was solely of the race's origin. It contained seafood meats mixed with vegetable greens and herbs and was completely compatible with human physiology.

She then noticed Kyle was still staring at his display. Neither had Michael selected anything. She placed her arm around Michael's little shoulder, reached over to Kyle's display, and touched a series of buttons. She selected a variety of Earth foods as well as a vitamin C cherry fruit drink, and all the food items instantly appeared on a plate, along with his drink.

Michael was staring up at her with a calm yet extremely observant face, having watched her select Kyle's food. She knew his body would no doubt be compatible with every food listed on the ship's menus, whether originating from Earth, the advanced race, or even other races. She decided to have him try Earth food for his first meal. She continued to stare down into his cute, sincere-looking face. "Go ahead and select the same food items and drink as Kyle," she said.

Michael did what she asked, and the items also suddenly appeared in front of him, along with metallic eating utensils and napkins. Now openly displayed in front of the boys was macaroni and cheese, lasagna with finely ground beef layered with cottage cheese, a side of green beans, and a slice of garlic bread. Steam rose up from the boys' plates, and Barbara was curious how hot their food might be, especially since Michael would not be able to judge what would be a normal temperature at which to eat food. Michael scooped up some macaroni and cheese, slowly brought it toward his mouth, placed it inside, and began analyzing its flavor. He stared up at his mother with a look of approval.

Barbara had figured Michael would like macaroni and cheese and felt reassured that the race would have never allowed food that would burn his mouth—especially for his first meal. She watched him next take a bite of lasagna and finally decided to try her own food. She sampled her casserole and found it was especially delicious, having a slight lobster and crab taste yet with a tinge of catfish. It was very unusual to be able to distinguish all three meat groups so easily, and the mouthwatering dish was stimulating to her taste buds. Jose had told her that the seafood meats had been created in molecularized form yet were an exact duplicate of the natural protein-enriched meats they enjoyed back home. Taking another bite, she noticed her husband and their three boys also enjoying their food, with Dan now visiting with the captain, his officers, and the geneticists.

On the other side of Barbara, Jose also witnessed Michael taking his first bites of American Earth food and grinned a little. "Michael will adjust just fine with your family," she said.

Her kind words made Barbara feel good. "Sure appears that way," she replied and then turned briefly to Dan, who was in an interesting conversation with the captain and his first officer.

To Dan's left, Jason was also enjoying his food, acting like a grown-up while listening to the interesting conversation between his father, Captain Donaldson, and the first officer. Captain Donaldson told his father there were over thirty-one thousand crew members aboard his ship, 31,208 to be exact, which included military and nonmilitary, some of whom also had their families with them. The captain also told his father the ship had 34,000 rooms and 510 levels, including a very large, magnificent room with plants and trees and a curved glass ceiling giving a nice view into outer space. The Valzarians had a special word in their language for these large rooms, but there was no exact English equivalent. Captain Donaldson explained that the rooms were similar to Earth atriums, arboretums, and conservatories, but the Valzarian rooms were different, as they contained running water, such as a stream, and, of course, the glass ceiling view into outer space. If a term existed in the English language for such rooms, they would be called plantariums or plantatriums. Jason sipped on his drink while looking around the table and turned back to his father, who was still talking to Captain Donaldson. He remained quiet with real interest about their conversation.

Dan quietly chewed his food and thought about the plantatrium and the size of the mother ship, including the number of personnel aboard. He took a sip of his drink. "This is truly an amazing ship," he said.

"Yes, it is," Captain Donaldson said, "and extremely powerful."

Dan was curious about his statement. "How powerful?"

Captain Donaldson stared across the table and then back to Dan. "Let's just say," he answered, "that the energy source that allows it to travel thousands of times the speed of light could power the country of the United States for decades."

Dan shook his head, flabbergasted. "From what source of nature are you obtaining that kind of energy?"

"From compressed gravity waves throughout our entire universe," Captain Donaldson said. "They are everywhere around us in some type of compression mode, carrying both potential and kinetic energies, as you call them on Earth, and are much more prevalent where space is compressed by a planetary body or a star's magnetic field, such as your sun. They are also all eventually focused back to black holes, regardless of whether the black hole is located at the center of the galaxy or not, as with all galaxies, or located where it has swallowed up portions of a galaxy in the form of a quasar, as your race calls the phenomenon." Captain Donaldson paused to see Dan quietly staring at him and added, "For your information and not to be known by your race, Dan, quasars are nothing more than unstable, supermassive black holes that have collapsed beyond their own quantum stability, continually extruding their magnetic field inward while at the same time constantly releasing and spewing energy outward from the depths of the universe itself."

Captain Donaldson paused a second time, noticing Dan still had a distant stare, like that of a child, and calmly added, "If you were, for instance, to orbit completely around a redshift quasar from an immense distance, you would find that it has a redshift in all spherical directions from its center. We have used probes to accomplish this feat, as well as sent staffed spacecraft into the event horizons of quasars, so that is why our race knows this to be a fact. It also agrees with our quasar quantum mathematics, not to mention our quasar computer models that back up our mathematical sciences with one hundred percent accuracy." Captain Donaldson let out a deep breath. "Now blueshift quasars," he continued, "are a different story and, by our race's standards, one of the greatest mysteries of our known universe, because they should act exactly opposite of redshift quasars, but they do not. In fact, they are only visible, optically, when you are within a distance of less than ten light-years of their outer magnetic field constraint horizon and space-force pressures. That is why they are so strange, because there is a compression of their energy back toward their center, causing every known energy type we understand not to be able to escape their quantum event horizon. This we know because about five of our centuries ago one of our crews traveled into the event horizon of one of these strange quasars. Despite using quantum gravity propulsion, they were lost and never heard from again. We now stay away from blueshift quasars and have even placed low-level technology warning beacons just outside their magnetic field event horizon—the spherical constraint of no return—to warn others not to approach any closer." Captain Donaldson paused.

Dan was extremely quiet, amazed and starry-eyed to hear all of this out of the blue. He never would have guessed that his question about how powerful the mother ship was would give him an explanation about aspects of the universe and quasars that had baffled Earth's scientists, but then, the advanced race did not understand wormhole technology and, surprisingly, blueshift quasars. Dan took another bite, wondering about that exact thing. He sipped on his tea and then set his glass down. "Has your race made any headway into wormhole technologies?"

Captain Donaldson paused. "No, we have not," he said, "but some of our scientists believe they know where the field resides in relation to time-warp-field quantum gravity technologies, but we have not yet been able to scratch the surface for the required gravity compression forces, including how to maintain them inside an envelope of new space-time perception of energy per circular-area units of space. That is especially true because we believe wormholes should be able to have curvatures to them, not just fixed straight tunnels, as used by our quantum gravity time-warp-field jumps or bursts."

Dan believed it was true the race did not understand wormholes; otherwise, the creation of Michael might not have happened. He glanced over at his wife, and she paused from telling Jose about her parents, who lived in Albany, New York. She instinctively knew Dan had something on his mind, especially after catching his brief conversation with the captain about wormholes. She wondered whether he was also thinking about a strange mystery on Earth within the top-secret communities, directly related to a rumor Dan had first heard about after working on some highly secretive projects for the government.

Dan turned his attention back to Captain Donaldson. "What does your race know about a man by the name of Dr. John Reed, who was possibly the smartest human to walk the planet, including the many unsubstantiated rumors surrounding his family?"

Captain Donaldson, his first officer, his science officer, and others sitting nearby showed a slight reaction to the question. It was rather quiet for a brief moment at their end of their table, and Dan raised his eyebrows, wondering whether there was more to it than just rumors.

Captain Donaldson glanced over at his first officer and then back to Dan. "We have heard about the many unsubstantiated rumors within your Earth's top-secret Majestic community, even from the above-top-secret government, regarding the human you have mentioned, but we also do not know with one hundred percent assurance what really happened."

Dan showed extreme interest. He was surprised to hear Captain Donaldson reference Earth's supersecretive Majestic 12 group, which covered up UFO encounters and helped safeguard all related advanced alien technologies in the possession of the human race, working to keep them out of private hands. "What are your rumors?" Dan asked.

Captain Donaldson shook his head in a negative manner. "I am not at liberty to discuss that," he said, "as it falls under your planet's

Majestic protocols, maybe even higher, and as such, what we suspect actually happened is still highly classified by our own race."

Dan realized he was probably not going to get any additional information about Dr. John Reed and his family.

Barbara was quiet because she, too, had heard about the many rumors surrounding Dr. John Reed and his family, not only from Dan, but also from others she used to work with in the top-secret community. They did not dare talk about those rumors outside of work or to anyone who did not carry the same level of compartmentalized top-secret clearance. She was now curious whether Michael might know the full details about Dr. John Reed.

Captain Donaldson looked down at Michael and then back to Dan. "Looks like your new son is going to have quite the appetite," he kidded.

Dan noticed Captain Donaldson was changing the subject. "Yes, it does," he replied.

Captain Donaldson briefly thought about the Reeds, especially John Reed, whose lineage could never be fully verified. He set his glass down and gave Dan a calm, relaxed look. "After dinner, in about four of your Earth hours," he said, "Jose, my officers, and I will come to your guest quarters and escort you to your new ship. I know you probably want to return home and take in everything that has transpired in what had to seem like a short span of time."

"You got that right," Dan said. "Do you care if we sightsee until then?"

"Not at all," Captain Donaldson said. "Some rooms will have restricted entry, but you'll quickly find that out, since our computers know everyone's exact cellular composition and will only open the doors to those who are authorized."

Dan nodded a little. "I understand. What's your plantatrium like?"

Dan's three boys perked up, waiting for the answer, and Captain Donaldson smiled a little. "It is a magnificent," he said, "and an important outlet for crew members, as sometimes we do not visit viable planets for weeks or months at a time—'viable' meaning planets with an atmosphere able to sustain carbon-based beings such as ourselves without the use of a special suit or force field. Anyway, the plantatrium is over fourteen stories high and filled with an abundance of plants and trees, with some of those trees almost reaching the ceiling. It has a running stream and a very large, beautiful waterfall. It is like a quiet walk in the park, as you say on Earth."

Dan grinned a little. "We'll definitely visit it, then," he said. "Thank you."

Captain Donaldson sipped his drink, set the glass down, and touched his flat display. An unusual-looking chocolate dessert appeared in front of him.

Dan eyed the delicious-looking dessert with intense interest. "What kind of dessert is that?"

Captain Donaldson paused. "In our world," he said, "we have many fruits not found on your planet. This particular dessert has a topping of chocolate, derived from a cocoa plant of our race's origin, and the fruit is from a naturally growing plant not found on your Earth. It would be called cherbanna in your native tongue, if it existed in your world, as it is a cross between a banana and a cherry. Believe it or not, but it contains some of the same plastid cells and carbon bonds of your bananas and cherries on Earth."

Dan was very interested to hear this. "Is that right? Does your race also have banana and cherry trees?"

"Yes, we do," Captain Donaldson said, "but our cherry and banana tree species are much larger than what is found on Earth, as are the fruits they bear. Our cherry fruits, for instance, are over sixty centimeters in diameter, and the trees bearing those fruits grow upwards of forty-five meters."

"Simply amazing," Dan blurted out. "I would not mind trying one of your cherbanna desserts."

"I will select you one," Captain Donaldson said. He touched

his console, and another cherbanna dessert, topped with chocolate, suddenly appeared in front of him. He then handed it to Dan.

The clear tulip-shaped glass cup was slightly larger than normal-sized cups on Earth and was filled with a yellowish-red dessert with a light-brown chocolate topping. Dan scooped up some of the chocolate dessert topping and slowly placed it in his mouth. As he relished its mild yet delicious and sweet taste, his mouth started to water. "This is excellent," he said. "It has an unusual flavor that I've never tasted in a chocolate."

"Yes, it does," Captain Donaldson agreed. "Our chocolates are much more refined than your Earth's chocolates. They have no caffeine for the quick buzz that you get from Earth's chocolates. They also have other natural ingredients that have been enhanced through genetic engineering over the centuries, all of which are now passed down from generation to generation during the natural breeding cycles of our cocoa trees."

Dan scooped up more of his dessert, just below the chocolate line and into the fruit filling. The predominant flavor of his second bite was cherry mixed with an underlying tinge of banana. It was amazing. On Earth, they would have to mix the two separate fruits together for the same effect, but they could probably never get the same amount of underlying banana flavor as a fruit that was molecularly carbon-bonded together as one plant.

He glanced briefly over at his wife and could tell she was having an enjoyable visit with Jose. Their three boys were now eating chocolate pudding desserts, but he figured they had heard him talking about the plantatrium with the captain, including its waterfall, and were surely antsy to visit it. Surveying the room, he noticed some of the crew members had already left, and others were just now leaving. As soon as the crew members stood up, their plates, glasses, silverware, napkins, and all uneaten food instantly disappeared, just like had happened earlier this morning after breakfast in the Jupiter family's guest quarters.

Barbara noticed their three boys were almost done with their desserts and were enjoying them immensely. She turned back to Jose, who was very pretty and who looked to be in her forties but was probably much older in human years. "Do you have children?"

"Yes, I do," she said. "I have a boy and a girl, six grandkids, and twelve great-grandchildren. My son resides on our home world as the spiritual counselor and adviser to the high council, which regulates and oversees our laws. My daughter is also a spiritual counselor and is a crew member aboard another mother ship just like this one."

Barbara continued to stare into Jose's pretty face. "The chief engineer," she said, "mentioned your home world planet is called Valzar and that you can thus be called Valzarians. Do you have words that equate to our terms *human*, *man*, and *woman*?"

Jose knew Barbara was going to ask the question. "Yes, we do," she said. "*Valzae* is our term for human. *Czae* would be an adult male and *czoe* an adult female."

"Interesting," Barbara said. "How about children?"

"It would be *czaee* for a male child and *czoee* for a female child," Jose answered.

Barbara was amazed at Jose's answer. The way the terms were pronounced was strange. She nodded, appreciative of the answer. "Do your children carry your telepathic abilities?"

"Yes, they do," Jose said.

Jose did not say much more about her children's telepathic abilities, and Barbara gave her a curious look.

Jose noticed this, read Barbara's mind again, and telepathically communicated to her, *Yes, telepathy is a strange science.*

Barbara grinned a little at the fact that Jose had read her mind and communicated with her using telepathy. It was strange to hear Jose's thoughts projected into her mind, as though an echo, while her lips did not move in the least bit, like a master ventriloquist. "What allows you to read and transmit thoughts?" she asked.

"Telepathic neurons," she said. "The more you have, the stronger your telepathic abilities."

"Is that right?" Barbara said, amazed. "Did your race always naturally carry those neurons, or have your genome systems just evolved over the years?"

Jose grinned a little. "Yes, our genomes have always carried them," she said, "but they have become much more pronounced over the past millennium or so. Your race also carries them to some degree, but your human physiologies and cultural ways of life generally keep them turned off. For our race, they have always been active, but then, telepathy is not a trait used that often by our populous for communication, except between friends and family members. Using telepathy too often, especially according to the number of active neurons, can lead to a mild form of temporary spiritual insanity."

Barbara thought she somewhat understood what Jose had just told her and now wondered about Michael's abilities, whether or not he had telepathic neurons, since it had never been brought up in the meeting with the geneticists. "How about for Michael?" she asked.

Jose paused. "Yes, he also has them," she said, "but they are currently dormant and should not start becoming active for nearly half a decade, in Earth years."

Barbara was especially interested by this new information and saw Dan was now done with his dessert. She turned back to Jose and said, "Interesting."

"Yes, it is," Jose said.

Dan also knew Barbara was done or nearly done with her dessert. "About ready to leave?" he asked her. "I'm looking forward to visiting the plantatrium, especially its waterfall."

"Yes, I am," she said, "and so am I."

Their boys perked up again at the mention of the plantatrium, particularly the waterfall. Dan slid his chair back, stood up, and looked around the table before staring directly down at Captain Donaldson with a warm, relaxed feeling inside his spirit. "It was an especially nice dinner, thank you," he said. "I could easily sit here all day and all night talking to you."

"I bet you could," Captain Donaldson said. He stood up and shook Dan's hand. "I'll see you in about four hours, then."

Dan stared across the table to the first officer, the other officers, and the chief geneticists. "Goodbye, everyone," he said. "It was nice to have met all of you."

"Likewise, Dan," Phil said.

"Yes," Neill said, "it was nice to have met you too. I know you'll enjoy raising Michael."

Dan suddenly felt extremely personable. "Thank you," he replied.

Brian and James noticed Dan's personable attitude. "Bye, Dan," they both said.

Barbara also stood up. "Thank you, Jose," she said. "Our conversation was enjoyable, not to mention extremely interesting."

Jose knew she was referring to their discussion of telepathy and associated telepathic neurons. "Anytime, and you're welcome, Barbara," she said, noticing that Jason, Kyle, and Michael were also now standing.

Dan and his family finally started to leave the table, but then Dan stopped and turned around to Captain Donaldson. "Is it okay if we keep the pressure suits we are wearing?"

Captain Donaldson gave him a small grin, knowing Michael had explained some of the suits' properties to them. He also knew after a brief telepathic reading that Dan and his family were planning to return to their quarters and change back into the clothing they'd been wearing when they first came aboard his ship. "Sure, Dan," he said. "Once you've changed back into your Earth clothing, the pressure suits will be transported to your ship, and yes, your ship's computer can create gloves and face mask helmets that are composed of the same exact molecular-based material."

"Thank you," Dan said, totally amazed that Captain Donaldson had read his mind so easily. He and his family slowly continued away from the table. He had to stare up again at the chandeliers that were suspended in midair directly above them. He was also now wondering how often Captain Donaldson and his crew wore similar pressure suits. Maybe they were standard for military personnel. "Interesting," he mumbled under his breath. He turned right and continued down another aisle, past two more tables. He knew quite a number of the remaining crew members were watching them, which was understandable, since they were the guests of honor.

The double doors vanished in front of them, and they continued out into the hallway and stopped, the double doors reappearing behind them. Dan looked down the hallway to his right, then to his left, and finally straight ahead down the corridor they'd taken to get to the ballroom. Suddenly, Michael reached up and grabbed his left hand. Dan knew Michael had seen Jason doing it earlier. Jason, after seeing this, reached up and grabbed Dan's other hand. Kyle grabbed his mother's right hand, and then Michael took hold of Kyle's remaining hand. They all now walked together as a family, all holding hands, forming a chain, spreading across most of the hallway they had previously traveled.

Along the way, Dan looked up at the ceiling nearly two meters above his head and noticed like before that it was brightly lit—no shadows evident anywhere. There were curvatures where the walls met the ceilings and floor, and Dan figured the entire ship had the same design characteristics. Up ahead, three large males, all in military attire and with calm demeanors, were walking in their direction. Dan and his family slowed and moved to the right as their two groups finally met in the hallway. "Hello, Dan and Barbara Jupiter," one of the males said in plain English. "Hope you enjoyed your dinner."

Dan and Barbara were again only mildly surprised the crew member knew who they were. "Yes, we did, thank you," Dan replied.

The males continued down the corridor away from them. Dan and Barbara felt good about their apparent popularity and what had to be a lot of talk about them aboard the mother ship. They could probably walk anywhere aboard the ship and it would be like being among thousands of friends. Still holding hands, the Jupiter family slowly continued toward the transporter elevator with Dan and Barbara becoming increasingly curious about the other rooms on this level of the ship, especially since they were near the large ballroom. Dan suddenly stopped in front of a large door just to his right without breaking his grip on Michael's or Jason's hands. Like a chain reaction through Michael and Kyle over to his wife, they all came to a complete stop. Dan then turned and faced the door, wondering whether or not it would open and allow them entry, considering what Captain Donaldson had just told him about how some doors would only open to those authorized.

Barbara was growing curious about what Dan was up to when the door in front of them suddenly vanished. Dan was surprised, and after letting loose of his sons' hands, he walked inside, followed by his wife and three boys. The room was very different from any they'd seen so far. It was easily over two hundred meters long by a hundred meters wide, having a ceiling of around five meters. There were hundreds of evenly spaced, metallic-colored bins in many different sizes. Dozens of computer consoles with a multitude of holographic images were projected above each console, each image with information. Crew members were positioned in front of each console, as though monitoring the many different holographic images.

Dan finally looked down at Michael, very curious. "Do you know what this room is used for?"

"Yes, I do, Daddy," he answered. "It is the ship's main storage and food processing center."

Dan was amazed. "Oh really?" he said, noticing one of the males in the room was headed in their direction—a military officer, based on his outfit, though Dan had no idea what rank. He looked down again to Michael. "What is in the metallic bins?"

"Molecularized minerals and compounds in compressed form," Michael answered.

"Interesting," Dan said.

The military officer walked up to where they were standing. He had a large frame and was easily over seven feet tall. The officer knew they were the Earth family but was a little surprised the door had opened for them, as it was a highly restricted area. That meant Captain Donaldson had given them a fairly high level of access.

"Hello," Dan said.

"Hello," the supervisory officer replied in perfect English. "Do you want a full tour of our food storage and molecular processing facility?"

Dan glanced at his wristwatch and thought about the plantatrium, which they definitely wanted to visit before leaving the spaceship. "I wish we had time," he said, "but we were planning to visit the plantatrium before returning to Earth."

"Very understandable," the tall male said, "but since you're already here, how about I give you a quick rundown of how this processing center functions aboard this ship?"

Dan perked up, as did Barbara, but Michael did not show much of a reaction, because everything that was about to be explained was simple knowledge. "That sounds great!" Dan said.

The tall male looked briefly to Barbara and down at Jason, Kyle, and Michael before turning back to Dan. "This room," he explained, "has a very large assortment of elements and compounds in compressed pure molecular form, elements and compounds that are essential for sustaining the physical well-being and health of everyone on this ship." The male paused and pointed over at one of the cylindrical metallic bins two meters in diameter by three meters tall. "For instance," he said, "that metal bin there contains pure sodium. In its present high-density, gravitationally compressed form, a bin of that size, if full, would weigh in excess of one hundred tons, but on this ship, because the bin's force field containment is directly associated to outer space and not this spaceship's field of gravity, it is virtually weightless."

Dan and Barbara stood quietly amazed and interested, knowing the sodium had to be compressed to a volume weight per square foot not normally possible. The bin's maximum capacity had to be around 250 cubic feet, so if the sodium were not compressed, a full bin would weigh close to seven tons. That meant, with compression, the bin's full capacity was around fifteen times normal. What the officer had said about the weight being associated to outer space and not to the overall weight of the mother ship was mind-boggling.

The male knew what they were thinking. "Some of the largest bins," he continued, "contain minerals, such as calcium, magnesium, zinc, iron, and phosphorus, to name a few, and many other compounds, such as salt, pectin, folic acid, glucose, riboflavin, and ascorbic acid. Some also have a variety of enzymes that allow the creation of multitudes of high-energy amino acid protein food cell structures. All bins contain a vacuum and are free of all possible oxidation and microbes. Whenever a food is selected anywhere on this ship, our computers combine all required ingredients to create highly nutritional compounds and then transport the final product to the designated location where it was selected. The creation process is then complete. Uneaten food is molecularly separated, purified, and then reconstituted back into its original forms. Those molecular constitutes are then returned to the bins from which they first originated. There is no food waste on this ship, nor is there on any of our spaceships, including back on our home world."

Dan and Barbara grinned a little. "Interesting," Dan said. "Where are your water supplies and liquids to mix with all those bin ingredients?"

"Another room on this floor," the male replied. "The hydrogen and oxygen molecules remain separated, gravitationally compressed into high-density molecular forms. For instance, where water in Earth's gravity environment has a mass volume of around sixty-two pounds per cubic foot, in our gravitational compressed forms, as used in the bins of this ship, at least after the two molecules are combined, the mass volume equivalency of our water would be over six thousand pounds per cubic foot. For our fruit drinks, such as vitamin C and similar constituents, all their biomacromolecules are derived from actual fruit and vegetable plants, hydrogenated, and then compressed into their own vacuum-chamber bins, completely free of oxidation and microbes." The male paused from his detailed explanations.

Dan, Barbara, and their boys remained quiet. Dan and Barbara were amazed by their preview of the food processing center. Barbara noticed her three boys staring over at the metallic bins and looked up to the tall, good-looking male, curious whether there were actual authentic fresh foods aboard the ship. "Does this ship have any vegetable or fruit gardens?" she asked.

"Yes, it does," the male said. "Those gardens are located on one of the levels near the centerline of the spaceship and encompass nearly a half square mile of fertile dirt that is highly energized with phosphorus, potassium, and nitrogen. In this garden are hundreds of acres of disease-, drought-, and frost-resistant, grain-bearing plants, similar to the wheat, corn, and sorghum plants on your planet. All our grain plants are also high-yield crops. For instance, our plants that are similar to your wheat produce over four hundred bushels per acre, and their kernels, especially their endosperms, are extremely dense by nature."

Dan and Barbara now knew the mother ship was self-sustaining and could support its entire crew for quite some time, at least as long as they had a water supply. Dan wondered whether their vegetables and grain crops were ever eaten fresh. "Do you also store whole-grain crops?"

The male nodded in the affirmative and briefly read Dan's and Barbara's minds. "Yes, we do," he said, "and as a matter of fact, they are also stored in compressed forms inside vacuum-chamber bins. Our gardens have a wide variety of vegetable and fruit crops, always harvested by our computers, and yes, freshly eaten on this ship. But then again, whether their molecular structures have been in storage for six months or sixty years, it is unrecognizable to those eating them due to the vacuum storage. We do use the oldest constituents first, though. The more popular the food or drink, then the more of its internal ingredients, or whole food structures, are retained in storage."

Dan realized the nice male had read his mind. "Does your garden also have coffee plants, such as Travanian coffee?" he asked.

The male grinned at the fact that Dan knew about their race's most popular coffee. "Of course," he said. "In fact, you'd be surprised how many different flowers, medicinal plants, and edible plants are scattered throughout this ship, inside crew members' quarters, and even your own guest quarters. Some of our plants even filter the air of contaminant particles as a food source, kind of like an ionic filter collector, in addition to their photosynthesis carbon dioxide–oxygen exchange cycle."

Dan and Barbara were amazed to hear about these plants and knew their room had a few plants in it. It seemed there was only one reason the mother ship would ever have to locate a viable planet with an Earth-type atmosphere—fresh water. Dan was still curious about that exact thing and made eye contact with the tall male. "How long can this ship go without having to replenish its water supplies?"

"Good question," the male said. "About one Earth year with it current number of crew members, not including emergency supplies, and only when its water and food bins are completely full and, of course, provided no crew members are placed into a room-temperature stasis field when supplies run low."

Barbara and Dan were truly interested again, and Barbara felt appreciative for the time the male had taken to explain a little about their food processing facility, including a few other secrets. "Thank you for your time, sir," she said.

The male knew they were itching to see the magnificent room of plants and trees and especially the waterfall. They would be amazed. "No problem at all," he said.

Dan nodded his head a little. "Yes, thank you," he said.

The male looked down briefly at Michael because he knew the little boy understood everything about the molecular conversion processes of the elements, minerals, and vitamins inside the bins, from their compressed states into their solid, unrestricted food groups, and vice versa, and probably even beyond. He watched Michael turn toward the exit with his new family. The door vanished in front of them, and they continued out into the hallway, turning right and disappearing behind the closed door.

Without a second thought, the Jupiter family continued toward the elevator transporter. Jason again grabbed his dad's right hand. Michael, after seeing this, did the same with his dad's other hand, and before long, all of them were holding hands again the same as before their surprising visit to the main food processing center.

As they walked to the transporter elevator just up ahead, Dan and Barbara thought about their dinner and the special memories they would always carry of it. There was Barbara's conversation with Jose about her home world and then Dan's conversation with Captain Donaldson about the mother ship and its advanced capabilities and about redshift and blueshift quasars. Dan wished he could tell Earth's scientists what the advanced race knew to be a fact, especially their computer models associated to redshift quasars, but he knew it could never happen.

The Jupiter family finally walked up to the transporter elevator. The door vanished, exposing an empty room, and the boys suddenly let loose of their parents' hands, quickly entering inside. Dan looked down the hallway to his left, then to his right, seeing a few crew members in the far distance and realizing again that the hallways extended beyond his vision. It reminded him again of the enormous size of the mother ship. He then followed his wife into the transporter elevator and turned around to see the door had already reappeared behind him. He looked down at the wall console and said, "Level eighteen, quadrant twenty."

The door to their transporter this time displayed a dark-blue hue right before it vanished. Like the previous times, Dan could not visually see their bodies vanish before his eyes while they were molecularly broken down and then reconstituted. The three boys, now wound up with excitement, exited into the hallway, turned right, and then vanished out of sight. Dan and Barbara also exited into the hallway and turned right. Their boys were already well ahead, Jason leading the way for his younger brothers, and they started to disappear around the curved section of the hallway.

Again, the boys were not projecting any shadows inside the brightly lit hallway that was lit by some strange photon-neutrino decay method—via photons piggybacked on neutrinos. Dan was still contemplating the photon-neutrino technology. He cupped his hands together against his chest to see whether there would be any darkness behind his hands. Slightly lifting his right thumb, he was surprised to find that the space behind his hands first appeared dark right before lighting up as though he were cupping a small light bulb. *That is so very strange,* he thought. *The ship must be transmitting those photons to all open areas of space, possibly through our bodies, but then, the neutrinos are surely not degenerating inside our bodies, or the photons would release immense amounts of energy and heat them up. If the space-time degeneration path of the photons was slightly altered in relation to the path of the neutrinos so that they would end up inside organic matter, that would possibly create one heck of a powerful and dangerous photon weapon. That is an amazing realization and surely a weapon this race possesses.*

Dan and Barbara started around the curved hallway. The boys still were not in sight and were possibly already inside their quarters, though why they were in such a hurry, Dan and Barbara did not know for certain, other than they would soon be visiting the plantatrium. The hallway straightened out, and knowing their quarters were just up ahead on the right, Dan and Barbara sped their pace a little. When they reached the door, it displayed a slight deep-green haze before it vanished before their eyes. They continued inside to find the boys sitting at the same table where Jason and Kyle had sat earlier. A three-dimensional spherical image was currently displayed in front of Jason. There were three distinct, slightly transparent spheres inside one another this time, instead of the two that had been displayed yesterday. The entire image was filled with an abundance of colored dots. After the door to their quarters reappeared behind them, Dan and Barbara let out deep sighs, and Dan, with a quick glance of his wristwatch, saw it was 1:30 p.m. "In about thirty minutes, boys," he announced, staring over at them, "we'll visit the plantatrium."

Jason showed noticeable excitement. "Can we go now?" he asked.

"No," Dan said. "Let's let our food first settle just a bit."

Jason felt brief disappointment, but it was quickly overshadowed by the game he was currently playing against both of his brothers now. Michael having joined them would make it extremely challenging. "Okay," he said.

Dan noticed Jason was intensely interested in the holographic image and thought about what they'd just experienced in the large ballroom, including the enjoyable visit with Captain Donaldson, his officers, and his crew members. The ballroom with its large chandeliers, all suspended in midair, had truly been a magnificent sight.

Dan and Barbara sat down on the couch, and Dan touched the screen on the table in front of him, trying to locate the ship's main plantatrium. As he systematically browsed through the English-language menus, to his surprise, he saw a weapons and countermeasures menu. He selected it with a quick glance over at his wife. "Look at this, would you?" he said.

The menu contained several categories: gravity, electron, proton, neutron, photon, black energy, and subspace, each with secondary categories of emissive, submissive, and disruptive. Barbara surmised the three categories might mean warning, neutralize, and destroy but was not sure. "Wow!" she said.

Dan touched the subspace disruptive submenu and was given four options: gravity, photon, microwave, and subsonic. He was amazed at not only the number of possible weapon combinations but also that subspace would be associated with subsonic, as that combination did not make any sense. *A subsonic subspace field?* he wondered. *How is that possible?*

Wanting to know what it meant, he selected the subsonic subcategory. The screen suddenly displayed "Access denied. Level 6 clearance required." Dan noticed his wife looked amazed. "That was a surprise, huh?" he said.

"Yes, it was," she said. "At least we now know what level of information access we currently do not have. Maybe we have to understand the technology first, before we are allowed to even view it?"

"Possibly," Dan said, "but the funny thing about it all is that I'm certain Michael understands every aspect of those weapons and could probably explain everything about them to us, regardless of our restrictions."

Barbara nodded, amazed at that prospect, and thought about her conversations with Jose. She turned to Dan with a relaxed face and said, "I found out from Jose that their race's equivalent to *human* is *valzae*. Males are *czaes*, and female are *czoes*."

"Is that right?" Dan replied.

Barbara smiled a little at his reaction.

Dan glanced down at the manuals and decided to give his mind a break and digest the enjoyable, interesting conversations during dinner, as well as the amazing information revealed at the food processing center. He relaxed back on the couch until they were about ready to leave to see the plantatrium.

# 21

## THE MOTHER SHIP'S MAGNIFICENT PLANTATRIUM

It was now 2:02 p.m., and Dan figured they might as well change into their Earth clothing. A set of twenty-first-century Earth clothing had been provided for Michael: jeans, a blue short-sleeved shirt, white tennis shoes, gray socks, and underwear, all appearing very similar to and of the same quality as what Jason and Kyle were wearing. Dan was curious whether the advanced race had placed any name-brand identifications on the clothing, mimicking his other two boys' clothing.

Dan walked up to his and Barbara's bed and picked up the jeans provided for Michael. He studied them and suddenly giggled under his breath. He then inspected the neckline of the flannel shirt. After closely looking at the underwear and the tennis shoes, he shook his head with almost uncontrollable laughter.

Barbara, who had been watching him curiously, quickly stood up at his reaction and headed over to the bed. "What's so funny?" she asked.

Dan calmly answered, "Oh, it's hilarious how this race is not preferential to any name brands. There are no markings whatsoever on Michael's clothing or his tennis shoes, yet they appear almost identical to Jason's and Kyle's clothes in every other respect."

Barbara also thought it was hilarious and picked up Michael's jeans, which were of the same quality of any Levi or Wrangler jeans. His little tennis shoes also appeared of the same quality as Reebok or Nike shoes. She next picked up and inspected Jason's jeans, which were clean with a fresh scent.

Dan picked up his own jeans and felt the left pocket to make sure the communicator and his pocket change were still there—they were. He felt the right pocket again for the moondust and found it was also still there, undisturbed. That moondust would become a topic of conversation for his kids, his wife, and maybe even the race's two families currently living on Earth. He felt Kyle's jeans for the rock that his son had picked up on the moon, and sure enough, it was also still in the pocket. He set the pants down and finally exited the bedroom to see the boys still entranced in their game. "Are you boys ready to see the plantatrium?"

Jason showed anticipation. "Yes, I am," he said.

Michael and Kyle also showed excitement. "Yes, Daddy, I am," Michael said.

"Me too," Kyle chimed in.

"Okay," Dan said, "but before we go, let's get dressed in the clothes we were wearing when we first arrived, and for you, Michael, you've been provided simulated Earth clothing."

As the three boys stood up, the holographic imaged diminished but did not completely disappear. Michael had an unusual look on his face, probably because he was getting to wear Earth-type clothing for the first time. When they finally arrived at the bed, Jason picked up his clothes and tennis shoes as his parents started to remove Kyle's and Michael's pressure suits. Jason headed to the bathroom and thought about their upcoming visit to the plantatrium, feeling as though he were about to visit Disneyland, or maybe even a zoo.

At the bed, Dan continued to undress Kyle. The fact he was

able to do so meant the zippers were not biologically interfaced to only the one wearing the suit, unlike the armbands, but they could be biologically interfaced to their family. Barbara helped Michael out of his pressure suit while he quietly stared up into her face. Dan had to smile a little at this mother-son interaction. Barbara finished removing Michael's suit, and the two little boys now stood naked in front of their parents without a second thought of their being nude. It was the first time Dan and Barbara had seen Michael naked, and they noticed he had the exact external anatomy of a little Earth boy who had been circumcised, though possibly he had been genetically engineered without a foreskin.

The two boys slipped into their underwear with Michael closely watching Kyle to know what to do. Dan then grabbed Kyle's jeans and helped him into them, while Barbara did the same with Michael. She then stood Michael up and slowly fastened the buttons on his shirt.

While Dan fastened Kyle's shirt, he noticed Barbara had already set Michael on the side of the bed. "You're just too fast," he kidded.

Barbara grinned a little while slipping on Michael's socks. Dan finally placed Kyle on the bed next to Michael while Barbara now helped Michael into his tennis shoes. They both knew Michael, with his intellect, would easily dress himself after just one example of how to do so.

Jason, changed into his Earth clothes, exited the bathroom and returned to his parents' bedroom to see his two brothers almost completely dressed. "I am ready to go," he said.

Barbara snugged Michael's last shoestring tight and looked over at her oldest son. "Yes, you are," she said. She looked down again into Michael's pretty blue eyes and gently touched his chin, squeezing it a couple of times. "You're so cute," she said.

Michael suddenly felt an extreme warm feeling inside toward his nice mom. She set him down on the floor, and after Dan finished tying Kyle's last shoestring and pulled it tight, he set Kyle down next to Michael. He then picked up his own clothes and tennis shoes.

Barbara did the same and noticed the three boys quietly staring up at them. "We'll be back in a little bit," she said, "and then we'll all go see the plantatrium."

Jason again perked up. "Okay, Mom," he said.

Dan picked his armband off the small bedside table and followed his wife to the bathroom.

Meanwhile, Jason, Michael, and Kyle returned to the table and the nearly half-meter-diameter spherical holographic image, which suddenly turned from dim to bright. Michael touched the image, resuming their game. It was Jason's turn, and he briefly analyzed the sphere and then touched one of the white dots. As he pulled his hand out of the holograph, the white dot changed to blue, as did some of the red and green dots throughout the entire sphere. The spherical image moved directly in front of Kyle, who reached up and touched a white dot. The selected dot turned green, as did a few of the blue and red dots. The image moved in front of Michael, who was still thinking about his parents leaving the room to change their clothes. Like before, he figured it was okay for young kids to undress in front of their parents, but apparently his parents did not want to change in front of him and his brothers. Even after realizing this privilege of his parents, he still did not understand why they would be ashamed of their bodies.

"Your turn, Michael," Jason said.

Michael regained his senses and looked up into their spherical holographic game, knowing the image also represented a dynamic spherical coordinate aspect of quantum gravity propulsion, where the nucleus equaled the inner sphere, which equaled light-space, nominalizing the speed of light and space. He finally extended his hand inside the holograph and touched one of the semitransparent white dots. After he'd removed his hand, the dot changed from white to red, followed by some of the green and blue dots changing to red. There was now a higher quantity of red dots than any of Jason's blue dots or Kyle's green dots.

Jason looked up into the holographic image with the analytical perception of an intrigued ten-year-old Earth boy. After playing the two-sphere game with Kyle last night and then again briefly this morning, he'd had a chance to think more about its lines and points and now knew how many points, or dots, as well as curved and straight lines were associated to each sphere and between each sphere, including to the center point, or nucleus. The new three-sphere matrix would just add to the totals from one of the spheres.

There were 5 latitudinal lines circling each sphere horizontally, one at the equator and two at 30 and 60 degrees away, both above and below the equator. On each of those latitudinal lines were 12 dots equally spaced 30 degrees apart, completing 360 degrees of rotation. 12 points times 5 lines equaled a total of 60 points. Plus there were 2 points at the top and bottom poles, for a grand total of 62 points per sphere. All 3 spheres combined, that was 186 points. Adding the center point, or nucleus, resulted in a grand total of 187 points within the entire three-sphere hologram. Jason did not have the slightest idea what the significance of this number, integer 187, was.

Each latitudinal (horizontal) curved line on each sphere was broken into 12 line segments by the 12 dots on each line, with the 2 points at the poles being unusable. So total, 12 line segments times 5 lines on each sphere equaled 60 latitudinal line segments per sphere. The total number of longitudinal (vertical) curved line segments connecting all 62 dots together, the 2 points at the poles now being usable, would equal 72 line segments, or 12 times 6. The total number of curved latitudinal (horizontal) and curved longitudinal (vertical) line segments on the surface of each sphere thus equaled 132 line segments, or 60 plus 72. When multiplied times 3, there was a total of 396 curved line segments within the three-sphere image.

What was unique about the game was that each dot, or point, on the surface of each of the three spheres, had a straight faint white line segment connecting it inward to the corresponding point of the next sphere, with all the points on the innermost sphere connected directly to the center point, or nucleus, by the same number of straight line segments. Adding the top and bottom poles, the outer and middle spheres had a total of 62 straight line segments connecting each of their points to the corresponding 62 points of the next inward sphere, and then the 62 points of the innermost sphere connected directly to the center point, or nucleus. Adding all these straight line segments together, there were 186 total straight line segments between all the dots within the spherical holographic image. Adding the 186 straight line segments to the 396 curved longitudinal and latitudinal line segments previously determined provided a grand total of 582 total line segments connecting all the dots together into one magnificent-looking spherical matrix overlay of three spheres—a large outer sphere, a medium middle sphere, and a smaller inner sphere, with one center point, which could also, in reality, be viewed as a small sphere with only one point. So with the center point, or nucleus, and all the points on the surface of each sphere, there were *187 points*, all connected together by *582 straight and curved line segments*. Jason did not know the full mathematical and scientific significance of these numbers—*integers 187 and 582*—but he could not wait to talk to Michael more about it later, as surely it had some relationship to the game strategy.

Jason finally reached up inside the sphere and touched one of the white dots on the innermost sphere. When he removed his hand, the dot changed from white to blue, followed by some of the red and green dots also changing to blue within all three spheres. The light-yellow center point did not change, but it did flash a few times, just like it did every other time any white dot was selected.

While the kids continued their game, Dan and Barbara removed their pressure suits and got dressed in their original Earth clothing. Sitting next to each other on a small chair, they both slowly slithered into their jeans. Barbara stood up, pulled her jeans up to her waist, fastened them, and then sat down again. She slipped into her socks and looked over at Dan with anticipation of visiting the plantatrium. "I feel like we are about to see something really beautiful," she said.

Dan grinned at his half-naked wife. "That's for sure," he said. "I wonder if our small spaceship has a similar room?"

"Good question," Barbara said. "I hope so. That would be nice."

Barbara was now fully dressed, and Dan slipped on his socks and grabbed his tennis shoes, curious what the ship they were about to be given would look like. Tying his shoelaces, he was additionally curious about its ability to travel thousands of times the speed of light in an angular flight path anywhere between 0 and 180 degrees of their forward momentum—at least that was how it had been explained to them. The fixed quantum gravity time-warp-field jump with a speed millions of times the speed of light was even more amazing. It was unconceivable, as it would seem to take an exponentially tremendous amount of energy, and it was still a mystery to Dan, though the chief engineer had alluded to that space-travel technique much more quickly draining the ship's unique power source, a power source that had to be immensely powerful. What had happened with the semifake armband at the Los Alamos labs, when Dan had witnessed it generate over one million watts of power with less than a hundred watts of input, was also strange, as the energy had to be pulled from somewhere, possibly even from Earth's magnetic field. On the other hand, maybe it had been pulled from the depths of the universe in the form of universal gravitational energy? Who knew? Tightening his last shoelace, Dan stood up and saw his wife staring into a mirror. "Yes, you're pretty," he said, flirting.

Barbara giggled. "Well, let's go see the plantatrium," she said.

"Okay, let's do it," Dan said. He picked up his armband and slowly and methodically moved it toward his left forearm, zeroing in on the three holes that it had previously created. As soon as the needles contacted his skin, the armband changed shape, tightening and piercing deep into his forearm. He did not feel any pain, though, and it seemed as if the armband might have automatically positioned itself to the location of the previous holes.

He followed his wife toward the exit. The door glowed with a beautiful, mind-stimulating red-and-white hue emblazoned against a bluish-green rectangle and then vanished. They continued through the doorway, amazed, because the visual display sort of reminded them of the American flag. At the table, their boys were staring up into the holographic image that was filled with an abundance of red, blue, and green dots along each sphere. There was a light-yellow dot at the very center, and faint white lines connected all the dots. The red dots seemed much more prevalent, so one of the kids was evidently winning the unusual game. "Let's go, boys," Dan said, grabbing his kids' attention.

Jason touched the console, and the holographic image quickly disappeared. The boys all stood up without any hesitation whatsoever and quickly met their parents at the door, excitement and anticipation visible all over their faces. Dan and Barbara realized again that Michael was quickly mimicking and learning the emotional traits of excitement from his brothers.

The three boys led the way into the hallway and turned left, back toward the transporter elevator. In the distance, two very tall, nice-looking males were headed their direction. They were dressed in attire not seen on any other crew member and seemed slightly taller than the rest of the crew members, well over eight feet, and they also had a skin tint not seen with anyone else aboard the ship—as if slightly glowing. There was just something about them that Dan and Barbara could not quite place their finger on, but immense feelings of respect suddenly filled their spirits. "Hello, Dan and Barbara," one of the males said in plain English. "Hope you are all doing well."

Dan thought he would be clever. "*Ναι, είμαστε*," he replied, which was Greek for "Yes, we are."

The two males smiled, as they understood all of Earth's languages. One of them calmly said, "*To pepromenon phugein adunaton.*"

Dan laughed as the males continued away from them.

Barbara understood a little Greek but did not fully understand the male's reply. "What was that all about?"

Dan was still grinning a little and replied, "Oh, I was just seeing how well they spoke other Earth languages, such as Greek. His statement definitely makes you stop and think."

"Oh really?" she said. "What did he say?"

"He said, 'It's impossible to escape from what is destined.'"

Barbara was amazed to hear this and suddenly laughed, now wondering whether the two males were part of the ship's security, though they were not dressed like security. Plus, their skin coloring was different and odd, as if they had a slight glow. Her instinctive respect toward them also seemed much stronger that what she'd felt with any other crew members, including Captain Donaldson. She wondered more about it but then saw Michael and Kyle a little ways ahead of them with Jason following behind. Dan had also felt immense respect for the two large, tall males. He took a quick peek behind him, and the two males were strangely no longer visible, as if suddenly transported out of the hallway to another room of the ship. He did not give it much more thought and now wondered about the holographic game his sons had been playing. "Jason," he said, "who was winning your game?"

Jason turned around. "Michael was," he said, "and I was in second."

Dan and Barbara found their oldest son's reply humorous. Dan's question had been slightly rhetorical, as he and Barbara knew Michael would be hard to beat in any mentally challenging game, regardless of whether it was of Earth origin or of the race that had created him. It would be strange but interesting to play Michael in any board game, especially the ones requiring strategy. They knew the chances of ever beating him, after he understood how the game was played, were slim to none. The hallway straightened out, and the boys were now nearly four meters ahead of their parents. Dan turned to his wife to talk to her about what they had already witnessed earlier this morning. "You know, we'll have to teach Michael to not get so excited at times, as evidenced by his walking ahead of us and being so trusting of his four-year-old brother's immature decision-making."

"True," Barbara agreed.

Their boys waited in front of the transporter elevator, as the entrance door had again not opened for them. Either the elevator was in use, or the ship's computers were not allowing their kids to roam around by themselves. Dan and Barbara finally arrived at the entrance, and the door vanished. The three boys walked inside first, followed by Barbara and then Dan, who turned around in time to watch the door reappear with a slight red glow before appearing solid. "Level two hundred, quadrant four," he said.

The transporter-elevator door again suddenly vanished, exposing another brightly lit hallway. The three boys exited, and Dan and Barbara followed. The hallway extended to the left and right. To the right, about twenty meters away, was a large lobby filled with an abundance of crew members relaxing and visiting—perhaps one of the ship's main lounges. Most of the crew members appeared nonmilitary, or least were not dressed in military attire, maybe off duty.

Just beyond the lounge was a very large opening easily over seven meters high by ten meters wide. It clearly led to the plantatrium, as beyond the entrance were large trees with an abundance of green and red leaves. Sunlight, possibly from Earth's sun, shone down into the large room, likely through the glass ceiling Captain Donaldson had mentioned, but then, the sunlight could have been artificially generated. This visual sight was breathtaking for all of them. The very tall, colorful trees had to be many stories high, just as the captain had said. Inside the plantatrium were crew members with children.

Dan and Barbara immediately led the way, entering the lounge area, which was over fifty meters wide by a few hundred meters long. The lighting in the lounge was not quite as bright as the hallway, which could only mean there were not as many photons riding on neutrinos—at least that was what Dan surmised.

They continued toward the plantatrium as if driven by a magnetic force of visual acuity. As they walked through the lounge, servers passed by, delivering drinks and food to the tables, which was surprising since the race had space-transport technology to instantly transport items.

As they approached the plantatrium entrance, Dan saw a couple of extremely colorful birds flying around. He turned to Barbara, again surprised. "Did you see that?"

"Yes, I did," she said. "I wonder what stops them from flying out of the room and into the lounge area, since it appears to be an open entrance."

Dan continued to stare into his pretty wife's eyes. "You know, I was wondering that myself," he said.

The Jupiter family walked up to within a few meters of the entrance with some crew members in the lounge watching them. With Jason leading the way, Michael and Kyle following close behind, the boys walked through the open entrance. Dan and Barbara witnessed a faint light-blue flash of light around their little bodies. Dan turned to his wife as they approached the opening. "The entrance must have a force field of some type, huh?" he said.

Barbara nodded to agree. "Possibly," she said while walking through the opening. Sure enough, a barely noticeable blue layer of light opened up around their bodies, yet neither felt anything. They figured the force field was slightly different from the one they'd experienced when walking off the small spaceship to the moon's surface.

Now inside and continuing behind their boys, Dan figured the force field was somehow constraining the birds. "I would be willing to bet," he said, "that the force field we just walked through is some kind of organic energy barrier that confines the animals."

"You're probably right," she said, "and if that is the case, it is interesting to think about how the ship's computer biologically differentiates between different beings, but then, I wonder if the force field would hurt the birds if they were to fly directly into it."

"Good question," Dan said. "I would say probably not, with this highly advanced, peaceful race."

Their boys had already trotted up to a small stream. The sound of the moving stream was calming to their senses. As Dan and Barbara walked up to the stream and stood next to the boys, they started to realize just how huge the plantatrium really was. Down in the running water, to their surprise, were hundreds of small, extremely colorful fish, more than likely not of Earth origin.

Dan again gazed up to the ceiling, which was at least sixty meters above his head. There were hundreds of large, curved windows, each easily over ten meters wide by twenty meters long. On the other side of the windows was an extremely clear view of outer space. Bright rays of sunlight were being cast down into the plantatrium and lighting up its many large trees, which had to be at least thirty meters tall, their trunks a meter or more in diameter. The huge trees cast shadows, so the plantatrium lighting appeared all-natural, much different from the photon-neutrino lighting used in the rest of the ship. More of a mystery than the nonuse of the photon-neutrino technology was whether any of the large trees had taproots. If so, where would they have spread? If they did not have taproots, what held them up, especially when their trunks and large branches surely weighed possibly hundreds of tons?

Dan continued to stare up at the large trees, which grew to within maybe five to ten meters of some of the ceiling windows. He noticed the windows slowly curved down to their right, so the center of the spaceship was possibly to their left. The plantatrium appeared to extend easily a quarter mile in both directions from where they currently stood. On the other side of the stream, the sun was shining down through the windows with the intensity of afternoon sunshine, yet above them toward the right, they could see a few stars in the far distance, like an early- to late-evening sunset. Dan realized the mother ship's outer hull had to be blocking part of the sun's rays, meaning the ship was not directly lined up with Earth and its sun and was creating a pseudo lunar eclipse on the ship. So therefore, the mother ship was not located directly in the shadow of Earth and was possibly even tens of thousands of miles away while maintaining an orbit similar to Earth's at a velocity around the sun of over ninety thousand kilometers per hour.

Barbara noticed Dan lost in his thoughts and stared down at the running water again. Some of the exotic fish were now next to the shoreline where the boys were standing. She surveyed the plantatrium's catatonic atmosphere. There were beautiful trees and also tables and benches along the walkways. In fact, there appeared to be benches throughout the entire large plantatrium, some with families and children sitting at them. She was amazed at what she saw, especially because it was aboard a large spaceship, and turned back to her husband, who was still staring at the exotic fish. "This plantatrium is truly magnificent," she said.

Dan caught his breath. "Most definitely," he said. He took another deep breath and exhaled to find the air quality was unusually invigorating, as if cleaned by an ionic cleaner—an atmosphere much like what you would sense or smell after a nice, soft rain. He could now hear what had to be the large waterfall Captain Donaldson had mentioned, the rustling sound echoing throughout the plantatrium. The waterfall sounded different from natural Earth waterfalls, with a much-higher volume. The prospect of seeing this waterfall perked up his interest immensely.

Barbara saw Dan take another deep breath. "The air in here seems amazingly fresh, huh?" she said.

Dan nodded in agreement. "Yes, it is."

The boys were still playing near the shoreline of the small stream, which was surely flowing out of another large body of water, possibly from the main pool fed by the waterfall. Dan continued to stare into his wife's eyes. "Let's go check out the waterfall," he said with anticipation in his voice. "It sounds as if it is bristling with unusual pressure."

Barbara had also already noticed the waterfall's unusual echoes. "Sounds good to me," she said.

The boys were now squatted down, appearing to be touching the exotic fish, which seemed to want to be fed.

"Let's go see the waterfall, boys," Dan said.

Jason stood up. "Okay, Dad."

Michael and Kyle also stood, and Dan noticed Michael's demeanor was that of a calm, peaceful-looking child. "How are you doing, Michael?"

"Good, Daddy," he answered.

Dan and his family continued down a walkway nearly three meters wide and composed of bricks inlaid with unusual designs. The walkway appeared to be following the stream, which was easily flowing over three miles per hour. There were birds flying above them and others perched in trees. Some were white, similar to doves, while others looked like pigeons but extremely colorful like Amazon parrots. Dan and Barbara had to figure there were hundreds of birds and many different species.

When Dan stared down again at the bricks, he noticed a yellow tint, possibly a solid inlaid into the indentation designs, along with light-red-and-blue candy striping. As he continued staring at the 125- to 130-centimeter-long bricks, he was drawn to their brilliance and beauty. Inlaid flush to the bricks' surfaces were glittering green, blue, red, and white stones that were possibly mirror-backed glass, but for all he knew, they could be real emeralds, sapphires, rubies, and diamonds. They sure sparkled, and if they were precious stones, each of the faceted gems would easily range from a few carats to a couple hundred. They were in abundance and in many different shapes—rectangle, square, round, marquise, and even triangle. The interesting thought to Dan was not only were there possibly billions of dollars in precious gems inlaid into the bricks they were currently walking on—stones that could be as common as glass to the advanced race of beings—but there were no birds pecking at these stones, trying to remove them. The stones' bright, sparkling colors would definitely be a temptation to most any fowl or animal, and he wondered whether there might be a thin organic energy shield directly above the bricks to keep the birds away. With this race, though, who knew, they could have possibly taught the birds to stay away from the walkway surfaces.

As they neared the waterfall, Dan looked down again at the bricks. This time he noticed next to the brilliant, vibrant stones were engraved designs, squiggly lines filled with a gold-colored material—possibly the precious metal gold found on Earth? He looked over to his wife, amazed. "What unusual and extremely beautiful bricks, huh?" he said.

Barbara had also noticed the bricks, but the sparkling stones with deep internal luminance were what really caught her attention. They were surely precious beryl and corundum gemstones. "Yes, they are," she said, "but it's not just the bricks that are beautiful; it's everything in general—the trees, the bushes, the walls, even beyond the windows, to the stars dotting the sky. It would cost a bundle to create an arboretum like this on Earth, let alone build it aboard a large mother ship."

"You're right there," Dan fully agreed. He knew a mother ship like this one would cost trillions of dollars on Earth, but his curiosity about the waterfall was overshadowing that fact.

As they started up a walkway that rose in elevation, about three meters to their left was what had to be one of the tallest trees. It had a nearly two-meter-diameter trunk that was dark green with circular red rings, none of which appeared to be touching. Dan pointed it out to his family. "Look at that magnificent tree," he said.

Barbara and the boys stared over at the eye-catching grain of the tree's bark. "Yes, it is nice, isn't it?" Barbara said.

"Yep," Dan said. "It's strange how the circular patterns do not touch, huh? I wonder if that tree grows naturally or if it was genetically engineered like they've done with so many other things."

"Good question," Barbara said as they continued along the

walkway, which was curving to the right. "We should ask one of the families in here."

Dan knew that was a good idea. As they rounded the ninety-degree turn in the walkway, headed down in their direction was a family, a tall male and female with a young boy and girl, maybe ten and eight years old, respectively. They finally met on the walkway, and the male and female expressed kind faces. "Hello, Dan and Barbara," the male said in English.

Dan and Barbara grinned a little at the fact the male was speaking English, not to mention that he knew they were the Earth family. Of course, they were wearing their twenty-first-century Earth clothing and were shorter than all of the adults in the advanced race. Dan returned a kind face. "Hello," he said.

The male noticed Dan wearing one of their biologically molecular-interfaced armbands. "Hope you're all enjoying yourselves," he said.

Dan nodded. "Yes, we are, thank you." He glanced briefly at the large tree with the circular rings before turning back to the tall male. "Are the trees in here natural genome, or have they been genetically engineered, especially the large tree with the circular rings?"

"They are natural trees," the male replied, "grown from saplings while the ship was being constructed."

"Interesting," Dan said. "How old are the largest trees?"

The male paused with a small grin. "About eight hundred and seventy-five years," he answered, "and the red-ringed tree is among the oldest."

Dan, Barbara, and Jason now knew the mother ship had to be around 1,700 Earth years old, since surely he was talking in his race's years. This ship could have possibly been one of the advanced race's fairly early ships, and with its amazing space-travel techniques, it had likely visited a multitude of galaxies and worlds. Dan showed additional interest. "What about the taproots of those trees?" he calmly asked. "Do they project down through the ship?"

"They project down only about twenty meters," the male replied, “and are actually suspended in their vertical heights by permanent self-sustaining gravity-beam supports, which then project their force pressures outside the spaceship’s hull into outer space.”

Dan thought about the answer and remembered the conversation inside the food processing center, which used the same overall internal inertial-force-eliminating convention, which was an amazing science in itself. He glanced at his wristwatch and looked back up to the nice male, knowing he could talk for hours on end with him too. “Interesting,” he said. “Thank you for your time, sir. I could easily talk with you for days.”

The male knew that was the case. “No problem, Dan,” the tall male said and watched the Earth family of five continue up the walkway that led directly to the main waterfall. They would be very surprised by what they were about to witness, not only with the large waterfall, but also with what was located in the very middle of the large pool of water.

Dan and his family continued their trek up the inclined walkway as it turned back to their left at a forty-five-degree angle. It then straightened out, and Dan stared down again at the brick walkway to see even more inlaid brilliant-colored gemstones. Anyone dishonest would surely try to pry them out and steal them, but then, he still did not know whether they were actual precious gems, gems possibly unknown to Earth, or just faceted, colorful mirrored glass. When he looked up again, there was a clearing in the distance and a beautiful large waterfall to their right. It was around two hundred meters away and was thirty meters high by ten meters wide. The water was falling magnificently down into the pool, as if being propelled out of a water source under high pressure.

The walkway finally leveled off, and they stopped a few meters from the nearly hundred-meter-wide pool at the base of the waterfall. The water appeared multicolored as it fell into the pool at what could have been a velocity of a few hundred miles per hour, causing tremendous turbulence and throwing a light mist up into the air.

The multicolored waterfall was almost hypnotic. Colored lights were shining through the water, and it was as if the light was also inside the water and sparkled up into the air with a hue the Jupiter family had never before seen. Dan wondered whether this lighting was yet another aspect of the race's photon-neutrino technology.

When he looked over to their left, what really caught his attention was a spherical water fountain ornament located at the very center of the pool. It was mounted on a pedestal nearly two meters in diameter and rose high into the air to around three stories. There was a halo suspended above it, and across the entire surface of the sphere were small holes, through which water squirted out in tight streams in all directions. The halo near the top flattened out some of the water streams, which dispersed outward to form a curved cylinder before falling back into the pool.

Dan finally caught his breath after the sight of the magnificent ornament and looked farther to his left to see the water from the large pool flowing down a series of smaller waterfalls that more than likely fed the rest of the plantatrium with smaller streams. The heights of the many waterfalls ranged between one to five meters below their vantage point. When Dan finally looked back to his wife and sons, he noticed they were staring at the large, multicolored waterfall as though in a trance. He had to take a closer look himself and this time noticed it was displaying the colors of the rainbow—red, orange, yellow, green, blue, indigo, and violet. The rainbow actually seemed projected from out of the water, like a holographic image, but clearly was not, as the lights remained inside the water as it fell down into the pool. As soon as the water made contact with the stationary pool of water, multicolored lights flashed brightly like a dancing laser light show, but it was confined to the immediate area of the waterfall. The laser lights were seemingly being transmitted no more than two to three meters above the surface of the water. Dan remembered again what Jose, as well as Michael, had told him about how there were photons piggybacked on neutrinos, but this piggybacking scheme in the waterfall had to be much different, as the transmission of the photons was not into open space but into space already filled with hydrogen and oxygen molecules. The piggybacking of the photons must now be on the hydrogen and oxygen water molecules themselves, and that was an amazing realization.

The boys walked up to the pool, and Dan couldn't help but again feel mentally captivated by the large spherical water fountain ornament. On the other side, families were standing around the pool's edge and also admiring the aesthetic ornament that surely had some underlying significance. Dan finally turned to his wife. "That ornament is interesting, huh?" he said.

"Yes, it is," she said. "I wonder what it actually represents?"

"Good question," Dan said.

There was a family about twenty meters away, an older-looking male and female with two little kids, and suddenly, the little boy threw an object into the pool. Dan turned back to Barbara, surprised. "Did you see that?"

"Yes, I did," she said.

"Well," Dan said, "it appears they act very much like humans and throw objects into their water fountains."

"Yes, it does," she said. "I wonder if it was a coin or a token."

"Good question," Dan said. "We still do not know a whole lot about their society in general beyond what the chief engineer told us last night."

"True," Barbara said and looked back to the family, which also had a little girl who was possibly a few years younger than the boy. She remembered Captain Donaldson telling them how most of their race spoke a multitude of languages, including over twenty Earth languages. "Let's go visit them," she said, "and find out what their little boy tossed into the pool."

"Okay," Dan said and walked with his wife in their direction. Stopping within a few meters of where the family stood, Dan turned around briefly, keeping a watchful eye on his three sons still near the water's edge, and then made eye contact with the alien-race family.

The family had already seen Dan and his wife headed their direction and knew they were the Earth family.

Barbara gave them a kind smile. "Hello," she said.

The female returned the kind gesture. "Hello," she replied in English.

Barbara relaxed a little at the female's reply in English and noticed she was at least six feet five inches tall. "My husband and I were wondering what your little boy threw into the water."

"He threw a metallic token," she answered.

"Oh, really?" Barbara said. "We were also wondering if you still use any type of money or have commerce in your society."

"No, we don't," the female replied. "Our race did away with money for trade and services about two thousand of your Earth years ago, soon after all forms of disease and sickness were eradicated from our society."

Barbara was surprised yet intensely interested to hear this and noticed the female's husband and their two young kids were quietly listening. Barbara made eye contact again with the female. "How does your society function without monetary exchange?"

The female glanced briefly at Jason, Michael, and Kyle near the water's edge and then back to Barbara. "It is sort of like one close community," she calmly answered, "where everyone contributes and is taken care of—there is no poverty, no hunger, only world peace, where everyone lives in harmony, advancing their intellect and raising their children without stress or worries in their lives."

Dan and Barbara now wore distant stares, and Barbara caught her breath. "I wish Earth could be like that someday," she said.

The female's husband, who had been quiet so far, nodded to agree, and the female thought about Barbara's comment. "Hopefully," she said, "someday in your Earth's distant future, your society will also gain that same level of world peace."

Barbara and Dan felt encouraged by her words. They wished it were possible sometime in their lifetimes but did not believe it would happen. Barbara was now curious how the two contributed to their society. "What are your occupations?" she asked.

The female paused with a telepathic look to her husband and then turned back to Barbara. "We are ambassadors," she said, "and not actually assigned to this ship. We were supposed to travel to another galaxy, but when Captain Donaldson got a call about your son, Michael, we decided to travel with him out of curiosity. Now here we are standing and talking to each other, out of pure coincidence."

Dan and Barbara were quietly surprised at whom they'd just met, as these two particular Valzarians seemed fairly important. It made them realize again how peaceful the race was to have two of their ambassadors walking around without any security, but then again, they were aboard an extremely large military ship, one with automated, highly advanced molecular computers.

The two ambassadors noticed Dan and Barbara lost in thought and knew they were curious about how many different races they may have visited and how many treaties they may have helped broker. The female ambassador said, "On the planet we were scheduled to visit, there is a race that we've had a peace treaty with for almost eight hundred Earth years."

Dan and Barbara were again extremely interested. "Are they as technologically advanced?" Barbara asked.

"No," the female ambassador answered, "they're about six hundred years behind, but they have reached the first stages of quantum gravity time-warp-field propulsion—a great milestone for any race."

Barbara noticed Dan had a look of intense interest and glanced briefly at Jason, Michael, and Kyle still near the water's edge before she turned back to the two ambassadors. They could talk for hours with the two nice ambassadors, but they only had so much time before they would leave the mother ship and return to Earth. "Well, it was nice to have met you both," she said. "I wish we could talk longer, but we're leaving this ship in a spaceship of our own in a few hours to return to Earth."

The czae (male) ambassador, who had been quiet the whole time, was one of their race's most senior ambassadors. He stared briefly at the armband on Dan's left forearm and knew what Dan and Barbara was thinking. "It was nice to have met you both," he said. "Maybe sometime in the distant future our two races can bridge the gap between our societies so that we might also have a peace treaty."

Dan and Barbara could tell by the firmness in his voice that he had been around quite some time and possibly brokered a multitude of treaties. Dan now had a calm, relaxed expression on his face. "That would be nice," he said.

"Yes, it would," the male ambassador said. "Hopefully, your son Michael might help take your race down that path."

"Thank you," Dan said. "We look forward to raising him, and we'll definitely keep that in mind."

The ambassador and his wife glanced briefly over at Jason, Kyle, and Michael and then back to Dan and Barbara. The male ambassador had a calm, relaxed demeanor. "It will be strange at first with your secret lives on Earth, but I am sure you'll both adjust just fine."

Dan continued to make eye contact with the male ambassador. "Thank you," he said and reached out to shake his hand.

The male ambassador shook Dan's hand, and the female ambassador shook Barbara's. She then shook Dan's hand, and Barbara did the same with the male ambassador's huge hand. "Thank you both for your time," she said.

"You're welcome," the female ambassador said. "Enjoy the rest of your time in our plantatrium."

The ambassadors and the two kids, who were their great-great-great-grandchildren, whose parents were also aboard the ship, quietly walked away.

Dan thought about the little boy who had thrown the token into the pool and turned to Barbara with a small grin. "Let's toss some coins into the water for luck," he kidded. "I have some pocket change, and it would definitely be the first Earth money ever thrown into the pool, at least by someone actually from Earth."

Barbara laughed. "Probably true," she said.

Dan pulled his pocket change out of his jeans—two Washington quarters, three Roosevelt dimes, and four Lincoln pennies. Their sons were still playing over at the pool's edge. "Boys," he called out, "do you want to throw some money into the water?"

Jason, Michael, and Kyle turned around. "Okay, Dad," Jason said and headed in their direction without hesitation, Kyle and Michael tagging close behind. Dan handed each of them a Lincoln penny. Michael, after receiving his shiny penny, looked down at the round coin in the palm of his hand, not understanding it or what the raised engravings meant. He stared up with curiosity. "What is this?" he asked.

Dan was surprised that he did not know. "It's a Lincoln cent, Michael," he answered.

Michael was slightly puzzled but knew "cent" meant it was money used for trade and commerce. Since his father had given it to him, he also knew it was money used on Earth, but he did not understand why his father would have him throw it away. On the coin was the profile of a bearded man facing right, with the word *liberty* to the left. Above the man's head was the inscription "In God we trust." Just to the right of the man's chest was a date of 1982. "Who is this man?" he asked.

Dan and Barbara realized the race had not added any memories about Earth's history into Michael's immense synaptic cell cerebral core, at least not about commerce. Dan thought about his new son's question and looked down with compassion. "The penny commemorates Abraham Lincoln, Michael," he replied, "who was the sixteenth president of the United States and one of our greatest presidents. Before you throw your coin into the pool, I want you to make a wish."

Michael nodded as if he understood. "Okay," he said.

Dan and Barbara knew Michael would have no problem learning about Earth's history, both that of the United States and around the world.

All three boys walked up to the pool's edge and stopped. Jason drew his right arm back and quickly threw his penny out into the pool, causing a soft splash nearly five meters away. Next, Kyle tossed his penny out into the pool, creating another soft splash, only about a meter away. Michael stood for a short moment, as though making a wish, and then suddenly hurled his penny out into the pool, making a soft splash nearly two meters away.

Dan had one last penny, two dimes, and two quarters. He handed the penny to his wife, kept one of the dimes for himself, and placed the rest of the change back into his jeans. When Dan and Barbara looked down into the water, they noticed what appeared to be hundreds of metallic-looking objects—round, rectangular, pentagonal, hexagonal, and an assortment of other unusual shapes—but had no way of knowing whether they were tokens, money, or keepsakes. It also appeared the pool had not been cleaned for quite some time—maybe even for centuries.

Barbara closed her eyes, lifted her right arm, and then hurled her penny out into the water. There was a light splash about four meters away, and she opened her eyes.

Dan stared down at the Roosevelt dime, dated 1999, now in the palm of his hand. It brought back the memory of when they visited the Franklin D. Roosevelt Library and Museum in Hyde Park, New York, about four years ago. They had made the visit on their way to Newburgh in preparation for their LaGuardia flight back to Los Alamos the next day. They'd had a nice, enjoyable visit with Barbara's parents in Albany, New York, in which they had introduced them to their newest grandson, Kyle, who was only about four weeks old at the time. Dan really liked Barbara's parents, as they were teachers at the Hudson Valley Community College in Albany, New York, her father teaching forensic science and her mother chemistry. Dan had decided to change their flight for later the next day so they could also visit the Statue of Liberty.

Dan stared over at his wife with a small, subtle smile. "This Roosevelt dime brings back memories. It is dated 1999. Can you guess what I'm remembering?"

Barbara suddenly wore a distant grin. "Yes, I can," she said. "We visited the Franklin D. Roosevelt Museum after we introduced my parents to their newest grandson. We had a lot of fun on that trip, didn't we?"

"Yes, we did," Dan said, remembering them riding a ferry by the Statue of Liberty, because they did not have enough time to go inside. Jason had been six years old at the time. Dan calmly stared down at his oldest son. "Remember when we saw the Statue of Liberty, Jason?"

"Yes, I do," Jason said.

"Remember what the seven spikes on her crown represent?" Dan asked.

Jason knew the answer and always would. "Yes, I do, Dad," he said. "They stand for either the seven seas or the seven continents on Earth."

"Very good," Dan said. "Well, I'm going to make a wish now and throw my coin into the pool."

Dan closed his eyes. He pulled his right arm behind his head and lifted his left leg high into the air, as if he were about to hurl a baseball from the outfield toward home plate. He then threw his coin with as much force as humanly possible. He heard a light clanging sound and finally opened his eyes, not having a clue where his coin had fallen. He did not want to know either, but based on the sound, he thought it might have hit the lower pedestal of the water fountain ornament. Barbara, Jason, Kyle, and Michael all knew that it had indeed hit the pedestal and ricocheted back into the water. It also seemed to them as though the dime had briefly sped up, as though drawn toward the sphere, before smacking the pedestal.

Dan finally looked over to his wife and three boys. Michael, after seeing what his dad had just done, stared up with curiosity. "What did you wish for, Dad?"

Dan paused with a slight grin. "You're not supposed to tell what you wish for, Michael," he said, "that is, if you want it to come true, anyway. Maybe when you're older, I will let you know."

Michael thought about his dad's explanation. "Okay," he said.

Just behind them, about fifteen feet away down the incline, was an open bench. Next to the bench were vibrant plants with yellow-and-purple foliage. The plants' large leaves, nearly ten centimeters in length, were complemented by deep-purple flowers shaped like carnations. Dan thought briefly about what he had wished for before tossing the dime into the water—it had been in relation to Michael's ability to take Earth toward peace. But then, Michael's true origin could never be known to the human race, a heartbreaking dilemma Dan would have to accept. Therefore, in his lifetime, he felt his wish was just that—wishful thinking. "Let's go sit for a while," he said to his wife, "and take in the surroundings of this magnificent plantatrium."

"Sounds good," she replied and noticed their three boys staring over at the waterfall, oblivious to what their dad had said. "Boys," she said, "your dad and I will be sitting at one of the benches, so be careful if you play near the pool."

"Okay, Mom," Jason said. "We'll be careful."

Barbara believed her oldest son and followed Dan down a small grassy hill layered in what appeared to be rich green bentgrass—similar to what was used on golf courses. Continuing up to the bench, they slowly turned around and then sat down. Dan grabbed his wife's hand with an extremely relaxed, peaceful feeling inside, staring at the trees and the hundreds of birds flying around. There were even insects that looked similar to butterflies.

With a quick peek over at the boys again, he thought about how their time aboard the mother ship had felt like a dream. Dan turned to his wife, who was staring off at the abundance of magnificent-looking trees, clearly daydreaming. "This has been quite the last few days, huh?" he said.

Barbara turned her head. "Yes, it has," she said, "simply amazing."

They continued to watch their boys, as well as other families. They understood why the race would have a plantatrium aboard the mother ship, as it did have a relaxing, tranquil atmosphere, a requirement if the crew members were traveling for weeks or months before finding a planet with a life-sustaining atmosphere, water, or plant life.

Dan saw by his wristwatch that it was 3:51 p.m., approximately an hour before they needed to return to their quarters for what would surely be a nice send-off by the captain and his officers. Looking up at the curved windows in the ceiling, he noticed again the sun's rays shining brightly down into the far side of the plantatrium.

Suddenly, two large birds glided down and landed on the ground directly in front of them, mildly surprising Dan and Barbara. The large, bipedal birds were not only extremely pretty but also definitely not of Earth origin. They were pentadactyl, their feet having five toes, four in front and one centered directly behind like a thumb—not the ornithological configuration of the perchers, swifts, or woodpeckers found on Earth. They had beaks like parrots yet stood nearly 120 centimeters (48 inches) tall, with nearly half of their height consisting of their long light-brown legs that were like a flamingo's but much more muscular. Brightly colored tail feathers in red, blue, green, and orange, similar to a green-winged macaw, complemented their bodies. Their heads were like that of an eagle, having large, round eyes that were a deep-blue hue that seemed to glow slightly.

Both birds continued to stare at Dan and Barbara before one of them audibly said something in a strange language. It sounded like the language Michael and Captain Donaldson had spoken when they'd first been taken aboard the mother ship. Dan and Barbara were even more surprised now. The birds, their vocal cords well developed, were even more like parrots than they'd first thought. "Hello," Dan said back to the bird.

"Hello ... Hello," both birds began saying.

Dan turned to Barbara, surprised that the birds had picked up on their language so quickly. The two clearly smart birds continued to stand a few meters away. Then one of them finally walked up to the end of the bench where Dan was sitting, grabbed the bench with its beak, and climbed up on the bench next to him. Dan was leery of the bird, because even though it looked friendly, it had talons, and its beak, being over twenty centimeters (eight inches) long, could easily break a finger and cause him severe physical injury. It suddenly occurred to him that the advanced race would never allow a bird in the plantatrium that would harm anyone, especially when there were kids present. He gingerly reached out with his right hand, and the bird gently took hold of his fingers. With Dan's fingers resting inside its mouth, the bird began touching his fingers with its soft red tongue and did not try to bite whatsoever. Its pupils dilated, and a light hum came from its chest, as though it was purring like a house cat.

Dan now knew the large, "purring" bird was completely harmless, its dilated pupils a good sign. It had possibly even been raised in captivity when very young. After gently pulling his fingers out of its mouth, he reached up to its crest and scratched its head, discovering its feathers were extremely soft, like goose down. "You pretty bird," Dan said.

"Pretty bird," the bird replied in English.

Dan continued to hold his wife's left hand, and the smart bird lowered its head next to Dan's leg, similar to a cat or dog yearning for affection. As he stared more closely at the bird, he realized even more how extremely beautiful it was. He guessed it had to weigh at least forty to fifty pounds. Its pretty deep-blue eyes were almost hypnotic, having both round irises and round black pupils similar to humans'. These birds would most definitely be highly sought after as pets on Earth.

Jason, Michael, and Kyle were now staring over in their parents' direction, having spotted the two colorful birds. All three boys quickly walked down the hill and up to the bird standing on the grass in front of their parents' bench. Michael said something in a strange language. The bird replied back with a short, soft syllable and then tilted its neck toward the ground. All three boys then walked up to the bird and began petting and scratching its back and head.

The boys were clearly fascinated by the oversize turkey-eagle-parrot birds. When Dan looked back up to the ceiling, he noticed other colorful birds flying around and some perched in trees, but he saw no other birds like the two currently visiting them. He was now curious how long their wingspan and flight feathers were, so he let loose of his wife's hand, gently grabbed the bird's left wing, and flexed it outward. It stretched across the entire bench, even encompassing his wife. The main and secondary flight feathers were extremely pretty, and the bird's wing appeared similar to those of birds on Earth, with maybe a few extra digits. One clear difference was that at the end of the wing's major digit was a sharp spike nearly 5 centimeters in diameter and maybe around 12 centimeters (five inches) in length that only exposed itself when the wing was flexed outward. Dan felt the base of the spike and figured that it was solid bone. He then lightly touched the pointed end, which was sharp like a needle. The spike was possibly a defensive weapon to be used if the bird was threatened. It could easily be a lethal weapon, poking a deep hole, like the fang of a biting cat. The sharp-spiked wings would definitely make the bird a formidable opponent against many predators. "Look at this," Dan said.

Barbara leaned forward just a bit, noticing the bird's flight feathers were at least a meter long. She could also see the spike Dan had pointed out. "That is amazing," she said.

"Yes, it is," Dan said, "and it is extremely sharp. This bird would be one heck of a watch animal. It would probably scare the bejesus out of any would-be intruder after they saw its large talons, beak, and especially those wing spikes, and if it did ever attack them, that would pretty much be all she wrote."

Barbara grinned a little at his comment, and he finally let loose of the bird's wing. It immediately retracted against the bird's body, and the bone spike was no longer visible. No doubt they could easily spend the entire evening in the plantatrium, relaxing and enjoying their time with the unusual birds, but according to Dan's wristwatch, it was now about ten minutes after four. "Well, I suppose we ought to head back to our room," he said.

Barbara stood up with Dan, and the bird on the bench then raised its body into the air, openly displaying the magnificently colored plumage on its breast. It jumped to the ground. "Bye, pretty bird," Dan said.

The bird suddenly looked up into Dan's face, as if it was going to miss him. "Goodbye," it said in plain English.

Dan and Barbara were surprised and wondered how it knew to say *goodbye* as opposed to just *bye*. The boys were still scratching and admiring the other bird. "Let's go, boys," Dan said, "so we can get prepared to leave the ship."

Jason stood up. "Okay, Dad," he said. "I'm ready."

"Me too," Michael said, with Kyle nodding his head up and down.

The bird that had been on the bench walked over to the other bird. The two birds, which Dan and Barbara figured were a mated pair, suddenly took flight, and the Jupiter family felt a slight wave of air pressure from their powerful wings. The birds ended up in one of the taller trees, staring down at them. Meeting this magnificent bird species would be forever ingrained in their memories.

The Jupiter family finally started their trek effortlessly down the hill and onto a new walkway. This new walkway also displayed hundreds of vibrant, magnificent gemstones inlaid into the bricks, the same as the other walkways. Whether the gemstones were real or simulated would be interesting to find out, as well as whether the gold-colored material was the precious metal found on Earth, also known as element 79, or the element having the atomic number 79, in Earth's periodic table.

Dan turned around briefly one more time for a quick glance of the halo near the top of the water fountain ornament before it completely disappeared from his sight. He was still somewhat curious about the halo's underlying meaning and, in fact, the underlying meaning for the entire ornament. When he turned back around, he saw the plantatrium's exit just ahead. As they continued down the decline, he didn't feel his body trying to speed up under the influence of gravity. Evidently, the gravity environment seemed to be changing in respect to the position of their bodies.

The vertical wall above the plantatrium's entrance/exit had to be at least sixty meters high, but more amazing was that the wall had an assortment of symmetrical windows, like the windows on a high-rise apartment building. If the windows in fact belonged to living quarters, they would allow for a very nice view into the plantatrium. Dan turned to his wife. "Those windows are interesting," he said. "That would be a magnificent view, huh?"

"Yes, it would," she said. "I wonder if they're guest rooms or lounge viewing rooms."

"Good question," Dan said.

As they finally exited the plantatrium, they experienced the same light-blue flashes around their bodies but did not feel any static electricity—not even a single strand of hair stood up on their skin.

As they walked through the large lounge, this time Dan and Barbara noticed how truly nice it appeared, its atmosphere bubbling with energy, talk, and laughter from its many patrons. To their left, nearly fifteen meters away, built into the walls, were large aquariums filled with colorful exotic fish and plant life. Each aquarium was at least seven meters long and about three meters tall and was about a half meter off the floor. The aquariums were also lit up, as if the lights were shining out of the water with an exhilarating glowing effect. Dan figured it was possibly another aspect of the alien race's advanced photon-neutrino space-transport technology. The boys were staring intently at the aquariums when Jason finally turned in Dan's direction. "Can we watch the fish in the aquariums for a little while, Dad?"

Dan figured they could spend a little time in the lounge. "Sure," he said, "but only about twenty minutes. The captain and his officers will arrive at our guest quarters in less than an hour."

# 22

# A SURPRISING CONVERSATION IN THE LOUNGE

Jason immediately trotted over to the aquariums with Michael and Kyle in tow. His little brothers were like tiny magnets attracted to a larger magnet. The boys stood in front of the largest aquarium, admiring its aquatic life. Michael pointed directly at it, and Dan and Barbara figured he was explaining the different types of aquatic life and possibly their places of origin.

Dan and Barbara began surveying the lounge. There was a bar on the far side, fitted with what appeared to be legless barstools and a countertop at least twelve meters in length. Waitresses and waiters were walking up to the countertop, placing drinks and food on platters, and then delivering them to patrons throughout the large lounge. This was again surprising to Dan and Barbara, as until this point, all the drinks and food they'd seen had instantly appeared after being selected from a computer screen. Most of the lounge patrons were dressed in colorful attire that did not look to be military clothing, or at least it was not like what Captain Donaldson and his officers wore. Dan finally turned to his wife with a good feeling inside. "How about we sit at the bar while the kids enjoy the aquariums?"

"Sure," she said and followed Dan over to the countertop, where two good-looking, large czae (male) bartenders were standing behind the bar. They looked to be in their late thirties to early forties and were both well over seven feet tall. Sitting at the bar with drinks were six extremely pretty czoes (females) who appeared to be flirting with the bartenders.

Dan and Barbra sat down at two open barstools about four meters away from the six females. The legless barstools were suspended in midair, so their feet now dangled, but luckily they had footrests. Suddenly, surprising them, their stools rose up so that their chests were now slightly above the countertop. Behind the bar were drink dispensers similar to the soft-drink dispensers that would be found on Earth, as well as bottles and taps like would be used for alcoholic drinks on Earth.

Dan stared over at one of the males behind the bar. He didn't know whether the bartenders spoke English but figured they did since everyone else spoke the language extremely well. One of the bartenders walked up to Dan and Barbara and asked in plain, well-spoken English, "What can I get you two?"

Dan and Barbara were only mildly surprised that the bartender seemed to know they were the Earth family, because who wouldn't be able to recognize them on the mother ship? Dan turned briefly to his wife. "Want to drink some Travanian coffee?"

"Sure," she said.

Dan made eye contact with the tall, large-framed bartender, and the good feeling inside his spirit continued. "How about two cups of Travanian coffee?" he asked.

"Sure," the bartender replied, knowing it was the chief engineer that had introduced Dan and Barbara to the coffee. He walked over to a dispenser near the back of the bar. There were not any pictures of coffee or coffee beans on the dispenser like there would be on Earth. The bartender touched a series of buttons on a computer screen, and two white ceramic cups suddenly appeared below the dispenser.

Two separate streams of steaming dark liquid then flowed out of the dispenser. When the cups were full, the dispenser shut off, and the bartender carried them over to where Dan and Barbara patiently waited, setting them down in front of them.

"Thank you," Dan said. "How do we pay for these?"

The bartender chuckled because he knew what Dan had just asked was out of Earth habit. "Everything is free, Dan," he said with a slight grin. "Raising Michael more than pays for it."

Dan and Barbara grinned at his comment, strange as it was. They wondered again why this particular lounge was so different, with food and drinks being carried to tables by hand. Dan made eye contact with the bartender. "Sir," he asked, "why not just transport our coffees to us instead of delivering them? And why are waitresses and waiters delivering drinks and food to the patrons, instead of just transporting them directly to their tables?"

The bartender could understand the question and answered, "Because our race learned many centuries ago that you need to slow down occasionally, remember the way it used to be, and not get into too much of a hurry. This lounge is one of a few aboard this ship that still operates this way."

Dan could understand this philosophy, as what the chief engineer had told them last night was along that same line of thought. "That's interesting," he said. He turned briefly to his wife and then back to the bartender, curious about the thousands of possibly rare gemstones in the bricks in the plantatrium. He did not know the bartender's fields of understanding, but the male was surely knowledgeable in a multitude of fields and at a much higher level than he or his wife. Dan now displayed a curious face. "In the plantatrium," he said, "we noticed thousands of gemstones inlaid into the brick walkways, each stone easily ranging from a few carats to hundreds of carats. Are those precious gemstones, such as emeralds, rubies, sapphires, and diamonds like would be found on Earth?"

The bartender telepathically understood that the captain had told

Dan of the term *plantatrium*, as the large room of trees and plants would be called in the English language. He also knew about Earth's history of gemstone sciences, including the history of the stones in the plantatrium walkways. "Yes, they are real gemstones," the bartender said, "except very few are natural gemstones like what would be found in the mantle and crust of a planet after immense temperatures and pressures. In fact, most all of the larger stones in the plantatrium are flawless gemstones created by our race under similar planetary forces. They are as real as authentic gemstones, except without inherited age."

Dan and Barbara were only mildly surprised the race could create natural gemstones so easily. Dan turned briefly to his wife and back to the bartender, immense curiosity now filling his mind. "How do you combine the aluminum, silicon, oxygen, and beryllium so easily to create emeralds, let's say?"

"It's actually a simple process," the bartender said, "because when you can manipulate gravity forces into faster-than-light compression fields, immense pressures can be easily achieved that will exceed any planetary-core pressure and temperature—pressures that will then create the necessary hexagonal ionic bonds of the beryl crystal structures, for instance. Not only that, but we can also add whatever amounts of chromium and iron we wish for depth of color. Our stones are also indistinguishable from any naturally created stone, because like I told you previously, they are created under similar temperature and pressure conditions."

Dan was quiet for a short moment. "Amazing," he said under his breath, because his assumption that the bartender would be extremely knowledgeable, probably multitudes smarter than both him and Barbara, had been correct. He then said, "Being able to configure the carbon atoms into their proper crystalline structures to form a specialized diamond must be interesting, huh?"

"Yes, it is," the bartender said. "For pure carbon inside a quantum spherical shell, whenever faster-than-light gravity forces are focused inward, which is well beyond the carbon's nuclear stability, it causes force density pressures tens of thousands of times the core of any planetary body." The bartender paused to see Dan and Barbara quietly listening. "These force pressures," he continued, "then form flawless single-stage bonded atoms that pack the crystals, tetrahedrally, beyond the limits of their own nuclear bonds. Each of the diamonds created in this manner contains zero defect planes, with no inclusions of other elements, unless purposely added, and is extremely dense. The equivalent to a one-carat stone on Earth would weigh over one kilogram using the maximum gravity-force pressure limits that we are able to obtain inside one of our spherical quantum gravity fields. These extremely dense diamonds are also the hardest material known to our race, at least in their static states and not taking into account force-reactive elements, such as those used in the hulls of our spaceships."

Dan and Barbara were amazed again, and Dan looked down at his armband, wondering about the bartender's last comment in the context of what he had witnessed at the Los Alamos labs with the fake armband, which was probably made of the same or similar material as his real armband, both of them with strengths and characteristics well beyond Earth's sciences. He looked back up into the bartender's face and made eye contact. "Are those diamonds stronger overall than the material of my armband?"

The male bartender stared down briefly at Dan's armband and knew what he was thinking. He recognized the silver-colored reactive metal alloy material that was electrically and molecularly interfaced to his body, allowing it to be completely immune to all planetary magnetospheric fluctuations. Armbands without the three interface pins were prone to not being completely reliable over vast distances. "Yes," he said, "those diamonds are harder than your armband, but only after factoring out the reactive state of the material in your armband, which can also become a generator of a massive amount of power, just as you found out at the Los Alamos labs with the simulated armband your son Jason gave you."

Dan had to grin that the bartender had read his mind, or perhaps that information was in a report accessible to certain crew members. "Does your race methodically facet those extremely dense, hard stones by hand or use computers?"

The bartender glanced briefly at Barbara and then back to Dan. "For our extremely dense diamonds above two thousand megapascals," he answered, "they can only be cut by our computers. Stones one thousand to two thousand megapascals can be cut by either method, but when done by hand, it takes immense precision and patience by a specialized jeweler, especially the closer they get to the maximum limit. Faceting these stones is actually a hobby to some of our race, to come up with unique diamond shapes and depth of color never before envisioned, especially when other elements, such as boron, nitrogen, oxygen, or argon, can be methodically positioned and substituted for any of the individual carbons atoms. You'd be amazed at the size of some of our gemstones, as well as the many different elemental coloring schemes possible within each hexagonally shaped and densely packed crystalline bond structure."

Dan knew that being able to precisely control the location and position of other elements within the hexagonal crystalline diamond structures was an amazing feat.

Barbara paused from sipping her coffee and stared up at the bartender, almost hypnotically interested. "What are your largest diamonds?" she asked.

"Upwards of one hundred and twenty-five thousand carats," he replied.

Dan and Barbara were quiet again, flabbergasted. The alien race's ability to create large diamonds was amazing, not to mention their ability to precisely intermix and specifically locate other elements within the carbon atom bonds so easily.

The bartender noticed Dan and Barbara were still kind of quiet and added, "Of course, the large faceted gemstones that I speak of are time exhaustive to create, even with our computers, and highly protected by our race. They can only be viewed in our museums."

Dan and Barbara continued their silence and could understand why the gemstones would be kept in museums and highly protected, as other races might try to steal them for immense profit. "While we were in the plantatrium," Dan said, "a couple of your ambassadors told us a little about how you have peace treaties with other races, at least races that have reached the first stage of quantum gravity time-warp-field propulsion. Does your race not have to worry about those societies trying to steal your large gemstones?"

"Nope," the bartender quickly responded. "I've accompanied ambassadors many times and have been on their negotiation teams, so I know our race does not make peace treaties with any race that still uses money in their society or any type of commerce for monetary gain. All individuals are the commodity and must contribute to their society. The end result preempts the need for any money. Intelligent races who have not reached this status of peace will never know of our race, because we will never make ourselves known. We basically secretly scout races without their knowledge before we decide to take the next step of a peace treaty."

Dan and Barbara were amazed to hear this but still did not understand how the advanced race could keep other intelligent races from discovering their home world, either by a probe, a satellite, or a spaceship. Such a discovery would surely cause them problems, and Dan just had to know the answer. "How do you keep other races from discovering your home world? You know, like with a probe or a spaceship?"

"Easy," the bartender answered. "We have sensors positioned around our sun's heliospheric bubble that record all objects entering our solar system. There are gravity-stream subspace transmissions from those sensors that continually communicate with our home world planet. Since the sensors encompass all outside space around the heliosphere, there is a continual analysis of all objects, such as a spaceship or probe, approaching our solar system, whether terrestrial or nonterrestrial. The sensors determine everything about each object—its place of origin, level of technology, and so forth. If it is a probe or satellite and determined to be inferior, we alter its course around our solar system, update the inertial navigational databases and recorders accordingly, even install false data that appears real, and send it on its way in the same path it was previously traveling, as though there were nothing in our solar system. For all extraterrestrial spaceships that approach our solar system, it is a similar process. If a spaceship is deemed to be from a race that hasn't reached our level of peace, even if they have attained the first stage of quantum gravity time-warp-field propulsion, we intercept it without their knowledge, place the occupants into a hypnotic state, and take their ship hundreds of thousands of light-years away. After we wake them up, again without their knowledge, we send their ship on its way, so that they're left thinking there was nothing of significance in the solar system that they believe they just visited."

Dan and Barbara were again flabbergasted at what they heard, and Dan was filled with additional amazement. "Interesting!" he said. "Has your race ever encountered spaceships from races that you could not successfully relocate?"

"No," the bartender answered bluntly, "because like I said, our sensors analyze their level of technology and their level of peace. If their technology is close to or above our level, then they are making their presence known to us. If they have reached our level of peace and just happened to enter into our solar system, they could very well be a lucky race, due to what technological advancements they might receive, at least after we have visited their home world and signed a peace treaty with them. Now, if they were much more advanced than us, then our sensors probably would not detect them in the first place, so it becomes a moot point."

Dan grinned at the detailed answer, realizing the race he and his family were now friends with lived in true secrecy, but he still could not see how they would be able to keep other races from detecting the spectral line emission shifts for the oxygen and nitrogen in the atmosphere of their home world planet. The bartender read Dan's curious mind. "Not only do we keep track of all terrestrial objects entering our solar system," he said, "but we also have satellites located in a spherical pattern around our planet at a predetermined distance and along the same ecliptic plane it rotates around its sun. These tens of thousands of satellites continually transmit electromagnetic frequency patterns that offset all oxygen, nitrogen, and carbon dioxide spectral emissions, as well as other elemental line frequencies, to fool all would-be optical sensors that are being referenced against the normal planes of space-time."

Dan and Barbara were again amazed. Dan knew the bartender had read his mind but did not care. "Interesting," he said while looking over at his wife, who was in a quiet daydream. He turned back to the extremely knowledgeable bartender, wondering about what was inlaid into the brick walkways, specifically whether it was the rare, noncorrosive Earth metal gold. "Is the material inlaid into the plantatrium's walkways gold?" he asked. "The element with atomic number seventy-nine in Earth's periodic table?"

"Yes, it is," the bartender said, "solid twenty-four-karat gold, the same seventy-ninth electron-proton-neutron-configured element that came into existence after our universe was first born billions upon billions, possibly even trillions, of years ago. Of course, the metal is only rare to your race, but in its natural form, yes, it is a fairly rare element for most planetary bodies. Creating gold is actually a very simple process of using another mass element, such as lead or mercury, and through use of their natural harmonic vibrations, a pure atmospheric containment field, and the vibratory states of the lower atomic number elements, we are able to convert both elements into pure gold using a process that would be called electron-proton-capture, neutron-disintegration inverse transmutation in your tongue."

Dan and Barbara raised their eyebrows. Dan picked up his Travanian coffee, took a sip, and set the cup down. "Amazing," he said, his mind filled with a sense of stupor at his next question. "How is the inverse-transmutation synthesis actually accomplished?"

The bartender was thinking about the simple answer that had been taught to him during his young teenage years when he noticed servers lining up at the bar and overloading the other bartender. "I'll be right back," he said. "Hold that thought."

Dan and Barbara sat with immense interest in what the bartender had told them, but both bartenders now appeared very busy as more patrons entered the lounge, filling up tables and starting to sit at the bar. It did not appear the bartender they'd been having an interesting conversation with would be returning anytime soon to deliver more amazing answers to their questions.

Dan was still amazed at the race's level of alchemy, but he was not completely surprised, considering their advancements in so many other fields of science. As his sons continued to look at the aquariums, Dan turned to his wife with an amazed face, realizing they could talk with the extremely smart bartender for hours. He wondered whether the bartender might really be a professor in multiple fields of science, only bartending for the fun of it as part of his contribution to his race's society. Curiosity got the best of Dan, who knew they were running out of time before they would have to return to their quarters.

The bartender finally returned about ten minutes later. "Sorry about that," he said, "but we seem to have gotten extremely busy all of a sudden."

"No problem," Dan said. "I don't think we have time to hear your full explanation about how gold is synthesized, but my wife and I were curious if you carry advanced degrees?"

The tall bartender grinned a little. "Of course," he said. "All adults in our race carry multiple advanced degrees in at least two to three different fields of science, degrees that are of course at a much-higher level than the PhDs granted on Earth. One of my doctorates is in the field of particle physics, as you have probably surmised."

"Yep," Dan said, smiling a little. "Are you a part of the civilian community or attached to the military division?"

"I'm a civilian assigned to this ship," the bartender answered, "and attached to the military division as a consultant. As you may have also surmised, our race does not have the number of research labs that you have on Earth, because there are just not as many secrets in this physical universe of ours that we have not already unlocked. Our highest priorities are to continually explore this huge universe for sciences we've not yet encountered, to discover races who are still progressing in their understanding of science, and to chart as much of this universe as possible. So in a sense, I guess you could say that our military mother ships are like large flying laboratories that take us all over this huge universe while at the same time ensuring an enormous amount of protection of life in general, not just sentient beings, such as ourselves, but all forms of life, which essentially causes our race to act like guardians of the universe, you might say."

Dan and Barbara both grinned. "What is your assignment on this ship, then?" Dan asked.

The bartender looked down at the six females, who were talking to the other bartender, and a couple of them suddenly looked over in his direction with flirtatious smiles. He returned a subtle, relaxed grin and turned back to Dan and Barbara. "I work on a few of the expedition teams," he replied, "even on some of the covert missions to planets that are populated with intelligent and nonintelligent life-forms. Of course, those beings never know we are there. In addition to this, I am also part of the group that liaisons with other races we have treaties with, as I've previously said. You'd be amazed at the beautiful planets populated with peaceful races, even though their numbers are small in comparison to the millions of galaxies out there, each galaxy filled with billions of stars."

Dan thought about the bartender's comment. "Interesting," he said. "Exploring our universe like that sounds fun."

"Yes, it is," the bartender said.

Dan and Barbara daydreamed about what it would be like to be a part of those expedition teams, as it would surely be like a getaway vacation while also meeting other intelligent beings and visiting their home worlds, with some of the beings never even knowing you were present among their populous. Dan felt extremely privileged to have met the nice bartender, who was probably a highly respected professor of his race. "What is your name?" Dan asked.

"My name is Dr. Erik Stratford in your language," he replied, "but you two can just call me Erik."

Barbara grinned slightly, and Dan looked back to Erik. "Well, I figure you already know I am Dan Jupiter and this is my wife, Barbara."

"Of course, Dan," Erik said. "I know all about your family."

Dan chuckled a little and thought about how Erik had opportunities to spend time with other races. He caught his breath. "Are there members of other races with whom you have treaties aboard this ship?"

"Yes," Erik answered. "Most of them will look just like us biophysically—in fact, very close in most every respect, as if we'd all been created from an identical image or force of universal nature."

"Interesting," Dan said. "What would be some of the differences?"

"Minor differences," Erik replied, "like the number of digits on their hands or feet, the number or types of joints, skin coloring and texture, or even differences in carbon-based internal construction. Some races have a specific eye color, for instance, or a certain type of skin texture, while others have the ability to see in the dark and so forth. Intelligent life, with the ability to think, reason, and question their existence, is not like what you'd see in your science fiction movies and television shows, such as *Star Trek*, *Star Wars*, and others, where the beings look like what you'd consider to be a monster and have inconsistent or inefficient physical attributes or designs. Such beings are all just that: fiction, in the realm of someone's imagination. Take it from a race that has explored this vast universe for well over a thousand of your years and has visited a multitude of different galaxies."

Dan and Barbara exhibited starry-eyed, imaginative faces. Dan exhaled. "Interesting," he said again.

"Yes, it is," Erik said. He calmly added, "Even though some of the races we have peace treaties with have been around longer than our race, our progression into the many fields of science was much faster. I guess you could say it is because our race's genome systems have denser-than-normal brain matter, leading to a much-higher number of active neurons at the cerebral core."

Dan and Barbara knew without doubt that everyone in the alien race was an extreme genius according to Earth standards and would easily score over 200 on IQ tests. Dan now thought about what he and his wife had discussed regarding the entire race seeming to be in good physical shape with well-toned bodies and no obesity evident. "What types of exercise do you have aboard this ship?" he asked.

"Well," Erik calmly answered, "there are natural physical activities, such as jogging or running, and that is on level 212. Then there are the unnatural states of workout as used within molecular data streams, located on level seventy-six."

The term *molecular data streams* was peculiar to Dan and Barbara, and Dan now stared at Erik with intense interest. "What do you mean by *data streams*?"

"What I mean," Erik said, "is that the cellular structures of the organic body in reference are molecularly broken down inside a molecular world. There is then a reconfiguration of that molecular world to the programming of the system. You can go mountain climbing, take a nice walk in a park, go swimming, or even jog along a warm ocean beach. It's essentially anything you can wish in your mind that is also within your body's normal physical ability. Your body will then go through the individual molecular cell adjustments accordingly, as if you'd actually exercised in physical form." Erik paused. "In other words, you can do anything you could do normally, but you cannot become Superman," he kidded.

Dan and Barbara laughed but then grew quiet again after the amazing information. Dan thought some more about it. "How are the molecular data streams related to the holodeck concepts in the science fiction television series *Star Trek*?"

Erik was familiar with Earth's twentieth- and twenty-first-century science fiction movies and series. "Nothing like it," he replied. "In the world of molecular data streams, your body is broken down molecularly, compressed, and then put inside an accumulator. It is fully controlled by our highly computational computers with only minor adjustments to the programming and is completely fail-proof, with it being impossible for anyone to ever be physically harmed while inside the accumulator."

Dan and Barbara were quiet again, Dan's eyes widened. "Simply amazing," he said, knowing again he and his wife could talk for hours, days, or even weeks with the nice, warmhearted male, but then again, who on the ship would they not enjoy talking to, especially since these advanced beings could very well be over two thousand technological years ahead of the human race?

Dan glanced at his watch to see it was now 4:55 p.m. He looked briefly to his wife before turning around to see the boys standing in front of one of the aquariums with a half dozen other young kids. Picking up his coffee, he finished it to the last drop and slowly placed it on the counter with sincere appreciation of the time Erik had spent visiting with them. "It was nice to have met you, Erik," he said, "especially with everything you have told us."

"Likewise," Erik said. "It was my pleasure, and it was fun to see you two acting like little schoolkids while listening to what I revealed."

Barbara giggled, and Dan grinned widely. She gulped down the last of her coffee and noticed, like before, that Erik was extremely good-looking and would be a heartthrob on Earth, as would any of the males of his race. "Yes, thank you for everything you've told us," she said and slid off her barstool, which had lowered itself toward the floor.

"No problem, Barbara," he replied. "That's why I am here—to chat with and listen to those who need it."

Dan and Barbara both grinned a little. Dan also stood up, and he and Barbara slowly walked away from the counter to the aquarium where their boys were standing. The same young kids, three little girls and four boys, were standing next to Jason and Kyle, all of them listening intently to Michael, who was standing in front of them like a speaker in front of an audience. When Michael finally saw his parents, he stopped his conversation and remained quiet. "Let's go, boys," Dan said. "The captain and his officers will be arriving at our quarters in less than five minutes."

"Okay, Dad," Jason said.

"Okay, Daddy," Michael responded, Kyle again only nodding his head up and down.

Jason, Kyle, and Michael waved goodbye to the other kids, and the Jupiter family left the lounge and headed back to the transporter elevator. Along the way, Dan and Barbara thought about what Erik had told them in reference to how easily his race could create rare gems that were as real as authentic gems—a most interesting field of gemology. No doubt their special gems would have comparable, if not greater, luminance than mined gems, especially since they were extremely dense. The way the race could also easily turn lead or mercury into gold, via a lower-ordered periodic table element, was additionally interesting. Even though they had not gotten to hear Erik's explanation of how the alchemic synthesis was actually accomplished, just hearing the name of the process by which it was done—electron-proton-capture, neutron-disintegration inverse transmutation—was tantalizing, especially since more information was likely in their ship's computer data banks, just waiting for them to read all about it.

As they were about to arrive at the elevator, Dan's and Barbara's anticipation for leaving the mother ship within the hour rose. They would soon be starting their new secret lives on Earth, something that would without doubt be unusual at first, especially with their ties to top-secret governmental agencies. The urge would always be there to reveal some of the advanced knowledge in particle and molecular physics to the top-secret side of the government, but it could never happen, as Michael would immediately become center stage. Dan and Barbara did not know whether the secret government would allow their family's continued association to the race, including to Michael, if they knew about it. Neither did Dan and Barbara plan on finding out. They would not reveal anything unless the race specifically allowed it, which did not seem a likely prospect.

At the transporter elevator, the door glowed with a light-yellow hue and then vanished, with no one waiting inside. The Jupiter family continued inside with Dan bringing up the rear. The door reappeared behind them, and Dan stared down at the wall console. "Level eighteen, quadrant twenty," he said.

The transporter door again vanished, and the three boys quickly exited, turned right down the hallway, and headed back toward their guest quarters, seemingly anxious and excited. Dan and Barbara slowly followed. The boys were already getting far ahead, but Dan and Barbara did not say anything this time. Like before, they found themselves anxious to return to their room for what could possibly be the last time, unless maybe they were to visit the mother ship again and stay in the same room. They looked forward to meeting with the race for the required debriefing in six months. Since Michael would have been in their lives for some time at that point, the race would no doubt be curious about his progress and how well their family had adjusted to living in secrecy within Earth's society.

Dan and Barbara continued to the left, and the tubular hallway finally started to straighten out, but the boys were not visible anywhere—most likely they were already waiting inside their quarters. As Dan and Barbara approached their guest quarters, their anticipation was still high for Captain Donaldson and his officers to escort them to their new spaceship. Learning how to fly the spaceship would be extremely interesting and challenging, especially with no formal training or schooling, but then, there were always the telepathic helmets to control the ship, as the chief engineer had mentioned. Michael would also be able to answer any questions and help immensely.

Dan and Barbara reached their guest quarters, and the door disappeared in front of them. They continued inside but still did not see the boys when suddenly Jason, Kyle, and Michael all jumped out from behind the table next to the door. "Boo!" Jason said.

Dan and Barbara were startled but then giggled about it, as Jason and his brothers had caught them off guard. Michael was staring up at them, seemingly still analyzing the emotional response Jason had just caused.

"Boo! Boo!" Michael suddenly said, not realizing that he could not get the same emotional reaction out of them simply by saying "Boo!"

Dan laughed under his breath, and Barbara grinned. As Dan stared down into Michael's sincere face, he knew he was going to enjoy raising their brilliant yet naive little boy and teaching him everything required to grow up into a responsible young man.

Barbara picked Michael up and affectionately hugged and kissed him for his sincere, innocent sweetness. Dan picked up Kyle, and they carried their two little boys over to the couch, Jason following alongside, and they all sat down, Jason between his mom and dad. Dan noticed the armbands on the table in front of them and figured his family might as well reinstall them before Captain Donaldson and his officers arrived. He picked up all four armbands and handed Jason and Barbara theirs but was clueless as to which armband was Kyle's and which was Michael's, as they looked to be the same. Staring over at Michael sitting calmly in his mom's lap, Dan again noticed there were no puncture wounds on his left forearm, nor any scars evident whatsoever. "Which armband is yours, Michael?"

"It is in your right hand, Daddy," Michael replied.

Dan was surprised. "How do you know?"

"Because of the slight differences on each end," he replied.

Dan looked more closely at the two armbands, and sure enough, there was a remarkable, extremely small difference in the end curvatures for Michael's armband, something that would have been easily overlooked, if not pointed out. Dan handed Kyle and Michael their armbands. Michael slowly, hesitantly positioned the armband on his left forearm. When the armband touched his skin, it quickly changed shape and pulled itself flush to his skin, piercing holes deep into the nerve fibers of his forearm. Momentary distress filled his face, but his look of pain quickly went away. "That hurt," he said.

Dan did not say anything. Jason had already reinstalled his armband on his left forearm, presumably interfaced to the same holes, as otherwise he would have had a reaction to the needle pricks. Barbara also expressed no reaction after reinstalling her armband. Kyle still held his after seeing how Michael had reacted and clearly remembering how his mother had reacted when installing hers for the first time.

Michael knew Kyle was hesitant. "It will be okay, Kyle," he said. "You still have puncture holes in your arm that have not healed, so you will feel no pain."

Kyle stared up into his father's eyes. "Can you put this on me, Daddy?"

"Sure, Son," Dan said, taking Kyle's armband. Firmly supporting his son's forearm, he slowly moved the armband close to the three previous holes, making sure the needles were somewhat lined up. The armband seemed to shift a little, then quickly changed shape, and the needles punctured deep into his skin, as if drawn to the original holes like a magnet. Kyle showed no distress or discomfort whatsoever.

They were all now wearing their armbands. Dan placed Kyle next to his oldest brother and then relaxed back with a calm sense of peace. Barbara positioned Michael on the couch next to Jason, and the three boys quietly waited with their parents for Captain Donaldson and his officers to arrive, knowing they would soon be leaving the mother ship in a spaceship of their own.

# 23

## LEAVING THE MOTHER SHIP

Dan saw by his wristwatch it was now 5:02 p.m. Captain Donaldson and his officers should be arriving anytime now. There was a light tone in the room that caused all the Jupiter family members to look over toward the entry door, where there was a flashing green light, as though projected against the wall—an indication someone was waiting outside their door. They figured it was Captain Donaldson and his officers. "Please come in," Dan called out.

The door vanished, and in walked Captain Donaldson, along with his first officer, chief science officer, chief medical officer, and spiritual advisor, Jose. It seemed fitting that it would be the same officers they'd first met who would escort them to their new spaceship.

Captain Donaldson noticed the Jupiter family sitting relaxed on the couch but with anticipation all over their faces. He expressed a kind, open face. "How was your sightseeing?"

"The plantatrium was magnificent," Dan said and then stood up with his family of five. "The laser light show that was created when the waterfall met the pool was a very nice touch."

"I agree," Captain Donaldson said. "There are plantatriums on all our ships, as they provide a physical and spiritual outlet to anyone who wishes to visit them."

Dan and Barbara knew his philosophical statement to be a fact. They, along with their boys, walked up to the officers by the doorway. Dan again noticed he was much shorter than Captain Donaldson and his officers, even Jose. He still felt privileged to be called their friend. He stared into Captain Donaldson's face and said, "You know, we met two of your ambassadors in the plantatrium."

"Yes, that's what they told me," Captain Donaldson said.

Dan and Barbara were curious about that conversation—surely it had been good. Dan continued to stare into Captain Donaldson's face. "We also met two very smart, beautiful birds there as well," he said.

Captain Donaldson grinned at little. "Was it the two that appeared to be a cross between your parrot, eagle, and turkey fowl species on Earth?"

Dan and Barbara were only partially surprised. "Yes, it was," Dan answered.

"That had to be special," Captain Donaldson said. "They are very popular pets back on our home world and extremely smart creatures. Those two—a mated pair—are the only ones in the plantatrium, so your meeting them was very fortunate, especially because they usually do not approach anyone they have not previously met or been introduced to. They could have been drawn to you out of curiosity about your twenty-first-century Earth clothing."

Dan thought about it. "Possibly," he said. "They told us 'goodbye' right before we left. How did they know to add the word *good* to *bye*?"

Captain Donaldson suddenly showed another small grin. "Our descriptive conversational computers transmitted the word in a frequency that only they could hear. If you were ever to meet them again, they would be able to use that word combination without the help of a computer. They are very smart and have an amazing long-term memory. They speak multiple languages and have a vocabulary that would rival many of your high school students on Earth."

Dan and Barbara were fascinated to hear this.

Captain Donaldson felt a small feeling of loss, but it was quickly overshadowed with a good feeling that the Jupiter family of five was prepared to start their new secret lives on Earth. "Are you ready to head home?"

"Yes, we are," Dan said.

"Good," Captain Donaldson said. "We'll walk you to your new ship."

Dan noticed the three manuals still on the table, and Captain Donaldson also saw them. "We'll transport those manuals to your ship."

"Thank you," Dan said.

They all continued into the hallway together and turned left. Jose turned to Barbara with a kind, open face. "Michael will adjust just fine to Earth's society."

The soft words made Barbara feel good, and she noticed Jason and Kyle staring at Michael, probably thinking about how Michael would get to grow up with them as their brother.

Everyone was now a little quiet as they continued down the hallway. Jason and Kyle did have Michael on their minds, but the small ship at their disposal also filled their young imaginations. Michael thought about his new parents, brothers, and upcoming life on Earth. Captain Donaldson was looking forward to wishing Dan Jupiter and his family goodbye, but in the back of his mind, he was still concerned about the space anomaly that had originated from the far reaches of the Milky Way, near the nebula. It was something their race had never encountered. Their large armada was continuing to scour the area for the origin of the energy beam that had started the entire chain of events leading up to their current situation. Their search for answers would continue nonstop.

Captain Donaldson did not want Dan and Barbara to be caught

off guard after their spaceship exited the cargo bay. "Do not be surprised, Dan," he said, "when this mother ship and its support ships suddenly disappear before your eyes soon after exiting the cargo bay."

Dan was a little puzzled. "Why is that?"

"Because," Captain Donaldson answered, "my contingent of ships is headed to a nebula in the far reaches of this galaxy to join our fleet investigating the origin of the beam that caused the cargo ship carrying Michael to impact your planet in a controlled fall."

Dan and Barbara were especially quiet, as it now seemed something even stranger and more mysterious was going on behind the scenes than what they'd been initially told. Dan's curiosity increased. "Is that anything for us to be concerned about?"

Captain Donaldson shook his head in the negative. "No, we do not believe so," he said, "as you will always be under our race's full protection. Besides that, if the race that caused the cargo ship to impact Earth actually wanted to take Michael, they would have already had him in their possession. There would have been nothing that we could have done to prevent it either."

"Why do you say that?" Dan asked.

"Because the sixty crew members who were aboard the cargo ship are still unaccounted for. There are many in our race who believe they are still alive and well, but where, we have no idea."

Dan and Barbara had intense looks on their faces.

"What's the first order of business when you return home?" Captain Donaldson asked.

Dan noticed Captain Donaldson was changing the subject. "Well, after a good night's rest, my wife and I were planning to create a set of rules for what is and is not acceptable in public and then start figuring out the timing of when to introduce Michael to our relatives and friends, especially his grandparents."

Captain Donaldson knew they had a good plan forward. As they neared the transporter just ahead, he said, "The guidelines you place in motion will eventually become commonplace for how you interact with others of your population."

Dan and Barbara appreciated his kind words. At the transporter elevator, the door slowly faded away. The Jupiters entered, followed by Captain Donaldson and then his four officers. The door reappeared behind them, and Dan looked around the semicylindrical room, a question forming in his eyes. Captain Donaldson knew what he was searching for.

"Where are the tiny waveguide horns?" Dan asked. "There have to be entry and exit points somewhere."

Captain Donaldson pointed up at the ceiling. "See those small, pin-sized holes in the decorative surfaces of the ceiling panels?"

Dan now noticed the tiny holes after staring intently at the ceiling. "Yes," he answered.

"Well," Captain Donaldson said, "those thousands of holes are the waveguide entrances and exits. Each hole has a hollow metallic conduit about the size of a twenty-gauge wire that is eventually interfaced to a primary molecular accumulator. All transporter-elevator waveguide tubes across the entire ship are interfaced to that same primary accumulator, via multiple secondary accumulators, according to the level on the ship. We enter one secondary accumulator, are transferred to the primary, and then, from there, are sent to another secondary accumulator right before our bodies are reconstituted."

Dan was thoroughly amazed. "That's interesting," he said and thought about what the chief engineer had told them. He had another question and was curious what the captain's answer would be. "Why not just use fiber-optic cables or even transport us directly between floors?"

"Because," Captain Donaldson replied, "fiber does not have the same unrestricted free-space aspect as hollow conduits, and though it would not be impossible to molecularly breakdown and reconstitute our bodies across fiber optics, it would be harder. But the main reason we do not very often transmit our bodies directly between floors, or from room to room, is due to the many foods, liquids, and other items that are being continually removed and reconstructed across the ship—it's a safety issue and a computer-processing issue. Plus, walking from room to room helps you gather your thoughts."

That all made complete sense to Dan.

Captain Donaldson finally stared down at the wall console. "Level five hundred and ten, quadrant two," he said in English.

The entry door suddenly vanished, and Dan and Barbara were amazed again how fast all of them had been transported nearly five hundred levels, or over two kilometers (more than one mile), through small, hollow conduits about three-hundredths of an inch in diameter. They all exited, turned left, and headed toward the large quadrant two cargo bay. As they approached the large double doors, Jason grabbed his father's left hand, wondering whether their new spaceship would look anything like Michael's little ship they'd used to travel to the moon.

Dan and Barbara also looked forward to seeing their new spaceship, which was nearly thirty meters (ninety-eight feet) in diameter, with advanced cloaking and quantum gravity space-travel capabilities. Dan gripped Jason's hand a little tighter. When they arrived at the large double doors, there was a subtle green glow before the doors vanished before they eyes. Now exposed was a very large cargo bay, along with a multitude of crew members and hundreds of spaceships ranging in size from ten meters to easily over sixty meters in diameter. Dan and his family followed Captain Donaldson and his officers inside, and Dan now realized how big the large cargo bay really was. It was maybe over six hundred meters deep, its ceiling at least eighty meters high. A very large spaceship could easily fit inside this particular cargo bay, but then, there was no visible outline of a cargo door or anything that could be considered an exit to outer space.

Following the lead of Captain Donaldson and his officers, Dan finally turned to Captain Donaldson with a sense of awe, wondering more about an aspect they'd witnessed in the cargo bay when first brought aboard the mother ship. "Why was the cargo bay void of crew members when we first came aboard your ship?"

Captain Donaldson smiled a little. "Precautionary procedure, Dan," he said, "just as Michael mostly guessed. Even though our race is immune to all Earth diseases and viruses, our computers still removed all unnecessary dormant retroviruses and bacteria that you and your family were carrying, especially those at the back of your throats and in your lymph nodes. We do not want to take any chances of a adenovirus or rhinovirus strain with unknown proteins, due to other races aboard on this ship, but the main reason we did not first show ourselves was because if we were to have taken Michael from you at that very moment, the less you saw and witnessed, the easier it would have been to regress your memories."

Dan and Barbara were extremely glad that had not happened but could understand the precautionary measures.

Most of the spaceships now before them had elliptical outer hulls, starting at a center band and extending up to the top and down to the bottom like two bowls facing each other. The ship they were about to receive might be shaped that way too, but then, some of the ships in the cargo bay were shaped a little differently, having flat bottoms with curvatures only on their top side. Dan finally turned to Captain Donaldson again, filled with curiosity, and pointed over at one of the flat-bottomed spaceships. "Why do some ships have flat bottoms?"

Captain Donaldson answered, "Because they do not use quantum gravity transitional time-warp fields—or jumps, for that matter. They have only a highly advanced gravity-propulsion system."

Dan thought about Captain Donaldson's answer, not recalling the flight manuals mentioning the reasoning behind the curvature of their ship's hull. "I take it that the curvature of the spaceship is directly related to the quantum gravity time-warp fields?"

"That is correct," Captain Donaldson said. "It's a mandatory shape against the planes of space-time, at least for extreme velocities well above light speed, so that the gravity element can be properly maintained while moving inside a field of kinetic quantum gravity that is also being continually converted into potential energy."

Dan was again amazed, as was Barbara. Dan suddenly noticed circular sections of a spaceship about a hundred meters away. The sections, which had once formed a long, tubular spacecraft, were laid up next to each other like slices of bread. Each circular section had to be close to fifteen meters in diameter, and some of the nearly two-meter-long tubular sections appeared to have had a hole cut into them while the ship was still intact.

When Jason and Michael saw the tubular spaceship sections, they knew the pieces belonged to the cargo ship that had impacted Earth and that had been carrying the small spaceship. Dan and Barbara were almost certain what they were viewing was the ship that had ferried Michael, but the ship being broken into smaller circular sections did not make complete sense. Dan turned to Captain Donaldson, curious about that exact thing. "Is that the cargo ship that was carrying Michael?"

"Yes, it is," Captain Donaldson said.

Dan and Barbara were also amazed the race had already recovered the ship, especially since it must have been stored in top-secret government facilities possibly including Area 51 and who knew what other highly secretive installations. Dan continued to stare at the destroyed cargo ship and finally turned back to Captain Donaldson, thinking about the mandatory hull shapes he'd just told them about. "Did the cargo ship also have a quantum gravity drive?"

"Yes, it did," Captain Donaldson said, "and like I earlier referenced, the hull curvatures of your ship and others like it are a requirement for extreme quantum gravity velocities reaching millions of times the speed of light. That particular cargo ship could not reach those same extreme velocities but still had the ability to surpass the speed of light by thousands of magnitudes."

Dan was amazed at the answer.

Captain Donaldson glanced down at the Jupiter family's armbands and finally stopped in front of a spaceship. No crew members were near this particular spaceship, which looked to be nearly thirty meters in diameter and maybe fifteen meters tall, just as they had already been told. Dan and Barbara figured this spaceship was the one the advanced race was giving to them. It looked magnificent. Of course, it only looked magnificent to them. There were quite a number of others in the cargo bay exactly like it, but to see the actual ship they would be using to travel back to Earth and even outside Earth's solar system one day made it take on a totally different look—it was kind of like getting your first new car or hot rod, except in this case, it was a highly advanced spaceship with quantum gravity propulsion.

Dan and his family continued to stare at their spaceship, mesmerized. Dan thought about how the cloaking field of the small spaceship they'd used to travel to the moon was sometimes unstable under certain acceleration thresholds. Curious, he turned to Captain Donaldson and asked, "Will the cloaking field of this particular spaceship briefly break down during immense acceleration or deceleration?"

Captain knew to what Dan was referring. "No, it will not," he answered. "Ships capable of quantum gravity time-warp-field propulsion are very different from flat-bottomed ships with only gravity propulsion, such as the one you took to the moon. Though the phase-matched cloaking fields of our flat-bottomed ships do break down occasionally under high velocities, or due to sudden changes in directional momentum, at least while inside the reference magnetic field of a planet, their flat bottoms require much less expenditure of gravitational propulsion energy while traveling below light-speed velocities. As far as their ability to reach the speed of light, it is impossible without a catastrophic meltdown of the spherical interactive dome encasing the gravity element."

Dan and Barbara were amazed again by the detailed answer, and Dan now closely examined their spaceship. Like some of the other ships in the cargo bay, its shape was like that of two bowls facing each other, with only one very small portion of the lower bowl's surface contacting the cargo bay floor. It seemed to him the ship would have a tendency to roll over onto one side or the other with only the smallest amount of weight off its center of mass—like being top heavy. Dan turned to Captain Donaldson, curious about that strange, mysterious sight. "How does the ship stay balanced in its present static state?" he asked. "You know … like keep from tipping over?"

"The ships are perfectly balanced," Captain Donaldson said, "and besides, most of their total mass is positioned at the very bottom and center of the ship. This is also where the gravity propulsion and quantum gravity time-warp-field drives reside, including the extremely dense spherical interactive dome that encases the gravity element and other rare earth elements. The cradle holding the highly reactive power supply is just above the dome and extends all the way down to the bottom of the ship. Since over ninety-eight percent of the ship's total mass is confined to this small area, you could say that these ships are extremely bottom heavy through their center of mass."

Dan and Barbara appreciated the detailed explanation, and Dan remembered from what he had read in the manual that there were gravitationally driven inertial damper compensators around the center compression ring to automatically correct for any abnormal directional or inertial force changes that might be felt inside the ship—a safety measure, kind of like a spinning top, except the only thing that was actually spinning were invisible rings of gravity. He also remembered reading about the spherical interactive dome but did not understand how it was able to focus an aperture of gravity so precisely to form a field of quantum gravity around the spaceship's outer hull for its immense propulsion velocities. What Captain Donaldson had just told him about the quantum gravity conversion from kinetic energy to potential energy was interesting.

Captain Donaldson read Dan's mind but did not comment any further on the spherical interactive dome or its highly advanced properties. He looked briefly at Barbara, the three boys, and then back to Dan. "Your armbands," he calmly said, "have been modified to allow direct interfaces to your spaceship's computer, as well as the smaller ship in its cargo bay."

Dan was now antsy to see their ship up close and personal. "Okay, thank you," he said.

Captain Donaldson looked down at Dan's armband a second time and calmly explained, "By pressing the square buttons on your armband in a combination of one-two-four, with button one being closest to your chest, the door to your ship will open, and a ramp will appear. Pressing a combination of one-three-two will set up a space transport of your bodies directly onto the ship, or off the ship, whichever you desire. Anybody in your near vicinity can transport with you by pressing the same buttons on their armbands, or you can have your ship's computer use automatic mode. Once this process is completed, just press button one on your armband, and the molecular transportation process will be finished. Everything I'm telling you can also be read in your ship's data banks." Captain Donaldson paused.

Dan took a short breath and looked down at his armband. He tilted his forearm toward his chest and, with his right hand, touched buttons one, two, and four in the sequence mentioned. Sure enough, an open doorway into their ship, maybe two to three meters above the cargo bay floor, suddenly appeared, as did a silver-colored ramp directly below it that was now contacting the cargo bay. Dan looked up inside the brightly lit spaceship and turned back to Captain Donaldson and his officers, realizing they were very close to leaving the mother ship.

Captain Donaldson knew this and stared down at Kyle and Michael, who were standing next to each other like twin brothers. "Bye, Kyle, bye, Michael," he calmly said, and with a gracious nod, he leaned his large, tall body down and shook their little hands.

"Goodbye, Captain," Michael replied, returning the handshake.

Kyle was thrilled to shake the hand of the captain of the large spaceship. "Goodbye, Captain," he also said.

Captain Donaldson knew the young Earth boy was a loved little boy and that Michael would learn emotional traits from him. The captain straightened and stared directly into Jason's eyes. It was Jason's bravery in heading to the cargo ship with no fear or second thought of his actions and then meeting Michael that had ultimately caused their race's friendship with his family. If the US government's top-secret military had confiscated the small spaceship, it could have complicated matters immensely, especially if Michael had come out of his stasis in the presence of another human being besides Jason, like someone within the US government. That might not have ended well for Michael. "Goodbye, Jason," Captain Donaldson graciously said and shook his hand.

Jason, with a disguised, distant grin, felt admiration and calmly returned the handshake. "Goodbye, Captain."

Captain Donaldson again straightened. As his four officers said goodbye to the three boys, he turned to Dan and Barbara with an immense feeling of contentment. "I have every confidence that you'll raise Michael and protect him with your lives as any parent would do for their son." He then reached out to shake their hands.

Dan knew that was a fact and returned the handshake. "Yes, we will," he said, "and thank you for all of your kindness, especially having confidence in us."

Barbara wore a kind, relaxed face and also shook the captain's hand. "Yes, thank you," she said.

Jose made eye contact with Dan. "We look forward to when all of you visit our home world. Your wife said she hopes it will be soon."

"Thank you for the invite," Dan said, "and yes, we'll do just that sometime in the very near future."

Captain Donaldson paused again with an extremely relaxed spirit. "Dan," he calmly said, "once you're situated in the cockpit, turn on the ship's gravity-propulsion system, and we'll transport you out of the cargo bay."

"Okay, thank you," Dan said. He let out a sigh, and they finally started up the ramp, Jason leading the way, followed by Michael, then Kyle, Barbara, and Dan. Once inside, Dan turned around, and after one last small wave, he continued into the ship, out of sight. He knew Captain Donaldson could have transported them directly to the cockpit, but he probably wanted them to use the doorway and ramp for their first time boarding the ship.

There was an open doorway about four meters away, and Dan recognized it as a transporter elevator. When he turned back around, the doorway into their ship was no longer there. Neither was there an outline to suggest a door ever existing, so he had to surmise that it was possible the open doorway had amazingly bonded back to the ship's outer hull.

Captain Donaldson and his officers now stood quietly, staring at the Jupiters' spaceship, realizing again that the Jupiter family was about to embark on a new secret life on Earth that would be filled with not only learning more about their race's technologies but also raising Michael, unbeknownst to the rest of the human race. It was a challenge the captain and officers felt Dan and Barbara Jupiter were prepared to take on without a second thought or hint of hesitation.

Inside the spaceship, Dan and his family had entered the transporter elevator. Everything appeared the same as on the mother ship. Dan looked down at the small wall console and said, "Cockpit."

The transporter-elevator door suddenly vanished before their eyes, and since there were no elevator shafts, Dan knew their bodies were molecularly broken down and transported through tiny, hollow conduits the size of 20-guage electrical wire. The instantaneous transport would no doubt take some getting used to, but since there would not be as many instantaneous matter transports aboard their ship as on the mother ship, they could probably just transport directly between floors. Dan exited the elevator alongside his family and found the first-floor cockpit level was very spacious. From what he had read in the manual, it had over one thousand square feet of usable floor space, consisting of five bedrooms, two bathrooms, and a family area. The ceiling at the very center, directly over the cockpit, was nearly four meters high, curving down toward the sides to match the upside-down bowl shape of the outer hull. Around the perimeter of the first floor, Dan and Barbara would be able to reach up and touch the ceiling, but it was still high enough that they did not have to stoop. There were curved windows throughout that matched the outer hull, some about two meters above the floor. Through a few of the windows they could see the hundreds of spaceship in the cargo bay.

In front of the cockpit, the floor was recessed nearly a half meter lower than the rest of the cockpit. There were three oval tables in this space, each with six tabletop displays, a cushioned chair in front of each display. In the middle of the cockpit, behind the tables and the recessed floor, were seven evenly centered, cushioned high-back chairs, positioned in a slightly curved row, each chair separated by about a half meter. The chair in the very center was a little larger than the rest—clearly the captain's chair. In front of each seat was a display and console, but there were no multidirectional control wheels for this particular spaceship, unlike the smaller ship they'd taken to the moon. It made Dan realize even more that the small ship was a child's spaceship, just as they had been told.

Dan and his family finally walked into the cockpit and continued toward the seven seats. Dan sat down in the captain's chair. Its soft armrests and seat felt like memory foam with a touch of bubble wrap. The armrests had an assortment of touch-activated buttons as well as roller balls on the ends. Dan knew from the manual that the roller balls had direct control of the spaceship's gravity-propulsion system. Barbara sat down to his left and Jason to his right. Kyle sat down next to Jason, and Michael sat just to Kyle's right. To Barbara's left were two empty seats.

Dan looked up through the two-meter-long rectangular window directly above them and finally turned to his wife and boys to see they were waiting for his next course of action. His front console suddenly lit up by itself, and he remembered what the flight manual had said as far as activating the gravity-propulsion system. "Well, here we go," he said and touched the red button on his flat-screen console.

Barbara sat in quiet, surreal anticipation.

Their ship's systems and subsystems immediately came on line. Dan's front console went from dim to bright, as did the consoles in front of his wife and sons, but the two consoles to Barbara's left remained unlit. The general lighting throughout the cockpit area seemed to have dimmed somewhat. Dan knew their ship's gravity-propulsion system was for sure now online, because their spaceship had just risen a few meters off the cargo bay floor—as evidenced by the spaceships in the cargo bay being a little farther below their vantage point.

Suddenly, there was a forward bump, and their spaceship began moving toward a rectangular opening in the cargo bay that had not been there previously. Outer space was clearly visible, with no apparent force field to isolate the cargo bay from the vacuum of outer space, though surely there must be an invisible shield of some type. They continued through the doorway and into outer space. Dan looked back through their windows and then down at what was displayed on his front console. Their ship was moving farther away from the mother ship at an extremely fast pace, inside what had to be another gravity tractor beam. Then, to Dan's amazement, their ship rotated 180 degrees while still inside the tractor beam, continuing to move farther away from the mother ship. They all again noticed how truly, immensely huge the mother ship was, as it still filled the entire view of their spaceship's front windows. They seemed to be speeding away from the mother ship at an even quicker rate. Then the opening in the side of the mother ship suddenly disappeared. Their ship continued farther away. According to Dan's front display, they were already at a distance of five kilometers, yet the mother ship still looked as though they were right next to it. There was another bump, a release of the tractor beam, and the Jupiters now stared hypnotically at the dozens of support ships that were like glowing dots, reflecting the sunlight, all of them in a stationary pattern in the vicinity of the mother ship. The support ships looked exactly like the spaceship they were currently aboard. Suddenly, half of the support ships vanished before their very eyes, then the mother ship, followed by the remainder of the support ships.

Dan turned to his wife, surprised, even after already knowing it was going to happen. He just hadn't expected it to happen so soon. Even more amazing was the fact the mother ship and its contingent of support ships were probably now traveling thousands of times the speed of light and would exit the sun's heliosphere and enter interstellar space in less than five seconds. If they were using a quantum gravity time-warp burst, then they would have left the sun's solar system nearly instantaneously. "Well, I guess we are finally on our own," Dan said and noticed Earth clearly in view, slightly to their left.

Barbara also noticed Earth in the far distance. "Looks that way," she said.

Michael already had something displayed on his front console and was now helping Kyle with his display. Jason touched his console, and Barbara started to fiddle with hers too. Dan finally reached down to his own console, which was slightly bigger than the other six. On the main menu was a button for cloaking countermeasures. He touched it, and another menu appeared, revealing the cloaking capabilities of their ship. Surprisingly, there were sixteen different cloaking schemes. Dan turned to his wife, amazed. "Would you look at this?" he said.

Barbara looked over at his display, also amazed at the number of cloaking countermeasures. The higher cloaking orders 10 through 16 had red dots next to them, and Barbara wondered whether the dots meant these cloaking schemes would be unavailable to them, remembering how the mother ship's computers had earlier prevented them from accessing and using certain options due to a lack of security clearance. But then, those red dots also could mean those cloaking schemes were dangerous. "That is amazing," she said.

"Yes, it is," Dan agreed. "Well, I had better just select the lowest cloaking level for now, at least until we have some understanding of what the higher-order cloaking schemes do to our immediate area of space. Those red dots surely mean a warning of some kind."

"True," Barbara said, fully agreeing, "but our ship's computer would also probably override any cloaking selection that is not required to shield us from Earth's radar technologies or the technologies of another race, for that matter. I believe that is what the chief engineer alluded to us."

Dan thought about it. "You're right," he said, "and since our ship's computer surely knows Earth's technologies, it probably wouldn't even allow a cloaking scheme that was overkill."

Barbara nodded to agree.

Dan selected the lowest cloaking level—phase-matched gravity field—and a new message appeared: "Ready to activate." He decided to wait until they were near Earth to cloak their ship.

Below his front display he saw the small telepathic helmet. It was strange to think about how he could control their ship by simply wearing this helmet and using his thoughts. There was a helmet in front of each console, and Dan turned to his wife. "Did you notice you also have a telepathic helmet?"

"Yes, I did," she said.

"Strange huh?"

"Yes, it is."

A distant look filled Dan's face, and he turned back to his wife. "I wonder if wearing our helmets at the same time would allow us to telepathically communicate."

Barbara showed a sudden, strange grin. "You know, that could be a possibility."

"Would definitely be different," Dan said and noticed she was now staring over at the boys. He touched his front screen again, activating their ship's main gravity drive, but felt nothing different.

Dan studied his front screen and saw there was a gravity field fully encompassing their ship that was shaped similar to an oblong sphere. In addition, his screen indicated there was rotational gravity, according to a specific harmonic, inside that same field that was directly related to the ship's quantum gravity capabilities. Not wanting to get engrossed in what he saw, he positioned his hands on his armrest control wheels, which were like the roller balls of a computer mouse. He slightly spun the left roller ball to his left. Their ship quickly moved sideways to their left, well over three hundred miles in a short time span, and then stopped. "Well, that didn't work very well," he mumbled under his breath. He spun the ball slightly to the right and toward him at the same time. Within seconds, their ship immediately moved four-hundred miles to their right and rotated at a one-hundred and forty-five-degree clockwise angle from their starting position. They were still pointed away from Earth. Dan removed his fingers from the roller balls, lifted his arms into the air, interlocking his fingers, and then stretched his arms, hands, and shoulders. He felt invigorated. "This will take some getting used to," he said.

Barbara only gave him a small grin.

Dan briefly clenched his fists, placed his left hand back on the roller ball, and gently spun it in an ever-so-smooth clockwise circular motion. Their ship rotated to the right. Earth finally came into full view with the sun to their right, and the cockpit windows immediately darkened as though filtering the bright ultraviolet sunlight. Dan removed his fingers from the roller ball while staring over at his wife. "These roller balls sure are sensitive. I must have moved the roller ball less than a centimeter to rotate our ship nearly ninety degrees."

"Amazing," Barbara said.

Dan stared at Earth's brilliant blue atmosphere, mesmerized to be looking at it from such a vast distance away, as though they were astronauts in an Earth-based craft returning from a voyage. On his front display, their distance to Earth was listed in both miles and kilometers—232,000 miles and 366,660 kilometers. It made him realize again that the mother ship had been orbiting around the sun to match Earth's orbital speed over the last few days while at the same time maintaining its perspective to Earth. It did appear though that the mother ship had moved to a new position that was ahead of Earth's orbital motion. A question suddenly displayed on his front screen: "Activate phase-matched gravity-field cloaking for the reference planet before entering its dipole magnetic field envelope?"

Dan knew the ship's computer was referencing Earth and now knew their cloaking field would automatically activate, but he was curious about the meaning of "magnetic field envelope," as Earth had many different planetary envelopes. He touched the Yes button and turned to his wife, who was still staring at Earth. "Well, let's head home," he said.

Barbara turned to Dan with an anxious feeling. "I am ready," she said.

Jason, Kyle, and Michael were also staring in Dan's direction. "Are you boys ready to go home?" he calmly asked.

"Yes, I am, Dad," Jason said.

"Yes, Daddy," Kyle replied.

"Me too, Daddy," Michael piped with visible excitement.

Dan thought it hilarious how his sons had responded.

# 24

## RETURNING HOME

According to Dan's wristwatch, it was 5:33 p.m., Los Alamos time. He selected the gravity-propulsion menu, and a flat holographic image suddenly appeared in front of him with what appeared to be an interactive numeric keypad. There was a red warning flag and message: "Maximum speed derated—planetary body ahead."

Dan was amazed by the warning, not to mention the flat holographic image, which had unusual depth, as though layered. Behind the flat holograph was a three-dimensional, color image of Earth, its latitudinal and longitudinal lines showing, along with a time of 5:34 p.m., which he knew to be the time in Los Alamos, New Mexico. According to information next to the spherical image of Earth, that reference time was on the sunward side of Earth and in a thirty-three-degree counterclockwise rotation from their ship's present location in space. On the holographic touch keypad, he entered the town of Los Alamos as the end coordinate point, followed by the number 200,000, amazed by how the holographic keypad was so interactive, like a semisolid display, even having a slight feel of pressure against his fingertips. A question suddenly popped up across the image: "200,000 kilometers per hour velocity. Is this correct?"

Dan touched the Yes button on the holographic image. It was as if the ship had read his mind to know that he was thinking kilometers per hour and not miles per hour.

Their spaceship's computer immediately forced a high-energy electromagnetic energy beam across the spherical interactive dome encasing the gravity element, forming a short aperture beam of kinetic energy across the hull of the spaceship. The end result was an immediate beam of potential gravitational energy projected toward Earth's magnetosphere. Dan and his family watched as the stars quickly changed their positions. Dan knew by what was now showing in the holographic image that they were already traveling two hundred thousand kilometers per hour. He did not feel any acceleration or inertial forces whatsoever, and their speed seemed almost instantaneous, taking only a few seconds at the most. Another flat holographic image appeared just to the right of the other holograph, displaying their estimated time of arrival, along with yet another spherical image of Earth in the background. This new spherical image displayed detailed information about Earth's magnetosphere, atmospheric composition, and electron-ion flow as Earth was affected by the sun's solar winds. There was other surprising planetary information, some of which he did not recognize. Their ETA was one hour and fifty minutes at their current speed.

Dan looked back through their front windows. He saw the sun just to the right of Earth and felt sudden déjà vu. This trip felt a lot like the trip a few days ago after visiting the moon, when they'd been intercepted by the advanced alien race on their way back to Earth. The familiarity was overshadowed by one immense difference: the fact they were now aboard a much-larger spaceship having quantum gravity propulsion. It was all strange to think about, especially all the unbelievable time they'd spent aboard the mother ship over the last few days. Dan stared back out the side windows, which seemed to be filtering the sun's bright ultraviolet rays, because he could look directly at the sun without having to squint, no special sunglasses required. He could also see amazing, enhanced details of the sun like he'd never before seen. "Our ship's window seems to have very strange filtering properties," he said while staring over at his wife. "Did you notice that we can look directly at the sun without having to squint?"

"Yes, I did," she said. "There is definitely some special automatic tinting or filtering while also having unusual light-enhancing properties, like in high definition."

"For sure," Dan agreed and noticed Michael looking at a holographic image. "What type of ultraviolet filtering is designed into the windows, Michael?"

Michael looked in his direction. "Ellipithelial molecular bonding," he said.

Dan and Barbara were surprised to hear the term *ellipithelial*, which seemed to indicate a molecular elliptical configuration in combination with an epithelial structure, epithelial referring to the tissue lining the inside and outside surfaces of a cell structure. Dan continued to stare at Michael, filled not only with immense curiosity but also anticipation for the answer to his next question. "What do you mean by ellipithelial?"

"Ellipithelial," Michael explained, "is in direct reference to the silica atoms and their cohesiveness to the cerium-barium nanocrystals, including the ability of each individual bond to rotate up to one hundred and eighty degrees, depending on the severity of light. It is equivalent to having both one-way and two-way mirrors within the window's molecular structures, Dad."

Dan continued to stare at Michael, shaking his head in amazement at this answer. Earth had been working on trying to use small mirrors inside displays, but nothing to the degree of what Michael had mentioned. "Interesting!" Dan said. "Are those internal reflective properties driven by external sensors and a power supply, or are they built into the glass itself as automatic tinting?"

"They have an external power source and sensors," Michael answered.

Dan continued to gaze into Michael's face. "Thank you for your explanation, Michael," he said.

Michael remained calm, with an extremely contented face, and turned back to his holographic image. Jason and Kyle were also now staring up at Michael's holograph.

Dan took hold of his wife's hand, and they relaxed back in their seats while their spaceship approached Earth at 200,000 kilometers per hour (a little over 124,000 miles per hour).

The boys left their seats, walked down a few steps into the recessed area, and sat at one of the oval tables about four meters away, with Michael sitting directly across from his two brothers. Michael touched the flat-screen tabletop display in front of him, and a highly detailed holographic image appeared directly above their table. It was an image of a sixteen-planet solar system with a large sun. He touched the console a couple more times and reached up into the image. It quickly changed in appearance, with the sixteen planets slowly rotating around the sun in their respective orbital patterns. One of the planets started becoming much larger, as if being zoomed in on.

Dan and Barbara figured that planet might be the race's home world planet, Valzar. There were now multiple moving images inside the holograph, possibly of the planet's history. Dan and Barbara heard Michael explaining the images to Jason and Kyle. As they continued to stare at the moving picture images, Dan squeezed his wife's hand a couple of times, and a flirty, kind expression suddenly crossed her face, because what they were now witnessing convinced them beyond doubt that Jason and Kyle would always respect Michael for what he had to tell them, even though Michael himself had a lot to learn emotionally while growing up into a young man on Earth.

Dan noticed it was now 5:43 p.m. At their current velocity, there was still well over an hour before reaching Earth. He touched a series of buttons on his front console to learn a little more about their spaceship and found it had four levels. On the second level were additional rooms, a few guest rooms, and a plantatrium with a vaulted ceiling that took up a portion of the top floor. The plantatrium was of interest, since he had not previously known for sure whether their ship would have one, though Captain Donaldson had alluded to the fact that all their spaceships did. On the third level were additional rooms and a laboratory, which he knew would contain a brain wave recording device.

Dan continued to study the layout, realizing the upper deck was considered level 1, the same as the mother ship, and the numbers counted down toward the bottom floor, or cargo hold. The cargo bay was on the fourth and bottom level, its contents consisting of only a small spaceship—in fact, the same spaceship they had taken to the moon. Below the cargo bay floor was the spherical interactive dome, its cradle, the powerful energy system, and the highly radioactive gravity element, including other rare isotopic elements Dan did not recognize. He finally relaxed back in his chair and turned to Barbara with a good feeling inside. "Want to sightsee around our ship until arriving home? There is a plantatrium on the second level."

"Is that right?" she replied.

"Yep," Dan said and noticed their kids still staring at the holographic moving picture images. He turned back to his wife. "How about we let the kids spend time together? It would definitely be a new experience for them while aboard our new ship and might help with their maturity."

Barbara knew that was a good idea and nodded to agree.

"Boys," Dan said, "your mother and I are going to walk around the ship. We'll return before reaching Earth."

"Okay, Dad," Jason said. "We'll be right here."

The holographic images in front of Dan suddenly disappeared. This was only mildly surprising to Dan and Barbara, as the same thing had happened to the holographic image above the small workstation on the small ship when they were traveling to the moon. Dan and Barbara finally stood up and headed to the transporter elevator filled with anticipation. The door disappeared in front of them and immediately reappeared as soon as they entered. Dan stared down at the wall console and said, "Level two, plantatrium."

The door vanished again, and they exited into the hallway, immediately spotting the plantatrium directly to their right. To their left, the hallway extended about ten meters, and there appeared to be at least four doorways. They could not help but be drawn toward the plantatrium. There were trees and lush vegetation and the sounds of a waterfall.

As they headed toward the plantatrium, Dan thought about the double-elliptical shape of their spaceship. With its four levels, he figured there could be three thousand square feet of livable space, not counting the cargo bay. That was an interesting thought, as they could easily entertain quite a few other passengers. As they walked up to the plantatrium, they were curious whether its waterfall might be similar to the mother ship's, with sparkling, multicolored water falling into the pool to create a stunning, shimmering, and unique laser light show. Continuing inside, they noticed three trees near the waterfall and a few more scattered throughout the plantatrium but no laser light show. The waterfall was flowing normally, like it would under Earth gravity. The water was being expelled out of a hole in one of the walls, which looked to be grayish-brown rock—possibly simulated rocks. The waterfall was close to three meters in height, ending in an oblong pool nearly four meters wide. Its soft rustling sound was soothing to their spirits. On the ceiling, about five meters above their heads, were dozens of large, curved windows, though they did not remember seeing those windows on the hull when the ship was in the cargo bay. Some of the trees were within a few meters of the windows, and rays of sunlight filtered down into the plantatrium.

With a deep breath, Dan felt invigorated by the fresh, oxygenated atmosphere that appeared similar to the mother ship's plantatrium. "This plantatrium is pretty nice, huh?" he said.

"Yes, it is," Barbara said, "fresh like after a soft rain."

Dan continued up to the pool's edge. The pool was about a meter deep, and there were two small streams flowing out of it. Where they ended was a mystery, so he and Barbara walked alongside one stream toward the other end of the plantatrium, where the stream suddenly stopped on the far wall. At this particular area, water was flowing down a hole like a bathtub drain, causing a slight whirlpool action. A fine silver-colored mesh covered the hole, and the water appeared to be flowing around two to three miles per hour. The mesh no doubt kept solid material out of the return, including any aquatic life.

They headed back toward the waterfall, not noticing any aquatic life whatsoever in the streams or in the pool. Dan turned to his wife. "Guess we'll be populating this pool, huh?" he kidded.

Barbara grinned a little. "Yes, we will," she said.

Dan glanced at his wristwatch and noticed there was less than twenty-seven minutes before reaching Earth. Looking around the plantatrium some more, they noticed six tables, each table with six chairs, that could easily accommodate dozens of visitors. "You know," Barbara finally said, "I can see why you would want to spend time here."

"For sure," Dan replied. "Let's sit and relax for a bit."

"Okay," she said and sat down at the table closest to the waterfall. Dan sat down next to her, knowing that these chairs, which faced the waterfall, would most likely become their favorite seats, especially since they were the first ones they sat down in—as though drawn to those exact chairs.

Dan stared more closely at the trees. Their leaves did not appear to be of Earth origin, nor did he recognize any of the plants, some of which had beautiful purple and green flowers similar to roses. Two different-colored flowers on the same plant was a breathtaking and amazing sight. The colorful plants were definitely not bushes, nor did they appear to have any thorns, so they could very well belong to the carnation class. The drain hole in the bottom of the streambed was also interesting, as it had to have some type of pumping system or possibly another advanced aspect of the race's space-displacement technology. Dan grabbed his wife's hand with an extremely serene feeling. Barbara followed his kindness by laying her head against his shoulder, and they both quietly stared at the waterfall, daydreaming, wondering, and contemplating their future on Earth, taking in the moment like a dream they'd never believed possible.

✦ ✦ ✦

In the cockpit, Michael had explained quite a lot about the planet Valzar, its three moons, and its solar system comprised of sixteen planetary bodies. Jason and Kyle listened intently, and Jason continued to stare directly over at Michael. "What's it like," he finally asked, "to understand where you came from without actually seeing it?"

Michael thought about this question, since the planet and its history were like deeply ingrained memories. "I'm not sure, Jason," he finally answered. "It is just something I know, sort of like the memory of a dream after waking up."

Kyle was confused by the answer, but Jason thought he understood and continued staring into Michael's face. "Will you now dream when you sleep?"

"Yes, I will," Michael said. "When I was in the second stasis, I remember dreaming about things that I had never experienced."

Kyle now understood Michael's previous statement. "I dream too," he blurted out.

Michael was curious. "What do you dream about?"

Kyle answered, "I dream about catching me a big fish and getting lots of toys on my birthday and at Christmas."

Michael understood Kyle's mention of a birthday, but he did not know exactly what day he had taken his first breath of life. He also did not understand what Kyle meant by *Christmas*. "What is Christmas?" he asked.

Jason knew Kyle did not know for sure how to reply and saw Michael waiting for an answer. "Christmas," Jason answered, "is when family or friends get together to exchange gifts and celebrate the season. It is also a religious holiday commemorating the birth of a man called Jesus, who walked this planet almost two thousand years ago."

Michael somewhat understood what Jason had told him, as there were a variety of religions on the planet Valzar, but he did not understand why Earthlings would be celebrating the birth of a man. "Who is Jesus?" he asked.

Jason glanced down at his little brother, who was listening intently, and then back to Michael. "Jesus was a religious leader and prophet, Michael," he said, "who walked the Earth as a man yet was also the son of a living spiritual God—a great and powerful being. Jesus taught much good in our world, and when he was a young man, the human race crucified him, even after he showed them many miraculous powers." Jason paused.

Michael was now confused. "Why would they kill him, then?"

"Because they would not accept him," Jason said. "He healed the sick with a touch of his hand, raised the dead, and was even able to raise himself from the dead three days after he was crucified. He died so that everyone might have a chance of everlasting life after our physical deaths."

Michael knew the man Jason referred to had to be from a higher power to perform those types of miracles and must have had a very high, pure level of spiritual DNA coursing through his veins, especially to be able to raise himself from the dead. Then he remembered what his new parents had talked about at the dinner table a few days ago regarding the suicide bomber who had killed a prominent Shiite cleric in the country called Iraq. He compared it to what Jason had just told him about the crucifixion of Jesus, and it seemed to him that some of the human race had not changed much in nearly two thousand years. "I think I understand," he said.

Jason felt happy at Michael's reply and noticed Earth getting much closer. "Let's return to our seats," he said.

"Okay," Michael said.

The boys returned to their same chairs, just to the right of their dad's captain's chair, and waited patiently for their parents to return. Jason grabbed his communicator to be safe. "Mom, Dad," he said, "Earth is getting pretty close."

There was silence.

"I know, Jason," their father finally replied through the communicator. "We are on our way back now."

"Okay," Jason said.

Michael was staring directly at Jason. "Our ship would have automatically slowed down even if Mom and Dad were not here."

"Why is that?" Jason asked.

"Because," Michael answered, "if our spaceship were to enter Earth's pressurized atmospheric space at its current speed, there would be a magnificent ball of fire and immense flash of light that most everyone on our side of Earth would notice, like an immensely huge meteor from outer space. There would also be an instantaneous temperature and differential pressure change against our ship's hull, including a possible inertial effect inside the ship."

Jason thought about what Michael had told them. "That's interesting," he said. "Would our ship's hull be damaged?"

"No," Michael said, "but we could be injured."

About that time, Dan and Barbara walked into the cockpit, saw the three boys sitting in their original chairs, and returned to their previous seats. Dan stared across his wife at the boys. "How are you all doing?"

"Good, Dad," Jason said.

"I am doing fine," Michael said.

"Me too," Kyle piped.

Dan now clearly saw through their front cockpit windows the magnificent blue planet Earth. Two holographic images suddenly appeared again directly in front of him, the right image spherical and the other image flat but with immaculate depth of perception. The right holograph listed Earth as 18,225 kilometers (11,324 miles) away, with an ETA a little over five minutes. Dan knew they'd entered into Earth's plasma sheet many kilometers ago and began studying the right image, which displayed Earth's dipole field and magnetotail, which currently showed an axial inclination tilt of 23.4393218 degrees to the sun. Also in the image was information about the planet's magnetic field, ionospheric layers, and ozone composition and thickness, along with a multitude of internal thermal configurations across its atmospheric layers. Their ship's computer had also identified dangerous areas in the stratospheric ozone layers—a small hole over Antarctica and a smaller hole near the North Pole. A few equations briefly displayed in the image, referencing polar-metric polarities, followed by a green message: "Phase-matched resonance cloaking *active*."

Dan did not fully understand the equations but did recognize the magnetic B-field polarities, just not how they were related to the ring currents. Another message, this time in red letters, suddenly appeared: "Entering ionosphere soon. ** Inertial effects possible. ** Automatic safeguards and overrides apply."

Dan now knew their ship would automatically slow down but decided to manually change the speed. He reached up into the holograph and selected a propulsion of 20,000 on the semi-invisible keypad, which again had a slight feel of pressure against his fingertips, and a question appeared: "Slow propulsion to 20,000 kilometers per hour?"

Dan touched Yes, and their ship suddenly decelerated to 20,000 kilometers per hour within a few seconds. Another message, in blue, appeared across the image: "Speed is acceptable to maintain full inertial control."

"That was strange, huh?" Barbara said.

"Yes, it was," Dan said. "Hard to believe our ship was traveling over fifty-five kilometers per second and decelerated nearly fifty of those kilometers within only a few seconds and without our bodies feeling any inertial forces."

"For sure," she replied.

Dan continued to stare at the two chest-level holographs. In the right image, their ship was shown as a small blue dot against the planet's sphere. Also displayed was the outer layer of the ionosphere, and he noticed their ship had already entered into the ionosphere's inner regions. When Dan looked over at his boys, Michael was showing Jason and Kyle another holographic image, so he turned his attention back to his own holographs. At their current speed, they would pass through the ionosphere and into Earth's thermosphere and mesosphere layers in less than ten seconds. A space-pressure change was definitely coming, and their ship would become like a small rock thrown into a large pool of water. He also did not know for certain what would happen to their ship's cloaking field and its hull, so he reached over and grabbed his wife's hand. "Mesosphere layer coming up," he said.

Barbara gently squeezed his hand and prepared herself for the fire and intense heat when their ship finally breached Earth's outer atmospheric layers.

Dan gazed over again at the three boys, who were now staring intently through the cockpit windows, and figured they were also getting ready for the display of intense heat against their ship's hull. He glanced back at his left holograph, which showed their ship's current position in direct reference to Earth: 35 degrees south latitude, 155 degrees east longitude, at an altitude of 240 kilometers. Dan knew this coordinate position was also referenced against Earth's equator as a latitudinal zero line, and the Prime Meridian, which was an imaginary longitudinal zero line that passed through Greenwich, England

Barbara also read what was on his holograph, including the time and date for their position—10:47 a.m., Saturday, September 13—as well as the closest large city below them, which was Sydney, Australia.

She calculated the time to arrive home in Los Alamos, taking into account daylight saving time and the GMT difference, and found it would be 6:47 p.m. on Friday evening. According to Dan's left holograph, the distance to Los Alamos on the other side of the planet, from their current positional altitude, was now a little over thirteen thousand kilometers (approximately eight thousand miles), at least after taking Earth's curvature and horizon into account.

All the Jupiter family members quietly watched as their ship continued to descend, when suddenly, extremely bright yellow-and-white flames appeared outside the cockpit windows, completely enveloping their ship. Dan worried the cloaking field was encountering intense heat and quickly reached into the right holographic image and entered a propulsion speed of zero. The flames immediately ceased, and their ship came to a complete stop. Only Michael knew their ship's reactive hull material had immediately dissipated any heat that had transferred through the gravity field onto its surfaces.

They now sat stationary inside the stratosphere at an altitude of almost forty-four kilometers (sixteen miles) above Earth's surface. Their ship was still pointed toward Earth, and on his front display, Dan selected the optical display menu. Their ship's advanced optical cameras pointed directly toward Australia, utilizing an optical dispersion view of six kilometers. His left holographic image now displayed Sydney and its South Pacific coastline—an absolutely magnificent, mind-stimulating view. To his surprise, their ship's longitudinal and latitudinal numbers weren't changing, not even a fraction of a percentile. Not only did their ship's gravity-propulsion system not care about the orientation of Earth's gravity, but their ship was also rotating at the exact rotational momentum as Earth, as though locked into a magnetic orbit. This was unusual, as their ship was inside the gravitational and torsional envelope of Earth, yet their spaceship's gravity field remained unaffected, with their bodies still pulled toward the floor of the ship, regardless of any gravity effects outside of the ship.

Barbara was curious why her husband had stopped their ship. "Now what?" she asked.

Dan glanced over at the boys and then back to his wife with a soft grin. "Oh, I thought we'd cruise home while trying out both the telepathic and manual controls of our ship."

Barbara showed a strange, anxious feeling. "Okay," she said.

Jason, Michael, and Kyle watched with interest as their father continued to stare at the holographic images. What was showing caused Dan to reminisce back to when he and his wife had visited Sydney nearly thirteen years ago on their honeymoon, after enjoying an immensely gratifying week in the Bahamas, where they had physically and spiritually bonded to each other as newlyweds. Because of his and his wife's top-secret clearances, the government had been well aware of their out-of-country trips, which had both been fully approved. The Bahamas had been more fun than they could have imagined and had been followed by an extremely interesting visit to Australia. Dan finally fixated his eyes on his wife. "Remember when we visited Australia?"

Barbara was starry-eyed, remembering. After their honeymoon in the Bahamas, they had visited the Australian Museum, the Powerhouse Museum, the Canberra Space Dome, and, lastly, the Canberra observatory, including a visit to its virtual reality theater. "Yes, I do," she said. "Our honeymoon in the Bahamas was extremely enjoyable, and our visit afterward to Australia was well spent, especially seeing the Zeiss star projector in the planetarium."

"Yes, it was," Dan said. "The forty-one-centimeter Newtonian telescope to gaze up at Mars was also interesting."

"For sure," she said, "but then, what we are currently witnessing easily trumps all of that by tenfold."

Dan smiled a little, knowing that to be a fact, and picked up the wireless telepathic helmet just below his console. He slowly positioned it on his head, and as soon as it was firmly in place, it tightened up just a bit. Small, round circles along the side of the helmet exposed his ears, and the front of the helmet stopped right below his eyebrows, leaving his eyes exposed.

Dan's thoughts suddenly appeared much clearer and focused—like in a dream with three-dimensional depth perception. He placed his hands on top of the roller balls, not sure whether the telepathic helmet and the manual roller balls were compatible.

He gently moved the left roller ball in a clockwise movement until their ship slowly rotated, now facing Earth's northern horizon at an altitude of 43.89 kilometers. Even-brighter rays of sunlight were now evident, but they still did not hurt their eyes. Looking up, they could still see deep outer space. Dan rotated the right roller ball clockwise, toward his right just a little, until their ship suddenly stopped, seemingly ignoring the roller ball commands. He realized the ship's computer had temporarily taken command, possibly from his own telepathic thoughts of wanting to be parallel to Earth's surface and pointed toward Los Alamos. Based on what was showing in the right holographic image, the bottom of their spaceship was now perfectly parallel to Earth's surface and oriented at a northeasterly bearing of 64.382 degrees, which would be an exact path toward Los Alamos from their position.

He briefly daydreamed about the Hoover Dam, which they'd visited a few years ago, but he wanted to make it home before dark. Since Los Alamos was over 13,000 straight-line kilometers away, they would need to travel over 13,000 kilometers per hour (8,200 miles per hour) to ensure they arrived home before the Friday-evening sunset. He then thought about how fast of a descent rate would be needed at their current altitude to drop their ship for an hour. *Our travel should be 13,000 kilometers per hour toward the northeast while dropping in altitude at a rate of three meters per second.*

Their ship's gravity-propulsion system immediately propelled them toward the northeast, the ship now under Dan's telepathic control. He felt assured the ship still had appropriate autopilot safeguards to override his telepathic thoughts, if necessary. Suddenly, a flat holographic image replaced the previous left image. It was a strange-looking Mercator projection he'd never seen before. The ninety-degree intersecting latitude and longitude lines had numbers beside them, and their ship was shown as a blue dot cruising across the Pacific Ocean toward the North American continent. The general lighting in the cockpit seemed to be getting brighter as they traveled toward the sunward side of Earth, traveling with Earth's rotation, not against it, in order for them to arrive home on Friday night. They would not be experiencing any nighttime space travel by crossing the Atlantic Ocean and East Coast of the United States in westward travel; instead, they would be crossing the Pacific Ocean and gaining eight solar hours. That was an interesting scenario to think about—either traveling minus sixteen solar hours against Earth's rotation or an equivalency of eight solar hours ahead of Earth's rotation into a late-evening sunset. Since they were doing the latter, it truly would be like gaining eight biological hours, minus the one hour for their travel, or seven hours in total, due to Earth's rotational mechanics.

Based on their ship's current propulsion speed, as shown on the left holograph, it would take them about fifty-five minutes to reach the West Coast of North America. On his front console, Dan checked their ship's cloaking field and found it was still active, so fortunately, they would not have to worry about being detected by NORAD's radars or satellites. Using his telepathic thoughts, he caused their ship to drop at an even-quicker pace. They passed through the tropopause and then into the tropospheric regions as if skating on ice. They continued through the atmosphere with no turbulence or vibrations being felt whatsoever, as though flying aboard an airplane in a calm, high-altitude pocket of air. It was also extremely quiet aboard their ship, with no wind noise or sound from their ship's gravity-propulsion drive, only the light sounds of their bodies as they gently moved around in their seats.

Their altitude was now nineteen kilometers (twelve miles) as they continued toward North America in a northeasterly path. Dan telepathically leveled out their ship at sixty thousand feet, knowing they were still well above the flight ceiling of all commercial jetliners and most military jets, except for a few, such as the F-15 Eagle, F-22 Raptor, Mikoyan MiG-31, SR-71 Blackbird, and the B-1 Bomber, to name a few.

Through the cockpit windows, Dan recognized the West Coast of the United States ahead and knew Los Angeles should be just to their northeast. Time sure seemed to be flying by when traveling at such a high rate of velocity, especially when in gravity-propulsion mode. After looking at the right holograph and their actual bearing, it came to his realization that their northeasterly path had not been on a direct 64.382-degree initial heading toward Los Alamos, as first thought, but closer to a 61-degree heading. He now realized their ship must be traveling toward the Hoover Dam, so subconsciously, deep down inside, he must have wanted to visit the large dam. It gave him a different perspective of the different telepathic levels. In the future, he would have to adjust and prioritize his thoughts accordingly.

Now visible to their south was what appeared to be a tropical storm brewing over the Pacific Ocean. All the Jupiters stared through the southern windows at the circular patterns of air high in the atmosphere. It was possibly a hurricane in its early stages that could be headed toward Southern California. Dan turned to his wife, who was also awed by this rare eastern-Pacific tropical storm. "What do you think about that storm?" he asked.

Barbara focused her attention away from the magnificent natural Earth phenomenon and to her husband. "It is amazing," she said. "Remember nearly six years ago when the West Coast had one of its strongest storms ever recorded in the eastern Pacific?"

Dan would always remember that powerful event of Mother Nature. "Yes, I do," he said. "Good thing the storm turned away before actually reaching the coast. Remember us feeling the brunt of some of its winds, which were upwards of one hundred eighty miles per hour?"

Barbara nodded in the affirmative, remembering it well. They had been staying with Dan's parents while on their summer vacation. His parents lived a few miles from San Diego and were still in the same house even to this day, so they would always have a place to stay if they again visited the San Diego area. Jason had had a lot of fun on that vacation, especially when they visited the San Diego Zoo, the San Diego Wild Animal Park, and then, to finish it off, SeaWorld Adventure Park. He had been only four years old, and their trip would always carry special memories with lots of pictures to back them up. Kyle had been years away from his first breath of life but had always been in their dreams. Now it appeared Michael must have been in their dreams too.

Barbara smiled a little at her vivid memories of six years ago and glanced over at the boys, who were staring intently at the tropical storm. "Jason," she calmly said, "remember when we visited the San Diego Zoo and SeaWorld?"

Jason turned to his mother with an amazed face. "Yes, I do, Mom," he said. "I would like to see them again."

Barbara turned briefly to Dan and then back to Jason. "Well, maybe our entire family will just have to visit them."

The three boys were visibly excited at that prospect, especially Kyle, as he had heard about SeaWorld and the San Diego Zoo from his older brother and had seen all the pictures. Michael was excited because he saw Jason and Kyle were excited, but the words *zoo* and *SeaWorld* were also intriguing, especially for his extremely brilliant, bioengineered mind. He had memories of zoos back on the advanced race's home planet, Valzar, and knew what they were, but he had never actually seen an animal up close or touched one until meeting the extremely smart and friendly birds in the mother ship's plantatrium.

Dan noticed the boys' reaction and knew one of the reasons his wife brought up the zoo and SeaWorld was so that they could also visit his parents and introduce them to their newest grandson. Michael would need to be acclimated to his four grandparents as soon as possible, so that it was no mystery to any of their relatives that they had a new son in their lives. They would have to give his grandparents some elaborate explanation for his adoption, maybe something along the lines of "He was found abandoned by the authorities, and since we were on the adoption list with two little boys, we were offered the opportunity to raise him until everything is sorted out." This excuse would not be far from the truth, at least as far as abandonment. Their parents would never imagine he was actually a new breed of alien child from an entirely different galaxy. Neither would their parents ever believe they had a spaceship with tremendous space-travel capabilities. They would be somewhat surprised that Dan and Barbara had never told them they were even contemplating adopting a child. If only they knew the real truth, as even Dan and Barbara had not known they would be adopting a little boy.

A small, subtle grin crossed Dan's face as he thought about those future scenarios. He then looked back at the highly detailed holographic Mercator map, which also had circular depth, quickly recognizing they'd already passed by the West Coast and were about to leave California. He glanced at his wristwatch. It was now 6:55 p.m. in Los Alamos. He telepathically dropped their ship's altitude to two kilometers with a continued assurance in his mind that their cloaked ship would still be invisible to all Earth-based radars and also could not be visually seen by anyone on the ground or in an airborne aircraft.

Hoover Dam was up ahead. The dam was over seven hundred feet tall, at least when measured to the bottom of the Colorado River, and its hydropower, turbine-driven generators produced nearly 2.8 million kilowatts of power. Their ship quickly flew by the dam at over eight thousand miles per hour. Thinking about the Hoover Dam generators briefly caused Dan to think about the fake armband he'd taken to the metallurgy lab and the conductivity test that he and Frank had carried out. When they'd applied 20,000 volts to the ends of the armband, it had blown the breakers in the lab, and the high-voltage, high-current arc had seemed to jump circuits, specifically the 460-volt breaker feeds. The armband could have had the capability to produce a power output comparable to the Hoover Dam—at least in relation to the amount of applied energy.

The Grand Canyon was now directly below them. The Colorado River's torrent of water was even more evident as it cut a deep path into Earth's crust right before flowing toward the Hoover Dam and then the Gulf of California. Dan telepathically slowed their spaceship to 2,600 kilometers per hour (1,600 miles per hour), and they rotated three degrees to the south for a direct flight path toward Los Alamos. He looked over to his sons and then pointed through the windows. "See the Grand Canyon down below us, boys?" he said. "We'll have to visit it sometime soon with our spaceship for a view only dreamed about." The suggestion clearly excited the boys.

Dan knew they were already in Arizona and passing by Grand Canyon National Park. At their current speed, they would leave Arizona in less than twelve minutes, enter New Mexico, and arrive at Los Alamos in less than seven minutes. He did not want to overshoot Los Alamos, but he realized their ship's computer probably would not allow it, since that was the original destination in his mind. His anticipation began to rise, as did his wife's, when it suddenly came to their realization that they were minutes away from finally arriving home. Dan telepathically dropped their ship even more, and they now flew in level flight at ninety-one meters. None of them felt any deceleration forces or altitude changes the entire time. Their altitude then dropped to fifty meters, and their ship's velocity slowed down immensely, to less than one hundred miles per hour.

Dan noticed the ship's computer was already altering their propulsion against his telepathic commands. It no doubt knew the exact magnetic field location of their house. He spotted their house and barns just ahead, and he turned to his wife with a deep sigh. "Well, we are finally home."

# 25

## THE JUPITERS' FIRST EVENING BACK ON EARTH

Barbara watched as Dan guided their spaceship using his mind, totally amazed by the telepathic interface and also the ship's ability to easily override those thoughts if needed. The alien race's understanding of how to interface telepathic thoughts, using dormant telepathic neurons, as Jose had told her, was still a mystery and reminded Barbara of their astounding understanding in a vast array of sciences.

Dan could now feel he was telepathically butting heads with their spaceship's computer, because it had more control of the spaceship than he did. Their ship finally stopped, hovering fifteen and a half meters above their house. The Lincoln Navigator was still where he'd left it, and the cover was still over the pool. Dan made a conscious decision in his mind to land their ship in the open field just behind the barn, approximately where the small ship had been. He decided to try navigating the ship both manually and telepathically and placed his fingers on the roller balls. As he tried to take control of the propulsion system, he was at first successful, but then the ship's computer quickly took complete control. Remarkably, he felt the telepathic link disconnect. His feeling of a three-dimensional dream diminished, and his level of mental clarity also faded.

With the computer now in full control, their ship continued over the large, tall elm tree west of the barn and into the open field. About sixty meters south of the barn, they finally started to descend. Dan watched the left holographic image closely as their altitude dropped—fifteen meters … ten meters … five meters … Touchdown!

None of the Jupiter family felt even the slightest bump when their ship finally came to a stop. Dan quickly removed the telepathic helmet and noticed Barbara staring at him. "How about we transport off the ship near the front porch?"

"Okay," she said.

The holographic images in front of Dan suddenly disappeared, and he reached down to his front console, surprised to find a space-displacement menu already showing, as if their ship's computer had been listening to what he'd just asked his wife. The ship's computer was way ahead of him, as the screen now displayed the message "Five armbands aboard this ship are currently interfaced to carbon-based bodies. Activate all five armbands for space transport?" Dan quickly touched Yes, and another message appeared: "All five armbands now active for space displacement through the cloaking field."

Dan and Barbara were even more amazed when a three-dimensional, high-definition holographic layout of the east side of their house suddenly appeared in front of Dan, along with the statement "Select transportation location." Dan reached up into the image and touched a location about five meters southeast of the porch stairs. A small diagram next appeared, displaying his armband's six square buttons, numbered 1 through 6 from left to right, with 1 being the closest to his chest. A statement followed: "Touch button combination 4-6-2 to turn on displacement and 3-3-2 to activate."

Dan made a mental note of the combinations. His sons were still sitting down, quietly staring at him. He did not know whether the computer would adjust their bodies from a sitting position to a standing position during the transport, but he figured they would be transported in the way they were currently positioned. He could not have them falling down on their butts right after the transport, as if someone had pulled the chairs out from under them. "Boys," he calmly said, "let's all stand near the back of the cockpit before transporting off the ship."

"Okay, Dad," Jason said and then stood up, with Michael and Kyle following his lead. All three boys patiently waited just behind their mom's and dad's chairs.

Dan and Barbara also slid out of their chairs, and they all now patiently waited. "Is everyone ready?" Dan asked.

"Yes," Barbara said. "How do you know any solid objects won't end up inside our bodies?"

"Most likely impossible," Dan said. "Remember what the chief engineer, Doug Clarke, told us about the space-transport equations and how all solid objects are calculated against two opposing gravity fields?"

"Yes," she said.

"Well," Dan continued, "I would say that our ship's molecular computer is much too smart to ever let a potentially fatal condition like that occur."

Barbara knew her husband was correct but asked, concerned, "What about insects or birds that might fly into the areas of space that our bodies will soon occupy?"

Dan paused. "Good question," he said, "but as I remember Doug also telling us, all biological and nonbiological matter is removed, and the space is then reserved." He stared down at Michael. "Can you elaborate on your mom's question, Michael?"

"Yes, I can," he said. "No object, whether it is a bird, an insect, or even a speck of dust, can occupy the end location of our bodies' space transport. This is because those areas of space are reserved, and all objects, even Earth's atmosphere, including photons, are blocked from entering. At the same time, anything currently occupying those spaces is expelled, essentially creating an empty area of space similar to a vacuum." Michael paused to see his mother and father still staring down at him, interest written all over their faces.

Dan and Barbara suddenly laughed at Michael's "grown-up" explanation. Filled with humor, Dan turned back to his wife. "How's that for an answer?"

Barbara shook her head with a slight grin. "Yes, I am satisfied," she said.

"Okay then, here we go," Dan said. He touched the number combination 4-6-2 on his armband. Nothing appeared to happen, so he followed with 3-3-2. The next moment they were all standing east of the front porch. At first, none of them recognized a change in their positions, until they noticed the setting sun. "That sure was quick," Dan said, wondering whether they had been transported through the barn or around it. "That seemed just like the transporter elevators on the mother ship."

Barbara saw the boys standing next to them. "Yes, it did," she said.

Dan also saw the boys were okay. "Well, I guess we can say that we are finally home," he said.

Barbara was extremely agreeable and noticed their sons staring up at them. "Are you boys all okay?" she asked.

"Yes, Mom," Jason said.

"Yes, Mommy," Kyle said.

Michael continued to stare up at his kind, caring mother. "Me too, Mommy," he finally said.

Barbara suddenly felt good inside and walked with her family up the east porch stairs, with the boys leading the way. Dan thought about the fact that their house only had three bedrooms. "I guess we'll have to turn the study into a temporary bedroom, at least until another bedroom is added, or maybe we could just have a basement installed under the house."

"Either one would be fine," Barbara said. "I am curious what Michael might hang on the walls of his bedroom."

Dan thought about that. "And so am I," he replied with a humorous face. "I'm especially looking forward to what technologically advanced toys he might build."

Barbara giggled a little at that very real possibility and noticed Michael pointing down at Kyle's armband. Just to the right of the front door, which was probably still locked, their two porch swings rocked softly back and forth from a northeasterly breeze. Jason turned back in his parents' direction with a clever grin. "Watch this, Mom and Dad," he said.

Jason faced the door, paused, and then walked straight through the solid wood door as though it were open, vanishing out of sight. Kyle looked up at his parents, hesitant, stared at the door, and then followed his brother, also vanishing. Michael slowly turned toward the door, and he, too, disappeared, as though the door were composed of a soft, pliable liquid.

Dan and Barbara were amazed to witness this firsthand and found they were now standing behind a closed, locked door. Dan touched the door and found it still had the same texture and feel of solid wood. "Well, that sure was different, huh?" he said. "Our ship must have caused the molecular construction of their bodies to vibrate at a much-higher rate than the door or maybe vice versa."

"True," Barbara said, "but we'll have to teach them to be careful when using their armbands and not use them as a toy."

"You're right," Dan agreed, removing the house key from his pants. "It would draw unnecessary attention to our family." He then unlocked the door, and they entered to find their three sons sitting on the couch and already watching television—*Star Trek: The Next Generation*. "Boys," he said, "your mom and I are going to get freshened up. We'll return in a few minutes to talk about some rules that must be strictly followed."

Jason turned his head. "Okay, Dad," he said.

Barbara suddenly remembered her cinnamon-crumb apple pie

on the kitchen countertop. "I'll check on the two-day-old apple pie," she kidded.

Dan grinned at her comment, as it reminded him of his question to Jason a few days ago about the simulated armband he'd taken to the Los Alamos labs. It was partly that question that had led to their current situation of having Michael permanently ingrained in their lives. Barbara continued into the kitchen out of sight, and Dan turned back to the boys. "How about we all sit on the porch and watch the stars while enjoying apple pie topped with vanilla ice cream?"

All three boys displayed excited anticipation. "Sure, Dad," Jason immediately replied.

"Okay, Daddy," Kyle chimed in.

"That's fine with me too, Dad," Michael said.

"Great!" Dan said with a relaxed grin. "Your mom and I will be back in a little bit."

Dan continued out of the room toward his bedroom and thought about the boys' reaction to what he'd just told them, especially Michael's. They might be excited for their family watching the stars together, or it might be for eating apple pie topped with vanilla ice cream. It really did not matter, as long as they were excited. Entering the bedroom, he pulled off his shirt and continued into the bathroom, immediately turning on the lights. Staring at the mirror over the two sinks, he analyzed the general lighting in the room, knowing it was from intense filament heat and thermal equilibrium, not like the photon-neutrino technology used by the advanced race. The two lighting schemes were not even remotely related, as the photon-neutrino technology was not macroscopic but microscopic, on the electron level, or rather the neutrino level.

Dan was a little grubby, so he put his electric shaver on top of the counter and turned on the faucet. After splashing warm water on his face, he placed a warm, damp washcloth over his eyes and face, enjoying the relaxing, warm moisture penetrating deep into his skin. It caused him to think about the past few days spent aboard the mother ship, as well as the secretive life his family would now have to live. Then there was their quantum gravity–capable spaceship and its many highly advanced technologies, all of which would have to be kept secret from the human race at all costs while they also maintained a clandestine friendship with the race that had created Michael. At least there were two families from that race living on Earth with whom they could interact, talk freely, and even become good friends.

Dan removed the washcloth and wiped himself down, even though he did not seem to have much body odor. After turning on his shaver, he heard his wife enter the bedroom. She continued into the bathroom and up to the adjacent sink, and Dan quickly turned off the shaver. "How was the apple pie?"

"It was fine," she said. "I can't wait to try it."

"And neither can I," Dan said. He then gave her a slight, suggestive grin. "How about we hop into the Jacuzzi later on?"

She let out a sexy giggle, because she knew exactly what was on his mind. "We'll see," she kidded in return. She grabbed another washcloth and began freshening up, curious what the boys might be thinking about at this very moment.

✦ ✦ ✦

In the living room, Jason, Kyle, and Michael continued watching the episode of *Star Trek: The Next Generation*, which was nearing its end. Michael looked around the room and stared briefly at his new brothers. He now completely understood what Jason meant by having a brother and mom and dad. When he turned back to the television, he was intrigued by its primitive cathode-ray tube (CRT) display method, with electron beams projected against the picture tube's phosphor background. Those beams, he knew, were then modified by horizontal and vertical deflection coils to produce an image of lines known as a raster.

Electron-beam technology was surely to start becoming obsolete in less than a decade, Michael figured, as Earth's sciences were already progressing quickly into flat and curved LCD, LED, and plasma displays, but then, Earth's sciences were at least a half dozen decades away from true three-dimensional television, where the holographic images were projected into free space—at least according to what his ship's computer had determined from radio and television transmissions as well as secret and top-secret laboratories scattered throughout the United States and the world. His ship's computer had easily decrypted those primitive twenty-first-century computer-protected encryption schemes without them ever knowing it.

Michael, understanding every aspect of advanced holographic imagery technology, knew that until humans mastered multi-interlaced time-compression scanning, at least as referenced to the speed of light in free space, they would never obtain the required holographic temporal resolution imagery he envisioned. The understanding and eventual use of this technology in the public domain could be even more distant, possibly centuries, and true bipolar interactive holographic imagery, where there was touch interaction, was much farther away. He looked back at the CRT television and thought about his new parents, his two brothers, and his growing up on Earth with them.

✦ ✦ ✦

In the bedroom, Dan stood next to the bed, where his wife was sitting half-naked. She had already laid out a new change of clothes for him—a light bluish-green short-sleeved polo shirt and relaxed-fit Levi jeans—and on the floor were the same tennis shoes he'd been wearing aboard the mother ship. Those tennis shoes, as well as the clothes he'd just changed out of, would always carry special memories, because they were technically his space suit for their first moonwalk.

Barbara finally stood up and noticed Dan now sitting on the bed in only his boxer shorts and socks, nicely displaying his well-toned, muscular body. "Yes," she said with a slight grin, "the Jacuzzi later on sounds good."

Dan shook his head, laughing, slipped on his shirt and jeans, and cinched his belt tight. After putting on his tennis shoes, he stood up and noticed his cell phone on top of the bed. He removed the communicator, his house keys, and all the remaining change from his old jeans. He grabbed a metal coffee can filled with change off his dresser and dumped it out on the bed. He then put the remaining change he'd had while aboard the mother ship into the can. He then turned out the right pants pocket of his old jeans over the coffee can, dumping as much moondust as possible into the can. The contents of the can would always serve as a memory of his family's first moonwalk and their time together aboard the mother ship, especially their visit to its plantatrium.

Dan felt a sudden relaxed spirit. "This moondust will always be cherished," he said.

Barbara completely understood, as who else on Earth would ever get the chance to walk on the moon inside a gravity environment comparable to Earth's, especially without the need for any space suits? She remembered Kyle picking up a small moon rock that had appeared igneous in composition. "I'll be sure to also place Kyle's moon rock into the can too," she said.

"Great idea," Dan said. "These souvenirs will forever serve as a memory of our first time there, but of course, we can always go back and get more moondust and rocks."

Barbara giggled a little, because it was very true.

Dan and Barbara headed to the kitchen, where Barbara had already neatly arranged five saucers with apple pie, with an ice-cream scoop next to the saucers. Dan continued over to the countertop, placed the three smaller pie pieces into the microwave, and pressed the Start button, curious about what might be going though Michael's head right now, especially since he was about to start a secret life on Earth. While he continued to daydream, Barbara removed a half-gallon container of vanilla ice cream from the freezer and placed it on the countertop next to him. The microwave beeped, and Dan removed the saucers and positioned them on the countertop. As Barbara placed a scoop of ice cream on each of the heated pies, he put the larger apple pie slices inside the microwave and again touched the Start button.

Barbara noticed the ice cream now melting on the boys' apple pie slices and thought about how Michael still had to learn the differences between hot and cold—just like a little baby would. "I hope the pie doesn't burn Michael," she said.

"Probably won't," Dan said, "but better warn him just in case."

Because Michael had a fast cellular regenerative healing process, even if he was burned, he would probably quickly heal within minutes, possibly even seconds, but Dan and Barbara still never wanted to see their new little boy go through any pain, if avoidable.

The microwave beeped again, and Dan removed their pies, set them on the countertop, and placed a large scoop of ice cream on each, followed by an additional scoop on his pie. Barbara then placed all five pies on a tray, along with forks and napkins. "Well, let's go watch the stars and eat apple pie," she said.

Dan grinned a little and placed the ice cream back into the freezer. He then followed her into the living room, to find the boys still watching television—*Stargate SG-1* now. Seeing the three boys sitting next to each other and bonding as brothers did caused Dan's and Barbara's hearts to again swell. Jason would no doubt always have a special bond to Michael no one else could ever have, and Kyle would develop his own special bond to Michael while always carrying an immense amount of brotherly respect. As for Michael, they suspected he would always look out for his younger brother and even his older brother, Jason.

Dan and Barbara stood for a short while longer and found themselves looking forward to learning more about the alien race's advanced technologies, if not from Michael, then surely from their spaceship's computer data banks. Dan turned to his wife and then back to their sons. "Boys," he said, "are you ready to watch the stars and enjoy apple pie topped with ice cream?"

All the boys again expressed excitement, filled with added anticipation. "Yes, I am," Jason said.

"Yes," Michael said.

"Me too," Kyle said.

The boys saw their mother holding the tray of cinnamon-crumb apple pies topped with vanilla ice cream and left the couch. Dan then made eye contact with his oldest son. "Jason, you and your brothers need to be consciously aware and as inconspicuous as possible when using your armbands and not use them as toys. We do not need unwanted attention. Understand?"

Jason understood. "Okay, Dad," he said.

Dan knew his oldest son did understand, as did Michael, but Kyle would have to learn about the dangers of openly exposing advanced technologies in view of the general public or anyone they did not know and trust.

Dan led his family to the front door, turned off the automatic porch light, and held the door open as they all exited, closing the door behind him. His sons took a seat together on the far west porch swing. Strangely, Michael's eyes were slightly glowing, as though a see-in-the-dark switch had turned on. Dan did not say anything about it, as it was possibly another aspect of Michael's bioengineered design not mentioned by the geneticists in any of the meetings.

Barbara laid the tray on the small table between the two porch swings, and Dan looked up into the heavens to see the moon shining brilliantly in the northeastern sky. He sat down on the east porch swing as his wife handed a saucer, a fork, and a napkin to each of their boys. "The pies could be hot, so be careful not to burn your mouths," she told them.

Barbara picked up the remaining saucers and handed the pie with two ice-cream scoops to Dan along with a fork and napkin. "Thank you," he said.

Barbara smiled a little and sat down next to her husband. "Did you notice Michael's eyes?" she calmly asked.

"Yes, I did," he said. "I assume it has to do with night vision. I wonder why the race did not tell us that he has the ability to see in the dark."

"Good question," Barbara said, "but the more amazing thing is that the glow faded away, as if he has the ability to turn it off like a switch. That being the case, his maculae must have unique photoreceptors with a special interface to his motor neurons, similar to moving a hand or finger. I am curious whether Captain Donaldson and his officers knew of this ability. Moreover, why the geneticists did not mention it is a mystery."

Dan cut off a piece of his pie. "Good question. Maybe they thought if the military knew about it, they would want it removed, and it was an attribute that could not have been easily changed."

"Possibly," Barbara said and cut off a piece of her own pie.

All the Jupiter family members now gently rocked their glider swings back and forth under a slight northeasterly breeze, enjoying the slight motion on the roller bearings with very little noise whatsoever—barely even a squeak. Continuing to enjoy their mouthwatering pies topped with ice cream, they all stared up into the night sky with serene feelings inside. For Jason, it reminded him of when he'd been watching the stars nearly four nights ago and had seen what he'd thought to be a shooting star, only to find out that it was much, much more.

Both swings gently came to a complete stop as they all continued to stare up into the heavens. The last few days aboard the mother ship had been amazing. It became unusually quiet. All that could be heard were crickets chirping and frogs croaking, seemingly in concert with the bristling wind against the trees. An owl suddenly hooted in a nearby tree, and a strange calmness filled the air. The Jupiter family looked back up into the heavens, wondering about the many mysteries of their universe, including their friendship with a race that lived in a completely different galaxy yet had two families living secretly on Earth.

Dan and Barbara looked very much forward to meeting those two families and continued to wonder about the race's home world, which was located in a solar system called the Andromeda System—the actual birthplace of Michael, the place where he had been biologically created as a new intelligent being, a superior biological entity to even the race that had created him. Dan and Barbara looked up again into the night sky and noticed how truly clear it was on this Friday night in Los Alamos, the stars seemingly brighter than normal and filled with unusual luster.

Dan located the Big Dipper star formation and pointed up at it. "Look how bright the Big Dipper shines over there," he said.

Barbara and the three boys looked to where he had pointed and saw the seven stars of the Big Dipper, three that formed a handle and four that formed a bowl. Dan and Barbara knew the Big Dipper was not a constellation by itself but a part of the Ursa Major constellation, also known as the Great Bear. They did not know whether Michael knew that or not, but he might.

Barbara smiled a little after seeing the three boys still staring at the Big Dipper. She looked back to Dan and grabbed his hand with an extremely relaxed, serene feeling inside, and Dan squeezed her hand a couple of times. He easily located the planet Mars, as it was the brightest celestial object in the eastern sky. "Over there is Mars," he said, pointing directly at it, "the fourth-closest planet to the sun in our solar system."

The boys and Barbara shifted their gaze to the eastern sky and spotted Mars. It looked like a small light bulb with a reddish tint, as its current orbit had brought it to within forty-eight million kilometers of Earth, something that had not happened in almost sixty thousand years.

Dan glanced briefly at his wife and then the boys, who were still staring at the red planet, and he now thought about their secret lives on Earth. He looked back up at Mars and then said out of the blue, "Wouldn't it be fun to travel to Mars and beyond?"

Barbara, Jason, Kyle, and Michael looked over in Dan's direction, curious about his comment. Barbara continued to stare at her husband. "When would you want to do that?"

"Oh, I don't know," he said. "Maybe when we go visit our new friends in the Small Magellanic Cloud galaxy."

Barbara wore a distant look, while Jason now stared intently at his father. "When, Dad?" he asked.

"I will have to figure that one out, Jason," Dan said.

Jason had anticipation inside like never before, as he had always wanted to fly to the stars and visit Mars especially. He looked briefly at his two brothers and stared back up into the heavens, still thinking about what his dad had just told them.

As they continued to gaze up into the night sky, surprisingly, a bright-colored object appeared in the northern sky, seemingly less than a half mile from their house. It was shrouded in a deep reddish-blue glow. The glow disappeared, and it started flashing in unusual multicolored sequences.

Speechless, Dan and Barbara knew the object was most likely an extraterrestrial spaceship. Dan peeked over at Michael, who was also staring at the object. "Is that one of the two families, Michael?" he asked.

Michael turned to his father. "Yes, it is," he answered.

"How do you know?" Dan asked.

"Their multicolored lights said so, Daddy," Michael said confidently.

Dan realized the flashing colored lights were a code that Michael understood. It was a code that he and his family would also need to learn. He noticed the ship was now glowing only light blue and turned back to Michael. "What did they have to say?"

"They wished us a warm welcome, Dad," he said.

Dan gave a small grin and saw his wife also staring at Michael, knowing she was as attached to him as their other boys. He focused his attention back to the spaceship and found himself very much looking forward to meeting the family aboard the spaceship, when all of a sudden, the spaceship glowed orange, turned bright red, and then vanished in the blink of an eye. It was a surprising display, and Dan naturally looked over to Michael. "Was that normal, Michael?"

"No, it wasn't," Michael said.

Out of nowhere, a white ball appeared in the sky in the proximity of where the other spaceship had once been visible. This new object was extremely different from the prior spaceship. It was a large, luminescent ball, like a spotlight in the sky, much bigger than the prior spaceship. In fact, it was extremely huge in comparison, seeming to fill the northern sky. It was now glowing bright silver, and the Jupiters were in awe, including Michael. It was particularly quiet on the porch at that moment.

Dan finally looked over in Michael's direction and knew something was not right. "What is that, Michael?"

"I do not know, Daddy," he answered.

Dan was puzzled. His wife and the boys continued to stare up at the luminescent ball as though in a hypnotic trance. When he looked back at the spherical object, he had a strange feeling. A blue beam of light appeared on the ground directly in front of them, and all of a sudden, there was a bright flash of light!

A strange calm filled the air around the Jupiters' home—no crickets chirping, no frogs croaking, no owls hooting. On the front porch, it was quiet, no familiar sounds to be heard. The moon continued to shine down on the two porch swings as they rocked gently back and forth in the breeze. Dan; his wife, Barbara; and their sons, Jason, Michael, and Kyle, were nowhere to be found—they had been taken aboard a mother ship from a far more advanced race.

# 26

## THE FOLLOWING DAY

At eight fifteen the next morning, Dan woke up next to his wife with the sun shining brightly and casting magnificent shadows throughout their entire bedroom. He thought about everything that had transpired last night after seeing the spaceship belonging to one of the alien race's two families living on Earth. Less than a minute after their spaceship had flashed its lights in a code Michael understood, wishing them a warm welcome, they had landed just east of the Jupiters' house. They had invited the Jupiters aboard for an enjoyable visit that had lasted well into the early-morning hours.

The family had a little boy seven Earth years old and a girl six Earth years old. It was actually the family Michael was supposed to have grown up with on Earth. Dan and Barbara would never tell Michael that, though. All five kids had played together while the parents had gotten to spend quality time with each other. The alien parents were using the assumed identities of John and Mary Stevens, and their two kids went by Scott and Julie, but then, Dan and Barbara had never bothered to ask whether their assumed names were actually the English equivalent to their names in their alien language.

John and Mary had been living on Earth for seven years on thirty acres of land about three miles north of Santa Fe, New Mexico, and ran a very successful certified computer-repair business out of their home. Their business was a good source of income, not that they really needed it. To them, the microprocessor systems were like toys for little children. When they'd said this, Dan and Barbara had laughed hilariously, because they knew how true it had to be, with how smart John and Mary were in relation to Earth's twenty-first-century sciences.

Dan sat up on the side of the bed with a small grin and looked down at his wife, who was understandably still sleeping, considering they'd visited with John and Mary until about three in the morning. His wife had hit it off with Mary, who was almost six feet six inches tall. Her husband, John, was close to seven feet two inches, and both were extremely nice. It had been interesting to hear about when they'd first started living on Earth, including how easily their race had manipulated the census databases and provided them with Social Security numbers, places of birth, and even cemeteries where their supposed parents were buried. All they'd needed to do was find parents who had no siblings, or whose kids had all passed away or quit visiting, and then manipulated the databases accordingly.

Dan looked forward to their continued friendship. They would visit quite often, like close relatives, since they only lived about thirty miles apart. John and Mary had told them about the other family, who had a residence on thirty acres of land just north of Washington, DC, near Columbia, Maryland. Dan and Barbara had made a decision to visit the other family next weekend, as John had told them they had two boys, aged eight and nine years old. Jason, Michael, and Kyle would no doubt enjoy interacting with their kids.

Dan stood up with an invigorated feeling, stretching his arms. The first order of the day was to make a fresh pot of coffee and start breakfast for his family.

✦ ✦ ✦

In Jason's bedroom, all three boys had slept together, having talked each other to sleep, with Michael leading most of the conversations. Michael woke up first, and when he finally opened his eyes, he stared up at the etchings of sunlight and relaxing bands of shadows cast against the ceiling. He thought back to their visit aboard John and Mary's spaceship with their two kids. He knew it had really happened, but for some reason, he could not remember their ship actually landing. He had been sitting on the porch next to his brothers and parents, watching John and Mary's spaceship in the northern sky, and the next moment, they had been walking over to their ship, which had landed just east of their house. He felt like he'd had a dream of being aboard a totally different spaceship than John and Mary's—a dream where he, his mom, his dad, Jason, Kyle, John, Mary, and their two kids all appeared to be sound asleep and suspended in midair on platforms. He could see another race of beings standing next to the platforms, their bodies shrouded in a shimmering white glow. They were much larger than the race that had created him. Michael figured it all had to be a vivid dream, because he had also been asleep on one of those platforms.

He finally peeked over at Jason and Kyle, who were still sound asleep. He stared out through the window again and then back to Jason with a feeling there was a hidden memory implanted deep inside in his head. He tried to analyze this memory but could not retrieve it no matter how hard he tried, so he nudged Jason's shoulder. "Jason, wake up," he said.

Jason moved his head around.

Michael nudged his shoulder a second time. "Jason, wake up," he said a little louder.

Jason finally opened his sleep-laden eyes and saw Michael sitting on the side of the bed, wide-awake, and staring down at him.

"Good morning, Jason," Michael said.

Jason grinned a little while opening his eyes a little more and lifted his arms in a big, mind-warming stretch. "What time is it?"

"Nine fifteen," Michael replied. "Dad said we would all go fishing at the creek later today, maybe even camp out under the stars. Remember?"

Jason rubbed his eyes. "Yes, I remember. Do you want to take a bath with me?"

Michael gave a strange look, as a *bath* was something he'd only heard Jason and Kyle doing. "Okay," he said.

Jason slowly rolled out of bed and stood up, Michael crawling off the bed after him. They went to the bathroom, and Jason turned on the light. Michael, standing in his underwear, quietly analyzed the bathroom—the sink, the mirror, the stool, even the bathtub. Jason walked over to the tub, flipped a small handle to close a drain valve, and then turned on the water. He placed his hand under the water and then stood back up.

Jason stared down at Michael, who was still quietly analyzing the layout of the bathroom. "Shouldn't be long now," he said.

✦ ✦ ✦

In the kitchen, Dan was cooking breakfast for his family—omelets and hash browns—and sipping on coffee. He'd already set the table for a family of five. Having a third child who was already five would take some getting used to, but he knew it would be no problem. He looked forward to watching their father-son relationship grow over the years, as his wife looked forward to their mother-son bonding. He started another omelet and was curious whether his wife or any of their boys were awake yet. Jason was an early riser sometimes and might be awake even though they had stayed up late into the morning hours while visiting with John and Mary and their two kids.

Dan stared over at the hash browns in the other skillet, turned the heat down on both burners, and left the kitchen to check on his wife. When he entered their bedroom, she was not in bed. He could hear her in the bathtub, so he continued into the bathroom to find her relaxed back in the tub with her hair tied up. "Good morning," he said.

Barbara looked up with a good feeling inside. "Good morning," she said. "What an unusual night last night, huh?"

"Yes, it was," he said, "and we thought being aboard a mother ship for nearly two days would be the end of our adventures."

"That's for sure," she said. "John and Mary were really nice."

"Yes, they were," Dan said. "You know, having those two families join us with their spaceships, maybe even riding aboard one of their spaceships, while traveling outside our solar system would be interesting."

Barbara paused with a dreamy look. "True," she said. "It would be like a small convoy if we were to all travel in separate ships."

"Very true," Dan calmly agreed, now curious what outer space would look like when their spaceship used quantum gravity time-warp-field propulsion, especially if there were other ships next to them also traveling thousands of times the speed of light, maybe even millions of times the speed of light, if a jump were used. He looked down again at his naked, pretty wife and thought about the time they'd spent in the Jacuzzi after the boys had gone to sleep. "That Jacuzzi was long overdue," he kidded.

Barbara giggled at his hidden innuendo.

Dan gave her a small, subtle grin. "I'll make sure the kids are up and around," he said. "Breakfast should be ready in about twenty minutes."

"Okay, I'll be ready."

Dan stared down again at his sexy wife and then headed toward Jason's bedroom, where he knew the three boys had slept together. When he opened his son's bedroom door, Kyle was still conked out in bed, but he could hear Jason and Michael in the bathtub. He continued up to the bathroom door, pushed it open slightly, and saw them sitting in the bathtub. "How are you two doing?"

"Good," Jason said.

It made Michael feel good that his father was seeing him take his first bath. "Good, Daddy," he also replied.

Dan realized Jason was already treating Michael the same as Kyle, but then, Michael would no doubt be an over-the-top, highly intellectual little brother. "Breakfast will be ready in about twenty minutes, boys," he said. "I'll wake your brother and have him join you. Jason, help your brothers get dressed, and I will see all of you at the dining room table."

"Okay, Dad," Jason said.

Dan left the bathroom and walked up to the bed, where his youngest son was still sound asleep like a little angel. He gently nudged Kyle's shoulder. "Wake up, sleepyhead," he said softly.

Kyle moved his head around.

Dan again gently nudged his shoulder. "Wake up, Son. We are about to eat breakfast and then go fishing at the creek." Dan knew his last comment might help wake his little boy.

Kyle finally opened his eyes, just a bit, and stared up into his dad's face. Dan gently lifted him off the bed. "Go take a bath with your brothers, Kyle," he said.

"Okay," he replied.

Dan pulled off Kyle's pajamas and carried him into the bathroom. After Dan set him down on the floor, Kyle removed his underwear without a second thought and crawled into the tub. Dan felt good inside, knowing his three sons would always remain close and develop a special bond that only brothers could form. "See you boys at breakfast," he said and left the bathroom.

Dan headed back to the kitchen and glanced briefly out the kitchen window at the gazebo over their Jacuzzi in the backyard. He then returned to the stove and flipped over the omelet. He turned the heat back up and removed the hash browns from the other skillet. He began wondering whether Michael was now listed in the US Census Bureau and whether he had a Social Security number and make-believe history for how he had supposedly been born in the

United States—a US citizen. Dan would log onto the internet after breakfast to find out. It would be interesting, especially because, due to his high-level top-secret clearance, some of his and his family's information was currently restricted by the government. Michael would also have to fall under those same restrictions, so classified electronic databases would need to be adjusted accordingly, even backup systems.

Barbara walked into the kitchen and noticed Dan lost in his thoughts. She continued up to where he stood and placed a small kiss against his lips. Dan followed the kiss with a warm hug.

"Omelets smell good," she said. "Need any help?"

"You might make the last omelet, while I start the toast."

"Sure," Barbara said. She removed the fourth omelet from the skillet and placed it on the platter next to the other omelets. She added more virgin olive oil to the skillet and then poured in the egg batter. After the egg batter started solidifying, she filled it with diced ham, diced onions, mushrooms, fully cooked bacon slices, and cheese. She then nicely folded the omelet's flaps across each other. Barbara knew even one omelet would be quite filling for any little boy's appetite.

Dan again wondered how Michael might be listed in the top-secret and general-public databases, including what his last name prior to their supposed adoption of him was—surely there were also now records of their having filed adoption papers. He turned to his wife, curious. "I look forward to seeing how Michael is listed in the databases—you know, like what adoption agency he came from, his Social Security number, supposed date of birth, and so on."

Barbara turned the omelet over. "Yes, that will be interesting," she said. "I also look forward to buying him new clothes tomorrow."

"Yes, that will be fun," Dan said. The toast popped up, and he began buttering it, curious how Michael might react to his first time out in public. He placed two more slices of bread in the toaster. He got a half-gallon jug of orange juice and a gallon jug of milk out of the refrigerator and carried them to the dining room table. The table being set for five, with a place for Michael between him and Kyle, caused him to grin slightly. Michael would be sitting at the table for the first time. It was extraordinary, especially since he and his wife had met Michael only two and a half days ago.

Dan slowly filled the five larger glasses with milk and the smaller glasses with orange juice and returned both jugs to the refrigerator. His wife was now buttering the toast, so he grabbed the jelly. He thought about what he'd told the boys about going fishing and turned to his wife, who looked to be in good spirits. "What time will you be joining us at the creek?"

"How about around two this afternoon?" she said. "I'll bring a lunch basket."

Dan nodded slightly. "Sounds good," he said. "I can't wait to see the expression on Michael's face after he catches his first fish."

"I hope I don't miss that," she said.

Dan returned to the dining room and placed the jelly on the table. Barbara removed the last omelet from the skillet and turned the burners off. He walked up behind her, placing his arms around her waist, followed by a soft kiss against the right side of her neck. "Do you want to have another baby?"

Barbara thought about his question. They had talked before about wanting to have another child but had not decided when. She figured he was bringing it up again now because of their new son, Michael. A newborn baby would help speed his transition into their family, giving him a little baby brother or sister to interact with and show affection to. "Sure," she said. "Let's have another child as soon as possible, and we'll just add two bedrooms instead of one."

Dan knew building a basement under the house was the most logical solution to four children. He kissed her again, just behind her right ear, this time with an extremely sensual feeling. "I'll check on the boys," he whispered.

His kiss gave Barbara a ticklish feeling deep inside her chest. She suddenly remembered the voice mail Frank Andrews had left on Dan's cell phone less than fifteen minutes ago. It had been very vague and sounded urgent, with Frank wanting Dan to call him as soon as possible. Even more surprising was the new text message she had gotten a few moments ago that only stated, "Pick up your mail," with no phone number or any clue where it had originated from. She wondered whether it might have come from the advanced race. "Okay," she said, "but can you go pick up the mail first?"

"Sure," Dan said and removed his arms from around her waist, somewhat curious about her request.

Barbara turned around. "I wasn't planning to mention anything before breakfast," she said, "but Frank Andrews called your cell phone about fifteen minutes ago and left a vague voice mail that seemed urgent. He said that he tried to call you yesterday but your cell phone had no service."

Dan thought about what he was told. "Oh really?" he said, somewhat surprised. "Did he allude to what it was all about?"

"No," she said.

"Okay," Dan said. "I'll call him on my way out to the mailbox. You might make sure the kids are dressed."

Barbara was now extremely curious about the phone call, but the contents of their mailbox were even more intriguing. "Okay," she said.

Dan left the kitchen, wondering again why his wife would have him retrieve the last two days of mail before breakfast and not wait until afterward. Continuing into the bedroom, he grabbed his cell phone and headed toward the front door but then stopped at the doorway to Jason's bedroom to see the boys were all now getting dressed. "Breakfast is about ready," he said. "I'm headed to the mailbox and will return shortly."

"Okay, Dad," Jason said. "We'll be waiting at the table."

Dan continued to the front door, becoming increasingly curious about Frank's phone call. He flipped his phone open and browsed the call logs to see that Frank had only called him once, and that had been this morning. He exited the front door, continued down the porch steps to the driveway, and then dialed Frank's cell phone number. He patiently waited as the phone rang. Frank answered after three rings.

"Dan," Frank quickly said, "am I ever glad to finally get in touch with you."

Dan stared ahead at his mailbox nearly fifty yards away. "Why is that?" he asked.

"Believe it or not," he said, "but government agents dressed in black showed up at the Los Alamos labs yesterday with authority like you would not believe. We were told not to ask them questions, and that came all the way from the top—the director of our facility. Remember that transformer that fried?"

A sudden strange feeling came over Dan. "Yes," he slowly answered.

"Well, I heard they now have it in their possession," Frank said.

Dan was surprised. "Is that right?"

"Yes," Frank said, "and it was removed from the premises quicker than any electrical contractor could have ever done."

Dan thought about the possible secret-government agents Frank had mentioned. "How did they ever find out about it?" he asked.

"I have no idea," Frank said.

"Did they interrogate you?" Dan asked.

Frank paused, his silence echoing into the phone. It gave Dan another strange feeling.

"Yes, they did," Frank finally answered, "but I told them that I did not know for sure what happened in the lab. I will say this, Dan, those government agents were scary. They were armed, carried unusual Secret Service NSA identifications, and acted like they owned the place."

Dan stopped at the mailbox, surprised at Frank's statement, and opened the mailbox to see Thursday and Friday's mail, along with a plain manila envelope with no return address. He removed the mail and envelope and closed the door. "I do not know for sure what to say, Frank," Dan said. "Did you mention my name to them?"

"No, I didn't," Frank said, "but they did bring you up and asked me if you might have brought any unusual artifacts to the labs lately. I told them that I've known you over twenty years and if you had brought anything to the labs, I would have been the first to know."

Dan started back toward his house and realized Frank had slyly sidestepped the government agent's question without having to lie to them. "Then what happened?" he calmly asked.

"Nothing more was mentioned," Frank said. "They left soon afterward."

Dan wondered whether the agents had not said anything else because Frank carried the same high-level top-secret clearance as Dan himself. He was now curious whether any of those agents had visited his house while he and his family were gone the last few days. If so, were the agents now curious about their whereabouts? He looked down at the manila envelope, extremely curious about its contents. It seemed to contain a manual or a booklet, and he had to speculate it was from the advanced race. He positioned his cell phone a little closer to his ear, but Frank was now a little quiet. "I will talk to you later, Frank," he said. "I am about to eat breakfast with my family. We just finalized the adoption of a new little boy into our family yesterday. He is about five years old, and you and your family will have to come over next week for dinner and meet him."

Frank was puzzled, as Dan had not mentioned they were even contemplating adopting, but he had taken a few days' vacation. "Sure, Dan," he said. "We'll do just that. What do we do about the government agents?"

"Absolutely nothing," Dan said. "Let's let everything cool down a bit and not talk anymore about it, especially using electronic devices."

"Okay, Dan, will do," he said. "I will talk to you later, then."

Dan slowed as he approached the front porch stairs. "Talk to you later, Frank."

"Bye, Dan."

Dan closed his phone and walked back inside. He set the mail and the manila envelope down on the front foyer table but then picked the manila envelope back up, as his curiosity about its contents was immense. He opened it on his way to the kitchen and surprisingly found it contained a manual nearly twenty pages long. It was a summary report from the alien race about Michael's new identity on Earth. Also in the envelope were his Social Security card, a paper birth certificate, and a birth certificate card with the official New Mexico state seal on the back. Dan left those in the envelope and opened the manual to the first page of Michael's supposed history, which included his birthdate, his place of birth, and the reasons for their adoption. Michael had supposedly been born in Santa Fe, New Mexico, and was the only child of a couple who had been involved in a fatal car accident and who had no living relatives.

Dan walked into the dining room to see his wife and sons sitting at the table, patiently waiting for his return. He placed the summary report on a small table. Jason was sitting to his mom's right in his usual chair. Michael and Kyle were across from Jason, with Kyle closest to his mother. Michael would be just to Dan's right. Nobody was wearing their armbands, and Dan again noticed that there were no triangular scars evident on Michael's forearm.

As Dan continued toward his chair, Barbara was curious not only about what Frank had called about but also, even more so, about what was in the manila envelope Dan had just laid down on the small table, as it did not have a return address. "What's in the envelope?" she asked.

Dan continued past Jason and sat down with a small grin. "Believe it or not," he said, "but it is a summary report from the alien race that explains in great detail Michael's supposed history on Earth prior to and after us adopting him."

Barbara raised her eyebrows. Even though Michael's true history and where he'd come from was fictional according to Earth's records and databases, it was as real as any other top-secret record hidden from the general public that could not be explained. "Oh really?" she said. "I can't wait to read it."

Dan looked directly at Michael and noticed an unusual look on his face. "You'll need to read it too, Michael, as it appears that your first breath of life many years ago directly correlates to the Earth day of July 4, or Independence Day. That is an amazing coincidence and actually one thing that will always be true about your birthday."

Michael continued to stare up at his nice father. He understood why his Earth history was fiction, but then, his actual birthday was not. "Okay, Daddy," he said. "But what is Independence Day?"

Dan grinned a little while staring across the table at his wife. He turned back to see sincerity all over Michael's face. "Independence Day," he explained, "is a day we celebrate this country's heritage and our independence from the country of Britain two hundred and twenty-seven years ago in 1776. Because it's the day we got our independence, it is now considered our country's birthday, and each year across this land it is celebrated with fireworks displays and family and friends getting together to watch those fireworks."

Michael was extremely interested, as it appeared he would celebrate his birthday the same day, which meant his birthday would always have fireworks.

Dan looked around the table again and knew his family was ready for breakfast. He still could not help but be amazed by how quickly Michael had accepted him and Barbara as his parents. He stared down at the food and then back to his wife with an immense feeling of love. He felt extremely blessed for their third son, even if he was from an entirely different galaxy. Of course, all Earth records would indicate he'd originated on Earth. It was amazing how things had worked out, as if a higher force had been at work. Dan had always believed in a higher intelligence called God, as taught to him by his own parents, and was now demonstrating those same beliefs and qualities for his own kids. How Michael would fit into the many different religions on Earth, he had no idea, nor did he presently care. All he cared about was that Michael was now a part of his life, his wife's life, and their two sons' lives. Blessing the food before each meal was something he'd always done, and he expected his sons would do the same when they were young men and starting their own families. He also had to figure Michael had heard him praying a few days ago when aboard his small spaceship, but it would surely be a new experience for him to now be inside their house, hearing and seeing it with his own two eyes and ears. Dan looked around the table again, took a deep breath, and exhaled. "Let's hold hands and say a prayer for our food, our new friendship with the race that created Michael, and a hope for world peace one day."

Dan then reached for Michael, who quickly grabbed his hand. Jason took hold of his dad's other hand and grabbed his mother's right hand, and Barbara held Kyle's right hand. Michael grabbed Kyle's other hand, and Dan, after seeing his family had completed a circle, said, "May this bond never be broken so that we will always remain a family, a family who looks after one another and a family who respects one another. Let's now bow our heads and pray."

Everyone bowed their heads. Dan closed his eyes, and a strange warmth of mental clarity suddenly filled his soul, as if from the Holy Spirit. "Our father in heaven, we come to you at this time on this special occasion, asking that you bless this family, watch over them, and keep them safe from harm. Be with Michael, who is like a gift, now a part of our family, that his purpose on Earth may be fulfilled according to your will. Oversee this world for what its future has in store that its people might come to understand its many problems and figure out how to solve them. Let all of its wars of the past and present, its racial tensions, hatreds, and conflicts between its many different religions be a reminder for all world leaders of what must change if there is ever a chance of world peace one day. Conflicts of purpose, conflicts of belief, conflicts of morals, and conflicts for what is right and wrong—may they be given the insight to see what is required to solve those conflicts, if not in my lifetime, then my kids' or grandkids'.

In closing, bless our food, so it will sustain our bodies, our minds, and our souls, allowing us to do good in the world and for the world. This we ask in your son's dear name, Jesus Christ ... Amen and shalom."

Dan lifted his head, opened his eyes, and noticed his family staring at him. He gently squeezed Jason's and Michael's hands and then let go to see his wife had also let go of Jason's and Kyle's hands. He knew Barbara appreciated his words and returned a gracious nod to her, whom he loved deeply. He then picked up the platter of omelets and placed an omelet on Michael's plate, Kyle's plate, and then his own. Jason took the platter, slid an omelet onto his plate, and passed the platter to his mom. Barbara took her omelet and then began passing the platter of hash browns, starting with Jason.

Everyone was still kind of quiet after Dan's mind-tantalizing prayer, and Michael was still looking up at Dan as if he had something on his mind. He suddenly asked, "Do you end all your prayers in the name of Jesus, Dad, because he died for us?"

Dan paused from spreading jelly on Michael's and Kyle's toast, a little surprised Michael was aware of Jesus and his crucifixion. "Yes, we do," he said. "How did you know that?"

"Jason told me while you and Mom were in the plantatrium on our way back to Earth."

Dan gave Jason an appreciative nod but was also curious about that conversation. "Whatever brought that up?"

Jason looked briefly at Michael and then to his father. "Kyle mentioned getting presents at Christmas, Dad, and Michael asked what Christmas was, so I explained why it was celebrated."

Dan was again appreciative of his oldest son. "Very good," he said and stared down at Michael with a compassionate heart. "A belief in something is always good, Michael. Even though God can never be seen, you have to believe that an almighty being had to have created our universe, including everything about its magnificent grand design."

Michael now understood more about how God, an almighty

being, should be viewed and blurted out, "I saw something that I believe."

Dan was unusually curious. "What?"

Michael turned briefly to his mother, glanced across the table at Jason, and then looked back to his father. "I dreamed we were aboard another large spaceship, as were John and Mary and their two kids, and we were all suspended in midair, sound asleep on horizontal platforms. There was another race next to the platforms that looked just like us, except they were glowing like angels."

Dan, Barbara, and Jason were surprised. They did not remember another spaceship, neither did Kyle, so Michael must have really had a dream. They all also knew Michael had to have an immense imagination beyond comprehension. Dan finally gave a humorous, small grin. "You have quite the imagination, Michael," he kidded.

"But it really happened," Michael stressed.

Barbara, Dan, and Jason giggled, as they could guess what kind of imagination and dreams Michael might have, especially with the amount of knowledge he had at his young age.

Jason grabbed the grape jelly with a continued grin. "You're funny, Michael," he said.

Michael was puzzled. "What do you mean?"

"It's your persistence about what you told us," Jason said. "It is funny to hear how much you believe your dream was real."

Michael now knew what Jason meant, and it caused him to grin a little.

"Thanks, Jason," Barbara said as he passed her the toast. "Can you also pass me the jelly?"

"Sure, Mom," he said.

Everyone now had a portion of everything that had been prepared, and Barbara relished her delicious omelet. Michael reached for his fork, but then it suddenly jumped off the table, straight up into his waiting fingers, as if attached to an invisible string. Barbara looked directly down the table to her husband, surprised. "Did you see that?"

Dan had missed it. "See what?"

"Michael's fork," she said. "It suddenly jumped off the table and into his waiting fingers."

"Is that right?" Dan said. "How did that happen, Michael?"

Michael continued his calm face. "I just thought about it, Dad, and it came to me."

Dan and Barbara were extremely surprised, as it appeared Michael had some telekinesis, but they had no idea of the extent or how powerful it was. The geneticists had not revealed that powerful mental ability either, and Dan and Barbara now wondered whether they even knew Michael had that special advanced attribute. Dan directed his gaze back to Michael. "You know what you just accomplished, Michael, is what we call telekinesis here on Earth?"

"Yes, I do," Michael said.

"Well," Dan said, "you will have to be very careful using that ability, especially in public around those you do not know. Telekinesis is not something openly used by this race. There is no acceptance of it in society, and very few, if any, have the ability. Do you understand?"

"Yes, I do, Dad," Michael said.

Dan stared down to the other end of the table, and his wife returned a calm, reassuring nod. They watched Michael cut a small piece of his omelet. What Barbara had just witnessed caused her to wonder about their cloaked spaceship behind the barn. Even though it could probably remained cloaked indefinitely while inside Earth's magnetic field, she did not know what effects it might have on surrounding vegetation and trees. She looked briefly at Michael, then to Dan. "What are we going to do about our ship?"

"What do you mean?" Dan asked.

"For instance," she said, "its active cloaking field. Could there be possible side effects to the surrounding vegetation and trees?"

Dan thought about her somewhat surprising question. "I really do not know," he said and noticed Michael already looking up at him. "Is that a possibility, Michael?"

"Yes, it is," Michael said. "The molecular structures of the plants and trees will slowly start to invert under magnetic induction the longer they're inside the cloaking field. If they were to remain inside the field too long and complete this molecular conversion, they would start to die once the cloaking field was removed, unless adjustments were made to their cellular structures, and Earth's sciences cannot readjust them, Dad."

Dan was surprised by Michael's explanation and very curious about it. "How long would those conversions normally take?"

"Seven to thirty Earth days," Michael said, "at least for ideal Earth temperatures. It takes longer when lower temperatures force hibernation growth."

Dan definitely did not want to keep their ship cloaked longer than seven days, but there was no large building in which to hide their ship. If they were to uncloak the ship, it would be easily visible from the skies. That was an interesting dilemma, and Dan expressed extreme curiosity with his next question. "Is there any way to hide our ship without cloaking it?"

"Yes, there is," Michael answered. "The hull of our ship also has the ability to take on the colors of its surroundings like a chameleon, at least once the function is programmed into the computer. Our ship could then sit in the field behind the barn, uncloaked, and would be unrecognizable from the air or ground, even using infrared or any other Earth technologies. There are special optical glasses we can wear that would allow us to see the residual energy patterns of our ship's outer hull."

Dan, Barbara, and Jason were amazed to hear about this "chameleon" capability of their spaceship. "That is amazing," Dan said while continuing to stare at his extremely smart son. "Can you program that function into our ship's computer after we eat and right before we go fishing?"

"Sure, Dad," Michael said.

Barbara grinned at Dan's interaction with their new son. She knew Michael would probably be more of a daddy's boy. Jason was definitely a daddy's boy too, and it had been evident even before he turned three. It was just the opposite with Kyle, who leaned more toward her. Yet, without doubt, all three boys had a deep attachment to both her and Dan.

Barbara then thought about Michael's birthplace, the race's home world, Valzar, located in an entirely different galaxy Earth called the Small Magellanic Cloud. She very much wanted to see it soon. "When would you want to visit Michael's birthplace?" she asked as Dan sipped on his orange juice.

All three boys perked up.

Dan paused at her question. It would be interesting traveling to an entirely new galaxy, but he always seemed to have a fairly busy work schedule. Christmas season was less than three months away, though, just around the corner, and there would be a closure of the labs over the holidays, except for a few security guards watching over the complex. "How about after Christmas?" he suggested.

Barbara noticed the boys transfixed by their dad's question. "Are you serious?" she asked.

"Yes, I am," Dan said. "When I go back to work Monday, I will request three weeks' vacation right after the holidays, starting the first week of January. That'll give us about a month to enjoy ourselves."

The boys were still staring up at their father, as if glued to what he'd just told them. Barbara turned her attention back to Dan, who was now relaxed back in his chair.

Dan actually felt immense anticipation for the opportunity of his family traveling to another galaxy. "Great!" he said. "We'll leave for the Small Magellanic Cloud galaxy on December 26."

"That would be a wonderful Christmas present," Barbara said.

"For sure," Dan said. "I am curious what it will be like leaving the boundaries of our galaxy and traveling into the dark matter between the galaxies."

"Me too," Barbara said.

Michael suddenly blurted out, "Traveling into the space between each galaxy is like traveling out of a bright, sunny day into a late-evening sunset, because the photon densities are not as high or held in place in the same manner."

Dan and Barbara continued to stare at Michael, and Dan finally grinned. "Is that right?" he said. "And how do you know that?"

"I just know," Michael said.

Dan thought Michael's quaint, casual attitude was amusing and could not wait to talk to him later about his full understanding of the photon densities mentioned, including dark matter space, or darkened space between the galaxies. The boys were almost finished with their breakfasts, and Barbara was looking at him with a curious face. "What was Frank's phone call about?" she asked.

Dan looked around the table. "I'll tell you later," he said.

Barbara knew it could not be good. "Okay," she said.

Jason gulped down his milk, wiped his hands, and set his napkin down. "Before we go fishing, Dad, I'm going to my bedroom."

"Sure, Son," Dan said.

Kyle suddenly stared up into his father's eyes. "Can I go to his bedroom too, Daddy?" he softly asked.

"Yes, you may," Dan said.

Michael was also staring up at him and sincerely asked, "Can I too?"

"Yes, you may also," Dan again answered.

The three boys stood up. Jason instinctively walked up to his mom and placed a small kiss against her cheek. Kyle did the same, and Michael beelined toward his mom as well. She leaned down and received a small kiss and hug from him too. "Thanks for breakfast, Mom," Michael said.

Dan felt warm inside to see this display of affection from all three boys, especially Michael, and knew Michael would show this love and affection to his new mother for the rest of her natural life. "Boys," Barbara said, "your dad cooked most of the breakfast, so thank him too."

Without hesitation, like a marching band, they walked to the other end of the table and one by one hugged their dad, followed by a small kiss and a "Thank you, Dad" before leaving the dining room, with Kyle and Michael like two little ducklings following behind Jason to his bedroom.

Barbara felt good inside. "Michael will act and grow up just like his brothers," she said.

"Appears that way," Dan said.

Barbara finished her orange juice and set the glass down. "What did Frank call about?"

"Believe it or not," he said, "but strange NSA Secret Service federal agents dressed in black showed up at the labs yesterday, and he was interrogated. My name was also mentioned."

Barbara's eyes widened. "Then what happened?"

"As far as I know, nothing," Dan said. "He did say they asked him whether I had brought any unusual artifacts to the labs."

Barbara remained quiet.

Dan noticed this and continued, "Frank worded his answer in a sly manner to indicate no while sidestepping their original question and technically telling the truth."

Barbara had a strange feeling inside, but she masked it with an unusual grin. "What do we do now? Those agents are possibly associated to the rumored highly secretive group Majestic 12."

Dan thought about it. "Yes, I know. Maybe we should try forming a secret pact with them. That way, not only would they leave us alone, but they could also help shield our family from public scrutiny."

"True," she said. "But would the alien race ever allow it?"

"Good question," Dan said. "We'll have to ask one of the families living here or contact their home world, just in case this highly secretive government agency determines something with our family isn't quite right."

Barbara nodded wholeheartedly and started picking up plates and glasses.

Dan stood up to help clear the table. With their hands now full, they continued up to the kitchen granite countertop. He stood quietly, wondering about the possible communication with the race's high council regarding what he and Barbara had just talked about. He made eye contact with his wife. "Let's say, for instance," he said, "that the high council does allow our association with their race to be known to this highly secretive government agency. That agency might be very surprised to find their electronic databases were easily manipulated without them ever realizing it."

"For sure," Barbara said while setting dishes in the sink, "but then, they also would have to be somewhat primed, because the cargo ship's broken tubular hull sections and all its contents were mysteriously taken from them, regardless of where they were hidden."

"No doubt," Dan said and returned to the dining room.

As Dan picked up the last of the dishes and wiped down the oak table, Barbara found herself curious what the boys might be doing.

Dan returned to the kitchen, wondering whether a pact with the top-secret government agency responsible for covering up and shielding advanced alien technologies from the general public was even possible. He placed the last of the dishes on the countertop. "Here you go," he said.

"Thank you," Barbara said.

As Dan returned the jelly and butter to the refrigerator, the boys came back to the kitchen. "Dad," Jason said, "we're going to the backyard for a little while before we go fishing, okay?"

"Sure, Son," Dan said.

Jason held the door for his two brothers as they exited onto the deck. All three boys then walked down the stairs and directly to one of their swing sets. Dan then walked up behind Barbara and placed his arms around her waist as they stared through the kitchen window at their boys sitting on swings next to each other and talking. He kissed her on the side of the neck. "The next few months will be interesting," he whispered.

A ticklish shiver shot up Barbara's back, and she gently laid her head against his chest. "Yes, it will," she softly replied.

They both now thought about the secret life they would have to live on Earth, as well as the trip they were planning to the Small Magellanic Cloud galaxy in less than four months. Barbara also thought about the possibility that she might be pregnant when they did travel to the race's home world. If that were the case, their unborn child would become a space traveler—at least from inside her womb. She turned around with a small grin and looked into Dan's eyes. "You know, carrying a baby on our trip to the race's home world is an interesting thought."

Dan held her a little tighter, knowing what she was referring to. "Yes, it is. Do you want a boy or a girl?"

"Definitely a girl," she said.

Dan placed a soft kiss against her lips. "Well, let's wish for a girl, then," he said.

Barbara held him a little tighter and dreamed some more about their raising Michael and the highly advanced spaceship at their disposal. Family vacations would now take on an entirely new meaning, at least whenever they involved using their spaceship. They could travel to any of the seven continents on Earth, to the tallest mountains, to the bottom of any of its major oceans, and possibly to the Pacific Ocean's Mariana Trench, with a depth of over thirty-six thousand feet. They could explore their solar system and the Milky Way galaxy, travel to any planet and its moons, and walk on any of those planetary bodies without the use of space suits—at least while inside an atmospheric gravity bubble. Was there life elsewhere inside their solar system besides just Earth? Maybe below the icy waters of Jupiter's moon Callisto?

Barbara placed another soft kiss against Dan's lips and whispered, "Our new lives will become more wonderful than can be imagined."

Dan pressed his face against her soft, scintillating cheek. "Yes, it will," he whispered back.

# ABBREVIATIONS

| | |
|---|---|
| AIDS | acquired immune deficiency syndrome |
| CAC | Common Access Card |
| CCME | cerebral core memory extractor |
| CIA | Central Intelligence Agency |
| $CO_2$ | carbon dioxide |
| CRT | cathode-ray tube |
| DNA | deoxyribonucleic acid |
| EDXRF | energy-dispersive x-ray fluorescence |
| EEG | electroencephalograph |
| EMP | electromagnetic pulse |
| ETA | estimated time of arrival |
| FBI | Federal Bureau of Investigation |
| HIV | human immunodeficiency virus |
| IMT | instantaneous matter transport |
| IQ | intelligence quotient |
| keV | kiloelectron volt or 1,000 electron volts |
| MJ-12 | Majestic 12 |

| | |
|---|---|
| MRI | magnetic resonance imaging |
| NSA | National Security Agency |
| NORAD | North American Aerospace Defense |
| REM | rapid eye movement |
| UFO | unidentified flying object |
| VAC | volts of alternating current |
| XRF | x-ray fluorescence |